Great Short Works

of

EDGAR ALLAN POE

Great Short Works

of

EDGAR ALLAN POE

Edited with an Introduction by

G. R. THOMPSON

PERENNIAL LIBRARY

Harper & Row, Publishers, New York
Grand Rapids, Philadelphia, St. Louis, San Francisco
London, Singapore, Sydney, Tokyo, Toronto

For My Grandparents
Mae Lapp and James Lapp
Frank Oxley
And For My Children
Hallie and Erin

GREAT SHORT WORKS OF EDGAR ALLAN POE

Copyright © 1970 by G. R. Thompson.

Printed in the United States of America.
All rights reserved.

First PERENNIAL CLASSIC edition published 1970
by Harper & Row, Publishers, Inc.,
10 East 53rd Street, New York, N.Y. 10022.

ISBN: 0-06-083093-X

99 00 01 OPM   34 35 36

SOURCES AND ACKNOWLEDGMENTS

POEMS: Text of the poems is from *Collected Works of Edgar Allan Poe*, edited by Thomas Olive Mabbott (Cambridge: Harvard University Press, 1969). Dates following poems indicate the year, or years, of first publication and, where differences occur, the date of publication of the texts used in this volume.

TALES: "Metzengerstein, A Tale in Imitation of the German" from *Southern Literary Messenger*, Vol. II, January 1836. "Loss of Breath. A Tale a la Blackwood" from *Southern Literary Messenger*, Vol. I, September 1835. "MS. Found in a Bottle" from *Broadway Journal*, Vol. II, October 11, 1845. "The Assignation" from *BJ*, Vol. I, June 7, 1845. "Berenice" from *BJ*, Vol. I, April 5, 1845. "Some Passages from the Life of a Lion" from *BJ*, Vol. I, March 15, 1845. "Shadow—A Parable" from *BJ*, Vol. I, May 31, 1845. "Silence—A Fable" from *BJ*, Vol. II, September 6, 1845. "Ligeia" from *BJ*, Vol. II, September 27, 1845. "How to Write a Blackwood Article. A Predicament" from *BJ*, Vol. II, July 12, 1845. "The Fall of the House of Usher," "The Man of the Crowd," "The Murders in the Rue Morgue," "A Descent Into the Maelström," "The Colloquy of Monos and Una," "The Black Cat," and "The Purloined Letter" from *Tales* (New York: Wiley & Putnam, 1845. Facsimile edition published by Charles E. Merrill Publishing Company, Columbus, Ohio, 1969). "William Wilson" from *BJ*, Vol. II, August 30, 1845. "Never Bet the Devil Your Head. A Tale with a Moral" from *BJ*, Vol. II, August 16, 1845. "The Oval Portrait" from *BJ*, Vol. I, April 26, 1845. "The Masque of the Red Death" from *BJ*, Vol. II, July 19, 1845. "The Pit and the Pendulum" from *BJ*, Vol. I, May 10, 1845. "The Tell-Tale Heart" from *BJ*, Vol. II, August 23, 1845. "A Tale of the Ragged Mountains" from *BJ*, Vol. II, November 29, 1845. "The Premature Burial" from *BJ*, Vol. I, June 14, 1845. "Some Words With A Mummy" from *BJ*, Vol. II, November 1, 1845. "The Imp of the Perverse" from *The Mayflower, for MDCCCXLVI*, Boston, 1846. "The Facts in the Case of M. Valdemar" from *Broadway Journal*, Vol. II, December 20, 1845. "The Sphinx" from *Arthur's Ladies' Magazine*, Vol. V, January 1846. "The Cask of Amontillado" from *Godey's Lady's Book*, Vol. XXXIII, November 1846. "Hop-Frog, or the Eight Chained Ourang-Outangs" from *The Flag of Our Union*, Vol. IV, March 17, 1849. Dates of the tales in the Table of Contents are those of first publication and, where differences occur, the date of publication of the texts used in this volume.

CRITICISM: "Review of 'Twice-Told Tales By Nathaniel Hawthorne,'" from *Graham's Lady's and Gentleman's Magazine*, Vol. XX, May 1842. "The Philosophy of Composition" from *Graham's Lady's and Gentleman's Magazine*, Vol. XXVIII, April 1846. Excerpts from "The Poetic Principle" from *Sartain's Union Magazine*, Vol. VII, October 1850.

The Tales and Criticism are printed from the original sources indicated above, with editorial correction of sure typographical errors only. Even these corrections have been kept to a minimum, for some of the seeming "errors" silently corrected in other editions have in fact been unsuspecting emendations of puns. For some of the tales, which Poe published in several versions during his career, earlier rather than the latest versions have been used because the satiric exaggerations stand out more clearly.

Thanks are due to Gayle Conrad, Judy Osowski, and Robert L. Marrs, for help with the physical manuscript, and Professor Conny E. Nelson for suggestions regarding the introductory matter.

CONTENTS

II TALES

III CRITICISM

INTRODUCTION

G. R. THOMPSON

I

Despite his desire to be remembered as a poet, it is, to use the words of a recent critic, as the arch-priest of the Gothic horror tale that we remember Edgar Allan Poe. Yet according to the temper of modern criticism generally, there are at least two major problems with Poe's short stories to prevent us from regarding him so.

First, his Gothic tales seem never *quite* to work; something is always out of keeping even in the best of them. Allen Tate, in an essay written for the centennial of Poe's death in 1949, catches the curious effect that Poe has on many insightful readers. On the one hand, Tate "confesses" that Poe's tales have "massive impact" and that "Poe's voice" is often "so near that I recoil a little lest he, Montressor, lead me into the cellar, address me as Fortunato, and wall me up alive." On the other hand, Tate observes that if we do feel Poe's power, we likely also feel a little guilty about our response, or at least feel oddly disappointed with Poe's oddly flawed tales, with their apparently overdone rhetoric, melodramatic situations, sudden shifts in tone, and seemingly inappropriate intrusions of the comic and absurd. " 'The Fall of the House of Usher'," Tate writes, "was a little spoiled for me even at fourteen by the interjection of the 'Mad Tryst of Sir Launcelot Canning'."

The second major problem with Poe's tales (actually another aspect of the first) is that as a single group they seem to lack consistency and wholeness; the body of his fiction splits disturbingly into two large, seemingly incon-

1

sistent, groups: flawed Gothic tales on the one hand, and flawed comic and satiric tales on the other. Poe's critics have found this duality disturbing not only because the humor of his comic stories seems unpleasantly morbid, really humorless, or finally pointless, but also because Poe has always seemed to them to be, first and last, a Gothic-Romantic writer. His many attempts at humor and satire, according to the Gothicist view of Poe, show not that he was a humorist, but only that humor was actually "alien" to his personality; when he tried to write humor, he was attempting to put on an incongruous mask out of keeping with his real self.

Indeed, it has come to be conventional to explain the curious incongruities in Poe's works by means of a psuedo-Freudian biographical approach, as proceeding from his lack of self-identity (Poe as the orphaned child of itinerant actors reared in the home of a tyrannical and unloving foster father). This lack of identity is supposed to have caused him to assume various unsuitable masks or guises and to spend his life in "role-playing." In this mode, one of the most coherent views of the diversity of Poe's career is the suggestion that Poe borrowed not only the literary symbols of English Romanticism, but also the very personalities of the English Romantic poets. Poe is supposed to have played Byron in his earliest poems, then Shelley, then Coleridge in his later poems. His "unattractive" satire and parody, according to this view, shows, in another dimension, how much he depended on imitation for literary inspiration. This imitative habit is supposed also to be part of Poe's "American" quality, derived from the "empirical" habit of mind in the American culture at large. This "empirical" strain in Poe is said to have completely taken over from the "Romantic" one in the early 1840s, when he wrote his first purely "ratiocinative" detective stories. His 1842 review of Hawthorne's *Twice-Told Tales*, in which he discussed the principle of complete unity and totality of effect, thus shows Poe systematizing a formula for the short story; and "The Philosophy of Composition" (1846), in which Poe explained in almost mechanical terms how he came to write "The Raven" step by rational step, shows Poe claiming as his own the analytic mind of M. Dupin, the rational French detective-hero of "Murders in the Rue Morgue" (1841), "The Mystery of Marie Roget" (1842), and "The Purloined Letter" (1844). The scheme falters a little at this point, however, for at the same time that Poe was playing, in the words of Leon Howard, the "coldly calculating emotional engineer" of "The Philosophy of Composition," he was also playing the bereaved Romantic hero of "The Raven" (1845), a role picked up shortly again in "Ulalume" (1847). Thus, we return to the easy Freudian view of Poe's inconsistencies: the "personal implications" of "The Raven" as poem along with the prose account of its composition, according to Howard, are "almost" schizophrenic. Howard does go on to say, however, that Poe's was not truly a "psychological" case, since even before 1846, in the Dupin stories, he was seeking a middle ground intellectually that is most clearly seen in the long philosophical essay *Eureka* (1848). Dupin is the man of reason *and* intuition, poet *and* mathematician, whose imagination provides a hypothesis, whose reason controls its application, and whose observation verifies it. This, Poe proposes in *Eureka*, is the true way to knowledge: instead of the creeping and crawling methods of induction and deduction, we must have leaps of intuition "corrected" by reason.

But this view of Poe's imaginative life, attractive and coherent though it may be, does not adequately account for the analytic criticism he practiced from the beginning, nor for the number of satiric and comic works that appeared throughout his twenty-year career in a pattern of loose alternation with the Gothic works. Poe's first published story, "Metzengerstein," is ostensibly a Gothic tale; but it was one of a group of five that Poe sent to the Philadelphia *Saturday Courier* in 1831, four of which ("The Duc de L'Omelette," "A Tale of Jerusalem," "Loss of Breath," and "Bon-Bon") are comic and satiric. These tales, published after "Metzengerstein" early in 1832, were followed in the next three years by four Gothic stories ("MS. Found in a Bottle," "The Assignation," "Berenice," and "Morella"). Then came three comic and satiric tales ("Lionizing," "Hans Phaal," and "King Pest") in the middle of 1835, followed by the Gothic tale, "Shadow." Then two more comic and satiric tales ("Four Beasts in One" in 1836 and "Mystification" in 1837) were followed by two more Gothic tales ("Silence" in 1837 and "Ligeia" in 1838). From the winter of 1838-39 to the winter of 1839-40, we find four satiric tales ("How to Write a Blackwood Article. A Predicament," "The Devil in the Belfry," and "The Man That Was Used Up") followed by three Gothic tales ("The Fall of the House of Usher," "William Wilson," "The Conversation of Eiros and Charmion"), followed in turn by another comic tale ("Why the Little Frenchman Wears His Hand in a Sling"). This loose pattern of alternation continues to the end of Poe's career, even suggesting conscious self-parody. The Dupin stories (1841-45) are burlesqued in the comic detective story " 'Thou Art the Man' " (1844); the suspended animation of "M. Valdemar" (1845) is made comic in Count Allamistakeo's resurrection in "Some Words With a Mummy" in the same year; the living burials of Madeline Usher and of Berenice are travestied in "The Premature Burial" (1844); the Gothic decor of "The Masque of the Red Death" (1842) and the revenge theme in "The Cask of Amontillado" (1846) become part of an absurd, though savage, fairy tale in "Hop-Frog" (1848).

When, at almost exactly the midpoint of his career,

Poe first collected his stories as *Tales of the Grotesque and Arabesque* (1840), the comic and satiric works outnumbered the ostensibly serious works by fourteen to eleven. Of the tales written after 1840, the serious outnumbered the comic and satiric by twenty-four to nineteen (though what is serious and what is comic in about a half dozen of these later tales may, initially, seem arguable). Thus, of the total of Poe's sixty-eight short tales, thirty-five are serious and thirty-three comic and satiric—a balancing off of the serious and the comic that can hardly be mere accident.

Another, more comprehensive explanation of these and other seeming "inconsistencies" in Poe's work focuses on the basic thesis of *Eureka* (1848), Poe's essay on the origin, meaning, and destiny of the Universe. In this book-length work, Poe begins with the proposition that existence implies ultimate annihilation—not only of the individual, but of all things, in a pointlessly pulsating cosmos which endlessly creates and destroys itself. Often self-consciously facing extinction, the forlorn Poe hero gives way to "hysterical" laughter. In Poe, writes Harry Levin, "the premise of knowledge" is that "all men are mortal, and the insights of tragedy culminate in the posture of dying. More than once . . . [Poe] reminds us that Tertullian's credo, 'I believe because it is absurd,' was inspired by the doctrine of resurrection. And though Poe's resurrections prove ineffectual or woefully incomplete, we are reminded by the Existentialists that the basis of man's plight is absurdity." Given Levin's existentialist context, Poe's Gothic works, implicitly based on a vision of absurdity, and the mad and half-mad Gothic figures which inhabit these works, seem clearly related to the fierce absurdity of his comic and satiric works.

Although this is a progressive explanation (except for the element of "hysteria") of the whole body of Poe's work and of its fascination for the modern reader, and while it points the way to a more just assessment of Poe, critics have been slow to re-examine thoroughly the corpus of Poe's work. The result has been an incomplete revaluation which has passively reinforced the older and now traditional view of Poe as merely the schizophrenic genius of the demoniac imagination. The apparent discrepancy between Poe's "unnatural" comic face and his "true" serious face remains a nagging problem for the modern reader. Moreover, even the reader who would allow Poe a natural diversity of interest finds himself faced with the problem of just how to read the works of a Gothic humorist—or the works, for that matter, of a humorous Gothicist.

What we need is a new way of reading Poe, a way just as informed as the new readings of Mark Twain and Herman Melville which in the last few decades have saved their works from consignment to the adolescent's bookshelf. We must divorce ourselves from the traditional Gothicist view of Poe, a view which includes not only the image of Poe as the mad genius of the macabre tale but also the contrary image of Poe as the dreamy poet of the "ideal" world of supernal Beauty. The "ideal" and the "demonic" are, of course, major elements in Poe's consciously developed image, but so too are the comic and satiric. The real questions are: how to develop a reading inclusive of these divergent tendencies, and how truly divergent are they, at last?

The key to this new style of reading Poe is to be found in the twentieth-century emphasis on the concepts of *tension* and *irony* characteristic of the "New Critics"— Brooks, Warren, Empson, Richards, Tate, and others. The contrast between the ideal and the demonic in Poe's works, between the serious and the comic, the Gothic and the satiric, and, thematically, between hope and despair, is a matter of the balance achieved by the dynamic *tension* of opposite forces. Flat statements or commitments in Poe are only seeming. Almost everything that Poe wrote is qualified by, indeed controlled by, a prevailing *irony* in which the artist presents us with slyly insinuated mockery of both ourselves as readers and himself as writer. The view of art (and life) informing both the tales and the poems, and to an extent the criticism, is that of skeptical dissembler and hoaxer, who complexly, ambivalently, and ironically explored the fads of the Romantic Age. All of Poe's fiction, and the poems as well, can be seen as one coherent piece—as the work of one of the greatest ironists of world literature.

II

In general, the word *irony*, historically and at present, points to some basic discrepancy between what is expected or apparent and what is actually the case. As a literary term, *irony* implies some deception, which becomes clear with the perception of discrepancy between the immediately apparent intention, or meaning, or circumstance, or stated belief, and a half-hidden meaning or reality. Literary irony is seen in a writer's verbal and structural mode of purporting to take seriously what he does not take seriously, or at least does not take with complete seriousness. In the implied contrasts the ironist sets up, there is often a sense of one term in some way mocking the other. Irony may also be a serious, non-comic, non-satiric attitude; in such a case irony may mean simply that an expressed attitude is somehow qualified, usually by its opposite possibility. In any event, although there are different ironic tones, irony is more often than not philosophically characterized by a "skepticism" engendered by seeing opposite possibilities in a situation, as is especially evident in the particularly complex, ambivalent and paradoxical skepticism of the strongly ironic poetry of the seventeenth and twentieth centuries. This style of irony is highly praised in modern literary criticism; and it is in this sense that the term *irony* describes Poe's characteristic mode of writing, his habit of mind, and even his style of Romantic idealism.

But Poe is not only an ironist, he is a satiric ironist. Satire, in general, makes fuller use of comic distortion than irony and is always immediately clearer, since the incongruities show more plainly. Satire distorts the characteristic features of an individual, or of a society, or of an artistic work in order to ridicule that which the satirist dislikes—usually (or avowedly) the vices and follies of mankind, the lamentable falling away from traditional ideals. When the satirist makes use of irony, he pretends to take his opponents seriously, accepting their premises and values and methods of reasoning in order eventually to expose their absurdity. The relationship of *irony* to *satire*, however, is complicated by the problem of emphasis, since either can be the weapon of the other, since either can provide the basic thrust of a work, and since both make use of distortion. But in addition to Poe's ironic and satiric styles, we must consider his closely related style as a hoaxer. Whereas satire makes use of comic surprises and contrasts, irony is usually subtler, and the essential deception involved in literary irony may be so subtle that the work becomes a hoax, and this is often the case in Poe. A *hoax* is usually thought of as an attempt to deceive others about the truth or reality of an event. But a literary hoax attempts to persuade the reader not merely of the reality of false events but of the reality of false literary intentions or circumstances—that a work is by a certain writer or of a certain age when it is not, or that one is writing a serious Gothic story when one is not. The laugh of the hoaxer is rather private, intended at best for a limited coterie. Just as the satirist limits his circle of understanding readers to those who can perceive the flaws of society, so the ironist limits his circle of understanding readers to those who can discriminate with more subtlety the complexities of art and life. At the extreme, the hoax can limit the circle of understanding readers to an audience of one. In such a case it can be seen as a kind of supreme irony in which the writer mocks even perceptive *eirons* like himself, and even, therefore, himself. Indeed, the German "Romantic Ironists" of the early nineteenth century, who had great influence on Poe, constructed theories of transcendence of one's mere "selfness" through almost this very means—what Friedrich Schlegel called "self-parody" and "transcendental buffoonery," which involves achieving a mystical sense of an "ideal" state beyond our limited earthly one by playing, as it were, a cosmic hoax on both the world and oneself.

It has been insufficiently recognized that it is this Continental movement or school that comprised Poe's basic intellectual, philosophical, and artistic milieu. In the last two decades of the eighteenth century and the first two decades of the nineteenth, writers like Friedrich Schlegel and his brother August Wilhelm Schlegel, J. M. R. Lenz, E. T. A. Hoffmann, Ludwig Tieck, and others had preceded Poe in the exploration of the twin mysteries of the psychological and occult—in the exploration of what they called the "night-side" of the mind and Nature. By Poe's time Romanticists generally had come to feel that the secrets of Nature lay deep within the human mind itself. But in their philosophical struggles with objectivity and subjectivity, and in their exploration of mental aberrations, many, especially the "gloomy Germans," became increasingly pessimistic about man's ability to free himself from the web of illusion that existence seemed to present. However, the small group of writers and thinkers we are concerned with developed a liberating if still rather gloomy theory of the darkly comic along with a philosophy of "Transcendental Irony," or more familiarly "Romantic Irony," which could, they felt, free the deep-thinking man from his agonies (at least temporarily). Modern critics look at historical "Romantic Irony" as an awkward and seemingly pointless breaking of dramatic illusion, such as having a stage "audience" interrupt a play with criticisms and even usurp the roles of the "actors," or having a character in a novel observe in Volume III that the lake he is now passing by is the very one he had fallen into in Volume I, page such and such. These techniques, of course, have been used frequently by twentieth-century expressionist playwrights—indeed, they seem to have been in some sense rediscovered by the practitioners of Theater of the Absurd in their attempt to present an empty, absurd, illusory world. In Poe's time, this kind of "irony" became (for Poe and the coterie of writers we are talking about) the highest creative, poetic, and philosophical activity, having as its aim the "annihilation" of apparent contradictions and earthly limitations through a liberating perception of the element of Absurdity in the mysterious contrarieties of the Universe. The Romantic Ironist strove, in his contrariness, deceptiveness, satire, and even self-mockery, to attain a penetrating view of existence from a subliminally Idealistic height—but always with an eye on the terrors of an ultimately incomprehensible, disconnected, absurd, or at best probably decaying and possibly malevolent Universe. The more usual Romanticist wished to penetrate beyond the sensory to the ultimate secrets that, as mentioned, Romantic writers increasingly felt lay within the mind itself. But for the "Dark Romanticist," especially for the Romantic Ironist, the only attainable harmony in all the deceptiveness and chaos which the world presented was a double vision, a double awareness, a double emotion, culminating in an ambivalent joy of stoical self-possession and intellectual control. This kind of Romantic artist-hero held the world together by the force of his own mind—or he watched the "world" and his own mind crumble under the stress of dark contrary forces. The result, in the works of these writers, is an ambivalent pessimism: a kind of black humor, or black irony, and also a skepticism engendered by the self-awareness of the subjective human mind insistently reaching out toward an illusive certainty.

The fiction and poetry resulting from such philosophical and artistic attitudes were sometimes called *grotesques*, sometimes *arabesques*, by the German (and French) writers of the day. These two words have complicated and intertwining histories; but clearly Poe was pointing out his philosophical and literary affinities with these writers when he remarked, albeit negatively, on the apparent "Germanism" of his tales in the Preface to his first collection of fiction, significantly titled *Tales of the Grotesque and Arabesque* (1840). This distinctively German genre of Romantic fiction (and poetry) is characterized by multiplicity of view and yet also by complete dramatization of the imagined world from the viewpoint of a single mind. Thus, in Poe's works, the limited perspective of the ever-present "I" in the tales has, carefully worked up around it, an intricate "arabesque" structure of illusion, misperception, perversity, and grotesque self-torment. Yet, in the complex structure and tone of the tales and poems, all is treated with a seldom recognized half-humorous ironic detachment from the plight of the "I" protagonist. This is true for both the apparently serious works and the comic and satiric works, though of course in the comic works the ironic and satiric distortions, or grotesqueries, are even clearer. Less clear is the presence of these ironic, mocking, comic elements in the poems, and it will be well to glance at the ironic patterns of some of Poe's supposedly dream-haunted and intensely Romantic poems before dealing more specifically with any of the Gothic tales.

III

Poe began his literary career as a poet when, at the age
of eighteen, he published the small volume, *Tamerlane
and Other Poems* (1827). Before his first work of fiction
was published, he had published two more volumes (or
augmented editions) of poems: *Al Aaraaf, Tamerlane, and
Minor Poems* (1829) and, more simply, *Poems* (1831).
He was not to collect his poetry again, however, for
another fifteen years, when he published *The Raven and
Other Poems* (1845). In his Preface to this volume he
claimed that, had he not been forced by worldly considerations to devote his energies to the (somewhat)
more profitable pursuits of editing, criticism, and tale-
writing, poetry would have been his first choice for a
career.

Although the 1845 volume included such works as "The
Coliseum," "Israfel," "The City in the Sea," "Sonnet—
Silence," "Sonnet—To Science," and "To Helen," Poe yet
remarked, perhaps in ironic self-defense, that the volume
contained nothing "of much value to the public or very
creditable to myself." This seemingly modest remark is
not at all characteristic of Poe, but the Preface concludes
more typically with the observation that "with me poetry
has been not a purpose, but a passion; and the passions
should be held in reverence; they must not—they cannot
at will be excited with an eye to the paltry compensations,
or the more paltry commendations, of mankind." Thus
his prefatory deprecation of his efforts in poetry is actually
an exaltation of the Poetic Ideal, which he elsewhere
suggested was a vision of "Supernal Beauty," an ideal
above the mundane considerations of deadlines and com-
merce.

This image of himself is in accord with Baudelaire's
conception of Poe. Yet it is probable that Poe actually did
feel that his achievement in poetry did not match his

achievements in editing, criticism, and fiction. Certainly, modern critical interest in his fiction tends to bear out this judgment, though the present age is perhaps congenitally unsympathetic to the Romantic ideal of rendering a visionary world "out of space—out of time," as Poe puts it in "Dream-Land" (1844). But many of his best-known poems do *not* so seek after the Transcendental Ideal, but instead present, as in his fiction, dramatically rendered (though extreme) psychological states. "The Raven" is a case in point; indeed, the poem became the test case for his critical theories of absolute craftsmanship and classical control over the recalcitrant materials of the visionary—the discipline of the *poeta* (maker, craftsman) shaping, modifying, controlling the wild visions of the *vates* (seer, prophet). In "The Raven," the most occult and Gothic materials are fully rendered as the dramatization of the extreme psychological state of the bereaved lover who absolutely revels in self-torment. And in "The Philosophy of Composition" (1846), Poe is at pains to point out the fact that the eerie appropriateness of the raven's one-word refrain, rather than a message from Beyond, is but the learned response of a dumb animal, and that the significance of the reply is totally the product of the brain of the distraught student. Such a precise dramatic and thematic conception of the psychological state of the bereaved lover is hardly that of the dream-bedazzled Romantic seer that readers have usually taken Poe the poet to be.

It must be admitted that in "The Raven" intense "passions" are indeed "reverenced," in their way, and that there is a distinct difference in imagery between the early "dream" poems before 1840 and the rather more dramatically conceived poems afterwards. But even such a poem as the early "Sonnet—To Science" (1829), which first stood as an introduction to "Al Aaraaf" (Poe's dream-vision of the far wandering star where poetic myths, banished from earthly realities, still have ethereal existence) is actually a very tough-minded work when looked at closely. "Sonnet—To Science" seems, on the surface, to lament the death of poetic vision at the hands of modern physics, chemistry, and astronomy; but insinuated into its surface pattern is an undercurrent of ironic meaning. The first lines, "Science! true daughter of Old Time thou art! / Who alterest all things with thy peering eyes," hint that since Science with its "dull realities" is but the daughter of Time itself, all things are mutable. It is not just that the scientific vision changes our conception of things: the very order of existence itself is mutable and capable of diverse conceptualizations of its form. This is why Science is the "true" daughter of Time. Then, with thematic wryness, Poe *recreates* in the last lines of the poem the older "poetic" or "imaginative" vision of the forces of the Universe in terms of hamadryads, naiads, and moon-goddesses, *despite* the current unvisionary, scientific explanations which the first part of the poem says have "preyed" upon the poetic sensibilities. The culminating irony, never sufficiently remarked by Poe's critics, lies in the consistency of feminine images employed throughout. To move from the unlovely but true "daughter" of Time who alters our perception of things to the lament for the lost poetic vision of nymphs and goddesses is finally to suggest that Science is, for its time in fashion, but another construct of the mind—less appealing than the old myths, but a "nymph" of the imagination nevertheless. Amid the beautifully melancholy recreation of the lost "summer dream beneath the tamarind tree," we find the ironic, subtle, and dramatically presented confrontation of the "I" narrator with total illusoriness, even with nothingness and void, as he muses on the "mythic" in poetry and science both.

This tough-minded complexity in Poe's melancholy Romantic dream-poems has yet another side—the satiric.

The poem that stood as the "Introduction" (also extant in shortened versions and called "Preface" and "Romance") to Poe's third volume of poetry (1831) exhibits the same kind of complexity and ironic self-knowledge as "Sonnet —To Science." Its first and last verses (as the poem usually is given in its shorter version) seem sentimental and self-pitying: "eternal Condor years" fall upon the visionary soul of the poet-narrator, robbing him of his ability to see the benign aspects of the world of spirit; even the few calm hours he occasionally has must be spent in passionate response to some dimly perceived horror lurking beneath. Paradoxically, this "celebration" of passion, of emotion, suggests that even horror or sorrow is better than "nothing" at all. The visionary perception of, first, childhood's natural predilection for the green-plumed parrot of Romance (no insignificant choice of bird), and second, the grown man's apprehension of dark "tumult" and "unquiet" in Nature, is better than what is hinted at in "The Raven," "Sonnet—Silence," "Sonnet—To Science," and other of the poems—Nothingness. There must be *something* beyond the illusory world, the poem seems to say; let it be perceived, even though it be demoniacally horrible. But the long middle section of "Introduction" presents a wry and ironically toned rendering of the "perversity" of the "visionary" spirit. This ironic portrait comes suspiciously close to self-mockery, and at the very least contains gentle mockery of all visionary Romantic spirits. After commenting that in the newly perceived "blackness of the general Heaven" there is at least in "the very blackness" yet "Light on the lightning's silver wing," the narrator further remarks (in eighteenth-century couplet style):

> For, being an idle boy lang syne,
> Who read Anacreon, and drank wine,
> I early found Anacreon rhymes

> Were almost passionate sometimes—
> And by strange alchemy of brain
> His pleasures always turned to pain. . . .
> And so being young, and dipt in folly,
> I fell in love with melancholy . . . .

It is, indeed, sometimes argued that because Poe was only eighteen when his first volume appeared, that it is not likely he *intended* any ironic serio-comic complexity. The test, of course, is the poetry itself. What, for example, are we to make of the poem "Fairy-Land," which appeared with "Sonnet—To Science" as early as 1829 when Poe was but twenty? This poem is either one of the worst Poe ever produced—or a spoof. We cannot tell for sure at the beginning whether the poem is serious or comic, for Poe's indefinite landscapes elsewhere are not unlike the

> Dim vales—and shadowy floods—
> And cloudy-looking woods,
> Whose forms we can't discover
> For the tears that drip all over.

But the awkward incantation of the waxing and waning of "huge moons" in this visionary landscape in the memorable line "Again—again—again—" can hardly be serious. When, a few lines later, the narrator is speaking of a moon "more filmy than the rest" and adds as a parenthetical aside "(A kind which, upon trial, / They have found to be the best)," the "they" referred to can hardly be other than Romantic poets in general. Thus the "forms" of vales and floods and woods that "we can't discover" in the first lines refers to the style of the Romantic poets, with their sentimental "tears that drip all over" obscuring everything. Again, another memorable incantation follows: this moon "comes down—still down—and down." And later the narrator comments: "And then, how deep!

—O deep" is the "passion" of the "drowsy" spirits of this fairy-land. When the spirits of the place rise, and their "moony covering" flies off into the skies, our narrator reaches intently for an appropriate Romantic metaphor (a satiric thrust at a line in Thomas Moore's *Lalla Rookh*): "Like—almost anything— / Or a yellow Albatross." The poetic spirits now "use that moon no more / For the same end as before," that is, as "a tent," an image and metaphor which, the narrator remarks, "I think extravagant." Subtly echoing Shelley's famous phrase "the desire of the moth for the star," Poe's narrator concludes by describing the "butterflies of Earth, who seek the skies" and bring down a "specimen" of Romance and moon and extravagant metaphor upon "their quivering wings," an example of which, we may assume, is the present poem. This parody of the Romanticist stance has for years been taken with a straight face by readers who have not caught Poe's complex sense of wit and irony, and who insist on hanging on to the sentimental picture of Poe as the youthful visionary dream-poet (who, alas, died so young).

But even Poe's earliest poem (indeed, his earliest-known work) was blatantly comic and satiric. Written just a year before the Byronic and seemingly self-indulgent emotionalism of *Tamerlane* (1827), this poem, "O, Tempora! O, Mores!" (1826), was a satirical sally in forty-six heroic couplets aimed at a dry goods clerk named Pitts, who was unsuccessfully wooing a Richmond, Virginia, belle. After an opening lament for the deterioration of the manners of the times, the speaker of the poem comically articulates what might indeed be the persistent philosophical and artistic question of Poe's entire career. Should one's philosophical stance (here engendered by the pitiable condition of the poor rejected Pitts) be that of Heraclitus or Democritus? The speaker of the poem wonders:

> I've been a thinking—isn't that the phrase?—
> I like your Yankee words and Yankee ways—
> I've been a thinking, whether it were best
> To take things seriously, or all in jest . . . .

Such may not be the "visionary" and ethereal poetry of "To Helen" or of "Israfel" (a poem which, however, has its sly ironic innuendo about the "bolder note" that *could* swell from the sky were the speaker of the poem in Israfel's place). But this other side of Poe—the comic, the ironic, the hoaxical—cannot be ignored, even in the poems. It may be that in the poems Poe presented us with his most intense feelings of loss and illusoriness, but given the possibility of ironic "self-transcendence," it would be well for the serious reader to look carefully at anything that seems a little too extravagant, or too visionary, or too intense in the poems. "Spirits of the Dead," "Evening Star," "A Dream within a Dream," "In Youth Have I Known," "The Happiest Day," "The Lake," "Ulalume," "The Bells," "Eldorado," "For Annie," as well as other poems, are not without their dramatic, structural, tonal, and thematic ironies.

IV

When we come to the tales, the comic and ironic side of Poe is clearer and more emphatic. And it is here, rather than among the poems, I believe, that we find the *great* works of Poe. (All of Poe's works, except his one novel, *Arthur Gordon Pym*, are "short.") His criticism, though historically interesting in its specificity and topicality, and the best of his time (barring only Coleridge's criticism), is valuable today mainly for its precise enunciation of principles of rational control over even the wildest materials—for its enunciation of a principle, not merely of "unity," but of "*totality* of effect." "If [the] very first sentence," Poe wrote in his 1847 review of Hawthorne's *Twice-Told Tales*, "tend not to the outbringing of this effect, then in his very first step has [the artist] committed a blunder. In the whole composition there should be no word written of which the tendency, direct *or indirect*, is not to the pre-established design" (my italics). This principle he observed in each and every one of his tales —and not only in the well-known Gothic tales and detective stories, but also in the underrated comic and satiric tales, even though in these he was "slapping" (as he said in a letter to Joseph Snodgrass in 1841) "left & right at things in general."

In Poe's characteristically intricate, even involuted patterns of dramatic irony, the apparent narrative "voice" which pervades the surface atmosphere of the work is also seen within a qualifying frame. Several of the tales (for example, "The Black Cat," "The Tell-Tale Heart," "Ligeia," "The Imp of the Perverse," "The Cask of Amontillado") involve a confessional element, wherein a first-person narrator, like Montresor, seems calmly or gleefully to recount horrible deeds, but which generally implies a listener to whom the agonized soul is revealing his torment. Especially revealing of the ironic structure thus achieved is Montresor in "The Cask of Amontillado." In the surface story, Montresor seems to be chuckling over his flawlessly executed revenge upon unfortunate "Fortunato" fifty years before. But a moment's reflection suggests that the indistinct "you" whom Montresor addresses in the first paragraph is probably his death-bed confessor—for if Montresor has murdered Fortunato fifty years before, he must now be some seventy to eighty years of age. None of this is explicitly stated; it is presented dramatically; and we get the double effect of feeling the coldly calculated murder at the same time that we see the larger point that Montresor, rather than having successfully taken his revenge "with impunity," as he says, has instead suffered a fifty-years' ravage of conscience. Likewise, many of Poe's Gothic tales seem to involve supernatural happenings; but insinuated into them, like clues in a detective story, are details which begin to construct dramatic frames around the narrative "voice" of the work. These dramatic frames suggest the delusiveness of the experience as the first-person narrator renders it. As in Henry James and Joseph Conrad, there is often in Poe a tale within a tale within a tale; and the meaning of the whole lies in the relationship of the various implied stories and their frames rather than in the explicit meaning given to the surface story by the dramatically involved narrator.

Only within the last ten to fifteen years have critics begun to examine Poe's narrators as characters in the total design of his tales and poems, and to suspect that even his most famous Gothic works—like "Usher" and "Ligeia" —have ironic double and triple perspectives playing upon them: supernatural from one point of view, psychological from another point of view, and often burlesque from yet a third. Not only is nearly half of Poe's fiction satiric and comic in an obvious way, but the Gothic tales contain within them satiric and comic elements thematically related to the macabre elements. Poe seems very carefully to have aimed at the ironic effect of touching his readers simultaneously on an archetypal irrational level of fear and on an (almost subliminal) level of intellectual and philosophical perception of the Absurd. The result in the Gothic tales, as in many of the poems, is a kind of ambivalent mockery. We can respond to Poe's scenes of horror or despair at the same time that we are aware of their caricatural quality.

Although not really one of Poe's complex tales and at the end ostensibly comic, "The Premature Burial" (1844) is probably the clearest example of Poe's double effect, of his Gothic irony. The hero, an avid reader of Gothic books about burial alive, relates horrifying "factual" histories for three-quarters of the tale. Terrified of being buried alive himself, especially since he is subject to cataleptic fits, the protagonist arranges for a special sepulchre, easily opened from within, and a special coffin, with a spring-lid and a hole through which a bell-pull is to be tied to the hand of his "corpse." When he awakes in a cramped, dark, earthy-smelling place, he is convinced that he has fallen into a trance while among strangers and that he has been:

> . . . thrust deep, deep, and for ever, into some solitary and nameless *grave* . . . this awful conviction forced itself, thus, into the innermost chambers of my soul . . . I once again struggled to cry aloud. And in this second endeavor I succeeded. A long, wild, and continuous shriek, or yell, of agony, resounded through the realms of the subterrene Night.
>
> "Hillo! hillo, there!" said a gruff voice in reply.

The Gothic terror is comically undercut by the reply, and it turns out that the hero has fallen asleep in the narrow berth of a ship, where he has sought refuge for the night, and he is rousted out of his bunk by the sailors he has awakened with his horrible cry. Once we see that this is by no means a straightforward Gothic tale, we can see also the comic exaggeration of the overwrought Gothic style, that is, of what conventionally are "flaws" for twentieth-century readers. The emphasized "deep, deep, and for ever," the italicized "*grave*," the punning meaning of "innermost chambers of my soul," the redundancy of "shriek, or yell," and the capitalized letter of "subterrene Night" are typical of the exaggerations elsewhere in the tale. There can be no doubt that these stylistic exaggerations are part of Poe's burlesque technique once we read the conclusion, for the incident just described strikes the narrator as so ludicrous that he is shocked into sanity:

> My soul acquired tone—acquired temper. I went abroad. I took vigorous exercise . . . . I thought upon other subjects than Death. I discarded my medical books. "Buchan" I burned. I read no "Night Thoughts"—no fustian about churchyards—no bugaboo tales—*such as this*.

The hero then tells us that "from that memorable night" his "charnel apprehensions" were "dismissed forever;" and with them "vanished the cataleptic disorder, of which, perhaps, they had been less the consequence than the cause."

The satiric irony of the tale is multiple. The narrator horrifies us with his chilling "factual" cases in the first three-quarters of the tale; and then *he* loses his charnel apprehensions quite suddenly, whereas we are still left entertaining the ghastly possibilities he has suggested. Moreover, the earnestness of his conversion suggests parody of didactic magazine fiction ("out of Evil proceeded Good : . . . very excess wrought in my spirit an inevitable revulsion"), especially when we remember Poe's formulation of the "Heresy of the Didactic" in "The Poetic Principle" and elsewhere. Finally, in the last paragraph, just as we are perhaps adjusting to the comic conclusion, the narrator reaffirms ("Alas!") that "sepulchral terrors cannot be regarded as altogether fanciful." The "imagination of man" cannot "explore with impunity its every cavern"; our "Demons" must be allowed to "sleep, or they will devour us." Thus, the final lines suggest with nice ambiguity both the psychological and the supernatural, and leave us entertaining the serious possibilities of the absurd situation.

Many critics, however, will grant Poe a unified complexity of symbolism supporting the madness of an *obviously* mad character, like Roderick Usher, but balk at seeing an ironic complexity governing the whole tale in the suggested madness of the narrators of spooky stories like "Usher" and "Ligeia." Edward Wagenknecht, for example, has written that the "absurd notion" that "Ligeia" is "not a story of the supernatural but a study in morbid psychology" requires that we "ignore the text except where it can be perverted" and that we substitute "the fashionable notions of a later period" for those of Poe's own time. "Neither aesthetically nor psychologically," Wagenknecht continues, does this twentieth-century Freudian reading allow us to read the tale as a nineteenth-century story:

> Abnormal as he is, the narrator is a fairly conventional type of Poe hero; if we are to assume that we see the whole story in a distorted mind in this instance, why should not the other stories be interpreted on the same basis? Indeed, once we have decided to ignore the author's intentions and the milieu out of which the story comes, there is no reason why we should confine ourselves to misrepresenting Poe; an unlimited field is opened up.

Wagenknecht's theoretical point is well taken, but his conclusion about Poe is in error for, given the psychological theories of the eighteenth and nineteenth centuries and the techniques of nineteenth-century Romantic fiction, especially in Germany and America, one is forced to conclude that the psychological reading of "Ligeia" is, for the proper audience, indeed a nineteenth-century reading. As Michael Allen has demonstrated in his *Poe and the British Magazine Tradition*, the concept of a coterie audience was an important element in the attitude of the writers of fiction for the influential *Blackwood's Edinburgh Magazine*, whose lead Poe seems to have followed, even though he also subjected that journal to satiric burlesque. There was, in the minds of these writers, on the one hand, a large mass audience addicted to the somewhat tawdry melodramas of people caught in impossible predicaments, such as being accidentally baked in an oven (or buried alive), and, on the other hand, a smaller coterie of more perceptive readers who could enjoy the sly satire insinuated into such tales.

On the surface, of course, "Ligeia" is a serious supernatural tale of metempsychosis. But it can *also* be read as the story of the ambiguous delusions of a guilt-ridden madman who has probably murdered his wife (perhaps two wives) and hallucinated a weird rationalization of his crimes in the "ghostly" return of his first wife. Moreover, the absurdist element in the tale is underscored in the opening paragraphs, wherein the narrator tells us that not only can he not remember where or how he met Ligeia, he cannot even remember her last name! The full name of his "second" wife, the Lady Rowena Trevanion, of Tremaine, he remembers with constrasting specificness, since her title is what prompts him to marry her in the first place. This contrast with the partially nameless Ligeia underscores her unreal quality and leads us back to the absurd situation described in the opening paragraphs, only now it is clear that the narrator has tried to put something over on us—or on himself. The facts that the narrator is a drug addict and that several of his descriptions of Ligeia are in terms of comparison with "opium-dreams," that he has prepared for Rowena not a bridal chamber but a funeral chamber, that he is aware of what he calls his own "incipient madness," and finally that Poe has very clearly provided us with the narrator's motive for murdering Rowena, should be enough evidence for anyone as to what were Poe's intentions in this "Gothic" tale.

Pursuing the matter of Poe's "intentions" further, we should note that the first several paragraphs of "Ligeia" are burlesqued almost phrase by phrase in the opening paragraphs of "The Man That Was Used Up. A Tale of the Late Bugaboo and Kickapoo Campaign" published in 1839, a year after "Ligeia." This comic tale presents a completely artificial man, Brevet Brigadier General A. B. C. Smith, severely (almost totally) wounded in the "Indian" Wars, but fully reconstructed by American technological know-how: he is fitted up with artificial limbs, artificial shoulders, an artificial chest, and artificial hair, eyes, teeth, and palate. When put all together, the General is a handsome figure of a man, over six feet tall, and altogether admirable. Of him, however, the narrator remarks that his appearance "gives force to the pregnant observation of Francis Bacon that 'there is no exquisite beauty existing in the world without a certain degree of *strangeness* in the expression'." This, of course, is just what the narrator of "Ligeia," also alluding to Francis Bacon, says of her beautifully strange face. The implications for Poe's detached, ironic attitude toward "Ligeia" are obvious; but Poe has also recorded his attitude in an ironic letter to P. P. Cooke the same year "The Man That Was Used Up" was published. Regarding "Ligeia" he told Cooke who, he professed to believe, understood "Ligeia" better than others (a doubtful matter): "As for the mob —let them talk on. I should be grieved if I thought they comprehended me here."

The effect of "Ligeia" is then double—for the coterie of the perceptive. The *rationale* of the tale is psychological (and who can deny that Poe was interested in abnormal psychology?), but its *primary impact* is spooky and weird. Yet this double impact is but part of Poe's irony, for the tale also contains under its primary structure of ghostly events, its secondary structure of psychological hallucination, its tertiary structure of absurdity, yet a fourth structure of satire aimed at the Transcendentalists (for that is what Ligeia is, a Transcendental list) and at the two kinds of horror materials to be found in the German and English brands of Gothicism (as certain twisted parallels to *Ivanhoe* suggest).

As to Poe's "intentions" in general, critics until recently have failed to consider with enough care several revealing documents in which Poe discusses his plans for a book-length series of burlesque tales, to be read at the monthly meeting of "The Folio Club." These "Folio Club Tales" (never published as such) included the ostensibly serious tales "Metzengerstein," "MS. Found in a Bottle," "The Assignation," "Berenice," "Morella," "Shadow," "Silence," and very probably "Ligeia." The first seventeen tales Poe published include these eight stories, along with nine obviously comic ones, and seventeen is the number of burlesques Poe mentions in a letter to an editor on September 2, 1836:

> At different times there has appeared in the Messenger a series of Tales, by myself—in all seventeen. They are of a bizarre and generally whimsical character . . . . I have prepared them for republication in book form, in the following manner. I imagine a company of 17 persons who call themselves the Folio Club. . . .

The Folio Club, according to Poe's "Introduction" (extant in manuscript) was a "Junto of *Dunderheadism*," formed on April first, the "settled intention" of which was "to abolish Literature, subvert the Press, and overturn the Government of Nouns and Pronouns." Among its seventeen members (the authors and narrators) were: Mr. Solomon Seadrift (apparently author of "MS. Found in A Bottle"), Mr. Horribile Dictu, with white eyelashes, who had graduated from Göttingen (apparently author of "Metzengerstein"), Mr. Blackwood Blackwood (apparently author of "Loss of Breath"). But even if we grant, for the sake of argument, that "Ligeia" is not a Folio Club tale, we still have a remarkable pattern: *all* of Poe's tales up to "Ligeia" were Folio Club burlesques or else clearly comic and satiric.

V

Of the tales included in this volume, only a half-dozen are comic and satiric in any obvious way. "Loss of Breath" (1832), for example, is a burlesque of "sensationist" and "predicament" stories appearing in *Blackwood's*, with side jabs at Transcendentalism (both German and American), though the tale is not without some grisly scenes of horror. The "predicament" of the narrator: he has lost his breath while cursing his wife. He tries to get along without the faculty of speech that his "loss" engenders by practicing the "Indian" dramas then popular on the American stage, for these plays require only "froglike" tones, looking asquint, showing of teeth, working of knees, shuffling of feet, and other "unmentionable graces which are justly considered the characteristics of a popular performer." While searching for his breath, the hero is beaten, accused of various crimes, hanged, partially dissected, and entombed—all the while conscious of his "sensations." A refinement of this satire on the *Blackwood's* tale appears six years later in the companion stories "How to Write a Blackwood Article" and "A Predicament" (1838), the title of the second being a kind of comment on the first. In "Blackwood Article," the litterateur Mr. Blackwood Blackwood, editor of an influential British journal, advises a Bluestocking litterateur on the publishing situation of the day; and his recommendations constitute Poe's burlesque assessment of the *Blackwood's* formulae, with comments on the "tone didactic," the "tone enthusiastic," the "tone natural," the "tone laconic," the "tone metaphysical," and the "tone elevated, diffusive, and interjectional," in the latter of which the "words must be all in a whirl, like a humming-top, and make a noise very similar, which answers remarkably well instead of meaning . . . the best of all possible styles where the writer is in too great a hurry to think." Blackwood gives the young lady (whose name is either Suky Snobbs or Psyche Zenobia, depending on the precision of one's pronunciation) several "piquant facts for similes" and "piquant expressions" which she is to introduce into her narrative. The companion tale is Miss Snobbs's (or Zenobia's) attempt to write in the *Blackwood's* style, replete with badly garbled versions of Blackwood's expressions. Suky (or Psyche) tells of her "sensations" when her head gets caught in a steeple clock: the clock hand comes down upon her neck while she is looking out of a hole in the clock-face; while she is inextricably caught in this predicament, her head is severed from her body—a circumstance which gives rise to profound thoughts on the nature of "identity."

In "Some Passages from the Life of a Lion" ("Lionizing," 1835), Poe, with indecent sexual innuendo, lampoons the "literati" of America and Great Britain, in particular, the British novelist Edward Bulwer-Lytton and the British patroness of the arts Lady Blessington, along with Thomas Moore (the Irish poet), Francis Jeffrey (the Scots editor of the *Edinburgh Review*), and Nathaniel P. Willis (an American editor). The narrator of the tale, having completed a treatise on "Nosology" is lionized by arty society, and at one point demands of an artist 1,000 pounds for the privilege of portraying his nose on canvas. Later, having been insulted by the men in the group, the hero shoots off the "nose" of a rival in a duel, a circumstance which makes his rival the new lion of the day, pursued ardently by the literary ladies. The thinly disguised motifs of impotence and perversion need little comment as satiric blasts at the litterateurs of his day.

In "Never Bet the Devil Your Head, A Tale with a

Moral" (1841), Poe "answers" the charge that his works are unmoral. Only the "moral" of this tale is a satiric slap at the high moralizing of the Transcendentalists and at their journal, the *Dial*. The shocking conclusion of the tale, wherein the narrator coldly plans to have the body of his friend Toby Dammit dug up for "dog's meat," has been pointed to by some critics as an example of the fierceness and basic uncongeniality of "humor" in Poe. But the tale takes on a different complexion when we see the clues to Dammit's true identity, first blatantly announced in the subtitle and then continued, detective-story-like, in his peculiar mannerisms: even as a youngster he wears moustaches, has a peculiar "style" of enunciation, and is constantly wiggling, leaping, running. The "moral" of the sad tale of Dammit, who prides himself on his nearly transcendental ability to "leap" to great heights, becomes absurdly clear when we see that a "moral tale" is for Poe (who detested works in which a moral overrides the artistry) an *animal* fable in the manner of Aesop and La Fontaine: the comic burlesque of the "dissolute" life of the "immoral" but transcendentally gifted Dammit which culminates in such profound "tragedy" for him becomes even more comically pointed when we see that it is merely the story of a boy and his dog.

"Some Words with a Mummy" (1845) comically presents Poe's dissatisfaction with mobocracy, with the already burgeoning American technology, and with the very concept of "Progress" which had become by 1845 dear to the hearts of his countrymen. An Egyptian noble-man, Count Allamistakeo, is resurrected by means of the Voltaic pile in nineteenth-century America and confronted with modern invention, science, government, and culture. But as the modern nineteenth-century gentlemen who have revived him question him about Egyptian life, they find themselves rather hard put to find areas in which their own culture is superior; increasingly they ignore the implications of Allamistakeo's words, preferring to think him a bit addled. They question him on phrenology, mesmerism, architecture, transportation, mechanics, steam power, metaphysics (from the *Dial*, a "chapter or two about something that is not very clear, but which' the Bostonians call the Great Movement of Progress"), and democracy (some Egyptian provinces had tried it but consolidated into "the most odious and insupportable despotism that was ever heard of upon the face of the earth" —the tyrant *Mob*). Finally, having failed on every count to demonstrate the superiority of nineteenth-century life, even in dress, the Americans confront Allamistakeo with "Ponnonner's lozenges" and "Brandeth's pills." At this, the defeated Egyptian blushes and hangs down his head. The narrator, however, unlike his friends, is more deeply disturbed by the experience, and comments at the end: "The truth is, I am heartily sick of this life and of the nineteenth century in general. I am convinced that everything is going wrong."

These tales are not so often anthologized as the Gothic tales, but they are representative of nearly half of Poe's fiction. Of the more sinister seeming tales included in this volume, "Metzengerstein" (1832) is a good example of a work Poe intended as a satiric parody of the supernatural horror tale, but which became his first Gothic hoax when his readers took the tale seriously. Its extended series of plot ironies, its caricatured fifteen-year-old Gothic villain, its "dunderheaded" Gothic narrator (who at one point praises death by consumption), and its melodramatic style all interweave to form a clear satiric pattern that mocks the few scenes of effective horror that Poe intrudes, as it were, into the satire. Moreover, the working out of an ominous prophecy is comically parodied by a confused curse, which also works out, ironically, in every detail, so that the plot as a whole becomes a kind of cosmic hoax, augmented by man's perverse propensity to act against his own best interests. The series of plot ironies culminates in the climax of the Gothic plot as the fiendish boy-villain rides to a fiery death at the very moment of his apparent triumph over what he considers his deadly enemy—a *horse!*

Poe's second "Gothic" tale, "MS. Found in a Bottle" (1833), on the surface a supernatural adventure story, not only parodies its literary type through blatant absurdities (such as the narrator's dabbing desultorily at a sail with a tar-brush only to discover that he has spelled out *destruction* and *discovery*) but also through an ironic distance between narrator and reader that mocks the narrator's supercilious conception of his unshakable rationality. At the beginning of the tale, the narrator, in a crisp and fact-filled style, insists on his unemotional and rational character. On a simple "Gothic" level, this emphasis seems to confirm the reality of the supernatural events to follow. But Poe immediately subjects his narrator to a terrifying storm; and in contrast to the stoicism of an old sailor whom he contemptuously calls "superstitious," the narrator himself becomes increasingly frenzied, and his style of narration highly cadenced and emotional. The machinations of fortune ironically preserve him from death at the very moment of apparent destruction by throwing him high into the air and into the rigging of a gigantic phantom ship, which we subsequently learn has been growing in the South Seas water like a living thing. The rest of the tale, in which the phantom ship with its silent statue-like crew sails into an opening at the pole and goes "down," is rendered with an atmosphere of dreaminess that, combined with the narrator's proven untrustworthiness, suggests that the incredible events are the delusion of a man driven mad. Seen as a voyage of "discovery," the ludicrous "supernatural" events act as a grotesquerie of the discovery of what lies beyond the normal world or beyond death, for the tale abruptly ends at the very verge of revelation in apparent final destruction and silence. Just as Arthur Gordon Pym journeys toward the great discovery of what lies "Beyond" only to find the white blankness of Nothingness, so the caricatured narrator of "MS. Found in a Bottle" discovers Nothing.

In "The Assignation" (1834), it is the perverse fortune of the laughing and crying Byronic stranger to become united with his beloved only in death. The tale has seemed to most critics one of Poe's most intensely "Romantic" productions. But under its Romantic surface is presented a coded satiric allegory of burlesque parallels and contrasts to Lord Byron's intrigue with the Countess Guiccioli, to Thomas Moore's adulatory account of his visit to Byron's Venice apartment in 1819, and to Moore's edition of Byron's letters in 1830. The cream of the jest and salient clue to the satiric hoax lies in an outrageous pun: "To die laughing," the mysterious Byronic stranger remarks to the narrator, "must be the most glorious of all glorious deaths! Sir Thomas More—a very fine man was Sir Thomas More—Sir Thomas More died laughing, you remember." The thrice-repeated name of the decapitated Sir Thomas More has no other function in the tale than to act as a pun on the name of the Romantic poet Tom Moore (whom Poe here subjects to satiric decapitation).

The fusion of the satiric and the sinister in the tale (characterized indirectly by the narrator himself as a "mingled tone of levity and solemnity," along with an excess of exclamation points, "ineffables," tear-stained pages, and submerged satiric puns) is imaged several times in the story: in the altar to laughter (the *only* monument to have survived in ancient Sparta); in the grinning masks at Persepolis (out of the eyes of which, however, adders writhe); in the comic incongruity of the furnishings of the Byronic stranger's apartment (with its gigantic paintings and fragile glassware); and in the fiery "arabesque" censers lighting his apartment. Like the censers' flames, his spirit, the Byronic stranger says, is "writhing in fire," a phrase which not only suggests his torment but also picks up the image of the writhing adders in the grinning masks at Persepolis. The tale is *both* a Romantic tale of dark passion *and* a burlesque. The imagery of dreams and the delirium of a spirit writhing in fire, combined with the satiric allegory, the altar to laughter, the melodramatic death, the death-jest and pun, and the writhing adders and grinning masks all together make "The Assignation" itself an emblem of the serio-comic, ironic ambivalence of Poe's "Gothic" fiction.

In "Berenice" (1835), another "serious" tale of compulsion which actually lampoons its literary type, it is the absurd obsession of the narrator with Berenice's *teeth* which leads to his grief, an obsession resulting from a temper of mind engendered by his grotesque birth and rearing. It has been his perverse misfortune to have been both born and brought up in his mother's *library*, and thus he has become totally imbued with the Gothic horrors and weird philosophical (Transcendental) mysticism of the day. "Shadow" (1835) and "Silence" (1837), under their seemingly mystic and intensely "poetic" surfaces, seem in substance and style to be parodies of pseudopoetic transcendental fictions, especially those of Bulwer-Lytton, De Quincey, and the other "psychological autobiographists" (perhaps including Emerson) indicated in Poe's subtitle to "Silence." "Shadow," after developing a sense of the finality of death concludes with an ironic turn in which the chilling *immortality* of the "shadows" of the narrator's friends is revealed to him though, since he and his companions are dead drunk, it is hard to tell how truly revealing the transcendental "sleep-waking" revelation is. "Silence" develops the theme of a deceptive and illusory world, with shrieking water-lilies, lowing

hippopotami, and graven rocks whose letters change. At
the end, a Demon laughs hysterically at a confused human
being, while a lynx stares steadily at the Demon's face.
That the lynx is a symbol of the ironic vision peering
unflinchingly into the face of perversity is suggested by
Poe's lynx metaphor in *Marginalia* (a series of brief
"filler" notes Poe printed in journals he edited in the
1840s), though the meaning of the lynx is only vaguely
felt in the satiric "confusion" of the tale. Poe writes in
Marginalia that "it is only the philosophical lynx-eye that,
through the indignity-mist of Man's life, can still discern
the dignity of man." These, then, are the "Gothic" tales,
published in the *Southern Literary Messenger* from 1835
to 1837, that Poe apparently intended to include in the
burlesque Folio Club series, tales that Poe considered
of a "bizarre and generally whimsical character."

Between 1838 and 1840, the middle years of his career,
Poe published three of his most famous Gothic stories:
"Ligeia," which we have already discussed, "The Fall
of the House of Usher," and "William Wilson." Like
"Ligeia," the other two tales involve "doubles" and
dramatize a weird universe as perceived by a subjective
mind. "Usher," despite the supernatural atmosphere, can
be read as the tale of the frenzied fantasies of *both* the
narrator and Usher, fantasies engendered by a vague fear
that something ominous *may* happen and by the disconnected, alien environment. The overriding theme is the
mechanism of fear itself, which has perversely operated
on Roderick Usher before the narrator arrives, and which
operates on the narrator *through* Usher afterwards. When
the narrator rides his horse up to the House of Usher
and gazes at its leaden-eyed aspect and at the tarn, with
its sickly white stems of dead plants sticking up through
the stagnant water, he is immediately seized by a vague
apprehension. Later in the tale, he remarks that the
"mental disorder" and "hysteria" of his friend Roderick

Usher "terrified" and "infected" him: "I felt creeping upon me, by slow yet certain degrees, the wild influences of his own fantastic yet impressive superstitions." The narrator's confrontation with (and submission to) a mind gone mad is imaged in the facelike appearance of the House itself, with its leaden-hued eyelike windows and its zigzag crack down the middle, and in the wild "arabesque" face of Roderick Usher. The poem "The Haunted Palace," which Usher has composed, is also a symbolic, indeed allegorical, portrait of a facelike structure. The "face" of the palace changes when the "Monarch Thought" topples from his throne within, and the palace comes to resemble the face of Usher and his House as the narrator has described them. Moreover, when the narrator first looks down into the tarn, what he should see of course is his own face since he is on its very brink, but instead he sees the inverted image of the "face" of the House of Usher. His next action is to go inside and meet Usher face to face. Immediately, his attention is arrested by certain details of Usher's face; though he does not articulate the resemblances, as such, the narrator so describes the weblike hair of Usher that we are compelled to remember the webwork of fungi about the eaves of the House.

By the time the narrator "sees" the "return" of Madeline Usher from her grave, the themes of narcissism and inversion are so clear that the relevance of the absurdist interlude, "The Mad Trist of Sir Lancelot Canning" to the story as a whole (that is, to the dramatic situation of the narrator rather than merely to Roderick's "trist" with his twin sister) is obvious. The tale is the story of the "mad trist" of the twin, hysterical personalities of the narrator and Usher. Finally, we do not know for sure *what* has happened for, as our narrator flees "aghast" from the scene, the face of the House splits apart and sinks into that tarn which first merged the images of the faces of both the House and the narrator. The tale has long been hailed as a masterpiece of Gothic horror; it is also a masterpiece of dramatic irony and structural symbolism.

"William Wilson" (1839), though lacking the complexity of "Ligeia" and "Usher," exhibits Poe's continuing use not only of the double but also of double perspective. Although apparently a straight Romantic tale of a man's confrontation, supernaturally, with his own soul, the tale can be read as the delusive but perversely persistent confrontation of a guilt-ridden mind with itself. Whether the second Wilson, twin of the narrator, exists as a supernatural spirit or as a construct of the mind of the narrator remains ambiguous, as in other Poe tales, though the clues for a double reading are carefully planted. Again, the world that we perceive as readers is what is filtered through the subjective mind of the narrator, and it is this structure, along with some absurdist motifs (such as the precise timing of the second Wilson's entrances and his recurrent whisper), that gives rise to the dramatic irony of the tale. Certainly, if the second Wilson is the product of the imagination of the first Wilson, the first Wilson's behavior must seem to his companions, if not comic, very *peculiar* indeed.

Poe's "serious" tales, clearly, are only apparently serious in the manner that they purport to be. The whole of Poe's Gothic fiction can be read not only as an ambivalent parody of the world of Gothic horror tales, but also as an extended grotesquerie of the human condition. Nothing quite works out for his heroes, even though they sometimes make superhuman efforts, and even though they are occasionally rescued from their predicaments. They undergo extended series of ironic reverses in fictional structures so ironically twisted that the form itself, even the very plot, approaches an absurd hoax perpetrated on the characters. The universe created in Poe's fiction is one in which the human mind tries vainly to perceive order and meaning. The universe is deceptive; its basic mode seems almost to be a constant shifting of appearances; reality is a flux variously interpreted, or even created, by the individual human mind. In its deceptiveness, the universe of Poe's Gothic fiction seems not so much malevolent as mocking or "perverse." The universe is much like a gigantic hoax that God has played on man, an idea which is the major undercurrent of Poe's essay on the universe, *Eureka*. Thus, the hoaxlike irony of Poe's technique has its parallel in the dramatic world in which his characters move.

The ultimate irony of this universe, however, is the "perversity" of man's own mind. The mind, and the mind only, seems to sustain Poe's heroes in their most desperate predicaments; yet in an instant the mind is capable of slipping into confusion, hysteria, madness— even while it seems most rational. From a more "Gothicist" point of view, Edward H. Davidson, without using the term *irony*, and without reading Poe's Gothic tales ironically or satirically, comes to much the same conclusion regarding Poe's universe. "Poe's nightmare universe," Davidson writes, "is one in which . . . people . . . are condemned to live as if they are in some long aftertime of belief and morality." The evil-doer is driven by "some maggot in the brain" that leaves him a kind of "moral freak" in a universe that also has some fantastic defect in it. In Poe's universe, Davidson suggests, evil and suffering are "the capacity and measure of man to feel and to know"; pain is the basis of life, and death is the only release from his "grotesque condition of 'perversity.'"

This view of Poe's "perverse" universe is, I think, essentially correct. Poe's fiction developed from a basically satiric mode into an ironic mode in which a tragic response to the perversities of fortune and to the treacheries of one's own mind is contrasted by a near-comic perception of the absurdity of man's condition in the universe.

Such a double perception, according to the German
Ironists, leads, through art, to a momentary transcendence
of the dark chaos of the universe. If the artist (and
through him the reader) can mock man's absurd condition at the same time that he feels it deeply, he transcends
earthly or finite limits in an artistic paralleling of God's
infinite perception. In Poe, however, such transcendence
is always at the expense of the less perceptive mind. Poe
plays a constant intellectual game with his readers; he
tries to draw the reader into the "Gothic" world of the
mind, but he is ready at any moment to mock the
simplistic Gothic vision (under the trappings of which
Poe saw man's real estrangement and isolation) that con-
temporary readers insisted on in the popular magazines.

VI

Of Poe's remaining fiction, nearly half (nineteen short
tales out of forty-two) are clearly comic; the twenty-three
Gothic and "philosophical" works, along with the novel
Pym, further extend the central theme of the subjective
deceptiveness of the world in terms of Nothingness and the
"perverse." "The Man of the Crowd" (1840), on the surface a tale of a lonely city wanderer, who is weirdly suggestive of what Hawthorne called the Outcast of the Universe (in his own dark "comedy," "Wakefeld"), may be
read also as the deluded romanticizing of the tipsy narrator, who perversely attributes a Romantic significance to
an old drunk who wanders from bistro to bistro. In "A
Descent Into the Maelström" (1841), Poe emphasizes
the traditional Western themes of transcendence from a
petty involvement with "self" and the need for submission to the larger design of Nature. Giving up all
sense of mere individual importance, the narrator feels a
positive *wish* to see what lies at the bottom of the whirlpool. Although he survives (probably by mere accident
rather than by his careful observation of and submission to

Nature, since the mechanics of the hydraulic effect on geometric forms is false), his incomplete confrontation with Nothingness at the center of the whirlpool (a "manifestation of God's power") yet turns his hair prematurely white. Thus the tale ironically inverts traditional Western belief: the narrator's mystical experience of the magnificence of God is one of horror rather than of beatitude.

"The Oval Portrait" (1842), a tale about the transfer of life from a living person to a painting, has a carefully constructed dramatic and ironic frame around it, so that the tale can also read as the dream of a man delirious from pain and lack of sleep. "The Masque of The Red Death" (1842), a tale of the supernatural visitation of Death himself, can also be read as a tone poem about hysteria, engendered by mood and setting, with a sarcastic concluding echo from Pope's *Dunciad*. Prince Prospero's sinister stronghold, of course, contrasts directly with the enchanted island of his namesake, Prospero, the magician in Shakespeare's *The Tempest*. The ironic theme of Poe's tale focuses on the grimly perverse joke of Prospero's having walled *in* death in a frenetic attempt to wall it out.

"The Pit and the Pendulum" (1842) is one of Poe's clearest dramatizations of the futile efforts of man's will to survive the malevolent perversity of the world and to make order out of chaos. The tale has sometimes been read as the escape from madness through a descent into madness. Although the hero is mentally tortured until he confesses to himself that "all is madness" and that his mind has been "nearly annihilated," he learns to rely on *primal* cunning, and an *instinctive* sense of danger. Under the razor-edge of the pendulum, he recovers his ratiocinative power: "for the first time during many hours—or perhaps days—I thought." But the narrator thinks of his avoidance of the pit as: "the merest of accidents, and I knew that surprise, or entrapment into torment, formed an important portion of all the grotesquerie of these dungeon deaths." Under the pendulum he becomes "frantically mad" and strains to force himself against the slowly descending blade. The irony, the grotesquerie of human dignity and rationality, here lies in the narrator's ultimately futile efforts to change his basic condition. He cannot hurry destruction and thus avoid the torment allotted to him. His mind suffers another radical shock and, ironically, his mind hysterically shifts to an opposite mode, moving toward the rational only because of his helplessness in madness (which is a clear rationale for the insanity of Poe's murders—to *survive* is man's only duty). Then, escaping from the pendulum, he is, ironically, again faced with the pit. The walls become heated, and for "a wild moment" the narrator's mind "refused to comprehend," although at length he says "it burned itself in upon my shuddering reason." Thinking of the cooling waters of the pit he rushes to its edge, only to stop short, again in horror of such a death. Then as the walls begin to close in, he realizes that he had been destined by his tormentors for the pit in the first place and that all his luck, all his cunning, and all his rgeained rationality have, ironically, trapped him into self-torment and increased his agony. The final irony comes with the sudden cessation of the movement of the walls, a rescue from outside that comes unexpectedly, independently, unconnected with his own personal fate at the last moment of his despair and defeat.

"The Tell-Tale Heart" (1843), a study in obsessive paranoia, is yet another story of the mind watching itself disintegrate under the stresses of delusion in an alienated world. It is the perverse fortune of the narrator to become fearful of the grotesque eye of a kindly old man, whom he says he loves. With a double perversity, he gives himself away to the police at the moment of success. Yet the narrator is caught in a weird world in which he loves the old man yet displays no real emotion toward him, in which he cannot let the "beloved" old man live and yet cannot kill him without remorse, in which he cannot expose his crime and yet must do so. Perhaps the final irony is that the apparent beating of his own heart which he mistakes as, first, the beating of the still-living heart of the old man, and which, second, seems to be an emblem of his own guilt (and which, finally, compels him to confess), may very well be initially the peculiar thumping sound of the wood-beetles gnawing at the walls. "The Black Cat" (1843) carries the same themes further and details more clearly the irrational desire, almost the ultimate irony, to act against oneself, with an ambiguous conclusion suggesting the agency of malevolent fortune at the same time that it suggests subconscious self-punishment. The major absurdist irony, perhaps, is that the murder which the narrator commits is the result of subconscious remorse over the *cat* he has previously mistreated. "A Tale of the Ragged Mountains" (1844), ostensibly a story of metempsychosis, is more probably a murder story in which all the characters (and possibly the murderer) are duped regarding the reality of events. The physician, Templeton, obsessively (though perhaps unconsciously) reenacts the murder of his friend Oldeb years before and (unwittingly perhaps) takes another life. Moreover, the tale has a number of twisted parallels to Charles Brockden Brown's *Edgar Huntley* (1799) which suggest a burlesque undercurrent to the hoaxlike "mystery" of the story.

"The Imp of the Perverse" (1845), seemingly more an essay than a tale, is a dark comedy of errors which clearly spells out Poe's fundamental conception that it is man's fate to act against his own best interests. But the dissertation on perversity has its dramatic irony, for the "rationality" of the narrator merely enmeshes him deeper in anxiety as he absurdly, helplessly, uses his imaginative intellect to will his own destruction by means of a mere whimsical thought. Having committed murder he reflects that he is "safe"—unless, of course, he be fool enough to confess. This foolish fancy immediately seizes him and he rushes out to confess his crime to passersby in the street. The recurrent confessional structure of other of Poe's tales is an operative factor here too, for the narrator has apparently confessed to a priest in his cell the night before his impending execution. In an attempt to explain his obsession with the possibility that some "Imp" in the structure of the universe has victimized him, the narrator succeeds in convincing us not of his rationality but of his irrationality. The long prologue in its "circumlocution" does not directly make his point but instead seems to obscure the more direct and succinct conclusions. But the point of this circumlocutious inventiveness becomes clear when the narrator finally reveals to us his anxiety about his execution; his imagination immediately foresees additional possibilities for perverse speculation: in death he will be free of his physical chains and his cell—but what new torments yet await him, he wonders, in what afterlife?

"The Facts in The Case of M. Valdemar" (1845), purportedly a serious Gothic tale of the horror of prolonging life beyond the proper point of death, not only was a hoax in the sense of fraudulent literal fact (it was taken for a time to be an actual case history), but also contains absurd comic details suggestive of Poe's intensely mocking attitude. For one thing, if we look closely at the details he gives us, we find that three-quarters of Valdemar's lungs has turned to bone! And what is left is a mass of adhesions and holes. Despite this rather extreme condition (and he also has an aneurism), Valdemar is sitting up writing. His literary efforts suggest an ironic doubleness as the underlying vision of the tale, for he has been translating on the one hand an heroic drama of Schiller and on the other a mock-heroic burlesque from Rabelais. Valdemar's very appearance suggests a symbolic doubleness—his black beard contrasts with his white hair: emblematic clues to the double-edged quality of the tale. Finally, after Valdemar's "life" has been preserved by modern "technology" (in this case, mesmerism), the last horrible details suggest the real, grisly finality of Death.

Two other darker tales of the late 'forties have similar "comic" undercurrents. "The Sphinx" (1846), comes quickly to a comic conclusion after a frightening and weird (but absurdly deceptive) vision of a monster that turns out to be a bug dangling only a fraction of an inch from the eye. "Hop-Frog" (1849) is a compellingly ludicrous tale of horrible revenge told almost sweetly in a fairy-tale style, at the conclusion of which the dwarf declares to the burning King and his ministers that their death is but his last "jest."

Poe's six ratiocinative tales of the 1840s represent the few successes of the acute mind in overcoming the bewildering deceptiveness of the perverse world. Five of the tales are ostensibly serious ("Murders in the Rue Morgue," "Marie Roget," "The Purloined Letter," "Goldbug," "Descent into the Maelström") and one is comic and suggests self-parody (" 'Thou Art the Man' "). The Dupin kind of mentality assumes a godlike omniscience, the "I" and the reader, the role of dull-witted dupes. The major ironies of these tales are consistent with Poe's more clearly Gothic tales: their basis is the discrepancy between appearance and actuality; and the ease of Dupin's solutions contrasts with our mystification.

The same concern with illusion, transitoriness, and death, and with absurd purpose and purposelessness, is to be found in the remainder of Poe's fiction. The four poetic "landscapes" (not included here), "Island of the Fay" (1844), "Landscape Garden" (1842), "Arnheim" (1847), and "Landor's Cottage" (1849), supposedly deal with the natural beauty God has created in the world but insinuate the melancholy facts of death, imperfection, purposelessness in contrast to man's futile imagining of an ideal state of harmony and beauty. Four philosophical dialogs, with and among bodiless spirits, including "The Colloquy of Monos and Una" (1841), follow the same pattern of asserting some mystical meaning inherent in existence while quietly undercutting the assertion. "The Colloquy of Monos and Una," like others of the "serious" tales, has the pattern of a detective story. Seemingly a "loving" and affirmative dialog between two disembodied Platonic "spirits" beyond death, this dialog, we are gradually compelled to see, takes place in the grave. The major subjects of the tale, time, consciousness, and corporeality, come together in a chilly ironic revelation of what is Beyond: the merging of the body with the elements in the slow process of decay, while the spirit is, all the while, *aware* of this decay as its own energy fades away to a mere "glow" and silence—a chilling conception of afterlife indeed.

Poe's concept of the "perverse" functioning as both a world view and a psychology is perhaps the ultimate grotesquerie to be found in his Gothic fiction. Poe's characters live in a cosmos in which there are few certainties beyond that of individual annihilation. In a deceptive universe that does not provide for individual immortality, Poe's heroes and heroines vainly struggle to find order and to preserve their lives. Yet they are at the same time fascinated with death as the ultimate fact of existence, and they perversely yearn for knowledge of the secret that lies beyond death. But in Poe's universe, there is nothing beyond death, nothing beyond this "life."

In a sense, the true horror, the true *Gothic* quality, of Poe's tales lies in their substantive irony, for Poe's tales are more than ironic in mode, more than supercilious hoaxes perpetrated on the unsuspecting devotees of the

Gothic romance, though such mockery certainly looms large. The insinuated burlesque, the ironic modes of language, and the ironic themes merge with ironies of plot and characterization in the creation of an absurd universe.

Poe's career is the history of his simultaneous exploration of the fearful and the ridiculous. This is not to deny the obsessive quality of his principal concerns. But his obsessive subjects and themes—the primal fact of death, the perverse fascination of death, the appalling possibility of complete annihilation into an ultimate Nothingness, the perverse mockery of fate, the horror of the inhuman and the dehumanized—and even the symbolization of subconscious feelings and the dramatization of a mind watching itself go to pieces—are indeed all done up, as more than one critic has suggested, in purple rhetoric, with ludicrous stage-Gothic decor, and with absurd interludes—but for a purpose.

In an attempt to suggest the depth and complexity of that purpose, the present anthology includes works which represent the range of Poe's imagination, from the best of his comic and satiric works to the best of his Gothic works. Unfortunately a few (though very few) of the famous Gothic tales have been excluded in preference for some of the much underrated satiric pieces. But the fundamental ironic and skeptical consistency informing the seemingly diverse performance collected here is a remarkable literary achievement—perhaps one of the most remarkable of the nineteenth century.

Washington State University
October, 1969

I

POEMS

DREAMS

Oh! that my young life were a lasting dream!
My spirit not awak'ning till the beam
Of an Eternity should bring the morrow:
Yes! tho' that long dream were of hopeless sorrow,
'Twere better than the dull reality
Of waking life to him whose heart shall be,
And hath been ever, on the chilly earth,
A chaos of deep passion from his birth!

But should it be—that dream eternally
Continuing—as dreams have been to me
In my young boyhood—should it thus be given,
'Twere folly still to hope for higher Heaven!
For I have revell'd, when the sun was bright
 In the summer sky; in dreamy fields of light,
And left unheedingly my very heart
In climes of mine imagining—apart
From mine own home, with beings that have been
Of mine own thought—what more could I have seen?

'Twas once and *only* once and the wild hour
From my remembrance shall not pass—some power
Or spell had bound me—'twas the chilly wind
Came o'er me in the night and left behind
Its image on my spirit, or the moon
Shone on my slumbers in her lofty noon
Too coldly—or the stars—howe'er it was
That dream was as that night wind—let it pass.

I have been happy—tho' but in a dream.
I have been happy—and I love the theme—
Dreams! in their vivid colouring of life—
As in that fleeting, shadowy, misty strife

Of semblance with reality which brings
To the delirious eye more lovely things
Of Paradise and Love—and all our own!
Than young Hope in his sunniest hour hath known.

[1827, 1828]

SPIRITS OF THE DEAD

I

Thy soul shall find itself alone
'Mid dark thoughts of the gray tomb-stone—
Not one, of all the crowd, to pry
Into thine hour of secrecy:

II

Be silent in that solitude,
   Which is not loneliness—for then
The spirits of the dead who stood
   In life before thee are again
In death around thee—and their will
Shall overshadow thee: be still.

III

The night—tho' clear—shall frown—
And the stars shall look not down,
From their high thrones in the heaven,
With light like Hope to mortals given—
But their red orbs, without beam,
To thy weariness shall seem
As a burning and a fever
Which would cling to thee for ever.

IV

Now are thoughts thou shalt not banish—
Now are visions ne'er to vanish—
From thy spirit shall they pass
No more—like dew-drop from the grass.

v

The breeze—the breath of God—is still—
And the mist upon the hill
Shadowy—shadowy—yet unbroken,
Is a symbol and a token—
How it hangs upon the trees,
A mystery of mysteries!—

[1827, 1839]

EVENING STAR

'Twas noontide of summer,
   And mid-time of night;
And stars, in their orbits,
   Shone pale, thro' the light
Of the brighter, cold moon,
   'Mid planets her slaves,
Herself in the Heavens,
   Her beam on the waves.
   I gaz'd awhile
   On her cold smile;
Too cold—too cold for me—
   There pass'd, as a shroud,
   A fleecy cloud,
And I turn'd away to thee,
   Proud Evening Star,
   In thy glory afar,
And dearer thy beam shall be;
   For joy to my heart
   Is the proud part
Thou bearest in Heav'n at night,
   And more I admire
   Thy distant fire,
Than that colder, lowly light.

[1827]

A DREAM WITHIN A DREAM

Take this kiss upon the brow!
And, in parting from you now,
Thus much let me avow—
You are not wrong, who deem
That my days have been a dream;
Yet if hope has flown away
In a night, or in a day,
In a vision, or in none,
Is it therefore the less *gone?*
All that we see or seem
Is but a dream within a dream.

I stand amid the roar
Of a surf-tormented shore,
And I hold within my hand
Grains of the golden sand—
How few! yet how they creep
Through my fingers to the deep,
While I weep—while I weep!
O God! can I not grasp
Them with a tighter clasp?
O God! can I not save
One from the pitiless wave?
Is *all* that we see or seem
But a dream within a dream?

[1827–1849]

STANZAS

How often we forget all time, when lone
Admiring Nature's universal throne;
Her woods—her wilds—her mountains—the intense
Reply of HERS to OUR intelligence!

1

In youth have I known one with whom the Earth
In secret communing held—as he with it,
In day light, and in beauty from his birth:
Whose fervid, flick'ring torch of life was lit
From the sun and stars, whence he had drawn forth
A passionate light—such for his spirit was fit—
And yet that spirit knew not—in the hour
Of its own fervor—what had o'er it power.

2

Perhaps it may be that my mind is wrought
To a ferver by the moon beam that hangs o'er,
But I will half believe that wild light fraught
With more of sov'reignty than ancient lore
Hath ever told—or is it of a thought
The unembodied essence, ånd no more
That with a quick'ning spell doth o'er us pass
As dew of the night-time, o'er the summer grass?

3

Doth o'er us pass, when, as th' expanding eye
To the loved object—so the tear to the lid
Will start, which lately slept in apathy?
And yet it need not be—(that object) hid
From us in life—but common—which doth lie
Each hour before us—but *then* only bid
With a strange sound, as of a harp-string broken
T'awake us—'Tis a symbol and a token,

4

Of what in other worlds shall be—and giv'n
In beauty by our God, to those alone
Who otherwise would fall from life and Heav'n
Drawn by their heart's passion, and that tone,
That high tone of the spirit which hath striv'n
Tho' not with Faith—with godliness—whose throne

With desp'rate energy 't hath beaten down;
Wearing its own deep feeling as a crown.

[1827]

A DREAM

In visions of the dark night
  I have dreamed of joy departed—
But a waking dream of life and light
  Hath left me broken-hearted.

Ah! what is not a dream by day
  To him whose eyes are cast
On things around him with a ray
  Turned back upon the past?

That holy dream—that holy dream,
  While all the world were chiding,
Hath cheered me as a lovely beam
  A lonely spirit guiding.

What though that light, thro' storm and night,
  So trembled from afar—
What could there be more purely bright
  In Truth's day-star?   [1827–1845]

THE HAPPIEST DAY

The happiest day—the happiest hour
  My sear'd and blighted heart hath known,
The highest hope of pride, and power,
  I feel hath flown.

Of power! said I? Yes! such I ween
  But they have vanish'd long alas!
The visions of my youth have been—
  But let them pass.

And, pride, what have I now with thee?
An other brow may ev'n inherit
The venom thou hast pour'd on me—
   Be still my spirit.

The happiest day—the happiest hour
   Mine eyes shall see—have ever seen
The brightest glance of pride and power
   I feel—have been:

But were that hope of pride and power
   Now offer'd, with the pain
Ev'n *then* I felt—that brightest hour
   I would not live again:

For on its wing was dark alloy
   And as it flutter'd—fell
An essence—powerful to destroy
   A soul that knew it well.   [1827]

THE LAKE—TO——

In spring of youth it was my lot
To haunt of the wide world a spot
The which I could not love the less—
So lovely was the loneliness
Of a wild lake, with black rock bound,
And the tall pines that towered around.

But when the Night had thrown her pall
Upon that spot, as upon all,
And the mystic wind went by
Murmuring in melody—
Then—ah then I would awake
To the terror of the lone lake.

Yet that terror was not fright,
But a tremulous delight—

A feeling not the jewelled mine
Could teach or bribe me to define—
Nor Love—although the Love were thine.

Death was in that poisonous wave,
And in its gulf a fitting grave
For him who thence could solace bring
To his lone imagining—
Whose solitary soul could make
An Eden of that dim lake.

[1827, 1845]

SONNET—TO SCIENCE

Science! true daughter of Old Time thou art!
    Who alterest all things with thy peering eyes.
Why preyest thou thus upon the poet's heart,
    Vulture, whose wings are dull realities?
How should he love thee? or how deem thee wise,
    Who wouldst not leave him in his wandering
To seek for treasure in the jewelled skies,
    Albeit he soared with an undaunted wing?
Hast thou not dragged Diana from her car?
    And driven the Hamadryad from the wood
To seek a shelter in some happier star?
    Hast thou not torn the Naiad from her flood,
The Elfin from the green grass, and from me
The summer dream beneath the tamarind tree?

[1829, 1845]

TO—

The bowers whereat, in dreams, I see
    The wantonest singing birds,

Are lips—and all thy melody
   Of lip-begotten words—

Thine eyes, in Heaven of heart enshrined
   Then desolately fall,
O God! on my funereal mind
   Like starlight on a pall—

Thy heart—*thy* heart!—I wake and sigh,
   And sleep to dream till day
Of the truth that gold can never buy—
   Of the baubles that it may.

                            [1829, 1845]

FAIRY-LAND

Dim vales—and shadowy floods—
And cloudy-looking woods,
Whose forms we can't discover
For the tears that drip all over.
Huge moons there wax and wane—
Again—again—again—
Every moment of the night—
Forever changing places—
And they put out the star-light
With the breath from their pale faces.
About twelve by the moon-dial
One more filmy than the rest
(A kind which, upon trial,
They have found to be the best)
Comes down—still down—and down
With its centre on the crown
Of a mountain's eminence,
While its wide circumference
In easy drapery falls
Over hamlets, over halls,
Wherever they may be—
O'er the strange woods—o'er the sea—

Over spirits on the wing—
Over every drowsy thing—
And buries them up quite
In a labyrinth of light—
And then, how deep!—O, deep!
Is the passion of their sleep.
In the morning they arise,
And their moony covering
Is soaring in the skies,
With the tempests as they toss,
Like—almost any thing—
Or a yellow Albatross.
They use that moon no more
For the same end as before—
Videlicet a tent—
Which I think extravagant:
Its atomies, however,
Into a shower dissever,
Of which those butterflies,
Of Earth, who seek the skies,
And so come down again
(Never-contented things!)
Have brought a specimen
Upon their quivering wings.

[1829, 1845]

INTRODUCTION

Romance, who loves to nod and sing,
With drowsy head and folded wing,
Among the green leaves as they shake
Far down within some shadowy lake,
To me a painted paroquet
Hath been—a most familiar bird—
Taught me my alphabet to say—
To lisp my very earliest word
While in the wild-wood I did lie
A child—with a most knowing eye.

Succeeding years, too wild for song,
Then roll'd like tropic storms along,
Where, tho' the garish lights that fly
Dying along the troubled sky,
Lay bare, thro' vistas thunder-riven,
The blackness of the general Heaven,
That very blackness yet doth fling
Light on the lightning's silver wing.

For, being an idle boy lang syne,
Who read Anacreon, and drank wine,
I early found Anacreon rhymes
Were almost passionate sometimes—
And by strange alchemy of brain
His pleasures always turn'd to pain—
His naivete to wild desire—
His wit to love—his wine to fire—
And so, being young and dipt in folly
I fell in love with melancholy,
And used to throw my earthly rest
And quiet all away in jest—
I could not love except where Death
Was mingling his with Beauty's breath—
Or Hymen, Time, and Destiny
Were stalking between her and me.

O, then the eternal Condor years
So shook the very Heavens on high,
With tumult as they thunder'd by;
I had no time for idle cares,
Thro' gazing on the unquiet sky!
Or if an hour with calmer wing
Its down did on my spirit fling,
That little hour with lyre and rhyme
To while away—forbidden thing!
My heart half fear'd to be a crime
Unless it trembled with the string.

But *now* my soul hath too much room—
Gone are the glory and the gloom—

The black hath mellow'd into grey,
And all the fires are fading away.

My draught of passion hath been deep—
I revell'd, and I now would sleep—
And after-drunkenness of soul
Succeeds the glories of the bowl—
An idle longing night and day
To dream my very life away:

But dreams—of those who dream as I,
Aspiringly, are damned, and die:
Yet should I swear I mean alone,
By notes so very shrilly blown,
To break upon Time's monotone,
While yet my vapid joy and grief
Are tintless of the yellow leaf—
Why not an imp the greybeard hath,
Will shake his shadow in my path—
And even the greybeard will o'erlook
Connivingly my dreaming-book.

[1829–1831]

ALONE

From childhood's hour I have not been
As others were—I have not seen
As others saw—I could not bring
My passions from a common spring—
From the same source I have not taken
My sorrow—I could not awaken
My heart to joy at the same tone—
And all I lov'd—I lov'd alone—
Then—in my childhood—in the dawn
Of a most stormy life—was drawn
From ev'ry depth of good and ill
The mystery which binds me still—

From the torrent, or the fountain—
From the red cliff of the mountain—
From the sun that 'round me roll'd
In its autumn tint of gold—
From the lightning in the sky
As it pass'd me flying by—
From the thunder, and the storm—
And the cloud that took the form
(When the rest of Heaven was blue)
Of a demon in my view—

[1829]

TO HELEN

Helen, thy beauty is to me
   Like those Nicéan barks of yore,
That gently, o'er a perfumed sea,
   The weary, way-worn wanderer bore
   To his own native shore.

On desperate seas long wont to roam,
   Thy hyacinth hair, thy classic face,
Thy Naiad airs have brought me home
   To the glory that was Greece,
And the grandeur that was Rome.

Lo! in yon brilliant window-niche
   How statue-like I see thee stand,
   The agate lamp within thy hand!
Ah, Psyche, from the regions which
   Are Holy-Land!

[1831, 1845]

ISRAFEL

And the angel Israfel, whose heart-strings are a lute, who has the sweetest voice of all God's creatures.—KORAN.

In Heaven a spirit doth dwell
  "Whose heart-strings are a lute;"
None sing so wildly well
As the angel Israfel,
And the giddy stars (so legends tell)
Ceasing their hymns attend the spell
  Of his voice all mute.

Tottering above
  In her highest noon,
  The enamoured moon
Blushes with love,
  While, to listen, the red levin
  (With the rapid Pleiads, even,
  Which were seven,
  Pauses in Heaven.

And they say (the starry choir
  And the other listening things)
That Israfeli's fire
Is owing to that lyre
  By which he sits and sings—
The trembling living wire
Of those unusual strings.

But the skies that angel trod,
  Where deep thoughts are a duty—
Where Love's a grown-up God—
  Where the Houri glances are—
Imbued with all the beauty
  Which we worship in yon star.

Therefore, thou art not wrong
   Israfeli, who despisest
An unimpassioned song;
To thee the laurels belong,
   Best bard, because the wisest!
Merrily live, and long!

The ecstacies above
   With thy burning measures suit—
Thy grief, thy joy, thy hate, thy love
   With the fervour of thy lute—
Well may the stars be mute!

Yes, Heaven is thine: but this
   Is a world of sweets and sours;
   Our flowers are merely—flowers,
And the shadow of thy perfect bliss
   Is the sunshine of ours.

If I did dwell
Where Israfel
   Hath dwelt, and he where I,
He might not sing so wildly well—
   A mortal melody,
One half as passionately,
While a bolder note than his might swell
From my lyre within the sky.

                        [1831–1845]

THE CITY IN THE SEA

Lo! Death has reared himself a throne
In a strange city lying alone
Far down within the dim West,
Where the good and the bad and the worst and the best
Have gone to their eternal rest.
There shrines and palaces and towers
 (Time-eaten towers that tremble not!)

Resemble nothing that is ours.
Around, by lifting winds forgot,
Resignedly beneath the sky
The melancholy waters lie.

No rays from the holy heaven come down
On the long night-time of that town;
But light from out the lurid sea
Streams up the turrets silently—
Gleams up the pinnacles far and free
Up domes—up spires—up kingly halls—
Up fanes—up Babylon-like walls—
Up shadowy long-forgotten bowers
Of sculptured ivy and stone flowers—
Up many and many a marvellous shrine
Whose wreathéd friezes intertwine
The viol, the violet, and the vine.

Resignedly beneath the sky
The melancholy waters lie.
So blend the turrets and shadows there
That all seem pendulous in air,
While from a proud tower in the town
Death looks gigantically down.

There open fanes and gaping graves
Yawn level with the luminous waves;
But not the riches there that lie
In each idol's diamond eye—
Not the gaily-jewelled dead
Tempt the water from their bed;
For no ripples curl, alas!
Along that wilderness of glass—
No swellings tell that winds may be
Upon some far-off happier sea—
No heaving hint that winds have been
On seas less hideously serene.

But lo, a stir is in the air!
The wave—there is a movement there!
As if the towers had thrust aside,

In slightly sinking, the dull tide—
As if their tops had feebly given
A void within the filmy Heaven.
The waves have now a redder glow—
The hours are breathing faint and low—
And when, amid no earthly moans,
Down, down that town shall settle hence,
Hell, rising from a thousand thrones,
Shall do it reverence.   [1831–1845]

THE SLEEPER

At midnight, in the month of June,
I stand beneath the mystic moon.
An opiate vapour, dewy, dim,
Exhales from out her golden rim,
And, softly dripping, drop by drop,
Upon the quiet mountain top,
Steals drowsily and musically
Into the universal valley.
The rosemary nods upon the grave;
The lily lolls upon the wave;
Wrapping the fog about its breast,
The ruin moulders into rest;
Looking like Lethë, see! the lake
A conscious slumber seems to take,
And would not, for the world, awake.
All Beauty sleeps!—and lo! where lies
Irenë, with her Destinies!

Oh, lady bright! can it be right—
This window open to the night?
The wanton airs, from the tree-top,
Laughingly through the lattice drop—
The bodiless airs, a wizard rout,
Flit through thy chamber in and out,
And wave the curtain canopy

So fitfully—so fearfully—
Above the closed and fringéd lid
'Neath which thy slumb'ring soul lies hid,
That, o'er the floor and down the wall,
Like ghosts the shadows rise and fall!
Oh, lady dear, hast thou no fear?
Why and what art thou dreaming here?
Sure thou art come o'er far-off seas,
A wonder to these garden trees!
Strange is thy pallor! strange thy dress!
Strange, above all, thy length of tress,
And this all solemn silentness!

The lady sleeps! Oh, may her sleep,
Which is enduring, so be deep!
Heaven have her in its sacred keep!
This chamber changed for one more holy,
This bed for one more melancholy,
I pray to God that she may lie
Forever with unopened eye,
While the pale sheeted ghosts go by!

My love, she sleeps! Oh, may her sleep,
As it is lasting, so be deep!
Soft may the worms about her creep!
Far in the forest, dim and old,
For her may some tall vault unfold—
Some vault that oft hath flung its black
And wingéd pannels fluttering back,
Triumphant, o'er the crested palls,
Of her grand family funerals—
Some sepulchre, remote, alone,
Against whose portal she hath thrown,
In childhood, many an idle stone—
Some tomb from out whose sounding door
She ne'er shall force an echo more,
Thrilling to think, poor child of sin!
It was the dead who groaned within.

[1831, 1849]

THE VALLEY OF UNREST

*Once,*it smiled a silent dell
Where the people did not dwell;
They had gone unto the wars,
Trusting to the mild-eyed stars,
Nightly, from their azure towers,
To keep watch above the flowers,
In the midst of which all day
The red sun-light lazily lay.
Now each visiter shall confess
The sad valley's restlessness.
Nothing there is motionless.
Nothing save the airs that brood
Over the magic solitude.
Ah, by no wind are stirred those trees
That palpitate like the chill seas
Around the misty Hebrides!
Ah, by no wind those clouds are driven
That rustle through the unquiet Heaven
Uneasily, from morn till even,
Over the violets there that lie
In myriad types of the human eye—
Over the lilies there that wave
And weep above a nameless grave!
They wave:—from out their fragrant tops
Eternal dews come down in drops.
They weep:—from off their delicate stems
Perennial tears descend in gems.

[1831–1845]

LENORE

Ah, broken is the golden bowl!
  The spirit flown forever!
Let the bell toll!—A saintly soul
  Glides down the Stygian river!
And let the burial rite be read—
  The funeral song be sung—
A dirge for the most lovely dead
  That ever died so young!
    And, Guy de Vere,
    Hast *thou* no tear?
      Weep now or nevermore!
    See, on yon drear
    And rigid bier,
      Low lies thy love Lenore!

"Yon heir, whose cheeks of pallid hue
  With tears are streaming wet,
Sees only, through
Their crocodile dew,
  A vacant coronet—
    False friends! ye loved her for her wealth
      And hated her for her pride,
    And, when she fell in feeble health,
      Ye blessed her—that she died.
        How *shall* the ritual, then, be read?
          The requiem *how* be sung
        For her most wrong'd of all the dead
          That ever died so young?"

Peccavimus!
But rave not thus!
  And let the solemn song
Go up to God so mournfully that *she* may feel no wrong!

The sweet Lenore
Hath "gone before"
  With young hope at her side,
    And thou art wild
    For the dear child
That should have been thy bride—
    For her, the fair
    And debonair,
That now so lowly lies—
The life still there
Upon her hair,
  The death upon her eyes.

"Avaunt!—to-night
My heart is light—
  No dirge will I upraise,
But waft the angel on her flight
  With a Pæan of old days!
    Let *no* bell toll!
    Lest her sweet soul,
      Amid its hallow'd mirth,
      Should catch the note
      As it doth float
      Up from the damned earth—
        To friends above, from fiends below,
          [th' indignant ghost is riven—
        From grief and moan
        To a gold throne
        Beside the King of Heaven!"

[1831–1843]

THE COLISEUM

Type of the antique Rome! Rich reliquary
Of lofty contemplation left to Time
By buried centuries of pomp and power!
At length—at length—after so many days

Of weary pilgrimage and burning thirst,
(Thirst for the springs of lore that in thee lie,)
I kneel, an altered and an humble man,
Amid thy shadows, and so drink within
My very soul thy grandeur, gloom, and glory!

Vastness! and Age! and Memories of Eld!
Silence! and Desolation! and dim Night!
I feel ye now—I feel ye in your strength—
O spells more sure than e'er Judæan king
Taught in the gardens of Gethsemane!
O charms more potent than the rapt Chaldee
Ever drew down from out the quiet stars!

Here, where a hero fell, a column falls!
Here, where the mimic eagle glared in gold,
A midnight vigil holds the swarthy bat!
Here, where the dames of Rome their gilded hair
Waved to the wind, now wave the reed and thistle!
Here, where on golden throne the monarch lolled,
Glides, spectre-like, unto his marble home,
Lit by the wan light of the hornéd moon,
The swift and silent lizard of the stones!

But stay! these walls—these ivy-clad arcades—
These mouldering plinths—these sad and blackened
    shafts—
These vague entablatures—this crumbling frieze—
These shattered cornices—this wreck—this ruin—
These stones—alas! these gray stones—are they all—
All of the famed, and the colossal left
By the corrosive Hours to Fate and me?

"Not all—the Echoes answer me—not all!
Prophetic sounds and loud, arise forever
From us, and from all Ruin, unto the wise,
As melody from Memmon to the Sun.
We rule the hearts of mightiest men—we rule
With a despotic sway all giant minds.
We are not impotent—we pallid stones.
Not all our power is gone—not all our fame—

Not all the magic of our high renown—
Not all the wonder that encircles us—
Not all the mysteries that in us lie—
Not all the memories that hang upon
And cling around about us as a garment,
Clothing us in a robe of more than glory."

[1833, 1850]

SONNET—SILENCE

There are some qualities—some incorporate things,
    That have a double life, life which thus is made
A type of that twin entity which springs
    From matter and light, evinced in solid and shade.
There is a two-fold *Silence*—sea and shore—
    Body and Soul. One dwells in lonely places,
    Newly with grass o'ergrown; some solemn graces,
Some human memories and tearful lore,
Render him terrorless: his name's "No more."
    He is the corporate Silence: dread him not!
    No power hath he of evil in himself;
But should some urgent fate (untimely lot!)
    Bring thee to meet his shadow (nameless elf,
That haunteth the lone regions where hath trod
No foot of man,) commend thyself to God!

[1839–1845]

DREAM-LAND

By a route obscure and lonely,
Haunted by ill angels only,
Where an Eidolon, named Night,
On a black throne reigns upright,
I have reached these lands but newly

From an ultimate dim Thule—
From a wild weird clime that lieth, sublime,
    Out of Space—out of Time.

Bottomless vales and boundless floods,
And chasms, and caves, and Titan woods,
With forms that no man can discover
For the dews that drip all over;
Mountains toppling evermore
Into seas without a shore;
Seas that restlessly aspire,
Surging, unto skies of fire;
Lakes that endlessly outspread
Their lone waters—lone and dead,—
Their still waters—still and chilly
With the snows of the lolling lily.

By the lakes that thus outspread
Their lone waters, lone and dead,—
Their sad waters, sad and chilly
With the snows of the lolling lily,—
By the mountains—near the river
Murmuring lowly, murmuring ever,—
By the grey woods,—by the swamp
Where the toad and the newt encamp,—
By the dismal tarns and pools
    Where dwell the Ghouls,—
By each spot the most unholy—
In each nook most melancholy,—
There the traveller meets aghast
Sheeted Memories of the Past—
Shrouded forms that start and sigh
As they pass the wanderer by—
White-robed forms of friends long given
In agony, to the Earth—and Heaven.

For the heart whose woes are legion
'Tis a peaceful, soothing region—
For the spirit that walks in shadow
O! it is an Eldorado!

But the traveller, travelling through it,
May not—dare not openly view it;
Never its mysteries are exposed
To the weak human eye unclosed;
So wills its King, who hath forbid
The uplifting of the fringed lid;
And thus the sad Soul that here passes
Beholds it but through darkened glasses.

By a route obscure and lonely,
Haunted by ill angels only,
Where an Eidolon, named NIGHT,
On a black throne reigns upright,
I have wandered home but newly
From this ultimate dim Thule.

[1844–1849]

THE RAVEN

Once upon a midnight dreary, while I pondered, weak
and weary,
Over many a quaint and curious volume of forgotten lore—
While I nodded, nearly napping, suddenly there came a
tapping,
As of some one gently rapping, rapping at my chamber
door—
" 'Tis some visiter," I muttered, "tapping at my chamber
door—
        Only this and nothing more."

Ah, distinctly I remember it was in the bleak December;
And each separate dying ember wrought its ghost upon the
floor.
Eagerly I wished the morrow;—vainly I had sought to
borrow
From my books surcease of sorrow—sorrow for the lost
Lenore—

For the rare and radiant maiden whom the angels name
Lenore—
> Nameless *here* for evermore.

And the silken, sad, uncertain rustling of each purple
curtain
Thrilled me—filled me with fantastic terrors never felt
before;
So that now, to still the beating of my heart, I stood repeating
" 'Tis some visiter entreating entrance at my chamber
door—
Some late visiter entreating entrance at my chamber
door;—
> This it is and nothing more."

Presently my soul grew stronger; hesitating then no longer,
"Sir," said I, "or Madam, truly your forgiveness I implore;
But the fact is I was napping, and so gently you came
rapping,
And so faintly you came tapping, tapping at my chamber
door,
That I scarce was sure I heard you"—here I opened wide
the door;———
> Darkness there and nothing more.

Deep into that darkness peering, long I stood there wonder-
ing, fearing,
Doubting, dreaming dreams no mortal ever dared to
dream before;
But the silence was unbroken, and the stillness gave no
token,
And the only word there spoken was the whispered word,
"Lenore?"
This I whispered, and an echo murmured back the word,
"Lenore!"
> Merely this and nothing more.

Back into the chamber turning, all my soul within me
burning,
Soon again I heard a tapping somewhat louder than before.

"Surely," said I, "surely that is something at my window
  lattice;
Let me see, then, what thereat is, and this mystery explore—
Let my heart be still a moment and this mystery explore;—
      'Tis the wind and nothing more!"

Open here I flung the shutter, when, with many a flirt and
  flutter,
In there stepped a stately Raven of the saintly days of
  yore;
Not the least obeisance made he; not a minute stopped
  or stayed he;
But, with mien of lord or lady, perched above my chamber
  door—
Perched upon a bust of Pallas just above my chamber
  door—
      Perched, and sat, and nothing more.

Then this ebony bird beguiling my sad fancy into smil-
  ing,
By the grave and stern decorum of the countenance it
  wore,
"Though thy crest be shorn and shaven, thou," I said, "art
  sure no craven,
Ghastly grim and ancient Raven wandering from the
  Nightly shore—
Tell me what thy lordly name is on the Night's Plutonian
  shore!"
      Quoth the Raven "Nevermore."

Much I marvelled this ungainly fowl to hear discourse so
  plainly,
Though its answer little meaning—little relevancy bore;
For we cannot help agreeing that no living human being
Ever yet was blessed with seeing bird above his chamber
  door—
Bird or beast upon the sculptured bust above his chamber
  door,
      With such name as "Nevermore."

But the Raven, sitting lonely on the placid bust, spoke only
That one word, as if his soul in that one word he did outpour.
Nothing farther then he uttered—not a feather then he
fluttered—
Till I scarcely more than muttered "Other friends have
flown before—
On the morrow *he* will leave me, as my Hopes have flown
before."
     Then the bird said "Nevermore."

Startled at the stillness broken by reply so aptly spoken,
"Doubtless," said I, "what it utters is its only stock and
store
Caught from some unhappy master whom unmerciful
Disaster
Followed fast and followed faster till his songs one burden
bore—
Till the dirges of his Hope that melancholy burden bore
     Of 'Never—nevermore.' "

But the Raven still beguiling my sad fancy into smiling,
Straight I wheeled a cushioned seat in front of bird, and
bust and door;
Then, upon the velvet sinking, I betook myself to linking
Fancy unto fancy, thinking what this ominous bird of
yore—
What this grim, ungainly, ghastly, gaunt, and ominous
bird of yore
     Meant in croaking "Nevermore."

This I sat engaged in guessing, but no syllable expressing
To the fowl whose fiery eyes now burned into my bosom's
core;
This and more I sat divining, with my head at ease reclining
On the cushion's velvet lining that the lamp-light gloated
o'er,
But whose velvet-violet lining with the lamp-light gloating
o'er,
     She shall press, ah, nevermore!

Then, methought, the air grew denser, perfumed from an
   unseen censer
Swung by seraphim whose foot-falls tinkled on the tufted
   floor.
"Wretch," I cried, "thy God hath lent thee—by these
   angels he hath sent thee
Respite—respite and nepenthe from thy memories of
   Lenore;
Quaff, oh quaff this kind nepenthe and forget this lost
   Lenore!"
            Quoth the Raven "Nevermore."

"Prophet!" said I, "thing of evil!—prophet still, if bird or
   devil!—
Whether Tempter sent, or whether tempest tossed thee
   here ashore,
Desolate yet all undaunted, on this desert land enchanted—
On this home by Horror haunted—tell me truly, I implore—
Is there—*is* there balm in Gilead?—tell me—tell me, I
   implore!"
            Quoth the Raven "Nevermore."

"Prophet!" said I, "thing of evil!—prophet still, if bird
   or devil!
By that Heaven that bends above us—by that God we
   both adore—
Tell this soul with sorrow laden if, within the distant
   Aidenn,
It shall clasp a sainted maiden whom the angels name
   Lenore—
Clasp a rare and radiant maiden whom the angels name
   Lenore."
            Quoth the Raven "Nevermore."

"Be that word our sign of parting, bird or fiend!" I
   shrieked, upstarting—
"Get thee back into the tempest and the Night's Plutonian
   shore!
Leave no black plume as a token of that lie thy soul hath
   spoken!

Leave my loneliness unbroken!—quit the bust above my
    door!
Take thy beak from out my heart, and take thy form from
    off my door!"
      Quoth the Raven "Nevermore."

And the Raven, never flitting, still is sitting, *still* is
    sitting
On the pallid bust of Pallas just above my chamber door;
And his eyes have all the seeming of a demon's that is
    dreaming,
And the lamp-light o'er him streaming throws his shadow
    on the floor;
And my soul from out that shadow that lies floating on
    the floor
      Shall be lifted—nevermore!

                                                [1845–1849]

ULALUME—A BALLAD

The skies they were ashen and sober;
   The leaves they were withering and sere:
   The leaves they were withering and sere:
It was night, in the lonesome October
   Of my most immemorial year:
It was hard by the dim lake of Auber,
   In the misty mid region of Weir:—
It was down by the dank tarn of Auber,
   In the ghoul-haunted woodland of Weir.

Here once, through an alley Titanic,
   Of cypress, I roamed with my Soul—
   Of cypress, with Psyche, my Soul.
These were days when my heart was volcanic
   As the scoriac rivers that roll—
   As the lavas that restlessly roll
Their sulphurous currents down Yaanek,
   In the ultimate climes of the Pole—

That groan as they roll down Mount Yaanek,
  In the realms of the Boreal Pole.

Our talk had been serious and sober,
  But our thoughts they were palsied and sere—
  Our memories were treacherous and sere;
For we knew not the month was October,
  And we marked not the night of the year—
  (Ah, night of all nights in the year!)
We noted not the dim lake of Auber,
  (Though once we had journeyed down here)
We remembered not the dank tarn of Auber,
  Nor the ghoul-haunted woodland of Weir.

And now, as the night was senescent,
  And star-dials pointed to morn—
  As the star-dials hinted of morn—
At the end of our path a liquescent
  And nebulous lustre was born,
Out of which a miraculous crescent
  Arose with a duplicate horn—
Astarte's bediamonded crescent,
  Distinct with its duplicate horn.

And I said—"She is warmer than Dian;
  She rolls through an ether of sighs—
  She revels in a region of sighs.
She has seen that the tears are not dry on
  These cheeks where the worm never dies,
And has come past the stars of the Lion,
  To point us the path to the skies—
  To the Lethean peace of the skies—
Come up, in despite of the Lion,
  To shine on us with her bright eyes—
Come up, through the lair of the Lion,
  With love in her luminous eyes."

But Psyche, uplifting her finger,
  Said—"Sadly this star I mistrust—
  Her pallor I strangely mistrust—

Ah, hasten!—ah, let us not linger!
  Ah, fly!—let us fly!—for we must."
In terror she spoke; letting sink her
  Wings till they trailed in the dust—
In agony sobbed; letting sink her
  Plumes till they trailed in the dust—
  Till they sorrowfully trailed in the dust.

I replied—"This is nothing but dreaming.
  Let us on, by this tremulous light!
  Let us bathe in this crystalline light!
Its Sibyllic splendor is beaming
  With Hope and in Beauty to-night—
  See!—it flickers up the sky through the night!
Ah, we safely may trust to its gleaming
  And be sure it will lead us aright—
We surely may trust to a gleaming
  That cannot but guide us aright
Since it flickers up to Heaven through the night."

Thus I pacified Psyche and kissed her,
  And tempted her out of her gloom—
  And conquered her scruples and gloom;
And we passed to the end of the vista—
  But were stopped by the door of a tomb—
  By the door of a legended tomb:—
And I said—"What is written, sweet sister,
  On the door of this legended tomb?"
  She replied—"Ulalume—Ulalume!—
  'T is the vault of thy lost Ulalume!"

Then my heart it grew ashen and sober
  As the leaves that were crispéd and sere—
  As the leaves that were withering and sere—
And I cried—"It was surely October,
  On *this* very night of last year,
  That I journeyed—I journeyed down here!—
  That I brought a dread burden down here—
  On this night, of all nights in the year,
  Ah, what demon hath tempted me here?

Well I know, now, this dim lake of Auber—
　　This misty mid region of Weir:—
Well I know, now, this dank tarn of Auber—
　　This ghoul-haunted woodland of Weir."

Said we, then—the two, then—"Ah, can it
　　Have been that the woodlandish ghouls—
　　The pitiful, the merciful ghouls,
To bar up our way and to ban it
　　From the secret that lies in these wolds—
　　From the thing that lies hidden in these wolds—
Have drawn up the spectre of a planet
　　From the limbo of lunary souls—
This sinfully scintillant planet
　　From the Hell of the planetary souls?"

　　　　　　　　　　　　　　　　[1847–1849]

THE BELLS

1.

　　Hear the sledges with the bells—
　　　　Silver bells!
What a world of merriment their melody foretells!
　　How they tinkle, tinkle, tinkle,
　　　　In the icy air of night!
　　While the stars that oversprinkle
　　All the Heavens, seem to twinkle
　　　　With a crystalline delight;
　　Keeping time, time, time,
　　In a sort of Runic rhyme,
To the tintinabulation that so musically wells
　　From the bells, bells, bells, bells,
　　　　Bells, bells, bells—
　　　　From the jingling and the tinkling of the bells.

2.

　　Hear the mellow wedding bells—
　　　　Golden bells!

What a world of happiness their harmony foretells!
    Through the balmy air of night
    How they ring out their delight!—
      From the molten-golden notes
        And all in tune,
      What a liquid ditty floats
To the turtle-dove that listens while she gloats
        On the moon!
      Oh, from out the sounding cells
What a gush of euphony voluminously wells!
        How it swells!
        How it dwells
      On the Future!—how it tells
      Of the rapture that impels
To the swinging and the ringing
      Of the bells, bells, bells!—
Of the bells, bells, bells, bells,
      Bells, bells, bells—
To the rhyming and the chiming of the bells!

3.

    Hear the loud alarum bells—
      Brazen bells!
What tale of terror, now, their turbulency tells!
    In the startled ear of Night
    How they scream out their affright!
      Too much horrified to speak,
      They can only shriek, shriek,
        Out of tune,
In a clamorous appealing to the mercy of the fire—
In a mad expostulation with the deaf and frantic fire,
      Leaping higher, higher, higher,
      With a desperate desire
    And a resolute endeavor
    Now—now to sit, or never,
    By the side of the pale-faced moon.
      Oh, the bells, bells, bells!
      What a tale their terror tells
        Of despair!

How they clang and clash and roar!
What a horror they outpour
In the bosom of the palpitating air!
      Yet the ear, it fully knows,
            By the twanging
            And the clanging,
      How the danger ebbs and flows:—
Yes, the ear distinctly tells,
            In the jangling
            And the wrangling,
      How the danger sinks and swells,
By the sinking or the swelling in the anger of the bells—
            Of the bells—
      Of the bells, bells, bells, bells,
            Bells, bells, bells—
      In the clamor and the clangor of the bells.

                    4

      Hear the tolling of the bells—
            Iron bells!
What a world of solemn thought their monody compels!
      In the silence of the night
      How we shiver with affright
At the melancholy meaning of the tone!
      For every sound that floats
      From the rust within their throats
            Is a groan.
         And the people—ah, the people
         They that dwell up in the steeple
            All alone,
      And who, tolling, tolling, tolling,
         In that muffled monotone,
      Feel a glory in so rolling
         On the human heart a stone—
They are neither man nor woman—
They are neither brute nor human,
            They are Ghouls:—
And their king it is who tolls:—
And he rolls, rolls, rolls, rolls
      A Pæan from the bells!

And his merry bosom swells
　　With the Pæan of the bells!
And he dances and he yells;
　Keeping time, time, time,
　In a sort of Runic rhyme,
　　To the Pæan of the bells—
　　　Of the bells:—
　Keeping time, time, time,
　In a sort of Runic rhyme,
　　To the throbbing of the bells—
Of the bells, bells, bells—
　　To the sobbing of the bells:—
　Keeping time, time, time,
　　As he knells, knells, knells,
　In a happy Runic rhyme,
　　To the rolling of the bells—
Of the bells, bells, bells:—
　　To the tolling of the bells—
Of the bells, bells, bells, bells,
　　Bells, bells, bells—
To the moaning and the groaning of the bells.

　　　　　　　　　　　　　　　　　　[1849]

ELDORADO

　Gaily bedight,
　A gallant knight,
In sunshine and in shadow,
　　Had journeyed long,
　　Singing a song,
In search of Eldorado.

　But he grew old—
　This knight so bold—
And o'er his heart a shadow
　　Fell, as he found
　　No spot of ground
That looked like Eldorado.

And, as his strength
    Failed him at length
He met a pilgrim shadow—
    "Shadow," said he,
    "Where can it be—
This land of Eldorado?"

"Over the Mountains
    Of the Moon,
Down the Valley of the Shadow,
    Ride, boldly ride,"
    The shade replied,—
"If you seek for Eldorado!"

[1849]

FOR ANNIE

Thank Heaven! the crisis—
    The danger is past,
And the lingering illness
    Is over at last—
And the fever called "Living"
    Is conquered at last.

Sadly, I know
    I am shorn of my strength,
And no muscle I move
    As I lie at full length—
But no matter!—I feel
    I am better at length.

And I rest so composedly,
    Now, in my bed,
That any beholder
    Might fancy me dead—
Might start at beholding me,
    Thinking me dead.

The moaning and groaning,
    The sighing and sobbing,
Are quieted now,
    With that horrible throbbing
At heart:—ah, that horrible,
    Horrible throbbing!

The sickness—the nausea—
    The pitiless pain—
Have ceased, with the fever
    That maddened my brain—
With the fever called "Living"
    That burned in my brain.

And oh! of all tortures
    That torture the worst
Has abated—the terrible
    Torture of thirst
For the napthaline river
    Of Passion accurst:—
I have drank of a water
    That quenches all thirst:—

Of a water that flows,
    With a lullaby sound,
From a spring but a very few
    Feet under ground—
From a cavern not very far
    Down under ground.

And ah! let it never
    Be foolishly said
That my room it is gloomy
    And narrow my bed;
For man never slept
    In a different bed—
And, to *sleep*, you must slumber
    In just such a bed.

My tantalized spirit
    Here blandly reposes,

Forgetting, or never
  Regretting its roses—
Its old agitations
  Of myrtles and roses:

For now, while so quietly
  Lying, it fancies
A holier odor
  About it, of pansies—
A rosemary odor,
  Commingled with pansies—
With rue and the beautiful
  Puritan pansies.

And so it lies happily,
  Bathing in many
A dream of the truth
  And the beauty of Annie—
Drowned in a bath
  Of the tresses of Annie.

She tenderly kissed me,
  She fondly caressed,
And then I fell gently
  To sleep on her breast—
Deeply to sleep
  From the heaven of her breast.

When the light was extinguished,
  She covered me warm,
And she prayed to the angels
  To keep me from harm—
To the queen of the angels
  To shield me from harm.

And I lie so composedly,
  Now, in my bed,
(Knowing her love)
  That you fancy me dead—
And I rest so contentedly,
  Now in my bed,

(With her love at my breast)
  That you fancy me dead—
That you shudder to look at me,
  Thinking me dead:—

But my heart it is brighter
  Than all of the many
Stars in the sky,
  For it sparkles with Annie—
It glows with the light
  Of the love of my Annie—
With the thought of the light
  Of the eyes of my Annie.

[1849]

ANNABEL LEE

It was many and many a year ago,
  In a kingdom by the sea,
That a maiden there lived whom you may know
  By the name of Annabel Lee;—
And this maiden she lived with no other thought
  Than to love and be loved by me.

I was a child and *she* was a child
  In this kingdom by the sea,
But we loved with a love that was more than love—
  I and my Annabel Lee—
With a love that the wingéd seraphs of Heaven
  Coveted her and me.

And this was the reason that, long ago,
  In this kingdom by the sea,
A wind blew out of a cloud, chilling
  My beautiful Annabel Lee;
So that her highborn kinsmen came
  And bore her away from me,

To shut her up in a sepulchre,
  In this kingdom by the sea.

The angels, not half so happy in Heaven,
  Went envying her and me—
Yes! that was the reason (as all men know,
  In this kingdom by the sea)
That the wind came out of the cloud by night,
  Chilling and killing my Annabel Lee.

But our love it was stronger by far than the love
  Of those who were older than we—
  Of many far wiser than we—
And neither the angels in Heaven above
  Nor the demons down under the sea
Can ever dissever my soul from the soul
  Of the beautiful Annabel Lee:—

For the moon never beams, without bringing me dreams
  Of the beautiful Annabel Lee;
And the stars never rise, but I feel the bright eyes
  Of the beautiful Annabel Lee:—
And so, all the night-tide, I lie down by the side
Of my darling—my darling—my life and my bride,
  In her sepulchre there by the sea—
  In her tomb by the sounding sea.

[May 1849]

II

TALES

METZENGERSTEIN

A TALE IN IMITATION OF THE GERMAN

Pestis eram vivus—moriens tua mors ero.—MARTIN LUTHER

Horror and Fatality have been stalking abroad in all ages. Why then give a date to the story I have to tell? I will not. Besides, I have other reasons for concealment. Let it suffice to say, that at the period of which I speak, there existed, in the interior of Hungary, a settled although hidden belief in the doctrines of the Metempsychosis. Of the doctrines themselves—that is, of their falsity, or of their probability—I say nothing. I assert, however, that much of our incredulity—as La Bruyére says of all our unhappiness—*"vient de ne pouvoir etre seuls."*

But there were some points in the Hungarian superstition which were fast verging to absurdity. They—the Hungarians—differed very essentially from their Eastern authorities. For example. *"The soul,"* said the former—I give the words of an acute and intelligent Parisian—*ne demeure qu'un seul fois dans un corps sensible: au reste— un cheval, un chien, un homme même n' est que la ressemblance peu tangible de ces animaux."*

*   *   *

The families of Berlifitzing and Metzengerstein had been at variance for centuries. Never before were two houses so illustrious mutually embittered by hostility so deadly. Indeed, at the era of this history, it was observed by an old crone of haggard and sinister appearance, that "fire and water might sooner mingle than a Berlifitzing clasp the hand of a Metzengerstein." The origin of this enmity seems to be found in the words of an ancient prophecy— "A lofty name shall have a fearful fall when, like the rider over his horse, the mortality of Metzengerstein shall triumph over the immortality of Berlifitzing."

To be sure the words themselves had little or no meaning. But more trivial causes have given rise—and that no long while ago—to consequences equally eventful. Besides, the estates, which were contiguous, had long exercised a rival influence in the affairs of a busy government. Moreover, near neighbors are seldom friends—and the inhabitants of the Castle Berlifitzing might look, from their lofty buttresses, into the very windows of the Chateau Metzengerstein. Least of all was the more than feudal magnificence thus discovered calculated to allay the irritable feelings of the less ancient and less wealthy Berlifitzings. What wonder, then, that the words, however silly, of that prediction, should have succeeded in setting and keeping at variance two families already predisposed to quarrel by every instigation of hereditary jealousy? The prophecy seemed to imply—if it implied any thing—a final triumph on the part of the already more powerful house; and was of course remembered with the more bitter animosity on the side of the weaker and less influential.

*   *   *

Wilhelm, Count Berlifitzing, although honorably and loftily descended, was, at the epoch of this narrative, an infirm and doting old man, remarkable for nothing but an inordinate and inveterate personal antipathy to the family of his rival, and so passionate a love of horses, and of hunting, that neither bodily infirmity, great age, nor mental incapacity, prevented his daily participation in the dangers of the chase.

Frederick, Baron Metzengerstein, was, on the other hand, not yet of age. His father, the Minister G——, died young. His mother, the Lady Mary, followed quickly after. Frederick was, at that time, in his fifteenth year. In a city fifteen years are no long period—a child may be still a child in his third lustrum: but in a wilderness—in so magnificent a wilderness as that old principality, fifteen years have a far deeper meaning.

The beautiful Lady Mary! How *could* she die?—and of consumption! But it is a path I have prayed to follow. I would wish all I love to perish of that gentle disease. How glorious! to depart in the hey-day of the young blood— the heart all passion—the imagination all fire—amid the remembrances of happier days—in the fall of the year— and so be buried up forever in the gorgeous autumnal leaves!

Thus died the Lady Mary. The young Baron Frederick stood without a living relative by the coffin of his dead mother. He placed his hand upon her placid forehead. No shudder came over his delicate frame—no sigh from his flinty bosom. Heartless, self-willed, and impetuous from his childhood, he had reached the age of which I speak through a career of unfeeling, wanton, and reckless dissipation; and a barrier had long since arisen in the channel of all holy thoughts and gentle recollections.

*   *   *

From some peculiar circumstances attending the administration of his father, the young Baron, at the decease of the former, entered immediately upon his vast possessions. Such estates were seldom held before by a nobleman of Hungary. His castles were without number—of these the chief in point of splendor and extent was the "Chateau Metzengerstein." The boundary line of his dominions was never clearly defined—but his principal park embraced a circuit of fifty miles.

Upon the succession of a proprietor so young—with a

character so well known—to a fortune so unparalleled—
little speculation was afloat in regard to his probable
course of conduct. And, indeed, for the space of three days
the behavior of the heir out-heroded Herod, and fairly
surpassed the expectations of his most enthusiastic ad-
mirers. Shameful debaucheries—flagrant treacheries—un-
heard-of atrocities—gave his trembling vassals quickly to
understand that no servile submission on their part—no
punctilios of conscience on his own—were thenceforward
to prove any security against the remorseless and bloody
fangs of a petty Caligula. On the night of the fourth day,
the stables of the Castle Berlifitzing were discovered to be
on fire: and the unanimous opinion of the neighborhood
instantaneously added the crime of the incendiary to the
already hideous list of the Baron's misdemeanors and
enormities.

But during the tumult occasioned by this occurrence,
the young nobleman himself sat, apparently buried in
meditation, in a vast and desolate upper apartment of the
family palace of Metzengerstein. The rich although faded
tapestry-hangings which swung gloomily upon the walls,
represented the shadowy and majestic forms of a thousand illustrious ancestors. *Here*, rich-ermined priests, and
pontifical dignitaries, familiarly seated with the autocrat
and the sovereign, put a veto on the wishes of a temporal
king—or restrained with the fiat of papal supremacy the
rebellious sceptre of the Arch-Enemy. *There*, the dark, tall
statures of the Princes Metzengerstein—their muscular
war-courses plunging over the carcass of a fallen foe—
startled the steadiest nerves with their vigorous expression:
and *here*, again, the voluptuous and swan-like figures of
the dames of days gone by, floated away in the mazes of
an unreal dance to the strains of imaginary melody.

But as the Baron listened, or affected to listen to the
gradually increasing uproar in the stables of Berlifitzing—
or perhaps pondered upon some more novel—some more

decided act of audacity—his eyes became unwittingly
rivetted to the figure of an enormous, and unnaturally
colored horse, represented in the tapestry as belonging to a
Saracen ancestor of the family of his rival. The horse
itself, in the foreground of the design, stood motionless
and statue-like—while farther back its discomfitted rider
perished by the dagger of a Metzengerstein.

On Frederick's lip arose a fiendish expression, as he became aware of the direction his glance had, without his
consciousness, assumed. Yet he did not remove it. On the
contrary he could by no means account for the singular,
intense, and overwhelming anxiety which appeared falling
like a shroud upon his senses. It was with difficulty that
he reconciled his dreamy and incoherent feelings with the
certainty of being awake. The longer he gazed, the more
absorbing became the spell—the more impossible did it
appear that he could ever withdraw his glance from the fascination of that tapestry. But the tumult without becoming
suddenly more violent, with a kind of compulsory and
desperate exertion he diverted his attention to the glare
of ruddy light thrown full by the flaming stables upon the
windows of the apartment.

The action, however, was but momentary—his gaze returned mechanically to the wall. To his extreme horror
and astonishment the head of the gigantic steed had, in
the meantime, altered its position. The neck of the animal,
before arched, as if in compassion, over the prostrate body
of its lord, was now extended, at full length, in the direction of the Baron. The eyes, before invisible, now wore an
energetic and human expression, while they gleamed with
a fiery and unusual red: and the distended lips of the
apparently enraged horse left in full view his sepulchral
and disgusting teeth.

Stupified with terror the young nobleman tottered to
the door. As he threw it open, a flash of red light streaming far into the chamber, flung his shadow with a clear

outline against the quivering tapestry; and he shuddered to perceive that shadow—as he staggered awhile upon the threshold—assuming the exact position, and precisely filling up the contour of the relentless and triumphant murderer of the Saracen Berlifitzing.

To lighten the depression of his spirits the Baron hurried into the open air. At the principal gate of the Chateau he encountered three equerries. With much difficulty, and at the imminent peril of their lives, they were restraining the unnatural and convulsive plunges of a gigantic and fiery-colored horse.

"Whose horse? Where did you get him?" demanded the youth in a querulous and husky tone of voice, as he became instantly aware that the mysterious steed in the tapestried chamber was the very counterpart of the furious animal before his eyes.

"He is your own property, Sire"—replied one of the equerries—"at least he is claimed by no other owner. We caught him flying, all smoking and foaming with rage, from the burning stables of the Castle Berlifitzing. Supposing him to have belonged to the old Count's stud of foreign horses, we led him back as an estray. But the grooms there disclaim any title to the creature—which is strange, since he bears evident marks of having made a narrow escape from the flames."

"The letters W. V. B. are also branded very distinctly on his forehead"—interrupted a second equerry—"I supposed them, of course, to be the initials of Wilhelm Von Berlifitzing—but all at the Castle are positive in denying any knowledge of the horse."

"Extremely singular!" said the young Baron, with a musing air, and apparently unconscious of the meaning of his words—"He is, as you say, a remarkable horse—a prodigious horse! although, as you very justly observe, of a suspicious and untractable character——Let him be mine, however," he added, after a pause—"perhaps a rider like Frederick of Metzengerstein, may tame even the devil from the stables of Berlifitzing."

"You are mistaken, my lord—the horse, as I think we mentioned, is *not* from the stables of the Count. If such were the case, we know our duty better than to bring him into the presence of a noble of your family."

"True!" observed the Baron drily—and at that instant a page of the bed chamber came from the Chateau with a heightened color, and precipitate step. He whispered into his master's ear an account of the miraculous and sudden disappearance of a small portion of the tapestry, in an apartment which he designated: entering, at the same time, into particulars of a minute and circumstantial character—but from the low tone of voice in which these latter were communicated, nothing escaped to gratify the excited curiosity of the equerries.

The young Frederick, during the conference, seemed agitated by a variety of emotions. He soon, however, recovered his composure, and an expression of determined malignancy settled upon his countenance, as he gave peremptory orders that a certain chamber should be immediately locked up, and the key placed in his own possession.

* * *

"Have you heard of the unhappy death of the old hunter Berlifitzing?" said one of his vassals to the Baron, as, after the affair of the page, the huge and mysterious steed which that nobleman had adopted as his own, plunged and curvetted, with redoubled and supernatural fury, down the long avenue which extended from the Chateau to the stables of Metzengerstein.

"No!"—said the Baron, turning abruptly towards the speaker—"dead! say you?"

"It is indeed true, my lord—and, to a noble of your name, will be, I imagine, no unwelcome intelligence."

A rapid smile of a peculiar and unintelligible meaning shot over the beautiful countenance of the listener—"How died he?"

"In his rash exertions to rescue a favorite portion of his hunting stud, he has himself perished miserably in the flames."

"I—n—d—e—e—d—!"—ejaculated the Baron, as if slowly and deliberately impressed with the truth of some exciting idea.

"Indeed"—repeated the vassal.

"Shocking!" said the youth calmly, and turned quietly into the Chateau.

*   *   *

From this date a marked alteration took place in the outward demeanor of the dissolute young Baron Frederick Von Metzengerstein. Indeed his behaviour disappointed every expectation, and proved little in accordance with the views of many a manœuvering mamma—while his habits and manners, still less than formerly, offered any thing congenial with those of the neighboring aristocracy. He was never to be seen beyond the limits of his own domain, and, in this wide and social world, was utterly companionless—unless, indeed, that unnatural, impetuous, and fiery-colored horse, which he henceforward continually bestrode, had any mysterious right to the title of his friend.

Numerous invitations on the part of the neighborhood for a long time, however, periodically came in—"Will the Baron honor our festivals with his presence?" "Will the Baron join us in a hunting of the boar?" "Metzengerstein does not hunt"—"Metzengerstein will not attend"—were the haughty and laconic answers.

These repeated insults were not to be endured by an imperious nobility. Such invitations became less cordial—less frequent—in time they ceased altogether. The widow of the unfortunate Count Berlifitzing, was even heard to express a hope—"that the Baron might be at home when he did not wish to be at home, since he disdained the company of his equals: and ride when he did not wish to ride, since he preferred the society of a horse." This to be sure was a very silly explosion of hereditary pique; and merely proved how singularly unmeaning our sayings are apt to become, when we desire to be unusually energetic.

The charitable, nevertheless, attributed the alteration in the conduct of the young nobleman to the natural sorrow of a son for the untimely loss of his parents—forgetting, however, his atrocious and reckless behavior during the short period immediately succeeding that bereavement. Some there were, indeed, who suggested a too haughty idea of self-consequence and dignity. Others again —among whom may be mentioned the family physician— did not hesitate in speaking of morbid melancholy, and hereditary ill-health: while dark hints, of a more equivocal nature, were current among the multitude.

Indeed the Baron's perverse attachment to his lately-acquired charger—an attachment which seemed to attain new strength from every fresh example of the animal's ferocious and demonlike propensities—at length became, in the eyes of all reasonable men, a hideous and unnatural fervor. In the glare of noon—at the dead hour of night—in sickness or in health—in calm or in tempest— in moonlight or in shadow—the young Metzengerstein seemed rivetted to the saddle of that colossal horse, whose intractable audacities so well accorded with the spirit of his own.

There were circumstances, moreover, which, coupled with late events, gave an unearthly and portentous character to the mania of the rider, and to the capabilities of the steed. The space passed over in a single leap had been accurately measured, and was found to exceed by an astounding difference, the wildest expectations of the most

imaginative. The Baron, besides, had no particular *name*
for the animal, although all the rest in his extensive collection were distinguished by characteristic appellations.
His stable, too, was appointed at a distance from the rest;
and with regard to grooming and other necessary offices,
none but the owner in person had ventured to officiate, or
even to enter the enclosure of that particular stall. It
was also to be observed, that although the three grooms,
who had caught the horse as he fled from the conflagration at Berlifitzing, had succeeded in arresting his course,
by means of a chain-bridle and noose—yet no one of the
three could with any certainty affirm that he had, during
that dangerous struggle, or at any period thereafter, actually placed his hand upon the body of the beast. Instances of peculiar intelligence in the demeanor of a
noble and high spirited steed are not to be supposed
capable of exciting unreasonable attention—especially
among men who, daily trained to the labors of the chase,
might appear well acquainted with the sagacity of a horse
—but there were certain circumstances which intruded
themselves per force, upon the most skeptical and phleg-
matic—and it is said there were times when this singular
and mysterious animal, caused the gaping crowd who
stood around to recoil in silent horror from the deep and
impressive meaning of his terrible stamp—times when
the young Metzengerstein turned pale and shrunk away
from the rapid and searching expression of his intense and
human-looking eye.

Among all the retinue of the Baron, however, none
were found to doubt the ardor of that extraordinary affection which existed on the part of the young nobleman
for the fiery qualities of his horse—at least, none but an
insignificant and misshapen little page, whose deformities
were in every body's way, and whose opinions were of the
least possible importance. He—if his ideas are worth
mentioning at all—had the effrontery to assert that his

master never vaulted into the saddle, without an unaccountable and almost imperceptible shudder—and that, upon his return from every long-continued and habitual ride, an expression of triumphant malignity distorted every muscle in his countenance.

One tempestuous night, Metzengerstein, awaking from a heavy and oppressive slumber, descended like a maniac from his chamber, and mounting in great haste, bounded away into the mazes of the forest. An occurrence so common attracted no particular attention—but his return was looked for with intense anxiety on the part of his domestics, when, after some hours' absence, the stupendous and magnificent battlements of the Chateau Metzengerstein, were discovered crackling and rocking to their very foundation, under the influence of a dense and livid mass of ungovernable fire.

As the flames, when first seen, had already made so terrible a progress that all efforts to save any portion of the building were evidently futile, the astonished neighborhood stood idly around in silent and apathetic wonder. But a new and fearful object soon rivetted the attention of the multitude, and proved how much more intense is the excitement wrought in the feelings of a crowd by the contemplation of human agony, than that brought about by the most appalling spectacles of inanimate matter.

Up the long avenue of aged oaks which led from the forest to the main entrance of the Chateau Metzengerstein, a steed, bearing an unbonneted and disordered rider, was seen leaping with an impetuosity which outstripped the very Demon of the Tempest, and extorted from every stupified beholder the ejaculation—"horrible!"

The career of the horseman was indisputably, on his own part, uncontrollable. The agony of his countenance—the convulsive struggle of his frame—gave evidence of superhuman exertion: but no sound, save a solitary shriek, escaped from his lacerated lips, which were bitten through and through in the intensity of terror. One instant, and the clattering of hoofs resounded sharply and shrilly above the roaring of the flames and the shrieking of the winds—another, and, clearing at a single plunge the gateway and the moat, the steed bounded far up the tottering staircases of the Palace, and, with its rider, disappeared amid the whirlwind of chaotic fire.

The fury of the tempest immediately died away, and a dead calm sullenly succeeded. A white flame still enveloped the building like a shroud, and, streaming far away into the quiet atmosphere, shot forth a glare of preternatural light; while a cloud of smoke settled heavily over the battlements in the distinct collossal figure of—a horse.

LOSS OF BREATH

A TALE A LA BLACKWOOD

O breathe not, &c.—Moore's Melodies

The most notorious ill-fortune must, in the end, yield to the untiring courage of philosophy—as the most stubborn city to the ceaseless vigilance of an enemy. Salmanezer, as we have it in the holy writings, lay three years before Samaria: yet it fell. Sardanapalus—see Diodorus—maintained himself seven in Nineveh: but to no purpose. Troy expired at the close of the second lustrum: and Azoth, as Aristæus declares upon his honor as a gentleman, opened at last her gates to Psammitticus, after having barred them for the fifth part of a century.

*   *   *

"Thou wretch!—thou vixen!—thou shrew!"—said I to my wife on the morning after our wedding—"thou witch! —thou hag!—thou whippersnapper!—thou sink of iniquity!—thou fiery-faced quintessence of all that is abominable!—thou—thou—" Here standing upon tiptoe, seizing her by the throat, and placing my mouth close to her ear, I was preparing to launch forth a new and more decided epithet of opprobrium which should not fail, if ejaculated, to convince her of her insignificance, when, to my extreme horror and astonishment, I discovered that I *had lost my breath.*

The phrases "I am out of breath," "I have lost my breath," &c. are often enough repeated in common conversation, but it had never occurred to me that the terrible accident of which I speak could *bonâ fide* and actually happen! Imagine—that is if you have a fanciful turn —imagine I say, my wonder—my consternation—my despair!

There is a good genius, however, which has never, at any time, entirely deserted me. In my most ungovernable moods I still retain a sense of propriety, *et le chemin des passions me conduit*—as Rousseau says it did him—*à la philosophie veritable.*

Although I could not at first precisely ascertain to what degree the occurrence had affected me, I unhesitatingly determined to conceal at all events the matter from my wife until farther experience should discover to me the extent of this my unheard of calamity. Altering my countenance, therefore, in a moment, from its bepuffed and distorted appearance, to an expression of arch and coquettish benignity, I gave my lady a pat on the one cheek, and a kiss on the other, and without saying one syllable, (Furies! I could not,) left her astonished at my drollery, as I pirouetted out of the room in a *Pas de Zephyr.*

Behold me then safely ensconced in my private *boudoir*, a fearful instance of the ill consequences attending upon irascibility—alive with the qualifications of the dead —dead with the propensities of the living—an anomaly on the face of the earth—being very calm, yet breathless.

Yes! breathless. I am serious in asserting that my breath was entirely gone. I could not have stirred with it a feather if my life had been at issue, or sullied even the delicacy of a mirror. Hard fate!—yet there was some alleviation to the first overwhelming paroxysm of my sorrow. I found upon trial that the powers of utterance which, upon my inability to proceed in the conversation with my wife, I then concluded to be totally destroyed, were in fact only partially impeded, and I discovered that had I, at that interesting crisis, dropped my voice to a singularly deep guttural, I might still have continued to her the communication of my sentiments; this pitch of voice (the guttural) depending, I find, not upon the current of the breath, but upon a certain spasmodic action of the muscles of the throat.

Throwing myself upon a chair, I remained for some time absorbed in meditation. My reflections, be sure, were of no consolatory kind. A thousand vague and lachrymatory fancies took possession of my soul—and even the phantom Suicide flitted across my brain; but it is a trait in the perversity of human nature to reject the obvious and the ready, for the far-distant and equivocal. Thus I shuddered at self-murder as the most decided of atrocities, while the tabby cat purred strenuously upon the rug, and the very water-dog wheezed assiduously under the table, each taking to itself much merit for the strength of its lungs, and all obviously done in derision of my own pulmonary incapacity.

Oppressed with a tumult of vague hopes and fears, I at length heard the footsteps of my wife descending the staircase. Being now assured of her absence, I returned with a palpitating heart to the scene of my disaster.

Carefully locking the door on the inside, I commenced a vigorous search. It was possible, I thought, that concealed in some obscure corner, or lurking in some closet or drawer, might be found the lost object of my inquiry.

It might have a vapory—it might even have a tangible form. Most philosophers, upon many points of philosophy, are still very unphilosophical. William Godwin, however, says in his "Mandeville," that "invisible things are the only realities." This, all will allow, is a case in point. I would have the judicious reader pause before accusing such asseverations of an undue quantum of absurdity. Anaxagoras—it will be remembered—maintained that snow is black. This I have since found to be the case.

Long and earnestly did I continue the investigation: but the contemptible reward of my industry and perseverance proved to be only a set of false teeth, two pair of hips, an eye, and a bundle of *billets-doux* from Mr. Windenough to my wife. I might as well here observe that this confirmation of my lady's partiality for Mr. W. occasioned me little uneasiness. That Mrs. Lacko'breath should admire any thing so dissimilar to myself was a natural and necessary evil. I am, it is well known, of a robust and corpulent appearance, and, at the same time somewhat diminutive in stature. What wonder then that the lath-like tenuity of my acquaintance, and his altitude which has grown into a proverb, should have met with all due estimation in the eyes of Mrs. Lacko'breath? It is by logic similar to this that true philosophy is enabled to set misfortune at defiance. But to return.

My exertions, as I have before said, proved fruitless. Closet after closet—drawer after drawer—corner after corner—were scrutinized to no purpose. At one time, however, I thought myself sure of my prize, having, in rummaging a dressing-case, accidentally demolished a bottle (I had a remarkably sweet breath) of Hewitt's "Seraphic and Highly-Scented Extract of Heaven or Oil of Archangels" —which, as an agreeable perfume, I here take the liberty of recommending.

With a heavy heart I returned to my *boudoir*—there to ponder upon some method of eluding my wife's penetration, until I could make arrangements prior to my leaving the country, for to this I had already made up my mind. In a foreign climate, being unknown, I might, with some probability of success, endeavor to conceal my unhappy calamity—a calamity calculated, even more than beggary, to estrange the affections of the multitude, and to draw down upon the wretch the well-merited indignation of the virtuous and the happy. I was not long in hesitation. Being naturally quick, I committed to memory the entire tragedies of ——, and ——. I had the good fortune to recollect that in the accentuation of these dramas, or at least of such portion of them as is allotted to their heroes, the tones of voice in which I found myself deficient were altogether unnecessary, and that the deep guttural was expected to reign monotonously throughout.

I practised for some time by the borders of a well-frequented marsh—herein, however, having no reference to a similar proceeding of Demosthenes, but from a design peculiarly and conscientiously my own. Thus armed at all points, I determined to make my wife believe that I was suddenly smitten with a passion for the stage. In this I succeeded to a miracle; and to every question or suggestion found myself at liberty to reply in my most frog-like and sepulchral tones with some passage from the tragedies, any portion of which, as I soon took great pleasure in observing, would apply equally well to any particular subject. It is not to be supposed, however, that in the delivery of such passages I was found at all deficient in the looking asquint —the showing my teeth—the working my knees—the shuffling my feet—or in any of those unmentionable graces which are now justly considered the characteristics of a popular performer. To be sure they spoke of confining me in a straight jacket—but good God! they never suspected me of having lost my breath.

Having at length put my affairs in order, I took my seat very early one morning in the mail stage for ——, giving it to be understood among my acquaintances that business of the last importance required my immediate personal attendance.

The coach was crammed to repletion—but in the uncertain twilight the features of my companions could not be distinguished. Without making any effectual resistance I suffered myself to be placed between two gentlemen of colossal dimensions; while a third, of a size larger, requesting pardon for the liberty he was about to take, threw himself upon my body at full length, and falling asleep in an instant, drowned all my guttural ejaculations for relief, in a snore which would have put to the blush the roarings of a Phalarian bull. Happily the state of my respiratory faculties rendered suffocation an accident entirely out of the question.

As however, the day broke more distinctly in our approach to the outskirts of the city, my tormentor arising and adjusting his shirt-collar, thanked me in a very friendly manner for my civility. Seeing that I remained motionless, (all my limbs were dislocated, and my head twisted on one side,) his apprehensions began to be excited; and arousing the rest of the passengers, he communicated, in a very decided manner, his opinion that a dead man had been palmed upon them during the night for a living *bond fide* and responsible fellow-traveller—here giving me a thump on the right eye, by way of evidencing the truth of his suggestion.

Thereupon all, one after another, (there were nine in company) believed it their duty to pull me by the ear. A young practising physician, too, having applied a pocket-mirror to my mouth, and found me without breath, the assertion of my persecutor was pronounced a true bill; and the whole party expressed their determination to endure tamely no such impositions for the future, and to proceed no farther with any such carcasses for the present.

I was here accordingly thrown out at the sign of the

"Crow," (by which tavern the coach happened to be passing) without meeting with any farther accident than the breaking of both my arms under the left hind wheel of the vehicle. I must besides do the driver the justice to state that he did not forget to throw after me the largest of my trunks, which, unfortunately falling on my head, fractured my skull in a manner at once interesting and extraordinary.

The landlord of the "Crow," who is a hospitable man, finding that my trunk contained sufficient to indemnify him for any little trouble he might take in my behalf, sent forthwith for a surgeon of his acquaintance, and delivered me to his care with a bill and receipt for five and twenty dollars.

The purchaser took me to his apartments and commenced operations immediately. Having, however, cut off my ears, he discovered signs of animation. He now rang the bell, and sent for a neighboring apothecary with whom to consult in the emergency. In case, however, of his suspicions with regard to my existence proving ultimately correct, he, in the meantime, made an incision in my stomach, and removed several of my viscera for private dissection.

The apothecary had an idea that I was actually dead. This idea I endeavored to confute, kicking and plunging with all my might, and making the most furious contortions—for the operations of the surgeon had, in a measure, restored me to the possession of my faculties. All, however, was attributed to the effects of a new Galvanic Battery, wherewith the apothecary, who is really a man of information, performed several curious experiments, in which, from my personal share in their fulfilment I could not help feeling deeply interested. It was a source of mortification to me nevertheless, that although I made several attempts at conversation, my powers of speech were so entirely *in abeyance*, that I could not even open my mouth;

much less then make reply to some ingenious but fanciful theories of which, under other circumstances, my minute acquaintance with the Hippocratian Pathology would have afforded me a ready confutation.

Not being able to arrive at a conclusion, the practitioners remanded me for further examination. I was taken up into a garret; and the surgeon's lady having accommodated me with drawers and stockings, the surgeon himself fastened my hands, and tied up my jaws with a pocket handkerchief—then bolted the door on the outside as he hurried to his dinner, leaving me alone to silence and to meditation.

I now discovered to my extreme delight that I could have spoken had not my mouth been tied up by the pocket-handkerchief. Consoling myself with this reflection, I was mentally repeating some passages of the ———, as is my custom before resigning myself to sleep, when two cats, of a greedy and vituperative turn, entering at a hole in the wall, leaped up with a flourish *à la Catalani*, and alighting opposite one another on my visage, betook themselves to unseemly and indecorous contention for the paltry consideration of my nose.

But, as the loss of his ears proved the means of elevating to the throne of Cyrus, the Magian or Mige-Gush of Persia, and as the cutting off his nose gave Zopyrus possession of Babylon, so the loss of a few ounces of my countenance proved the salvation of my body. Aroused by the pain, and burning with indignation, I burst, at a single effort, the fastenings and the bandage. Stalking across the room I cast a glance of contempt at the belligerents, and throwing open the sash to their extreme horror and disappointment, precipitated myself—very dexterously—from the window.

The mail-robber W———, to whom I bore a singular resemblance, was at this moment passing from the city jail to the scaffold erected for his execution in the suburbs.

His extreme infirmity and long-continued ill health, had obtained him the privilege of remaining unmanacled; and habited in his gallows costume—a dress very similar to my own—he lay at full length in the bottom of the hangman's cart (which happened to be under the windows of the surgeon at the moment of my precipitation)—without any other guard than the driver who was asleep, and two recruits of the sixth infantry, who were drunk.

As ill-luck would have it, I alit upon my feet within the vehicle. W——, who was an acute fellow, perceived his opportunity. Leaping up immediately he bolted out behind, and turning down an alley, was out of sight in the twinkling of an eye. The recruits aroused by the bustle, could not exactly comprehend the merits of the transaction. Seeing, however, a man, the precise counterpart of the felon, standing upright in the cart before their eyes, they were of opinion that "the rascal, (meaning W——) was after making his escape," (so they expressed themselves) and, having communicated this opinion to one another, they took each a dram, and then knocked me down with the but-ends of their muskets.

It was not long ere we arrived at the place of destination. Of course nothing could be said in my defence. Hanging was my inevitable fate. I resigned myself thereto, with a feeling half stupid, half acrimonious. Being little of a cynic, I had all the sentiments of a dog. The hangman, however, adjusted the noose about my neck. The drop fell. My convulsions were said to be extraordinary. Several gentlemen swooned, and some ladies were carried home in hysterics. Pinxit, too, availed himself of the opportunity to retouch, from a sketch taken upon the spot, his admirable painting of the "Marsyas flayed alive."

I will endeavor to depict my sensations upon the gallows. To write upon such a theme it is necessary to have been hanged. Every author should confine himself to matters of experience. Thus Mark Antony wrote a treatise upon drunkenness.

Die I certainly did not. The sudden jerk given to my neck upon the falling of the drop, merely proved a corrective to the unfortunate twist afforded me by the gentleman in the coach. ‚Although my body certainly *was*, I had, alas! no breath *to be* suspended; and but for the shaking of the rope, the pressure of the knot under my ear, and the rapid determination of blood to the brain, should, I dare say, have experienced very little inconvenience.

The latter feeling, however, grew momentarily more painful. I heard my heart beating with violence—the veins in my hands and wrists swelled nearly to bursting—my temples throbbed tempestuously—and I felt that my eyes were starting from their sockets. Yet when I say that in spite of all this my sensations were not absolutely intolerable, I will not be believed.

There were noises in my ears—first like the tolling of huge bells—then like the beating of a thousand drums—then, lastly, like the low, sullen murmurs of the sea. But these noises were very far from disagreeable.

Although, too, the powers of my mind were confused and distorted, yet I was—strange to say!—well aware of such confusion and distortion. I could, with unerring promptitude determine at will in what particulars my sensations were correct—and in what particulars I wandered from the path. I could even feel with accuracy *how far*—to *what very point*, such wanderings had misguided me, but still without the power of correcting my deviations. I took besides, at the same time, a wild delight in analyzing my conceptions.*

* The general reader will I dare say recognize, in these *sensations* of Mr. Lacko'breath, much of the absurd *metaphysicianism* of the redoubted Schelling.

Memory, which, of all other faculties, should have first taken its departure, seemed on the contrary to have been endowed with quadrupled power. Each incident of my past life flitted before me like a shadow. There was not a brick in the building where I was born—not a dog-leaf in the primer I had thumbed over when a child—not a tree in the forest where I hunted when a boy—not a street in the cities I had traversed when a man—that I did not at that time most palpably behold. I could repeat to myself entire lines, passages, names, acts, chapters, books, from the studies of my earlier days; and while, I dare say, the crowd around me were blind with horror, or aghast with awe, I was alternately with Æschylus, a demi-god, or with Aristophanes, a frog.

*   *   *

A dreamy delight now took hold upon my spirit, and I imagined that I had been eating opium, or feasting upon the Hashish of the old Assassins. But glimpses of pure, unadulterated reason—during which I was still buoyed up by the hope of finally escaping that death which hovered, like a vulture above me—were still caught occasionally by my soul.

By some unusual pressure of the rope against my face, a portion of the cap was chafed away, and I found to my astonishment that my powers of vision were not altogether destroyed. A sea of waving heads rolled around me. In the intensity of my delight I eyed them with feelings of the deepest commiseration, and blessed, as I looked upon the haggard assembly, the superior benignity of *my* proper stars.

I now reasoned, rapidly I believe—profoundly I am sure—upon principles of common law—propriety of that law especially, for which I hung—absurdities in political economy which till then I had never been able to acknowledge—dogmas in the old Aristotelians now generally denied, but not the less intrinsically true—detestable school formulæ in Bourdon, in Garnier, in Lacroix—synonymes in Crabbe—lunar-lunatic theories in St. Pierre—falsities in the Pelham novels—beauties in Vivian Grey—more than beauties in Vivian Grey—profundity in Vivian Grey—genius in Vivian Grey—every thing in Vivian Grey.

Then came, like a flood, Coleridge, Kant, Fichte, and Pantheism—then like a deluge, the Academie, Pergola, La Scala, San Carlo, Paul, Albert, Noblet, Ronzi Vestris, Fanny Bias, and Taglioni.

* * *

A rapid change was now taking place in my sensations. The last shadows of connection flitted away from my meditations. A storm—a tempest of ideas, vast, novel, and soul-stirring, bore my spirit like a feather afar off. Confusion crowded upon confusion like a wave upon a wave. In a very short time Schelling himself would have been satisfied with my entire loss of self-identity. The crowd became a mass of mere abstraction.

About this period I became aware of a heavy fall and shock—but, although the concussion jarred throughout my frame, I had not the slightest idea of its having been sustained in my own proper person; and thought of it as of an incident peculiar to some other existence—an idiosyncrasy belonging to some other Ens.

It was at this moment—as I afterwards discovered—that having been suspended for the full term of execution, it was thought proper to remove my body from the gallows—this, the more especially as the real culprit had now been retaken and recognized.

Much sympathy was now exercised in my behalf—and as no one in the city appeared to identify my body, it was ordered that I should be interred in the public sepulchre early in the following morning. I lay, in the meantime, without signs of life—although from the moment, I suppose, when the rope was loosened from my neck, a dim consciousness of my situation oppressed me like the night-mare.

I was laid out in a chamber sufficiently small, and very much encumbered with furniture—yet to me it appeared of a size to contain the universe. I have never before or since, in body or in mind, suffered half so much agony as from that single idea. Strange! that the simple conception of abstract magnitude—of infinity—should have been accompanied with pain. Yet so it was. "With how vast a difference," said I, "in life and in death—in time and in eternity—here and hereafter, shall our merest sensations be imbodied!"

The day died away, and I was aware that it was growing dark—yet the same terrible conceit still overwhelmed me. Nor was it confined to the boundaries of the apartment—it extended, although in a more definite manner, to all objects, and, perhaps I will not be understood in saying that it extended also to all *sentiments*. My fingers as they lay cold, clammy, stiff, and pressing helplessly one against another, were, in my imagination, swelled to a size according with the proportions of the Antœus. Every portion of my frame betook of their enormity. The pieces of money—I well remember—which being placed upon my eyelids, failed to keep them effectually closed, seemed huge, interminable chariot-wheels of the Olympia, or of the Sun.

Yet it is very singular that I experienced no sense of weight—of gravity. On the contrary I was put to much inconvenience by that buoyancy—that tantalizing *difficulty of keeping down*, which is felt by the swimmer in deep water. Amid the tumult of my terrors I laughed with a hearty internal laugh to think what incongruity there would be—could I arise and walk—between the elasticity of my motion, and the mountain of my form.

*   *   *

The night came—and with it a new crowd of horrors. The consciousness of my approaching interment, began to assume new distinctness, and consistency—yet never for one moment did I imagine *that I was not actually dead.*

"This then"—I mentally ejaculated—"this darkness which is palpable, and oppresses with a sense of suffocation—this—this—is indeed *death.* This is death—this is death the terrible—death the holy. This is the death undergone by Regulus—and equally by Seneca. Thus—thus, too, shall I always remain—always—always remain. Reason is folly, and Philosophy a lie. No one will know my sensations, my horror—my despair. Yet will men still persist in reasoning, and philosophizing, and making themselves fools. There is, I find, no hereafter but this. This—this—this—is the only Eternity!—and what, O Beelzebub!—*what* an Eternity!—to lie in this vast—this awful void—a hideous, vague, and unmeaning anomaly—motionless, yet wishing for motion—powerless, yet longing for power—forever, forever, and forever!"

But the morning broke at length—and with its misty and gloomy dawn arrived in triple horror the paraphernalia of the grave. Then—and not till then—was I fully sensible of the fearful fate hanging over me. The phantasms of the night had faded away with its shadows, and the actual terrors of the yawning tomb left me no heart for the bug-bear speculations of Transcendentalism.

I have before mentioned that my eyes were but imperfectly closed—yet as I could not move them in any degree, those objects alone which crossed the direct line of vision were within the 'sphere of my comprehension. But across that line of vision spectral and stealthy figures were continually flitting, like the ghosts of Banquo. They were making hurried preparations for my interment. First came the coffin which they placed quietly by my side. Then the undertaker with attendants and a screw-driver. Then a stout man whom I could distinctly see and who took hold of my feet—while one whom I could only feel lifted me by the head and shoulders. Together they placed me in the coffin, and drawing the shroud up over my face proceeded to fasten down the lid. One of the screws, missing its proper direction, was screwed by the carelessness of the undertaker deep—deep—down into my shoulder. A convulsive shudder ran throughout my frame. With what horror, with what sickening of heart did I reflect that one minute sooner a similar manifestation of life, would, in all probability, have prevented my inhumation. But alas! it was now too late, and hope died away within my bosom as I felt myself lifted upon the shoulders of men—carried down the stairway—and thrust within the hearse.

During the brief passage to the cemetery my sensations, which for some time had been lethargic and dull, assumed, all at once, a degree of intense and unnatural vivacity for which I can in no manner account. I could distinctly hear the rustling of the plumes—the whispers of the attendants —the solemn breathings of the horses of death. Confined as I was in that narrow and strict embrace, I could feel the quicker or slower movement of the procession—the restlessness of the driver—the windings of the road as it led us to the right or to the left. I could distinguish the peculiar odor of the coffin—the sharp acid smell of the steel screws. I could see the texture of the shroud as it lay close against my face; and was even conscious of the rapid variations in light and shade which the flapping to and fro of the sable hangings occasioned within the body of the vehicle.

In a short time however, we arrived at the place of sculpture, and I felt myself deposited within the tomb. The entrance was secured—they departed—and I was left alone. A line of Marston's "Malcontent,"

"Death's a good fellow and keeps open house,"

struck me at that moment as a palpable lie. Sullenly I lay at length, the quick among the dead—an *Anacharsis inter Scythas*.

From what I overheard early in the morning, I was led to believe that the occasions when the vault was made use of were of very rare occurrence. It was probable that many months might elapse before the doors of the tomb would be again unbarred—and even should I survive until that period, what means could I have more than at present, of making known my situation or of escaping from the coffin? I resigned myself, therefore, with much tranquillity to my fate, and fell, after many hours, into a deep and deathlike sleep.

How long I remained thus is to me a mystery. When I awoke my limbs were no longer cramped with the cramp of death—I was no longer without the power of motion. A very slight exertion was sufficient to force off the lid of my prison—for the dampness of the atmosphere had already occasioned decay in the woodwork around the screws.

My steps as I groped around the sides of my habitation were, however, feeble and uncertain, and I felt all the gnawings of hunger with the pains of intolerable thirst. Yet, as time passed away, it is strange that I experienced little uneasiness from these scourges of the earth, in comparison with the more terrible visitations of the fiend *Ennui*. Stranger still were the resources by which I endeavored to banish him from my presence.

The sepulchre was large and subdivided into many compartments, and I busied myself in examining the peculiarities of their construction. I determined the length and breadth of my abode. I counted and recounted the stones of the masonry. But there were other methods by which I endeavored to lighten the tedium of my hours. Feeling my way among the numerous coffins ranged in order around, I lifted them down, one by one, and breaking open their lids, busied myself in speculations about the mortality within.

"This," I reflected, tumbling over a carcass, puffy, bloated, and rotund—"this has been, no doubt, in every sense of the word, an unhappy—an unfortunate man. It has been his terrible lot not to walk, but to waddle—to pass through life not like a human being, but like an elephant—not like a man, but like a rhinoceros.

"His attempts at getting on have been mere abortions—and his circumgyratory proceedings a palpable failure. Taking a step forward, it has been his misfortune to take two towards the right, and three towards the left. His studies have been confined to the Philosophy of Crabbe.

"He can have had no idea of the wonders of a *Pirouette*. To him a *Pas de Papillon* has been an abstract conception.

"He has never ascended the summit of a hill. He has never viewed from any steeple the glories of a metropolis.

"Heat has been his mortal enemy. In the dog-days his days have been the days of a dog. Therein, he has dreamed of flames and suffocation—of mountains upon mountains—of Pelion upon Ossa.

"He was short of breath—to say all in a word—he was short of breath.

"He thought it extravagant to play upon wind instruments. He was the inventor of self moving fans—wind-sails—and ventilators. He patronized Du Pont the bellows-maker—and died miserably in attempting to smoke a cigar.

"His was a case in which I feel deep interest—a lot in which I sincerely sympathize."

"But here," said I—"here"—and I dragged spitefully from its receptacle a gaunt, tall, and peculiar-looking form, whose remarkable appearance struck me with a sense of unwelcome familiarity—"here," said I—"here is a wretch entitled to no earthly commiseration." Thus saying, in order to obtain a more distinct view of my subject, I applied my thumb and forefinger to his nose, and, causing him to assume a sitting position upon the ground, held him, thus, at the length of my arm, while I continued my soliloquy.

—"entitled," I repeated, "to no earthly commiseration. Who indeed would think of compassionating a shadow? Besides—has he not had his full share of the blessings of mortality? He was the originator of tall monuments—shot-towers—lightning-rods—lombardy-populars. His treatise upon 'Shades and Shadows' has immortalized him.

"He went early to college and studied Pneumatics. He then came home—talked eternally—and played upon the French horn.

"He patronized the bag-pipes. Captain Barclay, who walked against Time, would not walk against *him*. Windham and Allbreath were his favorite writers. He died gloriously while inhaling gas—*levique flatu corrumpitur*, like the *fama pudicitiæ* in Hieronymus.* He was indubitably a"———

"How *can* you?—how—*can*—you?"—interrupted the object of my animadversions, gasping for breath, and tearing off, with a desperate exertion, the bandage around his jaws—how *can* you, Mr. Lacko'breath, be so infernally cruel as to pinch me in that manner by the nose? Did you not see how they had fastened up my mouth—and you *must* know—if you know any thing—what a vast superfluity of breath I have to dispose of! If you do *not* know, however, sit down and you shall see. In my situation it is really a great relief to be able to open one's mouth—to be able to expatiate—to be able to communicate with a person like yourself who do not think yourself called upon at every period to interrupt the thread of a gentleman's discourse. Interruptions are annoying and should undoubtedly be abolished—don't you think so?—no reply, I

---

* *Tenera res in feminis fama pudicitiæ et quasi flos pulcherrimus, cito ad levem marcessit auram, levique flatu corrumpitur—maxime, &c.*—Hieronymus ad Salvinam.

beg you,—one person is enough to be speaking at a time.
I shall be done, by and by, and then you may begin. How
the devil, sir, did you get into this place?—not a word I
beseech you—been here some time myself—terrible accident!—heard of it I suppose—awful calamity!—walking
under your windows—some short while ago—about the
time you were stage-struck—horrible occurrence! heard of
'catching one's breath,' eh?—hold your tongue I tell you!
—I caught somebody else's!—had always too much of my
own—met Blab at the corner of the street—wouldn't give
me a chance for a word—couldn't get in a syllable edge-
ways—attacked, consequently, with Epilepsis—Blab made
his escape—damn all fools!—they took me up for dead,
and put me in this place—pretty doings all of them!—
heard all you said about me—every word a lie—horrible!—
wonderful!—outrageous!—hideous!—incomprehensible!—
et cetera—et cetera—et cetera—et cetera"———

It is impossible to conceive my astonishment at so unexpected a discourse; or the extravagant joy with which I
became gradually convinced that the breath so fortunately
caught by the gentleman—whom I soon recognized as
my neighbor Windenough—was, in fact, the identical
expiration mislaid by myself in the conversation with my
wife. Time—place—and incidental circumstances rendered
it a matter beyond question. I did not however, immediately release my hold upon Mr. W.'s proboscis—not
at least during the long period in which the inventor of
lombardy poplars continued to favor me with his explanations. In this respect I was actuated by that habitual
prudence which has ever been my predominating trait.

I reflected that many difficulties might still lie in the
path of my preservation which extreme exertion on my
part would be alone able to surmount. Many persons, I
considered, are prone to estimate commodities in their
possession—however valueless to the then proprietor—however troublesome, or distressing—in precise ratio with the

advantages to be derived by others from their attainment
—or by themselves from their abandonment. Might not
this be the case with Mr. Windenough? In displaying
anxiety for the breath of which he was at present so
willing to get rid, might I not lay myself open to the
exactions of his avarice? There are scoundrels in this world
—I remembered with a sigh—who will not scruple to take
unfair opportunities with even a next door neighbor—and
(this remark is from Epictetus) it is precisely at that time
when men are most anxious to throw off the burden of
their own calamities that they feel the least desirous of
relieving them in others.

Upon considerations similar to these, and still retaining
my grasp upon the nose of Mr. W., I accordingly thought
proper to model my reply.

"Monster!"—I began in a tone of the deepest indignation—"monster! and double-winded idiot!—Dost *thou*
whom, for thine iniquities, it has pleased Heaven to ac-
curse with a two-fold respiration—dost *thou*, I say, presume to address me in the familiar language of an old
acquaintance?—'I lie,' forsooth!—and 'hold my tongue,'
to be sure—pretty conversation, indeed, to a gentleman
with a single breath!—and all, this, too, when I have it
in my power to relieve the calamity under which thou
dost so justly suffer—to curtail the superfluities of thine
unhappy respiration." Like Brutus I paused for a reply—
with which, like a tornado, Mr. Windenough immediately
overwhelmed me. Protestation followed upon protestation, and apology upon apology. There were no terms
with which he was unwilling to comply, and there were
none of which I failed to take the fullest advantage.

Preliminaries being at length arranged, my acquaintance delivered me the respiration—for which—having
carefully examined it—I gave him afterwards a receipt.

I am aware that by many I shall be held to blame for
speaking in a manner so cursory of a transaction so im-

palpable. It will be thought that I should have entered more minutely into the details of an occurrence by which —and all this is very true—much new light might be thrown upon a highly interesting branch of physical philosophy.

To all this, I am sorry, that I cannot reply. A hint is the only answer which I am permitted to make. There were circumstances—but I think it much safer upon consideration to say as little as possible about an affair so delicate—so *delicate*, I repeat, and at the same time involving the interests of a third party whose resentment I have not the least desire, at this moment, of incurring.

We were not long after this necessary arrangement in effecting an escape from the dungeons of the sepulchre. The united strength of our resuscitated voices was soon efficiently apparent. Scissors, the Whig Editor, republished a treatise upon "the nature and origin of subterranean noises." A reply—rejoinder—confutation—and justification followed in the columns of an ultra Gazette. It was not until the opening of the vault to decide the controversy, that the appearance of Mr. Windenough and myself proved both parties to have been decidedly in the wrong.

I cannot conclude these details of some very singular passages in a life at all times sufficiently eventful, without again recalling to the attention of the reader the merits of that indiscriminate philosophy which is a sure and ready shield against those shafts of calamity which can be neither seen, felt, nor fully understood. It was in the spirit of this wisdom that, among the ancient Hebrews, it was believed the gates of Heaven would be inevitably opened to that sinner, or saint, who with good lungs and implicit confidence, should vociferate the word "*Amen!*" It was in the spirit of this wisdom that when a great plague raged at Athens, and every means had been in vain attempted for its removal, Epimenides—as Laertius relates in his second book of the life of that philosopher—advised the erection of a shrine and temple *to prostekonti Theo*— "to the proper God."

MS. FOUND IN A BOTTLE

Qui n'a plus qu'un moment à vivre
N'a plus rien à dissimuler.—*Quinault—Atys.*

Of my country and of my family I have little to say. Ill usage and length of years have driven me from the one, and estranged me from the other. Hereditary wealth afforded me an education of no common order, and a contemplative turn of mind enabled me to methodize the stores which early study very diligently garnered up.—Beyond all things, the works of the German moralists gave me great delight: not from any ill-advised admiration of their eloquent madness, but from that ease with which my habits of rigid thought enabled me to detect their falsities. I have often been reproached with the aridity of my genius; a deficiency of imagination has been imputed to me as a crime: and the Pyrrhonism of my opinions has at all times rendered me notorious. Indeed, a strong relish for physical philosophy has, I fear, tinctured my mind with a very common error of this age—I mean the habit of referring occurrences, even the least susceptible of such reference, to the principles of that science. Upon the whole, no person could be less liable than myself to be led away from the severe precincts of truth by the *ignes fatui* of superstition. I have thought proper to premise thus much, lest the incredible tale I have to tell should be considered rather the raving of a crude imagination, than the positive experience of a mind to which the reveries of fancy have been a dead letter and a nullity.

After many years spent in foreign travel, I sailed in the year 18—, from the port of Batavia, in the rich and populous island of Java, on a voyage to the Archipelago of the Sunda islands. I went as passenger—having no other inducement than a kind of nervous restlessness which haunted me as a fiend.

Our vessel was a beautiful ship of about four hundred tons, copper fastened, and built at Bombay of Malabar teak. She was freighted with cotton-wood and oil, from the Lachadive islands. We had also on board coir, jaggeree, ghee, cocoa-nuts, and a few cases of opium. The stowage was clumsily done, and the vessel consequently crank.

We got under way with a mere breath of wind, and for many days stood along the eastern coast of Java, without any other incident to beguile the monotony of our course than the occasional meeting with some of the small grabs of the Archipelago to which we were bound.

One evening, leaning over the taffrail, I observed a very singular, isolated cloud, to the N. W. It was remarkable, as well for its color, as from its being the first we had seen since our departure from Batavia. I watched it attentively until sunset, when it spread all at once to the eastward and westward, girting in the horizon with a narrow strip of vapor, and looking like a long line of low beach. My notice was soon afterwards attracted by the dusky-red appearance of the moon, and the peculiar character of the sea. The latter was undergoing a rapid change, and the water seemed more than usually transparent. Although I could distinctly see the bottom, yet, heaving the lead, I found the ship in fifteen fathoms. The air now became intolerably hot, and was loaded with spiral exhalations similar to those arising from heated iron. As night came on, every breath of wind died away, and a more entire calm it is impossible to conceive. The flame of a candle burned upon the poop without the least per-

ceptible motion, and a long hair, held between the finger
and thumb, hung without the possibility of detecting a
vibration. However, as the captain said he could perceive
no indication of danger, and as we were drifting in bodily
to shore, he ordered the sails to be furled, and the anchor
let go. No watch was set, and the crew, consisting principally of Malays, stretched themselves deliberately upon
deck. I went below—not without a full presentiment of
evil. Indeed, every appearance warranted me in appre-
hending a Simoom. I told the captain my fears: but he
paid no attention to what I said, and left me without deign-
ing to give a reply. My uneasiness, however, prevented me
from sleeping, and about midnight I went upon deck.—
As I placed my foot upon the upper step of the com-
panion-ladder, I was startled by a loud, humming noise,
like that occasioned by the rapid revolution of a mill-
wheel, and before I could ascertain its meaning, I found
the ship quivering to its centre. In the next instant, a
wilderness of foam hurled us upon our beam-ends, and,
rushing over us fore and aft, swept the entire decks from
stem to stern.

The extreme fury of the blast proved, in a great measure, the salvation of the ship. Although completely water-
logged, yet, as her masts had gone by the board, she rose,
after a minute, heavily from the sea, and, staggering awhile
beneath the immense pressure of the tempest, finally
righted.

By what miracle I escaped destruction, it is impossible
to say. Stunned by the shock of the water, I found myself,
upon recovery, jammed in between the stern-post and rud-
der. With great difficulty I gained my feet, and looking
dizzily around, was, at first, struck with the idea of our
being among breakers; so terrific, beyond the wildest imagination, was the whirlpool of mountainous and foaming
ocean within which we were engulfed. After a while, I
heard the voice of an old Swede, who had shipped with us

at the moment of our leaving port. I hallooed to him with all my strength, and presently he came reeling aft. We soon discovered that we were the sole survivors of the accident. All on deck, with the exception of ourselves, had been swept overboard;—the captain and mates must have perished as they slept, for the cabins were deluged with water. Without assistance, we could expect to do little for the security of the ship, and our exertions were at first paralyzed by the momentary expectation of going down. Our cable had, of course, parted like pack-thread, at the first breath of the hurricane, or we should have been instantaneously overwhelmed. We scudded with frightful velocity before the sea, and the water made clear breaches over us. The framework of our stern was shattered excessively, and, in almost every respect, we had received considerable injury; but to our extreme joy we found the pumps, unchoked, and that we had made no great shifting of our ballast.—Then main fury of the blast had already blown over, and we apprehended, little danger from the violence of the wind; but we looked forward to its total cessation with dismay; well believing, that, in our shattered condition, we should inevitably perish in the tremendous swell which would ensue. But this very just apprehension seemed by no means likely to be soon verified. For five entire days and nights—during which our only subsistence was a small quantity of jaggeree, procured with great difficulty from the forecastle—the hulk flew at a rate defying computation, before rapidly succeeding flaws of wind, which, without equalling the first violence of the Simoom, were still more terrific than any tempest I had before encountered. Our course for the first four days was, with trifling variations, S. E. and by S.; and we must have run down the coast of New Holland.—On the fifth day the cold became extreme, although the wind had hauled round a point more to the northward.— The sun arose with a sickly yellow lustre, and clambered a very few degrees above the horizon—emitting no decisive light. There were no clouds apparent, yet the wind was upon the increase, and blew with a fitful and unsteady fury. About noon, as nearly as we could guess, our attention was again arrested by the appearance of the sun. It gave out no light, properly so called, but a dull and sullen glow without reflection, as if all its rays were polarized. Just before sinking within the turgid sea, its central fires suddenly went out, as if hurriedly extinguished by some unaccountable power. It was a dim, silver-like rim, alone, as it rushed down the unfathomable ocean.

We waited in vain for the arrival of the sixth day— that day to me has not arrived—to the Swede, never did arrive. Thenceforward we were enshrouded in pitchy darkness, so that we could not have seen an object at twenty paces from the ship. Eternal night continued to envelop us, all unrelieved by the phosphoric sea-brilliancy to which we had been accustomed in the tropics. We observed too, that, although the tempest continued to rage with unabated violence, there was no longer to be discovered the usual appearance of surf, or foam, which had hitherto attended us. All around were horror, and thick gloom, and a black sweltering desert of ebony. Superstitious terror crept by degrees into the spirit of the old Swede, and my own soul was wrapped up in silent wonder. We neglected all care of the ship, as worse than useless, and securing ourselves, as well as possible, to the stump of the mizen-mast, looked out bitterly into the world of ocean. We had no means of calculating time, nor could we form any guess of our situation. We were, however, well aware of having made farther to the southward than any previous navigators, and felt great amazement at not meeting with the usual impediments of ice. In the meantime every moment threatened to be our last— every mountainous billow hurried to overwhelm us. The swell surpassed anything I had imagined possible, and that we were not instantly buried is a miracle. My companion spoke of the lightness of our cargo, and reminded me of the excellent qualities of our ship; but I could not help feeling the utter hopelessness of hope itself, and prepared myself gloomily for that death which I thought nothing could defer beyond an hour, as, with every knot of way the ship made, the swelling of the black stupendous seas became more dismally appalling. At times we gasped for breath at an elevation beyond the albatross—at times became dizzy with the velocity of our descent into some watery hell, where the air grew stagnant, and no sound disturbed the slumbers of the kraken.

We were at the bottom of one of these abysses, when a quick scream from my companion broke fearfully upon the night. "See! see!" cried he, shrieking in my ears, "Almighty God! see! see!" As he spoke, I became aware of a dull, sullen glare of red light which streamed down the sides of the vast chasm where we lay, and threw a fitful brilliancy upon our deck. Casting my eyes upwards, I beheld a spectacle which froze the current of my blood. At a terrific height directly above us, and upon the very verge of the precipitous descent, hovered a gigantic ship of, perhaps, four thousand tons. Although upreared upon the summit of a wave more than a hundred times her own altitude, her apparent size still exceeded that of any ship of the line or East Indiaman in existence. Her huge hull was of a deep dingy black, unrelieved by any of the customary carvings of a ship. A single row of brass cannon protruded from her open ports, and dashed from their polished surfaces the fires of innumerable battle-lanterns, which swung to and fro about her rigging. But what mainly inspired us with horror and astonishment, was that she bore up under a press of sail in the very teeth of that supernatural sea, and of that ungovernable hurricane. When we first discovered her, her bows were alone to be seen, as she rose slowly from the dim and horrible gulf beyond her. For a moment of intense terror she paused upon the giddy pinnacle, as if in contemplation of her own sublimity, then trembled and tottered, and—came down.

At this instant, I know not what sudden self-possession came over my spirit. Staggering as far aft as I could, I awaited fearlessly the ruin that was to overwhelm. Our own vessel was at length ceasing from her struggles, and sinking with her head to the sea. The shock of the descending mass struck her, consequently, in that portion of her frame which was already under water, and the inevitable result was to hurl me, with irresistible violence, upon the rigging of the stranger.

As I fell, the ship hove in stays, and went about; and to the confusion ensuing I attributed my escape from the notice of the crew. With little difficulty I made my way unperceived to the main hatchway, which was partially open, and soon found an opportunity of secreting myself in the hold. Why I did so I can hardly tell. An indefinite sense of awe, which at first sight of the navigators of the ship had taken hold of my mind, was perhaps the principle of my concealment. I was unwilling to trust myself with a race of people who had offered, to the cursory glance I had taken, so many points of vague novelty, doubt, and apprehension. I therefore thought proper to contrive a hiding-place in the hold. This I did by removing a small portion of the shifting-boards, in such a manner as to afford me a convenient retreat between the huge timbers of the ship.

I had scarcely completed my work, when a footstep in the hold forced me to make use of it. A man passed by my place of concealment with a feeble and unsteady gait. I could not see his face, but had an opportunity of observing his general appearance. There was about it an evidence of great age and infirmity. His knees tottered beneath a load of years, and his entire frame quivered under the burthen. He muttered to himself in a low broken

tone, some words of a language which I could not understand, and groped in .a corner among a pile of singular-
looking instruments, and decayed charts of navigation.
His manner was a wild mixture of the peevishness of second childhood, and the solemn dignity of a God. He at
length went on deck, and I saw him no more.

*   *   *

A feeling, for which I have no name, has taken possession of my soul—a sensation which will admit of no
analysis, to which the lessons of by-gone time are inade-
quate, and for which I fear futurity itself will offer me
no key. To a mind constituted like my own, the latter
consideration is an evil. I shall never—I know that I shall
never—be satisfied with regard to the nature of my conceptions. Yet it is not wonderful that these conceptions
are indefinite, since they have their origin in sources so
utterly novel. A new sense—a new entity is added to my
soul.

It is long since I first trod the deck of this terrible ship,
and the rays of my destiny are, I think, gathering to a
focus. Incomprehensible men! Wrapped up in meditations of a kind which I cannot divine, they pass me by
unnoticed. Concealment is utter folly on my part, for the
people *will not* see. It was but just now that I passed directly before the eyes of the mate—it was no long while
ago that I ventured into the captain's own private cabin,
and took thence the materials with which I write, and have
written. I shall from time to time continue this journal.
It is true that I may not find an opportunity of transmit-
ting it to the world, but I will not fail to make the endeavour. At the last moment I will enclose the MS. in a
bottle, and cast it within the sea.

*   *   *

An incident has occurred which has given me new room
for meditation. Are such things the operation of ungov-

erned Chance? I had ventured upon deck and thrown myself down, without attracting any notice, among a pile of ratlin-stuff and old sails, in the bottom of the yawl. While musing upon the singularity of my fate, I unwittingly daubed with a tar-brush the edges of a neatly-folded studding-sail which lay near me on a barrel. The studding-sail is now bent upon the ship, and the thoughtless touches of the brush are spread out into the word DISCOVERY.

*   *   *

I have made many observations lately upon the structure of the vessel. Although well armed, she is not, I think, a ship of war. Her rigging, build, and general equipment, all negative a supposition of this kind. What she is *not*, I can easily perceive—what she *is* I fear it is impossible to say. I know not how it is, but in scrutinizing her strange model and singular cast of spars, her huge size and overgrown suits of canvass, her severely simple bow and antiquated stern, there will occasionally flash across my mind a sensation of familiar things, and there is always mixed up with such indistinct shadows of recollection, an unaccountable memory of old foreign chronicles and ages long ago.

I have been looking at the timbers of the ship. She is built of a material to which I am a stranger. There is a peculiar character about the wood which strikes me as rendering it unfit for the purpose to which it has been applied. I mean its extreme *porousness*, considered independently of the worm-eaten condition which is a consequence of navigation in these seas, and apart from the rottenness attendant upon age. It will appear perhaps an observation somewhat over-curious, but this wood would have every characteristic of Spanish oak, if Spanish oak were distended by any unnatural means.

In reading the above sentence a curious apothegm of an old weather-beaten Dutch navigator comes full upon my recollection. "It is as sure," he was wont to say, when any doubt was entertained of his veracity, "as sure as there is a sea where the ship itself will grow in bulk like the living body of the seaman."

*   *   *

About an hour ago, I made bold to thrust myself among a group of the crew. They paid me no manner of attention, and, although I stood in the very midst of them all, seemed utterly unconscious of my presence. Like the one I had at first seen in the hold, they all bore about them the marks of a hoary old age. Their knees trembled with infirmity; their shoulders were bent double with decrepitude; their shrivelled skins rattled in the wind; their voices were low, tremulous and broken: their eyes glistened with the rheum of years; and their gray hairs streamed terribly in the tempest. Around them, on every part of the deck, lay scattered mathematical instruments of the most quaint and obsolete construction.

*   *   *

I mentioned some time ago the bending of a studding-sail. From that period the ship, being thrown dead off the wind, has continued her terrific course due south, with every rag of canvass packed upon her, from her trucks to her lower studding-sail booms, and rolling every moment her top-gallant yard-arms into the most appalling hell of water which it can enter into the mind of man to imagine. I have just left the deck, where I find it impossible to maintain a footing, although the crew seem to experience little inconvenience. It appears to me a miracle of miracles that our enormous bulk is not swallowed up at once and forever. We are surely doomed to hover continually upon the brink of Eternity, without taking a final plunge into the abyss. From billows a thousand times more stupendous than any I have ever seen, we glide away with the facility of the arrowy sea-gull; and the colossal waters rear their heads above us like demons of the deep, but like demons confined to simple threats and forbidden to destroy. I am led to attribute these frequent escapes to the only natural cause which can account for such effect.—I must suppose the ship to be within the influence of some strong current, or impetuous under-tow.

* * *

I have seen the captain face to face, and in his own cabin—but, as I expected, he paid me no attention. Although in his appearance there is, to a casual observer, nothing which might bespeak him more or less than man —still a feeling of irrepressible reverence and awe mingled with the sensation of wonder with which I regarded him. In stature he is nearly my own height; that is, about five feet eight inches. He is of a well-knit and compact frame of body, neither robust nor remarkably otherwise. But it is the singularity of the expression which reigns upon the face—it is the intense, the wonderful, the thrilling evidence of old age so utter, so extreme, which excites within my spirit a sense—a sentiment ineffable. His forehead, although little wrinkled, seems to bear upon it the stamp of a myriad of years.—His gray hairs are records of the past, and his grayer eyes are Sybils of the future. The cabin floor was thickly strewn with strange, iron-clasped folios, and mouldering instruments of science, and obsolete long-forgotten charts. His head was bowed down upon his hands, and he pored, with a fiery unquiet eye, over a paper which I took to be a commission, and which, at all events, bore the signature of a monarch. He muttered to himself, as did the first seaman whom I saw in the hold, some low peevish syllables of a foreign tongue, and although the speaker was close at my elbow, his voice seemed to reach my ears from the distance of a mile.

* * *

The ship and all in it are imbued with the spirit of Eld. The crew glide to and fro like the ghosts of buried centuries; their eyes have an eager and uneasy meaning; and when their figures fall athwart my path in the wild glare of the battle-lanterns, I feel as I have never felt before, although I have been all my life a dealer in antiquities, and have imbibed the shadows of fallen columns at Balbec, and Tadmor, and Persepolis, until my very soul has become a ruin.

* * *

When I look around me I feel ashamed of my former apprehensions. If I trembled at the blast which has hitherto attended us, shall I not stand aghast at a warring of wind and ocean, to convey any idea of which the words, tornado and simoom are trivial and ineffective! All in the immediate vicinity of the ship is the blackness of eternal night, and a chaos of foamless water; but, about a league on either side of us, may be seen, indistinctly and at intervals, stupendous ramparts of ice, towering away into the desolate sky, and looking like the walls of the universe.

* * *

As I imagined, the ship proves to be in a current; if that appellation can properly be given to a tide which, howling and shrieking by the white ice, thunders on to the southward with a velocity like the headlong dashing of a cataract.

* * *

To conceive the horror of my sensations is, I presume, utterly impossible; yet a curiosity to penetrate the mysteries of these awful regions, predominates even over my despair, and will reconcile me to the most hideous aspect of death. It is evident that we are hurrying onwards to some exciting knowledge—some never-to-be-imparted secret, whose attainment is destruction. Perhaps this current leads us to the southern pole itself. It must be confessed that a supposition apparently so wild has every probability in its favor.

* * *

The crew pace the deck with unquiet and tremulous step; but there is upon their countenances an expression more of the eagerness of hope than of the apathy of despair.

In the meantime the wind is still in our poop, and, as we carry a crowd of canvass, the ship is at times lifted bodily from out the sea————Oh, horror upon horror! the ice opens suddenly to the right, and to the left, and we are whirling dizzily, in immense concentric circles, round and round the borders of a gigantic amphitheatre, the summit of whose walls is lost in the darkness and the distance. But little time will be left me to ponder upon my destiny—the circles rapidly grow small—we are plunging madly within the grasp of the whirlpool—and amid a roaring, and bellowing, and thundering of ocean and of tempest, the ship is quivering, oh God! and—going down.

THE ASSIGNATION

Stay for me there! I will not fail
To meet thee in that hollow vale.

[*Exequy on the death of his wife, by Henry King, Bishop of Chichester.*]

Ill-fated and mysterious man!—bewildered in the brilliancy of thine own imagination, and fallen in the flames of thine own youth! Again in fancy I behold thee! Once more thy form hath risen before me!—not—oh not as thou art—in the cold valley and shadow—but as thou *shouldst be*—squandering away a life of magnificent meditation in that city of dim visions, thine own Venice—which is a star-beloved Elysium of the sea, and the wide windows of whose Palladian palaces look down with a deep and bitter meaning upon the secrets of her silent waters. Yes! I repeat it—as thou *shouldst be*. There are surely other worlds than this—other thoughts than the thoughts of the multitude—other speculations than the speculations of the sophist. Who then shall call thy conduct into question? who blame thee for thy visionary hours, or denounce those occupations as a wasting away of life, which were but the overflowings of thine everlasting energies?

It was at Venice, beneath the covered archway there called the *Ponte di Sospiri*, that I met for the third or fourth time the person of whom I speak. It is with a confused recollection that I bring to mind the circumstances of that meeting. Yet I remember—ah! how should I forget? —the deep midnight, the Bridge of Sighs, the beauty of woman, and the Genius of Romance that stalked up and down the narrow canal.

It was a night of unusual gloom. The great clock of the

Piazza had sounded the fifth hour of the Italian evening. The square of the Campanile lay silent and deserted, and the lights in the old Ducal Palace were dying fast away. I was returning home from the Piazzetta, by way of the Grand Canal. But as my gondola arrived opposite the mouth of the canal San Marco, a female voice from its recesses broke suddenly upon the night, in one wild, hysterical, and long continued shriek. Startled at the sound, I sprang upon my feet: while the gondolier, letting slip his single oar, lost it in the pitchy darkness beyond a chance of recovery, and we were consequently left to the guidance of the current which here sets from the greater into the smaller channel. Like some huge and sable-feathered condor, we were slowly drifting down towards the Bridge of Sighs, when a thousand flambeaux flashing from the windows, and down the staircases of the Ducal Palace, turned all at once that deep gloom into a livid and preternatural day.

A child, slipping from the arms of its own mother, had fallen from an upper window of the lofty structure into the deep and dim canal. The quiet waters had closed placidly over their victim; and, although my own gondola was the only one in sight, many a stout swimmer, already in the stream, was seeking in vain upon the surface, the treasure which was to be found, alas! only within the abyss. Upon the broad black marble flagstones at the entrance of the palace, and a few steps above the water, stood a figure which none who then saw can have ever since forgotten. It was the Marchesa Aphrodite—the adoration of all Venice—the gayest of the gay—the most lovely where all were beautiful—but still the young wife of the old and intriguing Mentoni, and the mother of that fair child, her first and only one, who now deep beneath the murky water, was thinking in bitterness of heart upon her sweet caresses, and exhausting its little life in struggles to call upon her name.

She stood alone. Her small, bare, and silvery feet gleamed in the black mirror of marble beneath her. Her hair, not as yet more than half loosened for the night from its ball-room array, clustered, amid a shower of diamonds, round and round her classical head, in curls like those of the young hyacinth. A snowy-white and gauze-like drapery seemed to be nearly the sole covering to her delicate form; but the mid-summer and midnight air was hot, sullen, and still, and no motion in the statue-like form itself, stirred even the folds of that raiment of very vapor which hung around it as the heavy marble hangs around the Niobe. Yet—strange to say!—her large lustrous eyes were not turned downwards upon that grave wherein her brightest hope lay buried—but riveted in a widely different direction! The prison of the Old Republic is, I think, the stateliest building in all Venice—but how could that lady gaze so fixedly upon it, when beneath her lay stifling her only child? Yon dark, gloomy niche, too, yawns right opposite her chamber window—what, then, *could* there be in its shadows—in its architecture—in its ivy-wreathed and solemn cornices—that the Marchesa di Mentoni had not wondered at a thousand times before? Nonsense!— Who does not remember that, at such a time as this, the eye, like a shattered mirror, multiplies the images of its sorrow, and sees in innumerable far off places, the woe which is close at hand?

Many steps above the Marchesa, and within the arch of the water-gate, stood, in full dress, the Satyr-like figure of Mentoni himself. He was occasionally occupied in thrumming a guitar, and seemed *ennuyé* to the very death, as at intervals he gave directions for the recovery of his child. Stupified and aghast, I had myself no power to move from the upright position I had assumed upon first hearing the shriek, and must have presented to the eyes of the agitated group a spectral and ominous appearance, as with pale countenance and rigid limbs, I floated down among them in that funereal gondola.

All efforts proved in vain. Many of the most energetic in the search were relaxing their exertions, and yielding to a gloomy sorrow. There seemed but little hope for the child; (how much less than for the mother!) but now, from the interior of that dark niche which has been already mentioned as forming a part of the Old Republican prison, and as fronting the lattice of the Marchesa, a figure muffled in a cloak, stepped out within reach of the light, and, pausing a moment upon the verge of the giddy descent, plunged headlong into the canal. As, in an instant afterwards, he stood with the still living and breathing child within his grasp, upon the marble flagstones by the side of the Marchesa, his cloak, heavy with the drenching water, became unfastened, and, falling in folds about his feet, discovered to the wonder-stricken spectators the graceful person of a very young man, with the sound of whose name the greater part of Europe was then ringing.

No word spoke the deliverer. But the Marchesa! She will now receive her child—she will press it to her heart—she will cling to its little form, and smother it with her caresses. Alas! *another's* arms have taken it from the stranger— *another's* arms have taken it away, and borne it afar off, unnoticed, into the palace! And the Marchesa! Her lip— her beautiful lip trembles: tears are gathering in her eyes— those eyes which, like Pliny's acanthus, are "soft and almost liquid." Yes! tears are gathering in those eyes—and see! the entire woman thrills throughout the soul, and the statue has started into life! The pallor of the marble countenance, the swelling of the marble bosom, the very purity of the marble feet, we behold suddenly flushed over with a tide of ungovernable crimson; and a slight shudder quivers about her delicate frame, as a gentle air at Napoli about the rich silver lilies in the grass.

Why *should* that lady blush! To this demand there is no answer—except that, having left, in the eager haste and terror of a mother's heart, the privacy of her own *boudoir*, she has neglected to enthral her tiny feet in their slippers, and utterly forgotten to throw over her Venitian shoulders that drapery which is their due. What other possible reason could there have been for her so blushing?—for the glance of those wild appealing eyes?—for the unusual tumult of that throbbing bosom?—for the convulsive pressure of that trembling hand?—that hand which fell, as Mentoni turned into the palace, accidentally, upon the hand of the stranger. What reason could there have been for the low—the singularly low tone of those unmeaning words which the lady uttered hurriedly in bidding him adieu? "Thou hast conquered"—she said, or the murmurs of the water deceived me—"thou hast conquered—one hour after sunrise—we shall meet—so let it be!"

*   *   *

The tumult had subsided, the lights had died away within the palace, and the stranger, whom I now recognized, stood alone upon the flags. He shook with inconceivable agitation, and his eye glanced around in search of a gondola. I could not do less than offer him the service of my own; and he accepted the civility. Having obtained an oar at the water-gate, we proceeded together to his residence, while he rapidly recovered his self-possession, and spoke of our former slight acquaintance in terms of great apparent cordiality.

There are some subjects upon which I take pleasure in being minute. The person of the stranger—let me call him by this title, who to all the world was still a stranger—the person of the stranger is one of these subjects. In height he might have been below rather than above the medium size: although there were moments of intense passion when his frame actually *expanded* and belied the assertion. The light, almost slender symmetry of his figure, promised more of that ready activity which he evinced at the Bridge of Sighs, than of that Herculean strength which he has been known to wield without an effort, upon occasions of more dangerous emergency. With the mouth and chin of a deity—singular, wild, full, liquid eyes, whose shadows varied from pure hazel to intense and brilliant jet—and a profusion of curling, black hair, from which a forehead of unusual breath gleamed forth at intervals all light and ivory—his were features than which I have seen none more classically regular, except, perhaps, the marble ones of the Emperor Commodus. Yet his countenance was, nevertheless, one of those which all men have seen at some period of their lives, and have never afterwards seen again. It had no peculiar—it had no settled predominant expression to be fastened upon the memory; a countenance seen and instantly forgotten—but forgotten with a vague and never-ceasing desire of recalling it to mind. Not that the spirit of each rapid passion failed, at any time, to throw its own distinct image upon the mirror of that face—but that the mirror, mirror-like, retained no vestige of the passion, when the passion had departed.

Upon leaving him on the night of our adventure, he solicited me, in what I thought an urgent manner, to call upon him *very* early the next morning. Shortly after sunrise, I found myself accordingly at his Palazzo, one of those huge structures of gloomy, yet fantastic pomp, which tower above the water of the Grand Canal in the vicinity of the Rialto. I was shown up a broad winding staircase of mosaics, into an apartment whose unparalleled splendor burst through the opening door with an actual glare, making me blind and dizzy with luxuriousness.

I knew my acquaintance to be wealthy. Report had spoken of his possessions in terms which I had even ventured to call terms of ridiculous exaggeration. But as I gazed about me, I could not bring myself to believe that the wealth of any subject in Europe could have supplied the princely magnificence which burned and blazed around.

Although, as I say, the sun had arisen, yet the room was still brilliantly lighted up. I judged from this circumstance, as well as from an air of exhaustion in the countenance of my friend, that he had not retired to bed during the whole of the preceding night. In the architecture and embellishments of the chamber, the evident design had been to dazzle and astound. Little attention had been paid to the *decora* of what is technically called *keeping*, or to the proprieties of nationality. The eye wandered from object to object, and rested upon none—neither the *grotesques* of the Greek painters, nor the sculptures of the best Italian days, nor the huge carvings of untutored Egypt. Rich draperies in every part of the room trembled to the vibration of low, melancholy music, whose origin was not to be discovered. The senses were oppressed by mingled and conflicting perfumes, reeking up from strange convolute censers, together with multitudinous flaring and flickering tongues of emerald and violet fire. The rays of the newly risen sun poured in upon the whole, through windows formed each of a single pane of crimson-tinted glass. Glancing to and fro, in a thousand reflections, from curtains which rolled from their cornices like cataracts of molten silver, the beams of natural glory mingled at length fitfully with the artificial light, and lay weltering in subdued masses upon a carpet of rich, liquid-looking cloth of Chile gold.

"Ha! ha! ha!—ha! ha! ha!"—laughed the proprietor, motioning me to a seat as I entered the room, and throwing himself back at full length upon an ottoman. "I see," said he, perceiving that I could not immediately reconcile myself to the *bienséance* of so singular a welcome—"I see you are astonished at my apartment—at my statues—

my pictures—my originality of conception in architecture
and upholstery—absolutely drunk, eh? with my magnificence. But pardon me, my dear sir, (here his tone of
voice dropped to the very spirit of cordiality,) pardon me
for my uncharitable laughter. You appeared so *utterly*
astonished. Besides, some things are so completely ludicrous that a man *must* laugh or die. To die laughing must
be the most glorious of all glorious deaths! Sir Thomas
More—a very fine man was Sir Thomas More—Sir
Thomas More died laughing, you remember. Also in the
Absurdities of Ravisius Textor, there is a long list of characters who came to the same magnificent end. Do you
know, however," continued he musingly, "that at Sparta
(which is now Palæochori), at Sparta, I say, to the west
of the citadel, among a chaos of scarcely visible ruins, is a
kind of *socle* upon which are still legible the letters
ΛΑΞΜ. They are undoubtedly part of ΓΕΛΑΞΜΑ. Now
at Sparta were a thousand temples and shrines to a thousand different divinities. How exceedingly strange that the
altar of Laughter should have survived all the others! But
in the present instance," he resumed, with a singular alteration of voice and manner, "I have no right to be merry
at your expense. You might well have been amazed. Europe cannot produce anything so fine as this, my little regal
cabinet. My other apartments are by no means of the
same order; mere *ultras* of fashionable inspidity. This is
better than fashion—is it not? Yet this has but to be seen
to become the rage—that is, with those who could afford
it at the cost of their entire patrimony. I have guarded,
however, against any such profanation. With one exception you are the only human being besides myself and
my *valet*, who has been admitted within the mysteries of
these imperial precincts, since they have been bedizzened
as you see!"

I bowed in acknowledgment: for the overpowering sense
of splendor and perfume, and music, together with the un-

expected eccentricity of his address and manner, prevented me from expressing, in words, my appreciation of what I might have construed into a compliment.

"Here," he resumed, arising and leaning on my arm as he sauntered around the apartment, "here are paintings from the Greeks to Cimabue, and from Cimabue to the present hour. Many are chosen, as you see, with little deference to the opinons of Virtû. They are all, however, fitting tapestry for a chamber such as this. Here too, are some *chéf d'œuvres* of the unknown great—and here un-finished designs by men, celebrated in their day, whose very names the perspicacity of the academies has left to silence and to me. What think you," said he, turning abruptly as he spoke—"what think you of this Madonna della Pietà?"

"It is Guido's own!" I said with all the enthusiasm of my nature, for I had been poring intently over its surpass-ing loveliness. "It is Guido's own!—how *could* you have obtained it?—she is undoubtedly in painting what the Venus is in sculpture."

"Ha!" said he thoughtfully, "the Venus—the beautiful Venus?—the Venus of the Medici?—she of the diminu-tive head and the gilded hair? Part of the left arm (here his voice dropped so as to be heard with difficulty), and all the right are restorations, and in the coquetry of that right arm lies, I think, the quintessence of all affectation. Give *me* the Canova! The Apollo, too!—is a copy—there can be no doubt of it—blind fool that I am, who cannot behold the boasted inspiration of the Apollo! I cannot help —pity me!—I cannot help preferring the Antinous. Was it not Socrates who said that the statuary found his statue in the block of marble? Then Michæl Angelo was by no means original in his couplet—

'Non ha l'ottimo artista alcun concetto
Chè un marmo solo in se non circunscriva.' "

It has been, or should be remarked, that in the manner of the true gentleman, we are always aware of a difference from the bearing of the vulgar, without being at once precisely able to determine in what such difference consists. Allowing the remark to have applied in its full force to the outward demeanor of my acquaintance, I felt it, on that eventful morning, still more fully applicable to his moral temperament and character. Nor can I better define that peculiarity of spirit which seemed to place him so essentially apart from all other human beings, than by calling it a *habit* of intense and continual thought, pervading even his most trivial actions—intruding upon his moments of dalliance—and interweaving itself with his very flashes of merriment—like adders which writhe from out the eyes of the grinning masks in the cornices around the temples of Persepolis.

I could not help, however, repeatedly observing, through the mingled tone of levity and solemnity with which he rapidly descanted upon matters of little importance, a certain air of trepidation—a degree of nervous *unction* in action and in speech—an unquiet excitability of manner which appeared to me at all times unaccountable, and upon some occasions even filled me with alarm. Frequently, too, pausing in the middle of a sentence whose commencement he had apparently forgotten, he seemed to be listening in the deepest attention, as if either in momentary expectation of a visiter, or to sounds which must have had existence in his imagination alone.

It was during one of these reveries or pauses of apparent abstraction, that, in turning over a page of the poet and scholar Politian's beautiful tragedy "The Orfeo," (the first native Italian tragedy,) which lay near me upon an ottoman, I discovered a passage underlined in pencil. It was a passage towards the end of the third act—a passage of the most heart-stirring excitement—a passage which, although tainted with impurity, no man shall read without a thrill of novel emotion—no woman without a sigh. The whole page was blotted with fresh tears, and, upon the opposite interleaf, were the following English lines, written in a hand so very different from the peculiar characters of my acquaintance, that I had some difficulty in recognising it as his own.

> Thou wast that all to me, love,
>   For which my soul did pine—
> A green isle in the sea, love,
>   A fountain and a shrine,
> All wreathed with fairy fruits and flowers;
>   And all the flowers were mine.
>
> Ah, dream too bright to last;
>   Ah, starry Hope that didst arise
> But to be overcast!
>   A voice from out the Future cries
> "Onward!"—but o'er the Past
>   (Dim gulf!) my spirit hovering lies,
> Mute, motionless, aghast!
>
> For alas! alas! with me
>   The light of life is o'er.
> "No more—no more—no more,"
> (Such language holds the solemn sea
>   To the sands upon the shore,)
> Shall bloom the thunder-blasted tree,
>   Or the stricken eagle soar!
>
> Now all my hours are trances;
>   And all my nightly dreams
> Are where thy dark eye glances,
>   And where thy footstep gleams,
> In what ethereal dances,
>   By what Italian streams.
>
> Alas! for that accursed time
>   They bore thee o'er the billow,

From Love to titled age and crime,
   And an unholy pillow—
From me, and from our misty clime,
   Where weeps the silver willow!

That these lines were written in English—a language with which I had not believed their author acquainted—afforded me little matter for surprise. I was too well aware of the extent of his acquirements, and of the singular pleasure he took in concealing them from observation, to be astonished at any similar discovery; but the place of date, I must confess, occasioned me no little amazement. It had been originally written *London,* and afterwards carefully overscored—not, however, so effectually as to conceal the word from a scrutinizing eye. I say this occasioned me no little amazement; for I well remember that, in a former conversation with my friend, I particularly inquired if he had at any time met in London the Marchesa di Mentoni, (who for some years previous to her marriage had resided in that city,) when his answer, if I mistake not, gave me to understand that he had never visited the metropolis of Great Britain. I might as well here mention, that I have more than once heard, (without of course giving credit to a report involving so many improbabilities,) that the person of whom I speak was not only by birth, but in education, an *Englishman.*

*   *   *

"There is one painting," said he, without being aware of my notice of the tragedy—"there is still one painting which you have not seen." And throwing aside a drapery, he discovered a full length portrait of the Marchesa Aphrodite.

Human art could have done no more in the delineation of her superhuman beauty. The same ethereal figure which stood before me the preceding night upon the steps

of the Ducal Palace, stood before me once again. But in
the expression of the countenance, which was beaming all
over with smiles, there still lurked (incomprehensible
anomaly!) that fitful stain of melancholy which will ever
be found inseparable from the perfection of the beautiful.
Her right arm lay folded over her bosom. With her left she
pointed downward to a curiously fashioned vase. One
small, fairy foot, alone visible, barely touched the earth—
and, scarcely discernible in the brilliant atmosphere which
seemed to encircle and enshrine her loveliness, floated
a pair of the most delicately imagined wings. My glance
fell from the painting to the figure of my friend, and the
vigorous words of Chapman's *Bussy D'Ambois* quivered
instinctively upon my lips:

> "He is up
> There like a Roman statue! He will stand
> Till Death hath made him marble!"

"Come!" he said at length, turning towards a table of
richly enamelled and massive silver, upon which were a
few goblets fantastically stained, together with two large
Etruscan vases, fashioned in the same extraordinary model
as that in the foreground of the portrait, and filled with
what I supposed to be Johannisberger. "Come!" he said
abruptly, "let us drink! It is early—but let us drink. It is
indeed early," he continued, musingly, as a cherub with
a heavy golden hammer, made the apartment ring with
the first hour after sunrise—"It is *indeed* early, but what
matters it? let us drink! Let us pour out an offering to yon
solemn sun which these gaudy lamps and censers are so
eager to subdue!" And, having made me pledge him in a
bumper, he swallowed in rapid succession several goblets
of the wine.

"To dream," he continued, resuming the tone of his
desultory conversation, as he held up to the rich light of a

censer one of the magnificent vases—"to dream has been the business of my life. I have therefore framed for myself, as you see, a bower of dreams. In the heart of Venice could I have erected a better? You behold around you, it is true, a medley of architectural embellishments. The chastity of Ionia is offended by antediluvian devices, and the sphynxes of Egypt are outstretched upon carpets of gold. Yet the effect is incongruous to the timid alone. Proprieties of place, and especially of time, are the bugbears which terrify mankind from the contemplation of the magnificent. Once I was myself a decorist: but that sublimation of folly has palled upon my soul. All this is now the fitter for my purpose. Like these arabesque censers, my spirit is writhing in fire, and the delirium of this scene is fashioning me for the wilder visions of that land of real dreams whither I am now rapidly departing." He here paused abruptly, bent his head to his bosom, and seemed to listen to a sound which I could not hear. At length, erecting his frame, he looked upwards and ejaculated the lines of the Bishop of Chichester:—

> *Stay for me there! I will not fail*
> *To meet thee in that hollow vale.*

In the next instant, confessing the power of the wine, he threw himself at full length upon an ottoman.

A quick step was now heard upon the staircase, and a loud knock at the door rapidly succeeded. I was hastening to anticipate a second disturbance, when a page of Mentoni's household burst into the room, and faltered out, in a voice choking with emotion, the incoherent words, "My mistress!—my mistress!—poisoned—poisoned! Oh beautiful—oh beautiful Aphrodite!"

Bewildered, I flew to the ottoman, and endeavored to arouse the sleeper to a sense of the startling intelligence. But his limbs were rigid—his lips were livid—his lately beaming eyes were riveted in *death*. I staggered back towards the table—my hand fell upon a cracked and blackened goblet—and a consciousness of the entire and terrible truth flashed suddenly over my soul.

BERENICE

Dicebant mihi sodales, si sepulchrum amicae visitarem, curas meas aliquantulum fore levatas.—*Ebn Zaiat.*

Misery is manifold. The wretchedness of earth is multiform. Overreaching the wide horizon as the rainbow, its hues are as various as the hues of that arch,—as distinct too, yet as intimately blended. Overreaching the wide horizon as the rainbow! How is it that from beauty I have derived a type of unloveliness?—from the covenant of peace a simile of sorrow? But as, in ethics, evil is a consequence of good, so, in fact, out of joy is sorrow born. Either the memory of past bliss is the anguish of to-day, or the agonies which have their origin in the ecstasies which *might have been*.

My baptismal name is Egæus; that of my family I will not mention. Yet there are no towers in the land more time-honored than my gloomy, gray, hereditary halls. Our line has been called a race of visionaries; and in many striking particulars—in the character of the family mansion—in the frescos of the chief saloon—in the tapestries of the dormitories—in the chiselling of some buttresses in the armory—but more especially in the gallery of antique paintings—in the fashion of the library chamber—and, lastly, in the very peculiar nature of the library's contents, there is more than sufficient evidence to warrant the belief.

The recollection of my earliest years are connected with that chamber, and with its volumes—of which latter I will say no more. Here died my mother. Herein was I born. But it is mere idleness to say that I had not lived before—that the soul has no previous existence. You deny it?—let us not argue the matter. Convinced myself, I seek not to convince. There is, however, a remembrance of aerial forms—of spiritual and meaning eyes—of sounds, musical yet sad—a remembrance which will not be excluded; a memory like a shadow, vague, variable, indefinite, unsteady; and like a shadow, too, in the impossibility of my getting rid of it while the sunlight of my reason shall exist.

In that chamber was I born. Thus awaking from the long night of what seemed, but was not, nonentity, at once into the very regions of fairy-land—into a palace of imagination—into the wild dominions of monastic thought and erudition—it is not singular that I gazed around me with a startled and ardent eye—that I loitered away my boyhood in books, and dissipated my youth in reverie; but it *is* singular that as years rolled away, and the noon of manhood found me still in the mansion of my fathers—it *is* wonderful what stagnation there fell upon the springs of my life—wonderful how total an inversion took place in the character of my commonest thought. The realities of the world affected me as visions, and as visions only, while the wild ideas of the land of dreams became, in turn,—not the material of my everyday existence—but in very deed that existence utterly and solely in itself.

* * *

Berenice and I were cousins, and we grew up together in my paternal halls. Yet differently we grew—I ill of health and buried in gloom—she agile, graceful, and overflowing with energy—hers the ramble on the hill-side —mine the studies of the cloister—I living within my own heart, and addicted body and soul to the most intense and painful meditation—she roaming carelessly through life with no thought of the shadows in her path, or the silent flight of the raven-winged hours. Berenice!— I call upon her name—Berenice!—and from the gray ruins of memory a thousand tumultuous recollections are startled at the sound! Ah! vividly is her image before me now, as in the early days of her light-heartedness and joy! Oh! gorgeous yet fantastic beauty! Oh! sylph amid the shrubberies of Arnheim!—Oh! Naiad among its fountains!—and then—then all is mystery and terror, and a tale which should not be told. Disease—a fatal disease— fell like the simoom upon her frame, and, even while I gazed upon her, the spirit of change swept over her, pervading her mind, her habits, and her character, and, in a manner the most subtle and terrible, disturbing even the identity of her person! Alas! the destroyer came and went, and the victim—where was she? I knew her not—or knew her no longer as Berenice.

Among the numerous train of maladies superinduced by that fatal and primary one which effected a revolution of so horrible a kind in the moral and physical being of my cousin, may be mentioned as the most distressing and obstinate in its nature, a species of epilepsy not unfrequently terminating in *trance* itself—trance very nearly resembling positive dissolution, and from which her manner of recovery was, in most instances, startlingly abrupt. In the mean time my own disease—for I have been told that I should call it by no other appellation—my own disease, then, grew rapidly upon me, and assumed finally a monomaniac character of a novel and extraordinary form —hourly and momently gaining vigor—and at length obtaining over me the most incomprehensible ascendancy. This monomania, if I must so term it, consisted in a morbid irritability of those properties of the mind in metaphysical science termed the *attentive*. It is more than probable that I am not understood; but I fear, indeed, that it is in no manner possible to convey to the mind of the merely general reader, an adequate idea of that nervous *intensity of interest* with which, in my case, the powers of meditation (not to speak technically) busied and buried themselves, in the contemplation of even the most ordinary objects of the universe.

To muse for long unwearied hours with my attention riveted to some frivolous device on the margin, or in the typography of a book; to become absorbed for the better part of a summer's day in a quaint shadow falling aslant upon the tapestry, or upon the floor; to lose myself for an entire night in watching the steady flame of a lamp, or the embers of a fire; to dream away whole days over the perfume of a flower; to repeat monotonously some common word, until the sound, by dint of frequent repetition, ceased to convey any idea whatever to the mind; to lose all sense of motion or physical existence, by means of absolute bodily quiescence long and obstinately persevered in:—such were a few of the most common and least pernicious vagaries induced by a condition of the mental faculties, not, indeed, altogether unparalleled, but certainly bidding defiance to anything like analysis or explanation.

Yet let me not be misapprehended.—The undue, earnest, and morbid attention thus excited by objects in their own nature frivolous, must not be confounded in character with that ruminating propensity common to all mankind, and more especially indulged in by persons of ardent imagination. It was not even, as might be at first supposed, an extreme condition, or exaggeration of such propensity, but primarily and essentially distinct and different. In the one instance, the dreamer, or enthusiast, being interested by an object usually *not* frivolous, imperceptibly loses sight of this object in a wilderness of deductions and suggestions issuing therefrom, until, at the conclusion of a day dream *often replete with luxury*, he finds the *incitamentum* or first cause of his musings entirely vanished and forgotten. In my case the primary object was *invariably frivolous*, although assuming, through the medium of my distempered vision, a refracted and unreal importance. Few deductions, if any, were made; and those few pertinaciously returning in upon the original object as a centre. The meditations were *never* pleasurable; and, at the termination of the reverie, the first cause, so far from being out of sight, had attained that supernaturally exaggerated interest which was the prevailing feature of the disease. In a word, the powers of mind more particularly exercised were, with me, as I have said before, the *attentive*, and are, with the day-dreamer, the *speculative*.

My books, at this epoch, if they did not actually serve to irritate the disorder, partook, it will be perceived, largely, in their imaginative and inconsequential nature, of the characteristic qualities of the disorder itself. I well remember, among others, the treatise of the noble Italian Cœlius Secundus Curio "*de Amplitudine Beati Regni Dei:*" St. Austin' great work, the "City of God"; and Tertullian's "*de Carne Christi,*" in which the paradoxical sentence "*Mortuus est Dei filius; credibile est quia ineplum est: et sepultus resurrexit; certum est quia impossibile est*" occupied my undivided time, for many weeks of laborious and fruitless investigation.

Thus it will appear that, shaken from its balance only by trivial things, my reason bore resemblance to that ocean-crag spoken of by Ptolemy Hephestion, which steadily resisting the attacks of human violence, and the fiercer fury of the waters and the winds, trembled only to the touch of the flower called Asphodel. And although, to a careless thinker, it might appear a matter beyond doubt, that the alteration produced by her unhappy malady, in the *moral* condition of Berenice, would afford me many objects for the exercise of that intense and abnormal meditation whose nature I have been at some trouble in explaining, yet such was not in any degree the case. In the lucid intervals of my infirmity, her calamity, indeed, gave me pain, and, taking deeply to heart that total wreck of her fair and gentle life, I did not fail to ponder frequently and bitterly upon the wonder-working means by which so strange a revolution had been so suddenly brought to pass. But these reflections partook not of the idiosyncrasy of my disease, and where such as would have occurred, under similar circumstances, to the ordinary mass of mankind. True to its own character, my disorder revelled in the less important but more startling changes wrought in the *physical* frame of Berenice—in the singular and most appalling distortion of her personal identity.

During the brightest days of her unparalleled beauty, most surely I had never loved her. In the strange anomaly of my existence, feelings with me, *had never been* of the heart, and my passions *always were* of the mind. Through the gray of the early morning—among the trellissed shadows of the forest at noon-day—and in the silence of my library at night, she had flitted by my eyes, and I had seen her—not as the living and breathing Berenice, but as the Berenice of a dream—not as a being of the earth, earthy, but as the abstraction of such a being—not as a thing to admire, but to analyze—not as an object of love, but as the theme of the most abstruse although desultory speculation. And *now*—now I shuddered in her presence, and grew pale at her approach; yet bitterly lamenting her fallen and desolate condition, I called to mind that she had loved me long, and, in an evil moment, I spoke to her of marriage.

And at length the period of our nuptials was approaching, when, upon an afternoon in the winter of the year,—one of those unseasonably warm, calm, and misty days which are the nurse of the beautiful Halcyon,*—I sat,

---

* For as Jove, during the winter season, gives twice seven days of warmth, men have called this element and temperate time the nurse of the beautiful Halcyon.—*Simonides.*

(and sat, as I thought, alone,) in the inner apartment of the library. But uplifting my eyes I saw that Berenice stood before me.

Was it my own excited imagination—or the misty influence of the atmosphere—or the uncertain twilight of the chamber—or the gray draperies which fell around her figure—that caused in it so vacillating and indistinct an outline? I could not tell. She spoke no word, and I—not for worlds could I have uttered a syllable. An icy chill ran through my frame; a sense of insufferable anxiety oppressed me, a consuming curiosity pervaded my soul; and sinking back upon the chair, I remained for some time breathless and motionless, with my eyes riveted upon her person. Alas! its emaciation was excessive, and not one vestige of the former being, lurked in any single line of the contour. My burning glances at length fell upon the face.

The forehead was high, and very pale, and singularly placid; and the once jetty hair fell partially over it, and overshadowed the hollow temples with innumerable ringlets now of a vivid yellow, and jarring discordantly, in their fantastic character, with the reigning melancholy of the countenance. The eyes were lifeless, and lustreless, and seemingly pupil-less, and I shrank involuntarily from their glassy stare to the contemplation of the thin and shrunken lips. They parted; and in a smile of peculiar meaning, *the teeth* of the changed Berenice disclosed themselves slowly to my view. Would to God that I had never beheld them, or that, having done so, I had died!

*   *   *

The shutting of a door disturbed me, and, looking up, I found that my cousin had departed from the chamber. But from the disordered chamber of my brain, had not, alas! departed, and would not be driven away, the white and ghastly *spectrum* of the teeth. Not a speck on their surface—not a shade on their enamel—not an indenture in their edges—but what that brief period of her smile had sufficed to brand in upon my memory. I saw them *now* even more unequivocally than I beheld them *then*. The teeth!—the teeth!—they were here, and there, and every where, and visibly and palpably before me; long, narrow, and excessively white, with the pale lips writhing about them, as in the very moment of their first terrible development. Then came the full fury of my *monomania*, and I struggled in vain against its strange and irresistible influence. In the multiplied objects of the external world I had no thoughts but for the teeth. For these I longed with a phrenzied desire. All other matters and all different interests became absorbed in their single contemplation. They—they alone were present to the mental eye, and they, in their sole individuality, became the essence of my mental life. I held them in every light. I turned them in every attitude. I surveyed their characteristics. I dwelt upon their peculiarities. I pondered upon their conformation. I mused upon the alteration in their nature. I shuddered as I assigned to them in imagination a sensitive and sentient power, and even when unassisted by the lips, a capability of moral expression. Of Mam'selle Sallé it has been well said, "*que tous ses pas etaient des sentiments,*" and of Berenice I more seriously believed *que tous ses dents etaient des idées. Des idées!*—ah here was the idiotic thought that destroyed me! *Des idées!*—ah *therefore* it was that I coveted them so madly! I felt that their possession could alone ever restore me to peace, in giving me back to reason.

And the evening closed in upon me thus—and then the darkness came, and tarried, and went—and the day again dawned—and the mists of a second night were now gathering around—and still I sat motionless in that solitary room, and still I sat buried in meditation, and still the *phantasma* of the teeth maintained its terrible ascendancy as, with the most vivid and hideous distinctness, it floated about amid the changing lights and shadows of the chamber. At length there broke in upon my dreams a cry as of horror and dismay; and thereunto, after a pause, succeeded the sound of troubled voices, intermingled with many low moanings of sorrow, or of pain. I arose from my seat, and, throwing open one of the doors of the library, saw standing out in the antechamber a servant maiden, all in tears, who told me that Berenice was—no more. She had been seized with epilepsy in the early morning, and now, at the closing in of the night the grave was ready for its tenant, and all the preparations for the burial were completed.

*   *   *

I found myself sitting in the library, and again sitting there alone. It seemed that I had newly awakened from a confused and exciting dream. I knew that it was now midnight, and I was well aware that since the setting of the sun Berenice had been interred. But of that dreary period which intervened I had no positive—at least no definite comprehension. Yet its memory was replete with horror—horror more horrible from being vague, and terror more terrible from ambiguity. It was a fearful page in the record of my existence, written all over with dim, and hideous, and unintelligible recollections. I strived to decypher them, but in vain; while ever and anon, like the spirit of a departed sound, the shrill and piercing shriek of a female voice seemed to be ringing in my ears. I had done a deed—what was it? I asked myself the question aloud, and the whispering echoes of the chamber answered me, *"what was it?"*

On the table beside me burned a lamp, and near it lay a little box. It was of no remarkable character, and I had seen it frequently before, for it was the property of the family physician: but how came it *there*, upon my table, and why did I shudder in regarding it? These things were in no manner to be accounted for, and my eyes at length dropped to the open pages of a book, and to a sentence underscored therein. The words were the singular but simple ones of the poet Ebn Zaiat. "*Dicebant mihi sodales, si sepulchrum amicae visitarem, curas meas aliquantulum fore levatas.*" Why then, as I perused them, did the hairs of my head erect themselves on end, and the blood of my body become congealed within my veins?

There came a light tap at the library door, and pale as the tenant of a tomb, a menial entered upon tiptoe. His looks were wild with terror, and he spoke to me in a voice tremulous, husky, and very low. What said he?—some broken sentences I heard. He told of a wild cry disturbing the silence of the night—of the gathering together of the household—of a search in the direction of the sound;—and then his tones grew thrillingly distinct as he whispered me of a violated grave—of a disfigured body enshrouded, yet still breathing, still palpitating, *still alive!*

He pointed to my garments;—they were muddy and clotted with gore. I spoke not, and he took me gently by the hand;—it was indented with the impress of human nails. He directed my attention to some object against the wall;—I looked at it for some minutes;—it was a spade. With a shriek I bounded to the table, and grasped the box that lay upon it. But I could not force it open; and in my tremor it slipped from my hands, and fell heavily, and burst into pieces; and from it, with a rattling sound, there rolled out some instruments of dental surgery, intermingled with thirty-two small, white and ivory-looking substances that were scattered to and fro about the floor.

SOME PASSAGES
IN THE LIFE OF A LION

——— All people went
Upon their ten toes in wild wonderment.
—*Bishop Hall's Satires.*

I am—that is to say I *was*—a great man; but I am neither
the author of Junius nor the man in the mask; for my
name, I believe, is Robert Jones, and I was born somewhere in the city of Fum-Fudge.

The first action of my life was the taking hold of my
nose with both hands. My mother saw this and called me
a genius:—my father wept for joy and presented me with
a treatise on Nosology. This I mastered before I was
breeched.

I now began to feel my way in the science; and soon
came to understand that, provided a man had a nose sufficiently conspicuous, he might, by merely following it, arrive at a Lionship. But my attention was not confined to
theories alone. Every morning I gave my proboscis a couple
of pulls and swallowed a half dozen of drams.

When I came of age my father asked me, one day, if I
would step with him into his study.

"My son," said he, when we were seated, "what is the
chief end of your existence?"

"My father," I answered, "it is the study of Nosology."

"And what, Robert," he inquired, "is Nosology?"

"Sir," I said, "it is the Science of Noses."

"And can you tell me," he demanded, "what is the
meaning of a nose?"

"A nose, my father," I replied, greatly softened, "has

been variously defined by about a thousand different authors." [Here I pulled out my watch.] "It is now noon or thereabouts—We shall have time enough to get through with them all before midnight. To commence then:—The nose, according to Bartholinus, is that protuberance—that bump—that excrescence—that—" —"Will do, Robert," interrupted the good old gentleman, "I am thunderstruck at the extent of your information—I am positively—upon my soul." [Here he closed his eyes and placed his hand upon his heart.] "Come here!" [Here he took me by the arm.] "Your education may now be considered as finished —it is high time you should scuffle for yourself—and you cannot do a better thing than merely follow your nose— so—so—so—" [Here he kicked me down stairs, and out of the door.]—"so get out of my house and God bless you!"

As I felt within me the divine *afflatus*, I considered this accident rather fortunate than otherwise. I resolved to be guided by the paternal advice. I determined to follow my nose. I gave it a pull or two upon the spot, and wrote a pamphlet on Nosology forthwith.

All Fum-Fudge was in an uproar.

"Wonderful genius!" said the Quarterly.

"Superb physiologist!" said the Westminster.

"Clever fellow!" said the Foreign.

"Fine writer!" said the Edinburgh.

"Profound thinker!" said the Dublin.

"Great man!" said Bentley.

"Divine soul!" said Fraser.

"One of us!" said Blackwood.

"Who can he be?" said Mrs. Bas-Bleu.

"What can he be?" said big Miss Bas-Bleu.

"Where can he be?" said little Miss Bas-Bleu.—But I paid these people no attention whatever—I just stepped into the shop of an artist.

The Duchess of Bless-my-soul was sitting for her portrait; the Marquis of So-and-So was holding the Duchess' poodle; the Earl of This-and-That was flirting with her salts; and his Royal Highness of Touch-me-Not was leaning upon the back of her chair.

I approached the artist and turned up my nose.

"Oh, beautiful!" sighed her Grace.

"Oh my!" lisped the Marquis.

"Oh shocking!" groaned the Earl.

"Oh abominable!" growled his Royal Highness.

"What will you take for it?" asked the artist.

"For his *nose!*" shouted her Grace.

"A thousand pounds," said I, sitting down.

"A thousand pounds?" inquired the artist, musingly.

"A thousand pounds," said I.

"Do you warrant it?" he asked, turning the nose to the light.

"I do," said I, blowing it well.

"Is it *quite* original?" inquired he, touching it with reverence.

"Humph!" said I, twisting it to one side.

"Has *no* copy been taken?" he demanded, surveying it through a microscope.

"None," said I, turning it up.

"*Admirable!*" he ejaculated, thrown quite off his guard by the beauty of the manœuvre.

"A thousand pounds," said I.

"A *thousand* pounds?" he said.

"Precisely," said I.

"A thousand *pounds?*" said he.

"Just so," said I.

"You shall have them," said he, "what a piece of *virtu!*" —So he drew me a check upon the spot, and took a sketch of my nose. I engaged rooms in Jermyn street, and sent her Majesty the ninty-ninth edition of the "Nosology" with a portrait of the proboscis. That sad little rake, the Prince of Wales, invited me to dinner.

We were all lions and *recherchés.*

There was a modern Platonist. He quoted Porphyry, Iamblicus, Plotinus, Proclus, Hierocles, Maximus Tyrius, and Syrianus.

There was a human-perfectibility man. He quoted Turgot, Price, Priestly, Condorcet, De Staël, and the "Ambitious Student in Ill Health."

There was Sir Positive Paradox. He observed that all fools were philosophers, and that all philosophers were fools.

There was Æstheticus Ethix. He spoke of fire, unity, and atoms; bi-part and pre-existent soul; affinity and discord; primitive intelligence and homōomeria.

There was Theologos Theology. He talked of Eusebius and Arianus; heresy and the Council of Nice; Puseyism and consubstantialism; Homousios and Homouioisios.

There was Fricassée from the Rocher de Cancale. He mentioned Muriton of red tongue; cauliflowers with velouté sauce; veal à la St. Menehoult; marinade à la St. Florentin; and orange jellies en mosàiques.

There was Bibulus O'Bumper. He touched upon Latour and Markbrünen; and Mousseux and Chambertin; upon Richbourg and St. George; upon Haubrion, Leonville, and Medoc; upon Barac and Preignac; upon Gràve, and upon St. Peray. He shook his head at Clos de Vougeot, and told, with his eyes shut, the difference between Sherry and Amontillado.

There was Signor Tintontintino from Florence. He discoursed of Cimbabué, Arpino, Carpaccio, and Argostino —of the gloom of Caravaggio, of the amenity of Albano, of the colors of Titian, of the frowns of Rubens, and of the waggeries of Jan Steen.

There was the President of the Fum-Fudge University. He was of opinion that the moon was called Bendis in Thrace, Bubastis in Egypt, Dian in Rome, and Artemis in Greece.

There was a grand Turk from Stamboul. He could not

help thinking that the angels were horses, cocks and bulls; that somebody in the sixth heaven had seventy thousand heads; and that the earth was supported by a sky-blue cow with an incalculable number of green horns.

There was Delphinus Polyglott. He told us what had become of the eighty-three lost tragedies of Æschylus; of the fifty-four orations of Isœus; of the three hundred and ninety-one speeches of Lysias; of the hundred and eighty treatises of Theophrastus; of the eighth book of the Conic Sections of Apollonius; of Pindar's hymns and dithyrambics; and of the five and forty tragedies of Homer Junior.

There was Ferdinand Fitz-Fossillus Feltspar. He informed us all about internal fires and tertiary formations; about āeriforms, fluidiforms, and solidiforms; about quartz and marl; about schist and schorl; about gypsum and trap; about talc and calc; about blende and horn-blende; about mica-slate and pudding-stone; about cyanite and lepidolite; about hœmatite and tremolite; about antimony and calcedony; about manganese and whatever you please.

There was myself. I spoke of myself;—of myself, of myself, of myself;—of Nosology, of my pamphlet, and of myself. I turned up my nose and spoke of myself.

"Marvellous clever man!" said the Prince.

"Superb!" said his guests; and next morning her Grace of Bless-my-soul paid me a visit.

"Will you go to Almacks, pretty creature?" she said, tapping me under the chin.

"Upon honor," said I.

"Nose and all?" she asked.

"As I live," I replied.

"Here then is a card, my life, shall I say you *will* be there?"

"Dear Duchess, with all my heart."

"Pshaw, no!—but with all your nose?"

"Every bit of it my love," said I:—so I gave it a twist or two and found myself at Almacks.

The rooms were crowded to suffocation.

"He is coming!" said somebody on the staircase.

"He is coming!" said somebody farther up.

"He is coming!" said somebody farther still.

"He is come!" exclaimed the Duchess—"he is come, the little love!"—and seizing me firmly by both hands, she kissed me thrice upon the nose.

A marked sensation immediately ensued.

"*Diavolo!*" cried Count Capricornutti.

"*Mille tonnerres!*" ejaculated the Prince de Grenouille.

"*Tousand teufel!*" growled the Elector of Bluddennuff.

This was not to be borne. I grew angry. I turned short upon Bluddennuff.

"Sir," said I, "you are a baboon."

"Sir," he replied, after a pause, "*Donner und Blitzen.*"

This was all that could be desired. We exchanged cards. At Chalk-Farm, the next morning, I shot off his nose—and then called upon my friends.

"*Bête!*" said the first.

"Fool!" said the second.

"Dolt!" said the third.

"Ass!" said the fourth.

"Ninny!" said the fifth.

"Noodle!" said the sixth.

"Be off!" said the seventh.

At all this I felt mortified, and so called upon my father.

"Father," I said, "what is the chief end of my existence?"

"My son," he replied, "it is still the study of Nosology; but in shooting off the Elector's nose you have overshot your mark. You have a fine nose, it is true; but then Bluddennuff has none. You are damned, and he has become the hero of the day. I grant you that in Fum-Fudge the greatness of a lion is in proportion to the size of his proboscis—but, Good Heavens! there is no competing with a lion who has no proboscis at all."

SHADOW—A PARABLE

Yea! though I walk through the valley of the *Shadow*:
                              —*Psalm of David.*

Ye who read are still among the living; but I who write
shall have long since gone my way into the region of
shadows. For indeed strange things shall happen, and
secret things be known, and many centuries shall pass
away, ere these memorials be seen of men. And, when
seen, there will be some to disbelieve, and some to doubt,
and yet a few who will find much to ponder upon in the
characters here graven with a stylus of iron.

The year had been a year of terror, and of feelings
more intense than terror for which there is no name
upon the earth. For many prodigies and signs had taken
place, and far and wide, over sea and land, the black wings
of the Pestilence were spread abroad. To those, nevertheless, cunning in the stars, it was not unknown that the
heavens wore an aspect of ill; and to me, the Greek Oinos,
among others, it was evident that now had arrived the
alternation of that seven hundred and ninety fourth year
when, at the entrance of Aries, the planet Jupiter is conjoined with the red ring of the terrible Saturnus. The
peculiar spirit of the skies, if I mistake not greatly, made
itself manifest, not only in the physical orb of the earth,
but in the souls, imaginations, and meditations of mankind.

Over some flasks of the red Chian wine, within the walls
of a noble hall, in a dim city called Ptolemais, we sat, at
night, a company of seven. And to our chamber there was
no entrance save by a lofty door of brass; and the door was
fashioned by the artizan Coriunos, and being of rare work-

manship, was fastened from within. Black draperies, likewise, in the gloomy room, shut out from our view the
moon, the lurid stars, and the peopleless streets—but the
boding and the memory of Evil, they would not be so excluded. There were things around us and about of which I
can render no distinct account—things material and
spiritual—heaviness in the atmosphere—a sense of suffocation—anxiety—and, above all, that terrible state of existence which the nervous experience when the senses are
keenly living and awake, and meanwhile the powers of
thought lie dormant. A dead weight hung upon us. It hung
upon our limbs—upon the household furniture—upon the
goblets from which we drank; and all things were depressed, and borne down thereby—all things save only
the flames of the seven iron lamps which illuminated our
revel. Uprearing themselves in tall slender lines of light,
they thus remained burning all pallid and motionless; and
in the mirror which their lustre formed upon the round
table of ebony at which we sat, each of us there assembled
beheld the pallor of his own countenance, and the unquiet
glare in the downcast eyes of his companions. Yet we
laughed and were merry in our proper way—which was
hysterical: and sang the songs of Anacreon—which are
madness; and drank deeply—although the purple wine reminded us of blood. For there was yet another tenant of
our chamber in the person of young Zoilus. Dead, and at
full length he lay, enshrouded;—the genius and the
demon of the scene. Alas! he bore no portion in our mirth,
save that his countenance, distorted with the plague and
his eyes in which Death had but half extinguished the
fire of the pestilence, seemed to take such interest in our
merriment as the dead may haply take in the merriment
of those who are to die. But although I, Oinos, felt that
the eyes of the departed were upon me, still I forced myself not to perceive the bitterness of their expression, and,
gazing down steadily into the depths of the ebony mirror,

sang with a loud and sonorous voice the songs of the son of Teios. But gradually my songs they ceased, and their echoes, rolling afar off among the sable draperies of the chamber, became weak, and undistinguishable, and so faded away. And lo! From among those sable draperies where the sounds of the song departed, there came forth a dark and undefined shadow—a shadow such as the moon, when low in heaven, might fashion from the figure of a man: but it was the shadow neither of man, nor of God, nor of any familiar thing. And, quivering awhile among the draperies of the room, it at length rested in full view upon the surface of the door of brass. But the shadow was vague, and formless, and indefinite, and was the shadow neither of man nor of God—neither God of Greece, nor God of Chaldæa, nor any Egyptian God. And the shadow rested upon the brazen doorway, and under the arch of the entablature of the door, and moved not, nor spoke any word, but there became stationary and remained. And the door whereupon the shadow rested was, if I remember aright, over against the feet of the young Zoilus enshrouded. But we, the seven there assembled, having seen the shadow as it came out from among the draperies, dared not steadily behold it, but cast down our eyes, and gazed continually into the depths of the mirror of ebony. And at length I, Oinos, speaking some low words, demanded of the shadow its dwelling and its appellation. And the shadow answered, "I am SHADOW, and my dwelling is near to the Catacombs of Ptolemais, and hard by those dim plains of Helusion which border upon the foul Charonian canal." And then did we, the seven, start from our seats in horror, and stand trembling, and shuddering, and aghast: for the tones in the voice of the shadow were not the tones of any one being, but of a multitude of beings, and, varying in their cadences from syllable to syllable, fell duskily upon our ears in the well remembered and familiar accents of many thousand departed friends.

SILENCE.—A FABLE

Ἐνδουσιν δ'ορεων κορυφαι τε και φαραγγες
Πρωνες τε και χαραδραι.—ALCMAN.

The mountain pinnacles slumber; valleys, crags and caves
are silent.

"Listen to *me*," said the Demon, as he placed his hand upon my head. "The region of which I speak is a dreary region in Libya, by the borders of the river Zäire. And there is no quiet there, nor silence.

"The waters of the river have a saffron and sickly hue; and they flow not onwards to the sea, but palpitate forever and forever beneath the red eye of the sun with a tumultuous and convulsive motion. For many miles on either side of the river's oozy bed is a pale desert of gigantic water-lilies. They sigh one unto the other in that solitude, and stretch towards the heaven their long and ghastly necks, and nod to and fro their everlasting heads. And there is an indistinct murmur which cometh out from among them like the rushing of subterrene water. And they sigh one unto the other.

"But there is a boundary to their realm—the boundary of the dark, horrible, lofty forest. There, like the waves about the Hebrides, the low underwood is agitated continually. But there is no wind throughout the heaven. And the tall primeval trees rock eternally hither and thither with a crashing and mighty sound. And from their high summits, one by one, drop everlasting dews. And at the roots strange poisonous flowers lie writhing in perturbed slumber. And overhead, with a rustling and loud noise, the gray clouds rush westwardly forever, until they roll, a cataract, over the fiery wall of the horizon. But there is no wind throughout the heaven. And by the shores of the river Zäire there is neither quiet nor silence.

"It was night, and the rain fell; and, falling, it was rain, but, having fallen, it was blood. And I stood in the morass among the tall lilies, and the rain fell upon my head—and the lilies sighed one unto the other in the solemnity of their desolation.

"And, all at once, the moon arose through the thin ghastly mist, and was crimson in color. And mine eyes fell upon a huge gray rock which stood by the shore of the river, and was lighted by the light of the moon. And the rock was gray, and ghastly, and tall,—and the rock was gray. Upon its front were characters engraven in the stone; and I walked through the morass of water-lilies, until I came close unto the shore, that I might read the characters upon the stone. But I could not decypher them. And I was going back into the morass, when the moon shone with a fuller red, and I turned and looked again upon the rock, and upon the characters;—and the characters were DESOLATION.

"And I looked upwards, and there stood a man upon the summit of the rock; and I hid myself among the water-lilies that I might discover the actions of the man. And the man was tall and stately in form, and was wrapped up from his shoulders to his feet in the toga of old Rome. And the outlines of his figure were indistinct—but his features were the features of a deity; for the mantle of the night, and of the mist, and of the moon, and of the dew, had left uncovered the features of his face. And his brow was lofty with thought, and his eye wild with care; and, in the few furrows upon his cheek I read the fables of sorrow, and weariness, and disgust with mankind, and a longing after solitude.

"And the man sat upon the rock, and leaned his head

upon his hand, and looked out upon the desolation. He looked down into the low unquiet shrubbery, and up into the tall primeval trees, and up higher at the rustling heaven, and into the crimson moon. And I lay close within shelter of the lilies, and observed the actions of the man. And the man trembled in the solitude;—but the night waned, and he sat upon the rock.

"And the man turned his attention from the heaven, and looked out upon the dreary river Zäire, and upon the yellow ghastly waters, and upon the pale legions of the water-lilies. And the man listened to the sighs of the water lilies, and to the murmur that came up from among them. And I lay close within my covert and observed the actions of the man. And the man trembled in the solitude; —but the night waned and he sat upon the rock.

"Then I went down into the recesses of the morass, and waded afar in among the wilderness of the lilies, and called unto the hippopotami which dwelt among the fens in the recesses of the morass. And the hippopotami heard my call, and came, with the behemoth, unto the foot of the rock, and roared loudly and fearfully beneath the moon. And I lay close within my covert and observed the actions of the man. And the man trembled in the solitude; —but the night waned and he sat upon the rock.

"Then I cursed the elements with the curse of tumult; and a frightful tempest gathered in the heaven where, before, there had been no wind. And the heaven became livid with the violence of the tempest—and the rain beat upon the head of the man—and the floods of the river came down—and the river was tormented into foam—and the water-lilies shrieked within their beds—and the forest crumbled before the wind—and the thunder rolled—and the lightning fell—and the rock rocked to its foundation. And I lay close within my covert and observed the actions of the man. And the man trembled in the solitude;—but the night waned and he sat upon the rock.

"Then I grew angry and cursed, with the curse of *silence*, the river, and the lilies, and the wind, and the forest, and the heaven, and the thunder, and the sighs of the water-lilies. And they became accursed, and *were still*. And the moon ceased to totter up its pathway to heaven —and the thunder died away—and the lightning did not flash—and the clouds hung motionless—and the waters sunk to their level and remained—and the trees ceased to rock—and the water-lilies sighed no more—and the murmur was heard no longer from among them, nor any shadow of sound throughout the vast illimitable desert. And I looked upon the characters of the rock, and they were changed;—and the characters were SILENCE.

"And mine eyes fell upon the countenance of the man, and his countenance was wan with terror. And, hurriedly, he raised his head from his hand, and stood forth upon the rock and listened. But there was no voice throughout the vast illimitable desert, and the characters upon the rock were SILENCE. And the man shuddered, and turned his face away, and fled afar off, in haste, so that I beheld him no more."

*   *   *

Now there are fine tales in the volumes of the Magi— in the iron-bound, melancholy volumes of the Magi. Therein, I say, are glorious histories of the Heaven, and of the Earth, and of the mighty sea—and of the Genii that over-ruled the sea, and the earth, and the lofty heaven. There was much lore too in the sayings which were said by the Sybils; and holy, holy things were heard of old by the dim leaves that trembled around Dodona—but, as Allah liveth, that fable which the demon told me as he sat by my side in the shadow of the tomb, I hold to be the most wonderful of all! And as the Demon made an end of his story, he fell back within the cavity of the tomb and laughed. And I could not laugh with the Demon, and he cursed me because I could not laugh. And the lynx which dwelleth forever in the tomb, came out therefrom, and lay down at the feet of the Demon, and looked at him steadily in the face.

LIGEIA

And the will therein lieth, which dieth not. Who knoweth the mysteries of the will, with its vigor? For God is but a great will pervading all things by nature of its intentness. Man doth not yield himself to the angels, nor unto death utterly, save only through the weakness of his feeble will.

—JOSEPH GLANVILL.

I cannot, for my soul, remember how, when, or even precisely where, I first became acquainted with the lady Ligeia. Long years have since elapsed, and my memory is feeble through much suffering. Or, perhaps, I cannot *now* bring these points to mind, because, in truth, the character of my beloved, her rare learning, her singular yet placid cast of beauty, and the thrilling and enthralling eloquence of her low musical language, made their way into my heart by paces so steadily and stealthily progressive that they have been unnoticed and unknown. Yet I believe that I met her first and most frequently in some large, old, decaying city near the Rhine. Of her family—I have surely heard her speak. That it is of a remotely ancient date cannot be doubted. Ligeia! Ligeia! Buried in studies of a nature more than all else adapted to deaden impressions of the outward world, it is by that sweet word alone—by Ligeia—that I bring before mine eyes in fancy the image of her who is no more. And now, while I write, a recollection flashes upon me that I have *never known* the paternal name of her who was my friend and my betrothed, and who became the partner of my studies, and finally the wife of my bosom. Was it a playful charge on the part of my Ligeia? or was it a test of my strength of affection, that I should institute no inquiries upon this point? or was it rather a caprice of my own—a wildly romantic offering on the shrine of the most passionate devotion? I but indistinctly recall the fact itself—what wonder that I have utterly forgotten the circumstances which originated or attended it? And, indeed, if ever that spirit which is entitled *Romance*—if ever she, the wan and the misty-winged *Ashtophet* of idolatrous Egypt, presided, as they tell, over marriages ill-omened, then most surely she presided over mine.

There is one dear topic, however, on which my memory fails me not. It is the *person* of Ligeia. In stature she was tall, somewhat slender, and, in her latter days, even emaciated. I would in vain attempt to portray the majesty, the quiet ease, of her demeanor, or the incomprehensible lightness and elasticity of her footfall. She came and departed as a shadow. I was never made aware of her entrance into my closed study save by the dear music of her low sweet voice, as she placed her marble hand upon my shoulder. In beauty of face no maiden ever equalled her. It was the radiance of an opium dream—an airy and spirit-lifting vision more wildly divine than the phantasies which hovered about the slumbering souls of the daughters of Delos. Yet her features were not of that regular mould which we have been falsely taught to worship in the classical labors of the heathen. "There is no exquisite beauty," says Bacon, Lord Verulam, speaking truly of all the forms and *genera* of beauty, "without some *strangeness* in the proportion." Yet, although I saw that the features of Ligeia were not of a classic regularity—although I perceived that her loveliness was indeed "exquisite," and felt

that there was much of "strangeness" pervading it, yet I
have tried in vain to detect the irregularity and to trace
home my own perception of "the strange." I examined the
contour of the lofty and pale forehead—it was faultless—
how cold indeed that word when applied to a majesty so
divine!—the skin rivalling the purest ivory, the commanding extent and repose, the gentle prominence of the
regions above the temple; and then the raven-black, the
glossy, the luxuriant and naturally-curling tresses, setting
forth the full force of the Homeric epithet, "hyacinthine!"
I looked at the delicate outlines of the nose—and nowhere
but in the graceful medallions of the Hebrews had I beheld a similar perfection. There were the same luxurious
smoothness of surface, the same scarcely perceptible tendency to the aquiline, the same harmoniously curved nostrils
speaking the free spirit. I regarded the sweet mouth. Here
was indeed the triumph of all things heavenly—the magnificent turn of the short upper lip—the soft, voluptuous
slumber of the under—the dimples which sported, and the
color which spoke—the teeth glancing back, with a brilliancy almost startling, every ray of the holy light which
fell upon them in her serene and placid, yet most exult-
ingly radiant of all smiles. I scrutinized the formation of
the chin—and here, too, I found the gentleness of breadth,
the softness and the majesty, the fullness and the spirituality, of the Greek—the contour which the God Apollo revealed but in a dream, to Cleomenes, the son of the
Athenian. And then I peered into the large eyes of Ligeia.

For eyes we have no models in the remotely antique.
It might have been, too, that in these eyes of my beloved
lay the secret to which Lord Verulam alludes. They were,
I must believe, far larger than the ordinary eyes of our
own race. They were even fuller than the fullest of the
gazelle eyes of the tribe of the valley of Nourjahad. Yet
it was only at intervals—in moments of intense excitement
—that this peculiarity became more than slightly notice-

able in Ligeia. And at such moments was her beauty—in my heated fancy thus it appeared perhaps—the beauty of beings either above or apart from the earth—the beauty of the fabulous Houri of the Turk. The hue of the orbs was the most brilliant of black, and, far over them, hung jetty lashes of great length. The brows, slightly irregular in outline, had the same tint. The "strangeness," however, which I found in the eyes, was of a nature distinct from the formation, or the color, or the brilliancy of the features, and must, after all, be referred to the *expression*. Ah, word of no meaning! behind whose vast latitude of mere sound we intrench our ignorance of so much of the spiritual. The expression of the eyes of Ligeia! How for long hours have I pondered upon it! How have I, through the whole of a midsummer night, struggled to fathom it! What was it—that something more profound than the well of Democritus—which lay far within the pupils of my beloved? What *was* it? I was possessed with a passion to discover. Those eyes! those large, those shining, those divine orbs! they became to me twin stars of Leda, and I to them devoutest of astrologers.

There is no point, among the many incomprehensible anomalies of the science of mind, more thrillingly exciting than the fact—never, I believe, noticed in the schools—that, in our endeavors to recall to memory something long forgotten, we often find ourselves *upon the very verge* of remembrance, without being able, in the end, to remember. And thus how frequently, in my intense scrutiny of Ligeia's eyes, have I felt approaching the full knowledge of their expression—felt it approaching—yet not quite be mine—and so at length entirely depart! And (strange, oh strangest mystery of all!) I found, in the commonest objects of the universe, a circle of analogies to that expression. I mean to say that, subsequently to the period when Ligeia's beauty passed into my spirit, there dwelling as in a shrine, I derived, from many existences in the material world, a sentiment such as I felt always abound within me by her large and luminous orbs. Yet not the more could I define that sentiment, or analyze, or even steadily view it. I recognized it, let me repeat, sometimes in the survey of a rapidly-growing vine—in the contemplation of a moth, a butterfly, a chrysalis, a stream of running water. I have felt it in the ocean; in the falling of a meteor. I have felt it in the glances of unusually aged people. And there are one or two stars in heaven—(one especially, a star of the sixth magnitude, double and changeable, to be found near the large star in Lyra) in a telescopic scrutiny of which I have been made aware of the feeling. I have been filled with it by certain sounds from stringed instruments, and not unfrequently by passages from books. Among innumerable other instances, I well remember something in a volume of Joseph Glanvill, which (perhaps merely from its quaintness—who shall say?) never failed to inspire me with the sentiment;—"And the will therein lieth, which dieth not. Who knoweth the mysteries of the will, with its vigor? For God is but a great will pervading all things by nature of its intentness. Man doth not yield himself to the angels, nor unto death utterly, save only through the weakness of his feeble will."

Length of years, and subsequent reflection, have enabled me to trace, indeed, some remote connection between this passage in the English moralist and a portion of the character of Ligeia. An *intensity* in thought, action, or speech, was possibly, in her, a result, or at least an index, of that gigantic volition which, during our long intercourse, failed to give other and more immediate evidence of its existence. Of all the women whom I have ever known, she, the outwardly calm, the ever-placid Ligeia, was the most violently a prey to the tumultuous vultures of stern passion. And of such passion I could form no estimate, save by the miraculous expansion of those eyes which at once so delighted and appalled me—by the almost magical melody, modulation, distinctness and placidity of her very low voice—and by the fierce energy (rendered doubly effective by contrast with her manner of utterance) of the wild words which she habitually uttered.

I have spoken of the learning of Ligeia: it was immense—such as I have never known in woman. In the classical tongues was she deeply proficient, and as far as my own acquaintance extended in regard to the modern dialects of Europe, I have never known her at fault. Indeed upon any theme of the most admired, because simply the most abstruse of the boasted erudition of the academy, have I *ever* found Ligeia at fault? How singularly—how thrillingly, this one point in the nature of my wife has forced itself, at this late period only, upon my attention! I said her knowledge was such as I have never known in woman—but where breathes the man who has traversed, and successfully, *all* the wide areas of moral, physical, and mathematical science? I saw not then what I now clearly perceive, that the acquisitions of Ligeia were gigantic, were astounding; yet I was sufficiently aware of her infinite supremacy to resign myself, with a child-like confidence, to her guidance through the chaotic world of metaphysical investigation at which I was most busily occupied during the earlier years of our marriage. With how vast a triumph—with how vivid a delight—with how much of all that is ethereal in hope—did I *feel*, as she bent over me in studies but little sought—but less known —that delicious vista by slow degrees expanding before me, down whose long, gorgeous, and all untrodden path, I might at length pass onward to the goal of a wisdom too divinely precious not to be forbidden!

How poignant, then, must have been the grief with which, after some years, I beheld my well-grounded expectations take wings to themselves and fly away! Without Ligeia I was but as a child groping benighted. Her presence, her reading alone, rendered vividly luminous the many mysteries of the transcendentalism in which we were immersed. Wanting the radiant lustre of her eyes, letters, lambent and golden, grew duller than Saturnian lead. And now those eyes shone less and less frequently upon the pages over which I pored. Ligeia grew ill. The wild eyes blazed with a too—too glorious effulgence; the pale fingers became of the transparent waxen hue of the grave, and the blue veins upon the lofty forehead swelled and sank impetuously with the tides of the most gentle emotion. I saw that she must die—and I struggled desperately in spirit with the grim Azrael. And the struggles of the passionate wife were, to my astonishment, even more energetic than my own. There had been much in her stern nature to impress me with the belief that, to her, death would have come without its terrors;—but not so. Words are impotent to convey any just idea of the fierceness of resistance with which she wrestled with the Shadow. I groaned in anguish at the pitiable spectacle. I would have soothed—I would have reasoned; but, in the intensity of her wild desire for life,—for life—*but* for life —solace and reason were alike the uttermost of folly. Yet not until the last instance, amid the most convulsive writhings of her fierce spirit, was shaken the external placidity of her demeanor. Her voice grew more gentle— grew more low—yet I would not wish to dwell upon the wild meaning of the quietly uttered words. My brain reeled as I hearkened entranced, to a melody more than mortal—to assumptions and aspirations which mortality had never before known.

That she loved me I should not have doubted; and I might have been easily aware that, in a bosom such as hers, love would have reigned no ordinary passion. But in death only, was I fully impressed with the strength of her affection. For long hours, detaining my hand, would she pour out before me the overflowing of a heart whose more than passionate devotion amounted to idolatry. How had I deserved to be so blessed by such confessions?—how had I deserved to be so cursed with the removal of my beloved in the hour of her making them? But upon this subject I cannot bear to dilate. Let me say only, that in Ligeia's more than womanly abandonment to a love, alas! all unmerited, all unworthily bestowed, I at length recognized the principle of her longing with so wildly earnest a desire for the life which was now fleeing so rapidly away. It is this wild longing—it is this eager vehemence of desire for life —*but* for life—that I have no power to portray—no utterance capable of expressing.

At high noon of the night in which she departed, beckoning me, peremptorily, to her side, she bade me repeat certain verses composed by herself not many days before. I obeyed her.—They were these:

> Lo! 'tis a gala night
>   Within the lonesome latter years!
> An angel throng, bewinged, bedight
>   In veils, and drowned in tears,
> Sit in a theatre, to see
>   A play of hopes and fears,
> While the orchestra breathes fitfully
>   The music of the spheres.
>
> Mimes, in the form of God on high,
>   Mutter and mumble low,
> And hither and thither fly—
>   Mere puppets they, who come and go
> At bidding of vast formless things
>   That shift the scenery to and fro,
> Flapping from out their Condor wings
>   Invisible Woe!

That motley drama!—oh, be sure
    It shall not be forgot!
With its Phantom chased forevermore,
    By a crowd that seize it not,
Through a circle that ever returneth in
    To the self-same spot,
And much of Madness and more of Sin,
    And Horror the soul of the plot.

But see, amid the mimic rout,
    A crawling shape intrude!
A blood-red thing that writhes from out
    The scenic solitude!
It writhes!—it writhes!—with mortal pangs
    The mimes become its food,
And the seraphs sob at vermin fangs
    In human gore imbued.

Out—out are the lights—out all!
    And over each quivering form,
The curtain, a funeral pall,
    Comes down with the rush of a storm,
And the angels, all pallid and wan,
    Uprising, unveiling, affirm
That the play is the tragedy, "Man,"
    And its hero the Conqueror Worm.

"O God!" half shrieked Ligeia, leaping to her feet and extending her arms aloft with a spasmodic movement, as I made an end of these lines—"O God! O Divine Father! —shall these things be undeviatingly so?—shall this Conqueror be not once conquered? Are we not part and parcel in Thee? Who—who knoweth the mysteries of the will with its vigor? Man doth not yield him to the angels, *nor unto death utterly*, save only through the weakness of his feeble will."

And now, as if exhausted with emotion, she suffered her

white arms to fall, and returned solemnly to her bed of Death. And as she breathed her last sighs, there came mingled with them a low murmur from her lips. I bent to them my ear and distinguished, again, the concluding words of the passage in Glanvill—"*Man doth not yield himself to the angels, nor unto death utterly, save only through the weakness of his feeble will.*"

She died;—and I, crushed into the very dust with sorrow, could no longer endure the lonely desolation of my dwelling in the dim and decaying city by the Rhine. I had no lack of what the world calls wealth. Ligeia had brought me far more, very far more than ordinarily falls to the lot of mortals. After a few months, therefore, of weary and aimless wandering, I purchased, and put in some repair, an abbey, which I shall not name, in one of the wildest and least frequented portions of fair England. The gloomy and dreary grandeur of the building, the almost savage aspect of the domain, the many melancholy and time-honored memories connected with both, had much in unison with the feelings of utter abandonment which had driven me into that remote and unsocial region of the country. Yet although the external abbey, with its verdant decay hanging about it, suffered but little alteration, I gave way, with a child-like perversity, and perchance with a faint hope of alleviating my sorrows, to a display of more than regal magnificence within.—For such follies, even in childhood, I had imbibed a taste and now they came back to me as if in the dotage of grief. Alas, I feel how much even of incipient madness might have been discovered in the gorgeous and fantastic draperies, in the solemn carvings of Egypt, in the wild cornices and furniture, in the Bedlam patterns of the carpets of tufted gold! I had become a bounden slave in the trammels of opium, and my labors and my orders had taken a coloring from my dreams. But these absurdities I must not pause to detail. Let me speak only of that one chamber, ever accursed, whither in a mo-

ment of mental alienation, I led from the altar as my bride
—as the successor of the unforgotten Ligeia—the fair-
haired and blue-eyed Lady Rowena Trevanion, of Tremaine.

There is no individual portion of the architecture and
decoration of that bridal chamber which is not now visibly
before me. Where were the souls of the haughty family
of the bride, when, through thirst of gold, they permitted
to pass the threshold of an apartment *so* bedecked, a
maiden and a daughter so beloved? I have said that I minutely remember the details of the chamber—yet I am
sadly forgetful on topics of deep moment—and here there
was no system, no keeping, in the fantastic display, to take
hold upon the memory. The room lay in a high turret of
the castellated abbey, was pentagonal in shape, and of
capacious size. Occupying the whole southern face of the
pentagon was the sole window—an immense sheet of unbroken glass from Venice—a single pane, and tinted of a
leaden hue, so that the rays of either the sun or moon,
passing through it, fell with a ghastly lustre on the objects within. Over the upper portion of this huge window,
extended the trellice-work of an aged vine, which clambered up the massy walls of the turret. The ceiling, of
gloomy-looking oak, was excessively lofty, vaulted, and
elaborately fretted with the wildest and most grotesque
specimens of a semi-Gothic, semi-Druidical device. From
out the most central recess of this melancholy vaulting,
depended, by a single chain of gold with long links, a
huge censer of the same metal, Saracenic in pattern, and
with many perforations so contrived that there writhed in
and out of them, as if endued with a serpent vitality, a
continual succession of parti-colored fires.

Some few ottomans and golden candelabra, of Eastern
figure, were in various stations about—and there was the
couch, too—the bridal couch—of an Indian model, and
low, and sculptured of solid ebony, with a pall-like canopy

above. In each of the angles of the chamber stood on end a gigantic sarcophagus of black granite, from the tombs of the kings over against Luxor, with their aged lids full of immemorial sculpture. But in the draping of the apartment lay, alas! the chief phantasy of all. The lofty walls, gigantic in height—even unproportionably so—were hung from summit to foot, in vast folds, with a heavy and massive-looking tapestry—tapestry of a material which was found alike as a carpet on the floor, as a covering for the ottomans and the ebony bed, as a canopy for the bed, and as the gorgeous volutes of the curtains which partially shaded the window. The material was the richest cloth of gold. It was spotted all over, at irregular intervals, with arabesque figures, about a foot in diameter, and wrought upon the cloth in patterns of the most jetty black. But these figures partook of the true character of the arabesque only when regarded from a single point of view. By a contrivance now common, and indeed traceable to a very remote period of antiquity, they were made changeable in aspect. To one entering the room, they bore the appearance of simple monstrosities; but upon a farther advance, this appearance gradually departed; and step by step, as the visiter moved his station in the chamber, he saw himself surrounded by an endless succession of the ghostly forms which belong to the superstition of the Norman, or arise in the guilty slumbers of the monk. The phantasmagoric effect was vastly heightened by the artificial introduction of a strong continual current of wind behind the draperies—giving a hideous and uneasy animation to the whole.

In halls such as these—in a bridal chamber such as this—I passed, with the Lady of Tremaine, the unhallowed hours of the first month of our marriage—passed them with but little disquietude. That my wife dreaded the fierce moodiness of my temper—that she shunned me and loved me but little—I could not help perceiving; but it gave me rather pleasure than otherwise. I loathed her with a hatred belonging more to demon than to man. My memory flew back, (oh, with what intensity of regret!) to Ligeia, the beloved, the august, the beautiful, the entombed. I revelled in recollections of her purity, of her wisdom, of her lofty, her ethereal nature, of her passionate, her idolatrous love. Now, then, did my spirit fully and freely burn with more than all the fires of her own. In the excitement of my opium dreams (for I was habitually fettered in the shackles of the drug) I would call aloud upon her name, during the silence of the night, or among the sheltered recesses of the glens by day, as if, through the wild eagerness, the solemn passion, the consuming ardor of my longing for the departed, ·I could restore her to the pathway she had abandoned—ah, *could* it be forever?—upon the earth.

About the commencement of the second month of the marriage, the Lady Rowena was attacked with sudden illness, for which her recovery was slow. The fever which consumed her rendered her nights uneasy; and in her perturbed state of half-slumber, she spoke of sounds, and of motions, in and about the chamber of the turret, which I concluded had no origin save in the distemper of her fancy, or perhaps in the phantasmagoric influences of the chamber itself. She became at length convalescent—finally well. Yet but a brief period elapsed, ere a second more violent disorder again threw her upon a bed of suffering; and from this attack her frame, at all times feeble, never altogether recovered. Her illnesses were, after this epoch, of alarming character, and of more alarming recurrence, defying alike the knowledge and the great exertions of her physicians. With the increase of the chronic disease which had thus, apparently, taken too sure hold upon her constitution to be eradicated by human means, I could not fail to observe a similar increase in the nervous irritation of her temperament, and in her excitability by trivial causes of fear. She spoke again, and now more frequently and pertinaciously, of the sounds—of the slight sounds—and of the unusual motions among the tapestries, to which she had formerly alluded.

One night, near the closing in of September, she pressed this distressing subject with more than usual emphasis upon my attention. She had just awakened from an unquiet slumber, and I had been watching, with feelings half of anxiety, half of a vague terror, the workings of her emaciated countenance. I sat by the side of her ebony bed, upon one of the ottomans of India. She partly arose, and spoke, in an earnest low whisper, of sounds which she *then* heard, but which I could not hear—of motions which she *then* saw, but which I could not perceive. The wind was rushing hurriedly behind the tapestries, and I wished to show her (what, let me confess it, I could not *all* believe) that those almost inarticulate breathings, and those very gentle variations of the figures upon the wall, were but the natural effects of that customary rushing of the wind. But a deadly pallor, overspreading her face, had proved to me that my exertions to reassure her would be fruitless. She appeared to be fainting, and no attendants were within call. I remembered where was deposited a decanter of light wine which had been ordered by her physicians, and hastened across the chamber to procure it. But, as I stepped beneath the light of the censer, two circumstances of a startling nature attracted my attention. I had felt that some palpable although invisible object had passed lightly by my person; and I saw that there lay upon the golden carpet, in the very middle of the rich lustre thrown from the censer, a shadow—a faint, indefinite shadow of angelic aspect—such as might be fancied for the shadow of a shade. But I was wild with the excitement of an immoderate dose of opium, and heeded these things but little, nor spoke of them to Rowena. Having found the wine, I recrossed the chamber, and poured out a goblet-ful,

which I held to the lips of the fainting lady. She had now
partially recovered, however, and took the vessel herself,
while I sank upon an ottoman near me, with my eyes
fastened upon her person. It was then that I became distinctly aware of a gentle foot-fall upon the carpet, and near
the coach; and in a second thereafter, as Rowena was in
the act of raising the wine to her lips, I saw, or may have
dreamed that I saw, fall within the goblet, as if from some
invisible spring in the atmosphere of the room, three or
four large drops of a brilliant and ruby colored fluid. If this
I saw—not so Rowena. She swallowed the wine unhesitatingly, and I forbore to speak to her of a circumstance
which must, after all, I considered, have been but the suggestion of a vivid imagination, rendered morbidly active by
the terror of the lady, by the opium, and by the hour.

Yet I cannot conceal it from my own perception that,
immediately subsequent to the fall of the ruby-drops, a
rapid change for the worse took place in the disorder of
my wife; so that, on the third subsequent night, the hands
of her menials prepared her for the tomb, and on the
fourth, I sat alone, with her shrouded body, in that fantastic chamber which had received her as my bride.—
Wild visions, opium-engendered, flitted, shadow-like, before me. I gazed with unquiet eye upon the sarcophagi
in the angles of the room, upon the varying figures of the
drapery, and upon the writhing of the parti-colored fires
in the censer overhead. My eyes then fell, as I called to
mind the circumstances of a former night, to the spot
beneath the glare of the censer where I had seen the faint
traces of the shadow. It was there, however, no longer;
and breathing with greater freedom, I turned my glances
to the pallid and rigid figure upon the bed. Then rushed
upon me a thousand memories of Ligeia—and then came
back upon my heart, with the turbulent violence of a
flood, the whole of that unutterable woe with which I had
regarded *her* thus enshrouded. The night waned; and still,

with a bosom full of bitter thoughts of the one only and supremely beloved, I remained gazing upon the body of Rowena.

It might have been midnight, or perhaps earlier, or later, for I had taken no note of time, when a sob, low, gentle, but very distinct, startled me from my revery.— I *felt* that it came from the bed of ebony—the bed of death. I listened in an agony of superstitious terror— but there was no repetition of the sound. I strained my vision to detect any motion in the corpse—but there was not the slightest perceptible. Yet I could not have been deceived. I *had* heard the noise, however faint, and my soul was awakened within me. I resolutely and perseveringly kept my attention riveted upon the body. Many minutes elapsed before any circumstance occurred tending to throw light upon the mystery. At length it became evident that a slight, a very feeble, and barely noticeable tinge of color had flushed up within the cheeks, and along the sunken small veins of the eyelids. Through a species of unutterable horror and awe, for which the language of mortality has no sufficiently energetic expression, I felt my heart cease to beat, my limbs grow rigid where I sat. Yet a sense of duty finally operated to restore my self-possession. I could no longer doubt that we had been precipitate in our preparations—that Rowena still lived. It was necessary that some immediate exertion be made; yet the turret was altogether apart from the portion of the abbey tenanted by the servants—there were none within call—I had no means of summoning them to my aid without leaving the room for many minutes—and this I could not venture to do. I therefore struggled alone in my endeavors to call back the spirit still hovering. In a short period it was certain, however, that a relapse had taken place; the color disappeared from both eyelid and cheek, leaving a wanness even more than that of marble; the lips became doubly shrivelled and pinched up in the ghastly expression of death; a repulsive clamminess and coldness overspread rapidly the surface of the body; and all the usual rigorous stiffness immediately supervened. I fell back with a shudder upon the couch from which I had been so startlingly aroused, and again gave myself up to passionate waking visions of Ligeia.

An hour thus elapsed when (could it be possible?) I was a second time aware of some vague sound issuing from the region of the bed. I listened—in extremity of horror. The sound came again—it was a sigh. Rushing to the corpse, I saw—distinctly saw—a tremor upon the lips. In a minute afterward they relaxed, disclosing a bright line of pearly teeth. Amazement now struggled in my bosom with the profound awe which had hitherto reigned there alone. I felt that my vision grew dim, that my reason wandered; and it was only by a violent effort that I at length succeeded in nerving myself to the task which duty thus once more had pointed out. There was now a partial glow upon the forehead and upon the cheek and throat; a perceptible warmth pervaded the whole frame; there was even a slight pulsation at the heart. The lady *lived*; and with redoubled ardor I betook myself to the task of restoration. I chafed and bathed the temples and the hands, and used every exertion which experience, and no little medical reading, could suggest. But in vain. Suddenly, the color fled, the pulsation ceased, the lips resumed the expression of the dead, and, in an instant afterward, the whole body took upon itself the icy chilliness, the livid hue, the intense rigidity, the sunken outline, and all the loathsome peculiarities of that which has been, for many days, a tenant of the tomb.

And again I sunk into visions of Ligeia—and again, (what marvel that I shudder while I write?) *again* there reached my ears a low sob from the region of the ebony bed. But why shall I minutely detail the unspeakable horrors of that night? Why shall I pause to relate how,

time after time, until near the period of the gray dawn,
this hideous drama of revivification was repeated; how
each terrific relapse was only into a sterner and apparently
more irredeemable death; how each agony wore the aspect of a struggle with some invisible foe; and how each
struggle was succeeded by I know not what wild change
in the personal appearance of the corpse? Let me hurry to
a conclusion.

The greater part of the fearful night had worn away,
and she who had been dead, once again stirred—and now
more vigorously than hitherto, although arousing from a
dissolution more appalling in its utter hopelessness than
any. I had long ceased to struggle or to move, and remained sitting rigidly upon the ottoman, a helpless prey
to a whirl of violent emotions, of which extreme awe
was perhaps the least terrible, the least consuming. The
corpse, I repeat, stirred, and now more vigorously than
before. The hues of life flushed up with unwonted energy
into the countenance—the limbs relaxed—and, save that
the eyelids were yet pressed heavily together, and that the
bandages and draperies of the grave still imparted their
charnel character to the figure, I might have dreamed
that Rowena had indeed shaken off, utterly, the fetters of
Death. But if this idea was not, even then, altogether
adopted, I could at least doubt no longer, when, arising
from the bed, tottering, with feeble steps, with closed
eyes, and with the manner of one bewildered in a dream,
the thing that was enshrouded advanced bodily and palpably into the middle of the apartment.

I trembled not—I stirred not—for a crowd of unutterable fancies connected with the air, the stature, the demeanor of the figure, rushing hurriedly through my brain,
had paralyzed—had chilled me into stone. I stirred not—
but gazed upon the apparition. There was a mad disorder
in my thoughts—a tumult unappeasable. Could it, indeed,
be the *living* Rowena who confronted me? Could it indeed

be Rowena *at all*—the fair-haired, the blue-eyed Lady Rowena Trevanion of Tremaine? Why, *why* should I doubt it? The bandage lay heavily about the mouth—but then might it not be the mouth of the breathing Lady of Tremaine? And the cheeks—there were the roses as in her noon of life—yes, these might indeed be the fair cheeks of the living Lady of Tremaine. And the chin, with its dimples, as in health, might it not be hers?—but *had she then grown taller since her malady?* What inexpressible madness seized me with that thought? One bound, and I had reached her feet! Shrinking from my touch, she let fall from her head the ghastly cerements which had confined it; and there streamed forth, into the rushing atmosphere of the chamber, huge masses of long and dishevelled hair; *it was blacker than the wings of the midnight!* And now slowly opened *the eyes* of the figure which stood before me. "Here then, at least," I shrieked aloud, "can I never—can I never be mistaken—these are the full, and the black, and the wild eyes—of my lost love—of the lady—of the LADY LIGEIA!"

HOW TO WRITE
A BLACKWOOD ARTICLE

"In the name of the Prophet—figs!!"
Cry of the Turkish fig-pedler.

I presume every body has heard of me. My name is the Signora Psyche Zenobia. This I know to be a fact. No body but my enemies ever calls me Suky Snobbs. I have been assured that Suky is but a vulgar corruption of Psyche, which is good Greek, and means "the soul" (that's me, I'm *all* soul) and sometimes "a butterfly," which latter meaning undoubtedly alludes to my appearance in my new crimson satin dress, with the sky-blue Arabian *mantelet*, and the trimmings of green *agraffas*, and the seven flounces of orange-colored *auriculas*. As for Snobbs—any person who should look at me would be instantly aware that my name was n't Snobbs. Miss Tabitha Turnip propagated that report through sheer envy. Tabitha Turnip indeed! Oh the little wretch! But what can we expect from a turnip? Wonder if she remembers the old adage about "blood out of a turnip, &c." [Mem: put her in mind of it the first opportunity.] [Mem again—pull her nose.] Where was I? Ah! I have been assured that Snobbs is a mere corruption of Zenobia, and that Zenobia was a queen —(So am I. Dr. Moneypenny always calls me the Queen of Hearts)—and that Zenobia, as well as Psyche, is good Greek, and that my father was "a Greek," and that consequently I have a right to our patronymic, which is Zenobia, and not by any means Snobbs. Nobody but Tabitha Turnip calls me Suky Snobbs. I am the Signora Psyche Zenobia.

As I said before, every body has heard of me. I am that very Signora Psyche Zenobia, so justly celebrated as corresponding secretary to the "*Philadelphia, Regular, Exchange, Tea, Total, Young, Belles, Lettres, Universal, Experimental, Bibliographical, Association, To, Civilize, Humanity.*" Dr. Moneypenny made the title for us, and says he chose it because it sounded big like an empty rumpuncheon. (A vulgar man that sometimes—but he's deep.) We all sign the initials of the society after our names, in the fashion of the R.S.A., Royal Society of Arts—the S.D.U.K., Society for the Diffusion of Useful Knowledge, &c. &c. Dr. Moneypenny says that S stands for *stale*, and that D.U.K. spells duck, (but it don't,) and that S.D.U.K. stands for Stale Duck, and not for Lord Brougham's society —but then Dr. Moneypenny is such a queer man that I am never sure when he is telling me the truth. At any rate we always add to our names the initials P.R.E.T.T.Y.-

B.L.U.E.B.A.T.C.H.—that is to say, Philadelphia Regular, Exchange, Tea, Total, Young, Belles, Lettres, Universal, Experimental, Bibliographical, Association, To,
Civilize, Humanity—one letter for each word, which is a
decided improvement upon Lord Brougham. Dr. Moneypenny will have it that our initials give our true character
—but for my life I can't see what he means.

Notwithstanding the good offices of the Doctor, and the
strenuous exertions of the association to get itself into
notice, it met with no very great success until I joined it.
The truth is, members indulged in too flippant a tone of
discussion. The papers read every Saturday evening were
characterized less by depth than buffoonery. They were all
whipped syllabub. There was no investigation of first
causes, first principles. There was no investigation of anything at all. There was no attention paid to that great
point the "fitness of things." In short there was no fine
writing like this. It was all low—very! No profundity, no
reading, no metaphysics—nothing which the learned call
spirituality, and which the unlearned choose to stigmatise
as cant. [Dr. M. says I ought to spell "cant" with a capital
K—but I know better.]

When I joined the society it was my endeavour to introduce a better style of thinking and writing, and all the
world knows how well I have succeeded. We get up as
good papers now in the P.R.E.T.T.Y.B.L.U.E.B.A.T.C.H.
as any to be found even in Blackwood. I say, Blackwood,
because I have been assured that the finest writing, upon
every subject, is to be discovered in the pages of that justly
celebrated Magazine. We now take it for our model upon
all themes, and are getting into rapid notice accordingly.
And, after all, it's not so very difficult a matter to compose
an article of the genuine Blackwood stamp, if one only
goes properly about it. Of course I don't speak of the
political articles. Every body knows how *they* are managed,
since Dr. Moneypenny explained it. Mr. Blackwood has a

pair of tailor's shears, and three apprentices who stand by him for orders. One hands him the "Times," another the "Examiner," and a third a "Gulley's New Compendium of Slang-Whang." Mr. B. merely cuts out and intersperses. It is soon done—nothing but Examiner, Slang-Whang, and Times—then Times, Slang-Whang, and Examiner—and then Times, Examiner, and Slang-Whang.

But the chief merit of the Magazine lies in its miscellaneous articles; and the best of these come under the head of what Dr. Moneypenny calls the *bizarreries* (whatever that may mean) and what every body else calls the *intensities*. This is a species of writing which I have long known how to appreciate, although it is only since my late visit to Mr. Blackwood (deputed by the society) that I have been made aware of the exact method of composition. This method is very simple, but not so much so as the politics. Upon my calling at Mr. B.'s, and making known to him the wishes of the society, he received me with great civility, took me into his study, and gave me a clear explanation of the whole process.

"My dear madam," said he, evidently struck with my majestic appearance, for I had on the crimson satin, with the green *agraffas*, and orange-coloured *auriculas*, "My *dear* madam," said he, "sit down. The matter stands thus. In the first place, your writer of intensities must have very black ink, and a very big pen, with a very blunt nib. And, mark me, Miss Psyche Zenobia!" he continued, after a pause, with the most impressive energy and solemnity of manner, "mark me!—*that pen—must—never be mended!* Herein, madam, lies the secret, the soul, of intensity. I assume it upon myself to say, that no individual, of however great genius, ever wrote with a good pen,—understand me,—a good article. You may take it for granted, that when manuscript can be read it is never worth reading. This is a leading principle in our faith, to which if you cannot readily assent, our conference is at an end."

He paused. But, of course, as I had no wish to put an end to the conference, I assented to a proposition so very obvious, and one, too, of whose truth I had all along been sufficiently aware. He seemed pleased, and went on with his instructions.

"It may appear invidious in me, Miss Psyche Zenobia, to refer you to any article, or set of articles, in the way of model or study: yet perhaps I may as well call your attention to a few cases. Let me see. There was 'T*he Dead Alive*,' a capital thing!—the record of a gentleman's sensations, of taste, terror, sentiment, metaphysics, and erudition, when entombed before the breath was out of his body—full. You would have sworn that the writer had been born and brought up in a coffin. Then we had the '*Confessions of an Opium-eater*'—fine, very fine!—glorious imagination—deep philosophy—acute speculation—plenty of fire and fury, and a good spicing of the decidedly unintelligible. That was a nice bit of flummery, and went down the throats of the people delightfully. They would have it that Coleridge wrote the paper—but not so. It was composed by my pet baboon, Juniper, over a rummer of Hollands and water, 'hot, without sugar.'" [This I could scarcely have believed had it been any body but Mr. Blackwood, who assured me of it.] "Then there was '*The Involuntary Experimentalist*,' all about a gentleman who got baked in an oven, and came out alive and well, although certainly done to a turn. And then there was '*The Diary of a Late Physician*,' where the merit lay in good rant, and indifferent Greek—both of them taking things, with the public. And then there was '*The Man in the Bell*,' a paper by-the-bye, Miss Zenobia, which I cannot sufficiently recommend to your attention. It is the history of a young person who goes to sleep under the clapper of a church bell, and is awakened by its tolling for a funeral. The sound drives him mad, and, accordingly, pulling out his tablets, he gives a record of his sensations. Sensations are the great things after all. Should you ever be drowned or hung, be sure and make a note of your sensations—they will be worth to you ten guineas a sheet. If you wish to write forcibly, Miss Zenobia, pay minute attention to the sensations.

"That I certainly will, Mr. Blackwood," said I.

"Good!" he replied. "I see you are a pupil after my own heart. But I must put you *au fait* to the details necessary in composing what may be denominated a genuine Blackwood article of the sensation stamp—the kind which you will understand me to say I consider the best for all purposes.

"The first thing requisite is to get yourself into such a scrape as no one ever got into before. The oven, for instance,—that was a good hit. But if you have no oven, or big bell, at hand, and if you cannot conveniently tumble out of a balloon, or be swallowed up in an earthquake, or get stuck fast in a chimney, you will have to be contented with simply imagining some similar misadventure. I should prefer, however, that you have the actual fact to bear you out. Nothing so well assists the fancy, as an experimental knowledge of the matter in hand. 'Truth is strange,' you know, 'stranger than fiction'—besides being more to the purpose."

Here I assured him I had an excellent pair of garters, and would go and hang myself forthwith.

"Good!" he replied, "do so;—although hanging is somewhat hacknied. Perhaps you might do better. Take a dose of Brandreth's pills, and then give us your sensations. However, my instructions will apply equally well to any variety of misadventure, and in your way home you may easily get knocked in the head, or run over by an omnibus, or bitten by a mad dog, or drowned in a gutter. But, to proceed.

"Having determined upon your subject, you must next consider the tone, or manner, of your narration. There is the tone didactic, the tone enthusiastic, the tone natural —all common-place enough. But then there is the tone laconic, or curt, which has lately come much into use. It consists in short sentences. Somehow thus. Can't be too brief. Can't be too snappish. Always a full stop. And never a paragraph.

"Then there is the tone elevated, diffusive, and interjectional. Some of our best novelists patronize this tone. The words must be all in a whirl, like a humming-top, and make a noise very similar, which answers remarkably well instead of meaning. This is the best of all possible styles where the writer is in too great a hurry to think.

"The tone metaphysical is also a good one. If you know any big words this is your chance for them. Talk of the Ionic and Eleatic schools—of Archytas, Gorgias and Alcmœon. Say something about objectivity and subjectivity. Be sure and abuse a man called Locke. Turn up your nose at things in general, and when you let slip anything a little too absurd, you need not be at the trouble of scratching it out, but just add a foot-note, and say that you are indebted for the above profound observation to the 'Kritik der reinem Vernunft,' or to the 'Metaphysische Anfangsgrunde der Naturwissenschaft.' This will look erudite and—and—and frank.

"There are various other tones of equal celebrity, but I shall mention only two more—the tone transcendental and the tone heterogeneous. In the former the merit consists in seeing into the nature of affairs a very great deal farther than any body else. This second sight is very efficient when properly managed. A little reading of the 'Dial' will carry you a great way. Eschew, in this case, big words; get them as small as possible, and write them upside down. Look over Channing's poems and quote what he says about a 'fat little man with a delusive show of Can.' Put in something about the Supernal Oneness. Don't say a syllable about the Infernal Twoness. Above all, study innuendo.

Hint every thing—assert nothing. If you feel inclined to say 'bread and butter' do not by any means say it outright. You may say anything and every thing *approaching* to 'bread and butter.' You may hint at buck-wheat cake, or you may even go so far as to insinuate oat-meal porridge, but if bread and butter be your real meaning, be cautious, my *dear* Miss Psyche, not on any account to say 'bread and butter!' "

I assured him that I should never say it again as long as I lived. He kissed me and continued:

"As for the tone heterogeneous, it is merely a judicious mixture, in equal proportions, of all the other tones in the world, and is consequently made up of everything deep, great, odd, piquant, pertinent, and pretty.

"Let us suppose now you have determined upon your incidents and tone. The most important portion,—in fact the soul of the whole business, is yet to be attended to— I allude to *the filling up*. It is not to be supposed that a lady or gentleman either has been leading the life of a bookworm. And yet above all things it is necessary that your article have an air of erudition, or at least afford evidence of extensive general reading. Now I'll put you in the way of accomplishing this point. See here!" (pulling down some three or four ordinary looking volumes, and opening them at random.) "By casting your eye down almost any page of any book in the world, you will be able to perceive at once a host of little scraps of either learning or *bel-esprit-ism*, which are the very thing for the spicing of a Blackwood article. You might as well note down a few while I read them to you. I shall make two divisions: first, *Piquant Facts for the Manufacture of Similes*; and second, *Piquant Expressions to be introduced as occasion may require*. Write now!—" and I wrote as he dictated.

"PIQUANT FACTS FOR SIMILES. 'There were originally but three Muses—Melete, Mneme, and Acœde—meditation, memory, and singing.' You may make a great deal of that little fact if properly worked. You see it is not generally known, and looks *recherché*. You must be careful and give something with a downright *improviso* air.

"Again. 'The river Alpheus passed beneath the sea, and emerged without injury to the purity of its waters.' Rather stale that, to be sure, but, if properly dressed and dished up, will look quite as fresh as ever.

"Here is something better. 'The Persian Iris appears to some persons to possess a sweet and very powerful perfume, while to others it is perfectly scentless.' Fine that, and very delicate! Turn it about a little, and it will do wonders. We'd have something else in the botanical line. There's nothing goes down so well, especially with the help of a little Lawn. Write!

"'*The Epidendrum Flos Aeris*, of Java, bears a very beautiful flower, and will live when pulled up by the roots. The natives suspend it by a cord from the ceiling, and enjoy its fragrance for years.' That's capital! That will do for the similes. Now for the Piquant Expressions.

"PIQUANT EXPRESSIONS. '*The venerable Chinese novel Ju-Kiao-Li.*' Good! By introducing these few words with dexterity you will evince your intimate acquaintance with the language and literature of the Chinese. With the aid of this you may possibly get along without either Arabic, or Sanscrit, or Chickasaw. There is no passing muster, however, without Spanish, Italian, German, Latin, and Greek. I must look you out a little specimen of each: Any scrap will answer, because you must depend upon your own ingenuity to make it fit into your article. Now write!

"'*Aussi tendre que Zaïre*'—as tender as Zaïre—French. Alludes to the frequent repetition of the phrase, *la tendre Zaïre*, in the French tragedy of that name. Properly introduced, will show not only your knowledge of the language, but your general reading and wit. You can say, for instance, that the chicken you were eating (write an article about being choked to death by a chicken-bone) was not altogether *aussi tendre que Zaïre*. Write!

> '*Van muerte tan escondida,*
> *Que no te sienta venir,*
> *Porque el plazer del morir*
> *No me torne a dar la vida.*'

That's Spanish—from Miguel de Cervantes. 'Come quickly O death! but be sure and don't let me see you coming, lest the pleasure I shall feel at your appearance should unfortunately bring me back again to life.' This you may slip in quite *à propos* when you are struggling in the last agonies with the chicken-bone. Write!

> '*Il pover 'huomo che non se'n era accorto,*
> *Andava combattendo, e era morto.*'

That's Italian, you perceive,—from Ariosto. It means that a great hero, in the heat of combat, not perceiving that he had been fairly killed, continued to fight valiantly, dead as he was. The application of this to your own case is obvious —for I trust, Miss Psyche, that you will not neglect to kick for at least an hour and a half after you have been choked to death by that chicken-bone. Please to write!

> '*Und sterb'ich doch, no sterb'ich denn*
> *Durch sie—durch sie!*'

That's German—from Schiller. 'And if I die, at least I die—for thee—for thee!' Here it is clear that you are apostrophising the *cause* of your disaster, the chicken. Indeed what gentleman (or lady either) of sense, *wouldn't* die, I should like to know, for a well fattened capon of the right Molucca breed, stuffed with capers and mushrooms, and served up in a salad-bowl, with orange-jellies *en mosàiques.* Write! (You can get them that way at Tortoni's)—Write, if you please!

"Here is a nice little Latin phrase, and rare too, (one can't be too *recherché* or brief in one's Latin, it's getting so common,)—*ignoratio elenchi.* He has committed an *ignoratio elenchi*—that is to say, he has understood the words of your proposition, but not the ideas. The man was *a fool,* you see. Some poor fellow whom you addressed while choking with that chicken-bone, and who therefore didn't precisely understand what you were talking about. Throw the *ignoratio elenchi* in his teeth, and, at once, you have him annihilated. If he dare to reply, you can tell him from Lucan (here it is) that speeches are mere *anemonae verborum,* anemone words. The anemone, with great brilliancy, has no smell. Or, if he begin to bluster, you may be down upon him with *insomnia Jovis,* reveries of Jupiter—a phrase which Silius Italicus (see here!) applies to thoughts pompous and inflated. This will be sure and cut him to the heart. He can do nothing but roll over and die. Will you be kind enough to write?

"In Greek we must have something pretty—from Demosthenes, for example. Ανερ ο φεογων και παλιν μαχεσεται. [Aner o pheogon kai palin makesetai.] There is a tolerably good translation of it in Hudibras—

> For he that flies may fight again,
> Which he can never do that's slain.

In a Blackwood article nothing makes so fine a show as your Greek. The very letters have an air of profundity about them. Only observe, madam, the astute look of that Epsilon! That Phi ought certainly to be a bishop! Was ever there a smarter fellow than that Omicron? Just twig that Tau! In short, there is nothing like Greek for a genuine sensation-paper. In the present case your application is the most obvious thing in the world. Rap out the sentence, with a huge oath, and by way of *ultimatum*, at the good-for-nothing dunder-headed villain who couldn't understand your plain English in relation to the chicken-bone. He'll take the hint and be off, you may depend upon it."

These were all the instructions Mr. B. could afford me upon the topic in question, but I felt they would be entirely sufficient. I was, at length, able to write a genuine Blackwood article, and determined to do it forthwith. In taking leave of me, Mr. B. made a proposition for the purchase of the paper when written; but as he could offer me only fifty guineas a sheet, I thought it better to let our society have it, than sacrifice it for so paltry a sum. Notwithstanding this niggardly spirit, however, the gentleman showed his consideration for me in all other respects, and indeed treated me with the greatest civility. His parting words made a deep impression upon my heart, and I hope I shall always remember them with gratitude.

"My dear Miss Zenobia," he said, while the tears stood in his eyes, "is there *any*thing else I can do to promote the success of your laudable undertaking? Let me reflect! It is just possible that you may not be able, so soon as convenient, to—to—get yourself drowned, or—choked with a chicken-bone, or—or hung—or—bitten by a—but stay! Now I think me of it, there are a couple of very excellent bull dogs in the yard—fine fellows, I assure you—savage, and all that—indeed just the thing for your money—they'll have you eaten up, *auriculas* and all, in less than five minutes (here's my watch!)—and then only think of the sensations! Here! I say—Tom!—Peter!—Dick, you villain!—let out those"—but as I was really in a great hurry, and had not another moment to spare, I was reluctantly forced to expedite my departure, and accordingly took leave *at once*—somewhat more abruptly, I admit, than strict courtesy would have, otherwise, allowed.

It was my primary object, upon quitting Mr. Blackwood, to get into some immediate difficulty, pursuant to his advice, and with this view I spent the greater part of the day in wandering about Edinburgh, seeking for desperate adventures—adventures adequate to the intensity of my feelings, and adapted to the vast character of the article I intended to write. In this excursion I was attended by my negro-servant Pompey, and my little lap-dog Diana, whom I had brought with me from Philadelphia. It was not, however, until late in the afternoon that I fully succeeded in my arduous undertaking. An important event then happened, of which the following Blackwood article, in the tone heterogeneous, is the substance and result.

A PREDICAMENT

What chance, good lady, hath bereft you thus?—COMUS.

It was a quiet and still afternoon when I strolled forth in the goodly city of Edina. The confusion and bustle in the streets were terrible. Men were talking. Women were screaming. Children were choking. Pigs were whistling. Carts they rattled. Bulls they bellowed. Cows they lowed. Horses they neighed. Cats they caterwauled. Dogs they danced. *Danced!* Could it then be possible? *Danced!* Alas, thought I, *my* dancing days are over! Thus it is ever. What a host of gloomy recollections will ever and anon be awakened in the mind of genius and imaginative contemplation, especially of a genius doomed to the everlasting, and eternal, and continual, and, as one might say, the—*continued*—yes, the *continued and continuous*, bitter, harassing, disturbing, and, if I may be allowed the expression, the *very* disturbing influence of the serene, and godlike, and heavenly, and exalting, and elevated, and purifying effect of what may be rightly termed the most enviable, the most *truly* enviable—nay! the most benignly beautiful, the most deliciously ethereal, and, as it were, the most *pretty* (if I may use so bold an expression) *thing* (pardon me, gentle reader!) in the word—but I am led away by my feelings. In *such* a mind, I repeat, what a host of recollections are stirred up by a trifle! The dogs danced! *I*—I *could* not! They frisked—I wept. They capered—I sobbed aloud. Touching circumstances! which cannot fail to bring to the recollection of the classical reader that exquisite passage in relation to the fitness of things, which is to be found in the commencement of the third volume of that admirable and venerable Chinese novel, the *Jo-Go-Slow*.

In my solitary walk through the city I had two humble but faithful companions. Diana, my poodle! sweetest of creatures! She had a quantity of hair over her one eye, and a blue ribband tied fashionably around her neck. Diana was not more than five inches in height, but her head was somewhat bigger than her body, and her tail, being cut off exceedingly close, gave an air of injured innocence to the interesting animal which rendered her a favorite with all.

And Pompey, my negro!—sweet Pompey! how shall I ever forget thee? I had taken Pompey's arm. He was three feet in height (I like to be particular) and about seventy or perhaps eighty, years of age. He had bow-legs and was corpulent. His mouth should not be called small, nor his ears short. His teeth, however; were like pearl, and his large full eyes were deliciously white. Nature had endowed him with no neck, and had placed his ankles (as usual with that race) in the middle of the upper portion of the feet. He was clad with a striking simplicity. His sole garments were a stock of nine inches in height, and a nearly-new drab overcoat which had formely been in the service of the tall, stately, and illustrious Dr. Moneypenny. It was a good overcoat. It was well cut. It was well made. The coat was nearly new. Pompey held it up out of the dirt with both hands.

There were three persons in our party, and two of them

have already been the subject of remark. There was a third—that third person was myself. I am the Signora Psyche Zenobia. I am *not* Suky Snobbs. My appearance is commanding. On the memorable occasion of which I speak I was habited in a crimson satin dress, with a sky-blue Arabian mantelet. And the dress had trimmings of green agraffas, and seven graceful flounces of the orange colored auricula. I thus formed the third of the party. There was the poodle. There was Pompey. There was myself. We were *three*. Thus it is said there were originally but three Furies—Melty, Nimmy and Hetty—Meditation, Memory, and Fiddling.

Leaning upon the arm of the gallant Pompey, and attended at a respectful distance by Diana, I proceeded down one of the populous and very pleasant streets of the now deserted Edina. On a sudden, there presented itself to view a church—a Gothic cathedral—vast, venerable, and with a tall steeple, which towered into the sky. What madness now possessed me? Why did I rush upon my fate? I was seized with an uncontrollable desire to ascend the giddy pinnacle, and thence survey the immense extent of the city. The door of the cathedral stood invitingly open. My destiny prevailed. I entered the ominous archway. Where then was my guardian angel?—if indeed such angels there be. *If!* Distressing monosyllable! what a world of mystery, and meaning, and doubt, and uncertainty is there involved in thy two letters! I entered the ominous archway! I entered; and without injury to my orange-colored auriculas, I passed beneath the portal, and emerged within the vestibule! Thus it is said the immense river Alfred passed, unscathed, and unwetted, beneath the sea.

I thought the staircases would never have an end. *Round!* Yes, they went round and up, and round and up and round and up, until I could not help surmising, with the sagacious Pompey, upon whose supporting arm I leaned in all the confidence of early affection—I *could* not help surmising that the upper end of the continuous spiral ladder had been accidentally, or perhaps designedly, removed. I paused for breath; and, in the meantime, an incident occurred of too momentous a nature in a moral, and also in a metaphysical point of view, to be passed over without notice. It appeared to me—indeed I was quite confident of the fact—I could not be mistaken—no! I had, for some moments, carefully and anxiously observed the motions my Diana—I say that I *could not be* mistaken— Diana *smelt a rat!* At once I called Pompey's attention to the subject, and he—he agreed with me. There was then no longer any reasonable room for doubt. The rat had been smelled—and by Diana. Heavens! shall I ever forget the intense excitement of that moment? Alas! what is the boasted intellect of man? The rat!—it was there— that is to say, it was somewhere. Diane smelled the rat. I—I *could* not! Thus it is said the Prussian Iris has, for some persons, a sweet and very powerful perfume, while to others it is perfectly scentless.

The staircase had been surmounted, and there were now only three or four more upward steps intervening between us and the summit. We still asended, and now only one step remained. One step! One little, little step! Upon one such little step in the great staircase of human life how vast a sum of human happiness or misery often depends! I thought of myself, then of Pompey, and then of the mysterious and inexplicable destiny which surrounded us. I thought of Pompey!—alas, I thought of love! I thought of the many *false steps* which have been taken, and may be taken again. I resolved to be more cautious, more reserved. I abandoned the arm of Pompey, and, without his assistance, surmounted the one remaining step, and gained the chamber of the belfry. I was followed immediately afterwards by my poodle. Pompey alone remained behind. I stood at the head of the staircase, and encouraged him to ascend. He stretched forth to me his hand, and unfortu-

nately in so doing was forced to abandon his firm hold
upon the overcoat. Will the gods never cease their persecu-
tion? The overcoat it dropped, and with one of his feet,
Pompey stepped upon the long and trailing skirt of the
overcoat. He stumbled and fell—this consequence was inevitable. He fell forwards, and, with his accursed head,
striking me full in the—in the breast, precipitated me
headlong, together with himself, upon the hard, filthy
and detestable floor of the belfry. But my revenge was sure,
sudden and complete. Seizing him furiously by the wool
with both hands, I tore out a vast quantity of the black,
and crisp, and curling material, and tossed it from me
with every manifestation of disdain. It fell among the ropes
of the belfry and remained. Pompey arose, and said no
word. But he regarded me piteously with his large eyes
and—sighed. Ye gods—that sigh! It sunk into my heart.
And the hair—the wool! Could I have reached that wool
I would have bathed it with my tears, in testimony of
regret. But alas! it was now far beyond my grasp. As it
dangled among the cordage of the bell, I fancied it still
alive. I fancied that it stood on end with indignation. Thus
the *happy dandy Fios Aeris* of Java, bears, it is said, a
beautiful flower, which will live when pulled up by the
roots. The natives suspend it by a cord from the ceiling
and enjoy its fragrance for years.

Our quarrel was now made up, and we looked about
the room for an aperture through which to survey the city
of Edina. Windows there were none. The sole light admitted into the gloomy chamber proceeded from a square
opening, about a foot in diameter, at a height of about
seven feet from the floor. Yet what will the energy of true
genius not effect? I resolved to clamber up to this hole.
A vast quantity of wheels, pinions, and other cabalistic-
looking machinery stood opposite the hole, close to it; and
through the hole there passed an iron rod from the machinery. Between the wheels and the wall where the hole

lay, there was barely room for my body—yet I was desperate, and determined to persevere. I called Pompey to my side.

"You perceive that aperture, Pompey. I wish to look through it. You will stand here just beneath the hole—so. Now, hold out one of your hands, Pompey, and let me step upon it—thus. Now, the other hand, Pompey, and with its aid I will get upon your shoulders."

He did everything I wished, and I found, upon getting up, that I could easily pass my head and neck through the aperture. The prospect was sublime. Nothing could be more magnificent. I merely paused a moment to bid Diana behave herself, and assure Pompey that I would be considerate and bear as lightly as possible upon his shoulders. I told him I would be tender of his feelings—*ossi tender que beefsteak.* Having done this justice to my faithful friend, I gave myself up with great zest and enthusiasm to the enjoyment of the scene which so obligingly spread itself out before my eyes.

Upon this subject, however, I shall forbear to dilate. I will not describe the city of Edinburgh. Every one has been to Edinburgh—the classic Edina. I will confine myself to the momentous details of my own lamentable adventure. Having, in some measure, satisfied my curiosity in regard to the extent, situation, and general appearance of the city, I had leisure to survey the church in which I was, and the delicate architecture of the steeple. I observed that the aperture through which I had thrust my head was an opening in the dial-plate of a gigantic clock, and must have appeared, from the street, as a large keyhole, such as we see in the face of French watches. No doubt the true object was to admit the arm of an attendant, to adjust, when necessary, the hands of the clock from within. I observed also, with surprise, the immense size of these hands, the longest of which could not have been less than ten feet in length, and, where broadest, eight or nine inches in breadth. They were of solid steel apparently, and their edges appeared to be sharp. Having noticed these particulars, and some others, I again turned my eyes upon the glorious prospect below, and soon became absorbed in contemplation.

From this, after some minutes, I was aroused by the voice of Pompey, who declared he could stand it no longer, and requested that I would be so kind as to come down. This was unreasonable, and I told him so in a speech of some length. He replied, but with an evident misunderstanding of my ideas upon the subject. I accordingly grew angry, and told him in plain words that he was a fool, that he had committed an *ignoramus e-clench-eye*, that his notions were mere *insommary Bovis*, and his words little better than *an enemywerryhor'em*. With this he appeared satisfied, and I resumed my contemplations.

It might have been half an hour after this altercation when, as I was deeply absorbed in the heavenly scenery beneath me, I was startled by something very cold which pressed with a gentle pressure upon the back of my neck. It is needless to say that I felt inexpressibly alarmed. I knew that Pompey was beneath my feet, and that Diana was sitting, according to my explicit directions, upon her hind legs in the farthest corner of the room. What could it be? Alas! I but too soon discovered. Turning my head gently to one side, I perceived to my extreme horror, that the huge, glittering, scimitar-like minute-hand of the clock, had, in the course of its hourly revolution, *descended upon my neck*. There was, I knew, not a second to be lost. I pulled back at once—but it was too late. There was no chance of forcing my head through the mouth of that terrible trap in which it was so fairly caught, and which grew narrower and narrower with a rapidity too horrible to be conceived. The agony of that moment is not to be imagined. I threw up my hands and endeavoured, with all my strength, to force upwards the ponderous iron bar. I might as well have tried to lift the cathedral itself. Down, down, down it came, closer and yet closer. I screamed to Pompey for aid: but he said that I had hurt his feelings by calling him "an ignorant old squint eye." I yelled to Diana; but she only said "bow-wow-wow," and that "I had told her on no account to stir from the corner." Thus I had no relief to expect from my associates.

Meantime the ponderous and terrific *Scythe of Time* (for I now discovered the literal import of that classical phrase) had not stopped, nor was it likely to stop, in its career. Down and still down, it came. It had already buried its sharp edge a full inch in my flesh, and my sensations grew indistinct and confused. At one time I fancied myself in Philadelphia with the stately Dr. Moneypenny, at another in the back parlor of Mr. Blackwood receiving his invaluable instructions. And then again the sweet recollection of better and earlier times came over me, and I thought of that happy period when the world was not all a desert, and Pompey not altogether cruel.

The ticking of the machinery amused me. *Amused me,* I say, for my sensations now bordered upon perfect happiness, and the most trifling circumstances afforded me pleasure. The eternal *click-clack, click-clack, click-clack,* of the clock was the most melodious of music in my ears, and occasionally even put me in mind of the grateful sermonic harangues of Dr. Ohapod. Then there were the great figures upon the dial-plate—how intelligent, how intellectual, they all looked! And presently they took to dancing the Mazurka, and I think it was the figure V who performed the most to my satisfaction. She was evidently a lady of breeding. None of your swaggerers, and nothing at all indelicate in her motions. She did the pirouette to admiration—whirling round upon her apex. I made an endeavor to hand her a chair, for I saw that she appeared fatigued with her exertions—and it was not until then that I fully perceived my lamentable situation.

Lamentable indeed! The bar had buried itself two inches in my neck. I was aroused to a sense of exquisite pain. I prayed for death, and, in the agony of the moment, could not help repeating those exquisite verses of the poet Miguel De Cervantes:

> Vanny Buren, tan escondida
> Query no te senty venny
> Pork and pleasure, delly morry
> Nommy, torny, darry, widdy!

But now a new horror presented itself, and one indeed sufficient to startle the strongest nerves. My eyes, from the cruel pressure of the machine, were absolutely starting from their sockets. While I was thinking how I should possibly manage without them, one actually tumbled out of my head, and, rolling down the steep side of the steeple, lodged in the rain gutter which ran along the eaves of the main building. The loss of the eye was not so much as the insolent air of independence and contempt with which it regarded me after it was out. There it lay in the gutter just under my nose, and the airs it gave itself would have been ridiculous had they not been disgusting. Such a winking and blinking were never before seen. This behaviour on the part of my eye in the gutter was not only irritating on account of its manifest insolence and shameful ingratitude, but was also exceedingly inconvenient on account of the sympathy which always exists between two eyes of the same head, however far apart. I was forced, in a manner, to wink and to blink, whether I would or not, in exact concert with the scoundrelly thing that lay just under my nose. I was presently relieved, however, by the dropping out of the other eye. In falling it took the same direction (possibly a concerted plot) as its fellow. Both rolled out of the gutter together, and in truth I was very glad to get rid of them.

The bar was now four inches and a half deep in my neck, and there was only a little bit of skin to cut through. My sensations were those of entire happiness, for I felt that in a few minutes, at farthest, I should be relieved from my disagreeable situation. And in this expectation I was not at all deceived. At twenty-five mintues past five in the afternoon precisely, the huge minute-hand had proceeded sufficiently far on its terrible revolution to sever the small remainder of my neck. I was not sorry to see the head which had occasioned me so much embarrassment at length make a final separation from my body. It first rolled down the side of the steeple, then lodged, for a few seconds, in the gutter, and then made its way, with a plunge, into the middle of the street.

I will candidly confess that my feelings were now of the most singular—nay of the most mysterious, the most perplexing and incomprehensible character. My senses were here and there at one and the same moment. With my head I imagined, at one time, that I the head, was the real Signora Psyche Zenobia—at another I felt convinced that myself, the body, was the proper identity. To clear my ideas upon this topic I felt in my pocket for my snuff-box, but, upon getting it, and endeavoring to apply a pinch of its grateful contents in the ordinary manner, I became immediately aware of my peculiar deficiency, and threw the box at once down to my head. It took a pinch with great satisfaction, and smiled me an acknowledgement in return. Shortly afterwards it made me a speech, which I could hear but indistinctly without ears. I gathered enough, however, to know that it was astonished at my wishing to remain alive under such circumstances. In the concluding sentences it quoted the noble words of Ariosto—

> *Il pover hommy che non sera corty*
> *And have a combat tenty erry morty.*

thus comparing me to the hero who, in the heat of the combat, not perceiving that he was dead, continued to contest the battle with inextinguishable valor. There was nothing now to prevent my getting down from my elevation, and I did so. What it was that Pompey saw so *very* peculiar in my appearance I have never yet been able to find out. The fellow opened his mouth from ear to ear, and shut his two eyes as if he were endeavoring to crack nuts between the lids. Finally, throwing off his overcoat, he made one spring for the staircase and disappeared. I hurled after the scoundrel those vehement words of Demosthenes—

Andrew O'Phlegethon, you really make haste to fly,

and then turned to the darling of my heart, to the one-eyed! the shaggy-haired Diana. Alas! what horrible vision affronted my eyes? *Was* that a rat I saw skulking into his hole? *Are* these the picked bones of the little angel who has been cruelly devoured by the monster? Ye Gods! and what *do* I behold—*is* that the departed spirit, the shade, the ghost of my beloved puppy, which I perceive sitting with a grace so melancholy, in the corner? Harken! for she speaks, and, heavens! it is in the German of Schiller—

> "Unt stubby duk, so stubby dun
> Duk shel duk shel!"

Alas!—and are not her words too true?

> And if I died at least I died
> For thee—for thee.

Sweet creature! she *too* has sacrificed herself in my behalf Dogless, niggerless, headless, what *now* remains for the unhappy Signora Psyche Zenobia? Alas—*nothing!* I have done.

THE FALL OF
THE HOUSE OF USHER

Son cœur est un luth suspendu;
Sitôt qu'on le touche il resonne.
—De Béranger.

During the whole of a dull, dark, and soundless day in the
autumn of the year, when the clouds hung oppressively
low in the heavens, I had been passing alone, on horse-
back, through a singularly dreary tract of country; and at
length found myself, as the shades of the evening drew
on, within view of the melancholy House of Usher. I know
not how it was—but, with the first glimpse of the building, a sense of insufferable gloom pervaded my spirit. I
say insufferable; for the feeling was unrelieved by any of
that half-pleasurable, because poetic, sentiment, with
which the mind usually receives even the sternest natural
images of the desolate or terrible. I looked upon the scene
before me—upon the mere house, and the simple landscape features of the domain—upon the bleak walls—
upon the vacant eye-like windows —upon a few rank sedges
—and upon a few white trunks of decayed trees—with an
utter depression of soul which I can compare to no earthly
sensation more properly than to the afterdream of the
reveller upon opium—the bitter lapse into everyday life—
the hideous dropping off of the veil. There was an iciness,
a sinking, a sickening of the heart—an unredeemed
dreariness of thought which no goading of the imagination could torture into aught of the sublime. What was it
—I paused to think—what was it that so unnerved me in
the contemplation of the House of Usher? It was a mystery
all insoluble; nor could I grapple with the shadowy fancies

that crowded upon me as I pondered. I was forced to fall back upon the unsatisfactory conclusion, that while, beyond doubt, there *are* combinations of very simple natural objects which have the power of thus affecting us, still the analysis of this power lies among considerations beyond our depth. It was possible, I reflected, that a mere different arrangement of the particulars of the scene, of the details of the picture, would be sufficient to modify, or perhaps to annihilate its capacity for sorrowful impression; and, acting upon this idea, I reined my horse to the precipitous brink of a black and lurid tarn that lay in unruffled lustre by the dwelling, and gazed down—but with a shudder even more thrilling than before—upon the the remodelled and inverted images of the gray sedge, and the ghastly tree-stems, and the vacant and eye-like windows.

Nevertheless, in this mansion of gloom I now proposed to myself a sojourn of some weeks. Its proprietor, Roderick Usher, had been one of my boon companions in boyhood; but many years had elapsed since our last meeting. A letter, however, had lately reached me in a distant part of the country—a letter from him—which, in its wildly importunate nature, had admitted of no other than a personal reply. The MS. gave evidence of nervous agitation. The writer spoke of acute bodily illness—of a mental disorder which oppressed him—and of an earnest desire to see me, as his best, and indeed his only personal friend, with a view of attempting, by the cheerfulness of my society, some alleviation of his malady. It was the manner in which all this, and much more, was said—it was the apparent *heart* that went with his request—which allowed me no room for hesitation; and I accordingly obeyed forthwith what I still considered a very singular summons.

Although, as boys, we had been even intimate associates, yet I really knew little of my friend. His reserve had been always excessive and habitual. I was aware, however, that his very ancient family had been noted, time out of mind, for a peculiar sensibility of temperament, displaying itself, through long ages, in many works of exalted art, and manifested, of late, in repeated deeds of munificent yet unobtrusive charity, as well as in a passionate devotion to the intricacies, perhaps even more than to the orthodox and easily recognisable beauties, of musical science. I had learned, too, the very remarkable fact, that the stem of the Usher race, all time-honored as it was, had put forth, at no period, any enduring branch; in other words, that the entire family lay in the direct line of descent, and had always, with very trifling and very temporary variation, so lain. It was this deficiency, I considered, while running over in thought the perfect keeping of the character of the premises with the accredited character of the people, and while speculating upon the possible influence which the one, in the long lapse of centuries, might have exercised upon the other—it was this deficiency, perhaps, of collateral issue, and the consequent undeviating transmission, from sire to son, of the patrimony with the name, which had, at length, so identified the two as to merge the original title of the estate in the quaint and equivocal appellation of the "House of Usher"—an appellation which seemed to include, in the minds of the peasantry who used it, both the family and the family mansion.

I have said that the sole effect of my somewhat childish experiment—that of looking down within the tarn—had been to deepen the first singular impression. There can be no doubt that the consciousness of the rapid increase of my superstition—for why should I not so term it?—served mainly to accelerate the increase itself. Such, I have long known, is the paradoxical law of all sentiments having terror as a basis. And it might have been for this reason only, that, when I again uplifted my eyes to the house itself, from its image in the pool, there grew in my mind a strange fancy—a fancy so ridiculous, indeed, that I but mention it to show the vivid force of the sensations which oppressed me. I had so worked upon my imagination as really to believe that about the whole mansion and domain there hung an atmosphere peculiar to themselves and their immediate vicinity—an atmosphere which had no affinity with the air of heaven, but which had reeked up from the decayed trees, and the gray wall, and the silent tarn—a pestilent and mystic vapor, dull, sluggish, faintly discernible, and leaden-hued.

Shaking off from my spirit what *must* have been a dream, I scanned more narrowly the real aspect of the building. Its principal feature seemed to be that of an excessive antiquity. The discoloration of ages had been great. Minute fungi overspread the whole exterior, hanging in a fine tangled web-work from the eaves. Yet all this was apart from any extaordinary dilapidation. No portion of the masonry had fallen; and there appeared to be a wild inconsistency between its still perfect adaptation of parts, and the crumbling condition of the individual stones. In this there was much that reminded me of the specious totality of old wood-work which has rotted for long years in some neglected vault, with no disturbance from the breath of the external air. Beyond this indication of extensive decay, however, the fabric gave little token of instability. Perhaps the eye of a scrutinizing observer might have discovered a barely perceptible fissure, which, extending from the roof of the building in front, made its way down the wall in a zigzag direction, until it became lost in the sullen waters of the tarn.

Noticing these things, I rode over a short causeway to the house. A servant in waiting took my horse, and I entered the Gothic archway of the hall. A valet, of stealthy step, thence conducted me, in silence, through many dark and intricate passages in my progress to the *studio* of his master. Much that I encountered on the way contributed, I know not how, to heighten the vague sentiments of which I have already spoken. While the objects around me—while the carvings of the ceilings, the sombre tapestries of the walls, the ebon blackness of the floors, and the phantasmagoric armorial trophies which rattled as I strode, were but matters to which, or to such as which, I had been accustomed from my infancy—while I hesitated not to acknowledge how familiar was all this—I still wondered to find how unfamiliar were the fancies which ordinary images were stirring up. On one of the staircases, I met the physician of the family. His countenance, I thought, wore a mingled expression of low cunning and perplexity. He accosted me with trepidation and passed on. The valet now threw open a door and ushered me into the presence of his master.

The room in which I found myself was very large and lofty. The windows were long, narrow, and pointed, and at so vast a distance from the black oaken floor as to be altogether inaccessible from within. Feeble gleams of encrimsoned light made their way through the trellissed panes, and served to render sufficiently distinct the more prominent objects around; the eye, however, struggled in vain to reach the remoter angles of the chamber, or the recesses of the vaulted and fretted ceiling. Dark draperies hung upon the walls. The general furniture was profuse, comfortless, antique, and tattered. Many books and musical instruments lay scattered about, but failed to give any vitality to the scene. I felt that I breathed an atmosphere of sorrow, An air of stern, deep, and irredeemable gloom hung over and pervaded all.

Upon my entrance, Usher arose from a sofa on which he had been lying at full length, and greeted me with a vivacious warmth which had much in it, I at first thought, of an overdone cordiality—of the constrained effort of the *ennuyé* man of the world. A glance, however, at his countenance, convinced me of his perfect sincerity. We sat down; and for some moments, while he spoke not, I gazed upon him with a feeling half of pity, half of awe. Surely, man had never before so terribly altered, in so brief a period, as had Roderick Usher! It was with difficulty that I could bring myself to admit the identity of the wan being before me with the companion of my early boyhood. Yet the character of his face had been at all times remarkable. A cadaverousness of complexion; an eye large, liquid, and luminous beyond comparison; lips somewhat thin and very pallid, but of a surpassingly beautiful curve; a nose of a delicate Hebrew model, but with a breadth of nostril unusual in similar formations; a finely moulded chin, speaking, in its want of prominence, of a want of moral energy; hair of a more than web-like softness and tenuity; these features, with an inordinate expansion above the regions of the temple, made up altogether a countenance not easily to be forgotten. And now in the mere exaggeration of the prevailing character of these features, and of the expression they were wont to convey, lay so much of change that I doubted to whom I spoke. The now ghastly pallor of the skin, and the now miraculous lustre of the eye, above all things startled and even awed me. The silken hair, too, had been suffered to grow all unheeded, and as, in its wild gossamer texture, it floated rather than fell about the face, I could not, even with effort, connect its Arabesque expression with any idea of simple humanity.

In the manner of my friend I was at once struck with an incoherence—an inconsistency; and I soon found this to arise from a series of feeble and futile struggles to overcome an habitual trepidancy—an excessive nervous agitation. For something of this nature I had indeed been prepared, no less by his letter, than by reminiscences of certain boyish traits, and by conclusions deduced from his peculiar physical conformation and temperament. His action was alternately vivacious and sullen. His voice varied rapidly from a tremulous indecision (when the animal spirits seemed utterly in abeyance) to that species of energetic concision—that abrupt, weighty, unhurried, and hollow-sounding enunciation—that leaden, self-balanced and perfectly modulated guttural utterance, which may be observed in the lost drunkard, or the irreclaimable eater of opium, during the periods of his most intense excitement.

It was thus that he spoke of the object of my visit, of his earnest desire to see me, and of the solace he expected me to afford him. He entered, at some length, into what he conceived to be the nature of his malady. It was, he said, a constitutional and a family evil, and one for which he despaired to find a remedy—a mere nervous affection, he immediately added, which would undoubtedly soon pass off. It displayed itself in a host of unnatural sensations. Some of these, as he detailed them, interested and bewildered me; although, perhaps, the terms, and the general manner of the narration had their weight. He suffered much from a morbid acuteness of the senses; the most insipid food was alone endurable; he could wear only garments of certain texture; the odors of all flowers were oppressive; his eyes were tortured by even a faint light; and there were but peculiar sounds, and these from stringed instruments, which did not inspire him with horror.

To an anomalous species of terror I found him a bounden slave. "I shall perish," said he, "I *must* perish in this deplorable folly. Thus, thus, and not otherwise, shall I be lost. I dread the events of the future, not in themselves, but in their results. I shudder at the thought of any, even the most trivial, incident, which may operate upon this intolerable agitation of soul. I have, indeed, no abhorrence of danger, except in its absolute effect—in terror. In this unnerved—in this pitiable condition—I feel that the period will sooner or later arrive when I must abandon life and reason together, in some struggle with the grim phantasm, FEAR."

I learned, moreover, at intervals, and through broken and equivocal hints, another singular feature of his mental condition. He was enchained by certain superstitious impressions in regard to the dwelling which he tenanted, and whence, for many years, he had never ventured forth —in regard to an influence whose supposititious force was conveyed in terms too shadowdy here to be re-stated—an influence which some peculiarities in the mere form and substance of his family mansion, had, by dint of long sufferance, he said, obtained over his spirit—an effect which the *physique* of the gray walls and turrets, and of the dim tarn into which they all looked down, had, at length, brought about upon the *morale* of his existence.

He admitted, however, although with hesitation, that much of the peculiar gloom which thus afflicted him could be traced to a more natural and far more palpable origin—to the severe and long-continued illness—indeed to the evidently approaching dissolution—of a tenderly beloved sister—his sole companion for long years—his last and only relative on earth. "Her decease," he said, with a bitterness which I can never forget, "would leave him (him the hopeless and the frail) the last of the ancient race of the Ushers." While he spoke, the lady Madeline (for so was she called) passed slowly through a remote portion of the apartment, and, without having noticed my presence, disappeared. I regarded her with an utter astonishment not unmingled with dread—and yet I found it impossible to account for such feelings. A sensation of stupor oppressed me, as my eyes followed her retreating steps. When a door, at length, closed upon her, my glance sought instinctively and eagerly the countenance of the brother—but he had buried his face in his hands, and I could only perceive that a far more than ordinary wanness had overspread the emaciated fingers through which trickled many passionate tears.

The disease of the lady Madeline had long baffled the skill of her physicians. A settled apathy, a gradual wasting away of the person, and frequent although transient affections of a partially cataleptical character, were the unusual diagnosis. Hitherto she had steadily borne up against the pressure of her malady, and had not betaken herself finally to bed; but, on the closing in of the evening of my arrival at the house, she succumbed (as her brother told me at night with inexpressible agitation) to the prostrating power of the destroyer; and I learned that the glimpse I had obtained of her person would thus probably be the last I should obtain—that the lady, at least while living, would be seen by me no more.

For several days ensuing, her name was unmentioned by either Usher or myself: and during this period I was busied in earnest endeavors to alleviate the melancholy of my friend. We painted and read together; or I listened, as if in a dream, to the wild improvisations of his speaking guitar. And thus, as a closer and still closer intimacy admitted me more unreservedly into the recesses of his spirit, the more bitterly did I perceive the futility of all attempt at cheering a mind from which darkness, as if an inherent positive quality, poured forth upon all objects of the moral and physical universe, in one unceasing radiation of gloom.

I shall ever bear about me a memory of the many solemn hours I thus spent alone with the master of the House of Usher. Yet I should fail in any attempt to convey an idea of the exact character of the studies, or of the occupations, in which he involved me, or led me the way. An excited and highly distempered ideality threw a sulphureous lustre over all. His long improvised dirges will ring forever in my ears. Among other things, I hold painfully in mind a certain singular perversion and amplification of the wild air of the last waltz of Von Weber. From the paintings over which his elaborate fancy brooded, and which grew, touch by touch, into vaguenesses at which I shuddered the more thrillingly, because I shuddered knowing not why;—from these paintings (vivid as their images now are before me) I would in vain endeavor to educe more than a small portion which should lie within the compass of merely written words. By the utter simplicity, by the nakedness of his designs, he arrested and overawed attention. If ever mortal painted an idea, that mortal was Roderick Usher. For me at least—in the circumstances then surrounding me—there arose out of the pure abstractions which the hypochondriac contrived to throw upon his canvass, an intensity of intolerable awe, no shadow of which felt I ever yet in the contemplation of the certainly glowing yet too concrete reveries of Fuseli.

One of the phantasmagoric conceptions of my friend, partaking not so rigidly of the spirit of abstraction, may be shadowed forth, although feebly, in words. A small picture presented the interior of an immensely long and rectangular vault or tunnel, with low walls, smooth, white, and without interruption or device. Certain accessory points of the design served well to convey the idea that this excavation lay at an exceeding depth below the surface of the earth. No outlet was observed in any portion of its vast extent, and no torch, or other artificial source of light was discernible; yet a flood of intense rays rolled throughout, and bathed the whole in a ghastly and inappropriate splendor.

I have just spoken of that morbid condition of the auditory nerve which rendered all music intolerable to the sufferer, with the exception of certain effects of stringed instruments. It was, perhaps, the narrow limits to which he thus confined himself upon the guitar, which gave birth, in great measure, to the fantastic character of his performances. But the fervid *facility* of his *impromptus* could not be so accounted for. They must have been, and were, in the notes, as well as in the words of his wild fantasias (for he not unfrequently accompanied himself with rhymed verbal improvisations), the result of that intense mental collectedness and concentration to which I have previously alluded as observable only in particular moments of the highest artificial excitement. The words of one of these rhapsodies I have easily remembered. I was, perhaps, the more forcibly impressed with it, as he gave it, because, in the under or mystic current of its meaning, I fancied that I perceived, and for the first time, a full consciousness on the part of Usher, of the tottering of his lofty reason upon her throne. The verses, which were entitled "The Haunted Palace," ran very nearly, if not accurately, thus:

I

In the greenest of our valleys,
  By good angels tenanted,
Once a fair and stately palace—
  Radiant palace—reared its head.
In the monarch Thought's dominion—
  It stood there!
Never seraph spread a pinion
  Over fabric half so fair.

II

Banners yellow, glorious, golden,
  On its roof did float and flow;
(This—all this—was in the olden
  Time long ago)
And every gentle air that dallied,
  In that sweet day,
Along the ramparts plumed and pallid,
  A winged odor went away.

III

Wanderers in that happy valley
   Through two luminous windows saw
Spirits moving musically
   To a lute's well-tunéd law,
Round about a throne, where sitting
   (Porphyrogene!)
In state his glory well befitting,
   The ruler of the realm was seen.

IV

And all with pearl and ruby glowing
   Was the fair palace door,
Through which came flowing, flowing, flowing,
   And sparkling evermore,
A troop of Echoes whose sweet duty
   Was but to sing,
In voices of surpassing beauty,
   The wit and wisdom of their king.

V

But evil things, in robes of sorrow,
   Assailed the monarch's high estate;
(Ah, let us mourn, for never morrow
   Shall dawn upon him, desolate!)
And, round about his home, the glory
   That blushed and bloomed
Is but a dim-remembered story
   Of the old time entombed.

VI

And travellers now within that valley,
   Through the red-litten windows, see
Vast forms that move fantastically
   To a discordant melody;

While, like a rapid ghastly river,
Through the pale door,
A hideous throng rush out forever,
And laugh—but smile no more.

I well remember that suggestions arising from this ballad, led us into a train of thought wherein there became
manifest an opinion of Usher's which I mention not so
much on account of its novelty, (for other men* have
thought thus,) as on account of the pertinacity with which
he maintained it. This opinion, in its general form, was
that of the sentience of all vegetable things. But, in his
disordered fancy, the idea had assumed a more daring
character, and trespassed, under certain conditions, upon
the kingdom of inorganization. I lack words to express
the full extent, or the earnest *abandon* of his persuasion.
The belief, however, was connected (as I have previously
hinted) with the gray stones of the home of his forefathers. The conditions of the sentience had been here,
he imagined, fulfilled in the method of collocation of these
stones—in the order of their arrangement, as well as in
that of the many *fungi* which overspread them, and of the
decayed trees which stood around—above all, in the long
undisturbed endurance of this arrangement, and in its
reduplication in the still waters of the tarn. Its evidence—
the evidence of the sentience—was to be seen, he said,
(and I here started as he spoke,) in the gradual yet certain condensation of an atmosphere of their own about
the waters and the walls. The result was discoverable, he
added, in that silent, yet importunate and terrible influence which for centuries had moulded the destinies of
his family, and which made *him* what I now saw him—
what he was. Such opinions need no comment, and I will
make none.

* Watson, Dr. Percival, Spallanzani, and especially the Bishop
of Landaff.—See "Chemical Essays," vol. v.

Our books—the books which, for years, had formed no small portion of the mental existence of the invalid—were, as might be supposed, in strict keeping with this character of phantasm. We pored together over such works as the *Ververt et Chartreuse* of Gresset; the *Belphegor* of Machiavelli; the *Heaven and Hell* of Swedenborg; the *Subterranean Voyage of Nicholas Klimm* by Holberg; the *Chiromancy* of Robert Flud, of Jean D'Indaginé, and of De la Chambre; the *Journey into the Blue Distance* of Tieck; and the *City of the Sun* of Campanella. One favorite volume was a small octavo edition of the *Directorium Inquisitorium*, by the Dominican Eymeric de Gironne; and there were passages in Pomponius Mela, about the old African Satyrs and Œgipans, over which Usher would sit dreaming for hours. His chief delight, however, was found in the perusal of an exceedingly rare and curious book in quarto Gothic—the manual of a forgotten church—the *Vigiliae Mortuorum secundum Chorum Ecclesiae Maguntinae*.

I could not help thinking of the wild ritual of this work, and of its probable influence upon the hypochondriac, when, one evening, having informed me abruptly that the lady Madeline was no more, he stated his intention of preserving her corpse for a fortnight, (previously to its final interment,) in one of the numerous vaults within the main walls of the building. The worldly reason, however, assigned for this singular proceeding, was one which I did not feel at liberty to dispute. The brother had been led to his resolution (so he told me) by consideration of the unusual character of the malady of the deceased, of certain obtrusive and eager inquiries on the part of her medical men, and of the remote and exposed situation of the burial-ground of the family. I will not deny that when I called to mind the sinister countenance of the person whom I met upon the staircase, on the day of my arrival at the house, I had no desire to oppose what I regarded as at best but a harmless, and by no means an unnatural, precaution.

At the request of Usher, I personally aided him in the arrangements for the temporary entombment. The body having been encoffined, we two alone bore it to its rest. The vault in which we placed it (and which had been so long unopened that our torches, half smothered in its oppressive atmosphere, gave us little opportunity for investigation) was small, damp, and entirely without means of admission for light; lying, at great depth, immediately beneath that portion of the building in which was my own sleeping apartment. It had been used, apparently, in remote feudal times, for the worst purposes of a donjon-keep, and, in later days, as a place of deposit for powder, or some other highly combustible substance, as a portion of its floor, and the whole interior of a long archway through which we reached it, were carefully sheathed with copper. The door, of massive iron, had been, also, similarly protected. Its immense weight caused an unusually sharp grating sound, as it moved upon its hinges.

Having deposited our mournful burden upon tressels within this region of horror, we partially turned aside the yet unscrewed lid of the coffin, and looked upon the face of the tenant. A striking similitude between the brother and sister now first arrested my attention; and Usher, divining, perhaps, my thoughts, murmured out some few words from which I learned that the deceased and himself had been twins, and that sympathies of a scarcely intelligible nature had always existed between them. Our glances, however, rested not long upon the dead—for we could not regard her unawed. The disease which had thus entombed the lady in the maturity of youth, had left, as usual in all maladies of a strictly cataleptical character, the mockery of a faint blush upon the bosom and the face, and that suspiciously lingering smile upon the lip which is so terrible in death. We replaced and screwed down the lid, and, having secured the door of iron, made our way, with toil, into the scarcely less gloomy apartments of the upper portion of the house.

And now, some days of bitter grief having elapsed, an observable change came over the features of the mental disorder of my friend. His ordinary manner had vanished. His ordinary occupations were neglected or forgotten. He roamed from chamber to chamber with hurried, unequal, and objectless step. The pallor of his countenance had assumed, if possible, a more ghastly hue—but the luminousness of his eye had utterly gone out. The once occasional huskiness of his tone was heard no more; and a tremulous quaver, as if of extreme terror, habitually characterized his utterance. There were times, indeed, when I thought his unceasingly agitated mind was laboring with some oppressive secret, to divulge which he struggled for the necessary courage. At times, again, I was obliged to resolve all into the mere inexplicable vagaries of madness, for I beheld him gazing upon vacancy for long hours, in an attitude of the profoundest attention, as if listening to some imaginary sound. It was no wonder that his condition terrified—that it infected me. I felt creeping upon me, by slow yet certain degrees, the wild influences of his own fantastic yet impressive superstitions.

It was, especially, upon retiring to bed late in the night of the seventh or eighth day after the placing of the lady Madeline within the donjon, that I experienced the full power of such feelings. Sleep came not near my couch—while the hours waned and waned away. I struggled to reason off the nervousness which had dominion over me. I endeavored to believe that much, if not all of what I felt, was due to the bewildering influence of the gloomy furniture of the room—of the dark and tattered draperies, which, tortured into motion by the breath of a rising tempest, swayed fitfully to and fro upon the walls, and rustled uneasily about the decorations of the bed. But my efforts were fruitless. An irrepressible tremor gradually pervaded my frame; and, at length, there sat upon my very heart an incubus of utterly causeless alarm. Shaking this off with a gasp and a struggle, I uplifted myself upon the pillows, and, peering earnestly within the intense darkness of the chamber, harkened—I know not why, except that an instinctive spirit prompted me—to certain low and indefinite sounds which came, through the pauses of the storm, at long intervals, I knew not whence. Overpowered by an intense sentiment of horror, unaccountable yet unendurable, I threw on my clothes with haste (for I felt that I should sleep no more during the night), and endeavored to arouse myself from the pitiable condition into which I had fallen, by pacing rapidly to and fro through the apartment.

I had taken but few turns in this manner, when a light step on an adjoining staircase arrested my attention. I presently recognised it as that of Usher. In an instant afterward he rapped, with a gentle touch, at my door, and entered, bearing a lamp. His countenance was, as usual, cadaverously wan—but, moreover, there was a species of mad hilarity in his eyes—an evidently restrained *hysteria* in his whole demeanor. His air appalled me—but anything was preferable to the solitude which I had so long endured, and I even welcomed his presence as a relief.

"And you have not seen it?" he said abruptly, after having stared about him for some moments in silence—"you have not then seen it?—but, stay! you shall." Thus speaking, and having carefully shaded his lamp, he hurried to one of the casements, and threw it freely open to the storm.

The impetuous fury of the entering gust nearly lifted us from our feet. It was, indeed, a tempestuous yet sternly beautiful night, and one wildly singular in its terror and its beauty. A whirlwind had apparently collected its force in our vicinity; for there were frequent and violent alterations in the direction of the wind; and the exceeding density of the clouds (which hung so low as to press upon the turrets of the house) did not prevent our perceiving the life-like velocity with which they flew careering from all points against each other, without passing away into the distance. I say that even their exceeding density did not prevent our perceiving this—yet we had no glimpse of the moon or stars—nor was there any flashing forth of the lightning. But the under surfaces of the huge masses of agitated vapor, as well as all terrestrial objects immediately around us, were glowing in the unnatural light of a faintly luminous and distinctly visible gaseous exhalation which hung about and enshrouded the mansion.

"You must not—you shall not behold this!" said I, shudderingly, to Usher, as I led him, with a gentle violence, from the window to a seat. "These appearances, which bewilder you, are merely electrical phenomena not uncommon—or it may be that they have their ghastly origin in the rank miasma of the tarn. Let us close this casement;—the air is chilling and dangerous to your frame. Here is one of your favorite romances. I will read, and you shall listen;—and so we will pass away this terrible night together."

The antique volume which I had taken up was the "Mad Trist" of Sir Launcelot Canning; but I had called it a favorite of Usher's more in sad jest than in earnest; for, in truth, there is little in its uncouth and unimaginative prolixity which could have had interest for the lofty and spiritual ideality of my friend. It was, however, the only book immediately at hand; and I indulged a vague hope that the excitement which now agitated the hypochondriac, might find relief (for the history of mental disorder is full of similar anomalies) even in the extremeness of the folly which I should read. Could I have judged, indeed, by the wild overstrained air of vivacity with which he harkened, or apparently harkened, to the words of the tale, I might well have congratulated myself upon the success of my design.

I had arrived at that well-known portion of the story where Ethelred, the hero of the Trist, having sought in vain for peaceable admission into the dwelling of the hermit, proceeds to make good an entrance by force. Here, it will be remembered, the words of the narrative run thus:

"And Ethelred, who was by nature of a doughty heart, and who was now mighty withal, on account of the powerfulness of the wine which he had drunken, waited no longer to hold parley with the hermit, who, in sooth, was of an obstinate and maliceful turn, but, feeling the rain upon his shoulders, and fearing the rising of the tempest, uplifted his mace outright, and, with blows, made quickly room in the plankings of the door for his gauntleted hand; and now pulling therewith sturdily, he so cracked, and ripped, and tore all asunder, that the noise of the dry and hollow-sounding wood alarummed and reverberated throughout the forest."

At the termination of this sentence I started, and for a moment, paused; for it appeared to me (although I at once concluded that my excited fancy had deceived me)—it appeared to me that, from some very remote portion of the mansion, there came, indistinctly, to my ears, what might have been, in its exact similarity of character, the echo (but a stifled and dull one certainly) of the very cracking and ripping sound which Sir Launcelot had so particularly described. It was, beyond doubt, the coincidence alone which had arrested my attention; for, amid the rattling of the sashes of the casements, and the ordinary commingled noises of the still increasing storm, the sound, in itself, had nothing, surely, which should have interested or disturbed me. I continued the story:

"But the good champion Ethelred, now entering within the door, was sore enraged and amazed to perceive no signal of the maliceful hermit; but, in the stead thereof, a dragon of a scaly and prodigious demeanor, and of a fiery tongue, which sate in guard before a palace of gold, with a floor of silver; and upon the wall there hung a shield of shining brass with this legend enwritten—

> Who entereth herein, a conqueror hath bin;
> Who slayeth the dragon, the shield he shall win;

And Ethelred uplifted his mace, and struck upon the head of the dragon, which fell before him, and gave up his pesty breath, with a shriek so horrid and harsh, and withal so piercing, that Ethelred had fain to close his ears with his hands against the dreadful noise of it, the like whereof was never before heard."

Here again I paused abruptly, and now with a feeling of wild amazement—for there could be no doubt whatever that, in this instance, I did actually hear (although from what direction it proceeded I found it impossible to say) a low and apparently distant, but harsh, protracted, and most unusual screaming or grating sound—the exact counterpart of what my fancy had already conjured up for the dragon's unnatural shriek as described by the romancer.

Oppressed, as I certainly was, upon the occurrence of this second and most extraordinary coincidence, by a thousand conflicting sensations, in which wonder and extreme terror were predominant, I still retained sufficient presence of mind to avoid exciting, by any observation, the sensitive nervousness of my companion. I was by no means certain that he had noticed the sounds in question; although, assuredly, a strange alteration had, during the last few minutes, taken place in his demeanor. From a position fronting my own, he had gradually brought round his chair, so as to sit with his face to the door of the chamber; and thus I could but partially perceive his features, although I saw that his lips trembled as if he were murmuring inaudibly. His head had dropped upon his breast

—yet I knew that he was not asleep, from the wide and rigid opening of the eye as I caught a glance of it in profile. The motion of his body, too, was at variance with this idea—for he rocked from side to side with a gentle yet constant and uniform sway. Having rapidly taken notice of all this, I resumed the narrative of Sir Launcelot, which thus proceeded:

"And now, the champion, having escaped from the terrible fury of the dragon, bethinking himself of the brazen shield, and of the breaking up of the enchantment which was upon it, removed the carcass from out of the way before him, and approached valorously over the silver pavement of the castle to where the shield was upon the wall; which in sooth tarried not for his full coming, but fell down at his feet upon the silver floor, with a mighty great and terrible ringing sound."

No sooner had these syllables passed my lips, than—as if a shield of brass had indeed, at the moment, fallen heavily upon a floor of silver—I became aware of a distinct, hollow, metallic, and clangorous, yet apparently muffled reverberation. Completely unnerved, I leaped to my feet; but the measured rocking movement of Usher was undisturbed. I rushed to the chair in which he sat. His eyes were bent fixedly before him, and throughout his whole countenance there reigned a stony rigidity. But, as I placed my hand upon his shoulder, there came a strong shudder over his whole person; a sickly smile quivered about his lips; and I saw that he spoke in a low, hurried, and gibbering murmur, as if unconscious of my presence. Bending closely over him, I at length drank in the hideous import of his words.

"Not hear it?—yes, I hear it, and *have* heard it. Long— long—long—many minutes, many hours, many days, have I heard it—yet I dared not—oh, pity me, miserable wretch that I am!—I dared not—I *dared* not speak! *We have put her living in the tomb!* Said I not that my senses were acute? I *now* tell you that I heard her first feeble movements in the hollow coffin. I heard them—many, many days ago—yet I dared not—*I dared not speak!* And now—to-night—Ethelred—ha! ha!—the breaking of the hermit's door, and the death-cry of the dragon, and the clangor of the shield!—say, rather, the rending of her coffin, and the grating of the iron hinges of her prison, and her struggles within the coppered archway of the vault! Oh whither shall I fly? Will she not be here anon? Is she not hurrying to upbraid me for my haste? Have I not heard her footstep on the stair? Do I not distinguish that heavy and horrible beating of her heart? Madman!"—here he sprang furiously to his feet, and shrieked out his syllables, as if in the effort he were giving up his soul—"*Madman! I tell you that she now stands without the door!*"

As if in the superhuman energy of his utterance there had been found the potency of a spell—the huge antique pannels to which the speaker pointed, threw slowly back, upon the instant, their ponderous and ebony jaws. It was the work of the rushing gust—but then without those doors there *did* stand the lofty and enshrouded figure of the lady Madeline of Usher. There was blood upon her white robes, and the evidence of some bitter struggle upon every portion of her emaciated frame. For a moment she remained trembling and reeling to and fro upon the threshold—then, with a low moaning cry, fell heavily inward upon the person of her brother, and in her violent and now final death-agonies, bore him to the floor a corpse, and a victim to the terrors he had anticipated.

From that chamber, and from that mansion, I fled aghast. The storm was still abroad in all its wrath as I found myself crossing the old causeway. Suddenly there shot along the path a wild light, and I turned to see whence a gleam so unusual could have issued; for the vast house and its shadows were alone behind me. The radiance was that of the full, setting, and blood-red moon, which now shone vividly through that once barely-discernible fissure, of which I have before spoken as extending from the roof of the building, in a zigzag direction, to the base. While I gazed, this fissure rapidly widened—there came a fierce breath of the whirlwind—the entire orb of the satellite burst at once upon my sight—my brain reeled as I saw the mighty walls rushing asunder—there was a long tumultuous shouting sound like the voice of a thousand waters—and the deep and dank tarn at my feet closed sullenly and silently over the fragments of the *"House of Usher."*

WILLIAM WILSON

What say of it? what say CONSCIENCE grim,
That spectre in my path?
—CHAMBERLAIN'S PHARRONIDA.

Let me call myself, for the present, William Wilson. The fair page now lying before me need not be sullied with my real appellation. This has been already too much an object for the scorn—for the horror—for the detestation of my race. To the uttermost regions of the globe have not the indignant winds bruited its unparalleled infamy? Oh, outcast of all outcasts most abandoned!—to the earth art thou not forever dead? to its honors, to its flowers, to its golden aspirations?—and a cloud, dense, dismal, and limitless, does it not hang eternally between thy hopes and heaven?

I would not, if I could, here or to-day, embody a record of my later years of unspeakable misery, and unpardonable crime. This epoch—these later years—took unto themselves a sudden elevation in turpitude, whose origin alone it is my present purpose to assign. Men usually grow base

by degrees. From me, in an instant, all virtue dropped
bodily as a mantle. From comparatively trivial wickedness
I passed, with the stride of a giant, into more than the
enormities of an Elah-Gabalus. What chance—what one
event brought this evil thing to pass, bear with me while
I relate. Death approaches; and the shadow which fore-
runs him has thrown a softening influence over my spirit.
I long, in passing through the dim valley, for the sympathy
—I had nearly said for the pity—of my fellow men. I
would fain have them believe that I have been, in some
measure, the slave of circumstances beyond human control. I would wish them to seek out for me, in the details
I am about to give, some little oasis of *fatality* amid a
wilderness of error. I would have them allow—what they
cannot refrain from allowing—that, although temptation
may have erewhile existed as great, man was never *thus*,
at least, tempted before—certainly, never *thus* fell. And is
it therefore that he has never thus suffered? Have I not
indeed been living in a dream? And am I not now dying
a victim to the horror and the mystery of the wildest of
all sublunary visions?

I am the descendant of a race whose imaginative and
easily excitable temperament has at all times rendered
them remarkable; and, in my earliest infancy, I gave
evidence of having fully inherited the family character. As
I advanced in years it was more strongly developed; becoming, for many reasons, a cause of serious disquietude
to my friends, and of positive injury to myself. I grew
self-willed, addicted to the wildest caprices, and a prey to
the most ungovernable passions. Weak-minded, and beset
with constitutional infirmities akin to my own, my parents
could do but little to check the evil propensities which
distinguished me. Some feeble and ill-directed efforts resulted in complete failure on their part, and, of course,
in total triumph on mine. Thenceforward my voice was a
household law; and at an age when few children have

abandoned their leading-strings, I was left to the guidance of my own will, and became, in all but name, the master of my own actions.

My earliest recollections of a school-life, are connected with a large, rambling, Elizabethan house, in a misty-looking village of England, where were a vast number of gigantic and gnarled trees, and where all the houses were excessively ancient. In truth, it was a dream-like and spirit-soothing place, that venerable old town. At this moment, in fancy, I feel the refreshing chilliness of its deeply-shadowed avenues, inhale the fragrance of its thousand shrubberies, and thrill anew with undefinable delight, at the deep hollow note of the church-bell, breaking, each hour, with sullen and sudden roar, upon the stillness of the dusky atmosphere in which the fretted Gothic steeple lay imbedded and asleep.

It gives me, perhaps, as much of pleasure as I can now in any manner experience, to dwell upon minute recollections of the school and its concerns. Steeped in misery as I am—misery, alas! only too real—I shall be pardoned for seeking relief, however slight and temporary, in the weakness of a few rambling details. These, moreover, utterly trivial, and even ridiculous in themselves, assume, to my fancy, adventitious importance, as connected with a period and a locality when and where I recognize the first ambiguous monitions of the destiny which afterwards so fully overshadowed me. Let me then remember.

The house, I have said, was old and irregular. The grounds were extensive, and a high and solid brick wall, topped with a bed of mortar and broken glass, encompassed the whole. This prison-like rampart formed the limit of our domain; beyond it we saw but thrice a week—once every Saturday afternoon, when, attended by two ushers, we were permitted to take brief walks in a body through some of the neighbouring fields—and twice during Sunday, when we were paraded in the same formal manner to the morning and evening service in the one church of the village. Of this church the principal of our school was pastor. With how deep a spirit of wonder and perplexity was I wont to regard him from our remote pew in the gallery, as, with step solemn and slow, he ascended the pulpit! This reverend man, with countenance so demurely benign, with robes so glossy and so clerically flowing, with wig so minutely powdered, so rigid and so vast,—could this be he who, of late, with sour visage, and in snuffy habiliments, administered, ferule in hand, the Draconian laws of the academy? Oh, gigantic paradox, too utterly monstrous for solution!

At an angle of the ponderous wall frowned a more ponderous gate. It was riveted and studded with iron bolts, and surmounted with jagged iron spikes. What impressions of deep awe did it inspire! It was never opened save for the three periodical egressions and ingressions already mentioned; then, in every creak of its mighty hinges, we found a plenitude of mystery—a world of matter for solemn remark, or for more solemn meditation.

The extensive enclosure was irregular in form, having many capacious recesses. Of these, three or four of the largest constituted the play-ground. It was level, and covered with fine hard gravel. I well remember it had no trees, nor benches, nor any thing similar within it. Of course it was in the rear of the house. In front lay a small parterre, planted with box and other shrubs; but through this sacred division, we passed only upon rare occasions indeed—such as a first advent to school or final departure thence, or perhaps, when a parent or friend having called for us, we joyfully took our way home for the Christmas or Midsummer holy-days.

But the house!—how quaint an old building was this! —to me how veritably a palace of enchantment! There was really no end to its windings—to its incomprehensible subdivisions. It was difficult, at any given time, to say with certainty upon which of its two stories one happened to be. From each room to every other there were sure to be found three or four steps either in ascent or descent. Then the lateral branches were innumerable—inconceivable—and so returning in upon themselves, that our most exact ideas in regard to the whole mansion were not very far different from those with which we pondered upon infinity. During the five years of my residence there, I was never able to ascertain with precision, in what remote locality lay the little sleeping apartment assigned to myself and some eighteen or twenty other scholars.

The school-room was the largest in the house—I could not help thinking, in the world. It was very long, narrow, and dismally low, with pointed Gothic windows and a ceiling of oak. In a remote and terror-inspiring angle was a square enclosure of eight or ten feet, comprising the *sanctum*, "during hours," of our principal, the Reverend Dr. Bransby. It was a solid structure, with massy door, sooner than open which in the absence of the "Dominie," we would all have willingly perished by the *peine forte et dure*. In other angles were two other similar boxes, far less reverenced, indeed, but still greatly matters of awe. One of these was the pulpit of the "classical" usher, one of the "English and mathematical." Interspersed about the room, crossing and re-crossing in endless irregularity, were innumerable benches and desks, black, ancient, and time-worn, piled desperately with much-bethumbed books, and so beseamed with initial letters, names at full length, grotesque figures, and other multiplied efforts of the knife, as to have entirely lost what little of original form might have been their portion in days long departed. A huge bucket with water stood at one extremity of the room, and a clock of stupendous dimensions at the other.

Encompassed by the massy walls of this venerable academy, I passed, yet not in tedium or disgust, the years of the third lustrum of my life. The teeming brain of childhood requires no external world of incident to occupy or amuse it; and the apparently dismal monotony of a school was replete with more intense excitement than my riper youth has derived from luxury, or my full manhood from crime. Yet I must believe that my first mental development had in it much of the uncommon—even much of the *outré*. Upon mankind at large the events of very early existence rarely leave in mature age any definite impression. All is gray shadow—a weak and irregular remembrance— an indistinct regathering of feeble pleasures and phantasmagoric pains. With me this is not so. In childhood I must have felt with the energy of a man what I now find stamped upon memory in lines as vivid, as deep, and as durable as the *exergues* of the Cathaginian medals.

Yet in fact—in the fact of the world's view—how little was there to remember! The morning's awakening, the nightly summons to bed; the connings, the recitations; the periodical half-holidays, and perambulations; the playground, with its broils, its pastimes, its intrigues;—these, by a mental sorcery long forgotten, were made to involve a wilderness of sensation, a world of rich incident, an universe of varied emotion, of excitement the most passionate and spirit-stirring. "*Oh, le bon temps, que ce siecle de fer!*"

In truth, the ardor, the enthusiasm, and the imperiousness of my disposition, soon rendered me a marked character among my schoolmates, and by slow, but natural gradations, gave me an ascendancy over all not greatly older than myself;—over all with a single exception. This exception was found in the person of a scholar, who, although no relation, bore the same Christian and surname as myself;—a circumstance, in fact, little remarkable; for, notwithstanding a noble descent, mine was one of those every-day appellations which seem, by prescriptive right, to have been, time out of mind, the common property of the mob. In this narrative I have therefore designated myself as William Wilson,—a fictitious title not very dissimilar to the real. My namesake alone, of those who in school phraseology constituted "our set" presumed to compete with me in the studies of the class—in the sports and broils of the play-ground—to refuse implicit belief in my assertions, and submission to my will—indeed, to interfere with my arbitrary dictation in any respect whatsoever. If there is on earth a supreme and unqualified despotism, it is the despotism of a master mind in boyhood over the less energetic spirits of its companions.

Wilson's rebellion was to me a source of the greatest embarrassment;—the more so as, in spite of the bravado with which in public I made a point of treating him and his pretensions, I secretly felt that I feared him, and could not help thinking the equality which he maintained so easily with myself, a proof of his true superiority; since not to be overcome cost me a perpetual struggle. Yet this superiority—even this equality—was in truth acknowledged by no one but myself; our associates, by some unaccountable blindness, seemed not even to suspect it. Indeed, his competition, his resistance, and especially his impertinent and dogged interference with my purposes, were not more pointed than private. He appeared to be destitute alike of the ambition which urged, and of the passionate energy of mind which enabled me to excel. In his rivalry he might have been supposed actuated solely by a whimsical desire to thwart, astonish, or mortify myself; although there were times when I could not help observing, with a feeling made up of wonder, abasement, and pique, that he mingled with his injuries, his insults, or his contradictions, a certain most inappropriate, and assuredly most unwelcome *affectionateness* of manner. I could only conceive this singular behavior to arise from a consummate self-conceit assuming the vulgar airs of patronage and protection.

Perhaps it was this latter trait in Wilson's conduct, conjoined with our identity of name, and the mere accident of our having entered the school upon the same day, which set afloat the notion that we were brothers, among the senior classes in the academy. These do not usually inquire with much strictness into the affairs of their juniors. I have before said, or should have said, that Wilson was not, in the most remote degree, connected with my family. But assuredly if we *had* been brothers we must have been twins; for, after leaving Dr. Bransby's, I casually learned that my namesake was born on the nineteenth of January, 1813—and this is a somewhat remarkable coincidence; for the day is precisely that of my own nativity.

It may seem strange that in spite of the continual anxiety occasioned me by the rivalry of Wilson, and his intolerable spirit of contradiction, I could not bring myself to hate him altogether. We had, to be sure, nearly every day a quarrel in which, yielding me publicly the palm of victory, he, in some manner, contrived to make me feel that it was he who had deserved it; yet a sense of pride on my part, and a veritable dignity on his own, kept us always upon what are called "speaking terms," while there were many points of strong congeniality in our tempers, operating to awake in me a sentiment which our position alone, perhaps, prevented from ripening into friendship. It is difficult, indeed, to define, or even to describe, my real feelings towards him. They formed a motley and heterogeneous admixture;—some petulant animosity, which was not yet hatred, some esteem, more respect, much fear, with a world of uneasy curiosity. To the moralist it will be unnecessary to say, in addition, that Wilson and myself were the most inseparable of companions.

It was no doubt the anomalous state of affairs existing between us, which turned all my attacks upon him, (and they were many, either open or covert) into the channel of banter or practical joke (giving pain while assuming the aspect of mere fun) rather than into a more serious and determined hostility. But my endeavours on this head were by no means uniformly successful, even when my plans were the most wittingly concocted; for my namesake had much about him, in character, of that unassuming and quiet austerity which, while enjoying the poignancy of its own jokes, has no heel of Achilles in itself, and absolutely refuses to be laughed at. I could find, indeed, but one vulnerable point, and that, lying in a personal peculiarity, arising, perhaps, from constitutional disease, would have been spared by any antagonist less at his wit's end than myself;—my rival had a weakness in the faucial or guttural organs, which precluded him from raising his voice at any time *above a very low whisper*. Of this defect I did not fail to take what poor advantage lay in my power.

Wilson's retaliations in kind were many; and there was one form of his practical wit that disturbed me beyond measure. How his sagacity first discovered at all that so petty a thing would vex me, is a question I never could solve; but, having discovered, he habitually practised the annoyance. I had always felt aversion to my uncourtly patronymic, and its very common, if not plebeian prænomen. The words were venom in my ears; and when, upon the day of my arrival, a second William Wilson came also to the academy, I felt angry with him for bearing the name, and doubly disgusted with the name because a stranger bore it, who would be the cause of its twofold repetition, who would be constantly in my presence, and whose concerns, in the ordinary routine of the school business, must inevitably, on account of the detestable coincidence, be often confounded with my own.

The feeling of vexation thus engendered grew stronger with every circumstance tending to show resemblance, moral or physical, between my rival and myself. I had not then discovered the remarkable fact that we were of the same age; but I saw that we were of the same height, and I perceived that we were even singularly alike in general contour of person and outline of feature. I was galled, too, by the rumor touching a relationship, which had grown current in the upper forms. In a word, nothing could more seriously disturb me, (although I scrupulously concealed such disturbance,) than any allusion to a similarity of mind, person, or condition existing between us. But, in truth, I had no reason to believe that (with the exception of the matter of relationship, and in the case of Wilson himself,) this similarity had ever been made a subject of comment, or even observed at all by our schoolfellows. That *he* observed it in all its bearings, and as fixedly as I, was apparent; but that he could discover in such circumstances so fruitful a field of annoyance, can only be attributed, as I said before, to his more than ordinary penetration.

His cue, which was to perfect an imitation of myself, lay both in words and in actions; and most admirably did he play his part. My dress it was an easy matter to copy; my gait and general manner were, without difficulty, appropriated; in spite of his constitutional defect, even my voice did not escape him. My louder tones were, of course, unattempted, but then the key, it was identical; *and his singular whisper, it grew the very echo of my own.*

How greatly this most exquisite portraiture harassed me, (for it could not justly be termed a caricature,) I will not now venture to describe. I had but one consolation—in the fact that the imitation, apparently, was noticed by myself alone, and that I had to endure only the knowing and strangely sarcastic smiles of my namesake himself. Satisfied with having produced in my bosom the intended effect, he seemed to chuckle in secret over the sting he had inflicted, and was characteristically disregardful of the public applause which the success of his witty endeavours might have so easily elicited. That the school, indeed, did not feel his design, perceive its accomplishment, and participate in his sneer, was, for many anxious months, a riddle I could not resolve. Perhaps the *gradation* of his copy rendered it not so readily perceptible; or, more possibly, I owed my security to the masterly air of the copyist, who, disdaining the letter, (which in a painting is all the obtuse can see,) gave but the full spirit of his original for my individual contemplation and chagrin.

I have already more than once spoken of the disgusting air of patronage which he assumed toward me, and of his frequent officious interference with my will. This interference often took the ungracious character of advice; advice not openly given, but hinted or insinuated. I received it with a repugnance which gained strength as I grew in years. Yet, at this distant day, let me do him the simple justice to acknowledge that I can recall no occasion when the suggestions of my rival were on the side of those errors or follies so usual to his immature age and seeming inexperience; that his moral sense, at least, if not his general talents and worldly wisdom, was far keener than my own; and that I might, to-day, have been a better, and thus a happier man, had I less frequently rejected the counsels embodied in those meaning whispers which I then but too cordially hated and too bitterly despised.

As it was, I at length grew restive in the extreme under his distasteful supervision, and daily resented more and more openly what I considered his intolerable arrogance. I have said that, in the first years of our connexion as schoolmates, my feelings in regard to him might have been easily ripened into friendship; but, in the latter months of my residence at the academy, although the intrusion of his ordinary manner had, beyond doubt, in some measure, abated, my sentiments, in nearly similar proportion, partook very much of positive hatred. Upon one occasion he saw this, I think, and afterwards avoided, or made a show of avoiding me.

It was about the same period, if I remember aright, that, in an altercation of violence with him, in which he was more than usually thrown off his guard, and spoke and acted with an openness of demeanor rather foreign to his nature, I discovered, or fancied I discovered, in his accent, his air, and general appearance, a something which first startled, and then deeply interested me, by bringing to mind dim visions of my earliest infancy—wild, confused and thronging memories of a time when memory herself was yet unborn. I cannot better describe the sensation which oppressed me than by saying that I could with difficulty shake off the belief of my having been acquainted with the being who stood before me, at some epoch very long ago—some point of the past even infinitely remote. The delusion, however, faded rapidly as it came; and I mention it at all but to define the day of the last conversation I there held with my singular namesake.

The huge old house, with its countless subdivisions, had several large chambers communicating with each other, where slept the greater number of the students. There were, however, (as must necessarily happen in a building so awkwardly planned,) many little nooks or recesses, the odds and ends of the structure; and these the economic ingenuity of Dr. Bransby had also fitted up as dormitories; although, being the merest closets, they were capable of accommodating but a single individual. One of these small apartments was occupied by Wilson.

One night, about the close of my fifth year at the school, and immediately after the altercation just mentioned, finding every one wrapped in sleep, I arose from bed, and, lamp in hand, stole through a wilderness of narrow passages from my own bedroom to that of my rival. I had long been plotting one of those ill-natured pieces of practical wit at his expense in which I had hitherto been so uniformly unsuccessful. It was my intention, now, to put my scheme in operation, and I resolved to make him feel the whole extent of the malice with which I was imbued. Having reached his closet, I noiselessly entered, leaving the lamp, with a shade over it, on the outside. I advanced a step, and listened to the sound of his tranquil breathing. Assured of his being asleep, I returned, took the light, and with it again approached the bed. Close curtains were around it, which, in the prosecution of my plan, I slowly and quietly withdrew, when the bright rays fell vividly upon the sleeper, and my eyes, at the same moment, upon his countenance. I looked;—and a numbness, an iciness of feeling instantly pervaded my frame. My breast heaved, my knees tottered, my whole spirit became possessed with an objectless yet intolerable horror. Gasping for breath, I lowered the lamp in still nearer proximity to the face. Were these—*these* the lineaments of William Wilson? I saw, indeed, that they were his, but I shook as if with a fit of the ague in fancying they were not. What *was* there about them to confound me in this manner? I gazed;—while my brain reeled with a multitude of incoherent thoughts. Not thus he appeared—assuredly not *thus*—in the vivacity of his waking hours. The same name! the same contour of person! the same day of arrival at the academy! And then his dogged and meaningless imitation of my gait, my voice, my habits, and my manner! Was it, in truth, within the bounds of human possibility, that what I now saw was the result, merely, of the habitual practice of this sarcastic imitation? Awestricken, and with a creeping shudder, I extinguished the lamp, passed silently from the chamber, and left, at once, the halls of that old academy, never to enter them again.

After a lapse of some months, spent at home in mere idleness, I found myself a student at Eton. The brief interval had been sufficient to enfeeble my remembrance of the events at Dr. Bransby's, or at least to effect a material change in the nature of the feelings with which I remembered them. The truth—the tragedy—of the drama was no more. I could now find room to doubt the evidence of my senses; and seldom called up the subject at all but with wonder at the extent of human credulity, and a smile at the vivid force of the imagination which I hereditarily

possessed. Neither was this species of skepticism likely
to be diminished by the character of the life I led at
Eton. The vortex of thoughtless folly into which I there
so immediately and so recklessly plunged, washed away all
but the froth of my past hours, engulfed at once every solid
or serious impression, and left to memory only the veriest
levities of a former existence.

I do not wish, however, to trace the course of my
miserable profligacy here—a profligacy which set at defiance
the laws, while it eluded the vigilance of the institution.
Three years of folly, passed without profit, had but given
me rooted habits of vice, and added, in a somewhat unusual degree, to my bodily stature, when, after a week of
soulless dissipation, I invited a small party of the most dissolute students to a secret carousal in my chambers. We
met at a late hour of the night; for our debaucheries were
to be faithfully protracted until morning. The wine flowed
freely, and there were not wanting other and perhaps more
dangerous seductions; so that the grey dawn had already
faintly appeared in the east, while our delirious extravagance was at its height. Madly flushed with cards and intoxication I was in the act of insisting upon a toast of
more than wonted profanity, when my attention was suddenly diverted by the violent, although partial unclosing
of the door of the apartment, and by the eager voice of a
servant from without. He said that some person, apparently
in great haste, demanded to speak with me in the hall.

Wildly excited with wine, the unexpected interruption
rather delighted than surprised me. I staggered forward
at once, and a few steps brought me to the vestibule of the
building. In this low and small room there hung no lamp;
and now no light at all was admitted, save that of the exceedingly feeble dawn which made its way through the
semi-circular window. As I put my foot over the threshold,
I became aware of the figure of a youth about my own
height, and habited in a white kerseymere morning frock,

cut in the novel fashion of the one I myself wore at the
moment. This the faint light enabled me to perceive; but
the features of his face I could not distinguish. Upon my
entering he strode hurriedly up to me, and, seizing me by
the arm with a gesture of petulant impatience, whispered
the words "William Wilson!" in my ear.

I grew perfectly sober in an instant.

There was that in the manner of the stranger, and in
the tremulous shake of his uplifted finger, as he held it
between my eyes and the light, which filled me with unqualified amazement; but it was not this which had so
violently moved me. It was the pregnancy of solemn ad-
monition in the singular, low hissing utterance; and, above
all, it was the character, the tone, *the key*, of those few,
simple, and familiar, yet *whispered* syllables, which came
with a thousand thronging memories of by-gone days,
and struck upon my soul with the shock of a galvanic battery. Ere I could recover the use of my senses he was gone.

Although this event failed not of a vivid effect upon my
disordered imagination, yet was it evanescent as vivid. For
some weeks, indeed, I busied myself in earnest inquiry, or
was wrapped in a cloud of morbid speculation. I did not
pretend to disguise from my perception the identity of the
singular individual who thus perseveringly interfered with
my affairs, and harassed me with his insinuated counsel.
But who and what was this Wilson?—and whence came
he?—and what were his purposes? Upon neither of these
points could I be satisfied; merely ascertaining, in regard
to him, that a sudden accident in his family had caused his
removal from Dr. Bransby's academy on the afternoon of
the day in which I myself had eloped. But in a brief
period I ceased to think upon the subject; my attention
being all absorbed in a contemplated departure for Oxford.
Thither I soon went; the uncalculating vanity of my
parents furnishing me with an outfit, and annual establish-
ment, which would enable me to indulge at will in the

luxury already so dear to my heart,—to vie in profuseness of expenditure with haughtiest heirs of the wealthiest earldoms in Great Britain.

Excited by such appliances to vice, my constitutional temperament broke forth with redoubled ardor, and I spurned even the common restraints of decency in the mad infatuation of my revels. But it were absurd to pause in the detail of my extravagance. Let it suffice, that among spend-thrifts I out-Heroded Herod, and that, giving name to a multitude of novel follies, I added no brief appendix to the long catalogue of vices then usual in the most dissolute university of Europe.

It could hardly be credited, however, that I had, even here, so utterly fallen from the gentlemanly estate, as to seek acquaintance with the vilest arts of the gambler by profession, and, having become an adept in his despicable science, to practise it habitually as a means of increasing my already enormous income at the expense of the weak-minded among my fellow collegians. Such, nevertheless, was the fact. And the very enormity of this offence against all manly and honourable sentiment proved, beyond doubt, the main if not the sole reason of the impunity with which it was commmitted. Who, indeed, among my most aban-doned associates, would not rather have disputed the clearest evidence of his senses, than have suspected of such courses the gay, the frank, the generous William Wilson—the noblest and most liberal commoner at Oxford—him whose follies (said his parasites) were but the follies of youth and unbridled fancy—whose errors but inimitable whim—whose darkest vice but a careless and dashing extravagance?

I had been now two years successfully busied in this way, when there came to the university a young *parvenu* nobleman, Glendinning—rich, said report, as Herodes Atticus—his riches, too, as easily acquired. I soon found him of weak intellect, and, of course, marked him as a fitting subject for my skill. I frequently engaged him in play, and contrived, with a gambler's usual art, to let him win considerable sums, the more effectually to entangle him in my snares. At length, my schemes being ripe, I met him (with the full intention that this meeting should be final and decisive) at the chambers of a fellow-commoner, (Mr. Preston,) equally intimate with both, but who, to do him justice, entertained not even a remote suspicion of my design. To give to this a better coloring, I had contrived to have assumed a party of some eight or ten, and was solicitiously careful that the introduction of cards should appear accidental, and originate in the proposal of my contemplated dupe himself. To be brief upon a vile topic, none of the low finesse was omitted, so customary upon similar occasions that it is a just matter for wonder how any are still found so besotted as to fall its victim.

We had protracted our sitting far into the night, and I had at length effected the manœuvre of getting Glendinning as my sole antagonist. The game, too, was my favorite *écarté*. The rest of the company, interested in the extent of our play, had abandoned their own cards, and were standing around us as spectators. The *parvenu*, who had been induced by my artifices in the early part of the evening, to drink deeply, now shuffled, dealt, or played, with a wild nervousness of manner for which his intoxication, I thought, might partially, but could not altogether account. In a very short period he had become my debtor to a large amount, when, having taken a long draught of port, he did precisely what I had been coolly anticipating— he proposed to double our already extravagant stakes. With a well-feigned show of reluctance, and not until after my repeated refusal had seduced him into some angry words which gave a color of *pique* to my compliance, did I finally comply. The result, of course, did but prove how entirely the prey was in my toils; in less than an hour he had quadrupled his debt. For some time his countenance had been losing the florid tinge lent it by the wine; but now, to my astonishment, I perceived that it had grown to a pallor truly fearful. I say to my astonishment. Glendinning had been represented to my eager inquiries as immeasurably wealthy; and the sums which he had as yet lost, although in themselves vast, could not, I supposed, very seriously annoy, much less so violently affect him. That he was overcome by the wine just swallowed, was the idea which most readily presented itself; and, rather with a view to the preservation of my own character in the eyes of my associates, than from any less interested motive, I was about to insist, peremptorily, upon a discontinuance of the play, when some expressions at my elbow from among the company, and an ejaculation evincing utter despair on the part of Glendinning, gave me to understand that I had effected his total ruin under circumstances which, rendering him an object for the pity of all, should have protected him from the ill offices even of a fiend.

What now might have been my conduct it is difficult to say. The pitiable condition of my dupe had thrown an air of embarrassed gloom over all; and, for some moments, a profound silence was maintained, during which I could not help feeling my cheeks tingle with the many burning glances of scorn or reproach cast upon me by the less abandoned of the party. I will even own that an intolerable weight of anxiety was for a brief instant lifted from my bosom by the sudden and extraordinary interruption which ensued. The wide, heavy folding doors of the apartment were all at once thrown open, to their full extent, with a vigorous and rushing impetuosity that extinguished, as if by magic, every candle in the room. Their light, in dying, enabled us just to perceive that a stranger had entered, about my own height, and closely muffled in a cloak. The darkness, however, was now total; and we could only *feel* that he was standing in our midst. Before any one of us could recover from the extreme astonishment into which this rudeness had thrown all, we heard the voice of the intruder.

"Gentlemen," he said, in a low, distinct, and never-to-be-forgotten *whisper* which thrilled to the very marrow of my bones, "Gentlemen, I make no apology for this behaviour, because in thus behaving, I am but fulfilling a duty. You are, beyond doubt, uninformed of the true character of the person who has to-night won at *écarté* a large sum of money from Lord Glendinning. I will therefore put you upon an expeditious and decisive plan of obtaining this very necessary information. Please to examine, at your leisure, the inner linings of the cuff of his left sleeve, and the several little packages which may be found in the somewhat capacious pockets of his embroidered morning wrapper."

While he spoke, so profound was the stillness that one might have heard a pin drop upon the floor. In ceasing, he departed at once, and as abruptly as he had entered. Can I—shall I describe my sensations?—must I say that I felt all the horrors of the damned? Most assuredly I had little time given for reflection. Many hands roughly seized me upon the spot, and lights were immediately reprocured. A search ensued. In the lining of my sleeve were found all the court cards essential in *écarté*, and, in the pockets of my wrapper, a number of packs, fac-similes of those used at our sittings, with the single exception that mine were of the species called, technically, *arrondées*; the honors being slightly convex at the ends, the lower cards slightly convex at the sides. In this disposition, the dupe who cuts, as customary, at the length of the pack, will invariably find that he cuts his antagonist an honor; while the gambler, cutting at the breadth, will, as certainly, cut nothing for his victim which may count in the records of the game.

Any burst of indignation upon this discovery would

have affected me less than the silent contempt, or the sarcastic composure, with which it was received.

"Mr. Wilson," said our host, stooping to remove from beneath his feet an exceedingly luxurious cloak of rare furs, "Mr. Wilson, this is your property." (The weather was cold; and, upon quitting my own room, I had thrown a cloak over my dressing wrapper, putting it off upon reaching the scene of play.) "I presume it is supererogatory to seek here (eyeing the folds of the garment with a bitter smile) for any farther evidence of your skill. Indeed, we have had enough. You will see the necessity, I hope, of quitting Oxford—at all events, of quitting instantly my chambers."

Abased, humbled to the dust as I then was, it is probable that I should have resented this galling language by immediate personal violence, had not my whole attention been at the moment arrested by a fact of the most startling character. The cloak which I had worn was of a rare description of fur; how rare, how extravagantly costly, I shall not venture to say. Its fashion, too, was of my own fantastic invention; for I was fastidious to an absurd degree of coxcombry, in matters of this frivolous nature. When, therefore, Mr. Preston reached me that which he had picked up upon the floor, and near the folding doors of the apartment, it was with an astonishment nearly bordering upon terror, that I perceived my own already hanging on my arm, (where I had no doubt unwittingly placed it,) and that the one presented me was but its exact counterpart in every, in even the minutest possible particular. The singular being who had so disastrously exposed me, had been muffled, I remembered, in a cloak; and none had been worn at all by any of the members of our party with the exception of myself. Retaining some presence of mind, I took the one offered me by Preston; placed it, unnoticed, over my own; left the apartment with a resolute scowl of defiance; and, next morning ere dawn of day, commenced a hurried journey from Oxford to the continent, in a perfect agony of horror and of shame.

I fled in vain. My evil destiny pursued me as if in exultation, and proved, indeed, that the exercise of its mysterious dominion had as yet only begun. Scarcely had I set foot in Paris ere I had fresh evidence of the detestable interest taken by this Wilson in my concerns. Years flew, while I experienced no relief. Villain!—at Rome, with how untimely yet with how spectral an officiousness, stepped he in between me and my ambition! At Vienna, too—at Berlin—and at Moscow! Where, in truth, had I *not* bitter cause to curse him within my heart? From his inscrutable tyranny did I at length flee, panic-stricken, as from a pestilence; and to the very ends of the earth *I fled in vain.*

And again, and again, in secret communion with my own spirit, would I demand the questions "Who is he?— whence came he?—and what are his objects?" But no answer was there found. And now I scrutinized, with a minute scrutiny, the forms, and the methods, and the leading traits of his impertinent supervision. But even here there was very little upon which to base a conjecture. It was noticeable, indeed, that, in no one of the multiplied instances in which he had of late crossed my path, had he so crossed it except to frustrate those schemes, or to disturb those actions, which, if fully carried out, might have resulted in bitter mischief. Poor justification this, in truth, for an authority so imperiously assumed! Poor indemnity for natural rights of self-agency so pertinaciously, so insultingly denied!

I had also been forced to notice that my tormentor, for a very long period of time, (while scrupulously and with miraculous dexterity maintaining his whim of an identity of apparel with myself,) had so contrived it, in the execution of his varied interference with my will, that I saw not, at any moment, the features of his face. Be Wilson what he might, *this*, at least, was but the veriest of affection, or of folly. Could he, for an instant, have supposed that, in my admonisher at Eton—in the destroyer of my honor at Oxford,—in him who thwarted my ambition at Rome, my revenge at Paris, my passionate love at Naples, or what he falsely termed my avarice in Egypt,—that in this, my arch-enemy and evil genius, I could fail to recognise the William Wilson of my schoolboy days,—the namesake, the companion, the rival,—the hated and dreaded rival at Dr. Bransby's? Impossible!—But let me hasten to the last eventful scene of the drama.

Thus far I had succumbed supinely to this imperious domination. The sentiment of deep awe with which I habitually regarded the elevated character, the majestic wisdom, the apparent omnipresence and omnipotence of Wilson, added to a feeling of even terror, with which certain other traits in his nature and assumptions inspired me, had operated, hitherto, to impress me with an idea of my own utter weakness and helplessness, and to suggest an implicit, although bitterly reluctant submission to his arbitrary will. But, of late days, I had given myself up entirely to wine; and its maddening influence upon my hereditary temper rendered me more and more impatient of control. I began to murmur,—to hesitate,—to resist. And was it only fancy which induced me to believe that, with the increase of my own firmness, that of my tormentor underwent a proportional diminution? Be this as it may, I now began to feel the inspiration of a burning hope, and at length nurtured in my secret thoughts a stern and desperate resolution that I would submit no longer to be enslaved.

It was at Rome, during the Carnival of 18—, that I attended a masquerade in the palazzo of the Neapolitan Duke Di Broglio. I had indulged more freely than usual in the excesses of the wine-table; and now the suffocating atmosphere of the crowded rooms irritated me beyond endurance. The difficulty, too, of forcing my way through the mazes of the company contributed not a little to the ruffling of my temper; for I was anxiously seeking, (let me not say with what unworthy motive) the young, the gay, the beautiful wife of the aged and doting Di Broglio. With a too unscrupulous confidence she had previously communicated to me the secret of the costume in which she would be habited, and now, having caught a glimpse of her person, I was hurrying to make my way into her presence.—At this moment I felt a light hand placed upon my shoulder, and that ever-remembered, low, damnable *whisper* within my ear.

In an absolute phrenzy of wrath, I turned at once upon him who had thus interrupted me, and seized him violently by the collar. He was attired, as I had expected, in a costume altogether similar to my own; wearing a Spanish cloak of blue velvet, begirt about the waist with a crimson belt sustaining a rapier. A mask of black silk entirely covered his face.

"Scoundrel!" I said, in a voice husky with rage, while every syllable I uttered seemed as new fuel to my fury, "scoundrel! impostor! accursed villain! you shall not— you *shall not* dog me unto death! Follow me, or I stab you where you stand!"—and I broke my way from the ball-room into a small ante-chamber adjoining—dragging him unresistingly with me as I went.

Upon entering, I thrust him furiously from me. He staggered against the wall, while I closed the door with an oath, and commanded him to draw. He hesitated but for an instant; then, with a slight sigh, drew in silence, and put himself upon his defence.

The contest was brief indeed. I was frantic with every species of wild excitement, and felt within my single arm the energy and power of a multitude. In a few seconds I forced him by sheer strength against the wainscoting, and thus, getting him at mercy, plunged my sword, with brute ferocity, repeatedly through and through his bosom.

At that instant some person tried the latch of the door. I hastened to prevent an intrusion, and then immediately returned to my dying antagonist. But what human language can adequately portray *that* astonishment, *that* horror which possessed me at the spectacle then presented to view? The brief moment in which I averted my eyes had been sufficient to produce, apparently, a material change in the arrangements at the upper or farther end of the room. A large mirror,—so at first it seemed to me in my confusion—now stood where none had been perceptible before; and, as I stepped up to it in extremity of terror, mine own image, but with features all pale and dabbled in blood, advanced to meet me with a feeble and tottering gait.

Thus it appeared I say, but was not. It was my antagonist—it was Wilson, who then stood before me in the agonies of his dissolution. His mask and cloak lay, where he had thrown them, upon the floor. Not a thread in all his raiment—not a line in all the marked and singular lineaments of his face which was not, even in the most absolute identity, *mine own!*

It was Wilson; but he spoke no longer in a whisper, and I could have fancied that I myself was speaking while he said:

"You have conquered, and I yield. Yet, henceforward art thou also dead—dead to the World, to Heaven and to Hope! In me didst thou exist—and, in my death, see by this image, which is thine own, how utterly thou hast murdered thyself."

THE MAN OF THE CROWD

Ce grand malheur, de ne pouvoir être seul.—La Bruyère.

It was well said of a certain German book that *"er lasst sich nicht lesen"*—it does not permit itself to be read. There are some secrets which do not permit themselves to be told. Men die nightly in their beds, wringing the hands of ghostly confessors, and looking them piteously in the eyes—die with despair of heart and convulsion of throat, on account of the hideousness of mysteries which will not *suffer themselves* to be revealed. Now and then, alas, the conscience of man takes up a burthen so heavy in horror that it can be thrown down only into the grave. And thus the essence of all crime is undivulged.

Not long ago, about the closing in of an evening in autumn, I sat at the large bow window of the D—— Coffee-House in London. For some months I had been ill in health, but was now convalescent, and, with returning strength, found myself in one of those happy moods which are so precisely the converse of *ennui*—moods of the keenest appetency, when the film from the mental vision departs—the αχλυς ος πριν επηεν—and the intellect, electrified, surpasses as greatly its every-day condition, as does the vivid yet candid reason of Leibnitz, the mad and flimsy rhetoric of Gorgias. Merely to breathe was enjoyment; and I derived positive pleasure even from many of the legitimate sources of pain. I felt a calm but inquisitive interest in every thing. With a cigar in my mouth and a newspaper in my lap, I had been amusing myself for the greater part of the afternoon, now in poring over advertisements, now in observing the promiscuous company in the room, and now in peering through the smoky panes into the street.

This latter is one of the principal thoroughfares of the city, and had been very much crowded during the whole day. But, as the darkness came on, the throng momently increased; and, by the time the lamps were well lighted, two dense and continuous tides of population were rushing past the door. At this particular period of the evening I had never before been in a similar situation, and the tumultuous sea of human heads filled me, therefore, with a delicious novelty of emotion. I gave up, at length, all care of things within the hotel, and became absorbed in contemplation of the scene without.

At first my observations took an abstract and generalizing turn. I looked at the passengers in masses, and thought of them in their aggregate relations. Soon, however, I descended to details, and regarded with minute interest the innumerable varieties of figure, dress, air, gait, visage, and expression of countenance.

By far the greater number of those who went by had a satisfied business-like demeanor, and seemed to be thinking only of making their way through the press. Their brows were knit, and their eyes rolled quickly; when pushed against by fellow-wayfarers they evinced no symptom of impatience, but adjusted their clothes and hurried on. Others, still a numerous class, were restless in their movements, had flushed faces, and talked and gesticulated to themselves, as if feeling in solitude on account of the very denseness of the company around. When impeded in their progress, these people suddenly ceased muttering, but redoubled their gesticulations, and awaited, with an absent and overdone smile upon the lips, the course of the persons impeding them. If jostled, they bowed profusely to the jostlers, and appeared overwhelmed with confusion. —There was nothing very distinctive about these two large classes beyond what I have noted. Their habiliments belonged to that order which is pointedly termed the decent. They were undoubtedly noblemen, merchants, attorneys, tradesmen, stock-jobbers—the Eupatrids and the common-places of society—men of leisure and men actively engaged in affairs of their own—conducting business upon their own responsibility. They did not greatly excite my attention.

The tribe of clerks was an obvious one and here I discerned two remarkable divisions. There were the junior clerks of flash houses—young gentlemen with tight coats, bright boots, well-oiled hair, and supercilious lips. Setting aside a certain dapperness of carriage, which may be termed *deskism* for want of a better word, the manner of these persons seemed to me an exact facsimile of what had been the perfection of *bon ton* about twelve or eighteen months before. They wore the cast-off graces of the gentry;—and this, I believe, involves the best definition of the class.

The division of the upper clerks of staunch firms, or of the "steady old fellows," it was not possible to mistake. These were known by their coats and pantaloons of black or brown, made to sit comfortably, with white cravats and waistcoats, broad solid-looking shoes, and thick hose or gaiters.—They had all slightly bald heads, from which the right ears, long used to penholding, had an odd habit of standing off on end. I observed that they always removed or settled their hats with both hands, and wore watches, with short gold chains of a substantial and ancient pattern. Theirs was the affectation of respectability; —if indeed there be an affectation so honorable.

There were many individuals of dashing appearance, whom I easily understood as belonging to the race of swell pick-pockets, with which all great cities are infested. I watched these gentry with much inquisitiveness, and found it difficult to imagine how they should ever be mistaken for gentlemen by gentlemen themselves. Their voluminousness of wristband, with an air of excessive frankness, should betray them at once.

The gamblers, of whom I descried not a few, were still more easily recognisable. They wore every variety of dress, from that of the desperate thimble-rig bully, with velvet waistcoat, fancy neckerchief, gilt chains, and fillagreed buttons, to that of the scrupulously inornate clergyman, than which nothing could be less liable to suspicion. Still all were distinguished by a certain sodden swarthiness of complexion, a filmy dimness of eye, and pallor and compression of lip. There were two other traits, moreover, by which I could always detect them;—a guarded lowness of tone in conversation, and a more than ordinary extension of the thumb in a direction at right angles with the fingers. —Very often, in company with these sharpers, I observed an order of men somewhat different in habits, but still birds of a kindred feather. They may be defined as the gentlemen who live by their wits. They seem to prey upon the public in two battalions—that of the dandies and that of the military men. Of the first grade the leading features are long locks and smiles; of the second frogged coats and frowns.

Descending in the scale of what is termed gentility, I found darker and deeper themes for speculation. I saw Jew pedlars, with hawk eyes flashing from countenances whose every other feature wore only an expression of abject humility; sturdy professional street beggars scowling upon mendicants of a better stamp, whom despair alone had driven forth into the night for charity; feeble and ghastly invalids, upon whom death had placed a sure hand, and who sidled and tottered through the mob, looking every one beseechingly in the face, as if in search of some chance consolation, some lost hope; modest young girls returning from long and late labor to a cheerless home, and shrinking more tearfully than indignantly from the glances of ruffians, whose direct contact, even, could not be avoided; women of the town of all kinds and of all ages —the unequivocal beauty in the prime of her womanhood, putting one in mind of the statue in Lucian, with the surface of Parian marble, and the interior filled with filth—the loathsome and utterly lost leper in rags—the wrinkled, bejewelled and paint-begrimed beldame, making a last effort at youth—the mere child of immature form, yet, from long association, an adept in the dreadful coquetries of her trade, and burning with a rabid ambition to be ranked the equal of her elders in vice; drunkards innumerable and indescribable—some in shreds and patches, reeling, inarticulate, with bruised visage and lack-lustre eyes—some in whole although filthy garments, with a slightly unsteady swagger, thick sensual lips, and hearty-looking rubicund faces—others clothed in materials which had once been good, and which even now were scrupulously well brushed—men who walked with a more than naturally firm and springy step, but whose countenances were fearfully pale, whose eyes hideously wild and red, and who clutched with quivering fingers, as they strode through the crowd, at every object which came within their reach; beside these, pie-men, porters, coal-heavers, sweeps; organ-grinders, monkey-exhibiters and ballad mongers, those who vended with those who sang; ragged artizans and exhausted laborers of every description, and all full of a noisy and inordinate vivacity which jarred discordantly upon the ear, and gave an aching sensation to the eye.

As the night deepened, so deepened to me the interest of the scene; for not only did the general character of the crowd materially alter (its gentler features retiring in the gradual withdrawal of the more orderly portion of the people, and its harsher ones coming out into bolder relief, as the late hour brought forth every species of infamy from its den,) but the rays of the gas-lamps, feeble at first in their struggle with the dying day, had now at length gained ascendancy, and threw over every thing a fitful and garish lustre. All was dark yet splendid—as that ebony to which has been likened the style of Tertullian.

The wild effects of the light enchained me to an examination of individual faces; and although the rapidity with which the world of light flitted before the window, prevented me from casting more than a glance upon each visage, still it seemed that, in my then peculiar mental state, I could frequently read, even in that brief interval of a glance, the history of long years.

With my brow to the glass, I was thus occupied in scrutinizing the mob, when suddenly there came into view a countenance (that of a decrepid old man, some sixty-five or seventy years of age,)—a countenance which at once arrested and absorbed my whole attention, on account of the absolute idiosyncrasy of its expression. Any thing even remotely resembling that expression I had never seen before. I well remember that my first thought, upon beholding it, was that Retzch, had he viewed it, would have greatly preferred it to his own pictural incarnations of the fiend. As I endeavored, during the brief minute of my original survey, to form some analysis of the meaning conveyed, there arose confusedly and paradoxically within my mind, the ideas of vast mental power, of caution, of penuriousness, of avarice, of coolness, of malice, of blood-thirstiness, of triumph, of merriment, of excessive terror, of intense—of supreme despair. I felt singularly aroused, startled, fascinated. "How wild a history," I said to myself, "is written within that bosom!" Then came a craving desire to keep the man in view—to know more of him. Hurriedly putting on an overcoat, and seizing my hat and cane, I made my way into the street, and pushed through the crowd in the direction which I had seen him take; for he had already disappeared. With some little difficulty I at length came within sight of him, approached, and followed him closely, yet cautiously, so as not to attract his attention.

I had now a good opportunity of examining his person. He was short in stature, very thin, and apparently very feeble. His clothes, generally, were filthy and ragged; but as he came, now and then, within the strong glare of a lamp, I perceived that his linen, although dirty, was of beautiful texture; and my vision deceived me, or, through a rent in a closely-buttoned and evidently second-handed *roquelaure* which enveloped him, I caught a glimpse both of a diamond and of a dagger. These observations heightened my curiosity, and I resolved to follow the stranger whithersoever he should go.

It was now fully night-fall, and a thick humid fog hung over the city, soon ending in a settled and heavy rain. This change of weather had an odd effect upon the crowd, the whole of which was at once put into new commotion, and overshadowed by a world of umbrellas. The waver, the jostle, and the hum increased in a tenfold degree. For my own part I did not much regard the rain—the lurking of an old fever in my system rendering the moisture somewhat too dangerously pleasant. Tying a handkerchief about my mouth, I kept on. For half an hour the old man held his way with difficulty along the great thoroughfare; and I here walked close at his elbow through fear of losing sight of him. Never once turning his head to look back, he did not observe me. By and by he passed into a cross street, which, although densely filled with people, was not quite so much thronged as the main one he had quitted. Here a change in his demeanor became evident. He walked more slowly and with less object than before —more hesitatingly. He crossed and re-crossed the way repeatedly without apparent aim; and the press was still so thick that, at every such movement, I was obliged to follow him closely. The street was a narrow and long one, and his course lay within it for nearly an hour, during

which the passengers had gradually diminished to about
that number which is ordinarily seen at noon in Broadway
near the Park—so vast a difference is there between a
London populace and that of the most frequented American city. A second turn brought us into a square, brilliantly lighted, and overflowing with life. The old manner of the stranger re-appeared. His chin fell upon his
breast, while his eyes rolled wildly from under his knit
brows, in every direction, upon those who hemmed him
in. He urged his way steadily and perseveringly. I was surprised, however, to find, upon his having made the circuit
of the square, that he turned and retraced his steps. Still
more was I astonished to see him repeat the same walk
several times—once nearly detecting me as he came round
with a sudden movement.

In this exercise he spent another hour, at the end of
which we met with far less interruption from passengers
than at first. The rain fell fast; the air grew cool; and the
people were retiring to their homes. With a gesture of impatience, the wanderer passed into a bye-street comparatively deserted. Down this, some quarter of a mile long, he
rushed with an activity I could not have dreamed of seeing in one so aged, and which put me to much trouble in
pursuit. A few minutes brought us to a large and busy
bazaar, with the localities of which the stranger appeared
well acquainted, and where his original demeanor again
became apparent, as he forced his way to and fro, without aim, among the host of buyers and sellers.

During the hour and a half, or thereabouts, which we
passed in this place, it required much caution on my part
to keep him within reach without attracting his observation. Luckily I wore a pair of caoutchouc over-shoes, and
could move about in perfect silence. At no moment did
he see that I watched him. He entered shop after shop,
priced nothing, spoke no word, and looked at all objects
with a wild and vacant stare. I was now utterly amazed at

his behaviour, and firmly resolved that we should not part until I had satisfied myself in some measure respecting him.

A loud-toned clock struck eleven, and the company were fast deserting the bazaar. A shop-keeper, in putting up a shutter, jostled the old man, and at the instant I saw a strong shudder come over his frame. He hurried into the street, looked anxiously around him for an instant, and then ran with incredible swiftness through many crooked and people-less lanes, until we emerged once more upon the great thoroughfare whence we had started—the street of the D—— Hotel. It no longer wore, however, the same aspect. It was still brilliant with gas; but the rain fell fiercely, and there were few persons to be seen. The stranger grew pale. He walked moodily some paces up the once populous avenue, then, with a heavy sigh, turned in the direction of the river, and, plunging through a great variety of devious ways, came out, at length, in view of one of the principal theatres. It was about being closed, and the audience were thronging from the doors. I saw the old man gasp as if for breath while he threw himself amid the crowd; but I thought that the intense agony of his countenance had, in some measure, abated. His head again fell upon his breast; he appeared as I had seen him at first. I observed that he now took the course in which had gone the greater number of the audience—but, upon the whole, I was at a loss to comprehend the way-wardness of his actions.

As he proceeded, the company grew more scattered, and his old uneasiness and vacillation were resumed. For some time he followed closely a party of some ten or twelve roisterers; but from this number one by one dropped off, until three only remained together, in a narrow and gloomy lane little frequented. The stranger paused, and, for a moment, seemed lost in thought; then, with every mark of agitation, pursued rapidly a route which brought us to the verge of the city, amid regions very different

from those we had hitherto traversed. It was the most
noisome quarter of London, where every thing wore the
worst impress of the most deplorable poverty, and of the
most desperate crime. By the dim light of an accidental
lamp, tall, antique, worm-eaten, wooden tenements were
seen tottering to their fall, in directions so many and
capricious that scarce the semblance of a passage was discernible between them. The paving-stones lay at random,
displaced from their beds by the rankly-growing grass. Horrible filth festered in the dammed-up gutters. The whole
atmosphere teemed with desolation. Yet, as we proceeded,
the sounds of human life revived by sure degrees, and at
length large bands of the most abandoned of a London
populace were seen reeling to and fro. The spirits of the
old man again flickered up, as a lamp which is near its
death-hour. Once more he strode onward with elastic
tread. Suddenly a corner was turned, a blaze of light burst
upon our sight, and we stood before one of the huge
suburban temples of Intemperance—one of the palaces of
the fiend, Gin.

It was now nearly day-break; but a number of wretched
inebriates still pressed in and out of the flaunting entrance.
With a half shriek of joy the old man forced a passage
within, resumed at once his original bearing, and stalked
backward and forward, without apparent object, among
the throng. He had not been thus long occupied, however, before a rush to the doors gave token that the host
was closing them for the night. It was something even
more intense than despair that I then observed upon the
countenance of the singular being whom I had watched
so pertinaciously. Yet he did not hesitate in his career,
but, with a mad energy, retraced his steps at once, to the
heart of the mighty London. Long and swiftly he fled,
while I followed him in the wildest amazement, resolute
not to abandon a scrutiny in which I now felt an interest
all-absorbing. The sun arose while we proceeded, and,

when we had once again reached that most thronged mart of the populous town, the street of the D—— Hotel, it presented an appearance of human bustle and activity scarcely inferior to what I had seen on the evening before. And here, long, amid the momently increasing confusion, did I persist in my pursuit of the stranger. But, as usual, he walked to and fro, and during the day did not pass from out the turmoil of that street. And, as the shades of the second evening came on, I grew wearied unto death, and, stopping fully in front of the wanderer, gazed at him steadfastly in the face. He noticed me not, but resumed his solemn walk, while I, ceasing to follow, remained absorbed in contemplation. "This old man," I said at length, "is the type and the genius of deep crime. He refuses to be alone. *He is the man of the crowd.* It will be in vain to follow; for I shall learn no more of him, nor of his deeds. The worst heart of the world is a grosser book than the 'Hortulus Animæ,' * and perhaps it is but one of the great mercies of God that *'er lasst sich nicht lesen.'*"

THE MURDERS
IN THE RUE MORGUE

What song the Syrens sang, or what name Achilles assumed when he hid himself among women, although puzzling questions, are not beyond *all* conjecture.

Sir Thomas Browne.

The mental features discoursed of as the analytical, are, in themselves, but little susceptible of analysis. We ap-

---

* The "*Hortulus Animæ cum Oratiunculis Aliquibus Superadditis*" of Grünninger.

preciate them only in their effects. We know of them, among other things, that they are always to their possessor, when inordinately possessed, a source of the liveliest enjoyment. As the strong man exults in his physical ability, delighting in such exercises as call his muscles into action, so glories the analyst in that moral activity which *disentangles*. He derives pleasure from even the most trivial occupations bringing his talent into play. He is fond of enigmas, of conundrums, of hieroglyphics; exhibiting in his solutions of each a degree of *acumen* which appears to the ordinary apprehension præternatural. His results brought about by the very soul and essence of method, have, in truth, the whole air of intuition.

The faculty of re-solution is possibly much invigorated by mathematical study, and especially by that highest branch of it which, unjustly, and merely on account of its retrograde operations, has been called, as if *par excellence*, analysis. Yet to calculate is not in itself to analyse. A chess-player, for example, does the one without effort at the other. It follows that the game of chess, in its effects upon mental character, is greatly misunderstood. I am not now writing a treatise, but simply prefacing a somewhat peculiar narrative by observations very much at random; I will, therefore, take occasion to assert that the higher powers of the reflective intellect are more decidedly and more usefully tasked by the unostentatious game of draughts than by all the elaborate frivolity of chess. In this latter, where the pieces have different and *bizarre* motions, with various and variable values, what is only complex is mistaken (a not unusual error) for what is profound. The *attention* is here called powerfully into play. If it flag for an instant, an oversight is committed, resulting in injury or defeat. The possible moves being not only manifold but involute, the chances of such oversights are multiplied; and in nine cases out of ten it is the more concentrative rather than the more acute player who conquers. In draughts, on the contrary, where the moves are *unique* and have but little variation, the probabilities of inadvertence are diminished, and the mere attention being left comparatively unemployed, what advantages are obtained by either party are obtained by superior *acumen*. To be less abstract—Let us suppose a game of draughts where the pieces are reduced to four kings, and where, of course, no oversight is to be expected. It is obvious that here the victory can be decided (the players being at all equal) only by some *recherché* movement, the result of some strong exertion of the intellect. Deprived of ordinary resources, the analyst throws himself into the spirit of his opponent, identifies himself therewith, and not unfrequently sees thus, at a glance, the sole methods (sometimes indeed absurdly simply ones) by which he may seduce into error or hurry into miscalculation.

Whist has long been noted for its influence upon what is termed the calculating power; and men of the highest order of intellect have been known to take an apparently unaccountable delight in it, while eschewing chess as frivolous. Beyond doubt there is nothing of a similar nature so greatly tasking the faculty of analysis. The best chess-player in Christendom *may* be little more than the best player of chess; but proficiency in whist implies capacity for success in all those more important undertakings where mind struggles with mind. When I say proficiency, I mean that perfection in the game which includes a comprehension of *all* the sources whence legitimate advantage may be derived. These are not only manifold but multiform, and lie frequently among recesses of thought altogether inaccessible to the ordinary understanding. To observe attentively is to remember distinctly; and, so far, the concentrative chess-player will do very well at whist; while the rules of Hoyle (themselves based upon the mere mechanism of the game) are sufficiently and generally comprehensible. Thus to have a retentive memory, and to proceed by "the book," are points commonly regarded as the sum total of good playing. But it is in matters beyond the limits of mere rule that the skill of the analyst is evinced. He makes, in silence, a host of observations and inferences. So, perhaps, do his companions; and the difference in the extent of the information obtained, lies not so much in the validity of the inference as in the quality of the observation. The necessary knowledge is that of *what* to observe. Our player confines himself not at all; nor, because the game is the object, does he reject deductions from things external to the game. He examines the countenance of his partner, comparing it carefully with that of each of his opponents. He considers the mode of assorting the cards in each hand; often counting trump by trump, and honor by honor, through the glances bestowed by their holders upon each. He notes every variation of face as the play progresses, gathering a fund of thought from the differences in the expression of certainty, of surprise, or triumph, or of chagrin. From the manner of gathering up a trick he judges whether the person taking it can make another in the suit. He recognises what is played through feint, by the air with which it is thrown upon the table. A casual or inadvertent word; the accidental dropping or turning of a card, with the accompanying anxiety or carelessness in regard to its concealment; the counting of the tricks, with the order of their arrangement; embarrassment, hesitation, eagerness or trepidation —all afford, to his apparently intuitive perception, indications of the true state of affairs. The first two or three rounds having been played, he is in full possession of the contents of each hand, and thenceforward puts down his cards with as absolute a precision of purpose as if the rest of the party had turned outward the faces of their own.

The analytical power should not be confounded with simple ingenuity; for while the analyst is necessarily ingenious, the ingenious man is often remarkably incapable of analysis. The constructive or combining power, by which ingenuity is usually manifested, and to which the phrenologists (I believe erroneously) have assigned a separate organ, supposing it a primitive faculty, has been so frequently seen in those whose intellect bordered otherwise upon idiocy, as to have attracted general observation among writers on morals. Between ingenuity and the analytic ability there exists a difference far greater, indeed, than that between the fancy and the imagination, but of a character very strictly analogous. It will be found, in fact, that the ingenious are always fanciful, and the *truly* imaginative never otherwise than analytic.

The narrative which follows will appear to the reader somewhat in the light of a commentary upon the propositions just advanced.

Residing in Paris during the spring and part of summer of 18—, I there became acquainted with a Monsieur C. Auguste Dupin. This young gentleman was of an excellent —indeed of an illustrious family, but, by a variety of untoward events, had been reduced to such poverty that the energy of his character succumbed beneath it, and he ceased to bestir himself in the world, or to care for the retrieval of his fortunes. By courtesy of his creditors, there still remained in his possession a small remnant of his patrimony; and, upon the income arising from this, he managed, by means of a rigorous economy, to procure the necessaries of life, without troubling himself about its superfluities. Books, indeed, were his sole luxuries, and in Paris these are easily obtained.

Our first meeting was at an obscure library in the Rue Montmartre, where the accident of our both being in search of the same very rare and very remarkable volume, brought us into closer communion. We saw each other again and again. I was deeply interested in the little family history which he detailed to me with all that candor which a Frenchman indulges whenever mere self is his theme. I was astonished, too, at the vast extent of his reading; and, above all, I felt my soul enkindled within me by the wild fervor, and the vivid freshness of his imagination. Seeking in Paris the objects I then sought, I felt that the society of such a man would be to me a treasure beyond price; and this feeling I frankly confided to him. It was at length arranged that we should live together during my stay in the city; and as my worldly circumstances were somewhat less embarrassed than his own, I was permitted to be at the expense of renting, and furnishing in a style which suited the rather fantastic gloom of our common temper, a time-eaten and grotesque mansion, long deserted through superstitions into which we did not inquire, and tottering to its fall in a retired and desolate portion of the Faubourg St. Germain.

Had the routine of our life at this place been known to the world, we should have been regarded as madmen—although, perhaps, as madmen of a harmless nature. Our seclusion was perfect. We admitted no visitors. Indeed the locality of our retirement had been carefully kept a secret from my own former associates; and it had been many years since Dupin had ceased to know or be known in Paris. We existed within ourselves alone.

It was a freak of fancy in my friend (for what else shall I call it?) to be enamored of the Night for her own sake; and into this *bizarrerie*, as into all his others, I quietly fell; giving myself up to his wild whims with a perfect *abandon*. The sable divinity would not herself dwell with us always; but we could counterfeit her presence. At the first dawn of the morning we closed all the massy shutters of our old building; lighting a couple of tapers which, strongly perfumed, threw out only the ghastliest and feeblest of rays. By the aid of these we then busied our souls in dreams—reading, writing, or conversing, until warned by the clock of the advent of the true Darkness. Then we sallied forth into the streets, arm in arm, continuing the topics of the day, or roaming far and wide until a late hour, seeking, amid the wild lights and shadows of the populous city, that infinity of mental excitement which quiet observation can afford.

At such times I could not help remarking and admiring (although from his rich ideality I had been prepared to expect it) a peculiar analytic ability in Dupin. He seemed, too, to take an eager delight in its exercise—if not exactly in its display—and did not hesitate to confess the pleasure thus derived. He boasted to me, with a low chuckling laugh, that most men, in respect to himself, wore windows in their bosoms, and was wont to follow up such assertions by direct and very startling proofs of his intimate knowledge of my own. His manner at these moments was frigid and abstract; his eyes were vacant in expression; while his voice, usually a rich tenor, rose into a treble which would have sounded petulantly but for the deliberateness and entire distinctness of the enunciation. Observing him in these moods, I often dwelt meditatively upon the old philosophy of the Bi-Part Soul, and amused myself with the fancy of a double Dupin—the creative and the resolvent.

Let it not be supposed, from what I have just said, that I am detailing any mystery, or penning any romance. What I have described in the Frenchman, was merely the result of an excited, or perhaps of a diseased intelligence. But of the character of his remarks at the periods in question an example will best convey the idea.

We were strolling one night down a long dirty street, in the vicinity of the Palais Royal. Being both, apparently, occupied with thought, neither of us had spoken a syllable for fifteen minutes at least. All at once Dupin broke forth with these words:

"He is a very little fellow, that's true, and would do better for the *Théâtre des Variétés*."

"There can be no doubt of that," I replied unwittingly,

and not at first observing (so much had I been absorbed in reflection) the extraordinary manner in which the speaker had chimed in with my meditations. In an instant afterward I recollected myself, and my astonishment was profound.

"Dupin," said I, gravely, "this is beyond my comprehension. I do not hesitate to say that I am amazed, and can scarcely credit my senses. How was it possible you should know I was thinking of————?" Here I paused, to ascertain beyond a doubt whether he really knew of whom I thought.

"————of Chantilly," said he, "why do you pause? You were remarking to yourself that his diminutive figure unfitted him for tragedy."

This was precisely what had formed the subject of my reflections. Chantilly was a *quondam* cobbler of the Rue St. Denis, who, becoming stage-mad, had attempted the *rôle* of Xerxes, in Crébillon's tragedy so called, and been notoriously Pasquinaded for his pains.

"Tell me, for Heaven's sake," I exclaimed, "the method —if method there is—by which you have been enabled to fathom my soul in this matter." In fact I was even more startled than I would have been willing to express.

"It was the fruiterer," replied my friend, "who brought you to the conclusion that the mender of soles was not of sufficient height for Xerxes *et id genus omne.*"

"The fruiterer!—you astonish me—I know no fruiterer whomsoever."

"The man who ran up against you as we entered the street—it may have been fifteen minutes ago."

I now remembered that, in fact, a fruiterer, carrying upon his head a large basket of apples, had nearly thrown me down, by accident, as we passed from the Rue C———— into the thoroughfare where we stood; but what this had to do with Chantilly I could not possibly understand.

There was not a particle of *charlatânerie* about Dupin. "I will explain," he said, "and that you may comprehend all clearly, we will first retrace the course of your meditations, from the moment in which I spoke to you until that of the *rencontre* with the fruiterer in question. The larger links of the chain run thus—Chantilly, Orion, Dr. Nichols, Epicurus, Stereotomy, the street stones, the fruiterer."

There are few persons who have not, at some period of their lives, amused themselves in retracing the steps by which particular conclusions of their own minds have been attained. The occupation is often full of interest; and he who attempts it for the first time is astonished by the apparently illimitable distance and incoherence between the starting-point and the goal. What, then, must have been my amazement when I heard the Frenchman speak what he had just spoken, and when I could not help acknowledging that he had spoken the truth. He continued:

"We had been talking of horses, if I remember aright, just before leaving the Rue C———. This was the last subject we discussed. As we crossed into this street, a fruiterer, with a large basket upon his head, brushing quickly past us, thrust you upon a pile of paving-stones collected at a spot where the causeway is undergoing repair. You stepped upon one of the loose fragments, slipped, slightly strained your ankle, appeared vexed or sulky, muttered a few words, turned to look at the pile, and then proceeded in silence. I was not particularly attentive to what you did; but observation has become with me, of late, a species of necessity.

"You kept your eyes upon the ground—glancing, with a petulant expression, at the holes and ruts in the pavement, (so that I saw you were still thinking of the stones,) until we reached the little alley called Lamartine, which has been paved, by way of experiment, with the overlapping and riveted blocks. Here your countenance brightened up, and, perceiving your lips move, I could not doubt that you murmured the word 'stereotomy,' a term very affectedly applied to this species of pavement. I knew that you could not say to yourself 'stereotomy' without being brought to think of atomies, and thus of the theories of Epicurus; and since, when we discussed this subject not very long ago, I mentioned to you how singularly, yet with how little notice, the vague guesses of that noble Greek had met with confirmation in the late nebular cosmogony, I felt that you could not avoid casting your eyes upward to the great *nebula* in Orion, and I certainly expected that you would do so. You did look up; and I was now assured that I had correctly followed your steps. But in that bitter *tirade* upon Chantilly, which appeared in yesterday's '*Musée*,' the satirist, making some disgraceful allusions to the cobbler's change of name upon assuming the buskin, quoted a Latin line about which we have often conversed. I mean the line

Perdidit antiquum litera prima sonum

I had told you that this was in reference to Orion, formerly written Urion; and, from certain pungencies connected with this explanation, I was aware that you could not have forgotten it. It was clear, therefore, that you would not fail to combine the two ideas of Orion and Chantilly. That you did combine them I saw by the character of the smile which passed over your lips. You thought of the poor cobbler's immolation. So far, you had been stooping in your gait; but now I saw you draw yourself up to your full height. I was then sure that you reflected upon the diminutive figure of Chantilly. At this point I interrupted your meditations to remark that as, in fact, he *was* a very little fellow—that Chantilly—he would do better at the *Théâtre des Variétés*."

Not long after this, we were looking over an evening edition of the "Gazette des Tribunaux," when the following paragraphs arrested our attention.

"EXTRAORDINARY MURDERS.—This morning, about three o'clock, the inhabitants of the Quartier St. Roch were aroused from sleep by a succession of terrific shrieks, issuing, apparently, from the fourth story of a house in the Rue Morgue, known to be in the sole occupancy of one Madame L'Espanaye, and her daughter, Mademoiselle Camille L'Espanaye. After some delay, occasioned by a fruitless attempt to procure admission in the usual manner, the gateway was broken in with a crowbar, and eight or ten of the neighbors entered, accompanied by two *gendarmes*. By this time the cries had ceased; but, as the party rushed up the first flight of stairs, two or more rough voices, in angry contention, were distinguished, and seemed to proceed from the upper part of the house. As the second landing was reached, these sounds, also, had ceased, and everything remained perfectly quiet. The party spread themselves, and hurried from room to room. Upon arriving at a large back chamber in the fourth story, (the door of which, being found locked, with the key inside, was forced open,) a spectacle presented itself which struck every one present not less with horror than with astonishment.

"The apartment was in the wildest disorder—the furniture broken and thrown about in all directions. There was only one bedstead; and from this the bed had been removed, and thrown into the middle of the floor. On a chair lay a razor, besmeared with blood. On the hearth were two or three long and thick tresses of grey human hair, also dabbled in blood, and seeming to have been pulled out by the roots. Upon the floor were found four Napoleons, an ear-ring of topaz, three large silver spoons, three smaller of *métal d'Alger*, and two bags, containing nearly four thousand francs in gold. The drawers of a *bureau,* which stood in one corner, were open, and had been, apparently, rifled, although many articles still remained in them. A small iron safe was discovered under the *bed* (not under the bedstead). It was open, with the key still in the door. It had no contents beyond a few old letters, and other papers of little consequence.

"Of Madame L'Espanaye no traces were here seen; but an unusual quantity of soot being observed in the fireplace, a search was made in the chimney, and (horrible to relate!) the corpse of the daughter, head downward, was dragged therefrom; it having been thus forced up the narrow aperture for a considerable distance. The body was quite warm. Upon examining it, many excoriations were perceived, no doubt occasioned by the violence with which it had been thrust up and disengaged. Upon the face were many severe scratches, and, upon the throat, dark bruises, and deep indentations of finger nails, as if the deceased had been throttled to death.

"After a thorough investigation of every portion of the house, without farther discovery, the party made its way into a small paved yard in the rear of the building, where lay the corpse of the old lady, with her throat so entirely cut that, upon an attempt to raise her, the head fell off. The body, as well as the head, was fearfully mutilated—the former so much so as scarcely to retain any semblance of humanity.

"To this horrible mystery there is not as yet, we believe, the slightest clew."

The next day's paper had these additional particulars.

"*The Tragedy in the Rue Morgue.* Many individuals have been examined in relation to this most extraordinary and frightful affair," [The word '*affaire*' has not yet, in France, that levity of import which it conveys with us.] "but nothing whatever has transpired to throw light upon it. We give below all the material testimony elicited.

"*Pauline Dubourg,* laundress, deposes that she has

known both the deceased for three years, having washed for them during that period. The old lady and her daughter seemed on good terms—very affectionate towards each other. They were excellent pay. Could not speak in regard to their mode or means of living. Believed that Madame L. told fortunes for a living. Was reputed to have money put by. Never met any persons in the house when she called for the clothes or took them home. Was sure that they had no servant in employ. There appeared to be no furniture in any part of the building except in the fourth story.

"Pierre Moreau, tobacconist, deposes that he has been in the habit of selling small quantities of tobacco and snuff to Madame L'Espanaye for nearly four years. Was born in the neighborhood, and has always resided there. The deceased and her daughter had occupied the house in which the corpses were found, for more than six years. It was formerly occupied by a jeweller, who under-let the upper rooms to various persons. The house was the property of Madame L. She became dissatisfied with the abuse of the premises by her tenant, and moved into them herself, refusing to let any portion. The old lady was childish. Witness had seen the daughter some five or six times during the six years. The two lived an exceedingly retired life—were reputed to have money. Had heard it said among the neighbors that Madame L. told fortunes—did not believe it. Had never seen any person enter the door except the old lady and her daughter, a porter once or twice, and a physician some eight or ten times.

"Many other persons, neighbors, gave evidence to the same effect. No one was spoken of as frequenting the house. It was not known whether there were any living connexions of Madame L. and her daughter. The shutters of the front windows were seldom open. Those in the rear were always closed, with the exception of the large back room, fourth story. The house was a good house —not very old.

"*Isidore Musèt, gendarme*, deposes that he was called to the house about three o'clock in the morning, and found some twenty or thirty persons at the gateway, endeavoring to gain admittance. Forced it open, at length, with a bayonet—not with a crowbar. Had but little difficulty in getting it open, on account of its being a double or folding gate, and bolted neither at bottom nor top. The shrieks were continued until the gate was forced—and then suddenly ceased. They seemed to be screams of some person (or persons) in great agony—were loud and drawn out, not short and quick. Witness led the way up stairs. Upon reaching the first landing, heard two voices in loud and angry contention—the one a gruff voice, the other much shriller—a very strange voice. Could distinguish some words of the former, which was that of a Frenchman. Was positive that it was not a woman's voice. Could distinguish the words '*sacré*' and '*diable*.' The shrill voice was that of a foreigner. Could not be sure whether it was the voice of a man or of a woman. Could not make out what was said, but believed the language to be Spanish. The state of the room and of the bodies was described by this witness as we described them yesterday.

"*Henri Duval*, a neighbor, and by trade a silver-smith, deposes that he was one of the party who first entered the house. Corroborates the testimony of Musèt in general. As soon as they forced an entrance, they reclosed the door, to keep out the crowd, which collected very fast, notwithstanding the lateness of the hour. The shrill voice, this witness thinks, was that of an Italian. Was certain it was not French. Could not be sure that it was a man's voice. It might have been a woman's. Was not acquainted with the Italian language. Could not distinguish the words, but was convinced by the intonation that the speaker was an Italian. Knew Madame L. and her daughter. Had conversed with both frequently. Was sure that the shrill voice was not that of either of the deceased.

"—— *Odenheimer, restaurateur*. This witness volunteered his testimony. Not speaking French, was examined through an interpreter. Is a native of Amsterdam. Was passing the house at the time of the shrieks. They lasted for several minutes—probably ten. They were long and loud—very awful and distressing. Was one of those who entered the building. Corroborated the previous evidence in every respect but one. Was sure that the shrill voice was that of a man—of a Frenchman. Could not distinguish the words uttered. They were loud and quick—unequal—spoken apparently in fear as well as in anger. The voice was harsh—not so much shrill as harsh. Could not call it a shrill voice. The gruff voice said repeatedly '*sacré*,' '*diable*,' and once '*mon Dieu.*'

"*Jules Mignaud*, banker, of the firm of Mignaud et Fils, Rue Deloraine. Is the elder Mignaud. Madame L'Espanaye had some property. Had opened an account with his banking house in the spring of the year —— (eight years previously). Made frequent deposits in small sums. Had checked for nothing until the third day before her death, when she took out in person the sum of 4000 francs. This sum was paid in gold, and a clerk sent home with the money.

"*Adolphe Le Bon*, clerk to Mignaud et Fils, deposes that on the day in question, about noon, he accompanied Madame L'Espanaye to her residence with the 4000 francs, put up in two bags. Upon the door being opened, Mademoiselle L. appeared and took from his hands one of the bags, while the old lady relieved him of the other. He then bowed and departed. Did not see any person in the street at the time. It is a bye-street—very lonely.

"*William Bird*, tailor, deposes that he was one of the party who entered the house. Is an Englishman. Has lived in Paris two years. Was one of the first to ascend the stairs. Heard the voices in contention. The gruff voice was that of a Frenchman. Could make out several words, but cannot now remember all. Heard distinctly '*sacré*' and '*mon Dieu.*' There was a sound at the moment as if of several persons struggling—a scraping and scuffling sound. The shrill voice was very loud—louder than the gruff one. Is sure that it was not the voice of an Englishman. Appeared to be that of a German. Might have been a woman's voice. Does not understand German.

"Four of the above-named witnesses, being recalled, deposed that the door of the chamber in which was found the body of Mademoiselle L. was locked on the inside when the party reached it. Every thing was perfectly silent—no groans or noises of any kind. Upon forcing the door no person was seen. The windows, both of the back and front room, were down and firmly fastened from within. A door between the two rooms was closed, but not locked. The door leading from the front room into the passage was locked, with the key on the inside. A small room in the front of the house, on the fourth story, at the head of the passage, was open, the door being ajar. This room was crowded with old beds, boxes, and so forth. These were carefully removed and searched. There was not an inch of any portion of the house which was not carefully searched. Sweeps were sent up and down the chimneys. The house was a four story one, with garrets (*mansardes*). A trap-door on the roof was nailed down very securely— did not appear to have been opened for years. The time elapsing between the hearing of the voices in contention and the breaking open of the room door, was variously stated by the witnesses. Some made it as short as three minutes—some as long as five. The door was opened with difficulty.

"*Alfonzo Garcio*, undertaker, deposes that he resides in the Rue Morgue. Is a native of Spain. Was one of the party who entered the house. Did not proceed up stairs. Is nervous, and was apprehensive of the consequences of agitation. Heard the voices in contention. The gruff voice was that of a Frenchman. Could not distinguish what was said. The shrill voice was that of an Englishman—is sure of this. Does not understand the English language, but judges by the intonation.

"*Alberto Montani*, confectioner, deposes that he was among the first to ascend the stairs. Heard the voices in question. The gruff voice was that of a Frenchman. Distinguished several words. The speaker appeared to be expostulating. Could not make out the words of the shrill voice. Spoke quick and unevenly. Thinks it the voice of a Russian. Corroborates the general testimony. Is an Italian. Never conversed with a native of Russia.

"Several witnesses, recalled, here testified that the chimneys of all the rooms on the fourth story were too narrow to admit the passage of a human being. By 'sweeps' were meant cylindrical sweeping-brushes, such as are employed by those who clean chimneys. These brushes were passed up and down every flue in the house. There is no back passage by which any one could have descended while the party proceeded up stairs. The body of Mademoiselle L'Espanaye was so firmly wedged in the chimney that it could not be got down until four or five of the party united their strength.

"*Paul Dumas*, physician, deposes that he was called to view the bodies about day-break. They were both then lying on the sacking of the bedstead in the chamber where Mademoiselle L. was found. The corpse of the young lady was much bruised and excoriated. The fact that it had been thrust up the chimney would sufficiently account for these appearances. The throat was greatly chafed. There were several deep scratches just below the chin, together with a series of livid spots which were evidently the impression of fingers. The face was fearfully discolored, and the eye-balls protruded. The tongue had been partially bitten through. A large bruise was discovered upon the pit of the stomach, produced, apparently, by the pressure of a knee. In the opinion of M. Dumas, Mademoiselle L'Espanaye had been throttled to death by some person or persons unknown. The corpse of the mother was horribly mutilated. All the bones of the right leg and arm were more or less shattered. The left *tibia* much splintered, as well as all the ribs of the left side. Whole body dreadfully bruised and discolored. It was not possible to say how the injuries had been inflicted. A heavy club of wood, or a broad bar of iron—a chair—any large, heavy, and obtuse weapon would have produced such results, if wielded by the hands of a very powerful man. No woman could have inflicted the blows with any weapon. The head of the deceased, when seen by witness, was entirely separated from the body, and was also greatly shattered. The throat had evidently been cut with some very sharp instrument—probably with a razor.

"*Alexandre Etienne*, surgeon, was called with M. Dumas to view the bodies. Corroborated the testimony, and the opinions of M. Dumas.

"Nothing farther of importance was elicited, although several other persons were examined. A murder so mysterious, and so perplexing in all its particulars, was never before committed in Paris—if indeed a murder has been committed at all. The police are entirely at fault—an unusual occurrence in affairs of this nature. There is not, however, the shadow of a clew apparent."

The evening edition of the paper stated that the greatest excitement still continued in the Quartier St. Roch—that the premises in question had been carefully re-searched, and fresh examinations of witnesses instituted, but all to no purpose. A postscript, however, mentioned that Adolphe Le Bon had been arrested and imprisoned—although nothing appeared to criminate him, beyond the facts already detailed. .

Dupin seemed singularly interested in the progress of

this affair—at least so I judged from his manner, for he made no comments. It was only after the announcement that Le Bon had been imprisoned, that he asked me my opinion respecting the murders.

I could merely agree with all Paris in considering them an insoluble mystery. I saw no means by which it would be possible to trace the murderer.

"We must not judge of the means," said Dupin, "by this shell of an examination. The Parisian police, so much extolled for *acumen*, are cunning, but no more. There is no method in their proceedings, beyond the method of the moment. They make a vast parade of measures; but, not unfrequently, these are so ill adapted to the objects proposed, as to put us in mind of Monsieur Jourdain's calling for his *robe-de-chambre—pour mieux entendre la musique*. The results attained by them are not unfrequently surprising, but, for the most part, are brought about by simple diligence and activity. When these qualities are unavailing, their schemes fail. Vidocq, for example, was a good guesser, and a persevering man. But, without educated thought, he erred continually by the very intensity of his investigations. He impaired his vision by holding the object too close. He might see, perhaps, one or two points with unusual clearness, but in so doing he, necessarily, lost sight of the matter as a whole. Thus there is such a thing as being too profound. Truth is not always in a well. In fact, as regards the more important knowledge, I do believe that she is invariably superficial. The depth lies in the valleys where we seek her, and not upon the mountain-tops where she is found. The modes and sources of this kind of error are well typified in the contemplation of the heavenly bodies. To look at a star by glances—to view it in a side-long way, by turning toward it the exterior portions of the *retina* (more susceptible of feeble impressions of light than the interior), is to behold the star distinctly—is to have the best appreciation of its lustre—a lustre which grows dim just in proportion as we turn our vision *fully* upon it. A greater number of rays actually fall upon the eye in the latter case, but, in the former, there is the more refined capacity for comprehension. By undue profundity we perplex and enfeeble thought; and it is possible to make even Venus herself vanish from the firmament by a scrutiny too sustained, too concentrated, or too direct.

"As for these murders, let us enter into some examinations for ourselves, before we make up an opinion respecting them. An inquiry will afford us amusement," [I thought this an odd term, so applied, but said nothing] "and, besides, Le Bon once rendered me a service for which I am not ungrateful. We will go and see the premises with our own eyes. I know G———, the Prefect of Police, and shall have no difficulty in obtaining the necessary permission."

The permission was obtained, and we proceeded at once to the Rue Morgue. This is one of those miserable thoroughfares which intervene between the Rue Richelieu and the Rue St. Roch. It was late in the afternoon when we reached it; as this quarter is at a great distance from that in which we resided. The house was readily found; for there were still many persons gazing up at the closed shutters, with an objectless curiosity, from the opposite side of the way. It was an ordinary Parisian house, with a gateway, on one side of which was a glazed watch-box, with a sliding panel in the window, indicating a *loge de concierge*. Before going in we walked up the street, turned down an alley, and then, again turning, passed in the rear of the building—Dupin, meanwhile, examining the whole neighborhood, as well as the house, with a minuteness of attention for which I could see no possible object.

Retracing our steps, we came again to the front of the dwelling, rang, and, having shown our credentials, were admitted by the agents in charge. We went up stairs—into the chamber where the body of Mademoiselle L'Espanaye had been found and where both the deceased still lay. The disorders of the room had, as usual, been suffered to exist. I saw nothing beyond what had been stated in the "Gazette des Tribunaux." Dupin scrutinized every thing—not excepting the bodies of the victims. We then went into the other rooms, and into the yard; a *gendarme* accompanying us throughout. The examination occupied us until dark, when we took our departure. On our way home my companion stepped in for a moment at the office of one of the daily papers.

I have said that the whims of my friend were manifold, and that *Je les ménagais:*—for this phrase there is no English equivalent. It was his humor, now, to decline all conversation on the subject of the murder, until about noon the next day. He then asked me, suddenly, if I had observed any thing *peculiar* at the scene of the atrocity.

There was something in his manner of emphasizing the word "peculiar," which caused me to shudder, without knowing why.

"No, nothing *peculiar*," I said; "nothing more, at least, than we both saw stated in the paper."

"The 'Gazette,'" he replied, "has not entered, I fear, into the unusual horror of the thing. But dismiss the idle opinions of this print. It appears to me that this mystery is considered insoluble, for the very reason which should cause it to be regarded as easy of solution—I mean for the *outré* character of its features. The police are confounded by the seeming absence of motive—not for the murder itself—but for the atrocity of the murder. They are puzzled, too, by the seeming impossibility of reconciling the voices heard in contention, with the facts that no one was discovered up stairs but the assassinated Mademoiselle L'Espanaye, and that there were no means of egress without the notice of the party ascending. The wild disorder of the room; the corpse thrust, with the head downward, up the chimney; the frightful mutilation of the body of the old lady; these considerations, with those just mentioned, and others which I need not mention, have sufficed to paralyze the powers, by putting completely at fault the boasted *acumen*, of the government agents. They have fallen into the gross but common error of confounding the unusual with the abstruse. But it is by these deviations from the plane of the ordinary, that reason feels its way, if at all, in its search for the true. In investigations such as we are now pursuing, it should not be so much asked 'what has occurred,' as 'what has occurred that has never occurred before.' In fact, the facility with which I shall arrive, or have arrived, at the solution of this mystery, is in the direct ratio of its apparent insolubility in the eyes of the police."

I stared at the speaker in mute astonishment.

"I am now awaiting," continued he, looking toward the door of our apartment—"I am now awaiting a person who, although perhaps not the perpetrator of these butcheries, must have been in some measure implicated in their perpetration. Of the worst portion of the crimes committed, it is probable that he is innocent. I hope that I am right in this supposition; for upon it I build my expectation of reading the entire riddle. I look for the man here—in this room—every moment. It is true that he may not arrive; but the probability is that he will. Should he come, it will be necessary to detain him. Here are pistols; and we both know how to use them when occasion demands their use."

I took the pistols, scarcely knowing what I did, or believing what I heard, while Dupin went on, very much as if in a soliloquy. I have already spoken of his abstract manner at such times. His discourse was addressed to myself; but his voice, although by no means loud, had that intonation which is commonly employed in speaking to some one at a great distance. His eyes, vacant in expression, regarded only the wall.

"That the voices heard in contention," he said, "by the party upon the stairs, were not the voices of the women themselves, was fully proved by the evidence. This relieves us of all doubt upon the question whether the old lady could have first destroyed the daughter, and afterward have committed suicide. I speak on this point chiefly for the sake of method; for the strength of Madame L'Espanaye would have been utterly unequal to the task of thrusting her daughter's corpse up the chimney as it was found; and the nature of the wounds upon her own person entirely preclude the idea of self-destruction. Murder, then, has been committed by some third party; and the voices of this third party were those heard in contention. Let me now advert—not to the whole testimony respecting these voices—but to what was *peculiar* in that testimony. Did you observe any thing peculiar about it?"

I remarked that, while all the witnesses agreed in supposing the gruff voice to be that of a Frenchman, there was much disagreement in regard to the shrill, or, as one individual termed it, the harsh voice.

"That was the evidence itself," said Dupin, "but it was not the peculiarity of the evidence. You have observed nothing distinctive. Yet there *was* something to be observed. The witnesses, as you remark, agreed about the gruff voice; they were here unanimous. But in regard to the shrill voice, the peculiarity is—not that they disagreed—but that, while an Italian, an Englishman, a Spaniard, a Hollander, and a Frenchman attempted to describe it, each one spoke of it as that *of a foreigner*. Each is sure that it was not the voice of one of his own countrymen. Each likens it—not to the voice of an individual of any nation with whose language he is conversant—but the converse. The Frenchman supposes it the voice of a Spaniard, and 'might have distinguished some words *had he been acquainted with the Spanish.*' The Dutchman maintains it to have been that of a Frenchman; but we find it stated that '*not understanding French this witness was examined through an interpreter.*' The Englishman thinks it the voice of a German, and '*does not understand German.*' The Spaniard 'is sure' that it was that of an Englishman, but 'judges by the intonation' altogether, '*as he has no knowledge of the English.*' The Italian believes it the voice of a Russian, but '*has never conversed with a native of Russia.*' A second Frenchman differs, moreover, with the first, and is positive that the voice was that of an Italian; but, '*not being cognizant of that tongue,*' is, like the Spaniard, 'convinced by the intonation.' Now, how strangely unusual must that voice have really been, about which such testimony as this *could* have been elicited!—in whose *tones*, even, denizens of the five great divisions of Europe could recognise nothing familiar! You will say that it might have been the voice of an Asiatic—of an African. Neither Asiatics nor Africans abound in Paris; but, without denying the inference, I will now merely call your attention to three points. The voice is termed by one witness 'harsh rather than shrill.' It is represented by two others to have been 'quick and *unequal.*' No words—no sounds resembling words—were by any witness mentioned as distinguishable.

"I know not," continued Dupin, "what impression I may have made, so far, upon your own understanding; but I do not hesitate to say that legitimate deductions even from this portion of the testimony—the portion respecting the gruff and shrill voices—are in themselves sufficient to engender a suspicion which should give direction to all farther progress in the investigation of the mystery. I said 'legitimate deductions'; but my meaning is not thus fully expressed. I designed to imply that the deductions are the *sole* proper ones, and that the suspicion arises *in-*

evitably from them as the single result. What the suspicion is, however, I will not say just yet. I merely wish you to bear in mind that, with myself, it was sufficiently forcible to give a definite form—a certain tendency—to my inquiries in the chamber.

"Let us now transport ourselves, in fancy, to this chamber. What shall we first seek here? The means of egress employed by the murderers. It is not too much to say that neither of us believe in præternatural events. Madame and Mademoiselle L'Espanaye were not destroyed by spirits. The doers of the deed were material, and escaped materially. Then how? Fortunately, there is but one mode of reasoning upon the point, and that mode *must* lead us to a definite decision.—Let us examine, each by each, the possible means of egress. It is clear that the assassins were in the room where Mademoiselle L'Espanaye was found, or at least in the room adjoining, when the party ascended the stairs. It is then only from these two apartments that we have to seek issues. The police have laid bare the floors, the ceilings, and the masonry of the walls, in every direction. No *secret* issues could have escaped their vigilance. But, not trusting to *their* eyes, I examined with my own. There were, then, *no* secret issues. Both doors leading from the rooms into the passage were securely locked, with the keys inside. Let us turn to the chimneys. These, although of ordinary width for some eight or ten feet above the hearths, will not admit, throughout their extent, the body of a large cat. The impossibility of egress, by means already stated, being thus absolute, we are reduced to the windows. Through those of the front room no one could have escaped without notice from the crowd in the street. The murderers *must* have passed, then, through those of the back room. Now, brought to this conclusion in so unequivocal a manner as we are, it is not our part, as reasoners, to reject it on account of apparent impossibilities. It is only left for us to prove that these apparent 'impossibilities' are, in reality, not such.

"There are two windows in the chamber. One of them is unobstructed by furniture, and is wholly visible. The lower portion of the other is hidden from view by the head of the unwieldy bedstead which is thrust close up against it. The former was found securely fastened from within. It resisted the utmost force of those who endeavored to raise it. A large gimlet-hole had been pierced in its frame to the left, and a very stout nail was found fitted therein, nearly to the head. Upon examining the other window, a similar nail was seen similarly fitted in it; and a vigorous attempt to raise this sash, failed also. The police were now entirely satisfied that egress had not been in these directions. And, *therefore*, it was thought a matter of supererogation to withdraw the nails and open the windows.

"My own examination was somewhat more particular, and was so for the reason I have just given—because here it was, I knew, that all apparent impossibilities *must* be proved to be not such in reality.

"I proceeded to think thus—*à posteriori*. The murderers *did* escape from one of these windows. This being so, they could not have re-fastened the sashes from the inside, as they were found fastened;—the consideration which put a stop, through its obviousness, to the scrutiny of the police in this quarter. Yet the sashes *were* fastened. They *must*, then, have the power of fastening themselves. There was no escape from this conclusion. I stepped to the unobstructed casement, withdrew the nail with some difficulty, and attempted to raise the sash. It resisted all my efforts, as I had anticipated. A concealed spring must, I now knew, exist; and this corroboration of my idea convinced me that my premises, at least, were correct, however mysterious still appeared the circumstances attending the nails. A careful search soon brought to light the hidden spring. I pressed it, and, satisfied with the discovery, forbore to upraise the sash.

"I now replaced the nail and regarded it attentively. A person passing out through this window might have reclosed it, and the spring would have caught—but the nail could not have been replaced. The conclusion was plain, and again narrowed in the field of my investigations. The assassins *must* have escaped through the other window. Supposing, then, the springs upon each sash to be the same, as was probable, there *must* be found a difference between the nails, or at least between the modes of their fixture. Getting upon the sacking of the bedstead, I looked over the head-board minutely at the second casement. Passing my hand down behind the board, I readily discovered and pressed the spring, which was, as I had supposed, identical in character with its neighbor. I now looked at the nail. It was as stout as the other, and apparently fitted in the same manner—driven in nearly up to the head.

"You will say that I was puzzled; but, if you think so, you must have misunderstood the nature of the inductions. To use a sporting phrase, I had not been once 'at fault.' The scent had never for an instant been lost. There was no flaw in any link of the chain. I had traced the secret to its ultimate result,—and that result was *the nail*. It had, I say, in every respect, the appearance of its fellow in the other window; but this fact was an absolute nullity (conclusive as it might seem to be) when compared with the consideration that here, at this point, terminated the clew. 'There *must* be something wrong,' I said, 'about the nail.' I touched it; and the head, with about a quarter of an inch of the shank, came off in my fingers. The rest of the shank was in the gimlet-hole, where it had been broken off. The fracture was an old one (for its edges were incrusted with rust), and had apparently been accomplished by the blow of a hammer, which had partially imbedded, in the top of the bottom sash, the head portion of the nail. I now carefully replaced this head portion in the indentation whence I had taken it, and the resemblance to a perfect nail was complete—the fissure was invisible. Pressing the spring, I gently raised the sash for a few inches; the head went up with it, remaining firm in its bed. I closed the window, and the semblance of the whole nail was again perfect.

"The riddle, so far, was now unriddled. The assassin had escaped through the window which looked upon the bed. Dropping of its own accord upon his exit (or perhaps purposely closed), it had become fastened by the spring; and it was the retention of this spring which had been mistaken by the police for that of the nail,—farther inquiry being thus considered unnecessary.

"The next question is that of the mode of descent. Upon this point I had been satisfied in my walk with you around the building. About five feet and a half from the casement in question there runs a lightning-rod. From this rod it would have been impossible for any one to reach the window itself, to say nothing of entering it. I observed, however, that the shutters of the fourth story were of the peculiar kind called by Parisian carpenters *ferrades*—a kind rarely employed at the present day, but frequently seen upon very old mansions at Lyons and Bourdeaux. They are in the form of an ordinary door, (a single, not a folding door) except that the upper half is latticed or worked in open trellis—thus affording an excellent hold for the hands. In the present instance these shutters are fully three feet and a half broad. When we saw them from the rear of the house, they were both about half open—that is to say, they stood off at right angles from the wall. It is probable that the police, as well as myself, examined the back of the tenement; but, if so, in looking at these *ferrades* in the line of their breadth (as they must have done), they did not perceive this great breadth itself, or, at all events, failed to take it into due consideration. In fact, having once satisfied themselves that no egress could have been made in this quarter, they would naturally bestow here a very cursory examination. It was clear to me, however, that the shutter belonging to the window at the head of the bed, would, if swung fully back to the wall, reach to within two feet of the lightning-rod. It was also evident that, by exertion of a very unusual degree of activity and courage, an entrance into the window, from the rod, might have been thus effected.—By reaching to the distance of two feet and a half (we now suppose the shutter open to its whole extent) a robber might have taken a firm grasp upon the trellis-work. Letting go, then, his hold upon the rod, placing his feet securely against the wall, and springing boldly from it, he might have swung the shutter so as to close it, and, if we imagine the window open at the time, might even have swung himself into the room.

"I wish you to bear especially in mind that I have spoken of a *very* unusual degree of activity as requisite to success in so hazardous and so difficult a feat. It is my design to show you, first, that the thing might possibly have been accomplished:—but, secondly and *chiefly*, I wish to impress upon your understanding the *very extraordinary*— the almost præternatural character of that agility which could have accomplished it.

"You will say, no doubt, using the language of the law, that 'to make out my case,' I should rather undervalue, than insist upon a full estimation of the activity required in this matter. This may be the practice in law, but it is not the usage of reason. My ultimate object is only the truth. My immediate purpose is to lead you to place in juxta-position, that *very unusual* activity of which I have just spoken, with that *very peculiar* shrill (or harsh) and *unequal* voice, about whose nationality no two persons

could be found to agree, and in whose utterance no syllabification could be detected."

At these words a vague and half-formed conception of
the meaning of Dupin flitted over my mind. I seemed to
be upon the verge of comprehension, without power to
comprehend—as men, at times, find themselves upon the
brink of remembrance, without being able, in the end, to
remember. My friend went on with his discourse.

"You will see," he said, "that I have shifted the question from the mode of egress to that of ingress. It was
my design to convey the idea that both were effected in
the same manner, at the same point. Let us now revert to
the interior of the room. Let us survey the appearances
here. The drawers of the bureau, it is said, had been rifled,
although many articles of apparel still remained within
them. The conclusion here is absurd. It is a mere guess
—a very silly one—and no more. How are we to know
that the articles found in the drawers were not all these
drawers had originally contained? Madame L'Espanaye
and her daughter lived an exceedingly retired life—saw no
company—seldom went out—had little use for numerous
changes of habiliment. Those found were at least of as
good quality as any likely to be possessed by these ladies.
If a thief had taken any, why did he not take the best—
why did he not take all? In a word, why did he abandon
four thousand francs in gold to encumber himself with a
bundle of linen? The gold *was* abandoned. Nearly the
whole sum mentioned by Monsieur Mignaud, the banker,
was discovered, in bags, upon the floor. I wish you, therefore, to discard from your thoughts the blundering idea of
motive, engendered in the brains of the police by that
portion of the evidence which speaks of money delivered
at the door of the house. Coincidences ten times as remarkable as this (the delivery of the money, and murder
committed within three days upon the party receiving it),
happen to all of us every hour of our lives, without attract-

ing even momentary notice. Coincidences, in general, are
great stumbling-blocks in the way of that class of thinkers
who have been educated to know nothing of the theory
of probabilities—that theory to which the most glorious
objects of human research are indebted for the most
glorious of illustration. In the present instance, had the
gold been gone, the fact of its delivery three days before
would have formed something more than a coincidence.
It would have been corroborative of this idea of motive.
But, under the real circumstances of the case, if we are to
suppose gold the motive of this outrage, we must also
imagine the perpetrator so vacillating an idiot as to have
abandoned his gold and his motive together.

"Keeping now steadily in mind the points to which I
have drawn your attention—that peculiar voice, that unusual agility, and that startling absence of motive in a
murder so singularly atrocious as this—let us glance at
the butchery itself. Here is a woman strangled to death by
manual strength, and thrust up a chimney, head downward. Ordinary assassins employ no such modes of murder
as this. Least of all, do they thus dispose of the murdered.
In the manner of thrusting the corpse up the chimney,
you will admit that there was something *excessively outré*
—something altogether irreconcilable with our common
notions of human action, even when we suppose the actors
the most depraved of men. Think, too, how great must
have been that strength which could have thrust the body
up such an aperture so forcibly that the united vigor of
several persons was found barely sufficient to drag it
down!

"Turn, now, to other indications of the employment of
a vigor most marvellous. On the hearth were thick tresses
—very thick tresses—of grey human hair. These had been
torn out by the roots. You are aware of the great force
necessary in tearing thus from the head even twenty or
thirty hairs together. You saw the locks in question as

well as myself. Their roots (a hideous sight!) were clotted
with fragments of the flesh of the scalp—sure token of
the prodigious power which had been exerted in uproot-
ing perhaps half a million of hairs at a time. The throat
of the old lady was not merely cut, but the head absolutely severed from the body: the instrument was a mere
razor. I wish you also to look at the *brutal* ferocity of
these deeds. Of the bruises upon the body of Madame
L'Espanaye I do not speak. Monsieur Dumas, and his
worthy coadjutor Monsieur Etienne, have pronounced that
they were inflicted by some obtuse instrument; and so far
these gentlemen are very correct. The obtuse instrument
was clearly the stone pavement in the yard, upon which
the victim had fallen from the window which looked in
upon the bed. This idea, however simple it may now seem,
escaped the police for the same reason that the breadth
of the shutters escaped them—because, by the affair of
the nails, their perceptions had been hermetically sealed
against the possibility of the windows having ever been
opened at all.

"If now, in addition to all these things, you have
properly reflected upon the odd disorder of the chamber,
we have gone so far as to combine the ideas of an agility
astounding, a strength superhuman, a ferocity brutal, a
butchery without motive, a *grotesquerie* in horror absolutely alien from humanity, and a voice foreign in tone
to the ears of men of many nations, and devoid of all
distinct or intelligible syllabification. What result, then,
has ensued? What impression have I made upon your
fancy?"

I felt a creeping of the flesh as Dupin asked me the
question. "A madman," I said, "has done this deed—
some raving maniac, escaped from a neighboring *Maison
de Santé*."

"In some respects," he replied, "your idea is not irrelevant. But the voices of madmen, even in their wildest

paroxysms, are never found to tally with that peculiar voice heard upon the stairs. Madmen are of some nation, and their language, however incoherent in its words, has always the coherence of syllabification. Besides, the hair of a madman is not such as I now hold in my hand. I disentangled this little tuft from the rigidly clutched fingers of Madame L'Espanaye. Tell me what you can make of it."

"Dupin!" I said, completely unnerved; "this hair is most unusual—this is no *human* hair."

"I have not asserted that it is," said he; "but, before we decide this point, I wish you to glance at the little sketch I have here traced upon this paper. It is a *fac-simile* drawing of what has been described in one portion of the testimony as 'dark bruises, and deep indentations of finger nails,' upon the throat of Mademoiselle L'Espanaye, and in another, (by Messrs. Dumas and Etienne,) as a 'series of livid spots, evidently the impression of fingers.'

"You will perceive," continued my friend, spreading out the paper upon the table before us, "that this drawing gives the idea of a firm and fixed hold. There is no *slipping* apparent. Each finger has retained—possibly until the death of the victim—the fearful grasp by which it originally imbedded itself. Attempt, now, to place all your fingers, at the same time, in the respective impressions as you see them."

I made the attempt in vain.

"We are possibly not giving this matter a fair trial," he said. "The paper is spread out upon a plane surface; but the human throat is cylindrical. Here is a billet of wood, the circumference of which is about that of the throat. Wrap the drawing around it, and try the experiment again."

I did so; but the difficulty was even more obvious than before. "This," I said, "is the mark of no human hand."

"Read now," replied Dupin, "this passage from Cuvier."

It was a minute anatomical and generally descriptive

account of the large fulvous Ourang-Outang of the East Indian Islands. The gigantic stature, the prodigious strength and activity, the wild ferocity, and the imitative propensities of these mammalia are sufficiently well known to all. I understood the full horror of the murders at once.

"The description of the digits," said I, as I made an end of reading, "is in exact accordance with this drawing. I see that no animal but an Ourang-Outang, of the species here mentioned, could have impressed the indentations as you have traced them. This tuft of tawny hair, too, is identical in character with that of the beast of Cuvier. But I cannot possibly comprehend the particulars of this frightful mystery. Besides, there were *two* voices heard in contention, and one of them was unquestionably the voice of a Frenchman."

"True; and you will remember an expression attributed almost unanimously, by the evidence, to this voice,—the expression, '*mon Dieu!*' This, under the circumstances, has been justly characterized by one of the witnesses (Montani, the confectioner,) as an expression of remonstrance or expostulation. Upon these two words, therefore, I have mainly built my hopes of a full solution of the riddle. A Frenchman was cognizant of the murder. It is possible —indeed it is far more than probable—that he was innocent of all participation in the bloody transactions which took place. The Ourang-Outang may have escaped from him. He may have traced it to the chamber; but, under the agitating circumstances which ensued, he could never have re-captured it. It is still at large. I will not pursue these guesses—for I have no right to call them more— since the shades of reflection upon which they are based are scarcely of sufficient depth to be appreciable by my own intellect, and since I could not pretend to make them intelligible to the understanding of another. We will call them guesses then, and speak of them as such. If the Frenchman in question is indeed, as I suppose, innocent of this atrocity, this advertisement, which I left last night, upon our return home, at the office of 'Le Monde,' (a paper devoted to the shipping interest, and much sought by sailors,) will bring him to our residence."

He handed me a paper, and I read thus:

CAUGHT—*In the Bois de Boulogne, early in the morning of the ——— inst., (the morning of the murder,) a very large, tawny Ourang-Outang of the Bornese species. The owner, (who is ascertained to be a sailor, belonging to a Maltese vessel,) may have the animal again, upon identifying it satisfactorily, and paying a few charges arising from its capture and keeping. Call at No.———, Rue———, Faubourg St. Germain—au troisiême.*

"How was it possible," I asked, "that you should know the man to be a sailor, and belonging to a Maltese vessel?"

"I do *not* know it," said Dupin. "I am not *sure* of it. Here, however, is a small piece of ribbon, which from its form, and from its greasy appearance, has evidently been used in tying the hair in one of those long *queues* of which sailors are so fond. Moreover, this knot is one which few besides sailors can tie, and is peculiar to the Maltese. I picked the ribbon up at the foot of the lighting-rod. It could not have belonged to either of the deceased. Now if, after all, I am wrong in my induction from this ribbon, that the Frenchman was a sailor belonging to a Maltese vessel, still I can have done no harm in saying what I did in the advertisement. If I am in error, he will merely suppose that I have been misled by some circumstance into which he will not take the trouble to inquire. But if I am right, a great point is gained. Cognizant although innocent of the murder, the Frenchman will naturally hesitate about replying to the advertisement—about demanding the Ourang-Outang. He will reason thus:—'I am innocent; I am poor; my Ourang-Outang is of great value—to one in my circumstances a fortune of itself—why should I lose it through idle apprehensions of danger? Here it is, within my grasp. It was found in the Bois de Boulogne—at a vast distance from the scene of that butchery. How can it ever be suspected that a brute beast should have done the deed? The police are at fault—they have failed to procure the slightest clew. Should they even trace the, animal, it would be impossible to prove me cognizant of the murder, or to implicate me in guilt on account of that cognizance. Above all, *I am known*. The advertiser designates me as the possessor of the beast. I am not sure to what limit his knowledge may extend. Should I avoid claiming a property of so great value, which it is known that I possess, I will render the animal at least, liable to suspicion. It is not my policy to attract attention either to myself or to the beast. I will answer the advertisement, get the Ourang-Outang, and keep it close until this matter has blown over.' "

At this moment we heard a step upon the stairs.

"Be ready," said Dupin, "with your pistols, but neither use them nor show them until at a signal from myself."

The front door of the house had been left open, and the visiter had entered, without ringing, and advanced several steps upon the staircase. Now, however, he seemed to hesitate. Presently we heard him descending. Dupin was moving quickly to the door, when we again heard him coming up. He did not turn back a second time, but stepped up with decision, and rapped at the door of our chamber.

"Come in," said Dupin, in a cheerful and hearty tone.

A man entered. He was a sailor, evidently,—a tall, stout, and muscular-looking person, with a certain dare-devil expression of countenance, not altogether unprepossessing. His face, greatly sunburnt, was more than half hidden by whisker and *mustachio*. He had with him a huge oaken cudgel, but appeared to be otherwise unarmed. He bowed awkwardly, and bade us "good evening," in French accents, which, although somewhat Neufchatelish, were still sufficiently indicative of a Parisian origin.

"Sit down, my friend," said Dupin. "I suppose you have called about the Ourang-Outang. Upon my word, I almost envy you the possession of him; a remarkably fine, and no doubt a very valuable animal. How old do you suppose him to be?"

The sailor drew a long breath, with the air of a man relieved of some intolerable burden, and then replied, in an assured tone: "I have no way of telling—but he can't be more than four or five years old. Have you got him here?"

"Oh no; we had no conveniences for keeping him here. He is at a livery stable in the Rue Dubourg, just by. You can get him in the morning. Of course you are prepared to identify the property?"

"To be sure I am, sir."

"I shall be sorry to part with him," said Dupin.

"I don't mean that you should be at all this trouble for nothing, sir," said the man. "Couldn't expect it. Am very willing to pay a reward for the finding of the animal—that is to say, any thing in reason."

"Well," replied my friend, "that is all very fair, to be sure. Let me think!—what should I have? Oh! I will tell you. My reward shall be this. You shall give me all the information in your power about these murders in the Rue Morgue."

Dupin said the last words in a very low tone, and very quietly. Just as quietly, too, he walked toward the door, locked it, and put the key in his pocket. He then drew a pistol from his bosom and placed it, without the least flurry, upon the table.

The sailor's face flushed up as if he were struggling with suffocation. He started to his feet and grasped his cudgel; but the next moment he fell back into his seat, trembling violently, and with the countenance of death itself. He spoke not a word. I pitied him from the bottom of my heart.

"My friend," said Dupin, in a kind tone, "you are alarming yourself unnecessarily—you are indeed. We mean you no harm whatever. I pledge you the honor of a gentleman, and of a Frenchman, that we intend you no injury. I perfectly well know that you are innocent of the atrocities in the Rue Morgue. It will not do, however, to deny that you are in some measure implicated in them. From what I have already said, you must know that I have had means of information about this matter—means of which you could never have dreamed. Now the thing stands thus. You have done nothing which you could have avoided—nothing, certainly, which renders you culpable. You were not even guilty of robbery, when you might have robbed with impunity. You have nothing to conceal. You have no reason for concealment. On the other hand, you are bound by every principle of honor to confess all you know. An innocent man is now imprisoned, charged with that crime of which you can point out the perpetrator."

The sailor had recovered his presence of mind, in a great measure, while Dupin uttered these words; but his original boldness of bearing was all gone.

"So help me God," said he, after a brief pause, "I *will* tell you all I know about this affair;—but I do not expect you to believe one half I say—I would be a fool indeed if I did. Still, I *am* innocent, and I will make a clean breast if I die for it."

What he stated was, in substance, this. He had lately made a voyage to the Indian Archipelago. A party, of which he formed one, landed at Borneo, and passed into the interior on an excursion of pleasure. Himself and a companion had captured the Ourang-Outang. This companion dying, the animal fell into his own exclusive possession. After great trouble, occasioned by the intractable ferocity of his captive during the home voyage, he at length succeeded in lodging it safely at his own residence in Paris, where, not to attract toward himself the unpleasant curiosity of his neighbors, he kept it carefully secluded, until such time as it should recover from a wound in the foot, received from a splinter on board ship. His ultimate design was to sell it.

Returning home from some sailors' frolic on the night, or rather in the morning of the murder, he found the beast occupying his own bed-room, into which it had broken from a closet adjoining, where it had been, as was thought, securely confined. Razor in hand, and fully lathered, it was sitting before a looking-glass, attempting the operation of shaving, in which it had no doubt previously watched its master through the key-hole of the closet. Terrified at the sight of so dangerous a weapon in the possession of an animal so ferocious, and so well able to use it, the man, for some moments, was at a loss what to do. He had been accustomed, however, to quiet the creature, even in its fiercest moods, by the use of a whip, and to this he now resorted. Upon sight of it, the Ourang-Outang sprang at once through the door of the chamber, down the stairs, and thence, through a window, unfortunately open, into the street.

The Frenchman followed in despair; the ape, razor still in hand, occasionally stopping to look back and gesticulate at its pursuer, until the latter had nearly come up with it. It then again made off. In this manner the chase continued for a long time. The streets were profoundly quiet, as it was nearly three o'clock in the morning. In passing down an alley in the rear of the Rue Morgue, the fugitive's attention was arrested by a light gleaming from the open window of Madame L'Espanaye's chamber, in the fourth story of her house. Rushing to the building, it perceived the lightning-rod, clambered up with inconceivable agility, grasped the shutter, which was thrown fully back against the wall, and, by its means, swung itself directly upon the headboard of the bed. The whole feat did not occupy a minute. The shutter was kicked open again by the Ourang-Outang as it entered the room.

The sailor, in the meantime, was both rejoiced and perplexed. He had strong hopes of now recapturing the brute, as it could scarcely escape from the trap into which it had ventured, except by the rod, where it might be intercepted as it came down. On the other hand, there was much cause for anxiety as to what it might do in the house. This latter reflection urged the man still to follow the fugitive. A lightning-rod is ascended without difficulty, especially by a sailor; but, when he had arrived as high as the window, which lay far to his left, his career was stopped; the most that he could accomplish was to reach over so as to obtain a glimpse of the interior of the room. At this glimpse he nearly fell from his hold through excess of horror. Now it was that those hideous shrieks arose upon the night, which had startled from slumber the inmates of the Rue Morgue. Madame L'Espanaye and her daughter, habited in their night clothes, had apparently been occupied in arranging some papers in the iron chest already mentioned, which had been wheeled into the middle of the room. It was open, and its contents lay beside it on the floor. The victims must have been sitting with their backs toward the window; and, from the time elapsing between the ingress of the beast and the screams, it seems probable that it was not immediately perceived. The flapping-to of the shutter would naturally have been attributed to the wind.

As the sailor looked in, the gigantic animal had seized Madame L'Espanaye by the hair, (which was loose, as she had been combing it,) and was flourishing the razor about her face, in imitation of the motions of a barber. The daughter lay prostrate and motionless; she had swooned. The screams and struggles of the old lady (during which the hair was torn from her head) had the effect of changing the probably pacific purposes of the Ourang-Outang into those of wrath. With one determined sweep of its muscular arm it nearly severed her head from her body. The sight of blood inflamed its anger into phrenzy. Gnashing its teeth, and flashing fire from its eyes, it flew upon the body of the girl, and imbedded its fearful talons in her throat, retaining its grasp until she expired. Its wandering and wild glances fell at this moment upon the head of the bed, over which the face of its master, rigid with horror, was just discernible. The fury of the beast, who no doubt bore still in mind the dreaded whip, was instantly converted into fear. Conscious of having deserved punishment, it seemed desirous of concealing its bloody deeds, and skipped about the chamber in an agony of nervous agitation; throwing down and breaking the furniture as it moved, and dragging the bed from the bedstead. In conclusion, it seized first the corpse of the daughter, and thrust it up the chimney, as it was found; then that of the old lady, which it immediately hurled through the window headlong.

As the ape approached the casement with its mutilated burden, the sailor shrank aghast to the rod, and, rather gliding than clambering down it, hurried at once home—dreading the consequences of the butchery, and gladly abandoning, in his terror, all solicitude about the fate of the Ourang-Outang. The words heard by the party upon the staircase were the Frenchman's exclamations of horror and affright, commingled with the fiendish jabberings of the brute.

I have scarcely anything to add. The Ourang-Outang must have escaped from the chamber, by the rod, just before the breaking of the door. It must have closed the window as it passed through it. It was subsequently caught by the owner himself, who obtained for it a very large sum at the *Jardin des Plantes*. Le Bon was instantly released, upon our narration of the circumstances (with some comments from Dupin) at the *bureau* of the Prefect of Police. This functionary, however well disposed to my friend, could not altogether conceal his chagrin at the turn which affairs had taken, and was fain to indulge in a sarcasm or two, about the propriety of every person minding his own business.

"Let him talk," said Dupin, who had not thought it necessary to reply. "Let him discourse; it will ease his conscience. I am satisfied with having defeated him in his own castle. Nevertheless, that he failed in the solution of this mystery, is by no means that matter for wonder which he supposes it; for, in truth, our friend the Prefect is somewhat too cunning to be profound. In his wisdom is no *stamen*. It is all head and no body, like the pictures of the Goddess Laverna,—or, at best, all head and shoulders, like a codfish. But he is a good creature after all. I like him especially for one master stroke of cant, by which he has attained his reputation for ingenuity. I mean the way he has '*de nier ce qui est, et d'expliquer ce qui n'est pas.*' "*

A DESCENT INTO THE MAELSTRÖM

The ways of God in Nature, as in Providence, are not as our ways; nor are the models that we frame any way commensurate to the vastness, profundity, and unsearchableness of His works, *which have a depth in them greater than the well of Democritus.*

—*Joseph Glanville.*

We had now reached the summit of the loftiest crag. For some minutes the old man seemed too much exhausted to speak.

* Rousseau—*Nouvelle Heloise.*

"Not long ago," said he at length, "and I could have guided you on this route as well as the youngest of my sons; but, about three years past, there happened to me an event such as never happened before to mortal man—or at least such as no man ever survived to tell of—and the six hours of deadly terror which I then endured have broken me up body and soul. You suppose me a *very* old man—but I am not. It took less than a single day to change these hairs from a jetty black to white, to weaken my limbs, and to unstring my nerves, so that I tremble at the least exertion, and am frightened at a shadow. Do you know I can scarcely look over this little cliff without getting giddy?"

The "little cliff," upon whose edge he had so carelessly thrown himself down to rest that the weightier portion of his body hung over it, while he was only kept from falling by the tenure of his elbow on its extreme and slippery edge—this "little cliff" arose, a sheer unobstructed precipice of black shining rock, some fifteen or sixteen hundred feet from the world of crags beneath us. Nothing would have tempted me to within half a dozen yards of its brink. In truth so deeply was I excited by the perilous position of my companion, that I fell at full length upon the ground, clung to the shrubs around me, and dared not even glance upward at the sky—while I struggled in vain to divest myself of the idea that the very foundations of the mountain were in danger from the fury of the winds. It was long before I could reason myself into sufficient courage to sit up and look out into the distance.

"You must get over these fancies," said the guide, "for I have brought you here that you might have the best possible view of the scene of that event I mentioned—and to tell you the whole story with the spot just under your eye."

"We are now," he continued, in that particularizing manner which distinguished him—"we are now close upon

the Norwegian coast—in the sixty-eighth degree of latitude
—in the great province of Nordland—and in the dreary
district of Lofoden. The mountain upon whose top we
sit is Helseggen, the Cloudy. Now raise yourself up a
little higher—hold on to the grass if you feel giddy—so
—and look out, beyond the belt of vapor beneath us, into
the sea."

I looked dizzily, and beheld a wide expanse of ocean,
whose waters wore so inky a hue as to bring at once to my
mind the Nubian geographer's account of the *Mare
Tenebrarum*. A panorama more deplorably desolate no
human imagination can conceive. To the right and left, as
far as the eye could reach, there lay outstretched, like
ramparts of the world, lines of horridly black and beetling
cliff, whose character of gloom was but the more forcibly
illustrated by the surf which reared high up against it
its white and ghastly crest, howling and shrieking for ever.
Just opposite the promontory upon whose apex we were
placed, and at a distance of some five or six miles out at
sea, there was visible a small, bleak-looking island; or, more
properly, its position was discernible through the wilderness of surge in which it was enveloped. About two miles
nearer the land, arose another of smaller size, hideously
craggy and barren, and encompassed at various intervals
by a cluster of dark rocks.

The appearance of the ocean, in the space between the
more distant island and the shore, had something very
unusual about it. Although, at the time, so strong a gale
was blowing landward that a brig in the remote offing lay
to under a double-reefed trysail, and constantly plunged
her whole hull out of sight, still there was here nothing like
a regular swell, but only a short, quick, angry cross dashing of water in every direction—as well in the teeth of
the wind as otherwise. Of foam there was little except in
the immediate vicinity of the rocks.

"The island in the distance," resumed the old man, "is

called by the Norwegians Vurrgh. The one midway is
Moskoe. That a mile to the northward is Ambaaren.
Yonder are Islesen, Hotholm, Keildhelm, Suarven, and
Buckholm. Farther off—between Moskoe and Vurrgh—are
Otterholm, Flimen, Sandflesen, and Stockholm. These are
the true names of the places—but why it has been thought
necessary to name them at all, is more than either you or
I can understand. Do you hear any thing? Do you see any
change in the water?"

We had now been about ten minutes upon the top of
Helseggen, to which we had ascended from the interior
of Lofoden, so that we had caught no glimpse of the sea
until it had burst upon us from the summit. As the old
man spoke, I became aware of a loud and gradually increasing sound, like the moaning of a vast herd of buffaloes
upon an American prairie; and at the same moment I
perceived that what seamen term the *chopping* character
of the ocean beneath us, was rapidly changing into a
current which set to the eastward. Even while I gazed,
this current acquired a monstrous velocity. Each moment
added to its speed—to its headlong impetuosity. In five
minutes the whole sea, as far as Vurrgh, was lashed into
ungovernable fury; but it was between Moskoe and the
coast that the main uproar held its sway. Here the vast bed
of the waters, seamed and scarred into a thousand conflicting channels, burst suddenly into phrensied convulsion
—heaving, boiling, hissing—gyrating in gigantic and innumerable vortices, and all whirling and plunging on to the
eastward with a rapidity which water never elsewhere
assumes except in precipitous descents.

In a few minutes more, there came over the scene another radical alteration. The general surface grew somewhat
more smooth, and the whirlpools, one by one, disappeared,
while prodigious streaks of foam became apparent where
none had been seen before. These streaks, at length,
spreading out to a great distance, and entering into com-

bination, took unto themselves the gyratory motion of the subsided vortices, and seemed to form the germ of another more vast. Suddenly—very suddenly—this assumed a distinct and definite existence, in a circle of more than half a mile in diameter. The edge of the whirl was represented by a broad belt of gleaming spray; but no particle of this slipped into the mouth of the terrific funnel, whose interior, as far as the eye could fathom it, was a smooth, shining, and jet-black wall of water, inclined to the horizon at an angle of some forty-five degrees, speeding dizzily round and round with a swaying and sweltering motion, and sending forth to the winds an appalling voice, half shriek, half roar, such as not even the mighty cataract of Niagara ever lifts up in its agony to Heaven.

The mountain trembled to its very base, and the rock rocked. I threw myself upon my face, and clung to the scant herbage in an excess of nervous agitation.

"This," said I at length, to the old man—"this *can* be nothing else than the great whirlpool of the Maelström."

"So it is sometimes termed," said he. "We Norwegians call it the Moskoe-ström, from the island of Moskoe in the midway."

The ordinary accounts of this vortex had by no means prepared me for what I saw. That of Jonas Ramus, which is perhaps the most circumstantial of any, cannot impart the faintest conception either of the magnificence, or of the horror of the scene—or of the wild bewildering sense of *the novel* which confounds the beholder. I am not sure from what point of view the writer in question surveyed it, nor at what time; but it could neither have been from the summit of Helseggen, nor during a storm. There are some passages of his description, nevertheless, which may be quoted for their details, although their effect is exceedingly feeble in conveying an impression of the spectacle.

"Between Lofoden and Moskoe," he says, "the depth

of the water is between thirty-six and forty fathoms; but on the other side, toward Ver (Vurrgh) this depth decreases so as not to afford a convenient passage for a vessel, without the risk of splitting on the rocks, which happens even in the calmest weather. When it is flood, the stream runs up the country between Lofoden and Moskoe with a boisterous rapidity; but the roar of its impetuous ebb to the sea is scarce equalled by the loudest and most dreadful cataracts; the noise being heard several leagues off, and the vortices or pits are of such an extent and depth, that if a ship comes within its attraction, it is inevitably absorbed and carried down to the bottom, and there beat to pieces against the rocks; and when the water relaxes, the fragments thereof are thrown up again. But these intervals of tranquillity are only at the turn of the ebb and flood, and in calm weather, and last but a quarter of an hour, its violence gradually returning. When the stream is most boisterous, and its fury heightened by a storm, it is dangerous to come within a Norway mile of it. Boats, yachts, and ships have been carried away by not guarding against it before they were within its reach. It likewise happens frequently, that whales come too near the stream, and are overpowered by its violence; and then it is impossible to describe their howlings and bellowings in their fruitless struggles to disengage themselves. A bear once, attempting to swim from Lofoden to Moskoe, was caught by the stream and borne down, while he roared terribly, so as to be heard on shore. Large stocks of firs and pine trees, after being absorbed by the current, rise again broken and torn to such a degree as if bristles grew upon them. This plainly shows the bottom to consist of craggy rocks, among which they are whirled to and fro. This stream is regulated by the flux and reflux of the sea—it being constantly high and low water every six hours. In the year 1645, early in the morning of Sexagesima Sunday, it raged with such noise and impetuosity that the very stones of the houses on the coast fell to the ground."

In regard to the depth of the water, I could not see how this could have been ascertained at all in the immediate vicinity of the vortex. The "forty fathoms" must have reference only to portions of the channel close upon the shore either of Moskoe or Lofoden. The depth in the centre of the Moskoe-ström must be immeasurably greater; and no better proof of this fact is necessary than can be obtained from even the sidelong glance into the abyss of the whirl which may be had from the highest crag of Helseggen. Looking down from this pinnacle upon the howling Phlegethon below, I could not help smiling at the simplicity with which the honest Jonas Ramus records, as a matter difficult of belief, the anecdotes of the whales and the bears; for it appeared to me, in fact, a self-evident thing, that the largest ship of the line in existence, coming within the influence of that deadly attraction, could resist it as little as a feather the hurricane, and must disappear bodily and at once.

The attempts to account for the phenomenon—some of which, I remember, seemed to me sufficiently plausible in perusal—now wore a very different and unsatisfactory aspect. The idea generally received is that this, as well as three smaller vortices among the Ferroe islands, "have no other cause than the collision of waves rising and falling, at flux and reflux, against a ridge of rocks and shelves, which confines the water so that it precipitates itself like a cataract; and thus the higher the flood rises, the deeper must the fall be, and the natural result of all is a whirlpool or vortex, the prodigious suction of which is sufficiently known by lesser experiments."—These are the words of the Encyclopædia Britannica. Kircher and others imagine that in the centre of the channel of the Maelström is an abyss penetrating the globe, and issuing in some very remote part—the Gulf of Bothnia being somewhat decidedly named in one instance. This opinion, idle in itself, was the one to which, as I gazed, my imagination most readily assented; and, mentioning it to the guide, I was rather surprised to hear him say that, although it was the view almost universally entertained of the subject by the Norwegians, it nevertheless was not his own. As to the former notion he confessed his inability to comprehend it; and here I agreed with him—for, however conclusive on paper, it becomes altogether unintelligible, and even absurd, amid the thunder of the abyss.

"You have had a good look at the whirl now," said the old man, "and if you will creep round this crag, so as to get in its lee, and deaden the roar of the water, I will tell you a story that will convince you I ought to know something of the Moskoeström."

I placed myself as desired, and he proceeded.

"Myself and my two brothers once owned a schooner-rigged smack of about seventy tons burthen, with which we were in the habit of fishing among the islands beyond Moskoe, nearly to Vurrgh. In all violent eddies at sea there is good fishing, at proper opportunities, if one has only the courage to attempt it; but among the whole of the Lofoden coastmen, we three were the only ones who made a regular business of going out to the islands, as I tell you. The usual grounds are a great way lower down to the southward. There fish can be got at all hours, without much risk, and therefore these places are preferred. The choice spots over here among the rocks, however, not only yield the finest variety, but in far greater abundance; so that we often got in a single day, what the more timid of the craft could not scrape together in a week. In fact, we made it a matter of desperate speculation—the risk of life standing instead of labor, and courage answering for capital.

"We kept the smack in a cove about five miles higher up the coast than this; and it was our practice, in fine weather, to take advantage of the fifteen minutes' slack to push across the main channel of the Moskoe-ström, far above the pool, and then drop down upon anchorage somewhere near Otterholm, or Sandflesen, where the eddies are not so violent as elsewhere. Here we used to remain until nearly time for slack-water again, when we weighed and made for home. We never set out upon this expedition without a steady side wind for going and coming—one that we felt sure would not fail us before our return—and we seldom made a mis-calculation upon this point. Twice, during six years, we were forced to stay all night at anchor on account of a dead calm, which is a rare thing indeed just about here; and once we had to remain on the grounds nearly a week, starving to death, owing to a gale which blew up shortly after our arrival, and made the channel too boisterous to be thought of. Upon this occasion we should have been driven out to sea in spite of everything, (for the whirlpools threw us round and round so violently, that, at length, we fouled our anchor and dragged it) if it had not been that we drifted into one of the innumerable cross currents—here to-day and gone to-morrow—which drove us under the lee of Flimen, where, by good luck, we brought up.

"I could not tell you the twentieth part of the difficulties we encountered 'on the grounds'—it is a bad spot to be in, even in good weather—but we made shift always to run the gauntlet of the Moskoe-ström itself without accident; although at times my heart has been in my mouth when we happened to be a minute or so behind or before the slack. The wind sometimes was not as strong as we thought it at starting, and then we made rather less way than we could wish, while the current rendered the smack unmanageable. My eldest brother had a son eighteen years old, and I had two stout boys of my own. These would have been of great assistance at such times, in using the sweeps, as well as afterward in fishing—but, somehow, although we ran the risk ourselves, we had not the heart to let the young ones get into the danger—for, after all is said and done, it *was* a horrible danger, and that is the truth.

"It is now within a few days of three years since what I am going to tell you occurred. It was on the tenth day of July, 18—, a day which the people of this part of the world will never forget—for it was one in which blew the most terrible hurricane that ever came out of the heavens. And yet all the morning, and indeed until late in the afternoon, there was a gentle and steady breeze from the south-west, while the sun shone brightly, so that the oldest seaman among us could not have foreseen what was to follow.

"The three of us—my two brothers and myself—had crossed over to the island about two o'clock P.M., and had soon nearly loaded the smack with fine fish, which, we all remarked, were more plenty that day than we had ever known them. It was just seven, *by my watch*, when we weighed and started for home, so as to make the worst of the Ström at slack water, which we knew would be at eight.

"We set out with a fresh wind on our starboard quarter, and for some time spanked along at a great rate, never dreaming of danger, for indeed we saw not the slightest reason to apprehend it. All at once we were taken aback by a breeze from over Helseggen. This was most unusual— something that had never happened to us before—and I began to feel a little uneasy, without exactly knowing why. We put the boat on the wind, but could make no head-way at all for the eddies, and I was upon the point of proposing to return to the anchorage, when, looking astern, we saw the whole horizon covered with a singular copper-colored cloud that rose with the most amazing velocity.

"In the meantime the breeze that had headed us off fell away, and we were dead becalmed, drifting about in every direction. This state of things, however, did not last long enough to give us time to think about it. In less than a minute the storm was upon us—in less than two the sky was entirely overcast—and what with this and the driving spray, it became suddenly so dark that we could not see each other in the smack.

"Such a hurricane as then blew it is folly to attempt describing. The oldest seaman in Norway never experienced any thing like it. We had let our sails go by the run before it cleverly took us; but, at the first puff, both our masts went by the board as if they had been sawed off—the mainmast taking with it my youngest brother, who had lashed himself to it for safety.

"Our boat was the lightest feather of a thing that ever sat upon water. It had a complete flush deck, with only a small hatch near the bow, and this hatch it had always been our custom to batten down when about to cross the Ström, by way of precaution against the chopping seas. But for this circumstance we should have foundered at once—for we lay entirely buried for some moments. How my elder brother escaped destruction I cannot say, for I never had an opportunity of ascertaining. For my part, as soon as I had let the foresail run, I threw myself flat on deck, with my feet against the narrow gunwale of the bow, and with my hands grasping a ring-bolt near the foot of the foremast. It was mere instinct that prompted me to do this—which was undoubtedly the very best thing I could have done—for I was too much flurried to think.

"For some moments we were completely deluged, as I say, and all this time I held my breath, and clung to the bolt. When I could stand it no longer I raised myself upon my knees, still keeping hold with my hands, and thus got my head clear. Presently our little boat gave herself a shake, just as a dog does in coming out of the water, and thus rid herself, in some measure, of the seas. I was now trying to get the better of the stupor that had come over me, and to collect my senses so as to see what was to be done, when I felt somebody grasp my arm. It was my elder brother, and my heart leaped for joy, for I had made sure that he was overboard—but the next moment all this joy was turned into horror—for he put his mouth close to my ear, and screamed out the word 'Moskoe-ström!'

"No one ever will know what my feelings were at that moment. I shook from head to foot as if I had had the most violent fit of the ague. I knew what he meant by that one word well enough—I knew what he wished to make me understand. With the wind that now drove us on, we were bound for the whirl of the Ström, and nothing could save us!

"You perceive that in crossing the Ström channel, we always went a long way up above the whirl, even in the calmest weather, and then had to wait and watch carefully for the slack—but now we were driving right upon the pool itself, and in such a hurricane as this! 'To be sure,' I thought, 'we shall get there just about the slack—there is some little hope in that'—but in the next moment I cursed myself for being so great a fool as to dream of hope at all. I knew very well that we were doomed, had we been ten times a ninety-gun ship.

"By this time the first fury of the tempest had spent itself, or perhaps we did not feel it so much, as we scudded before it, but at all events the seas, which at first had been kept down by the wind, and lay flat and frothing, now got up into absolute mountains. A singular change, too, had come over the heavens. Around in every direction it was still as black as pitch, but nearly overhead there burst out, all at once, a circular rift of clear sky—as clear as I ever saw—and of a deep bright blue—and through it there blazed forth the full moon with a lustre that I never before knew her to wear. She lit up every thing about us with the greatest distinctness—but, oh God, what a scene it was to light up!

"I now made one or two attempts to speak to my brother

—but, in some manner which I could not understand, the din had so increased that I could not make him hear a single word, although I screamed at the top of my voice in his ear. Presently he shook his head, looking as pale as death, and held up one of his fingers, as if to say '*listen!*'

"At first I could not make out what he meant—but soon a hideous thought flashed upon me. I dragged my watch from its fob. It was not going. I glanced at its face by the moonlight, and then burst into tears as I flung it far away into the ocean. *It had run down at seven o'clock! We were behind the time of the slack, and the whirl of the Ström was in full fury!*

"When a boat is well built, properly trimmed, and not deep laden, the waves in a strong gale, when she is going large, seem always to slip from beneath her—which appears very strange to a landsman—and this is what is called *riding*, in sea phrase. Well, so far we had ridden the swells very cleverly; but presently a gigantic sea happened to take us right under the counter, and bore us with it as it rose—up—up—as if into the sky. I would not have believed that any wave could rise so high. And then down we came with a sweep, a slide, and a plunge, that made me feel sick and dizzy, as if I was falling from some lofty mountain-top in a dream. But while we were up I had thrown a quick glance around—and that one glance was all sufficient. I saw our exact position in an instant. The Moskoe-ström whirlpool was about a quarter of a mile dead ahead—but no more like the every-day Moskoe-ström, than the whirl as you now see it is like a mill-race. If I had not known where we were, and what we had to expect, I should not have recognised the place at all. As it was, I involuntarily closed my eyes in horror. The lids clenched themselves together as if in a spasm.

"It could not have been more than two minutes afterward until we suddenly felt the waves subside, and were enveloped in foam. The boat made a sharp half turn to larboard, and then shot off in its new direction like a thunderbolt. At the same moment the roaring noise of the water was completely drowned in a kind of shrill shriek— such a sound as you might imagine given out by the waste-pipes of many thousand steam-vessels, letting off their steam all together. We were now in the belt of surf that always surrounds the whirl; and I thought, of course, that another moment would plunge us into the abyss—down which we could only see indistinctly on account of the amazing velocity with which we were borne along. The boat did not seem to sink into the water at all, but to skim like an air-bubble upon the surface of the surge. Her starboard side was next the whirl, and on the larboard arose the world of ocean we had left. It stood like a huge writhing wall between us and the horizon.

"It may appear strange, but now, when we were in the very jaws of the gulf, I felt more composed than when we were only approaching it. Having made up my mind to hope no more, I got rid of a great deal of that terror which unmanned me at first. I suppose it was despair that strung my nerves.

"It may look like boasting—but what I tell you is truth —I began to reflect how magnificent a thing it was to die in such a manner, and how foolish it was in me to think of so paltry a consideration as my own individual life, in view of so wonderful a manifestation of God's power. I do believe that I blushed with shame when this idea crossed my mind. After a little while I became possessed with the keenest curiosity about the whirl itself. I positively felt a *wish* to explore its depths, even at the sacrifice I was going to make; and my principal grief was that I should never be able to tell my old companions on shore about the mysteries I should see. These, no doubt, were singular fancies to occupy a man's mind in such extremity —and I have often thought since, that the revolutions of the boat around the pool might have rendered me a little light-headed.

"There was another circumstance which tended to restore my self-possession; and this was the cessation of the wind, which could not reach us in our present situation—for, as you saw yourself, the belt of surf is considerably lower than the general bed of the ocean, and this latter now towered above us, a high, black, mountainous ridge. If you have never been at sea in a heavy gale, you can form no idea of the confusion of mind occasioned by the wind and spray together. They blind, deafen, and strangle you, and take away all power of action or reflection. But we were now, in a great measure, rid of these annoyances—just as death-condemned felons in prison are allowed petty indulgences, forbidden them while their doom is yet uncertain.

"How often we made the circuit of the belt it is impossible to say. We careered round and round for perhaps an hour, flying rather than floating, getting gradually more and more into the middle of the surge, and then nearer and nearer to its horrible inner edge. All this time I had never let go of the ring-bolt. My brother was at the stern, holding on to a small empty water-cask which had been securely lashed under the coop of the counter, and was the only thing on deck that had not been swept overboard when the gale first took us. As we approached the brink of the pit he let go his hold upon this, and made for the ring, from which, in the agony of his terror, he endeavored to force my hands, as it was not large enough to afford us both a secure grasp. I never felt deeper grief than when I saw him attempt this act—although I knew he was a madman when he did it—a raving maniac through sheer fright. I did not care, however, to contest the point with him. I thought it could make no difference whether either of us held on at all; so I let him have the bolt, and went astern to the cask. This there was no great difficulty in doing; for the smack flew round steadily enough, and upon an even keel—only swaying to and fro, with the immense sweeps and swelters of the whirl. Scarcely had I secured myself in my new position, when we gave a wild lurch to starboard, and rushed headlong into the abyss. I muttered a hurried prayer to God, and thought all was over.

"As I felt the sickening sweep of the descent, I had instinctively tightened my hold upon the barrel, and closed my eyes. For some seconds I dared not open them—while I expected instant destruction, and wondered that I was not already in my death-struggles with the water. But moment after moment elapsed. I still lived. The sense of falling had ceased; and the motion of the vessel seemed much as it had been before while in the belt of foam, with the exception that she now lay more along. I took courage, and looked once again upon the scene.

"Never shall I forget the sensations of awe, horror, and admiration with which I gazed about me. The boat appeared to be hanging, as if by magic, midway down, upon the interior surface of a funnel vast in circumference, prodigious in depth, and whose perfectly smooth sides might have been mistaken for ebony, but for the bewildering rapidity with which they spun around, and for the gleaming and ghastly radiance they shot forth, as the rays of the full moon, from that circular rift amid the clouds which I have already described, streamed in a flood of golden glory along the black walls, and far away down into the inmost recesses of the abyss.

"At first I was too much confused to observe anything accurately. The general burst of terrific grandeur was all that I beheld. When I recovered myself a little, however, my gaze fell instinctively downward. In this direction I was able to obtain an unobstructed view, from the manner in which the smack hung on the inclined surface of the pool. She was quite upon an even keel—that is to say, her deck lay in a plane parallel with that of the water—but this latter sloped at an angle of more than forty-five degrees, so that we seemed to be lying upon our beam-ends. I could not help observing, nevertheless, that I had scarcely more difficulty in maintaining my hold and footing in this situation, than if we had been upon a dead level; and this, I suppose, was owing to the speed at which we revolved.

"The rays of the moon seemed to search the very bottom of the profound gulf; but still I could make out nothing distinctly, on account of a thick mist in which everything there was enveloped, and over which there hung a magnificent rainbow, like that narrow and tottering bridge which Mussulmen say is the only pathway between Time and Eternity. This mist, or spray, was no doubt occasioned by the clashing of the great walls of the funnel, as they all met together at the bottom—but the yell that went up to the Heavens from out of that mist, I dare not attempt to describe.

"Our first slide into the abyss itself, from the belt of foam above, had carried us a great distance down the slope; but our farther descent was by no means proportionate. Round and round we swept—not with any uniform movement—but in dizzying swings and jerks, that sent us sometimes only a few hundred feet—sometimes nearly the complete circuit of the whirl. Our progress downward, at each revolution, was slow, but very perceptible.

"Looking about me upon the wide waste of liquid ebony on which we were thus borne, I perceived that our boat was not the only object in the embrace of the whirl. Both above and below us were visible fragments of vessels, large masses of building timber and trunks of trees, with many smaller articles, such as pieces of house furniture, broken boxes, barrels and staves. I have already described the unnatural curiosity which had taken the place of my original terrors. It appeared to grow upon me as I drew nearer and nearer to my dreadful doom. I now began to watch, with a strange interest, the numerous things that floated in our company. I *must* have been delirious—for I even sought *amusement* in speculating upon the relative velocities of their several descents toward the foam below. 'This fir tree,' I found myself at one time saying, 'will certainly be the next thing that takes the awful plunge and disappears,'—and then I was disappointed to find that the wreck of a Dutch merchant ship overtook it and went down before. At length, after making several guesses of this nature, and being deceived in all—this fact—the fact of my invariable miscalculation—set me upon a train of reflection that made my limbs again tremble, and my heart beat heavily once more.

"It was not a new terror that thus affected me, but the dawn of a more exciting *hope*. This hope arose partly from memory, and partly from present observation. I called to mind the great variety of buoyant matter that strewed the coast of Lofoden, having been absorbed and then thrown forth by the Moskoe-ström. By far the greater number of the articles were shattered in the most extraordinary way—so chafed and roughened as to have the appearance of being stuck full of splinters—but then I distinctly recollected that there were *some* of them which were not disfigured at all. Now I could not account for this difference except by supposing that the roughened fragments were the only ones which had been *completely absorbed*—that the others had entered the whirl at so late a period of the tide, or, for some reason, had descended so slowly after entering, that they did not reach the bottom before the turn of the flood came, or of the ebb, as the case might be. I conceived it possible, in either instance, that they might thus be whirled up again to the level of the ocean, without undergoing the fate of those which had been drawn in more early, or absorbed more rapidly. I made, also, three important observations. The first was, that, as a general rule, the larger the bodies were, the more rapid their descent; the second, that, between two masses of equal extent, the one spherical, and the other *of any other shape*, the superiority in speed of descent was with the sphere; the third, that, between two masses of equal size, the one cylindrical, and the other of any other shape, the cylinder was absorbed the more slowly. Since my escape, I have had several conversations on this subject with an old school-master of the district; and it was from him that I learned the use of the words 'cylinder' and 'sphere.' He explained to me—although I have forgotten the explanation—how what I observed was, in fact, the natural consequence of the forms of the floating fragments—and showed me how it happened that a cylinder, swimming in a vortex, offered more resistance to its suction, and was drawn in with greater difficulty than an equally bulky body, of any form whatever.*

"There was one startling circumstance which went a great way in enforcing these observations, and rendering me anxious to turn them to account, and this was that, at every revolution, we passed something like a barrel, or else the broken yard or the mast of a vessel, while many of these things, which had been on our level when I first opened my eyes upon the wonders of the whirlpool, were now high up above us, and seemed to have moved but little from their original station.

"I no longer hesitated what to do. I resolved to lash myself securely to the water cask upon which I now held, to cut it loose from the counter, and to throw myself with it into the water. I attracted my brother's attention by signs, pointed to the floating barrels that came near us, and did everything in my power to make him understand what I was about to do. I thought at length that he comprehended my design—but, whether this was the case or not, he shook his head despairingly, and refused to move

* See Archimedes, "*De Incidentibus in Fluido.*"—lib. 2.

from his station by the ring-bolt. It was impossible to force him; the emergency admitted no delay; and so, with a bitter struggle, I resigned him to his fate, fastened myself to the cask by means of the lashings which secured it to the counter, and precipitated myself with it into the sea, without another moment's hesitation.

"The result was precisely what I had hoped it might be. As it is myself who now tell you this tale—as you see that I *did* escape—and as you are already in possession of the mode in which this escape was effected, and must therefore anticipate all that I have farther to say—I will bring my story quickly to conclusion. It might have been an hour, or thereabout, after my quitting the smack, when, having descended to a vast distance beneath me, it made three or four wild gyrations in rapid succession, and, bearing my loved brother with it, plunged headlong, at once and forever, into the chaos of foam below. The cask to which I was attached sank very little farther than half the distance between the bottom of the gulf and the spot at which I leaped overboard, before a great change took place in the character of the whirlpool. The slope of the sides of the vast funnel became momently less and less steep. The gyrations of the whirl grew, gradually, less and less violent. By degrees, the froth and the rainbow disappeared, and the bottom of the gulf seemed slowly to uprise. The sky was clear, the winds had gone down, and the full moon was setting radiantly in the west, when I found myself on the surface of the ocean, in full view of the shores of Lofoden, and above the spot where the pool of the Moskoeström *had been*. It was the hour of the slack—but the sea still heaved in mountainous waves from the effects of the hurricane. I was borne violently into the channel of the Ström, and in a few minutes was hurried down the coast into the 'grounds' of the fishermen. A boat picked me up—exhausted from fatigue—and (now that the danger was removed) speechless from the memory of its horror.

Those who drew me on board were my old mates and daily companions—but they knew me no more than they would have known a traveller from the spirit-land. My hair which had been raven-black the day before, was as white as you see it now. They say too that the whole expression of my countenance had changed. I told them my story. They did not believe it. I now tell it to *you*—and I can scarcely expect you to put more faith in it than did the merry fishermen of Lofoden."

THE COLLOQUY
OF MONOS AND UNA

Μελλοντα ταυτα

Sophocles—Antig:

These things are in the future.

Una. "Born again?"

Monos. Yes, fairest and best beloved Una, "born again." These were the words upon whose mystical meaning I had so long pondered, rejecting the explanations of the priesthood, until Death himself resolved for me the secret.

Una. Death!

Monos. How strangely, sweet Una, you echo my words! I observe, too, a vacillation in your step—a joyous inquietude in your eyes. You are confused and oppressed by the majestic novelty of the Life Eternal. Yes, it was of Death I spoke. And here how singularly sounds that word which of old was wont to bring terror to all hearts—throwing a mildew upon all pleasures!

Una. Ah, Death, the spectre which sate at all feasts! How often, Monos, did we lose ourselves in speculations upon its nature! How mysteriously did it act as a check

to human bliss—saying unto it "thus far, and no farther!"
That earnest mutual love, my own Monos, which burned
within our bosoms—how vainly did we flatter ourselves,
feeling happy in its first upspringing, that our happiness
would strengthen with its strength! Alas! as it grew, so
grew in our hearts the dread of that evil hour which was
hurrying to separate us forever! Thus, in time, it became
painful to love. Hate would have been mercy then.

Monos. Speak not here of these griefs, dear Una—mine,
mine forever now!

Una. But the memory of past sorrow—is it not present
joy? I have much to say yet of the things which have been.
Above all, I burn to know the incidents of your own
passage through the dark Valley and Shadow.

Monos. And when did the radiant Una ask anything of
her Monos in vain? I will be minute in relating all—but at
what point shall the weird narrative begin?

Una. At what point?

Monos. You have said.

Una. Monos, I comprehend you. In Death we have both
learned the propensity of man to define the indefinable.
I will not say, then, commence with the moment of life's
cessation—but commence with that sad, sad instant when,
the fever having abandoned you, you sank into a breathless
and motionless torpor, and I pressed down your pallid eyelids with the passionate fingers of love.

Monos. One word first, my Una, in regard to man's
general condition at this epoch. You will remember that
one or two of the wise among our forefathers—wise in fact,
although not in the world's esteem—had ventured to
doubt the propriety of the term "improvement," as applied to the progress of our civilization. There were periods in each of the five or six centuries immediately preceding our dissolution, when arose some vigorous intellect,
boldly contending for those principles whose truth appears
now, to our disenfranchised reason, so utterly obvious—

principles which should have taught our race to submit to the guidance of the natural laws, rather than attempt their control. At long intervals some master-minds appeared, looking upon each advance in practical science as a retrogradation in the true utility. Occasionally the poetic intellect—that intellect which we now feel to have been the most exalted of all—since those truths which to us were of the most enduring importance could only be reached by that *analogy* which speaks in proof-tones to the imagination alone, and to the unaided reason bears no weight—occasionally did this poetic intellect proceed a step farther in the evolving of the vague idea of the philosophic, and find in the mystic parable that tells of the tree of knowledge, and of its forbidden fruit, death-producing, a distinct intimation that knowledge was not meet for man in the infant condition of his soul. And these men—the poets—living and perishing amid the scorn of the "utilitarians"—of rough pedants, who arrogated to themselves a title which could have been properly applied only to the scorned—these men, the poets, pondered piningly, yet not unwisely, upon the ancient days when our wants were not more simple than our enjoyments were keen—days when *mirth* was a word unknown, so solemnly deep-toned was happiness—holy, august and blissful days, when blue rivers ran undammed, between hills unhewn, into far forest solitudes, primæval, odorous, and unexplored.

Yet these noble exceptions from the general misrule served but to strengthen it by opposition. Alas! we had fallen upon the most evil of all our evil days. The great "movement"—that was the cant term—went on: a diseased commotion, moral and physical. Art—the Arts—arose supreme, and, once enthroned, cast chains upon the intellect which had elevated them to power. Man, because he could not but acknowledge the majesty of Nature, fell into childish exultation at his acquired and still-increasing dominion over her elements. Even while he stalked a God in his own fancy, an infantine imbecility came over him. As might be supposed from the origin of his disorder, he grew infected with system, and with abstraction. He enwrapped himself in generalities. Among other odd ideas, that of universal equality gained ground; and in the face of analogy and of God—in despite of the loud warning voice of the laws of *gradation* so visibly pervading all things in Earth and Heaven—wild attempts at an omni-prevalent Democracy were made. Yet this evil sprang necessarily from the leading evil, Knowledge. Man could not both know and succumb. Meantime huge smoking cities arose, innumerable. Green leaves shrank before the hot breath of furnaces. The fair face of Nature was deformed as with the ravages of some loathsome disease. And methinks, sweet Una, even our slumbering sense of the forced and of the far-fetched might have arrested us here. But now it appears that we had worked out our own destruction in the perversion of our *taste*, or rather in the blind neglect of its culture in the schools. For, in truth, it was at this crisis that taste alone—that faculty which, holding a middle position between the pure intellect and the moral sense, could never safely have been disregarded—it was now that taste alone could have led us gently back to Beauty, to Nature, and to Life. But alas for the pure contemplative spirit and majestic intuition of Plato! Alas for the μονσικη which he justly regarded as an all-sufficient education for the soul! Alas for him and for it!—since both were most desperately needed when both were most entirely forgotten or despised.*

* "It will be hard to discover a better [method of education] than that which the experience of so many ages has already discovered; and this may be summed up as consisting in gymnastics for the body, and *music* for the soul."—Repub. lib. 2. "For this reason is a musical education most essential; since it causes Rhythm and Harmony to penetrate most intimately into the soul, taking the strongest hold upon it, filling it with *beauty* and making the man *beautiful-minded*. . . . . He will praise and admire *the beautiful*; will receive it with joy into his soul, will

Pascal, a philosopher whom we both love, has said, how truly!—*"que tout notre raisonnement se rèduit à céder au sentiment"*; and it is not impossible that the sentiment of the natural, had time permitted it, would have regained its old ascendancy over the harsh mathematical reason of the schools. But this thing was not to be. Prematurely induced by intemperance of knowledge, the old age of the world drew on. This the mass of mankind saw not, or, living lustily although unhappily, affected not to see. But, for myself, the Earth's records had taught me to look for widest ruin as the price of highest civilization. I had imbibed a prescience of our Fate from comparison of China the simple and enduring, with Assyria the architect, with Egypt the astrologer, with Nubia, more crafty than either, the turbulent mother of all Arts. In history† of these regions I met with a ray from the Future. The individual artificialities of the three latter were local diseases of the Earth, and in their individual overthrows we had seen local remedies applied; but for the infected world at large I could anticipate no regeneration save in death. That man, as a race, should not become extinct, I saw that he must be *"born again."*

And now it was, fairest and dearest, that we wrapped our spirits, daily, in dreams. Now it was that, in twilight, we discoursed of the days to come, when the Art-scarred surface of the Earth, having undergone that purification* which alone could efface its rectangular obscenities, should

---

feed upon it, and *assimilate his own condition with it.*"—Ibid. lib. 3. Music (μουσικη) had, however, among the Athenians, a far more comprehensive signification than with us. It included not only the harmonies of time and of tune, but the poetic diction, sentiment and creation, each in its widest sense. The study of *music* was with them, in fact, the general cultivation of the taste —of that which recognizes the beautiful—in contra-distinction from reason, which deals with only the true.

† "History," from ιστορειν, to contemplate.

* The word *"purification"* seems here to be used with reference to its root in the Greek πυρ, fire.

clothe itself anew in the verdure and the mountain-slopes and the smiling waters of Paradise, and be rendered at length a fit dwelling-place for man:—for man the Death-purged—for man to whose now exalted intellect there should be poison in knowledge no more—for the redeemed, regenerated, blissful, and now immortal, but still for the *material*, man.

Una. Well do I remember these conversations, dear Monos; but the epoch of the fiery overthrow was not so near at hand as we believed, and as the corruption you indicate did surely warrant us in believing. Men lived; and died individually. You yourself sickened, and passed into the grave; and thither your constant Una speedily followed you. And though the century which has since elapsed, and whose conclusion brings us thus together once more, tortured our slumbering senses with no impatience of duration, yet, my Monos, it was a century still.

Monos. Say, rather, a point in the vague infinity. Unquestionably, it was in the Earth's dotage that I died. Wearied at heart with anxieties which had their origin in the general turmoil and decay, I succumbed to the fierce fever. After some few days of pain, and many of dreamy delirium replete with ecstasy, the manifestations of which you mistook for pain, while I longed but was impotent to undeceive you—after some days there came upon me, as you have said, a breathless and motionless torpor; and this was termed *Death* by those who stood around me.

Words are vague things. My condition did not deprive me of sentience. It appeared to me not greatly dissimilar to the extreme quiescence of him, who, having slumbered long and profoundly, lying motionless and fully prostrate in a midsummer noon, begins to steal slowly back into consciousness, through the mere sufficiency of his sleep, and without being awakened by external disturbances.

I breathed no longer. The pulses were still. The heart had ceased to beat. Volition had not departed, but was powerless. The senses were unusually active, although eccentrically so—assuming often each other's functions at random. The taste and the smell were inextricably confounded, and became one sentiment, abnormal and intense. The rose-water with which your tenderness had moistened my lips to the last, affected me with sweet fancies of flowers—fantastic flowers, far more lovely than any of the old Earth, but whose prototypes we have here blooming around us. The eyelids, transparent and bloodless, offered no complete impediment to vision. As volition was in abeyance, the balls could not roll in their sockets—but all objects within the range of the visual hemisphere were seen with more or less distinctness; the rays which fell upon the external retina, or into the corner of the eye, producing a more vivid effect than those which struck the front or interior surface. Yet, in the former instance, this effect was so far anomalous that I appreciated it only as *sound*—sound sweet or discordant as the matters presenting themselves at my side were light or dark in shade —curved or angular in outline. The hearing, at the same time, although excited in degree, was not irregular in action—estimating real sounds with an extravagance of precision, not less than of sensibility. Touch had undergone a modification more peculiar. Its impressions were tardily received, but pertinaciously retained, and resulted always in the highest physical pleasure. Thus the pressure of your sweet fingers upon my eyelids, at first only recognised through vision, at length, long after their removal, filled my whole being with a sensual delight immeasurable. I say with a sensual delight. *All* my perceptions were purely sensual. The materials furnished the passive brain by the senses were not in the least degree wrought into shape by the deceased understanding. Of pain there was some little; of pleasure there was much; but of moral pain or pleasure none at all. Thus your wild sobs floated into my ear with all their mournful cadences, and were appreciated in their every variation of sad tone; but they were soft musical sounds and no more; they conveyed to the extinct reason no intimation of the sorrows which gave them birth; while the large and constant tears which fell upon my face, telling the bystanders of a heart which broke, thrilled every fibre of my frame with ecstasy alone. And this was in truth the *Death* of which these bystanders spoke reverently, in low whispers—you, sweet Una, gaspingly, with loud cries.

They attired me for the coffin—three or four dark figures which flitted busily to and fro. As these crossed the direct line of my vision they affected me as *forms*; but upon passing to my side their images impressed me with the idea of shrieks, groans, and other dismal expressions of terror, of horror, or of woe. You alone, habited in a white robe, passed in all directions musically about me.

The day waned; and, as its light faded away, I became possessed by a vague uneasiness—an anxiety such as the sleeper feels when sad real sounds fall continuously within his ear—low distant bell-tones, solemn, at long but equal intervals, and commingling with melancholy dreams. Night arrived; and with its shadows a heavy discomfort. It oppressed my limbs with the oppression of some dull weight, and was palpable. There was also a moaning sound, not unlike the distant reverberation of surf, but more continuous, which, beginning with the first twilight, had grown in strength with the darkness. Suddenly lights were brought into the room, and this reverberation became forthwith interrupted into frequent unequal bursts of the same sound, but less dreary and less distinct. The ponderous oppression was in a great measure relieved; and, issuing from the flame of each lamp, (for there were many,) there flowed unbrokenly into my ears a strain of melodious monotone. And when now, dear Una, approaching the bed upon which I lay outstretched, you sat gently by my side, breathing odor from your sweet lips, and pressing them upon my brow, there arose tremulously within my bosom, and mingling with the merely physical sensations which circumstances had called forth, a something akin to sentiment itself—a feeling that, half appreciating, half responded to your earnest love and sorrow; but this feeling took no root in the pulseless heart, and seemed indeed rather a shadow than a reality, and faded quickly away, first into extreme quiescence, and then into a purely sensual pleasure as before.

And now, from the wreck and the chaos of the usual senses, there appeared to have arisen within me a sixth, all perfect. In its exercise I found a wild delight—yet a delight still physical, inasmuch as the understanding had in it no part. Motion in the animal frame had fully ceased. No muscle quivered; no nerve thrilled; no artery throbbed. But there seemed to have sprung up in the brain, *that* of which no words could convey to the merely human intelligence even an indistinct conception. Let me term it a mental pendulous pulsation. It was the moral embodiment of man's abstract idea of *Time*. By the absolute equalization of this movement—or of such as this—had the cycles of the firmamental orbs themselves, been adjusted. By its aid I measured the irregularities of the clock upon the mantel, and of the watches of the attendants. Their tickings came sonorously to my ears. The slightest deviations from the true proportion—and these deviations were omni-prævalent —affected me just as violations of abstract truth were wont, on earth, to affect the moral sense. Although no two of the time-pieces in the chamber struck the individual seconds accurately together, yet I had no difficulty in holding steadily in mind the tones, and the respective momentary errors of each. And this—this keen, perfect, self-existing sentiment of *duration*—this sentiment existing (as man could not possibly have conceived it to exist) independently of any succession of events—this idea—this sixth sense, upspringing from the ashes of the rest, was the first obvious and certain step of the intemporal soul upon the threshold of the temporal Eternity.

It was midnight; and you still sat by my side. All others had departed from the chamber of Death. They had deposited me in the coffin. The lamps burned flickeringly; for this I knew by the tremulousness of the monotonous strains. But, suddenly these strains diminished in distinctness and in volume. Finally they ceased. The perfume in my nostrils died away. Forms affected my vision no longer. The oppression of the Darkness uplifted itself from my bosom. A dull shock like that of electricity pervaded my frame, and was followed by total loss of the idea of contact. All of what man has termed sense was merged in the sole consciousness of entity, and in the one abiding sentiment of duration. The mortal body had been at length stricken with the hand of the deadly *Decay*.

Yet had not all of sentience departed; for the consciousness and the sentiment remaining supplied some of its functions by a lethargic intuition. I appreciated the direful change now in operation upon the flesh, and, as the dreamer is sometimes aware of the bodily presence of one who leans over him, so, sweet Una, I still dully felt that you sat by my side. So, too, when the noon of the second day came, I was not unconscious of those movements which displaced you from my side, which confined me within the coffin, which deposited me within the hearse, which bore me to the grave, which lowered me within it, which heaped heavily the mould upon me, and which thus left me, in blackness and corruption, to my sad and solemn slumbers with the worm.

And here, in the prison-house which has few secrets to disclose, there rolled away days and weeks and months; and the soul watched narrowly each second as it flew, and, without effort, took record of its flight—without effort and without object.

A year passed. The consciousness of *being* had grown hourly more indistinct, and that of mere *locality* had, in great measure, usurped its position. The idea of entity was becoming merged in that of *place*. The narrow space immediately surrounding what had been the body, was now growing to be the body itself. At length, as often happens to the sleeper (by sleep and its world alone is *Death* imaged)—at length, as sometimes happened on Earth to the deep slumberer, when some flitting light half startled him into awakening, yet left him half enveloped in dreams—so to me, in the strict embrace of the *Shadow*, came *that* light which alone might have had power to startle—the light of enduring *Love*. Men toiled at the grave in which I lay darkling. They upthrew the damp earth. Upon my mouldering bones there descended the coffin of Una.

And now again all was void. That nebulous light had been extinguished. That feeble thrill had vibrated itself into quiescence. Many *lustra* had supervened. Dust had returned to dust. The worm had food no more. The sense of being had at length utterly departed, and there reigned in its stead—instead of all things—dominant and perpetual—the autocrats *Place* and *Time*. For *that* which *was not*—for that which had no form—for that which had no thought—for that which had no sentience—for that which was soulless, yet of which matter formed no portion—for all this nothingness, yet for all this immortality, the grave was still a home, and the corrosive hours, co-mates.

NEVER BET THE DEVIL YOUR HEAD

A TALE WITH A MORAL.

"Con tal que las costumbres de un autor," says Don Thomas De Las Torres, in the preface to his "Amatory Poems" *"sean puras y castas, importo muy poco que no sean igualmente severas sus obras"*—meaning, in plain English, that, provided the morals of an author are pure, personally, it signifies nothing what are the morals of his books. We presume that Don Thomas is now in Purgatory for the assertion. It would be a clever thing, too, in the way of poetical justice, to keep him there until his "Amatory Poems" get out of print, or are laid definitely upon the shelf through lack of readers. Every fiction *should have* a moral; and, what is more to the purpose, the critics have discovered that every fiction *has*. Philip Melancthon, some time ago, wrote a commentary upon the "Batrachomyomachia" and proved that the poet's object was to excite a distaste for sedition. Pierre La Seine, going a step farther, shows that the intention was to recommend to young men temperance in eating and drinking. Just so, too, Jacobus Hugo has satisfied himself that, by Euenis, Homer meant to insinuate John Calvin; by Antinöus, Martin Luther; by the Lotophagi, Protestants in general; and, by the Harpies, the Dutch. Our more modern Scholiasts are equally acute. These fellows demonstrate a hidden meaning in "The Antediluvians," a parable in "Powhatan," new views in "Cock Robin," and transcendentalism in "Hop O' My Thumb." In short, it has been shown that no man can sit down to write with-

out a very profound design. Thus to authors in general much trouble is spared. A novelist, for example, need have no care of his moral. It is there—that is to say it is somewhere—and the moral and the critics can take care of themselves. When the proper time arrives, all that the gentleman intended, and all that he did not intend, will be brought to light, in the "Dial," or the "Down-Easter," together with all that he ought to have intended, and the rest that he clearly meant to intend:—so that it will all come very straight in the end.

There is no just ground, therefore, for the charge brought against me by certain ignoramuses—that I have never written a moral tale, or, in more precise words, a tale with a moral. They are not the critics predestined to bring me out, and *develop* my morals:—that is the secret. By and by the "North American Quarterly Humdrum" will make them ashamed of their stupidity. In the meantime, by way of staying execution—by way of mitigating the accusations against me—I offer the sad history appended;—a history about whose obvious moral there can be no question whatever, since he who runs may read it in the large capitals which form the title of the tale. I should have credit for this arrangement—a far wiser one than that of La Fontaine and others, who reserve the impression to be conveyed until the last moment, and thus sneak it in at the fag end of their fables.

Defuncti injuriá ne afficiantur was a law of the twelve tables, and *De mortuis nil nisi bonum* is an excellent injunction—even if the dead in question be nothing but dead small beer. It is not my design, therefore, to vituperate my deceased friend, Toby Dammit. He was a sad dog, it is true, and a dog's death it was that he died; but he himself was not to blame for his vices. They grew out of a personal defect in his mother. She did her best in the way of flogging him while an infant—for duties to her well-regulated mind were always pleasures, and babies, like tough steaks, or the modern Greek olive trees, are invariably the better for beating—but, poor woman! she had the misfortune to be left-handed, and a child flogged left-handedly had better be left unflogged. The world revolves from right to left. It will not do to whip a baby from left to right. If each blow in the proper direction drives an evil propensity out, it follows that every thump in an opposite one knocks its quota of wickedness in. I was often present at Toby's chastisements, and, even by the way in which he kicked, I could perceive that he was getting worse and worse every day. At last I saw, through the tears in my eyes, that there was no hope of the villain at all, and one day when he had been cuffed until he grew so black in the face that one might have mistaken him for a little African, and no effect had been produced beyond that of making him wriggle himself into a fit, I could stand it no longer, but went down upon my knees forthwith, and, uplifting my voice, made prophecy of his ruin.

The fact is that his precocity in vice was awful. At five months of age he used to get into such passions that he was unable to articulate. At six months, I caught him gnawing a pack of cards. At seven months he was in the constant habit of catching and kissing the female babies. At eight months he peremptorily refused to put his signature to the Temperance pledge. Thus he went on increasing in iniquity, month after month, until, at the close of the first year, he not only insisted upon wearing *moustaches*, but had contracted a propensity for cursing and swearing, and for backing his assertions by bets.

Through this latter most ungentlemanly practice, the ruin which I had predicted to Toby Dammit overtook him at last. The fashion had "grown with his growth and strengthened with his strength," so that, when he came to be a man, he could scarcely utter a sentence without interlarding it with a proposition to gamble. Not that he actually *laid* wagers—no. I will do my friend the justice to say that he would as soon have laid eggs. With him the thing was a mere formula—nothing more. His expressions on this head had no meaning attached to them whatever. They were simple if not altogether innocent expletives— imaginative phrases wherewith to round off a sentence. When he said "I'll bet you so and so," nobody ever thought of taking him up; but still I could not help thinking it my duty to put him down. The habit was an immoral one, and so I told him. It was a vulgar one—this I begged him to believe. It was discountenanced by society —here I said nothing but the truth. It was forbidden by act of Congress—here I had not the slightest intention of telling a lie. I remonstrated—but to no purpose. I demonstrated—in vain. I entreated—he smiled. I implored—he laughed. I preached—he sneered. I threatened—he swore. I kicked him—he called for the police. I pulled his nose— he blew it, and offered to bet the Devil his head that I would not venture to try that experiment again.

Poverty was another vice which the peculiar physical deficiency of Dammit's mother had entailed upon her son. He was detestably poor; and this was the reason, no doubt, that his expletive expressions about betting, seldom took a pecuniary turn. I will not be bound to say that I ever heard him make use of such a figure of speech as "I'll bet you a dollar." It was usually "I'll bet you what you please," or "I'll bet you what you dare," or "I'll bet you a trifle," or else, more significantly still, *"I'll bet the Devil my head."*

This latter form seemed to please him best:—perhaps because it involved the least risk; for Dammit had become excessively parsimonious. Had any one taken him up, his head was small, and thus his loss would have been small too. But these are my own reflections, and I am by no means sure that I am right in attributing them to him. At all events the phrase in question grew daily in favor, notwithstanding the gross impropriety of a man's betting his brains like banknotes:—but this was a point which my friend's perversity of disposition would not permit him to comprehend. In the end, he abandoned all other forms of wager, and gave himself up to *"I'll bet the Devil my head,"* with a pertinacity and exclusiveness of devotion that displeased not less than it surprised me. I am always displeased by circumstances for which I cannot account. Mysteries force a man to think, and so injure his health. The truth is, there was something in *the air* with which Mr. Dammit was wont to give utterance to his offensive expression—something in his *manner* of enunciation—which at first interested, and afterwards made me very uneasy—something which, for want of a more definite term at present, I must be permitted to call *queer*; but which Mr. Coleridge would have called mystical, Mr. Kant pantheistical, Mr. Carlyle twistical, and Mr. Emerson hyperquizzitistical. I began not to like it at all. Mr. Dammit's soul was in a perilous state. I resolved to bring all my eloquence into play to save it. I vowed to serve him as St. Patrick, in the Irish chronicle, is said to have served the toad, that is to say, "awaken him to a sense of his situation." I addressed myself to the task forthwith. Once more I betook myself to remonstrate. Again I collected my energies for a final attempt at expostulation.

When I had made an end of my lecture, Mr. Dammit indulged himself in some very equivocal behaviour. For some moments he remained silent, merely looking me inquisitively in the face. But presently he threw his head to one side, and elevated his eyebrows to great extent. Then he spread out the palms of his hands and shrugged up his shoulders. Then he winked with the right eye. Then he repeated the operation with the left. Then he shut them both up very tight. Then he opened them both so very wide that I became seriously alarmed for the consequences. Then, applying his thumb to his nose, he thought proper to make an indescribable movement with the rest of his fingers. Finally, setting his arms a-kimbo, he condescended to reply.

I can call to mind only the heads of his discourse. He would be obliged to me if I would hold my tongue. He wished none of my advice. He despised all my insinuations. He was old enough to take care of himself. Did I still think him baby Dammit? Did I mean to say anything against his character? Did I intend to insult him? Was I a fool? Was my maternal parent aware, in a word, of my absence from the domiciliary residence? He would put this latter question to me as to a man of veracity, and he would bind himself to abide by my reply. Once more he would demand explicitly if my mother knew that I was out. My confusion, he said, betrayed me, and he would be willing to bet the Devil his head that she did not.

Mr. Dammit did not pause for my rejoinder. Turning upon his heel, he left my presence with undignified precipitation. It was well for him that he did so. My feelings had been wounded. Even my anger had been aroused. For once I would have taken him up upon his insulting wager. I would have won for the Arch-Enemy Mr. Dammit's little head—for the fact is, my mamma *was* very well aware of my merely temporary absence from home.

But *Khoda shefa midêhed*—Heaven gives relief—as the Musselmen say when you tread upon their toes. It was in pursuance of my duty that I had been insulted, and I bore the insult like a man. It now seemed to me, however, that I had done all that could be required of me, in the case of this miserable individual, and I resolved to trouble him no longer with my counsel, but to leave him to his conscience and himself. But although I forebore to intrude with my advice, I could not bring myself to give up his society altogether. I even went so far as to humor some of his less reprehensible propensities; and there were times when I found myself lauding his wicked jokes, as epicures do mustard, with tears in my eyes:—so profoundly did it grieve me to hear his evil talk.

One fine day, having strolled out together arm in arm, our route led us in the direction of a river. There was a bridge, and we resolved to cross it. It was roofed over, by way of protection from the weather, and the arch-way, having but few windows, was thus very uncomfortably dark. As we entered the passage, the contrast between the external glare, and the interior gloom, struck heavily upon my spirits. Not so upon those of the unhappy Dammit, who offered to bet the Devil his head that I was hipped. He seemed to be in an unusual good humor. He was excessively lively—so much so that I entertained I know not what of uneasy suspicion. It is not impossible that he was affected with the transcendentals. I am not well enough versed, however, in the diagnosis of this disease to speak with decision upon the point; and unhappily there were none of my friends of the "Dial" present. I suggest the idea, nevertheless, because of a certain species of austere Merry-Andrewism which seemed to beset my poor friend, and caused him to make quite a Tom-Fool of himself. Nothing would serve him but wriggling and skipping about under and over everything that came in his way; now shouting out, and now lisping out, all manner of odd little and big words, yet preserving the gravest face in the world all the time. I really could not make up my mind whether to kick or to pity him. At length, having passed nearly across the bridge, we approached the termination of the foot-way, when our progress was impeded by a turnstile of some height. Through this I made my way quietly, pushing it around as usual. But this turn would not serve the turn of Mr. Dammit. He insisted upon leaping the stile, and said he could cut a pigeon-wing over it in the air. Now this, con-

scientiously speaking, I did not think he could do. The
best pigeon-winger over all kinds of style, was my friend
Mr. Carlyle, and as I knew *he* could not do it, I would
not believe it could be done by Toby Dammit. I therefore
told him, in so many words, that he was a braggadocio,
and could not do what he said. For this, I had reason to
be sorry afterwards;—for he straightway offered to *bet the
Devil his head* that he could.

I was about to reply, notwithstanding my previous
resolutions, with some remonstrance against his impiety,
when I heard, close at my elbow, a slight cough, which
sounded very much like the ejaculation *"ahem!"* I started,
and looked about me in surprise. My glance at length
fell into a nook of the frame-work of the bridge, and
upon the figure of a little lame old gentleman of venerable
aspect. Nothing could be more reverend than his whole
appearance; for he not only had on a full suit of black,
but his shirt was perfectly clean and the collar turned
very neatly down over a white cravat, while his hair was
parted in front like a girl's. His hands were clasped pen-
sively together over his stomach, and his two eyes were
carefully rolled up into the top of his head.

Upon observing him more closely, I perceived that he
wore a black silk apron over his small-clothes; and this
was a thing which I thought very odd. Before I had time
to make any remark, however, upon so singular a circumstance, he interrupted me with a second *"ahem!"*

To this observation I was not immediately prepared to
reply. The fact is, remarks of this laconic nature are nearly
unanswerable. I have known a Quarterly Review *non-
plused* by the word *"Fudge!"* I am not ashamed to say,
therefore, that I turned to Mr. Dammit for assistance.

"Dammit," said I, "what are you about? don't you
hear?—the gentleman says *'ahem!'* " I looked sternly at
my friend while I thus addressed him; for to say the truth,

I felt particularly puzzled, and when a man is particularly puzzled he must knit his brows and look savage, or else he is pretty sure to look like a fool.

"Dammit," observed I—although this sounded very much like an oath, than which nothing was farther from my thoughts—"Dammit," I suggested—"the gentleman says '*ahem!*' "

I do not attempt to defend my remark on the score of profundity; I did not think it profound myself; but I have noticed that the effect of our speeches is not always proportionate with their importance in our own eyes; and if I had shot Mr. D. through and through with a Paixhan bomb, or knocked him in the head with the "Poets and Poetry of America," he could hardly have been more discomfited than when I addressed him with those simple words—"Dammit, what are you about?—don't you hear? —the gentleman says '*ahem!*' "

"You don't say so?" gasped he at length, after turning more colors than a pirate runs up, one after the other, when chased by a man-of-war. "Are you quite sure he said *that?* Well, at all events I am in for it now, and may as well put a bold face upon the matter. Here goes, then —*ahem!*"

At this the little old gentleman seemed pleased—God only knows why. He left his station at the nook of the bridge, limped forward with a gracious air, took Dammit by the hand and shook it cordially, looking all the while straight up in his face with an air of the most unadulterated benignity which it is possible for the mind of man to imagine.

"I am quite sure you will win it, Dammit," said he with the frankest of all smiles, "but we are obliged to have a trial you know, for the sake of mere form."

"Ahem!" replied my friend, taking off his coat with a deep sigh, tying a pocket-hankerchief around his waist, and producing an unaccountable alteration in his coun-

tenance by twisting up his eyes, and bringing down the
corners of his mouth—"ahem!" And "ahem," said he
again, after a pause; and not another word more than
"ahem!" did I ever know him to say after that. "Aha!"
thought I, without expressing myself aloud—"this is quite
a remarkable silence on the part of Toby Dammit, and
is no doubt a consequence of his verbosity upon a previous occasion. One extreme induces another. I wonder
if he has forgotten the many unanswerable questions
which he propounded to me so fluently on the day when
I gave him my last lecture? At all events, he is cured of
the transcendentals."

"Ahem!" here replied Toby, just as if he had been
reading my thoughts, and looking like a very old sheep
in a reverie.

The old gentleman now took him by the arm, and led
him more into the shade of the bridge—a few paces back
from the turnstile. "My good fellow," said he, "I make it
a point of conscience to allow you this much run. Wait
here, till I take my place by the stile, so that I may see
whether you go over it handsomely, and transcendentally,
and don't omit any flourishes of the pigeon-wing. A mere
form, you know. I will say 'one, two, three, and away.'
Mind you start at the word 'away.' " Here he took his
position by the stile, paused a moment as if in profound
reflection, then *looked up* and, I thought, smiled very
slightly, then tightened the strings of his apron, then took
a long look at Dammit, and finally gave the word as
agreed upon—

One—two—three—and away!

Punctually, at the word "away," my poor friend set off
in a strong gallop. The stile was not very high, like Mr.
Lord's—nor yet very low, like that of Mr. Lord's reviewe-
ers, but upon the whole I made sure that he would clear
it. And then what if he did not?—ah, that was the ques-

tion—what if he did not? "What right," said I, "had the old gentleman to make any other gentleman jump? The little old dot-and-carry-one! who is *he*? If he asks *me* to jump, I won't do it, that's flat, and I don't care who *the devil he is*." The bridge, as I say, was arched and covered in, in a very ridiculous manner, and there was a most uncomfortable echo about it at all times—an echo which I never before so particularly observed as when I uttered the four last words of my remark.

But what I said, or what I thought, or what I heard, occupied only an instant. In less than five seconds from his starting, my poor Toby had taken the leap. I saw him run nimbly, and spring grandly from the floor of the bridge, cutting the most awful flourishes with his legs as he went up. I saw him high in the air, pigeon-winging it to admiration just over the top of the stile; and of course I thought it an unusually singular thing that he did not *continue* to go over. But the whole leap was the affair of a moment, and, before I had a chance to make any profound reflection, down came Mr. Dammit on the flat of his back, on the same side of the stile from which he had started. In the same instant I saw the old gentleman limping off at the top of his speed, having caught and wrapped up in his apron something that fell heavily into it from the darkness of the arch just over the turnstile. At all this I was much astonished; but I had no leisure to think, for Mr. Dammit lay particularly still, and I concluded that his feelings had been hurt, and that he stood in need of my assistance. I hurried up to him and found that he had received what might be termed a serious injury. The truth is, he had been deprived of his head, which after a close search I could not find anywhere;—so I determined to take him home, and send for the homœopathists. In the mean time a thought struck me, and I threw open an adjacent window of the bridge; when the sad truth flashed upon me at once. About five feet just above the top of the turnstile, and crossing the arch of the foot-path so as to constitute a brace, there extended a flat iron bar, lying with its breadth horizontally, and forming one of a series that served to strengthen the structure throughout its extent. With the edge of this brace it appeared evident that the neck of my unfortunate friend had come precisely in contact.

He did not long survive his terrible loss. The homœopathists did not give him little enough physic, and what little they did give him he hesitated to take. So in the end he grew worse, and at length died, a lesson to all riotous livers. I bedewed his grave with my tears, worked a *bar sinister* on his family escutcheon, and, for the general expenses of his funeral, sent in my very moderate bill to the transcendentalists. The scoundrels refused to pay it, so I had Mr. Dammit dug up at once, and sold him for dog's meat.

THE OVAL PORTRAIT

The chateau into which my valet had ventured to make forcible entrance, rather than permit me, in my desperately wounded condition, to pass a night in the open air, was one of those piles of commingled gloom and grandeur which have so long frowned among the Appenines, not less in fact than in the fancy of Mrs. Radcliffe. To all appearance it had been temporarily and very lately abandoned. We established ourselves in one of the smallest and least sumptuously furnished apartments. It lay in a remote turret of the building. Its decorations were rich, yet tattered and antique. Its walls were hung with tapestry and bedecked with manifold and multiform armorial trophies, together with an unusually great number of very spirited modern paintings in frames of rich golden arabesque. In these paintings, which depended from the walls not only in their main surfaces, but in very many nooks which the bizarre architecture of the chateau rendered necessary—in these paintings my incipient delirium, perhaps, had caused me to take deep interest; so that I bade Pedro to close the heavy shutters of the room—since it was already night—to light the tongues of a tall candelabrum which stood by the head of my bed—and to throw open far and wide the fringed curtains of black velvet which enveloped the bed itself. I wished all this done that I might resign myself, if not to sleep, at least alternately to the contemplation of these pictures, and the perusal of a small volume which had been found upon the pillow, and which purported to criticise and describe them.

Long—long I read—and devoutly, devotedly I gazed. Rapidly and gloriously the hours flew by, and the deep midnight came. The position of the candelabrum displeased me, and outreaching my hand with difficulty, rather than disturb my slumbering valet, I placed it so as to throw its rays more fully upon the book.

But the action produced an effect altogether unanticipated. The rays of the numerous candles (for there were many) now fell within a niche of the room which had hitherto been thrown into deep shade by one of the bedposts. I thus saw in vivid light a picture all unnoticed before. It was the portrait of a young girl just ripening into womanhood. I glanced at the painting hurriedly, and then closed my eyes. Why I did this was not at first apparent even to my own perception. But while my lids remained thus shut, I ran over in mind my reason for so shutting them. It was an impulsive movement to gain time for thought—to make sure that my vision had not deceived me—to calm and subdue my fancy for a more sober and more certain gaze. In a very few moments I again looked fixedly at the painting.

That I now saw aright I could not and would not doubt; for the first flashing of the candles upon that canvas had seemed to dissipate the dreamy stupor which was stealing over my senses, and startle me at once into waking life.

The portrait, I have already said, was that of a young girl. It was a mere head and shoulders, done in what is technically termed a *vignette* manner; much in the style of the favorite heads of Sully. The arms, the bosom and even the ends of the radiant hair, melted imperceptibly into the vague yet deep shadow which formed the background of the whole. The frame was oval, richly gilded and filagreed in *Moresque*. As a thing of art nothing could be more admirable than the painting itself. But it could have been neither the execution of the work, nor the immortal beauty of the countenance, which had so suddenly and so vehemently moved me. Least of all, could it have been that my fancy, shaken from its half slumber, had mistaken the head for that of a living person. I saw at once that the peculiarities of the design, of the *vignetting*, and of the frame, must have instantly dispelled such idea —must have prevented even its momentary entertainment. Thinking earnestly upon these points, I remained, for an hour perhaps, half sitting, half reclining, with my vision riveted upon the portrait. At length, satisfied with the true secret of its effect, I fell back within the bed. I had found the spell of the picture in an absolute *lifelikeliness* of expression, which at first startling, finally confounded, subdued and appalled me. With deep and reverent awe I replaced the candelabrum in its former position. The cause of my deep agitation being thus shut from view, I sought eagerly the volume which discussed the paintings and their histories. Turning to the number which designated the oval portrait, I there read the vague and quaint words which follow:

"She was a maiden of rarest beauty, and not more

lovely than full of glee. And evil was the hour when she saw, and loved, and wedded the painter. He, passionate, studious, austere, and having already a bride in his Art: she a maiden of rarest beauty, and not more lovely than full of glee: all light and smiles, and frolicksome as the young fawn: loving and cherishing all things: hating only the Art which was her rival: dreading only the pallet and brushes and other untoward instruments which deprived her of the countenance of her lover. It was thus a terrible thing for this lady to hear the painter speak of his desire to portray even his young bride. But she was humble and obedient, and sat meekly for many weeks in the dark high turret-chamber where the light dripped upon the pale canvas only from overhead. But he, the painter, took glory in his work, which went on from hour to hour and from day to day. And he was a passionate, and wild and moody man, who became lost in reveries; so that he *would* not see that the light which fell so ghastlily in that lone turret withered the health and the spirits of his bride, who pined visibly to all but him. Yet she smiled on and still on, uncomplainingly, because she saw that the painter, (who had high renown,) took a fervid and burning pleasure in his task, and wrought day and night to depict her who so loved him, yet who grew daily more dispirited and weak. And in sooth some who beheld the portrait spoke of its resemblance in low words, as of a mighty marvel, and a proof not less of the power of the painter than of his deep love for her whom he depicted so surpassingly well. But at length, as the labor drew nearer to its conclusion, there were admitted none into the turret; for the painter had grown wild with the ardor of his work, and turned his eyes from the canvas rarely, even to regard the countenance of his wife. And he *would* not see that the tints which he spread upon the canvas were drawn from the cheeks of her who sate beside him. And when many weeks had passed, and but little remained to do, save one brush upon the mouth and one tint upon the eye, the spirit of the lady again flickered up as the flame within the socket of the lamp. And then the brush was given, and then the tint was placed; and, for one moment, the painter stood entranced before the work which he had wrought; but in the next, while he yet gazed, he grew tremulous and very pallid, and aghast, and crying with a loud voice, "This is indeed *Life* itself!" turned suddenly to regard his beloved:—*She was dead.*"

THE MASQUE OF THE RED DEATH

The "Red Death" had long devastated the country. No pestilence had ever been so fatal, or so hideous. Blood was its Avator and its seal—the redness and the horror of blood. There were sharp pains, and sudden dizziness, and then profuse bleeding at the pores, with dissolution. The scarlet stains upon the body and especially upon the face of the victim, were the pest ban which shut him out from the aid and from the sympathy of his fellow-men. And the whole seizure, progress and termination of the disease, were the incidents of half an hour.

But the Prince Prospero was happy and dauntless and sagacious. When his dominions were half depopulated, he summoned to his presence a thousand hale and light-hearted friends from among the knights and dames of his court, and with these retired to the deep seclusion of one of his castellated abbeys. This was an extensive and magnificent structure, the creation of the prince's own eccentric yet august taste. A strong and lofty wall girdled it in. This wall had gates of iron. The courtiers, having entered, brought furnaces and massy hammers and welded the bolts. They resolved to leave means neither of ingress or egress to the sudden impulses of despair or of frenzy from within. The abbey was amply provisioned. With such precautions the courtiers might bid defiance to contagion. The external world could take care of itself. In the meantime it was folly to grieve, or to think. The prince had provided all the appliances of pleasure. There were buffoons, there were improvisatori, there were ballet-dancers, there were musicians, there was Beauty, there was wine. All these and security were within. Without was the "Red Death."

It was toward the close of the fifth or sixth month of his seclusion, and while the pestilence raged most furiously abroad, that the Prince Prospero entertained his thousand friends at a masked ball of the most unusual magnificence.

It was a voluptuous scene, that masquerade. But first let me tell of the rooms in which it was held. There were seven—an imperial suite. In many palaces, however, such suites form a long and straight vista, while the folding doors slide back nearly to the walls on either hand, so that the view of the whole extent is scarcely impeded. Here the case was very different; as might have been expected from the duke's love of the *bizarre*. The apartments were so irregularly disposed that the vision embraced but little more than one at a time. There was a sharp turn at every twenty or thirty yards, and at each turn a novel effect. To the right and left, in the middle of each wall, a tall and narrow Gothic window looked out upon a closed corridor which pursued the windings of the suite. These windows were of stained glass whose color varied in accordance with the prevailing hue of the decorations of the chamber into which it opened. That at the eastern extremity was hung, for example, in blue—and vividly blue were its windows. The second chamber was purple in its ornaments and tapestries, and here the panes were purple. The third was green throughout, and so were the casements. The fourth was furnished and lighted with orange—the fifth with white—the sixth with violet. The seventh apartment was closely shrouded in black velvet tapestries that hung all over the ceiling and down the walls, falling in heavy folds upon a carpet of the same material and hue. But in this chamber only, the color of the windows failed to correspond with the decorations. The panes here were scarlet—a deep blood color. Now in no one of the seven apartments was there any lamp or candelabrum, amid the profusion of golden ornaments that lay scattered to and fro or depended from the roof. There was no light of any kind emanating from lamp or candle within the suite of chambers. But in the corridors that followed the suite, there stood, opposite to each window, a heavy tripod, bearing a brazier of fire that projected its rays through the tinted glass and so glaringly illumined the room. And thus were produced a multitude of gaudy and fantastic appearances. But in the western or black chamber the effect of the fire-light that streamed upon the dark hangings through the blood-tinted panes, was ghastly in the extreme, and produced so wild a look upon the countenances of those who entered, that there were few of the company bold enough to set foot within its precincts at all.

It was in this apartment, also, that there stood against the western wall, a gigantic clock of ebony. Its pendulum swung to and fro with a dull, heavy, monotonous clang; and when the minute-hand made the circuit of the face, and the hour was to be stricken, there came from the brazen lungs of the clock a sound which was clear and loud and deep and exceedingly musical, but of so peculiar a note and emphasis that, at each lapse of an hour, the musicians of the orchestra were constrained to pause, momentarily, in their performance, to harken to the sound; and thus the waltzers perforce ceased their evolutions, and there was a brief disconcert of the whole gay company; and, while the chimes of the clock yet rang, it was observed that the giddiest grew pale, and the more aged and sedate passed their hands over their brows as if in confused reverie or meditation. But when the echoes had fully ceased, a light laughter at once pervaded the assembly; the musicians looked at each other and smiled as if at their own nervousness and folly, and made whispering vows, each to the other, that the next chiming of the clock should produce in them no similar emotion; and then, after the lapse of sixty minutes, (which embrace three thousand and six hundred seconds of the Time that flies,) there came yet another chiming of the clock, and then were the same disconcert and tremulousness and meditation as before.

But, in spite of these things, it was a gay and magnificent revel. The tastes of the duke were peculiar. He had a fine eye for colors and effects. He disregarded the *decora* of mere fashion. His plans were bold and fiery, and his conceptions glowed with barbaric lustre. There are some who would have thought him mad. His followers felt that he was not. It was necessary to hear and see and touch him to be *sure* that he was not.

He had directed, in great part, the moveable embellishments of the seven chambers, upon occasion of this great *fete*; and it was his own guiding taste which had given character to the masqueraders. Be sure they were grotesque. There were much glare and glitter and piquancy and phantasm—much of what has been since seen in "Hernani." There were arabesque figures with unsuited limbs and appointments. There were delirious fancies such as the madman fashions. There was much of the beautiful, much of the wanton, much of the *bizarre*, something of the terrible, and not a little of that which might have excited disgust. To and fro in the seven chambers there stalked, in fact, a multitude of dreams. And these—the dreams—writhed in and about, taking hue from the rooms, and causing the wild music of the orchestra to seem as the echo of their steps. And, anon, there strikes the ebony clock which stands in the hall of the velvet. And then, for a moment, all is still, and all is silent save the voice of the clock. The dreams are stiff-frozen as they stand. But the echoes of the chime die away—they have endured but an instant—and a light, half-subdued laughter floats after them as they depart. And now again the music swells, and the dreams live, and writhe to and fro more merrily than ever, taking hue from the many tinted windows through which stream the rays from the tripods. But to the chamber which lies most westwardly of the seven, there are now none of the maskers who venture: for the night is waning away; and there flows a ruddier light through the blood-colored panes; and the blackness of the sable drapery appalls; and to him whose foot falls upon the sable carpet, there comes from the near clock of ebony a muffled peal more solemnly emphatic than any which reaches *their* ears who indulge in the more remote gaieties of the other apartments.

But these other apartments were densely crowded, and in them beat feverishly the heart of life. And the revel went whirlingly on, until at length there commenced the sounding of midnight upon the clock. And then the music ceased, as I have told; and the evolutions of the waltzers were quieted; and there was an uneasy cessation of all things as before. But now there were twelve strokes to be sounded by the bell of the clock; and thus it happened, perhaps, that more of thought crept, with more of time, into the meditations of the thoughtful among those who revelled. And thus, too, it happened, perhaps, that before the last echoes of the last chime had utterly sunk into silence, there were many individuals in the crowd who had found leisure to become aware of the presence of a masked figure which had arrested the attention of no single individual before. And the rumor of this new presence having spread itself whisperingly around, there arose at length from the whole company a buzz, or murmur, expressive of disapprobation and surprise—then, finally, of terror, of horror, and of disgust.

In an assembly of phantasms such as I have painted, it may well be supposed that no ordinary appearance could have excited such sensation. In truth the masquerade license of the night was nearly unlimited; but the figure in question had out-Heroded Herod, and gone beyond the bounds of even the prince's indefinite decorum. There are chords in the hearts of the most reckless which cannot be touched without emotion. Even with the utterly lost, to whom life and death are equally jests, there are matters of which no jest can be made. The whole company, indeed, seemed now deeply to feel that in the costume and bearing of the stranger neither wit nor propriety existed. The figure was tall and gaunt, and shrouded from head to foot in the habiliments of the grave. The mask which concealed the visage was made so nearly to resemble the countenance of a stiffened corpse that the closest scrutiny must have had difficulty in detecting the cheat. And yet all this might have been endured, if not approved, by the mad revellers around. But the mummer had gone so far as to assume the type of the Red Death. His vesture was dabbled in *blood*—and his broad brow, with all the features of the face, was besprinkled with the scarlet horror.

When the eyes of Prince Prospero fell upon this spectral image (which with a slow and solemn movement, as if more fully to sustain its *rôle*, stalked to and fro among the waltzers) he was seen to be convulsed, in the first moment, with a strong shudder either of terror or distaste; but, in the next, his brow reddened with rage.

"Who dares?" he demanded hoarsely of the courtiers who stood near him—"who dares insult us with this blasphemous mockery? Seize him and unmask him—that we may know whom we have to hang at sunrise, from the battlements!"

It was in the eastern or blue chamber in which stood the Prince Prospero as he uttered these words. They rang throughout the seven rooms loudly and clearly—for the prince was a bold and robust man, and the music had become hushed at the waving of his hand.

It was in the blue room where stood the prince, with a group of pale courtiers by his side. At first, as he spoke, there was a slight rushing movement of this group in the direction of the intruder, who at the moment was also near at hand, and now, with deliberate and stately step, made closer approach to the speaker. But from a certain nameless awe with which the mad assumptions of the mummer had inspired the whole party, there were found none who put forth hand to seize him; so that, unimpeded, he passed within a yard of the prince's person; and, while the vast assembly, as if with one impulse, shrank from the centres of the rooms to the walls, he made his way uninterruptedly, but with the same solemn and measured step which had distinguished him from the first, through the blue chamber to the purple—through the purple to the green—through the green to the orange—through this again to the white—and even thence to the violet, ere a decided movement had been made to arrest him. It was then, however, that the Prince Prospero, maddening with rage and the shame of his own momentary cowardice, rushed hurriedly through the six chambers, while none followed him on account of a deadly terror that had seized upon all. He bore aloft a drawn dagger, and had approached, in rapid impetuosity, to within three or four feet of the retreating figure, when the latter, having attained the extremity of the velvet apartment, turned suddenly and confronted his pursuer. There was a sharp cry—and the dagger dropped gleaming upon the sable carpet, upon which, instantly afterwards, fell prostrate in death the Prince Prospero. Then, summoning the wild courage of despair, a throng of the revellers at once threw themselves into the black apartment, and, seizing the mummer, whose tall figure stood erect and motionless within the shadow of the ebony clock, gasped in unutterable horror at finding the grave-cerements and corpse-like mask which they handled with so violent a rudeness, untenanted by any tangible form.

And now was acknowledged the presence of the Red Death. He had come like a thief in the night. And one by one dropped the revellers in the blood-bedewed halls of their revel, and died each in the despairing posture of his fall. And the life of the ebony clock went out with that of the last of the gay. And the flames of the tripods expired. And Darkness and Decay and the Red Death held illimitable dominion over all.

THE PIT AND THE PENDULUM

Impia tortorum longas hic turba furores
Sanguinis innocui, non satinta, aluit.
Sospite nunc patria, fracto nunc funeris antro,
Mors ubi dira fuit vita salusque patent.

[*Quatrain composed for the gates of a Market to be erected upon the site of the Jacobin Club House at Paris.*]

I was sick—sick unto death with that long agony; and when they at length unbound me, and I was permitted to sit, I felt that my senses were leaving me. The sentence —the dread sentence of death—was the last of distinct accentuation which reached my ears. After that, the sound of the inquisitorial voices seemed merged in one dreamy indeterminate hum. It conveyed to my soul the idea of *revolution*—perhaps from its association in fancy with the burr of a mill-wheel. This only for a brief period; for presently I heard no more. Yet, for a while, I saw; but with how terrible an exaggeration! I saw the lips of the black-robed judges. They appeared to me white—whiter than the sheet upon which I trace these words—and thin even to grotesqueness; thin with the intensity of their expression of firmness—of immoveable resolution—of stern contempt of human torture. I saw that the decrees of what to me was Fate, were still issuing from those lips. I saw them writhe with a deadly locution. I saw them fashion the syllables of my name; and I shuddered because no sound succeeded. I saw, too, for a few moments of delirious horror, the soft and nearly imperceptible waving of the sable draperies which enwrapped the walls of the apartment. And then my vision fell upon the seven tall candles upon the table. At first they wore the aspect of charity, and seemed white slender angels who would save me; but then, all at once, there came a most deadly nausea over my spirit, and I felt every fibre in my frame thrill as if I had touched the wire of a galvanic battery, while the angel forms became meaningless spectres, with heads of flame, and I saw that from them there would be no help. And then there stole into my fancy, like a rich musical note, the thought of what sweet rest there must be in the grave. The thought came gently and stealthily, and it seemed long before it attained full appreciation; but just as my spirit came at length properly to feel and entertain it, the figures of the judges vanished, as if magically, from before me; the tall candles sank into nothingness; their flames went out utterly; the blackness of darkness supervened; all sensations appeared swallowed up in a mad rushing descent as of the soul into Hades. Then silence, and stillness, and night were the universe.

I had swooned; but still will not say that all of consciousness was lost. What of it there remained I will not attempt to define, or even to describe; yet all was not lost. In the deepest slumber—no! In delirium—no! In a swoon—no! In death—no! even in the grave all *is not* lost. Else there is no immortality for man. Arousing from the most profound of slumbers, we break the gossamer web of *some* dream. Yet in a second afterward, (so frail may that web have been) we remember not that we have dreamed. In the return to life from the swoon there are two stages; first, that of the sense of mental or spiritual; secondly, that of the sense of physical, existence. It seems probable that if, upon reaching the second stage, we could recall the impressions of the first, we should find these impressions eloquent in memories of the gulf beyond. And that gulf is—what? How at least shall we distinguish its shadows from those of the tomb? But if the impressions of what I have termed the first stage, are not, at will, recalled, yet, after long interval, do they not come unbidden, while we marvel whence they come? He who has swooned, is not he who finds strange palaces and wildly familiar faces in coals that glow; is not he who beholds floating in mid-air the sad visions that the many may not view; is not he who ponders ever the perfume of some novel flower—is not he whose brain grows bewildered with the meaning of some musical cadence which has never before arrested his attention.

Amid frequent and thoughtful endeavors to remember; amid earnest struggles to regather some token of the state of seeming nothingness into which my soul had lapsed, there have been moments when I have dreamed of success; there have been brief, very brief periods when I have conjured up remembrances which the lucid reason of a later epoch assures me could have had reference only to that condition of seeming unconsciousness. These shadows of memory tell, indistinctly, of tall figures that

lifted and bore me in silence down—down—still down—
till a hideous dizziness oppressed me at the mere idea of
the interminableness of the descent. They tell also of a
vague horror at my heart, on account of that heart's unnatural stillness. Then comes a sense of sudden motionlessness throughout all things; as if those who bore me
(a ghastly train!) had outrun, in their descent, the limits
of the limitless, and paused from the wearisomeness of
their toil. After this I call to mind flatness and dampness;
and then all is *madness*—the madness of a memory which
busies itself among forbidden things.

Very suddenly there came back to my soul motion and
sound—the tumultuous motion of the heart, and, in my
ears, th esound of its beating. Then a pause in which all is
blank. Then again sound, and motion, and touch—a
tingling sensation pervading my frame. Then the mere
consciousness of existence, without thought—a condition
which lasted long. Then, very suddenly, *thought*, and
shuddering terror, and earnest endeavor to comprehend
my true state. Then a strong desire to lapse into insensibility. Then a rushing revival of soul and a successful
effort to move. And now a full memory of the trial, of
the judges, of the sable draperies, of the sentence, of the
sickness, of the swoon. Then entire forgetfulness of all
that followed; of all that a later day and much earnestness
of endeavor have enabled me vaguely to recall.

So far, I had not opened my eyes. I felt that I lay upon
my back, unbound. I reached out my hand, and it fell
heavily upon something damp and hard. There I suffered it to remain for many minutes, while I strove to
imagine where and *what* I could be. I longed, yet dared
not to employ my vision. I dreaded the first glance at
objects around me. It was not that I feared to look upon
things horrible, but that I grew aghast lest there should
be *nothing* to see. At length, with a wild desperation at
heart, I quickly unclosed my eyes. My worst thoughts,

then, were confirmed. The blackness of eternal night encompassed me. I struggled for breath. The intensity of the darkness seemed to oppress and stifle me. The atmosphere was intolerably close. I still lay quietly, and made effort to exercise my reason. I brought to mind the inquisitorial proceedings, and attempted from that point to deduce my real condition. The sentence had passed; and it appeared to me that a very long interval of time had since elapsed. Yet not for a moment did I suppose myself actually dead. Such a supposition, notwithstanding what we read in fiction, is altogether inconsistent with real existence;—but where and in what state was I? The condemned to death, I knew, perished usually at the *auto-dafes*, and one of these had been held on the very night of the day of my trial. Had I been remanded to my dungeon, to await the next sacrifice, which would not take place for many months? This I at once saw could not be. Victims had been in immediate demand. Moreover, my dungeon, as well as all the condemned cells at Toledo, had stone floors, and light was not altogether excluded.

A fearful idea now suddenly drove the blood in torrents upon my heart, and for a brief period, I once more relapsed into insensibility. Upon recovering, I at once started to my feet, trembling convulsively in every fibre. I thrust my arms wildly above and around me in all directions. I felt nothing; yet dreaded to move a step, lest I should be impeded by the walls of a *tomb*. Perspiration burst from every pore, and stood in cold big beads upon my forehead. The agony of suspense, grew at length intolerable, and I cautiously moved forward, with my arms extended, and my eyes straining from their sockets, in the hope of catching some faint ray of light. I proceeded for many paces; but still all was blackness and vacancy. I breathed more freely. It seemed evident that mine was not, at least, the most hideous of fates.

And now, as I still continued to step cautiously onward, there came thronging upon my recollection a thousand vague rumors of the horrors of Toledo. Of the dungeons there had been strange things narrated—fables I had always deemed them—but yet strange, and too ghastly to repeat, save in a whisper. Was I left to perish of starvation in this subterranean world of darkness; or what fate, perhaps even more fearful, awaited me? That the result would be death, and a death of more than customary bitterness, I knew too well the character of my judges to doubt. The mode and the hour were all that occupied or distracted me.

My outstretched hands at length encountered some solid obstruction. It was a wall, seemingly of stone masonry—very smooth, slimy, and cold. I followed it up; stepping with all the careful distrust with which certain antique narratives had inspired me. This process, however, afforded me no means of ascertaining the dimensions of my dungeon; as I might make its circuit, and return to the point whence I set out, without being aware of the fact; so perfectly uniform seemed the wall. I therefore sought the knife which had been in my pocket, when led into the inquisitorial chamber; but it was gone; my clothes had been exchanged for a wrapper of coarse serge. I had thought of forcing the blade in some minute crevice of the masonry, so as to identify my point of departure. The difficulty, nevertheless, was but trivial; although, in the disorder of my fancy, it seemed at first insuperable. I tore a part of the hem from the robe and placed the fragment at full length, and at right angles to the wall. In groping my way around the prison, I could not fail to encounter this rag upon completing the circuit. So, at least I thought: but I had not counted upon the extent of the dungeon, or upon my own weakness. The ground was moist and slippery. I staggered onward for some time, when I stumbled and fell. My excessive fatigue induced me to remain prostrate; and sleep soon overtook me as I lay.

Upon awaking, and stretching forth an arm, I found beside me a loaf and a pitcher with water. I was too much exhausted to reflect upon this circumstance, but ate and drank with avidity. Shortly afterward, I resumed my tour around the prison, and with much toil, came at last upon the fragment of the serge. Up to the period when I fell I had counted fifty-two paces, and upon resuming my walk, I had counted forty-eight more;— when I arrived at the rag. There were in all, then, a hundred paces; and, admitting two paces to the yard, I presumed the dungeon to be fifty yards in circuit. I had met, however, with many angles in the wall, and thus I could form no guess at the shape of the vault; for vault I could not help supposing it to be.

I had little object—certainly no hope—in these researches; but a vague curiosity prompted me to continue them. Quitting the wall, I resolved to cross the area of the enclosure. At first I proceeded with extreme caution, for the floor, although seemingly of solid material, was treacherous with slime. At length, however, I took courage, and did not hesitate to step firmly; endeavoring to cross in as direct a line as possible, I had advanced some ten or twelve paces in this manner, when the remnant of the torn hem of my robe became entangled between my legs. I stepped on it, and fell violently on my face.

In the confusion attending my fall, I did not immediately apprehend a somewhat startling circumstance, which yet, in a few seconds afterward, and while I still lay prostrate, arrested my attention. It was this—my chin rested upon the floor of the prison, but my lips and the upper portion of my head, although seemingly at a less elevation than the chin, touched nothing. At the same time my forehead seemed bathed in a clammy vapor, and the peculiar smell of decayed fungus arose to my nostrils. I put forward my arm, and shuddered to find that I had fallen at the very brink of a circular pit, whose extent, of course, I had no means of ascertaining at the moment. Groping about the masonry just below the margin, I succeeded in dislodging a small fragment, and let it fall into the abyss. For many seconds I hearkened to its reverberations as it dashed against the sides of the chasm in its descent; at length there was a sullen plunge into water, succeeded by loud echoes. At the same moment there came a sound resembling the quick opening, and as rapid closing of a door overhead, while a faint gleam of light flashed suddenly through the gloom, and as suddenly faded away.

I saw clearly the doom which had been prepared for me, and congratulated myself upon the timely accident by which I had escaped. Another step before my fall, and the world had seen me no more. And the death just avoided, was of that very character which I had regarded as fabulous and frivolous in the tales respecting the Inquisition. To the victims of its tyranny, there was the choice of death with its direst physical agonies, or death with its most hideous moral horrors. I had been reserved for the latter. By long suffering my nerves had been unstrung, until I trembled at the sound of my own voice, and had become in every respect a fitting subject for the species of torture which awaited me.

Shaking in every limb, I groped my way back to the wall; resolving there to perish rather than risk the terrors of the wells, of which my imagination now pictured many in various positions about the dungeon. In other conditions of mind I might have had courage to end my misery at once by a plunge into one of these abysses; but now I was the veriest of cowards. Neither could I forget what I had read of these pits—that the *sudden* extinction of life formed no part of their most horrible plan.

Agitation of spirit kept me awake for many long hours; but at length I again slumbered. Upon arousing, I found by my side, as before, a loaf and a pitcher of water. A burning thirst consumed me, and I emptied the vessel at a draught. It must have been drugged; for scarcely had I drunk, before I became irresistibly drowsy. A deep sleep fell upon me—a sleep like that of death. How long it lasted of course, I know not; but when, once again, I unclosed my eyes, the objects around me were visible. By a wild sulphurous lustre, the origin of which I could not at first determine, I was enabled to see the extent and aspect of the prison.

In its size I had been greatly mistaken. The whole circuit of its walls did not exceed twenty-five yards. For some minutes this fact occasioned me a world of vain trouble; vain indeed! for what could be of less importance, under the terrible circumstances which environed me, than the mere dimensions of my dungeon? But my soul took a wild interest in trifles, and I busied myself in endeavors to account for the error I had committed in my measurement. The truth at length flashed upon me. In my first attempt at exploration I had counted fifty-two paces, up to the period when I fell; I must then have been within a pace or two of the fragment of serge; in fact, I had nearly performed the circuit of the vault. I then slept, and upon awaking, I must have returned upon my steps—thus supposing the circuit nearly double what it actually was. My confusion of mind prevented me from observing that I began my tour with the wall to the left, and ended it with the wall to the right.

I had been deceived, too, in respect to the shape of the enclosure. In feeling my way I had found many angles, and thus deduced an idea of great irregularity; so potent is the effect of total darkness upon one arousing from lethargy or sleep! The angles were simply those of a few slight depressions, or niches, at odd intervals. The general shape of the prison was square. What I had taken for masonry seemed now to be iron, or some other metal, in huge plates, whose sutures or joints occasioned the depression. The entire surface of this metallic enclosure was rudely daubed in all the hideous and repulsive devices to which the charnel superstition of the monks has given rise. The figures of fiends in aspects of menace, with skeleton forms, and other more really fearful images, overspread and disfigured the walls. I observed that the outlines of these monstrosities were sufficiently distinct, but that the colors seemed faded and blurred, as if from the effects of a damp atmosphere. I now noticed the floor, too, which was of stone. In the centre yawned the circular pit from whose jaws I had escaped; but it was the only one in the dungeon.

All this I saw indistinctly and by much effort: for my personal condition had been greatly changed during slumber. I now lay upon my back, and at full length, on a species of low framework of wood. To this I was securely bound by a long strap resembling a surcingle. It passed in many convolutions about my limbs and body, leaving at liberty only my head, and my left arm to such extent that I could, by dint of much exertion, supply myself with food from an earthen dish which lay by my side on the floor. I saw, to my horror, that the pitcher had been removed. I say to my horror; for I was consumed with intolerable thirst. This thirst it appeared to be the design of my persecutors to stimulate: for the food in the dish was meat pungently seasoned.

Looking upward, I surveyed the ceiling of my prison. It was some thirty or forty feet overhead, and constructed much as the side walls. In one of its panels a very singular figure riveted my whole attention. It was the painted figure of Time as he is commonly represented, save that, in lieu of a scythe, he held what, at a casual glance, I supposed to be the pictured image of a huge pendulum such as we see on antique clocks. There was something, however, in the appearance of this machine which caused me to regard it more attentively. While I gazed directly upward at it (for its position was immediately over my own) I fancied that I saw it in motion. In an instant afterward the fancy was confirmed. Its sweep was brief and of course slow. I watched it for some minutes, somewhat in fear, but more in wonder. Wearied at length with observing its dull movement, I turned my eyes upon the other objects in the cell.

A slight noise attracted my notice, and, looking to the floor, I saw several enormous rats traversing it. They had issued from the well, which lay just within view to my right. Even then, while I gazed, they came up in troops hurriedly, with ravenous eyes, allured by the scent of the meat. From this it required much effort and attention to scare them away.

It might have been half an hour, perhaps even an hour, (for I could take but imperfect note of time) before I again cast my eyes upward. What I then saw confounded and amazed me. The sweep of the pendulum had increased in extent by nearly a yard. As a natural consequence, its velocity was also much greater. But what mainly disturbed me was the idea that it had perceptibly *descended*. I now observed—with what horror it is needless to say—that its nether extremity was formed of a crescent of glittering steel, about a foot in length from horn to horn; the horns upward, and the under edge evidently as keen as that of a razor. Like a razor also, it seemed massy and heavy, tapering from the edge into a solid and broad structure above. It was appended to a weighty rod of brass, and the whole *hissed* as it swung through the air.

I could no longer doubt the doom prepared for me by

monkish ingenuity in torture. My cognizance of the pit had become known to the inquisitorial agents—*the pit* whose horrors had been destined for so bold a recusant as myself—*the pit*, typical of hell, and regarded by rumor as the Ultima Thule of all their punishments. The plunge into this pit I had avoided by the merest of accidents, and I knew that surprise, or entrapment into torment, formed an important portion of all the grotesquerie of these dungeon deaths. Having failed to fall, it was no part of the demon plan to hurl me into the abyss; and thus (there being no alternative) a different and a milder destruction awaited me. Milder! I half smiled in my agony as I thought of such application of such a term.

What boots it to tell of the long, long hours of horror more than mortal, during which I counted the rushing vibrations of the steel! Inch by inch—line by line—with a descent only appreciable at intervals that seemed ages— down and still down it came! Days passed—it might have been that many days passed—ere it swept so closely over me as to fan me with its acrid breath. The odor of the sharp steel forced itself into my nostrils. I prayed—I wearied heaven with my prayer for its more speedy descent. I grew frantically mad, and struggled to force myself upward against the sweep of the fearful scimitar. And then I fell suddenly calm, and lay smiling at the glittering death, as a child at some rare bauble.

There was another interval of utter insensibility; it was brief; for, upon again lapsing into life there had been no perceptible descent in the pendulum. But it might have been long; for I knew there were demons who took note of my swoon, and who could have arrested the vibration at pleasure. Upon my recovery, too, I felt very—oh, inexpressibly sick and weak, as if through long inanition. Even amid the agonies of that period, the human nature craved food. With painful effort I outstretched my left arm as far as my bonds permitted, and took possession of the small remnant which had been spared me by the rats. As I put a portion of it within my lips, there rushed to my mind a half formed thought of joy—of hope. Yet what business had I with hope? It was, as I say, a half formed thought —man has many such which are never completed. I felt that it was of joy—of hope; but I felt also that it had perished in its formation. In vain I struggled to perfect—to retain it. Long suffering had nearly annihilated all my ordinary powers of mind. I was an imbecile—an idiot.

The vibration of the pendulum was at right angles to my length. I saw that the crescent was designed to cross the region of the heart. It would fray the serge of my robe—it would return and repeat its operations—again—and again. Notwithstanding its terrifically wide sweep (some thirty feet or more) and the hissing vigor of its descent, sufficient to sunder these very walls of iron, still the fraying of my robe would be all that, for several minutes, it would accomplish. And at this thought I paused. I dared not go farther than this reflection. I dwelt upon it with a pertinacity of attention—as if, in so dwelling, I could arrest *here* the descent of the steel. I forced myself to ponder upon the sound of the crescent as it should pass across the garment—upon the peculiar thrilling sensation which the friction of cloth produces on the nerves. I pondered upon all this frivolity until my teeth were on edge.

Down—steadily down it crept. I took a frenzied pleasure in contrasting its downward with its lateral velocity. To the right—to the left—far and wide—with the shriek of a damned spirit; to my heart with the stealthy pace of the tiger! I alternately laughed and howled as the one or the other idea grew predominant.

Down—certainly, relentlessly down! It vibrated within three inches of my bosom! I struggled violently, furiously, to free my left arm. This was free only from the elbow to the hand. I could reach the latter, from the platter beside me, to my mouth, with great effort, but no farther. Could

I have broken the fastenings above the elbow, I would have seized and attempted to arrest the pendulum. I might as well have attempted to àrrest an avalanche!

Down—still unceasingly—still inevitably down! I gasped and struggled at each vibration. I shrunk convulsively at its every sweep. My eyes followed its outward or upward whirls with the eagerness of the most unmeaning despair; they closed themselves spasmodically at the descent, although death would have been a relief, oh! how unspeakable! Still I quivered in every nerve to think how slight a sinking of the machinery would precipitate that keen, glistening axe upon my bosom. It was *hope* that prompted the nerve to quiver—the frame to shrink. It was *hope*—the hope that triumphs on the rack—that whispers to the death-condemned even in the dungeons of the Inquisition.

I saw that some ten or twelve vibrations would bring the steel in actual contact with my robe, and with this observation there suddenly came over my spirit all the keen, collected calmness of despair. For the first time during many hours—or perhaps days—I *thought*. It now accurred to me that the bandage, or surcingle, which enveloped me, was *unique*. I was tied by no separate cord. The first stroke of the razor-like crescent athwart any portion of the band, would so detach it that it might be unwound from my person by means of my left hand. But how fearful, in that case, the proximity of the steel! The result of the slightest struggle how deadly! Was it likely, moreover, that the minions of the torturer had not foreseen and provided for this possibility! Was it probable that the bandage crossed my bosom in the track of the pendulum? Dreading to find my faint, and, as it seemed, my last hope frustrated, I so far elevated my head as to obtain a distinct view of my breast. The surcingle enveloped my limbs and body close in all directions—*save in the path of the destroying crescent*.

Scarcely had I dropped my head back into its original
position, when there flashed upon my mind what I cannot better describe than as the unformed half of that idea
of deliverance to which I have previously alluded, and of
which a moiety only floated indeterminately through my
brain when I raised food to my burning lips. The whole
thought was now present—feeble, scarcely sane, scarcely
definite,—but still entire. I proceeded at once, with the
nervous energy of despair, to attempt its execution.

For many hours the immediate vicinity of the low frame-
work upon which I lay, had been literally swarming with
rats. They were wild, bold, ravenous; their red eyes glaring
upon me as if they waited but for motionlessness on my
part to make me their prey. "To what food," I thought,
"have they been accustomed in the well."

They had devoured, in spite of all my efforts to prevent
them, all but a small remnant of the contents of the dish.
I had fallen into an habitual see-saw, or wave of the hand
about the platter: and, at length, the unconscious uni-
formity of the movement deprived it of effect. In their
voracity the vermin frequently fastened their sharp fangs
in my fingers. With the particles of the oily and spicy
viand which now remained, I thoroughly rubbed the
bandage wherever I could reach it; then, raising my hand
from the floor, I lay breathlessly still.

At first the ravenous animals were startled and terrified
at the change—at the cessation of movement. They shrank
alarmedly back; many sought the well. But this was only
for a moment. I had not counted in vain upon their
voracity. Observing that I remained without motion, one
or two of the boldest leaped upon the frame-work, and
smelt at the surcingle. This seemed the signal for a general rush. Forth from the well they hurried in fresh troops.
They clung to the wood—they overran it, and leaped in
hundreds upon my person. The measured movement of
the pendulum disturbed them not at all. Avoiding its

strokes they busied themselves with the anointed bandage. They pressed—they swarmed upon me in ever accumulating heaps. They writhed upon my throat; their cold lips sought my own; I was half stifled by their thronging pressure; disgust, for which the world has no name, swelled my bosom, and chilled, with a heavy clamminess, my heart. Yet one minute, and I felt that the struggle would be over. Plainly I perceived the loosening of the bandage. I knew that in more than one place it must be already severed. With a more than human resolution I lay *still*.

Nor had I erred in my calculations—nor had I endured in vain. I at length felt that I was *free*. The surcingle hung in ribands from my body. But the stroke of the pendulum already pressed upon my bosom. It had divided the serge of the robe. It had cut through the linen beneath. Twice again it swung, and a sharp sense of pain shot through every nerve. But the moment of escape had arrived. At a wave of my hand my deliverers hurried tumultuously away. With a steady movement—cautious, sidelong, shrinking, and slow—I slid from the embrace of the bandage and beyond the reach of the scimitar. For the moment, at least, *I was free*.

Free!—and in the grasp of the Inquisition! I had scarcely stepped from my wooden bed of horror upon the stone floor of the prison, when the motion of the hellish machine ceased and I beheld it drawn up, by some invisible force, through the ceiling. This was a lesson which I took desperately to heart. My every motion was undoubtedly watched. Free!—I had but escaped death in one form of agony, to be delivered unto worse than death in some other. With that thought I rolled my eyes nervously around on the barriers of iron that hemmed me in. Something unusual—some change which, at first, I could not appreciate distinctly—it was obvious, had taken place in the apartment. For many minutes of a dreamy and trembling abstraction I busied myself in vain, unconnected conjecture.

During this period, I became aware, for the first time, of the origin of the sulphurous light which illumined the cell. It proceeded from a fissure, about half an inch in width, extending entirely around the prison at the base of the walls, which thus appeared, and were, completely separated from the floor. I endeavored, but of course in vain, to look through the aperture.

As I arose from the attempt, the mystery of the alteration in the chamber broke at once upon my understanding. I have observed that, although the outlines of the figures upon the walls were sufficiently distinct, yet the colors seemed blurred and indefinite. These colors had now assumed, and were momentarily assuming, a startling and most intense brilliancy, that gave to the spectral and fiendish portraitures an aspect that might have thrilled even firmer nerves than my own. Demon eyes, of a wild and ghastly vivacity, glared upon me in a thousand directions, where none had been visible before, and gleamed with the lurid lustre of a fire that I could not force my imagination to regard as unreal.

Unreal!—Even while I breathed there came to my nostrils the breath of the vapour of heated iron! A suffocating odour pervaded the prison! A deeper glow settled each moment in the eyes that glared at my agonies! A richer tint of crimson diffused itself over the pictured horrors of blood. I panted! I gasped for breath! There could be no doubt of the design of my tormentors—oh! most unrelenting! oh! most demoniac of men! I shrank from the glowing metal to the centre of the cell. Amid the thought of the fiery destruction that impended, the idea of the coolness of the well came over my soul like balm. I rushed to its deadly brink. I threw my straining vision below. The glare from the enkindled roof illumined its inmost recesses. Yet, for a wild moment, did my spirit refuse to comprehend the meaning of what I saw. At length it forced —it wrestled its way into my soul—it burned itself in upon my shuddering reason.—Oh! for a voice to speak!—oh! horror!—oh! any horror but this! With a shriek, I rushed from the margin, and buried my face in my hands—weeping bitterly.

The heat rapidly increased, and once again I looked up, shuddering as with a fit of the ague. There had been a second change in the cell—and now the change was obviously in the *form*. As before, it was in vain that I, at first, endeavoured to appreciate or understand what was taking place. But not long was I left in doubt. The Inquisitorial vengeance had been hurried by my two-fold escape, and there was to be no more dallying with the King of Terrors. The room had been square. I saw that two of its iron angles were now acute—two, consequently, obtuse. The fearful difference quickly increased with a low rumbling or moaning sound. In an instant the apartment had shifted its form into that of a lozenge. But the alteration stopped not here—I neither hoped nor desired it to stop. I could have clasped the red walls to my bosom as a garment of eternal peace. "Death," I said, "any death but that of the pit!" Fool! might I have not known that *into the pit* it was the object of the burning iron to urge me? Could I resist its glow? or, if even that, could I withstand its pressure? And now, flatter and flatter grew the lozenge, with a rapidity that left me no time for contemplation. Its centre, and of course, its greatest width, came just over the yawning gulf. I shrank back—but the closing walls pressed me resistlessly onward. At length for my seared and writhing body there was no longer an inch of foothold on the firm floor of the prison. I struggled no more, but the agony of my soul found vent in one loud, long, and final scream of despair. I felt that I tottered upon the brink—I averted my eyes—

There was a discordant hum of human voices! There was a loud blast as of many trumpets! There was a harsh grating as of a thousand thunders! The fiery walls rushed back!

An outstretched arm caught my own as I fell, fainting, into the abyss. It was that of General Lasalle. The French army had entered Toledo. The Inquisition was in the hands of its enemies.

THE TELL-TALE HEART

True!—nervous—very, very dreadfully nervous I had been and am; but why *will* you say that I am mad? The disease had sharpened my senses—not destroyed—not dulled them. Above all was the sense of hearing acute. I heard all things in the heaven and in the earth. I heard many things in hell. How, then, am I mad? Hearken! and observe how healthily—how calmly I can tell you the whole story.

It is impossible to say how first the idea entered my brain; but once conceived, it haunted me day and night. Object there was none. Passion there was none. I loved the old man. He had never wronged me. He had never given me insult. For his gold I had no desire. I think it was his eye! yes, it was this! He had the eye of a vulture—a pale blue eye, with a film over it. Whenever it fell upon me, my blood ran cold; and so by degrees—very gradually—I made up my mind to take the life of the old man, and thus rid myself of the eye forever.

Now this is the point. You fancy me mad. Madmen know nothing. But you should have seen *me*. You should have seen how wisely I proceeded—with what caution—with what foresight—with what dissimulation I went to work! I was never kinder to the old man than during the whole week before I killed him. And every night, about midnight, I turned the latch of his door and opened it—oh so gently! And then, when I had made an opening sufficient for my head, I put in a dark lantern, all closed, closed, so that no light shone out, and then I thrust in my head. Oh, you would have laughed to see how cunningly I thrust it in! I moved it slowly—very, very slowly, so that I might not disturb the old man's sleep. It took me an hour to place my whole head within the opening so far that I could see him as he lay upon his bed. Ha!—would a madman have been so wise as this? And then, when my head was well in the room, I undid the lantern cautiously —oh, so cautiously—cautiously (for the hinges creaked) —I undid it just so much that a single thin ray fell upon the vulture eye. And this I did for seven long nights— every night just at midnight—but I found the eye always closed; and so it was impossible to do the work; for it was not the old man who vexed me, but his Evil Eye. And every morning, when the day broke, I went boldly into the chamber, and spoke courageously to him, calling him by name in a hearty tone, and inquiring how he had passed the night. So you see he would have been a very profound old man, indeed, to suspect that every night, just at twelve, I looked in upon him while he slept.

Upon the eighth night I was more than usually cautious in opening the door. A watch's minute hand moves more quickly than did mine. Never before that night, had I *felt* the extent of my own powers—of my sagacity. I could scarcely contain my feelings of triumph. To think that there I was, opening the door, little by little, and he not even to dream of my secret deeds or thoughts. I fairly chuckled at the idea; and perhaps he heard me; for he moved on the bed suddenly, as if startled. Now you may think that I drew back—but no. His room was as black as pitch with the thick darkness, (for the shutters were close fastened, through fear of robbers,) and so I knew that he could not see the opening of the door, and I kept pushing it on steadily, steadily.

I had my head in, and was about to open the lantern,

when my thumb slipped upon the tin fastening, and the old man sprang up in the bed, crying out—"Who's there?"

I kept quite still and said nothing. For a whole hour I did not move a muscle, and in the meantime I did not hear him lie down. He was still sitting up in the bed listening;—just as I have done, night after night, hearkening to the death watches in the wall.

Presently I heard a slight groan, and I knew it was the groan of mortal terror. It was not a groan of pain or of grief—oh, no!—it was the low stifled sound that arises from the bottom of the soul when overcharged with awe. I knew the sound well. Many a night, just at midnight, when all the world slept, it has welled up from my own bosom, deepening, with its dreadful echo, the terrors that distracted me. I say I knew it well. I knew what the old man felt, and pitied him, although I chuckled at heart. I knew that he had been lying awake ever since the first slight noise, when he had turned in the bed. His fears had been ever since growing upon him. He had been trying to fancy them causeless, but could not. He had been saying to himself—"It is nothing but the wind in the chimney—it is only a mouse crossing the floor," or "it is merely a cricket which has made a single chirp." Yes, he had been trying to comfort himself with these suppositions: but he had found all in vain. *All in vain*; because Death, in approaching him, had stalked with his black shadow before him, and enveloped the victim. And it was the mournful influence of the unperceived shadow that caused him to feel—although he neither saw nor heard—to *feel* the presence of my head within the room.

When I had waited a long time, very patiently, without hearing him lie down, I resolved to open a little—a very, very little crevice in the lantern. So I opened it—you cannot imagine how stealthily, stealthily—until, at length a single dim ray, like the thread of the spider, shot from out the crevice and fell full upon the vulture eye.

It was open—wide, wide open—and I grew furious as I gazed upon it. I saw it with perfect distinctness—all a dull blue, with a hideous veil over it that chilled the very marrow in my bones; but I could see nothing else of the old man's face or person: for I had directed the ray as if by instinct, precisely upon the damned spot.

And have I not told you that what you mistake for madness is but over acuteness of the senses?—now, I say, there came to my ears a low, dull, quick sound, such as a watch makes when enveloped in cotton. I knew *that* sound well, too. It was the beating of the old man's heart. It increased my fury, as the beating of a drum stimulates the soldier into courage.

But even yet I refrained and kept still. I scarcely breathed. I held the lantern motionless. I tried how steadily I could maintain the ray upon the eye. Meantime the hellish tattoo of the heart increased. It grew quicker and quicker, and louder and louder every instant. The old man's terror *must* have been extreme! It grew louder, I say, louder every moment!—do you mark me well? I have told you that I am nervous: so I am. And now at the dead hour of the night, amid the dreadful silence of that old house, so strange a noise as this excited me to uncontrollable terror. Yet, for some minutes longer I refrained and stood still. But the beating grew louder, louder! I thought the heart must burst. And now a new anxiety seized me— the sound would be heard by a neighbour! The old man's hour had come! With a loud yell, I threw open the lantern and leaped into the room. He shrieked once—once only. In an instant I dragged him to the floor, and pulled the heavy bed over him. I then smiled gaily, to find the deed so far done. But, for many minutes, the heart beat on with a muffled sound. This, however, did not vex me; it would not be heard through the wall. At length it ceased. The old man was dead. I removed the bed and examined the corpse. Yes, he was stone, stone dead. I placed my hand upon the heart and held it there many minutes. There was no pulsation. He was stone dead. His eye would trouble me no more.

If still you think me mad, you will think so no longer when I describe the wise precautions I took for the concealment of the body. The night waned, and I worked hastily, but in silence. First of all I dismembered the corpse. I cut off the head and the arms and the legs.

I then took up three planks from the flooring of the chamber, and deposited all between the scantlings. I then replaced the boards so cleverly, so cunningly, that no human eye—not even *his*—could have detected any thing wrong. There was nothing to wash out—no stain of any kind—no blood-spot whatever. I had been too wary for that. A tub had caught all—ha! ha!

When I had made an end of these labors, it was four o'clock—still dark as midnight. As the bell sounded the hour, there came a knocking at the street door. I went down to open it with a light heart,—for what had I *now* to fear? There entered three men, who introduced themselves, with perfect suavity, as officers of the police. A shriek had been heard by a neighbour during the night; suspicion of foul play had been aroused; information had been lodged at the police office, and they (the officers) had been deputed to search the premises.

I smiled,—for *what* had I to fear? I bade the gentlemen welcome. The shriek, I said, was my own in a dream. The old man, I mentioned, was absent in the country. I took my visitors all over the house. I bade them search—search *well*. I led them, at length, to *his* chamber. I showed them his treasures, secure, undisturbed. In the enthusiasm of my confidence, I brought chairs into the room, and desired them *here* to rest from their fatigues, while I myself, in the wild audacity of my perfect triumph, placed my own seat upon the very spot beneath which reposed the corpse of the victim.

The officers were satisfied. My *manner* had convinced them. I was singularly at ease. They sat, and while I answered cheerily, they chatted of familiar things. But, ere long, I felt myself getting pale and wished them gone. My head ached, and I fancied a ringing in my ears: but still they sat and still chatted. The ringing became more distinct:—it continued and became more distinct: I talked more freely to get rid of the feeling: but it continued and gained definitiveness—until, at length, I found that the noise was *not* within my ears.

No doubt I now grew *very* pale;—but I talked more fluently, and with a heightened voice. Yet the sound increased—and what could I do? It was *a low, dull, quick sound—much such a sound as a watch makes when enveloped in cotton.* I gasped for breath—and yet the officers heard it not. I talked more quickly—more vehemently; but the noise steadily increased. I arose and argued about trifles, in a high key and with violent gesticulations; but the noise steadily increased. Why *would* they not be gone? I paced the floor to and fro with heavy strides, as if excited to fury by the observations of the men—but the noise steadily increased. Oh God! what *could* I do? I foamed—I raved—I swore! I swung the chair upon which I had been sitting, and grated it upon the boards, but the noise arose over all and continually increased. It grew louder—louder—*louder!* And still the men chatted pleasantly, and smiled. Was it possible they heard not? Almighty God!—no, no! They heard!—they suspected!—they *knew!*—they were making a mockery of my horror! —this I thought, and this I think. But anything was better than this agony! Anything was more tolerable than this derision! I could bear those hypocritical smiles no longer! I felt that I must scream or die!—and now— again!—hark! louder! louder! louder! *louder!*

"Villains!" I shrieked, "dissemble no more! I admit the deed!—tear up the planks!—here, here!—it is the beating of his hideous heart!"

THE BLACK CAT

For the most wild, yet most homely narrative which I am about to pen, I neither expect nor solicit belief. Mad indeed would I be to expect it, in a case where my very senses reject their own evidence. Yet, mad am I not—and very surely do I not dream. But to-morrow I die, and to-day I would unburthen my soul. My immediate purpose is to place before the world, plainly, succinctly, and without comment, a series of mere household events. In their consequences, these events have terrified—have tortured—have destroyed me. Yet I will not attempt to expound them. To me, they have presented little but Horror—to many they will seem less terrible than *barroques*. Hereafter, perhaps, some intellect may be found which will reduce my phantasm to the common-place—some intellect more calm, more logical, and far less excitable than my own, which will perceive, in the circumstances I detail with awe, nothing more than an ordinary succession of very natural causes and effects.

From my infancy I was noted for the docility and humanity of my disposition. My tenderness of heart was even so conspicuous as to make me the jest of my companions. I was especially fond of animals, and was indulged by my parents with a great variety of pets. With these I spent most of my time, and never was so happy as when feeding and caressing them. This peculiarity of character grew with my growth, and, in my manhood, I derived from it one of my principal sources of pleasure. To those who have cherished an affection for a faithful and sagacious dog, I need hardly be at the trouble of explaining the nature or the intensity of the gratification thus derivable. There is something in the unselfish and self-sacrificing love of a brute, which goes directly to the heart of him who has had frequent occasion to test the paltry friendship and gossamer fidelity of mere *Man*.

I married early, and was happy to find in my wife a disposition not uncongenial with my own. Observing my partiality for domestic pets, she lost no opportunity of procuring those of the most agreeable kind. We had birds, gold-fish, a fine dog, rabbits, a small monkey, and *a cat*.

This latter was a remarkably large and beautiful animal, entirely black, and sagacious to an astonishing degree. In speaking of his intelligence, my wife, who at heart was not a little tinctured with superstition, made frequent allusion to the ancient popular notion, which regarded all black cats as witches in disguise. Not that she was ever *serious* upon this point—and I mention the matter at all for no better reason than that it happens, just now, to be remembered.

Pluto—this was the cat's name—was my favorite pet and playmate. I alone fed him, and he attended me wherever I went about the house. It was even with difficulty that I could prevent him from following me through the streets.

Our friendship lasted, in this manner, for several years, during which my general temperament and character—through the instrumentality of the Fiend Intemperance—had (I blush to confess it) experienced a radical alteration for the worse. I grew, day by day, more moody, more irritable, more regardless of the feelings of others. I suffered myself to use intemperate language to my wife. At length, I even offered her personal violence. My pets, of course, were made to feel the change in my disposition. I not only neglected, but ill-used them. For Pluto, however, I still retained sufficient regard to restrain me from maltreating him, as I made no scruple of maltreating the rabbits, the monkey, or even the dog, when by accident, or through affection, they came in my way. But my disease grew upon me—for what disease is like Alcohol!—and at length even Pluto, who was now becoming old, and consequently somewhat peevish—even Pluto began to experience the effects of my ill temper.

One night, returning home, much intoxicated, from one of my haunts about town, I fancied that the cat avoided my presence. I seized him; when, in his fright at my violence, he inflicted a slight wound upon my hand with his teeth. The fury of a demon instantly possessed me. I knew myself no longer. My original soul seemed, at once, to take its flight from my body; and a more than fiendish malevolence, gin-nurtured, thrilled every fibre of my frame. I took from my waistcoat-pocket a pen-knife, opened it, grasped the poor beast by the throat, and deliberately cut one of its eyes from the socket! I blush, I burn, I shudder, while I pen the damnable atrocity.

When reason returned with the morning—when I had slept off the fumes of the night's debauch—I experienced a sentiment half of horror, half of remorse, for the crime of which I had been guilty; but it was, at best, a feeble and equivocal feeling, and the soul remained untouched. I again plunged into excess, and soon drowned in wine all memory of the deed.

In the meantime the cat slowly recovered. The socket of the lost eye presented, it is true, a frightful appearance, but he no longer appeared to suffer any pain. He went about the house as usual, but, as might be expected, fled in extreme terror at my approach. I had so much of my old heart left, as to be at first grieved by this evident dislike on the part of a creature which had once so loved me. But this feeling soon gave place to irritation. And then came, as if to my final and irrevocable overthrow, the spirit of PERVERSENESS. Of this spirit philosophy takes no account. Yet I am not more sure that my soul lives, than I am that perverseness is one of the primitive impulses of the human heart—one of the indivisible primary faculties, or sentiments, which give direction to the character of Man. Who has not, a hundred times, found himself committing a vile or a silly action, for no other reason than because he knows he should *not*? Have we not a perpetual inclination, in the teeth of our best judgment, to violate that which is *Law*, merely because we understand it to be such? This spirit of perverseness, I say, came to my final overthrow. It was this unfathomable longing of the soul *to vex itself*—to offer violence to its own nature—to do wrong for the wrong's sake only—that urged me to continue and finally to consummate the injury I had inflicted upon the unoffending brute. One morning, in cool blood, I slipped a noose about its neck and hung it to the limb of a tree;—hung it with the tears streaming from my eyes, and with the bitterest remorse at my heart;—hung it *because* I knew that it had loved me, and *because* I felt it had given me no reason of offence;—hung it *because* I knew that in so doing I was committing a sin—a deadly sin that would so jeopardize my immortal soul as to place it—if such a thing were possible—even beyond the reach of the infinite mercy of the Most Merciful and Most Terrible God.

On the night of the day on which this cruel deed was done, I was aroused from sleep by the cry of fire. The curtains of my bed were in flames. The whole house was blazing. It was with great difficulty that my wife, a servant, and myself, made our escape from the conflagration. The destruction was complete. My entire worldly wealth was swallowed up, and I resigned myself thenceforward to despair.

I am above the weakness of seeking to establish a sequence of cause and effect, between the disaster and the atrocity. But I am detailing a chain of facts—and wish not to leave even a possible link imperfect. On the day succeeding the fire, I visited the ruins. The walls, with one exception, had fallen in. This exception was found in a compartment wall, not very thick, which stood about the middle of the house, and against which had rested the head of my bed. The plastering had here, in great measure, resisted the action of the fire—a fact which I attributed to its having been recently spread. About this wall a dense crowd were collected, and many persons seemed to be examining a particular portion of it with very minute and eager attention. The words "strange!" "singular!" and other similar expressions, excited my curiosity. I approached and saw, as if graven in *bas relief* upon the white surface, the figure of a gigantic *cat*. The impression was given with an accuracy truly marvellous. There was a rope about the animal's neck.

When I first beheld this apparition—for I could scarcely regard it as less—my wonder and my terror were extreme. But at length reflection came to my aid. The cat, I remembered, had been hung in a garden adjacent to the house. Upon the alarm of fire, this garden had been immediately filled by the crowds—by some one of whom the animal must have been cut from the tree and thrown, through an open window, into my chamber. This had probably been done with the view of arousing me from sleep. The falling of other walls had compressed the victim of my cruelty into the substance of the freshly-spread plaster; the lime of which, with the flames, and the *ammonia* from the carcass, had then accomplished the portraiture as I saw it.

Although I thus readily accounted to my reason, if not altogether to my conscience, for the startling fact just detailed, it did not the less fail to make a deep impression upon my fancy. For months I could not rid myself of the phantasm of the cat; and, during this period, there came back into my spirit a half-sentiment that seemed, but was not, remorse. I went so far as to regret the loss of the animal, and to look about me, among the vile haunts which I now habitually frequented, for another pet of the same species, and of somewhat similar appearance, with which to supply its place.

One night as I sat, half stupified, in a den of more than infamy, my attention was suddenly drawn to some black object, reposing upon the head of one of the immense hogsheads of Gin, or of Rum, which constituted the chief furniture of the apartment. I had been looking steadily at the top of this hogshead for some minutes, and what now caused me surprise was the fact that I had not sooner perceived the object thereupon. I approached it, and touched it with my hand. It was a black cat—a very large one— fully as large as Pluto, and closely resembling him in every respect but one. Pluto had not a white hair upon any portion of his body; but this cat had a large, although indefinite splotch of white, covering nearly the whole region of the breast.

Upon my touching him, he immediately arose, purred loudly, rubbed against my hand, and appeared delighted with my notice. This, then, was the very creature of which I was in search. I at once offered to purchase it of the landlord; but this person made no claim to it—knew nothing of it—had never seen it before.

I continued my caresses, and, when I prepared to go home, the animal evinced a disposition to accompany me. I permitted it to do so; occasionally stooping and patting it as I proceeded. When it reached the house it domesticated itself at once, and became immediately a great favorite with my wife.

For my own part, I soon found a dislike to it arising within me. This was just the reverse of what I had anticipated; but—I know not how or why it was—its evident fondness for myself rather disgusted and annoyed. By slow degrees, these feelings of disgust and annoyance rose into the bitterness of hatred. I avoided the creature; a certain sense of shame, and the remembrance of my former deed of cruelty, preventing me from physically abusing it. I did not, for some weeks, strike, or otherwise violently ill use it; but gradually—very gradually—I came to look upon it with unutterable loathing, and to flee silently from its odious presence, as from the breath of a pestilence.

What added, no doubt, to my hatred of the beast, was the discovery, on the morning after I brought it home, that, like Pluto, it also had been deprived of one of its eyes. This circumstance, however, only endeared it to my wife, who, as I have already said, possessed, in a high degree, that humanity of feeling which had once been my distinguishing trait, and the source of many of my simplest and purest pleasures.

With my aversion to this cat, however, its partiality for myself seemed to increase. It followed my footsteps with a pertinacity which it would be difficult to make the reader comprehend. Whenever I sat, it would crouch beneath my chair, or spring upon my knees, covering me with its loathsome caresses. If I arose to walk it would get between my feet and thus nearly throw me down, or, fastening its long and sharp claws in my dress, clamber, in this manner, to my breast. At such times, although I longed to destroy it with a blow, I was yet withheld from so doing, partly by a memory of my former crime, but chiefly —let me confess it at once—by absolute *dread* of the beast.

This dread was not exactly a dread of physical evil—and yet I should be at a loss how otherwise to define it. I am almost ashamed to own—yes, even in this felon's cell, I am almost ashamed to own—that the terror and horror with which the animal inspired me, had been heightened by one of the merest chimæras it would be possible to conceive. My wife had called my attention, more than once, to the character of the mark of white hair, of which I have spoken, and which constituted the sole visible difference between the strange beast and the one I had destroyed. The reader will remember that this mark, although large, had been originally very indefinite; but, by slow degrees—degrees nearly imperceptible, and which for a long time my Reason struggled to reject as fanciful—it had, at length, assumed a rigorous distinctness of outline. It was now the representation of an object that I shudder to name—and for this, above all, I loathed, and dreaded, and would have rid myself of the monster *had I dared*—it was now, I say, the image of a hideous—of a ghastly thing—of the GALLOWS!—oh, mournful and terrible engine of Horror and of Crime—of Agony and of Death!

And now was I indeed wretched beyond the wretchedness of mere Humanity. And *a brute beast*—whose fellow I had contemptuously destroyed—*a brute beast* to work out for *me*—for me a man, fashioned in the image of the High God—so much of insufferable woe! Alas! neither by day nor by night knew I the blessing of Rest any more! During the former the creature left me no moment alone; and, in the latter, I started, hourly, from dreams of unutterable fear, to find the hot breath of *the thing* upon my face, and its vast weight—an incarnate Night-Mare that I had no power to shake off—incumbent eternally upon my *heart!*

Beneath the pressure of torments such as these, the feeble remnant of the good within me succumbed. Evil thoughts became my sole intimates—the darkest and most evil of thoughts. The moodiness of my usual temper increased to hatred of all things and of all mankind; while from the sudden, frequent, and ungovernable outbursts of a fury to which I now blindly abandoned myself, my uncomplaining wife, alas! was the most usual and the most patient of sufferers.

One day she accompanied me, upon some household errand, into the cellar of the old building which our poverty compelled us to inhabit. The cat followed me down the steep stairs, and, nearly throwing me headlong, exasperated me to madness. Uplifting an axe, and forgetting, in my wrath, the childish dread which had hitherto stayed my hand, I aimed a blow at the animal which, of course, would have proved instantly fatal had it descended as I wished. But this blow was arrested by the hand of my wife. Goaded, by the interference, into a rage more than demoniacal, I withdrew my arm from her gasp and buried the axe in her brain. She fell dead upon the spot, without a groan.

This hideous murder accomplished, I set myself forthwith, and with entire deliberation, to the task of concealing the body. I knew that I could not remove it from the house, either by day or by night, without the risk of being observed by the neighbors. Many projects entered my mind. At one period I thought of cutting the corpse into minute fragments, and destroying them by fire. At another, I resolved to dig a grave for it in the floor of the cellar. Again, I deliberated about casting it in the well in the yard—about packing it in a box, as if merchandize, with the usual arrangements, and so getting a porter to take it from the house. Finally I hit upon what I considered a far better expedient than either of these. I determined to wall it up in the cellar—as the monks of the middle ages are recorded to have walled up their victims.

For a purpose such as this the cellar was well adapted. Its walls were loosely constructed, and had lately been plastered throughout with a rough plaster, which the dampness of the atmosphere had prevented from hardening. Moreover, in one of the walls was a projection, caused by a false chimney, or fireplace, that had been filled up, and made to resemble the rest of the cellar. I made no doubt that I could readily displace the bricks at this point, insert the corpse, and wall the whole up as before, so that no eye could detect any thing suspicious.

And in this calculation I was not deceived. By means of

a crow-bar I easily dislodged the bricks, and, having carefully deposited the body against the inner wall, I propped it in that position, while, with little trouble, I re-laid the whole structure as it originally stood. Having procured mortar, sand, and hair, with every possible precaution, I prepared a plaster which could not be distinguished from the old, and with this I very carefully went over the new brick-work. When I had finished, I felt satisfied that all was right. The wall did not present the slightest appearance of having been disturbed. The rubbish on the floor was picked up with the minutest care. I looked around triumphantly, and said to myself—"Here at least, then, my labor has not been in vain."

My next step was to look for the beast which had been the cause of so much wretchedness; for I had, at length, firmly resolved to put it to death. Had I been able to meet with it, at the moment, there could have been no doubt of its fate; but it appeared that the crafty animal had been alarmed at the violence of my previous anger, and forebore to present itself in my present mood. It is impossible to describe, or to imagine, the deep, the blissful sense of relief which the absence of the detested creature occasioned in my bosom. It did not make its appearance during the night—and thus for one night at least, since its introduction into the house, I soundly and tranquilly slept; aye, *slept* even with the burden of murder upon my soul!

The second and third day passed, and still my tormentor came not. Once again I breathed as a freeman. The monster, in terror, had fled the premises forever! I should behold it no more! My happiness was supreme! The guilt of my dark deed disturbed me but little. Some few inquiries had been made, but these had been readily answered. Even a search had been instituted—but of course nothing was to be discovered. I looked upon my future felicity as secured.

Upon the fourth day of the assassination, a party of the police came, very unexpectedly, into the house, and proceeded again to make rigorous investigation of the premises. Secure, however, in the inscrutability of my place of concealment, I felt no embarrassment whatever. The officers bade me accompany them in their search. They left no nook or corner unexplored. At length, for the third or fourth time, they descended into the cellar. I quivered not in a muscle. My heart beat calmly as that of one who slumbers in innocence. I walked the cellar from end to end. I folded my arms upon my bosom, and roamed easily to and fro. The police were thoroughly satisfied and prepared to depart. The glee at my heart was too strong to be restrained. I burned to say if but one word, by way of triumph, and to render doubly sure their assurance of my guiltlessness.

"Gentlemen," I said at last, as the party ascended the steps, "I delight to have allayed your suspicions. I wish you all health, and a little more courtesy. By the bye, gentlemen, this—this is a very well constructed house." [In the rabid desire to say something easily, I scarcely knew what I uttered at all.]—"I may say an *excellently* well constructed house. These walls—are you going, gentlemen?—these walls are solidly put together;" and here, through the mere phrenzy of bravado, I rapped heavily, with a cane which I held in my hand, upon that very portion of the brick-work behind which stood the corpse of the wife of my bosom.

But may God shield and deliver me from the fangs of the Arch-Fiend! No sooner had the reverberation of my blows sunk into silence, than I was answered by a voice from within the tomb!—by a cry, at first muffled and broken, like the sobbing of a child, and then quickly swelling into one long, loud, and continuous scream, utterly anomalous and inhuman—a howl—a wailing shriek, half of horror and half of triumph, such as might have arisen only out of hell, conjointly from the throats of the damned in their agony and of the demons that exult in the damnation.

Of my own thoughts it is folly to speak. Swooning, I staggered to the opposite wall. For one instant the party upon the stairs remained motionless, through extremity of terror and of awe. In the next, a dozen stout arms were toiling at the wall. It fell bodily. The corpse, already greatly decayed and clotted with gore, stood erect before the eyes of the spectators. Upon its head, with red extended mouth and solitary eye of fire, sat the hideous beast whose craft had seduced me into murder, and whose informing voice had consigned me to the hangman. I had walled the monster up within the tomb!

A TALE OF THE RAGGED MOUNTAINS

During the fall of the year 1827, while residing near Charlottesville, Virginia, I casually made the acquaintance of Mr. Augustus Bedloe. This young gentleman was remarkable in every respect, and excited in me a profound interest and curiosity. I found it impossible to comprehend him either in his moral or his physical relations. Of his family I could obtain no satisfactory account. Whence he came, I never ascertained. Even about his age—although I call him a young gentleman—there was something which perplexed me in no little degree. He certainly *seemed* young—and he made a point of speaking about his youth—yet there were moments when I should have had little trouble in imagining him a hundred years of age. But in no regard was he more peculiar than in his

personal appearance. He was singularly tall and thin. He
stooped much. His limbs were exceedingly long and emaciated. His forehead was broad and low. His complexion
was absolutely bloodless. His mouth was large and flexible,
and his teeth were more wildly uneven, although sound,
than I had ever before seen teeth in a human head. The
expression of his smile, however, was by no means un-
pleasing, as might be supposed; but it had no variation
whatever. It was one of profound melancholy—of a phase-
less and unceasing gloom. His eyes were abnormally large,
and round like those of a cat. The pupils, too, upon any
accession or diminution of light, underwent contraction or
dilation, just such as is observed in the feline tribe. In moments of excitement the orbs grew bright to a degree
almost inconceivable; seeming to emit luminous rays, not
of a reflected, but of an intrinsic lustre, as does a candle or
the sun; yet their ordinary condition was so totally vapid,
filmy and dull, as to convey the idea of the eyes of a long-
interred corpse.

These peculiarities of person appeared to cause him
much annoyance, and he was continually alluding to them
in a sort of half explanatory, half apologetic strain, which,
when I first heard it, impressed me very painfully. I soon,
however, grew accustomed to it, and my uneasiness wore
off. It seemed to be his design rather to insinuate than
directly to assert that, physically, he had not always
been what he was—that a long series of neuralgic attacks
had reduced him from a condition of more than usual
personal beauty, to that which I saw. For many years
past he had been attended by a physician, named Templeton—an old gentleman, perhaps seventy years of age—
whom he had first encountered at Saratoga, and from
whose attention, while there, he either received, or fancied
that he received, great benefit. The result was that Bedloe,
who was wealthy, had made an arrangement with Doctor
Templeton, by which the latter, in consideration of a

liberal annual allowance, had consented to devote his time and medical experience exclusively to the care of the invalid.

Doctor Templeton had been a traveller in his younger days, and, at Paris, had become a convert, in great measure, to the doctrines of Mesmer. It was altogether by means of magnetic remedies that he had succeeded in alleviating the acute pains of his patient; and this success had very naturally inspired the latter with a certain degree of confidence in the opinions from which the remedies had been educed. The Doctor, however, like all enthusiasts, had struggled hard to make a thorough convert of his pupil, and finally so far gained his point as to induce the sufferer to submit to numerous experiments.—By a frequent repetition of these, a result had arisen, which of late days has become so common as to attract little or no attention, but which, at the period of which I write, had very rarely been known in America. I mean to say, that between Doctor Templeton and Bedloe there had grown up, little by little, a very distinct and strongly marked *rapport*, or magnetic relation. I am not prepared to assert, however, that this *rapport* extended beyond the limits of the simple sleep-producing power; but this power itself had attained great intensity. At the first attempt to induce the magnetic somnolency, the mesmerist entirely failed. In the fifth or sixth he succeeded very partially, and after long continued effort. Only at the twelfth was the triumph complete. After this the will of the patient succumbed rapidly to that of the physician, so that, when I first became acquainted with the two, sleep was brought about almost instantaneously, by the mere volition of the operator, even when the invalid was unaware of his presence. It is only now, in the year 1845, when similar miracles are witnessed daily by thousands, that I dare venture to record this apparent impossibility as a matter of serious fact.

The temperature [temperament] of Bedloe was, in the highest degree, sensitive, excitable, enthusiastic. His imagination was singularly vigorous and creative; and no doubt it derived additional force from the habitual use of morphine, which he swallowed in great quantity, and without which he would have found it impossible to exist. It was his practice to take a very large dose of it immediately after breakfast, each morning—or rather immediately after a cup of strong coffee, for he ate nothing in the forenoon—and then set forth alone, or attended only by a dog, upon a long ramble among the chain of wild and dreary hills that lie westward and southward of Charlottesville, and are there dignified by the title of the Ragged Mountains.

Upon a dim, warm, misty day, toward the close of November, and during the strange *interregnum* of the seasons which in America is termed the Indian Summer, Mr. Bedloe departed, as usual, for the hills. The day passed, and still he did not return.

About eight o'clock at night, having become seriously alarmed at his protracted absence, we were about setting out in search of him, when he unexpectedly made his appearance, in health no worse than usual, and in rather more than ordinary spirits. The account which he gave of his expedition, and of the events which had detained him, was a singular one indeed.

"You will remember," said he, "that it was about nine in the morning when I left Charlottesville. I bent my steps immediately to the mountains, and, about ten, entered a gorge which was entirely new to me. I followed the windings of this pass with much interest.—The scenery which presented itself on all sides, although scarcely entitled to be called grand, had about it an indescribable, and to me, a delicious aspect of dreary desolation. The solitude seemed absolutely virgin. I could not help believing that the green sods and the gray rocks upon which I trod, had been trodden never before by the foot of a human being. So entirely secluded, and in fact inaccessible, except through a series of accidents, is the entrance of the ravine, that it is by no means impossible that I was indeed the first adventurer—the very first and sole adventurer who had ever penetrated its recesses.

"The thick and peculiar mist, or smoke, which distinguishes the Indian Summer, and which now hung heavily over all objects, served, no doubt, to deepen the vague impressions which these objects created. So dense was this pleasant fog, that I could at no time see more than a dozen yards of the path before me. This path was excessively sinuous, and as the sun could not be seen, I soon lost all idea of the direction in which I journeyed. In the meantime the morphine had its customary effect—that of enduing all the external world with an intensity of interest. In the quivering of a leaf—in the hue of a blade of grass—in the shape of a trefoil—in the humming of a bee —in the gleaming of a dew-drop—in the breathing of the wind—in the faint odors that came from the forest— there came a whole universe of suggestion—a gay and motely train of rhapsodical and immethodical thought.

"Busied in this, I walked on for several hours, during which the mist deepened around me to so great an extent, that at length I was reduced to an absolute groping of the way. And now an indescribable uneasiness possessed me— a species of nervous hesitation and tremor.—I feared to tread, lest I should be precipitated into some abyss. I remembered, too, strange stories told about these Ragged Hills, and of the uncouth and fierce races of men who tenanted their groves and caverns. A thousand vague fancies oppressed and disconcerted me—fancies the more distressing because vague. Very suddenly my attention was arrested by the loud beating of a drum.

"My amazement was, of course, extreme. A drum in these hills was a thing unknown. I could not have been more surprised at the sound of the trump of the Archangel. But a new and still more astounding source of interest and perplexity arose. There came a wild rattling or jingling sound, as if of a bunch of large keys—and upon the instant a dusky-visaged and half-naked man rushed past me with a shriek. He came so close to my person that I felt his hot breath upon my face. He bore in one hand an instrument composed of an assemblage of steel rings, and shook them vigorously as he ran. Scarcely had he disappeared in the mist, before, panting after him, with open mouth and glaring eyes, there darted a huge beast. I could not be mistaken in its character. It was a hyena.

"The sight of this monster rather relieved than heightened my terrors—for I now made sure that I dreamed, and endeavored to arouse myself to waking consciousness. I stepped boldly and briskly forward. I rubbed my eyes. I called aloud. I pinched my limbs. A small spring of water presented itself to my view, and here, stooping, I bathed my hands and my head and neck. This seemed to dissipate the equivocal sensations which had hitherto annoyed me. I arose, as I thought, a new man, and proceeded steadily and complacently on my unknown way.

"At length, quite overcome by exertion, and by a certain oppressive closeness of the atmosphere, I seated myself beneath a tree. Presently there came a feeble gleam of sunshine, and the shadow of the leaves of the tree fell faintly but definitely upon the grass. At this shadow I gazed wonderingly for many minutes. Its character stupified me with astonishment. I looked upward. The tree was a palm.

"I now arose hurriedly, and in a state of fearful agitation—for the fancy that I dreamed would serve me no longer. I saw—I felt that I had perfect command of my senses—and these senses now brought to my soul a world of novel and singular sensation. The heat became all at once intolerable. A strange odor loaded the breeze.— A low continuous murmur, like that arising from a full, but gently-flowing river, came to my ears, intermingled with the peculiar hum of multitudinous human voices.

"While I listened in an extremity of astonishment which I need not attempt to describe, a strong and brief gust of wind bore off the incumbent fog as if by the wand of an enchanter.

"I found myself at the foot of a high mountain, and looking down into a vast plain, through which wound a majestic river. On the margin of this river stood an Eastern-looking city, such as we read of in the Arabian Tales, but of a character even more singular than any there described. From my position, which was far above the level of the town, I could perceive its every nook and corner, as if delineated on a map. The streets seemed innumerable, and crossed each other irregularly in all directions, but were rather long winding alleys than streets, and absolutely swarmed with inhabitants. The houses were wildly picturesque. On every hand was a wilderness of balconies, of verandahs, of minarets, of shrines, and fantastically carved oriels. Bazaars abounded; and in these were displayed rich wares in infinite variety and profusion—silks, muslins, the most dazzling cutlery, the most magnificent jewels and gems. Besides these things, were seen, on all sides, banners and palanquins, litters with stately dames close veiled, elephants gorgeously caparisoned, idols grotesquely hewn, drums, banners and gongs, spears, silver and gilded maces. And amid the crowd, and the clamor, and the general intricacy and confusion—amid the million of black and yellow men, turbaned and robed, and of flowing beard, there roamed a countless multitude of holy filleted bulls, while vast legions of the filthy but sacred ape clambered, chattering and shrieking, about the cornices of the mosques, or clung to the minarets and oriels. From the swarming streets to the banks of the river, there descended innumerable flights of steps leading to bathing places, while the river itself seemed to force a passage with difficulty through the vast fleets of deeply-burthened ships that far and wide encumbered its surface. Beyond the limits of the city arose, in frequent majestic groups, the palm and the cocoa, with other gigantic and weird trees of vast age; and here and there might be seen a field of rice, the thatched hut of a peasant, a tank, a stray temple, a gypsy camp, or a solitary graceful maiden taking her way, with a pitcher upon her head, to the banks of the magnificent river.

"You will say now, of course, that I dreamed; but not so. What I saw—what I heard—what I felt—what I thought—had about it nothing of the unmistakeable idiosyncrasy of the dream. All was rigorously self-consistent. At first, doubting that I was really awake, I entered into a series of tests, which soon convinced me that I really was. Now, when one dreams, and, in the dream, suspects that he dreams, the suspicion *never fails to confirm itself*, and the sleeper is almost immediately aroused.—Thus Novalis errs not in saying that 'we are near waking when we dream that we dream.' Had the vision occurred to me as I describe it, without my suspecting it as a dream, then a dream it might absolutely have been, but, occurring as it did, and suspected and tested as it was, I am forced to class it among other phenomena."

"In this I am not sure that you are wrong," observed Dr. Templeton, "but proceed. You arose and descended into the city."

"I arose," continued Bedloe, regarding the Doctor with an air of profound astonishment, "I arose, as you say, and descended into the city. On my way, I fell in with an immense populace, crowding, through every avenue, all in the same direction, and exhibiting in every action the wildest excitement. Very suddenly, and by some inconceivable impulse, I became intensely imbued with personal interest in what was going on. I seemed to feel that I had an important part to play, without exactly understanding what it was. Against the crowd which environed me, however, I experienced a deep sentiment of animosity. I shrank from amid them, and, swiftly, by a circuitous path, reached and entered the city. Here all was the wildest tumult and contention. A small party of men, clad in garments half-Indian half European, and officered by gentlemen in a uniform partly British, were engaged, at great odds, with the swarming rabble of the alleys. I joined the weaker party, arming myself with the weapons of a fallen officer, and fighting I knew not whom with the nervous ferocity of despair. We were soon overpowered by numbers, and driven to seek refuge in a species of kiosk. Here we barricaded ourselves, and, for the present, were secure. From a loop-hole near the summit of the kiosk, I perceived a vast crowd, in furious agitation, surrounding and assaulting a gay palace that overhung the river. Presently, from an upper window of this palace, there descended an effeminate-looking person, by means of a string made of the turbans of his attendants. A boat was at hand, in which he escaped to the opposite bank of the river.

"And now a new object took possession of my soul. I spoke a few hurried but energetic words to my companions, and, having succeeded in gaining over a few of them to my purpose, made a frantic sally from the kiosk. We rushed amid the crowd that surrounded it. They retreated, at first, before us. They rallied, fought madly, and retreated again. In the mean time we were borne far from the kiosk, and became bewildered and entangled among the narrow streets of tall overhanging houses, into the recesses of which the sun had never been able to shine. The rabble pressed impetuously upon us, harassing us with their spears, and overwhelming us with flights of arrows. These latter were very remarkable, and resembled in some respects the writhing creese of the Malay. They were made to imitate the body of a creeping serpent, and were long and black, with a poisoned barb. One of them struck me upon the right temple. I reeled and fell. An instantaneous and deadly sickness seized me. I struggled —I gasped—I died."

"You will hardly persist *now*," said I, smiling, "that the whole of your adventure was not a dream. You are not prepared to maintain that you are dead?"

When I said these words, I of course expected some lively sally from Bedloe in reply; but, to my astonishment, he hesitated, trembled, became fearfully pallid, and remained silent. I looked towards Templeton. He sat erect and rigid in his chair—his teeth chattered, and his eyes were starting from their sockets. "Proceed!" he at length said hoarsely to Bedloe.

"For many minutes," continued the latter, "my sole sentiment—my sole feeling—was that of darkness and nonentity, with the consciousness of death. At length, there seemed to pass a violent and sudden shock through my soul, as if of electricity. With it came the sense of elasticity and of light. This latter I felt—not saw. In an instant I seemed to rise from the ground. But I had no bodily, no visible, audible, or palpable presence. The crowd had departed. The tumult had ceased. The city was in comparative repose. Beneath me lay my corpse, with the arrow in my temple, the whole head greatly swollen and disfigured. But all these things I felt—not saw. I took interest in nothing. Even the corpse seemed a matter in which I had no concern. Volition I had none, but appeared to be impelled into motion, and flitted buoyantly out of the city, retracing the circuitous path by which I had entered it. When I had attained that point of the ravine in the mountains, at which I had encountered the hyena, I again experienced a shock as of a galvanic battery; the sense of weight, of volition, of substance, returned. I became my original self, and bent my steps eagerly homewards—but the past had not lost the vividness of the real—and not now, even for an instant, can I compel my understanding to regard it as a dream."

"Nor was it," said Templeton, with an air of deep solemnity, "yet it would be difficult to say how otherwise it should be termed. Let us suppose only, that the soul of the man of to-day is upon the verge of some stupendous psychal discoveries. Let us content ourselves with this supposition. For the rest I have some explanation to make. Here is a water-colour drawing, which I should have shown you before, but which an unaccountable sentiment of horror has hitherto prevented me from showing."

We looked at the picture which he presented. I saw nothing in it of an extraordinary character; but its effect upon Bedloe was prodigious. He nearly fainted as he gazed. And yet it was but a miniature portrait—a miraculously accurate one, to be sure—of his own very remarkable features. At least this was my thought as I regarded it.

"You will perceive," said Templeton, "the date of this picture—it is here, scarcely visible, in this corner—1780. In this year was the portrait taken. It is the likeness of a dead friend—a Mr. Oldeb—to whom I became much attached at Calcutta, during the administration of Warren Hastings. I was then only twenty years old.—When I first saw you, Mr. Bedloe, at Saratoga, it was the miraculous similarity which existed between yourself and the painting, which induced me to accost you, to seek your friendship, and to bring about those arrangements which resulted in my becoming your constant companion. In accomplishing this point, I was urged partly, and perhaps principally, by a regretful memory of the deceased, but also, in part, by an uneasy, and not altogether horrorless curiosity respecting yourself.

"In your detail of the vision which presented itself to you amid the hills, you have described, with the minutest accuracy, the Indian city of Benares, upon the Holy River.

The riots, the combats, the massacre, were the actual events of the insurrection of Cheyte Sing, which took place in 1780, when Hastings was put in imminent peril of his life. The man escaping by the string of turbans, was Cheyte Sing himself. The party in the kiosk were sepoys and British officers, headed by Hastings. Of this party I was one, and did all I could to prevent the rash and fatal sally of the officer who fell, in the crowded alleys, by the poisoned arrow of a Bengalee. That officer was my dearest friend. It was Oldeb. You will perceive by these manuscripts," (here the speaker produced a note-book in which several pages appeared to have been freshly written) "that at the very period in which you fancied these things amid the hills, I was engaged in detailing them upon paper here at home."

In about a week after this conversation, the following paragraphs appeared in a Charlottesville paper.

"We have the painful duty of announcing the death of Mr. Augustus Bedlo, a gentleman whose amiable manners and many virtues have long endeared him to the citizens of Charlottesville.

"Mr. B., for some years past, has been subject to neuralgia, which has often threatened to terminate fatally; but this can be regarded only as the mediate cause of his decease. The proximate cause was one of especial singularity. In an excursion to the Ragged Mountains, a few days since, a slight cold and fever were contracted, attended with great determination of blood to the head. To relieve this, Dr. Templeton resorted to topical bleeding. Leeches were applied to the temples. In a fearfully brief period the patient died, when it appeared that, in the jar containing the leeches, had been introduced, by accident, one of the venomous vermicular sangsues which are now and then found in the neighboring ponds. This creature fastened itself upon a small artery in the right temple. Its close resemblance to the medicinal leech caused the mistake to be overlooked until too late.

"N.B. The poisonous sangsue of Charlottesville may always be distinguished from the medicinal leech by its blackness, and especially by its writhing or vermicular motions, which very nearly resemble those of a snake."

I was speaking with the editor of the paper in question, upon the topic of this remarkable accident, when it occurred to me to ask how it happened that the name of the deceased had been given as Bedlo.

"I presume," said I, "you have authority for this spelling, but I have always supposed the name to be written with an *e* at the end."

"Authority?—no," he replied. "It is a mere typographical error. The name is Bedlo with an *e*, all the world over, and I never knew it to be spelt otherwise in my life."

"Then," said I mutteringly, as I turned upon my heel, "then indeed has it come to pass that one truth is stranger than any fiction—for Bedlo, without the *e*, what is it but Oldeb conversed? And this man tells me it is a typographical error."

THE PREMATURE BURIAL

There are certain themes of which the interest is all-absorbing, but which are too entirely horrible for the purposes of legitimate fiction. These the mere romanticist must eschew, if he do not wish to offend, or to disgust. They are with propriety handled, only when the severity and majesty of Truth sanctify and sustain them. We thrill, for example, with the most intense of "pleasurable pain," over the accounts of the Passage of the Beresina, of the

Earthquake at Lisbon, of the Plague at London, of the Massacre of St. Bartholomew, or of the stifling of the hundred and twenty-three prisoners in the Black Hole at Calcutta. But, in these accounts, it is the fact—it is the reality—it is the history which excites. As inventions, we should regard them with simple abhorrence.

I have mentioned some few of the more prominent and august calamities on record; but, in these, it is the extent, not less than the character of the calamity, which so vividly impresses the fancy. I need not remind the reader that, from the long and weird catalogue of human miseries, I might have selected many individual instances more replete with essential suffering than any of these vast generalities of disaster. The true wretchedness, indeed—the ultimate woe—is particular, not diffuse. That the ghastly extremes of agony are endured by man the unit, and never by man the mass—for this let us thank a merciful God!

To be buried while alive, is, beyond question, the most terrific of these extremes which has ever fallen to the lot of mere mortality. That it has frequently, very frequently, so fallen, will scarcely be denied by those who think. The boundaries which divide Life from Death, are at best shadowy and vague. Who shall say where the one ends, and where the other begins? We know that there are diseases in which occur total cessations of all the apparent functions of vitality, and yet in which these cessations are merely suspensions, properly so called. They are only temporary pauses in the incomprehensible mechanism. A certain period elapses, and some unseen mysterious principle again sets in motion the magic pinions and the wizard wheels. The silver cord was not forever loosed, nor the golden bowl irreparably broken. But where, meantime, was the soul?

Apart, however, from the inevitable conclusion, *à priori*, that such causes must produce such effects—that the well known occurrence of such cases of suspended animation

must naturally give rise, now and then, to premature interments—apart from this consideration, we have the
direct testimony of medical and ordinary experience, to
prove that a vast number of such interments have actually
taken place. I might refer at once, if necessary, to a hundred well authenticated instances. One of very remarkable
character, and of which the circumstances may be fresh
in the memory of some of my readers, occurred, not very
long ago, in the neighboring city of Baltimore, where it
occasioned a painful, intense, and widely extended excitement. The wife of one of the most respectable citizens—a
lawyer of eminence and a member of Congress—was seized
with a sudden and unaccountable illness, which completely baffled the skill of her physicians. After much suffering she died, or was supposed to die. No one suspected,
indeed, or had reason to suspect, that she was not actually
dead. She presented all the ordinary appearances of death.
The face assumed the usual pinched and sunken outline.
The lips were of the usual marble pallor. The eyes were
lustreless. There was no warmth. Pulsation had ceased.
For three days the body was preserved unburied, during
which it had acquired a stony rigidity. The funeral, in
short, was hastened, on account of the rapid advance of
what was supposed to be decomposition.

The lady was deposited in her family vault, which, for
three subsequent years, was undisturbed. At the expiration
of this term, it was opened for the reception of a sacro-
phagus;—but, alas! how fearful a shock awaited the husband, who, personally, threw open the door. As its portals
swung outwardly back, some white-apparrelled object fell
rattling within his arms. It was the skeleton of his wife
in her yet unmouldered shroud.

A careful investigation rendered it evident that she had
revived within two days after her entombment—that her
struggles within the coffin had caused it to fall from a
ledge, or shelf, to the floor, where it was so broken as to

permit her escape. A lamp which had been accidentally left, full of oil, within the tomb, was found empty; it might have been exhausted, however, by evaporation. On the uppermost of the steps which led down into the dread chamber, was a large fragment of the coffin, with which it seemed that she had endeavored to arrest attention, by striking the iron door. While thus occupied, she probably swooned, or possibly died, through sheer terror; and, in falling, her shroud became entangled in some iron-work which projected interiorly. Thus she remained, and thus she rotted, erect.

In the year 1810, a case of living inhumation happened in France, attended with circumstances which go far to warrant the assertion that truth is, indeed, stranger than fiction. The heroine of the story was a Mademoiselle Victorine Lafourcade, a young girl of illustrious family, of wealth, and of great personal beauty. Among her numerous suitors was Julien Bossuet, a poor *littérateur*, or journalist, of Paris. His talents and general amiability had recommended him to the notice of the heiress, by whom he seems to have been truly beloved; but her pride of birth decided her, finally, to reject him, and to wed a Monsieur Rénelle, a banker, and a diplomatist of some eminence. After marriage, however, this gentleman neglected, and, perhaps, even more positively ill-treated her. Having passed with him some wretched years, she died,—at least her condition so closely resembled death as to deceive every one who saw her. She was buried—not in a vault—but in an ordinary grave in the village of her nativity. Filled with despair, and still inflamed by the memory of a profound attachment, the lover journeys from the capital to the remote province in which the village lies, with the romantic purpose of disinterring the corpse, and possessing himself of its luxuriant tresses. He reaches the grave. At midnight he unearths the coffin, opens it, and is in the

act of detaching the hair, when he is arrested by the unclosing of the beloved eyes. In fact, the lady had been
buried alive. Vitality had not altogether departed; and she
was aroused, by the caresses of her lover, from the lethargy
which had been mistaken for death. He bore her frantically
to his lodgings in the village. He employed certain powerful restoratives suggested by no little medical learning. In
fine, she revived. She recognized her preserver. She remained with him until, by slow degrees, she fully recovered
her original health. Her woman's heart was not adamant,
and this last lesson of love sufficed to soften it. She bestowed it upon Bossuet. She returned no more to her husband, but concealing from him her resurrection, fled with
her lover to America. Twenty years afterwards, the two returned to France, in the persuasion that time had so
greatly altered the lady's appearance that her friends would
be unable to recognize her. They were mistaken, however;
for, at the first meeting, Monsieur Rénelle did actually
recognize and make claim to his wife. This claim she resisted; and a judicial tribunal sustained her in her resistance; deciding that the peculiar circumstances, with the
long lapse of years, had extinguished, not only equitably
but legally, the authority of the husband.

The "Chirurgical Journal" of Leipsic—a periodical, of
high authority and merit, which some American book-
seller would do well to translate and republish—records, in
a late number, a very distressing event of the character in
question.

An officer of artillery, a man of gigantic stature and of
robust health, being thrown from an unmanageable horse,
received a very severe contusion upon the head, which
rendered him insensible at once; the skull was slightly
fractured; but no immediate danger was apprehended.
Trepanning was accomplished successfully. He was bled,
and many other of the ordinary means of relief were

adopted. Gradually, however, he fell into a more and more hopeless state of stupor; and, finally, it was thought that he died.

The weather was warm; and he was buried, with indecent haste, in one of the public cemeteries. His funeral took place on Thursday. On the Sunday following, the grounds of the cemetery were, as usual, much thronged with visiters; and, about noon, an intense excitement was created by the declaration of a peasant that, while sitting upon the grave of the officer, he had distinctly felt a commotion of the earth, as if occasioned by some one struggling beneath. At first little attention was paid to the man's asseveration; but his evident terror, and the dogged obstinacy with which he persisted in his story, had, at length, their natural effect upon the crowd. Spades were hurriedly procured, and the grave, which was shamefully shallow, was, in a few minutes, so far thrown open that the head of its occupant appeared. He was then, seemingly, dead; but he sat nearly erect within his coffin, the lid of which, in his furious struggles, he had partially uplifted.

He was forthwith conveyed to the nearest Hospital, and there pronounced to be still living, although in an asphytic condition. After some hours he revived, recognized individuals of his acquaintance, and, in broken sentences, spoke of his agonies in the grave.

From what he related, it was clear that he must have been conscious of life for more than an hour, while inhumed, before lapsing into insensibility. The grave was carelessly and loosely filled with an exceedingly porous soil; and thus some air was necessarily admitted. He heard the footsteps of the crowd overhead, and endeavored to make himself heard in turn. It was the tumult within the grounds of the cemetery, he said, which appeared to awaken him from a deep sleep—but no sooner was he awake than he became fully aware of the awful horrors of his position.

This patient, it is recorded, was doing well, and seemed

to be in a fair way of ultimate recovery, but fell a victim to the quackeries of medical experiment. The galvanic battery was applied; and he suddenly expired in one of those ecstatic paroxysms which, occasionally, it super-induces.

The mention of the galvanic battery, nevertheless, re-calls to my memory a well known and very extraordinary case in point, where its action proved the means of restor-ing to animation a young attorney of London who had been interred for two days. This occurred in 1831, and created, at the time, a very profound sensation wherever it was made the subject of converse.

The patient, Mr. Edward Stapleton, had died, ap-parently, of typhus fever, accompanied with some anoma-lous symptoms which had excited the curiosity of his medi-cal attendants. Upon his seeming decease, his friends were requested to sanction a *post mortem* examination, but declined to permit it. As often happens when such re-fusals are made, the practitioners resolved to disinter the body and dissect it at leisure, in private. Arrangements were easily effected with some of the numerous corps of body-snatchers with which London abounds; and, upon the third night after the funeral, the supposed corpse was unearthed from a grave eight feet deep, and deposited in the operating chamber of one of the private hospitals.

An incision of some extent had been actually made in the abdomen, when the fresh and undecayed appearance of the subject suggested an application of the battery. One experiment succeeded another, and the customary effects supervened, with nothing to characterize them in any respect, except, upon one or two occasions, a more than ordinary degree of life-likeliness in the convulsive action.

It grew late. The day was about to dawn; and it was thought expedient, at length, to proceed at once to the dissection. A student, however, was especially desirous of testing a theory of his own, and insisted upon applying the battery to one of the pectoral muscles. A rough gash was made, and a wire hastily brought in contact; when the patient, with a hurried but quite unconvulsive movement, arose from the table, stepped into the middle of the floor, gazed about him uneasily for a few seconds, and then— spoke. What he said was unintelligible; but words were uttered; the syllabification was distinct. Having spoken, he fell heavily to the floor.

For some moments all were paralyzed with awe—but the urgency of the case soon restored them their presence of mind. It was seen that Mr. Stapleton was alive, although in a swoon. Upon exhibition of ether he revived and was rapidly restored to health, and to the society of his friends —from whom, however, all knowledge of his resuscitation was withheld, until a relapse was no longer to be apprehended. Their wonder—their rapturous astonishment— may be conceived.

The most thrilling peculiarity of this incident, nevertheless, is involved in what Mr. S. himself asserts. He declares that at no period was he altogether insensible—that, dully and confusedly, he was aware of every thing which happened to him, from the moment in which he was pronounced *dead* by his physicians, to that in which he fell swooning to the floor of the Hospital. "I am alive" were the uncomprehended words which, upon recognizing the locality of the dissecting-room, he had endeavored, in his extremity, to utter.

It was an easy matter to multiply such histories as these —but I forbear—for, indeed, we have no need of such to establish the fact that premature interments occur. When we reflect how very rarely, from the nature of the case, we have it in our power to detect them, we must admit that they may *frequently* occur without our cognizance. Scarcely, in truth, is a graveyard ever encroached upon, for any purpose, to any great extent, that skeletons are not found in postures which suggest the most fearful of suspicions.

Fearful indeed the suspicion—but more fearful the doom! It may be asserted, without hesitation, that no event is so terribly well adapted to inspire the supremeness of bodily and of mental distress, as is burial before death. The unendurable oppression of the lungs—the stifling fumes from the damp earth—the clinging of the death garments —the rigid embrace of the narrow house—the blackness of the absolute Night—the silence like a sea that overwhelms —the unseen but palpable presence of the Conqueror Worm—these things, with thoughts of the air and grass above, with memory of dear friends who would fly to save us if but informed of our fate, and with consciousness that of this fate they can *never* be informed—that our hopeless portion is that of the really dead—these considerations, I say, carry into the heart, which still palpitates, a degree of appalling and intolerable horror from which the most daring imagination must recoil. We know of nothing so agonizing upon Earth—we can dream of nothing half so hideous in the realms of the nethermost Hell. And thus all narratives upon this topic have an interest profound; an interest, nevertheless, which, through the sacred awe of the topic itself, very properly and very peculiarly depends upon our conviction of the *truth* of the matter narrated. What I have now to tell, is of my own actual knowledge— of my own positive and personal experience.

For several years I had been subject to attacks of the singular disorder which physicians have agreed to term catalepsy, in défault of a more definitive title. Although both the immediate and the predisposing causes, and even the actual diagnosis, of this disease, are still mysteries, its obvious and apparent character is sufficiently well understood. Its variations seem to be chiefly of degree. Sometimes the patient lies, for a day only, or even for a shorter period, in a species of exaggerated lethargy. He is senseless and externally motionless; but the pulsation of the heart is still faintly perceptible; some traces of warmth remain; a slight color lingers within the centre of the cheek; and, upon application of a mirror to the lips, we can detect a torpid, unequal, and vacillating action of the lungs. Then again the duration of the trance is for weeks —even for months; while the closest scrutiny, and the most rigorous medical tests, fail to establish any material distinction between the state of the sufferer and what we conceive of absolute death. Very usually, he is saved from premature interment solely by the knowledge of his friends that he has been previously subject to catalepsy, by the consequent suspicion excited, and, above all, by the nonappearance of decay. The advances of the malady are, luckily, gradual. The first manifestations, although marked, are unequivocal. The fits grow successively more and more distinctive, and endure each for a longer term than the preceding. In this lies the principal security from inhumation. The unfortunate whose *first* attack should be of the extreme character which is occasionally seen, would almost inevitably be consigned alive to the tomb.

My own case differed in no important particular from those mentioned in medical books. Sometimes, without any apparent cause, I sank, little by little, into a condition of hemi-syncope, or half swoon; and, in this condition, without pain, without ability to stir, or, strictly speaking, to think, but with a dull lethargic consciousness of life and of the presence of those who surrounded my bed, I remained, until the crisis of the disease restored me, suddenly, to perfect sensation. At other times I was quickly and impetuously smitten. I grew sick, and numb, and chilly, and dizzy, and so fell prostrate at once. Then, for weeks, all was void, and black, and silent, and Nothing became the universe. Total annihilation could be no more. From these latter attacks I awoke, however, with a gradation slow in proportion to the suddenness of the seizure. Just as the day dawns to the friendless and houseless beggar who roams the streets throughout the long desolate winter night—just so tardily—just so wearily—just so cheerily came back the light of the Soul to me.

Apart from the tendency to trance, however, my general health appeared to be good; nor could I perceive that it was at all affected by the one prevalent malady—unless, indeed, an idiosyncrasy in my ordinary *sleep* may be looked upon as superinduced. Upon awaking from slumber, I could never gain, at once, thorough possession of my senses, and always remained, for many minutes, in much bewilderment and perplexity;—the mental faculties in general, but the memory in especial, being in a condition of absolute abeyance.

In all that I endured there was no physical suffering, but of moral distress an infinitude. My fancy grew charnal. I talked "of worms, of tombs and epitaphs." I was lost in reveries of death, and the idea of premature burial held continual possession of my brain. The ghastly Danger to which I was subjected, haunted me day and night. In the former, the torture of meditation was excessive—in the latter, supreme. When the grim Darkness overspread the Earth, then, with very horror of thought, I shook—shook as the quivering plumes upon the hearse. When Nature could endure wakefulness no longer, it was with a struggle that I consented to sleep—for I shuddered to reflect that, upon awaking, I might find myself the tenant of a grave. And when, finally, I sank into slumber, it was only to rush at once into a world of phantasms, above which, with vast, sable, overshadowing wings, hovered, predominant, the one sepulchral Idea.

From the innumerable images of gloom which thus oppressed me in dreams, I select for record but a solitary vision. Methought I was immersed in a cataleptic trance of more than usual duration and profundity. Suddenly

424 Great Short Works of Edgar Allan Poe

there came an icy hand upon my forehead, and an impatient, gibbering voice whispered the word "Arise!" within my ear.

I sat erect. The darkness was total. I could not see the figure of him who had aroused me. I could call to mind neither the period at which I had fallen into the trance, nor the locality in which I then lay. While I remained motionless, and busied in endeavors to collect my thoughts, the cold hand grasped me fiercely by the wrist, shaking it petulantly, while the gibbering voice said again:

"Arise! did I not bid thee arise?"

"And who," I demanded, "art thou?"

"I have no name in the regions which I inhabit," replied the voice mournfully: "I was mortal, but am fiend. I was merciless, but am pitiful. Thou dost feel that I shudder.— My teeth chatter as I speak, yet it is not with the chilliness of the night—of the night without end. But this hideousness is insufferable. How canst *thou* tranquilly sleep? I cannot rest for the cry of these great agonies. These sights are more than I can bear. Get thee up! Come with me into the outer Night, and let me unfold to thee the graves. Is not this a spectacle of woe?—Behold!"

I looked; and the unseen figure, which still grasped me by the wrist, had caused to be thrown open the graves of all mankind; and from each issued the faint phosphoric radiance of decay; so that I could see into the innermost recesses, and there view the shrouded bodies in their sad and solemn slumbers with the worm. But, alas! the real sleepers were fewer, by many millions, than those who slumbered not at all; and there was a feeble struggling; and there was a general sad unrest; and from out the depths of the countless pits there came a melancholy rustling from the garments of the buried. And, of those who seemed tranquilly to repose, I saw that a vast number had changed, in a greater or less degree, the rigid and uneasy position in which they had originally been entombed. And the voice again said to me, as I gazed:

"Is it not—oh, is it *not* a pitiful sight?"—but, before I could find words to reply, the figure had ceased to grasp my wrist, the phosphoric lights expired, and the graves were closed with a sudden violence, while from out them arose a tumult of despairing cries, saying again—"Is it not—oh, God! is it *not* a very pitiful sight?"

Phantasies such as these, presenting themselves at night, extended their terrific influence far into my waking hours. —My nerves became thoroughly unstrung, and I fell a prey to perpetual horror. I hesitated to ride, or to walk, or to indulge in any exercise that would carry me from home. In fact I no longer dared trust myself out of the immediate presence of those who were aware of my proneness to catalepsy, lest, falling into one of my usual fits, I should be buried before my real condition could be ascertained. I doubted the care, the fidelity of my dearest friends. I dreaded that, in some trance of more than customary duration, they might be prevailed upon to regard me as irrecoverable. I even went so far as to fear that, as I occasioned much trouble, they might be glad to consider any very protracted attack as sufficient excuse for getting rid of me altogether. It was in vain they endeavored to reassure me by the most solemn promises. I exacted the most sacred oaths, that under no circumstances they would bury me until decomposition had so materially advanced as to render farther preservation impossible. And, even then, my mortal terrors would listen to no reason—would accept no consolation. I entered into a series of elaborate precautions. Among other things, I had the family vault so remodelled as to admit of being readily opened from within. The slightest pressure upon a long lever that extended far into the tomb would cause the iron portals to fly back. There were arrangements also for the free admission of air and light, and convenient receptacles for food and water, within immediate reach of the coffin intended for my reception. This coffin was warmly and softly padded, and was provided with a lid, fashioned upon the principle of the vault-door, with the addition of springs so contrived that the feeblest movement of the body would be sufficient to set it at liberty. Besides all this, there was suspended from the roof of the tomb, a large bell, the rope of which, it was designed, should extend through a hole in the coffin, and so be fastened to one of the hands of the corpse. But, alas! what avails the vigilance against the Destiny of man? Not even these well contrived securities sufficed to save from the uttermost agonies of living inhumation, a wretch to these agonies foredoomed!

There arrived an epoch—as often before there had arrived—in which I found myself emerging from total unconsciousness into the first feeble and indefinite sense of existence.—Slowly—with a tortoise gradation—approached the faint gray dawn of the psychal day. A torpid uneasiness. An apathetic endurance of dull pain. No care—no hope—no effort. Then, after long interval, a ringing in the ears; then, after a lapse still longer, a pricking or tingling sensation in the extremities; then a seemingly eternal period of pleasurable quiescence, during which the awakening feelings are struggling into thought; then a brief re-sinking into non-entity; then a sudden recovery. At length the slight quivering of an eyelid, and immediately thereupon, an electric shock of a terror, deadly and indefinite, which sends the blood in torrents from the temples to the heart. And now the first positive effort to think. And now the first endeavor to remember. And now a partial and evanescent success. And now the memory has so far regained its dominion that, in some measure, I am cognizant of my state. I feel that I am not awaking from ordinary sleep. I recollect that I have been subject to catalepsy. And now, at last, as if by the rush of an ocean, my shuddering spirit is overwhelmed by the one grim Danger—by the one spectral and ever-prevalent Idea.

For some minutes after this fancy possessed me, I remained without motion. And why? I could not summon courage to move. I dared not make the effort which was to satisfy me of my fate—and yet there was something at my heart which whispered to me *it was sure*. Despair—such as no other species of wretchedness ever calls into being—despair alone urged me, after long irresolution, to uplift the heavy lids of my eyes. I uplifted them. It was dark—all dark. I knew that the fit was over. I knew that the crisis of my disorder had long passed. I knew that I had now fully recovered the use of my visual faculties—and yet it was dark—all dark—the intense and utter raylessness of the Night that endureth for evermore.

I endeavored to shriek; and my lips and my parched tongue moved convulsively together in the attempt—but no voice issued from the cavernous lungs, which, oppressed as if by the weight of some incumbent mountain, gasped and palpitated, with the heart, at every elaborate and struggling inspiration.

The movement of the jaws, in this effort to cry aloud, showed me that they were bound up, as is usual with the dead. I felt, too, that I lay upon some hard substance; and by something similar my sides were, also, closely compressed. So far, I had not ventured to stir any of my limbs—but now I violently threw up my arms, which had been lying at length, with the wrists crossed. They struck a solid wooden substance, which extended above my person at an elevation of not more than six inches from my face. I could no longer doubt that I reposed within a coffin at last.

And now, amid all my infinite miseries, came sweetly the cherub Hope—for I thought of my precautions. I writhed, and made spasmodic exertions to force open the lid: it would not move. I felt my wrists for the bell-rope: it was not to be found. And now the Comforter fled forever, and a still sterner Despair reigned triumphant; for I could not help perceiving the absence of the paddings which I had so carefully prepared—and then, too, there came suddenly to my nostrils the strong peculiar odor of moist earth. The conclusion was irresistible. I was *not* within the vault. I had fallen into a trance while absent from home—while among strangers—when, or how, I could not remember—and it was they who had buried me as a dog—nailed up in some common coffin—and thrust, deep, deep, and forever, into some ordinary and nameless *grave*.

As this awful conviction forced itself, thus, into the innermost chambers of my soul, I once again struggled to cry aloud. And in this second endeavor I succeeded. A long, wild, and continuous shriek, or yell, of agony, resounded through the realms of the subterrene Night.

"Hillo! hillo, there!" said a gruff voice in reply.

"What the devil's the matter now?" said a second.

"Get out o' that!" said a third.

"What do you mean by yowling in that ere kind of style, like a cattymount?" said a fourth; and hereupon I was seized and shaken without ceremony, for several minutes, by a junto of very rough-looking individuals. They did not arouse me from my slumber—for I was wide awake when I screamed—but they restored me to the full possession of my memory.

This adventure occurred near Richmond, in Virginia. Accompanied by a friend, I had proceeded, upon a gunning expedition, some miles down the banks of James River. Night approached, and we were overtaken by a storm. The cabin of a small sloop lying at anchor in the stream, and laden with garden mould, afforded us the only available shelter. We made the best of it, and passed the night on board. I slept in one of the only two berths in the vessel —and the berths of a sloop of sixty or seventy tons, need scarcely be described. That which I occupied had no bedding of any kind. Its extreme width was eighteen inches. The distance of its bottom from the deck overhead, was precisely the same. I found it a matter of exceeding difficulty to squeeze myself in. Nevertheless, I slept soundly; and the whole of my vision—for it was no dream, and no nightmare—arose naturally from the circumstances of my position—from my ordinary bias of thought—and from the difficulty, to which I have alluded, of collecting my senses, and especially of regaining my memory, for a long time after awaking from slumber. The men who shook me were the crew of the sloop, and some laborers engaged to unload it. From the load itself came the earthy smell. The bandage about the jaws was a silk handkerchief in which I had bound up my head, in default of my customary nightcap.

The tortures endured, however, were indubitably quite equal, for the time, to those of actual sepulture. They were fearfully—they were inconceivably hideous; but out of Evil proceeded Good; for their very excess wrought in my spirit an inevitable revulsion. My soul acquired tone—acquired temper. I went abroad. I took vigorous exercise. I breathed the free air of Heaven. I thought upon other subjects than Death. I discarded my medical books. "Buchan" I burned: I read no "Night Thoughts"—no fustian about churchyards—no bugaboo tales—*such as this*. In short, I became a new man, and lived a man's life. From that memorable night, I dismissed forever my charnal apprehensions, and with them vanished the cataleptic disorder, of which, perhaps, they had been less the consequence than the cause.

There are moments when, even to the sober eye of Reason, the world of our sad Humanity may assume the semblance of a Hell—but the imagination of man is no Carathis, to explore with impunity its every cavern. Alas! the grim legion of sepulchral terrors cannot be regarded as altogether fanciful—but, like the Demons in whose company Afrasiab made his voyage down the Oxus, they must sleep, or they will devour us—they must be suffered to slumber, or we perish.

THE PURLOINED LETTER

Nil sapientiae odiosius acumine nimio.

—*Seneca*

At Paris, just after dark one gusty evening in the autumn of 18—, I was enjoying the twofold luxury of meditation and a meerschaum, in company with my friend C. Auguste Dupin, in his little back library, or book-closet, *au troisième*, No. 33, *Rue Dunôt, Faubourg St. Germain.* For one hour at least we had maintained a profound silence; while each, to any casual observer, might have seemed intently and exclusively occupied with the curling eddies of smoke that oppressed the atmosphere of the chamber. For myself, however, I was mentally discussing certain topics which had formed matter for conversation between us at an earlier period of the evening; I mean the affair of the Rue Morgue, and the mystery attending the murder of Marie Rogêt. I looked upon it, therefore, as something of a coincidence, when the door of our apartment was thrown open and admitted our old acquaintance, Monsieur G——, the Prefect of the Parisian police.

We gave him a hearty welcome; for there was nearly half as much of the entertaining as of the contemptible about the man, and we had not seen him for several years. We had been sitting in the dark, and Dupin now arose for the purpose of lighting a lamp, but sat down again, without doing so, upon G.'s saying that he had called to consult us, or rather to ask the opinion of my friend, about some official business which had occasioned a great deal of trouble.

"If it is any point requiring reflection," observed Dupin, as he forebore to enkindle the wick, "we shall examine it to better purpose in the dark."

"That is another of your odd notions," said the Prefect, who had a fashion of calling every thing "odd" that was beyond his comprehension, and thus lived amid an absolute legion of "oddities."

"Very true," said Dupin, as he supplied his visiter with a pipe, and rolled towards him a comfortable chair.

"And what is the difficulty now?" I asked. "Nothing more in the assassination way, I hope?"

"Oh no; nothing of that nature. The fact is, the business is *very* simple indeed, and I make no doubt that we can manage it sufficiently well ourselves; but then I thought Dupin would like to hear the details of it, because it is so excessively *odd*."

"Simple and odd," said Dupin.

"Why, yes; and not exactly that, either. The fact is, we have all been a good deal puzzled because the affair *is* so simple, and yet baffles us altogether."

"Perhaps it is the very simplicity of the thing which puts you at fault," said my friend.

"What nonsense you *do* talk!" replied the Prefect, laughing heartily.

"Perhaps the mystery is a little *too* plain," said Dupin.

"Oh, good heavens! who ever heard of such an idea?"

"A little *too* self-evident."

"Ha! ha! ha!—ha! ha! ha!—ho! ho! ho!" roared our visiter, profoundly amused, "oh, Dupin, you will be the death of me yet!"

"And what, after all, *is* the matter on hand?" I asked.

"Why, I will tell you," replied the Prefect, as he gave a long, steady, and contemplative puff, and settled himself in his chair. "I will tell you in a few words; but, before I begin, let me caution you that this is an affair demanding the greatest secrecy, and that I should most probably lose the position I now hold, were it known that I confided it to any one."

"Proceed," said I.

"Or not," said Dupin.

"Well, then; I have received personal information, from a very high quarter, that a certain document of the last importance, has been purloined from the royal apartments. The individual who purloined it is known; this beyond a doubt; he was seen to take it. It is known, also, that it still remains in his possession."

"How is this known?" asked Dupin.

"It is clearly inferred," replied the Prefect, "from the nature of the document, and from the non-appearance of certain results which would at once arise from its passing *out* of the robber's possession;—that is to say, from his employing it as he must design in the end to employ it."

"Be a little more explicit," I said.

"Well, I may venture so far as to say that the paper gives its holder a certain power in a certain quarter where such power is immensely valuable." The Prefect was fond of the cant of diplomacy.

"Still I do not quite understand," said Dupin.

"No? Well; the disclosure of the document to a third person, who shall be nameless, would bring in question the honor of a personage of most exalted station; and this fact gives the holder of the document an ascendancy over the illustrious personage whose honor and peace are so jeopardized."

"But this ascendancy," I interposed, "would depend upon the robber's knowledge of the loser's knowledge of the robber. Who would dare—"

"The thief," said G., "is the Minister D———, who dares all things, those unbecoming as well as those becom-

ing a man. The method of the theft was not less ingenious than bold. The document in question—a letter, to
be frank—had been received by the personage robbed while
alone in the royal *boudoir*. During its perusal she was suddenly interrupted by the entrance of the other exalted
personage from whom especially it was her wish to conceal it. After a hurried and vain endeavor to thrust it in
a drawer, she was forced to place it, open as it was, upon
a table. The address, however, was uppermost, and, the
contents thus unexposed, the letter escaped notice. At this
juncture enters the Minister D———. His lynx eye immediately perceives the paper, recognizes the handwriting
of the address, observes the confusion of the personage addressed, and fathoms her secret. After some business transactions, hurried through in his ordinary manner, he produces a letter somewhat similar to the one in question,
opens it, pretends to read it, and then places it in close
juxtaposition to the other. Again he converses, for some
fifteen minutes, upon the public affairs. At length, in taking leave, he takes also from the table the letter to which
he had no claim. Its rightful owner saw, but, of course,
dared not call attention to the act, in the presence of the
third personage who stood at her elbow. The minister de-
camped; leaving his own letter—one of no importance—
upon the table."

"Here, then," said Dupin to me, "you have precisely
what you demand to make the ascendancy complete—the
robber's knowledge of the loser's knowledge of the robber."

"Yes," replied the Prefect; "and the power thus attained
has, for some months past, been wielded, for political purposes, to a very dangerous extent. The personage robbed
is more thoroughly convinced, every day, of the necessity
of reclaiming her letter. But this, of course, cannot be done
openly. In fine, driven to despair, she has committed the
matter to me."

"Than whom," said Dupin, amid a perfect whirlwind of smoke, "no more sagacious agent could, I suppose, be desired, or even imagined."

"You flatter me," replied the Prefect; "but it is possible that some such opinion may have been entertained."

"It is clear," said I, "as you observe, that the letter is still in possession of the minister; since it is this possession, and not any employment of the letter, which bestows the power. With the employment the power departs."

"True," said G., "and upon this conviction I proceeded. My first care was to make thorough search of the minister's hotel; and here my chief embarrassment lay in the necessity of searching without his knowledge. Beyond all things, I have been warned of the danger which would result from giving him reason to suspect our design."

"But," said I, "you are quite *au fait* in these investigations. The Parisian police have done this thing often before."

"O yes; and for this reason I did not despair. The habits of the minister gave me, too, a great advantage. He is frequently absent from home all night. His servants are by no means numerous. They sleep at a distance from their master's apartment, and, being chiefly Neapolitans, are readily made drunk. I have keys, as you know, with which I can open any chamber or cabinet in Paris. For three months a night has not passed, during the greater part of which I have not been engaged, personally, in ransacking the D—— Hotel. My honor is interested, and, to mention a great secret, the reward is enormous. So I did not abandon the search until I had become fully satisfied that the thief is a more astute man than myself. I fancy that I have investigated every nook and corner of the premises in which it is possible that the paper can be concealed."

"But is it not possible," I suggested, "that although the letter may be in possession of the minister, as it unquestionably is, he may have concealed it elsewhere than upon his own premises?"

"This is barely possible," said Dupin. "The present peculiar condition of affairs at court, and especially of those intrigues in which D——— is known to be involved, would render the instant availability of the document—its susceptibility of being produced at a moment's notice—a point of nearly equal importance with its possession."

"Its susceptibility of being produced?" said I.

"That is to say, of being *destroyed*," said Dupin.

"True," I observed; "the paper is clearly then upon the premises. As for its being upon the person of the minister, we may consider that as out of the question."

"Entirely," said the Prefect. "He has been twice way-laid, as if by footpads, and his person rigorously searched under my own inspection."

"You might have spared yourself this trouble," said Dupin. "D———, I presume, is not altogether a fool, and, if not, must have anticipated these waylayings, as a matter of course."

"Not *altogether* a fool," said G., "but then he's a poet, which I take to be only one remove from a fool."

"True," said Dupin, after a long and thoughtful whiff from his meerschaum, "although I have been guilty of certain doggrel myself."

"Suppose you detail," said I, "the particulars of your search."

"Why the fact is, we took our time, and we searched *every where*. I have had long experience in these affairs. I took the entire building, room by room; devoting the nights of a whole week to each. We examined, first, the furniture of each apartment. We opened every possible drawer; and I presume you know that, to a properly trained police agent, such a thing as a *secret* drawer is impossible. Any man is a dolt who permits a 'secret' drawer to escape him in a search of this kind. The thing is so plain. There is a certain amount of bulk—of space—to be accounted for in every cabinet. Then we have accurate rules. The fiftieth part of a line could not escape us. After the cabinets we took the chairs. The cushions we probed with the fine long needles you have seen me employ. From the tables we removed the tops."

"Why so?"

"Sometimes the top of a table, or other similarly arranged piece of furniture, is removed by the person wishing to conceal an article; then the leg is excavated, the article deposited within the cavity, and the top replaced. The bottoms and tops of bedposts are employed in the same way."

"But could not the cavity be detected by sounding?" I asked.

"By no means, if, when the article is deposited, a sufficient wadding of cotton be placed around it. Besides, in our case, we were obliged to proceed without noise."

"But you could not have removed—you could not have taken to pieces *all* articles of furniture in which it would have been possible to make a deposit in the manner you mention. A letter may be compressed into a thin spiral roll, not differing much in shape or bulk from a large knitting-needle, and in this form it might be inserted into the rung of a chair, for example. You did not take to pieces all the chairs?"

"Certainly not; but we did better—we examined the rungs of every chair in the hotel, and, indeed, the jointings of every description of furniture, by the aid of a most powerful microscope. Had there been any traces of recent disturbance we should not have failed to detect it instantly. A single grain of gimlet-dust, for example, would have been as obvious as an apple. Any disorder in the glueing—any unusual gaping in the joints—would have sufficed to insure detection."

"I presume you looked to the mirrors, between the boards and the plates, and you probed the beds and the bed-clothes, as well as the curtains and carpets."

"That of course; and when we had absolutely completed every particle of the furniture in this way, then we examined the house itself. We divided its entire surface into compartments, which we numbered, so that none might be missed; then we scrutinized each individual square inch throughout the premises, including the two houses immediately adjoining, with the microscope, as before."

"The two houses adjoining!" I exclaimed; "you must have had a great deal of trouble."

"We had; but the reward offered is prodigious."

"You include the *grounds* about the houses?"

"All the grounds are paved with brick. They gave us comparatively little trouble. We examined the moss between the bricks, and found it undisturbed."

"You looked among D———'s papers, of course, and into the books of the library?"

"Certainly; we opened every package and parcel; we not only opened every book, but we turned over every leaf in each volume, not contenting ourselves with a mere shake, according to the fashion of some of our police officers. We also measured the thickness of every book-cover, with the most accurate admeasurement, and applied to each the most jealous scrutiny of the microscope. Had any of the bindings been recently meddled with, it would have been utterly impossible that the fact should have escaped observation. Some five or six volumes, just from the hands of the binder, we carefully probed, longitudinally, with the needles."

"You explored the floors beneath the carpets?"

"Beyond doubt. We removed every carpet, and examined the boards with the microscope."

"And the paper on the walls?"

"Yes."

"You looked into the cellars?"

"We did."

"Then," I said, "you have been making a miscalculation, and the letter is *not* upon the premises, as you suppose."

"I fear you are right there," said the Prefect. "And now, Dupin, what would you advise me to do?"

"To make a thorough re-search of the premises."

"That is absolutely needless," replied G————. "I am not more sure that I breathe than I am that the letter is not at the Hotel."

"I have no better advice to give you," said Dupin. "You have, of course, an accurate description of the letter?"

"Oh yes!"—And here the Prefect, producing a memorandum-book, proceeded to read aloud a minute account of the internal, and especially of the external appearance of the missing document. Soon after finishing the perusal of this description, he took his departure, more entirely depressed in spirits than I had ever known the good gentleman before.

In about a month afterwards he paid us another visit, and found us occupied very nearly as before. He took a pipe and a chair and entered into some ordinary conversation. At length I said,—

"Well, but G————, what of the purloined letter? I presume you have at last made up your mind that there is no such thing as overreaching the Minister?"

"Confound him, say I—yes; I made the re-examination, however, as Dupin suggested—but it was all labor lost, as I knew it would be."

"How much was the reward offered, did you say?" asked Dupin.

"Why, a very great deal—a *very* liberal reward—I don't like to say how much, precisely; but one thing I *will* say, that I wouldn't mind giving my individual check for fifty

thousand francs to any one who could obtain me that
letter. The fact is, it is becoming of more and more
importance every day; and the reward has been lately
doubled. If it were trebled, however, I could do no more
than I have done."

"Why, yes," said Dupin, drawlingly, between the
whiffs of his meerschaum, "I really—think, G——,
you have not exerted yourself—to the utmost in this
matter. You might—do a little more, I think, eh?"

"How?—in what way?"

"Why—puff, puff—you might—puff, puff—employ
counsel in the matter, eh?—puff, puff, puff. Do you remember the story they tell of Abernethy?"

"No; hang Abernethy!"

"To be sure! hang him and welcome. But, once upon a
time, a certain rich miser conceived the design of spong-
ing upon this Abernethy for a medical opinion. Getting
up, for this purpose, an ordinary conversation in a private
company, he insinuated his case to the physician, as that
of an imaginary individual.

" 'We will suppose,' said the miser, 'that his symptoms
are such and such; now, doctor, what would *you* have
directed him to take?'

" 'Take!' said Abernethy, 'why, take *advice*, to be
sure.' "

"But," said the Prefect, a little discomposed, "I am
perfectly willing to take advice, and to pay for it. I would
really give fifty thousand francs to any one who would aid
me in the matter."

"In that case," replied Dupin, opening a drawer, and
producing a check-book, "you may as well fill me up a
check for the amount mentioned. When you have signed
it, I will hand you the letter."

I was astounded. The Prefect appeared absolutely
thunderstricken. For some minutes he remained speechless and motionless, looking incredulously at my friend

with open mouth, and eyes that seemed starting from their sockets; then, apparently recovering himself in some measure, he seized a pen, and after several pauses and vacant stares, finally filled up and signed a check for fifty thousand francs, and handed it across the table to Dupin. The latter examined it carefully and deposited it in his pocket-book; then, unlocking an *escritoire*, took thence a letter and gave it to the Prefect. This functionary grasped it in a perfect agony of joy, opened it with a trembling hand, cast a rapid glance at its contents, and then, scrambling and struggling to the door, rushed at length unceremoniously from the room and from the house, without having uttered a syllable since Dupin had requested him to fill up the check.

When he had gone, my friend entered into some explanations.

"The Parisian police," he said, "are exceedingly able in their way. They are persevering, ingenious, cunning, and thoroughly versed in the knowledge which their duties seem chiefly to demand. Thus, when G—— detailed to us his mode of searching the premises at the Hotel D——, I felt entire confidence in his having made a satisfactory investigation—so far as his labors extended."

"So far as his labors extended?" said I.

"Yes," said Dupin. "The measures adopted were not only the best of their kind, but carried out to absolute perfection. Had the letter been deposited within the range of their search, these fellows would, beyond a question, have found it."

I merely laughed—but he seemed quite serious in all that he said.

"The measures, then," he continued, "were good in their kind, and well executed; their defect lay in their being inapplicable to the case, and to the man. A certain set of highly ingenious resources are, with the Prefect, a sort of Procrustean bed, to which he forcibly adapts his

designs. But he perpetually errs by being too deep or too
shallow, for the matter in hand; and many a schoolboy is
a better reasoner than he. I knew one about eight years
of age, whose success at guessing in the game of 'even
and odd' attracted universal admiration. This game is
simple, and is played with marbles. One player holds in
his hand a number of these toys, and demands of another
whether that number is even or odd. If the guess is right,
the guesser wins one; if wrong, he loses one. The boy to
whom I allude won all the marbles of the school. Of
course he had some principle of guessing; and this lay in
mere observation and admeasurement of the astuteness
of his opponents. For example, an arrant simpleton is his
opponent, and, holding up his closed hand, asks, 'are they
even or odd?' Our schoolboy replies, 'odd,' and loses; but
upon the second trial he wins, for he then says to himself,
'the simpleton had them even upon the first trial, and
his amount of cunning is just sufficient to make him have
them odd upon the second; I will therefore guess odd;'—
he guesses odd, and wins. Now, with a simpleton a degree
above the first, he would have reasoned thus: 'This fellow
finds that in the first instance I guessed odd, and, in the
second, he will propose to himself, upon the first impulse,
a simple variation from even to odd, as did the first
simpleton; but then a second thought will suggest that
this is too simple a variation, and finally he will decide
upon putting it even as before. I will therefore guess even;'
—he guesses even, and wins. Now this mode of reasoning in the schoolboy, whom his fellows termed 'lucky,'—
what, in its last analysis, is it?"

"It is merely," I said, "an identification of the reasoner's intellect with that of his opponent."

"It is," said Dupin; "and, upon inquiring of the boy by
what means he effected the *thorough* identification in
which his success consisted, I received answer as follows:
'When I wish to find out how wise, or how stupid, or

how good, or how wicked is any one, or what are his thoughts at the moment, I fashion the expression of my face, as accurately as possible, in accordance with the expression of his, and then wait to see what thoughts or sentiments arise in my mind or heart, as if to match or correspond with the expression.' This reponse of the schoolboy lies at the bottom of all the spurious profundity which has been attributed to Rochefoucault, to La Bougive, to Machiavelli, and to Campanella."

"And the identification," I said, "of the reasoner's intellect with that of his opponent, depends, if I understand you aright, upon the accuracy with which the opponent's intellect is admeasured."

"For its practical value it depends upon this," replied Dupin; "and the Prefect and his cohort fail so frequently, first, by default of this identification, and, secondly, by ill-admeasurement, or rather through non-admeasurement, of the intellect with which they are engaged. They consider only their *own* ideas of ingenuity; and, in searching for anything hidden, advert only to the modes in which *they* would have hidden it. They are right in this much— that their own ingenuity is a faithful representative of that of *the mass*; but when the cunning of the individual felon is diverse in character from their own, the felon foils them, of course. This always happens when it is above their own, and very usually when it is below. They have no variation of principle in their investigations; at best, when urged by some unusual emergency—by some extraordinary reward—they extend or exaggerate their old modes of *practice*, without touching their principles. What, for example, in this case of D———, has been done to vary the principle of action? What is all this boring, and probing, and sounding, and scrutinizing with the microscope, and dividing the surface of the building into registered square inches—what is it all but an exaggeration *of the application* of the one principle or set of principles of search, which are based upon the one set of notions regarding human ingenuity, to which the Prefect, in the long routine of his duty, has been accustomed? Do you not see he has taken it for granted that *all* men proceed to conceal a letter,—not exactly in a gimlet-hole bored in a chair-leg—but, at least, in *some* out-of-the-way hole or corner suggested by the same tenor of thought which would urge a man to secrete a letter in a gimlet-hole bored in a chair-leg? And do you not see also, that such *recherchés* nooks for concealment are adapted only for ordinary occasions, and would be adopted only by ordinary intellects; for, in all cases of concealment, a disposal of the article concealed—a disposal of it in this *recherché* manner,—is, in the very first instance, presumable and presumed; and thus its discovery depends, not at all upon the acumen, but altogether upon the mere care, patience, and determination of the seekers; and where the case is of importance—or, what amounts to the same thing in the policial eyes, when the reward is of magnitude,—the qualities in question have *never* been known to fail. You will now understand what I meant in suggesting that, had the purloined letter been hidden any where within the limits of the Prefect's examination—in other words, had the principle of its concealment been comprehended within the principles of the Prefect—its discovery would have been a matter altogether beyond question. This functionary, however, has been thoroughly mystified; and the remote source of his defeat lies in the supposition that the Minister is a fool, because he has acquired renown as a poet. All fools are poets; this the Prefect *feels*; and he is merely guilty of a *non distributio medii* in thence inferring that all poets are fools."

"But is this really the poet?" I asked. "There are two brothers, I know; and both have attained reputation in letters. The Minister I believe has written learnedly on the

Differential Calculus. He is a mathematician, and no poet."

"You are mistaken; I know him well; he is both. As poet *and* mathematician, he would reason well; as mere mathematician, he could not have reasoned at all, and thus would have been at the mercy of the Prefect."

"You surprise me," I said, "by these opinions, which have been contradicted by the voice of the world. You do not mean to set at naught the well-digested idea of centuries. The mathematical reason has long been regarded as *the* reason *par excellence*."

" '*Il ya à parièr*,' " replied Dupin, quoting from Chamfort, " '*que toute idée publique, toute convention reçue, est une sottise, car elle a convenue au plus grand nombre.*' The mathematicians, I grant you, have done their best to promulgate the popular error to which you allude, and which is none the less an error for its promulgation as truth. With an art worthy a better cause, for example, they have insinuated the term 'analysis' into application to algebra. The French are the originators of this particular deception; but if a term is of any importance—if words derive any value from applicability—then 'analysis' conveys 'algebra' about as much as, in Latin, '*ambitus*' implies 'ambition,' '*religio*' 'religion,' or '*homines honesti*,' a set of *honorable* men."

"You have a quarrel on hand, I see," said I, "with some of the algebraists of Paris; but proceed."

"I dispute the availability, and thus the value, of that reason which is cultivated in any especial form other than the abstractly logical. I dispute, in particular, the reason educed by mathematical study. The mathematics are the science for form and quantity; mathematical reasoning is merely logic applied to observation upon form and quantity. The great error lies in supposing that even the truths of what is called *pure* algebra, are abstract or general truth. And this error is so egregious that I am confounded at the universality with which it has been received. Mathematical axioms are *not* axioms of general truth. What is true of *relation*—of form and quantity—is often grossly false in regard to morals, for example. In this latter science it is very usually *un*true that the aggregated parts are equal to the whole. In chemistry also the axiom fails. In the consideration of motive it fails; for two motives, each of a given value, have not, necessarily, a value when united, equal to the sum of their values apart. There are numerous other mathematical truths which are only truths within the limits of *relation*. But the mathematician argues, from his *finite truths*, through habit, as if they were of an absolutely general applicability—as the world indeed imagines them to be. Bryant, in his very learned 'Mythology,' mentions an analogous source of error, when he says that 'although the Pagan fables are not believed, yet we forget ourselves continually, and make inferences from them as existing realities.' With the algebraists, however, who are Pagans themselves, the 'Pagan fables' *are* believed, and the inferences are made, not so much through lapse of memory, as through an unaccountable addling of the brains. In short, I never yet encountered the mere mathematician who could be trusted out of equal roots, or one who did not clandestinely hold it as a point of his faith that $x^2 + px$ was absolutely and unconditionally equal to q. Say to one of these gentlemen, by way of experiment, if you please, that you believe occasions may occur where $x^2 + px$ is *not* altogether equal to q, and, having made him understand what you mean, get out of his reach as speedily as convenient, for, beyond doubt, he will endeavor to knock you down.

"I mean to say," continued Dupin, while I merely laughed at his last observations, "that if the Minister had been no more than a mathematician, the Prefect would have been under no necessity of giving me this check. I knew him, however, as both mathematician and poet, and my measures were adapted to his capacity, with reference to the circumstances by which he was surrounded. I knew him as a courtier, too, and as a bold *intriguant*. Such a man, I considered, could not fail to be aware of the ordinary policial modes of action. He could not have failed to anticipate—and events have proved that he did not fail to anticipate—the waylayings to which he was subjected. He must have foreseen, I reflected, the secret investigations of his premises. His frequent absences from home at night, which were hailed by the Prefect as certain aids to his success, I regarded only as *ruses*, to afford opportunity for thorough search to the police, and thus the sooner to impress them with the conviction to which G——, in fact, did finally arrive—the conviction that the letter was not upon the premises. I felt, also, that the whole train of thought, which I was at some pains in detailing to you just now, concerning the invariable principle of policial action in searches for articles concealed—I felt that this whole train of thought would necessarily pass through the mind of the Minister. It would imperatively lead him to despise all the ordinary *nooks* of concealment. *He* could not, I reflected, be so weak as not to see that the most intricate and remote recess of his hotel would be as open as his commonest closets to the eyes, to the probes, to the gimlets, and to the microscopes of the Prefect. I saw, in fine, that he would be driven, as a matter of course, to *simplicity*, if not deliberately induced to it as a matter of choice. You will remember, perhaps, how desperately the Prefect laughed when I suggested, upon our first interview, that it was just possible this mystery troubled him so much on account of its being so *very* self-evident."

"Yes," said I, "I remember his merriment well. I really thought he would have fallen into convulsions."

"The material world," continued Dupin, "abounds with very strict analogies to the immaterial; and thus some color of truth has been given to the rhetorical dogma, that metaphor, or simile, may be made to strengthen an argument, as well as to embellish a description. The principle of the *vis inertiæ*, for example, seems to be identical in physics and metaphysics. It is not more true in the former, that a large body is with more difficulty set in motion than a smaller one, and that its subsequent *momentum* is commensurate with this difficulty, than it is, in the latter, that intellects of the vaster capacity, while more forcible, more constant, and more eventful in their movements than those of inferior grade, are yet the less readily moved, and more embarrassed and full of hesitation in the first few steps of their progress. Again: have you ever noticed which of the street signs, over the shop-doors, are the most attractive of attention?"

"I have never given the matter a thought," I said.

"There is a game of puzzles," he resumed, "which is played upon a map. One party playing requires another to find a given word—the name of town, river, state or empire—any word, in short, upon the motley and perplexed surface of the chart. A novice in the game generally seeks to embarrass his opponents by giving them the most minutely lettered names; but the adept selects such words as stretch, in large characters, from one end of the chart to the other. These, like the over-largely lettered signs and placards of the street, escape observation by dint of being excessively obvious; and here the physical oversight is precisely analogous with the moral inapprehension by which the intellect suffers to pass unnoticed those considerations which are too obtrusively and too palpably self-evident. But this is a point, it appears, somewhat above or beneath the understanding of the Prefect. He never once thought it probable, or possible, that the Minister had deposited the letter immediately beneath the nose of the whole world, by way of best preventing any portion of that world from perceiving it.

"But the more I reflected upon the daring, dashing, and discriminating ingenuity of D———; upon the fact that the document must always have been *at hand*, if he intended to use it to good purpose; and upon the decisive evidence, obtained by the Prefect, that it was not hidden within the limits of that dignitary's ordinary search—the more satisfied I became that, to conceal this letter, the Minister had resorted to the comprehensive and sagacious expedient of not attempting to conceal it at all.

"Full of these ideas, I prepared myself with a pair of green spectacles, and called one fine morning, quite by accident, at the Ministerial hotel. I found D——— at home, yawning, lounging, and dawdling, as usual, and pretending to be in the last extremity of *ennui*. He is, perhaps, the most really energetic human being now alive —but that is only when nobody sees him.

"To be even with him, I complained of my weak eyes, and lamented the necessity of the spectacles, under cover of which I cautiously and thoroughly surveyed the apartment, while seemingly intent only upon the conversation of my host.

"I paid especial attention to a large writing-table near which he sat, and upon which lay confusedly, some miscellaneous letters and other papers, with one or two musical instruments and a few books. Here, however, after a long and very deliberate scrutiny, I saw nothing to excite particular suspicion.

"At length my eyes, in going the circuit of the room, fell upon a trumpery fillagree card-rack of pasteboard, that hung dangling by a dirty blue ribbon, from a little brass knob just beneath the middle of the mantel-piece. In this rack, which had three or four compartments, were five or six visiting cards and a solitary letter. This last was much soiled and crumpled. It was torn nearly in two, across the middle—as if a design, in the first instance, to tear it entirely up as worthless, had been altered, or stayed, in the second. It had a large black seal, bearing the D—— cipher *very* conspicuously, and was addressed, in a diminutive female hand, to D——, the minister, himself. It was thrust carelessly, and even, as it seemed, contemptuously, into one of the upper divisions of the rack.

"No sooner had I glanced at this letter, than I concluded it to be that of which I was in search. To be sure, it was, to all appearance, radically different from the one of which the Prefect had read us so minute a description. Here the seal was large and black, with the D—— cipher; there it was small and red, with the ducal arms of the S—— family. Here, the address, to the Minister, was diminutive and feminine; there the superscription, to a certain royal personage, was markedly bold and decided; the size alone formed a point of correspondence. But, then, the *radicalness* of these differences, which was excessive; the dirt; the soiled and torn condition of the paper, so inconsistent with the *true* methodical habits of D——, and so suggestive of a design to delude the beholder into an idea of the worthlessness of the document; these things, together with the hyperobtrusive situation of this document, full in the view of every visiter, and thus exactly in accordance with the conclusions to which I had previously arrived; these things, I say, were strongly corroborative of suspicion, in one who came with the intention to suspect.

"I protracted my visit as long as possible, and, while I maintained a most animated discussion with the Minister, on a topic which I knew well had never failed to interest and excite him, I kept my attention really riveted upon the letter. In this examination, I committed to memory its external appearance and arrangement in the rack; and also fell, at length, upon a discovery which set at rest whatever trivial doubt I might have entertained. In scrutinizing the edges of the paper, I observed them to be more *chafed* than seemed necessary. They presented the *broken* appearance which is manifested when a stiff paper, having been once folded and pressed with a folder, is refolded in a reversed direction, in the same creases or edges which had formed the original fold. This discovery was sufficient. It was clear to me that the letter had been turned, as a glove, inside out, re-directed, and re-sealed. I bade the Minister good morning, and took my departure at once, leaving a gold snuff-box upon the table.

"The next morning I called for the snuff-box, when we resumed, quite eagerly, the conversation of the preceding day. While thus engaged, however, a loud report, as if of a pistol, was heard immediately beneath the windows of the hotel, and was succeeded by a series of fearful screams, and the shoutings of a mob. D——— rushed to a casement, threw it open, and looked out. In the meantime, I stepped to the card-rack, took the letter, put it in my pocket, and replaced it by a *fac-simile,* (so far as regards externals,) which I had carefully prepared at my lodgings; imitating the D——— cipher, very readily, by means of a seal formed of bread.

"The disturbance in the street had been occasioned by the frantic behavior of a man with a musket. He had fired it among a crowd of women and children. It proved, however, to have been without ball, and the fellow was suffered to go his way as a lunatic or a drunkard. When he had gone, D——— came from the window, whither I had followed him immediately upon securing the object in view. Soon afterwards I bade him farewell. The pretended lunatic was a man in my own pay."

"But what purpose had you," I asked, "in replacing the letter by a *fac-simile?* Would it not have been better, at the first visit, to have seized it openly, and departed?"

"D———," replied Dupin, "is a desperate man, and a man of nerve. His hotel, too, is not without attendants devoted to his interests. Had I made the wild attempt you suggest, I might never have left the Ministerial presence alive. The good people of Paris might have heard of me no more. But I had an object apart from these considerations. You know my political prepossessions. In this matter, I act as a partisan of the lady concerned. For eighteen months the Minister has had her in his power. She has now him in hers; since, being unaware that the letter is not in his possession, he will proceed with his exactions as if it was. Thus will he inevitably commit himself, at once, to his political destruction. His downfall, too, will not be more precipitate than awkward. It is all very well to talk about the *facilis descensus Averni;* but in all kinds of climbing, as Catalani said of singing, it is far more easy to get up than to come down. In the present instance I have no sympathy—at least no pity—for him who descends. He is that *monstrum horrendum,* an unprincipled man of genius. I confess, however, that I should like very well to know the precise character of his thoughts, when, being defied by her whom the Prefect terms 'a certain personage,' he is reduced to opening the letter which I left for him in the card-rack."

"How? did you put any thing particular in it?"

"Why—it did not seem altogether right to leave the interior blank—that would have been insulting. D———, at Vienna once, did me an evil turn, which I told him, quite good-humoredly, that I should remember. So, as I knew he would feel some curiosity in regard to the identity of the person who had outwitted him, I thought it a pity not to give him a clue. He is well acquainted with my MS., and I just copied into the middle of the blank sheet the words—

——— Un dessein si funeste,
S'il n'est digne d'Atrée, est digne de Thyeste.

They are to be found in Crébillon's 'Atrée.'"

SOME WORDS WITH A MUMMY

The symposium of the preceding evening had been a little too much for my nerves. I had a wretched head-ache, and was desperately drowsy. Instead of going out, therefore, to spend the evening as I had proposed, it occurred to me that I could not do a wiser thing than just eat a mouthful of supper and go immediately to bed.

A *light* supper of course. I am exceedingly fond of Welsh rabbit. More than a pound at once, however, may not at all times be advisable. Still, there can be no material objection to two. And really between two and three, there is merely a single unit of difference. I ventured, perhaps, upon four. My wife will have it five;—but, clearly, she has confounded two very distinct affairs. The abstract number, five, I am willing to admit; but, con-cretely, it has reference to bottles of Brown Stout, with-out which, in the way of condiment, Welsh rabbit is to be eschewed.

Having thus concluded a frugal meal, and donned my night-cap, with the serene hope of enjoying it till noon the next day, I placed my head upon the pillow, and through the aid of a capital conscience, fell into a pro-found slumber forthwith.

But when were the hopes of humanity fulfilled? I could not have completed my third snore when there came a furious ringing at the street-door bell, and then an impatient thumping at the knocker, which awakened me at once. In a minute afterward, and while I was still rubbing my eyes, my wife thrust in my face a note from my old friend, Doctor Ponnonner. It ran thus:

Come to me by all means, my dear good friend, as soon

as you receive this. Come and help us to rejoice. At last, by long perseyering diplomacy, I have gained the assent of the Directors of the City Museum, to my examination of the Mummy—you know the one I mean. I have permission to unswathe it and open it, if desirable. A few friends only will be present—you, of course. The Mummy is now at my house, and we shall begin to unroll it at eleven to-night.

Yours ever,

PONNONNER.

By the time I had reached the "Ponnonner," it struck me that I was as wide awake as a man need be. I leaped out of bed in an ecstasy, overthrowing all in my way; dressed myself with a rapidity truly marvellous; and set off, at the top of my speed, for the Doctor's.

There I found a very eager company assembled. They had been awaiting me with much impatience; the Mummy was extended upon the dining table; and the moment I entered, its examination was commenced.

It was one of a pair brought, several years previously, by Captain Arthur Sabretash, a cousin of Ponnonner's, from a tomb near Eleithias, in the Lybian Mountains, a considerable distance above Thebes on the Nile. The grottoes at this point, although less magnificent than the Theban sepulchres, are of higher interest, on account of affording more numerous illustrations of the private life of the Egyptians. The chamber from which our specimen was taken, was said to be very rich in such illustrations; the walls being completely covered with fresco paintings and bas-reliefs, while statues, vases, and mosaic work of rich patterns, indicated the vast wealth of the deceased.

The treasure had been deposited in the Museum precisely in the same condition in which Captain Sabretash had found it;—that is to say, the coffin had not been disturbed. For eight years it had thus stood, subject only externally to public inspection. We had now, therefore, the complete Mummy at our disposal; and to those who are aware how very rarely the unransacked antique reaches our shores, it will be evident, at once, that we had great reason to congratulate ourselves upon our good fortune.

Approaching the table, I saw on it a large box, or case, nearly seven feet long, and perhaps three feet wide, by two feet and a half deep. It was oblong—not coffin-shaped. The material was at first supposed to be the wood of the sycamore (*platanus*), but, upon cutting into it, we found it to be pasteboard, or more properly, *papier mache*, composed of papyrus. It was thickly ornamented with paintings, representing funeral scenes, and other mournful subjects, interspersed among which in every variety of position, were certain series of hieroglyphical characters intended, no doubt, for the name of the departed. By good luck, Mr. Gliddon formed one of our party; and he had no difficulty in translating the letters, which were simply phonetic, and represented the word, *Allamistakeo*.

We had some difficulty in getting this case open without injury, but, having at length accomplished the task, we came to a second, coffin-shaped, and very considerably less in size than the exterior one, but resembling it precisely in every other respect. The interval between the two was filled with resin, which had, in some degree, defaced the colors of the interior box.

Upon opening this latter (which we did quite easily,) we arrived at a third case, also coffin-shaped, and varying from the second one in no particular, except in that of its material, which was cedar, and still emitted the peculiar and highly aromatic odor of that wood. Between the second and the third case there was no interval; the one fitting accurately within the other.

Removing the third case, we discovered and took out

the body itself. We had expected to find it, as usual, enveloped in frequent rolls, or bandages, of linen, but, in place of these, we found a sort of sheath, made of papyrus, and coated with a layer of plaster, thickly gilt and painted. The paintings represented subjects connected with the various supposed duties of the soul, and its presentation to different divinities, with numerous identical human figures, intended, very probably, as portraits of the persons embalmed. Extending from head to foot, was a columnar, or perpendicular inscription in phonetic hieroglyphics, giving again his name and titles, and the names and titles of his relations.

Around the neck thus ensheathed, was a collar of cylindrical glass beads, diverse in color, and so arranged as to form images of deities, of the scarabæus, etc., with the winged globe. Around the small of the waist was a similar collar, or belt.

Stripping off the papyrus, we found the flesh in excellent preservation, with no perceptible odor. The color was reddish. The skin was hard, smooth and glossy. The teeth and hair were in good condition. The eyes (it seemed) had been removed, and glass ones substituted, which were very beautiful and wonderfully life-like, with the exception of somewhat too determined a stare. The fingers and the nails were brilliantly gilded.

Mr. Gliddon was of opinion, from the redness of the epidermis, that the embalmment had been effected altogether by asphaltum; but, on scraping the surface with a steel instrument, and throwing into the fire some of the powder thus obtained, the flavor of camphor and other sweet-scented gums became apparent.

We searched the corpse very carefully for the usual openings through which the entrails are extracted, but, to our surprise, we could discover none. No member of the party was at that period aware that entire or unopened mummies are not unfrequently met. The brain it

was customary to withdraw through the nose; the in-
testines through an incision in the side; the body was
then shaved, washed, and salted; then laid aside for several weeks, when the operation of embalming, properly
so called, began.

As no trace of an opening could be found, Doctor
Ponnonner was preparing his instruments for dissection,
when I observed that it was then past two o'clock.
Hereupon it was agreed to postpone the internal examination until the next evening; and we were about to
separate for the present, when some one suggested an
experiment or two with the Voltaic pile.

The application of electricity to a Mummy three or
four thousand years old at the least, was an idea, if not
very sage, still sufficiently original, and we all caught
at it at once. About one tenth in earnest and nine tenths
in jest, we arranged a battery in the Doctor's study, and
conveyed thither the Egyptian.

It was only after much trouble that we succeeded in
laying bare some portions of the temporal muscle which
appeared of less stony rigidity than other parts of the
frame, but which, as we had anticipated, of course, gave
no indication of galvanic susceptibility when brought in
contact with the wire. This the first trial, indeed,
seemed decisive, and, with a hearty laugh at our own
absurdity, we were bidding each other good night, when
my eyes, happening to fall upon those of the Mummy,
were there immediately riveted in amazement. My brief
glance, in fact, had sufficed to assure me that the orbs
which we had all supposed to be glass, and which were
originally noticeable for a certain wild stare, were now
so far covered by the lids that only a small portion of
the *tunica albuginea* remained visible.

With a shout I called attention to the fact, and it became immediately obvious to all.

I cannot say that I was *alarmed* at the phenomenon,

because "alarmed" is, in my case, not exactly the word. It is possible, however, that, but for the Brown Stout, I might have been a little nervous. As for the rest of the company, they really made no attempt at concealing the downright fright which possessed them. Doctor Ponnonner was a man to be pitied. Mr. Gliddon, by some peculiar process, rendered himself invisible. Mr. Silk Buckingham, I fancy, will scarcely be so bold as to deny that he made his way, upon all fours, under the table.

After the first shock of astonishment, however, we resolved, as a matter of course, upon farther experiment forthwith. Our operations were now directed against the great toe of the right foot. We made an incision over the outside of the exterior *os sesamoideum pollicis pedis*, and thus got at the root of the *abductor* muscle. Re-adjusting the battery, we now applied the fluid to the bisected nerves—when, with a movement of exceeding life-likeness, the Mummy first drew up its right knee so as to bring it nearly in contact with the abdomen, and then, straightening the limb with inconceivable force, bestowed a kick upon Doctor Ponnonner which had the effect of discharging that gentleman, like an arrow from a catapult, through a window into the street below.

We rushed out *en masse* to bring in the mangled remains of the victim, but had the happiness to meet him upon the staircase, coming up in an unaccountable hurry, brimfull of the most ardent philosophy, and more than ever impressed with the necessity of prosecuting our experiments with rigor and with zeal.

It was by his advice, accordingly, that we made, upon the spot, a profound incision into the tip of the subject's nose, while the Doctor himself, laying violent hands upon it, pulled it into vehement contact with the wire.

Morally and physically—figuratively and literally—was the effect electric. In the first place, the corpse opened its eyes and winked very rapidly for several minutes, as does Mr. Barnes in the pantomime; in the second place, it sneezed; in the third, it sat upon end; in the fourth, it shook its fist in Doctor Ponnonner's face; in the fifth, turning to Messieurs Gliddon and Buckingham, it addressed them, in very capital Egyptian, thus:

"I must say, gentlemen, that I am as much surprised as I am mortified, at your behaviour. Of Doctor Ponnonner nothing better was to be expected. He is a poor little fat fool who *knows* no better. I pity and forgive him. But you, Mr. Gliddon—and you, Silk—who have travelled and resided in Egypt until one might imagine you to the manor born—you, I say, who have been so much among us that you speak Egyptian fully as well, I think, as you write your mother tongue—you, whom I have always been led to regard as the firm friend of the mummies—I really did anticipate more gentlemanly conduct from *you*. What am I to think of you standing quietly by and seeing me thus unhandsomely used? What am I to suppose by your permitting Tom, Dick and Harry to strip me of my coffins, and my clothes, in this wretchedly cold climate? In what light (to come to the point) am I to regard your aiding and abetting that miserable little villain, Doctor Ponnonner, in pulling me by the nose?"

It will be taken for granted, no doubt, that upon hearing this speech under the circumstances, we all either made for the door, or fell into violent hysterics, or went off in a general swoon. One of these three things was, I say, to be expected. Indeed each and all of these lines of conduct might have been very plausibly pursued. And, upon my word, I am at a loss to know how or why it was that we pursued neither the one or the other. But, perhaps, the true reason is to be sought in the spirit of the age, which proceeds by the rule of contraries altogether, and is now usually admitted as the solution of everything in the way of paradox and impossibility. Or, perhaps, after all, it was only the Mummy's exceedingly natural and matter-of-course air that divested his words of the terrible. However this may be, the facts are clear, and no member of our party betrayed any very particular trepidation, or seemed to consider that any thing had gone very especially wrong.

For my part I was convinced it was all right, and merely stepped aside, out of the range of the Egyptian's fist. Doctor Ponnonner thrust his hands into his breeches' pockets, looked hard at the Mummy, and grew excessively red in the face. Mr. Gliddon stroked his whiskers and drew up the collar of his shirt. Mr. Buckingham hung down his head, and put his right thumb into the left corner of his mouth.

The Egyptian regarded him with a severe countenance for some minutes, and at length, with a sneer, said:

"Why don't you speak, Mr. Buckingham? Did you hear what I asked you, or not? *Do* take your thumb out of your mouth!"

Mr. Buckingham, hereupon, gave a slight start, took his right thumb out of the left corner of his mouth, and, by way of indemnification, inserted his left thumb in the right corner of the aperture above-mentioned.

Not being able to get an answer from Mr. B., the figure turned peevishly to Mr. Gliddon, and, in a peremptory tone, demanded in general terms what we all meant.

Mr. Gliddon replied at great length, in phonetics; and but for the deficiency of American printing-offices in hieroglyphical type, it would afford me much pleasure to record here, in the original, the whole of his very excellent speech.

I may as well take this occasion to remark, that all the subsequent conversation in which the Mummy took a part, was carried on in primitive Egyptian, through the medium (so far as concerned myself and other untravelled members of the company)—through the medium,

I say, of Messieurs Gliddon and Buckingham, as interpreters. These gentlemen spoke the mother-tongue of the mummy with inimitable fluency and grace; but I could not help observing that (owing, no doubt, to the introduction of images entirely modern, and, of course, entirely novel to the stranger,) the two travelers were reduced, occasionally, to the employment of sensible forms for the purpose of conveying a particular meaning. Mr. Gliddon, at one period, for example, could not make the Egyptian comprehend the term "politics," until he sketched upon the wall, with a bit of charcoal, a little carbuncle-nosed gentleman, out at elbows, standing upon a stump, with his left leg drawn back, his right arm thrown forward, with the fist shut, the eyes rolled up toward Heaven, and the mouth open at an angle of ninety degrees. Just in the same way Mr. Buckingham failed to convey the absolutely modern idea, "wig," until, (at Doctor Ponnonner's suggestion,) he grew very pale in the face, and consented to take off his own.

It will be readily understood that Mr. Gliddon's discourse turned chiefly upon the vast benefits accruing to science from the unrolling and disembowelling of mummies; apologizing, upon this score, for any disturbance that might have been occasioned *him*, in particular, the individual Mummy called Allamistakeo; and concluding with a mere hint, (for it could scarcely be considered more) that, as these little matters were now explained, it might be as well to proceed with the investigation intended. Here Doctor Ponnonner made ready his instruments.

In regard to the latter suggestions of the orator, it appears that Allamistakeo had certain scruples of conscience, the nature of which I did not distinctly learn; but he expressed himself satisfied with the apologies tendered, and, getting down from the table, shook hands with the company all round.

When this ceremony was at an end, we immediately busied ourselves in repairing the damages which our subject had sustained from the scalpel. We sewed up the wound in his temple, bandaged his foot, and applied a square inch of black plaster to the tip of his nose.

It was now observed that the Count, (this was the title, it seems, of Allamistakeo,) had a slight fit of shivering—no doubt from the cold. The doctor immediately repaired to his wardrobe, and soon returned with a black dress coat, made in Jennings' best manner, a pair of sky-blue plaid pantaloons with straps, a pink gingham *chemise*, a flapped vest of brocade, a white sack overcoat, a walking cane with a hook, a hat with no brim, patent-leather boots, straw-colored kid gloves, an eye-glass, a pair of whiskers, and a waterfall cravat. Owing to the disparity of size between the Count and doctor, (the proportion being as two to one,) there was some little difficulty in adjusting these habiliments upon the person of the Egyptian; but when all was arranged, he might have been said to be dressed. Mr. Gliddon, therefore, gave him his arm, and led him to a comfortable chair by the fire, while the doctor rang the bell upon the spot and ordered a supply of cigars and wine.

The conversation soon grew animated. Much curiosity was, of course, expressed in regard to the somewhat remarkable fact of Allamistakeo's still remaining alive.

"I should have thought," observed Mr. Buckingham, "that it is high time you were dead."

"Why," replied the Count, very much astonished, "I am little more than seven hundred years old! My father lived a thousand, and was by no means in his dotage when he died."

Here ensued a brisk series of questions and computations, by means of which it became evident that the antiquity of the Mummy had been grossly misjudged. It had been five thousand and fifty years, and some months,

since he had been consigned to the catacombs at Eleithias.

"But my remark," resumed Mr. Buckingham, "had
no reference to your age at the period of interment; (I
am willing to grant, in fact, that you are still a young
man,) and my allusion was to the immensity of time
during which, by your own showing, you must have been
done up in asphaltum."

"In what?" said the Count.

"In asphaltum," persisted Mr. B.

"Ah, yes; I have some faint notion of what you mean;
it might be made to answer, no doubt,—but in my time
we employed scarcely anything else than the Bichloride
of Mercury."

"But what we are especially at a loss to understand,"
said Doctor Ponnonner, "is how it happens that, having
been dead and buried in Egypt five thousand years ago,
you are here to-day all alive, and looking so delightfully
well."

"Had I been, as you say, *dead*," replied the Count, "it
is more than probable that dead I should still be; for I
perceive you are yet in the infancy of Galvanism, and
cannot accomplish with it what was a common thing
among us in the old days. But the fact is, I fell into
catalepsy, and it was considered by my best friends that
I was either dead or should be; they accordingly embalmed me at once—I presume you are aware of the
chief principle of the embalming process?"

"Why, not altogether."

"Ah, I perceive;—a deplorable condition of ignorance!
Well, I cannot enter into details just now: but it is necessary to explain that to embalm, (properly speaking,)
in Egypt, was to arrest indefinitely *all* the animal functions subjected to the process. I use the word "animal"
in its widest sense, as including the physical not more
than the moral and *vital* being. I repeat that the lead-

ing principle of embalmment consisted, with us, in the immediately arresting, and holding in perpetual *abeyance*, *all* the animal functions subjected to the process. To be brief, in whatever condition the individual was, at the period of embalmment, in that condition he remained. Now, as it is my good fortune to be of the blood of the Scarabæus, I was embalmed *alive*, as you see me at present."

"The blood of the Scarabæus!" exclaimed Doctor Ponnonner.

"Yes. The Scarabæus was the *insignium*, or the "arms," of a very distinguished and a very rare patrician family. To be "of the blood of the Scarabæus," is merely to be one of that family of which the Scarabæus is the *insignium*. I speak figuratively."

"But what has this to do with your being alive?"

"Why it is the general custom, in Egypt, to deprive a corpse, before embalmment, of its bowels and brains; the race of the Scarabæi alone did not coincide with the custom. Had I not been a Scarabæus, therefore, I should have been without bowels and brains; and without either it is inconvenient to live."

"I perceive that;" said Mr. Buckingham, "and I presume that all the *entire* mummies that come to hand are of the race of Scarabœi."

"Beyond doubt."

"I thought," said Mr. Gliddon very meekly, "that the Scarabæus was one of the Egyptian gods."

"One of the Egyptian *what?*" exclaimed the Mummy, starting to its feet.

"Gods!" repeated the traveler.

"Mr. Gliddon I really am ashamed to hear you talk in this style," said the Count, resuming his chair. "No nation upon the face of the earth has ever acknowledged more than *one* god. The Scarabæus, the Ibis, etc., were with us, (as similar creatures have been with others) the symbols, or *media,* through which we offered worship to a Creator too august to be more directly approached."

There was here a pause. At length the colloquy was renewed by Doctor Ponnonner.

"It is not improbable, then, from what you have explained," said he, "that among the catacombs near the Nile, there may exist other mummies of the Scaraboeus tribe, in a condition of vitality."

"There can be no question of it," replied the Count; all the Scarabœi embalmed accidentally while alive, are alive now. Even some of those *purposely* so embalmed, may have been overlooked by their executors, and still remain in the tombs."

"Will you be kind enough to explain," I said, "what you mean by 'purposely so embalmed?'"

"With great pleasure," answered the Mummy, after surveying me leisurely through his eye-glass—for it was the first time I had ventured to address him a direct question.

"With great pleasure," said he. "The usual duration of man's life, in my time, was about eight hundred years. Few men died, unless by most extraordinary accident, before the age of six hundred; few lived longer than a decade of centuries; but eight were considered the natural term. After the discovery of the embalming principle, as I have already described it to you, it occurred to our philosophers that a laudable curiosity might be gratified, and, at the same time, the interests of science much advanced, by living this natural term in instalments. In the case of history, indeed, experience demonstrated that something of this kind was indispensable. An historian, for example, having attained the age of five hundred, would write a book with great labor and then get himself carefully embalmed; leaving instructions to his executors *pro tem.*, that they should cause him to be revivified after the lapse of a certain period say, five or six hundred years. Resuming existence at the expiration of this term, he would invariably find his great work converted into a species of hap-hazard note-book—that is to say, into a kind of literary arena for the conflicting guesses, riddles, and personal squabbles of whole herds of exasperated commentators. These guesses, etc. which passed under the name of annotations or emandations, were found so completely to have enveloped, distorted, and overwhelmed the text, that the author had to go about with a lantern to discover his own book. When discovered, it was never worth the trouble of the search. After re-writing it throughout, it was regarded as the bounden duty of the historian to set himself to work, immediately, in correcting from his own private knowledge and experience, the traditions of the day concerning the epoch at which he had originally lived. Now this process of re-scription and personal rectification, pursued by various individual sages, from time to time had the effect of preventing our history from degenerating into absolute fable."

"I beg your pardon," said Doctor Ponnonner at this point, laying his hand gently upon the arm of the Egyptian—"I beg your pardon, sir, but may I presume to interrupt you for one moment?"

"By all means, *sir*," replied the Count, drawing up.

"I merely wished to ask you a question," said the Doctor. "You mentioned the historian's personal correction of *traditions* respecting his own epoch. Pray, sir, upon an average, what proportion of these Kabbala were usually found to be right?"

"The Kabbala, as you properly term them, sir, were generally discovered to be precisely on a par with the facts recorded in the un-re-written histories themselves;

—that is to say, not one individual iota of either, was ever known, under any circumstances, to be not totally and radically wrong."

"But since it is quite clear," resumed the Doctor, "that at least five thousand years have elapsed since your entombment, I take it for granted that your histories at that period, if not your traditions, were sufficiently explicit on that one topic of universal interest, the Creation, which took place, as I presume you are aware, only about ten centuries before."

"Sir!" said Count Allamistakeo.

The Doctor repeated his remarks, but it was only after much additional explanation, that the foreigner could be made to comprehend them. The latter at length said, hesitatingly:

"The ideas you have suggested are to me, I confess, utterly novel. During my time I never knew any one to entertain so singular a fancy as that the universe (or this world if you will have it so) ever had a beginning at all. I remember, once, and once only, hearing something remotely hinted, by a man of many speculations, concerning the origin of *the human race*; and by this individual the very word *Adam* (or Red Earth), which you make use of, was employed. He employed it, however, in a generical sense, with reference to the spontaneous germination from rank soil (just as a thousand of the lower *genera* of creatures are germinated)—the spontaneous germination, I say, of five vast hordes of men, simultaneously upspringing in five distinct and nearly equal divisions of the globe."

Here, in general, the company shrugged their shoulders, and one or two of us touched our foreheads with a very significant air. Mr. Silk Buckingham, first glancing slightly at the occiput and then at the siniciput of Allamistakeo, spoke as follows:—

"The long duration of human life in your time, together with the occasional practice of passing it, as you have explained, in instalments, must have had, indeed, a strong tendency to the general development and conglomeration of knowledge. I presume, therefore, that we are to attribute the marked inferiority of the old Egyptians in all particulars of science, when compared with the moderns, and more especially with the Yankees, altogether to the superior solidity of the Egyptian skull."

"I confess again," replied the Count with much suavity, "that I am somewhat at a loss to comprehend you; pray, to what particulars of science do you allude?"

Here our whole party, joining voices, detailed, at great length, the assumptions of phrenology and the marvels of animal magnetism.

Having heard us to an end, the Count proceeded to relate a few anecdotes, which rendered it evident that prototypes of Gall and Spurzheim had flourished and faded in Egypt so long ago as to have been nearly forgotten, and that the manœuvres of Mesmer were really very contemptible tricks when put in collation with the positive miracles of the Theban *savans*, who created lice and a great many other similar things.

I here asked the Count if his people were able to calculate eclipses. He smiled rather contemptuously, and said they were.

This put me a little out, but I began to make other inquiries in regard to his astronomical knowledge, when a member of the company, who had never as yet opened his mouth, whispered in my ear that, for information on this head, I had better consult Ptolemy, (whoever Ptolemy is) as well as one Plutarch *de facie lunæ*.

I then questioned the Mummy about burning-glasses and lenses, and, in general, about the manufacture of glass; but I had not made an end of my queries before the silent member again touched me quietly on the elbow, and begged me for God's sake to take a peep at Diodorus

Siculus. As for the Count, he merely asked me, in the way of reply, if we moderns possessed any such microscopes as would enable us to cut cameos in the style of the Egyptians. While I was thinking how I should answer this question, little Doctor Ponnonner committed himself in a very extraordinary way.

"Look at our architecture!" he exclaimed, greatly to the indignation of both the travelers, who pinched him black and blue to no purpose.

"Look," he cried with enthusiasm, "at the Bowling-Green Fountain in New York! or if this be too vast a contemplation, regard for a moment the Capitol at Washington, D.C.!"—and the good little medical man went on to detail very minutely the proportions of the fabric to which he referred. He explained that the portico alone was adorned with no less than four and twenty columns, five feet in diameter, and ten feet apart.

The Count said that he regretted not being able to remember, just at that moment, the precise dimensions of any one of the principal buildings of the city of Aznac, whose foundations were laid in the night of Time, but the ruins of which were still standing, at the epoch of his entombment, in a vast plain of sand to the westward of Thebes. He recollected, however, (talking of porticoes) that one affixed to an inferior palace in a kind of suburb called Carnac, consisted of a hundred and forty-four columns, thirty-seven feet each in circumference, and twenty-five feet apart. The approach to this portico, from the Nile, was through an avenue two miles long, composed of sphynxes, statues and obelisks, twenty, sixty, and a hundred feet in height. The palace itself (as well as he could remember) was, in one direction, two miles long, and might have been, altogether, about seven in circuit. Its walls were richly painted all over, within and without, with hieroglyphics. He would not pretend to *assert* that even fifty or sixty of the Doctor's Capitols might have been built within these walls, but he was by no means sure that two or three hundred of them might not have been squeezed in with some trouble. That palace at Carnac was an insignificant little building after all. He (the Count), however, could not conscientiously refuse to admit the ingenuity, magnificence, and superiority of the Fountain at the Bowling-Green, as described by the Doctor. Nothing like it, he was forced to allow, had ever been seen in Egypt or elsewhere.

I here asked the Count what he had to say to our railroads.

"Nothing," he replied, "in particular." They were rather slight, rather ill-conceived, and clumsily put together. They could not be compared, of course, with the vast, level, direct, iron-grooved causeways, upon which the Egyptians conveyed entire temples and solid obelisks of a hundred and fifty feet in altitude.

I spoke of our gigantic mechanical forces.

He agreed that we knew something in that way, but inquired how I should have gone to work in getting up the imposts on the lintels of even the little palace at Carnac.

This question I concluded not to hear, and demanded if he had any idea of Artesian wells; but he simply raised his eye-brows; while Mr. Gliddon, winked at me very hard, and said, in a low tone, that one had been recently discovered by the engineers employed to bore for water in the Great Oasis.

I then mentioned our steel; but the foreigner elevated his nose, and asked me if our steel could have executed the sharp curved work seen on the obelisks, and which was wrought altogether by edge-tools of copper.

This disconcerted us so greatly that we thought it advisable to vary the attack to Metaphysics. We sent for a copy of a book called the "Dial," and read out of it a chapter or two about something which is not very clear, but which the Bostonians call the Great Movement or Progress.

The Count merely said that Great Movements were awfully common things in his day, and as for Progress it was at one time quite a nuisance, but it never progressed.

We then spoke of the great beauty and importance of Democracy, and were at much trouble in impressing the Count with a due sense of the advantages we enjoyed in living where there was suffrage *ad libitum*, and no king.

He listened with marked interest, and in fact seemed not a little amused. When we had done, he said that, a great while ago, there had occurred something of a very similar sort. Thirteen Egyptian provinces determined all at once to be free, and so set a magnificent example to the rest of mankind. They assembled their wise men, and concocted the most ingenious constitution it is possible to conceive. For a while they managed remarkably well; only their habit of bragging was prodigious. The thing ended, however, in the consolidation of the thirteen states, with some fifteen or twenty others, into the most odious and insupportable despotism that ever was heard of upon the face of the Earth.

I asked what was the name of the usurping tyrant.

As well as the Count could recollect, it was *Mob*.

Not knowing what to say to this, I raised my voice, and deplored the Egyptian ignorance of steam.

The Count looked at me with much astonishment, but made no answer. The silent gentleman, however, gave me a violent nudge in the ribs with his elbows—told me I had sufficiently exposed myself for once—and demanded if I was really such a fool as not to know that the modern steam engine is derived from the invention of Hero, through Solomon de Caus.

We were now in imminent danger of being discomfited; but, as good luck would have it, Doctor Ponnonner, having rallied, returned to our rescue, and inquired if the people of Egypt would seriously pretend to rival the moderns in the all-important particular of dress.

The Count, at this, glanced downward to the straps of his pantaloons, and then, taking hold of the end of one of his coat-tails; held it up close to his eyes for some minutes. Letting it fall, at last, his mouth extended itself very gradually from ear to ear; but I do not remember that he said anything in the way of reply.

Hereupon we recovered our spirits, and the Doctor, approaching the mummy with great dignity, desired it to say candidly, upon its honor as a gentleman, if the Egyptians had comprehended, at *any* period, the manufacture of either Ponnonner's lozenges, or Brandreth's pills.

We looked, with profound anxiety, for an answer;—but in vain. It was not forthcoming. The Egyptian blushed and hung down his head. Never was triumph more consummate; never was defeat borne with so ill a grace. Indeed I could not endure the spectacle of the poor Mummy's mortification. I reached my hat, bowed to him stiffly, and took leave.

Upon getting home I found it past four o'clock, and went immediately to bed. It is now ten, A. M. I have been up since seven, penning these memoranda for the benefit of my family and of mankind. The former I shall behold no more. My wife is a shrew. The truth is, I am heartily sick of this life and of the nineteenth century in general. I am convinced that everything is going wrong. Besides, I am anxious to know who will be President in 2045. As soon, therefore, as I shave and swallow a cup of coffee, I shall just step over to Ponnonner's and get embalmed for a couple of hundred years.

THE IMP OF THE PERVERSE

In the consideration of the faculties and impulses of the *prima mobilia* of the human soul, the phrenologists have failed to make room for a propensity, which, although obviously existing as a radical, primitive, irreducible sentiment, has been equally overlooked by all the moralists who have preceded them. In the pure arrogance of the reason, we have all overlooked it. We have suffered its existence to escape our senses, solely through want of belief—of faith;—whether it be faith in Revelation, or faith in the Kabbala. The idea of it has never occurred to us, simply because of its seeming supererogation. We saw no *need* of the impulse—for the propensity. We could not perceive its necessity. We could not understand, that is to say, we could not have understood, had the notion of this *primum mobile* ever obtruded itself;—we could not have understood in what manner it might be made to further the objects of humanity, either temporal or eternal. It cannot be denied that phrenology, and in great measure, all metaphysicianism, have been concocted *à priori*. The intellectual or logical man, rather than the understanding or observant man, set himself to imagine designs—to dictate purposes to God. Having thus fathomed to his satisfaction the intentions of Jehovah, out of these intentions he built his innumerable systems of mind. In the matter of phrenology, for example, we first determined, naturally enough, that it was the design of the Deity that man should eat. We then assigned to man an organ of alimentiveness, and this organ is the scourge with which the Deity compels man, will-I nill-I, into eating. Secondly, having settled it to be God's will that man should continue his species, we discovered an organ of amativeness, forthwith. And so with combativeness, with ideality, with causality, with constructiveness,—so, in short, with every organ, whether representing a propensity, a moral sentiment, or a faculty of the pure intellect. And in these arrangements of the *principia* of human action, the Spurzheimites, whether right or wrong, in part, or upon the whole, have but followed, in principle, the footsteps of their predecessors; deducing and establishing everything from the preconceived destiny of man, and upon the ground of the objects of his Creator.

It would have been wiser, it would have been safer to classify, (if classify we must,) upon the basis of what man usually or occasionally did, and was always occasionally doing, rather than upon the basis of what we took it for granted the Deity intended him to do. If we cannot comprehend God in his visible works, how then in his inconceivable thoughts, that call the works into being? If we cannot understand him in his objective creatures, how then in his substantive moods and phases of creation?

Induction, *à posteriori*, would have brought phrenology to admit, as an innate and primitive principle of human action, a paradoxical something, which we may call *perverseness*, for want of a more characteristic term. In the sense I intend, it is, in fact, a *mobile* without motive, a motive not *motivirt*. Through its promptings we act without comprehensible object; or, if this shall be understood as a contradiction in terms, we may so far modify the proposition as to say, that through its promptings we act, for the reason that we should *not*. In theory, no reason can be more unreasonable; but, in fact, there is none more strong. With certain minds, under certain conditions, it becomes absolutely irresistible. I am not more certain that I breathe, than that the assurance of the wrong or error of any action is often the one unconquerable *force* which impels us, and alone impels us, to its prosecution. Nor will this overwhelming tendency to do wrong for the wrong's sake, admit of analysis, or resolution into ulterior elements. It is a radical, a primitive impulse—elementary. It will be said, I am aware, that when we persist in acts because we feel we should *not* persist in them, our conduct is but a modification of that which ordinarily springs from the *combativeness* of phrenology. But a glance will show the fallacy of this idea. The phrenological combativeness has for its essence, the necessity of self-defence. It is our safeguard against injury. Its principle regards our well-being; and thus the desire to be well, is excited simultaneously with its development. It follows, that the desire to be well must be excited simultaneously with any principle which shall be merely a modification of combativeness, but in the case of that something which I term *perverseness*, the desire to be well is not only not aroused, but a strongly antagonistical sentiment exists.

An appeal to one's own heart is, after all, the best reply to the sophistry just noticed. No one who trustingly consults and thoroughly questions his own soul, will be disposed to deny the entire radicalness of the propensity in question. It is not more incomprehensible than distinctive. There lives no man who at some period, has not been tormented, for example, by an earnest desire to tantalize a listener by circumlocution. The speaker is aware that he displeases; he has every intention to please; he is usually curt, precise, and clear; the most laconic and luminous language is struggling for utterance upon his tongue; it is only with difficulty that he restrains himself from giving it flow; he dreads and deprecates the anger of him whom he addresses; yet, the thought strikes him, that by certain involutions and parentheses, this anger may be engendered. That single thought is enough. The impulse increases to a wish, the wish to a desire, the desire to an uncontrollable longing, and the longing (to the deep regret and mortifica-

tion of the speaker, and in defiance of all consequences,)
is indulged.

We have a task before us which must be speedily performed. We know that it will be ruinous to make delay.
The most important crisis of our life calls, trumpet-
tongued, for immediate energy and action. We glow, we
are consumed with eagerness to commence the work, with
the anticipation of whose glorious result our whole souls
are on fire. It must, it shall be undertaken to-day, and yet
we put it off until to-morrow; and why? There is no answer,
except that we feel *perverse*, using the word with no
comprehension of the principle. To-morrow arrives, and
with it a more impatient anxiety to do our duty, but with
this very increase of anxiety arrives, also, a nameless, a
positively fearful, because unfathomable craving for delay. This craving gathers strength as the moments fly. The
last hour for action is at hand. We tremble with the
violence of the conflict within us,—of the definite with
the indefinite—of the substance with the shadow. But, if
the contest have proceeded thus far, it is the shadow which
prevails,—we struggle in vain. The clock strikes, and is the
knell of our welfare. At the same time, it is the chanticleer-
note to the ghost that has so long over-awed us. It flies—
it disappears—we are free. The old energy returns. We
will labor *now*. Alas, it is *too late!*

We stand upon the brink of a precipice. We peer into
the abyss—we grow sick and dizzy. Our first impulse is to
shrink from the danger. Unaccountably we remain. By
slow degrees our sickness, and dizziness, and horror, become merged in a cloud of unnameable feeling. By gradations, still more imperceptible, this cloud assumes shape,
as did the vapor from the bottle out of which arose the
genius in the Arabian Nights. But out of this *our* cloud
upon the precipice's edge, there grows into palpability, a
shape, far more terrible than any genius, or any demon of

a tale, and yet it is but a thought, although a fearful one, and one which chills the very marrow of our bones with the fierceness of the delight of its horror. It is merely the idea of what would be our sensations during the sweeping precipitancy of a fall from such a height. And this fall —this rushing annihilation—for the very reason that it involves that one most ghastly and loathsome of all the most ghastly and loathsome images of death and suffering which have ever presented themselves to our imagination—for this very cause do we now the most vividly desire it. And because our reason violently deters us from the brink, *therefore*, do we the more impetuously approach it. There is no passion in nature so demoniacally impatient, as that of him, who shuddering upon the edge of a precipice, thus meditates a plunge. To indulge for a moment, in any attempt at *thought*, is to be inevitably lost; for reflection but urges us to forbear, and *therefore* it is, I say, that we *cannot*. If there be no friendly arm to check us, or if we fail in a sudden effort to prostrate ourselves backward from the abyss, we plunge, and are destroyed.

Examine these and similar actions as we will, we shall find them resulting solely from the spirit of the *Perverse*. We perpetrate them merely because we feel that we should *not*. Beyond or behind this, there is no intelligible principle. And we might, indeed, deem this perverseness a direct instigation of the Arch-Fiend, were it not occasionally known to operate in furtherance of good.

I have said thus much, that in some measure I may answer your question, that I may explain to you why I am here, that I may assign to you something that shall have at least the faint aspect of a cause for my wearing these fetters, and for my tenanting this cell of the condemned. Had I not been thus prolix, you might either have misunderstood me altogether; or with the rabble, you might have fancied me mad. As it is, you will easily perceive that I am one of the many uncounted victims of the Imp of the Perverse.

It is impossible that any deed could have been wrought with a more thorough deliberation. For weeks, for months, I pondered upon the means of the murder. I rejected a thousand schemes because their accomplishment involved a *chance* of detection. At length, in reading some French Memoirs, I found an account of a nearly fatal illness that occurred to Madame Pilau, through the agency of a candle accidentally poisoned. The idea struck my fancy at once. I knew my victim's habit of reading in bed. I knew, too, that his apartment was narrow and ill ventilated. But I need not vex you with impertinent details. I need not describe the easy artifices by which I substituted, in his bed-room candlestand, a wax-light of my own making, for the one which I there found. The next morning he was discovered dead in his bed, and the Coroner's verdict was, "Death by the visitation of God."

Having inherited his estate, all went well with me for years. The idea of detection never once entered my brain. Of the remains of the fatal taper, I had myself carefully disposed. I had left no shadow of a clue by which it would be possible to convict, or even to suspect me of the crime. It is inconceivable how rich a sentiment of satisfaction arose in my bosom as I reflected upon my absolute security. For a very long period of time, I was accustomed to revel in this sentiment. It afforded me more real delight than all the mere worldly advantages accruing from my sin. But there arrived at length an epoch, from which the pleasurable feeling grew, by scarcely perceptible gradations, into a haunting and harassing thought. It harassed because it haunted. I could scarcely get rid of it for an instant. It is quite a common thing to be thus annoyed with the ringing in our ears, or rather in our memories, of the burthen of some ordinary song, or some unimpressive snatches from an opera. Nor will we be the less tormented if the song in itself be good, or the opera air meritorious. In this manner, at last, I would perpetually catch myself pondering upon my security, and repeating, in a low undertone, the phrase, "I am safe."

One day, whilst sauntering along the streets, I arrested myself in the act of murmuring, half aloud, these customary syllables. In a fit of petulance, I remodelled them thus:—"I am safe—I am safe—yes—if I be not fool enough to make open confession!"

No sooner had I spoken these words, than I felt an icy chill creep to my heart. I had had some experience in these fits of perversity, whose nature I have been at some trouble to explain, and I remembered well, that in no instance, I had successfully resisted their attacks. And now my own casual self-suggestion, that I might possibly be fool enough to confess the murder of which I had been guilty, confronted me, as if the very ghost of him whom I had murdered—and beckoned me on to death.

At first, I made an effort to shake off this nightmare of the soul. I walked vigorously—faster—still faster—at length I ran. I felt a maddening desire to shriek aloud. Every succeeding wave of thought overwhelmed me with new terror, for, alas! I well, too well understood that, to *think*, in my situation, was to be lost. I still quickened my pace. I bounded like a madman through the crowded thoroughfares. At length, the populace took the alarm, and pursued me. I felt *then* the consummation of my fate. Could I have torn out my tongue, I would have done it, but a rough voice resounded in my ears—a rougher grasp seized me by the shoulder. I turned—I gasped for breath. For a moment, I experienced all the pangs of suffocation; I became blind, and deaf, and giddy; and then, some invisible fiend, I thought, struck me with his broad palm upon the back. The long imprisoned secret burst forth from my soul.

They say that I spoke with a distinct enunciation, but with marked emphasis, and passionate hurry, as if in dread of interruption before concluding the brief, but pregnant sentences that consigned me to the hangman, and to hell.

Having related all that was necessary for the fullest judicial conviction, I fell prostrate in a swoon.

But why shall I say more? To-day I wear these chains, and am *here!* To-morrow I shall be fetterless!—*but where?*

THE FACTS IN THE CASE
OF M. VALDEMAR

An article of ours, thus entitled, was published in the last number of Mr. Colton's "American Review," and has given rise to some discussion—especially in regard to the truth or falsity of the statements made. It does not become *us*, of course, to offer one word on the point at issue. We have been requested to reprint the article, and do so with pleasure. We leave it to speak for itself. We may observe, however, that there are a certain class of people who pride themselves upon Doubt, as a profession. —*Ed. B. J.* [*Broadway Journal*]

Of course I shall not pretend to consider it any matter for wonder, that the extraordinary case of M. Valdemar has excited discussion. It would have been a miracle had it not —especially under the circumstances. Through the desire of all parties concerned, to keep the affair from the public, at least for the present, or until we had farther opportunities for investigation—through our endeavors to effect this—a garbled or exaggerated account made its way into society, and became the source of many unpleasant misrepresentations, and, very naturally, of a great deal of disbelief.

It is now rendered necessary that I give the *facts*—as far as I comprehend them myself. They are, succinctly, these:

My attention, for the last three years, had been repeatedly drawn to the subject of Mesmerism; and, about nine months ago, it occurred to me, quite suddenly, that in the series of experiments made hitherto, there had been a very remarkable and most unaccountable omission:— no person had as yet been mesmerized *in articulo mortis*. It remained to be seen, first, whether in such condition, there existed in the patient any susceptibility to the magnetic influence; secondly, whether, if any existed, it was impaired or increased by the condition; thirdly, to what extent, or for how long a period, the encroachments of Death might be arrested by the process. There were other points to be ascertained, but these most excited my curiosity—the last in especial, from the immensely important character of its consequences.

In looking around me for some subject by whose means I might test these particulars, I was brought to think of my friend, M. Ernest Valdemar, the well-known compiler of the "Bibliotheca Forensica," and author (under the *nom de plume* of Issachar Marx) of the Polish versions of "Wallenstein" and "Gargantua." M. Valdemar, who has resided principally at Harlem, N. Y., since the year 1839, is (or was) particularly noticeable for the extreme spareness of his person—his lower limbs much resembling those of John Randolph; and, also, for the whiteness of his whiskers, in violent contrast to the blackness of his hair— the latter, in consequence, being very generally mistaken for a wig. His temperament was markedly nervous, and rendered him a good subject for mesmeric experiment. On two or three occasions I had put him to sleep with little difficulty, but was disappointed in other results which his peculiar constitution had naturally led me to anticipate. His will was at no period positively, or thoroughly, under my control, and in regard to *clairvoyance*, I could accomplish with him nothing to be relied upon. I always attributed my failure at these points to the disordered state of his health. For some months previous to my becoming acquainted with him, his physicians had declared him in a confirmed phthisis. It was his custom, indeed, to speak calmly of his approaching dissolution, as of a matter neither to be avoided nor regretted.

When the ideas to which I have alluded first occurred to me, it was of course very natural that I should think of M. Valdemar. I knew the steady philosophy of the man too well to apprehend any scruples from *him*; and he had no relatives in America who would be likely to interfere. I spoke to him frankly upon the subject; and, to my surprise, his interest seemed vividly excited. I say to my surprise; for, although he had always yielded his person freely to my experiments, he had never before given me any tokens of sympathy with what I did. His disease was of that character which would admit of exact calculation in respect to the epoch of its termination in death; and it was finally arranged between us that he would send for me about twenty-four hours before the period announced by his physicians as that of his decease.

It is now rather more than seven months since I received, from M. Valdemar himself, the subjoined note:

My dear P——,

You may as well come *now*. D—— and F—— are agreed that I cannot hold out beyond to-morrow midnight; and I think they have hit the time very nearly.

Valdemar.

I received this note within half an hour after it was written, and in fifteen minutes more I was in the dying man's chamber. I had not seen him for ten days, and was appalled by the fearful alteration which the brief interval had wrought in him. His face wore a leaden hue; the eyes were utterly lustreless; and the emaciation was so extreme that the skin had been broken through by the cheek-bones. His expectoration was excessive. The pulse was barely perceptible. He retained, nevertheless, in a very remarkable manner, both his mental power and a certain degree of physical strength. He spoke with distinctness—took some palliative medicines without aid—and, when I entered the room, was occupied in penciling memoranda in a pocketbook. He was propped up in the bed by pillows. Doctors D——— and F——— were in attendance.

After pressing Valdemar's hand, I took these gentlemen aside, and obtained from them a minute account of the patient's condition. The left lung had been for eighteen months in a semi-osseous or cartilaginous state, and was, of course, entirely useless for all purposes of vitality. The right, in its upper portion, was also partially, if not thoroughly, ossified, while the lower region was merely a mass of purulent tubercles, running one into another. Several extensive perforations existed; and, at one point, permanent adhesion to the ribs had taken place. These appearances in the right lobe were of comparatively recent date. The ossification had proceeded with very unusual rapidity; no sign of it had been discovered a month before, and the adhesion had only been observed during the three previous days. Independently of the phthisis, the patient was suspected of aneurism of the aorta; but on this point the osseous symptoms rendered an exact diagnosis impossible. It was the opinion of both physicians that M. Valdemar would die about midnight on the morrow (Sunday). It was then seven o'clock on Saturday evening.

On quitting the invalid's bed-side to hold conversation with myself, Doctors D——— and F——— had bidden him a final farewell. It had not been their intention to return; but, at my request, they agreed to look in upon the patient about ten the next night.

When they had gone, I spoke freely with M. Valdemar on the subject of his approaching dissolution, as well as, more particularly, of the experiment proposed. He still professed himself quite willing and even anxious to have it made, and urged me to commence it at once. A male and a female nurse were in attendance; but I did not feel myself altogether at liberty to engage in a task of this character with no more reliable witnesses than these people, in case of sudden accident, might prove. I therefore postponed operations until about eight the next night, when the arrival of a medical student with whom I had some acquaintance, (Mr. Theodore L———l,) relieved me from farther embarrassment. It had been my design, originally, to wait for the physicians; but I was induced to proceed, first, by the urgent entreaties of M. Valdemar, and secondly, by my conviction that I had not a moment to lose, as he was evidently sinking fast.

Mr. L———l was so kind as to accede to my desire that he would take notes of all that occurred; and it is from his memoranda that what I now have to relate is, for the most part, either condensèd or copied *verbatim*.

It wanted about five minutes of eight when, taking the patient's hand, I begged him to state, as distinctly as he could, to Mr. L———l, whether he (M. Valdemar) was entirely willing that I should make the experiment of mesmerizing him in his then condition.

He replied feebly, yet quite audibly, "Yes, I wish to be mesmerized"—adding immediately afterwards, "I fear you have deferred it too long."

While he spoke thus, I commenced the passes which I had already found most effectual in subduing him. He was evidently influenced with the first lateral stroke of my hand across his forehead; but although I exerted all my powers, no farther perceptible effect was induced until some minutes after ten o'clock, when Doctors D——— and F——— called, according to appointment. I explained to them, in a few words, what I designed, and as they opposed no objection, saying that the patient was already in the death agony, I proceeded without hesitation—exchanging, however, the lateral passes for downward ones, and directing my gaze entirely into the right eye of the sufferer.

By this time his pulse was imperceptible and his breathing was stertorous, and at intervals of half a minute.

This condition was nearly unaltered for a quarter of an hour. At the expiration of this period, however, a natural although a very deep sigh escaped the bosom of the dying man, and the stertorous breathing ceased—that is to say, its stertorousness was no longer apparent; the intervals were undiminished. The patient's extremities were of an icy coldness.

At five minutes before eleven I perceived unequivocal signs of the mesmeric influence. The glassy roll of the eye was changed for that expression of uneasy *inward* examination which is never seen except in cases of sleep-waking, and which it is quite impossible to mistake. With a few rapid lateral passes I made the lids quiver, as in incipient sleep, and with a few more I closed them altogether. I was not satisfied, however, with this, but continued the manipulations vigorously, and with the fullest exertion of the will, until I had completely stiffened the limbs of the slumberer, after placing them in a seemingly easy position. The legs were at full length; the arms were nearly so, and reposed on the bed at a moderate distance from the loins. The head was very slightly elevated.

When I had accomplished this, it was fully midnight, and I requested the gentlemen present to examine M. Valdemar's condition. After a few experiments, they admitted him to be in an unusually perfect state of mesmeric trance. The curiosity of both the physicians was greatly excited. Dr. D—— resolved at once to remain with the patient all night, while Dr. F—— took leave with a promise to return at day-break. Mr. L———l and the nurses remained.

We left M. Valdemar entirely undisturbed until about three o'clock in the morning, when I approached him and found him in precisely the same condition as when Dr. F——— went away—that is to say, he lay in the same position; the pulse was imperceptible; the breathing was gentle (scarcely noticeable, unless through the application of a mirror to the lips); the eyes were closed naturally; and the limbs were as rigid and as cold as marble. Still, the general appearance was certainly not that of death.

As I approached M. Valdemar I made a kind of half effort to influence his right arm into pursuit of my own, as I passed the latter gently to and fro above his person. In such experiments with this patient I had never perfectly succeeded before, and assuredly I had little thought of succeeding now; but to my astonishment, his arm very readily, although feebly, followed every direction I assigned it with mine. I determined to hazard a few words of conversation.

"M. Valdemar," I said, "are you asleep?" He made no answer, but I perceived a tremor about the lips, and was thus induced to repeat the question, again and again. At its third repetition, his whole frame was agitated by a very slight shivering; the eye-lids unclosed themselves so far as to display a white line of the ball; the lips moved sluggishly, and from between them, in a barely audible whisper, issued the words:

"Yes;—asleep now. Do not wake me!—let me die so!"

I here felt the limbs and found them as rigid as ever. The right arm, as before, obeyed the direction of my hand. I questioned the sleep-waker again:

"Do you still feel pain in the breast, M. Valdemar?"

The answer now was immediate, but even less audible than before:

"No pain—I am dying."

I did not think it advisable to disturb him farther just

then, and nothing more was said or done until the arrival of Dr. F———, who came a little before sunrise, and expressed unbounded astonishment at finding the patient still alive. After feeling the pulse and applying a mirror to the lips, he requested me to speak to the sleep-waker again. I did so, saying:

"M. Valdemar, do you still sleep?"

As before, some minutes elapsed ere a reply was made; and during the interval the dying man seemed to be collecting his energies to speak. At my fourth repetition of the question, he said very faintly, almost inaudibly:

"Yes; still asleep—dying."

It was now the opinion, or rather the wish, of the physicians, that M. Valdemar should be suffered to remain undisturbed in his present apparently tranquil condition, until death should supervene—and this, it was generally agreed, must now take place within a few minutes. I concluded, however, to speak to him once more, and merely repeated my previous question.

While I spoke, there came a marked change over the countenance of the sleep-waker. The eyes rolled themselves slowly open, the pupils disappearing upwardly; the skin generally assumed a cadaverous hue, resembling not so much parchment as white paper; and the circular hectic spots which, hitherto, had been strongly defined in the centre of each cheek, *went out* at once. I use this expression, because the suddenness of their departure put me in mind of nothing so much as the extinguishment of a candle by a puff of the breath. The upper lip, at the same time, writhed itself away from the teeth, which it had previously covered completely; while the lower jaw fell with an audible jerk, leaving the mouth widely extended, and disclosing in full view the swollen and blackened tongue. I presume that no member of the party then present had been unaccustomed to death-bed horrors; but so hideous beyond conception was the appearance of M. Valdemar at this moment, that there was a general shrinking back from the region of the bed.

I now feel that I have reached a point of this narrative at which every reader will be startled into positive disbelief. It is my business, however, simply to proceed.

There was no longer the faintest sign of vitality in M. Valdemar; and concluding him to be dead, we were consigning him to the charge of the nurses, when a strong vibratory motion was observable in the tongue. This continued for perhaps a minute. At the expiration of this period, there issued from the distended and motionless jaws a voice—such as it would be madness in me to attempt describing. There are, indeed, two or three epithets which might be considered as applicable to it in part; I might say, for example, that the sound was harsh, and broken and hollow; but the hideous whole is indescribable, for the simple reason that no similar sounds have ever jarred upon the ear of humanity. There were two particulars, nevertheless, which I thought then, and still think, might fairly be stated as characteristic of the intonation— as well adapted to convey some idea of its unearthly peculiarity. In the first place, the voice seemed to reach our ears—at least mine—from a vast distance, or from some deep cavern within the earth. In the second place, it impressed me (I fear, indeed, that it will be impossible to make myself comprehended) as gelatinous or glutinous matters impress the sense of touch.

I have spoken both of "sound" and of "voice." I mean to say that the sound was one of distinct—or even wonderfully, thrillingly distinct—syllabification. M. Valdemar *spoke*—obviously in reply to the question I had propounded to him a few minutes before. I had asked him, it will be remembered, if he still slept. He now said:

"Yes;—no;—I *have been* sleeping—and now—now—I *am dead.*"

No person present even affected to deny, or attempted to

repress, the unutterable, shuddering horror which these few words, thus uttered, were so well calculated to convey. Mr. L———l (the student) swooned. The nurses immediately left the chamber, and could not be induced to return. My own impressions I would not pretend to render intelligible to the reader. For nearly an hour, we busied ourselves, silently—without the utterance of a word—in endeavors to revive Mr. L———l. When he came to himself, we addressed ourselves again to an investigation of M. Valdemar's condition.

It remained in all respects as I have last described it, with the exception that the mirror no longer afforded evidence of respiration. An attempt to draw blood from the arm failed. I should mention, too, that this limb was no farther subject to my will. I endeavored in vain to make it follow the direction of my hand. The only real indication, indeed, of the mesmeric influence, was now found in the vibratory movement of the tongue, whenever I addressed M. Valdemar a question. He seemed to be making an effort at reply, but had no longer sufficient volition. To queries put to him by any other person than myself he seemed utterly insensible—although I endeavored to place each member of the company in mesmeric *rapport* with him. I believe that I have now related all that is necessary to an understanding of the sleep-waker's state at this epoch. Other nurses were procured; and at ten o'clock I left the house in company with the two physicians and Mr. L———l.

In the afternoon we all called again to see the patient. His condition remained precisely the same. We had now some discussion as to the propriety and feasibility of awakening him; but we had little difficulty in agreeing that no good purpose would be served by so doing. It was evident that, so far, death (or what is usually termed death) had been arrested by the mesmeric process. It seemed clear to us all that to awaken M. Valdemar would be merely to insure his instant, or at least his speedy dissolution.

From this period until the close of last week—*an interval of nearly seven months*—we continued to make daily calls at M. Valdemar's house, accompanied, now and then, by medical and other friends. All this time the sleep-waker remained *exactly* as I have last described him. The nurses' attentions were continual.

It was on Friday last that we finally resolved to make the experiment of awakening, or attempting to awaken him; and it is the (perhaps) unfortunate result of this latter experiment which has given rise to so much discussion in private circles—to so much of what I cannot help thinking unwarranted popular feeling.

For the purpose of relieving M. Valdemar from the mesmeric trance, I made use of the customary passes. These, for a time, were unsuccessful. The first indication of revival was afforded by a partial descent of the iris. It was observed, as especially remarkable, that this lowering of the pupil was accompanied by the profuse out-flowing of a yellowish ichor (from beneath the lids) of a pungent and highly offensive odor.

It now was suggested that I should attempt to influence the patient's arm, as heretofore. I made the attempt and failed. Dr. F—— then intimated a desire to have me put a question. I did so as follows:

"M. Valdemar, can you explain to us what are your feelings or wishes now?"

There was an instant return of the hectic circles on the cheeks; the tongue quivered, or rather rolled violently in the mouth (although the jaws and lips remained rigid as before;) and at length the same hideous voice which I have already described, broke forth:

"For God's sake!—quick!—quick!—put me to sleep—or, quick!—waken me!—quick!—*I say to you that I am dead!*"

I was thoroughly unnerved, and for an instant remained undecided what to do. At first I made an endeavor to recompose the patient; but, failing in this through total abeyance of the will, I retraced my steps and as earnestly struggled to awaken him. In this attempt I soon saw that I should be successful—or at least I soon fancied that my success would be complete—and I am sure that all in the room were prepared to see the patient awaken.

For what really occurred, however, it is quite impossible that any human being could have been prepared.

As I rapidly made the mesmeric passes, amid ejaculations of "dead! dead!" absolutely *bursting* from the tongue and not from the lips of the sufferer, his whole frame at once—within the space of a single minute, or even less, shrunk—crumbled—absolutely *rotted* away beneath my hands. Upon the bed, before that whole company, there lay a nearly liquid mass of loathsome—of detestable putridity.

THE SPHINX

During the dread reign of the Cholera in New York, I had accepted the invitation of a relative to spend a fortnight with him in the retirement of his *cottage ornée* on the banks of the Hudson. We had here around us all the ordinary means of summer amusement; and what with rambling in the woods, sketching, boating, fishing, bathing, music and books, we should have passed the time pleasantly enough, but for the fearful intelligence which reached us every morning from the populous city. Not a day elapsed which did not bring us news of the decease of some acquaintance. Then, as the fatality increased, we learned to expect daily the loss of some friend. At length we trembled at the approach of every messenger. The very air from the South seemed to us redolent with death. That palsying thought, indeed, took entire possession of my soul. I could neither speak, think, nor dream of any thing else. My host was of a less excitable temperament, and, although greatly depressed in spirits, exerted himself to sustain my own. His richly philosophical intellect was not at any time affected by unrealities. To the substances of terror he was sufficiently alive, but of its shadows he had no apprehension.

His endeavors to arouse me from the condition of abnormal gloom into which I had fallen, were frustrated in great measure, by certain volumes which I had found in his library. These were of a character to force into germination whatever seeds of hereditary superstition lay latent in my bosom. I had been reading these books without his knowledge, and thus he was often at a loss to account for the forcible impressions which had been made upon my fancy.

A favorite topic with me was the popular belief in omens—a belief which, at this one epoch of my life, I was almost seriously disposed to defend. On this subject we had long and animated discussions—he maintaining the utter groundlessness of faith in such matters.—I contending that a popular sentiment arising with absolute spontaneity—that is to say without apparent traces of suggestion—had in itself the unmistakeable elements of truth, and was entitled to as much respect as that intuition which is the idiosyncrasy of the individual man of genius.

The fact is, that soon after my arrival at the cottage, there had occurred to myself an incident so entirely inexplicable, and which had in it so much of the portentious character, that I might well have been excused for regarding it as an omen. It appalled, and at the same time so confounded and bewildered me, that many days elapsed before I could make up my mind to communicate the circumstance to my friend.

Near the close of an exceedingly warm day, I was sitting, book in hand, at an open window, commanding, through a long vista of the river banks, a view of a distant hill, the face of which nearest my position, had been denuded, by what is termed a land-slide, of the principal portion of its trees. My thoughts had been long wandering from the volume before me to the gloom and desolation of the neighboring city. Uplifting my eyes from the page, they fell upon the naked face of the hill, and upon an object—upon some living monster of hideous conformation, which very rapidly made its way from the summit to the bottom, disappearing finally in the dense forest below. As this creature first came in sight, I doubted my own sanity—or at least the evidence of my own eyes; and many minutes passed before I succeeded in convincing myself that I was neither mad nor in a dream. Yet when I describe the monster (which I distinctly saw, and calmly surveyed through the whole period of its progress,) my readers, I fear, will feel more difficulty in being convinced of these points than even I did, myself.

Estimating the size of the creature by comparison with the diameter of the large trees near which it passed—the few giants of the forest which had escaped the fury of the land-slide—I concluded it to be far larger than any ship of the line in existence. I say ship of the line, because the shape of the monster suggested the idea—the hull of one of our seventy-fours might convey a very tolerable conception of the general outline. The mouth of the animal was situated at the extremity of a proboscis some sixty or seventy feet in length, and about as thick as the body of an ordinary elephant. Near the root of this trunk was an immense quantity of black shaggy hair— more than could have been supplied by the coats of a score of buffalos; and projecting from this hair downwardly and laterally, sprang two gleaming tusks not unlike those of the wild boar, but of infinitely greater dimension. Extending forward, parallel with the proboscis, and on each side of it was a gigantic staff, thirty or forty feet in length, formed seemingly of pure crystal, and in shape a perfect prism:—it reflected in the most gorgeous manner the rays of the declining sun. The trunk was fashioned like a wedge with the apex to the earth. From it there were outspread two pairs of wings—each wing nearly one hundred yards in length—one pair being placed above the other, and all thickly covered with metal scales; each scale apparently some ten or twelve feet in diameter. I observed that the upper and lower tiers of wings were connected by a strong chain. But the chief peculiarity of this horrible thing, was the representation of a *Death's Head*, which covered nearly the whole surface of its breast, and which was as accurately traced in glaring white, upon the dark ground of the body, as if it had been there carefully designed by an artist. While I regarded this terrific animal, and more especially the appearance on its breast, with a feeling of horror and awe—with a sentiment of forthcoming evil, which I found it impossible to quell by any effort of the reason, I perceived the huge jaws at the extremity of the proboscis, suddenly expand themselves, and from them there proceeded a sound so loud and so expressive of woe, that it struck upon my nerves like a knell, and as the monster disappeared at the foot of the hill, I fell at once, fainting to the floor.

Upon recovering, my first impulse of course was to inform my friend of what I had seen and heard—and I can scarcely explain what feeling of repugnance it was, which, in the end, operated to prevent me.

At length, one evening, some three or four days after the occurrence, we were sitting together in the room in which I had seen the apparition—I occupying the same seat at the same window, and he lounging on a sofa near at hand. The association of the place and time impelled me to give him an account of the phenomenon. He heard me to the end—at first laughed heartily—and then lapsed into an excessively grave demeanor, as if my insanity was a thing beyond suspicion. At this instant I again had a distinct view of the monster—to which, with a shout of absolute terror, I now directed his attention. He looked eagerly— but maintained that he saw nothing—although I designated minutely the course of the creature, as it made its way down the naked face of the hill.

I was now immeasurably alarmed, for I considered the vision either as an omen of my death, or, worse, as the fore-runner of an attack of mania. I threw myself passionately back in my chair, and for some moments buried my face in my hands. When I uncovered my eyes, the apparition was no longer apparent.

My host, however, had in some degree resumed the calmness of his demeanor, and questioned me very vigorously in respect to the conformation of the visionary creature. When I had fully satisfied him on this head, he sighed deeply, as if relieved of some intolerable burden, and went on to talk, with what I thought a cruel calmness of various points of speculative philosophy, which had heretofore formed subject of discussion between us. I remember his insisting very especially (among other things) upon the idea that a principal source of error in all human investigations, lay in the liability of the understanding to under-rate or to over-value the importance of an object, through mere mis-admeasurement of its propinquity. "To estimate properly, for example," he said, "the influence to be exercised on mankind at large by the thorough diffusion of Democracy, the distance of the epoch at which such diffusion may possibly be accomplished, should not fail to form an item in the estimate. Yet can you tell me one writer on the subject of government, who has ever thought this particular branch of the subject worthy of discussion at all?"

He here paused for a moment, stepped to a bookcase,

and brought forth one of the ordinary synopses of Natural History. Requesting me then to exchange seats with him, that he might the better distinguish the fine print of the volume, he took my arm chair at the window, and, opening the book, resumed his discourse very much in the same tone as before.

"But for your exceeding minuteness," he said, "in describing the monster, I might never have had it in my power to demonstrate to you what it was. In the first place, let me read to you a school boy account of the genus *Sphinx*, of the family *Crepuscularia*, of the order of *Lepidoptera*, of the class of *Insecta*—or insects. The account runs thus:

" 'Four membranous wings covered with little colored scales of a metallic appearance; mouth forming a rolled proboscis, produced by an elongation of the jaws, upon the sides of which are found the rudiments of mandibles and downy palpi; the inferior wings retained to the superior by a stiff hair; antennæ in the form of an elongated club, prismatic; abdomen pointed. The Death's-headed Sphinx has occasioned much terror among the vulgar, at times, by the melancholy kind of cry which it utters, and the insignia of death which it wears upon its corslet.' "

He here closed the book and leaned forward in the chair, placing himself accurately in the position which I had occupied at the moment of beholding "the monster."

"Ah, here it is!" he presently exclaimed—"it is reascending the face of the hill, and a very remarkable looking creature, I admit it to be. Still, it is by no means so large or so distant as you imagined it; for the fact is that as it wriggles its way up this hair, which some spider has wrought along the window-sash, I find it to be about the sixteenth of an inch in its extreme length, and also about the sixteenth of an inch distant from the pupil of my eye!"

THE CASK OF AMONTILLADO

The thousand injuries of Fortunato I had borne as I best could, but when he ventured upon insult I vowed revenge. You, who so well know the nature of my soul, will not suppose, however, that I gave utterance to a threat. At *length* I would be avenged; this was a point definitively settled—but the very definitiveness with which it was resolved precluded the idea of risk. I must not only punish but punish with impunity. A wrong is unredressed when retribution overtakes its redresser. It is equally unredressed when the avenger fails to make himself felt as such to him who has done the wrong.

It must be understood that neither by word nor deed had I given Fortunato cause to doubt my good will. I continued, as was my wont, to smile in his face, and he did not perceive that my smile *now* was at the thought of his immolation.

He had a weak point—this Fortunato—although in other regards he was a man to be respected and even feared. He prided himself upon his connoisseurship in wine. Few Italians have the true virtuoso spirit. For the most part their enthusiasm is adopted to suit the time and opportunity, to practice imposture upon the British and Austrian *millionaires*. In painting and gemmary, Fortunato, like his countrymen, was a quack, but in the matter of old wines he was sincere. In this respect I did not differ from him materially;—I was skilful in the Italian vintages myself, and bought largely whenever I could.

It was about dusk, one evening during the supreme madness of the carnival season, that I encountered my friend. He accosted me with excessive warmth, for he had been drinking much. The man wore motley. He had on a tight-fitting partistriped dress, and his head was surmounted by the conical cap and bells. I was so pleased to see him that I thought I should never have done wringing his hand.

I said to him—"My dear Fortunato, you are luckily met. How remarkably well you are looking to-day. But I have received a pipe of what passes for Amontillado, and I have my doubts."

"How?" said he. "Amontillado? A pipe? Impossible! And in the middle of the carnival!"

"I have my doubts," I replied; "and I was silly enough to pay the full Amontillado price without consulting you in the matter. You were not to be found, and I was fearful of losing a bargain."

"Amontillado!"

"I have my doubts."

"Amontillado!"

"And I must satisfy them."

"Amontillado!"

"As you are engaged, I am on my way to Luchresi. If any one has a critical turn it is he. He will tell me———"

"Luchresi cannot tell Amontillado from Sherry."

"And yet some fools will have it that his taste is a match for your own."

"Come, let us go."

"Whither?"

"To your vaults."

"My friend, no; I will not impose upon your good nature. I perceive you have an engagement. Luchresi———"

"I have no engagement;—come."

"My friend, no. It is not the engagement, but the severe cold with which I perceive you are afflicted. The vaults are insufferably damp. They are encrusted with nitre."

"Let us go, nevertheless. Th ecold is merely nothing. Amontillado! You have been imposed upon. And as for Luchresi, he cannot distinguish Sherry from Amontillado."

Thus speaking, Fortunato possessed himself of my arm; and putting on a mask of black silk and drawing a *roquelaure* closely about my person, I suffered him to hurry me to my palazzo.

There were no attendants at home; they had absconded to make merry in honour of the time. I had told them that I should not return until the morning, and had given them explicit orders not to stir from the house. These orders were sufficient, I well knew, to insure their immediate disappearance, one and all, as soon as my back was turned.

I took from their sconces two flambeaux, and giving one to Fortunato, bowed him through several suites of rooms to the archway that led into the vaults. I passed down a long and winding staircase, requesting him to be cautious as he followed. We came at length to the foot of the descent, and stood together upon the damp ground of the catacombs of the Montresors.

The gait of my friend was unsteady, and the bells upon his cap jingled as he strode.

"The pipe," said he.

"It is farther on," said I; "but observe the white web-work which gleams from these cavern walls."

He turned towards me, and looked into my eyes with two filmy orbs that distilled the rheum of intoxication.

"Nitre?" he asked, at length.

"Nitre," I replied. "How long have you had that cough?"

"Ugh! ugh! ugh!—ugh! ugh! ugh!—ugh! ugh! ugh!—ugh! ugh! ugh!—ugh! ugh! ugh!"

My poor friend found it impossible to reply for many minutes.

"It is nothing," he said, at last.

"Come," I said, with decision, "we will go back; your

health is precious. You are rich, respected, admired, beloved; you are happy, as once I was. You are a man to be missed. For me it is no matter. We will go back; you will be ill, and I cannot be responsible. Besides, there is Luchresi——"

"Enough," he said: "the cough is a mere nothing; it will not kill me. I shall not die of a cough."

"True—true," I replied; "and, indeed, I had no intention of alarming you unnecessarily—but you should use all proper caution. A draught of this Medoc will defend us from the damps."

Here I knocked off the neck of a bottle which I drew from a long row of its fellows that lay upon the mould.

"Drink," I said, presenting him the wine.

He raised it to his lips with a leer. He paused and nodded to me familiarly, while his bells jingled.

"I drink," he said, "to the buried that repose around us."

"And I to your long life."

He again took my arm, and we proceeded.

"These vaults," he said, "are extensive."

"The Montresors," I replied, "were a great and numerous family."

"I forget your arms."

"A huge human foot d'or, in a field azure; the foot crushes a serpent rampant whose fangs are imbedded in the heel."

"And the motto?"

"*Nemo me impune lacessit.*"

"Good!" he said.

The wine sparkled in his eyes and the bells jingled. My own fancy grew warm with the Medoc. We had passed through long walls of piled skeletons, with casks and puncheons intermingling, into the inmost recesses of the catacombs. I paused again, and this time I made bold to seize Fortunato by an arm above the elbow.

"The nitre!" I said; "see, it increases. It hangs like moss upon the vaults. We are below the river's bed. The drops of moisture trickle among the bones. Come, we will go back ere it is too late. Your cough————"

"It is nothing," he said; "let us go on. But first, another draught of the Medoc."

I broke and reached him a flacon of De Grâve. He emptied it at a breath. His eyes flashed with a fierce light. He laughed and threw the bottle upwards with a gesticulation I did not understand.

I looked at him in surprise. He repeated the movement —a grotesque one.

"You do not comprehend?" he said.

"Not I," I replied.

"Then you are not of the brotherhood."

"How?"

"You are not of the masons."

"Yes, yes," I said; "yes, yes."

"You? Impossible! A mason?"

"A mason," I replied.

"A sign," he said, "a sign."

"It is this," I answered, producing from beneath the folds of my *roquelaure* a trowel.

"You jest," he exclaimed, recoiling a few paces. "But let us proceed to the Amontillado."

"Be it so," I said, replacing the tool beneath the cloak and again offering him my arm. He leaned upon it heavily. We continued our route in search of the Amontillado. We passed through a range of low arches, descended, passed on, and descending again, arrived at a deep crypt, in which the foulness of the air caused our flambeaux rather to glow than flame.

At the most remote end of the crypt there appeared another less spacious. Its walls had been lined with human remains, piled to the vault overhead, in the fashion of the great catacombs of Paris. Three sides of this interior crypt were still ornamented in this manner. From the fourth side the bones had been thrown down, and lay promiscuously upon the earth, forming at one point a mount of some size. Within the wall thus exposed by the displacing of the bones, we perceived a still interior crypt or recess, in depth about four feet, in width three, in height six or seven. It seemed to have been constructed for no especial use within itself, but formed merely the interval between two of the colossal supports of the roof of the catacombs, and was backed by one of their circumscribing walls of solid granite.

It was in vain that Fortunato, uplifting his dull torch, endeavoured to pry into the depth of the recess. Its termination the feeble light did not enable us to see.

"Proceed," I said; "herein is the Amontillado. As for Luchresi——"

"He is an ignoramus," interrupted my friend, as he stepped unsteadily forward, while I followed immediately at his heels. In an instant he had reached the extremity of the niche, and finding his progress arrested by the rock, stood stupidly bewildered. A moment more and I had fettered him to the granite. In its surface were two iron staples, distant from each other about two feet, horizontally. From one of these depended a short chain, from the other a padlock. Throwing the links about his waist, it was but the work of a few seconds to secure it. He was too much astounded to resist. Withdrawing the key I stepped back from the recess.

"Pass your hand," I said, "over the wall; you cannot help feeling the nitre. Indeed, it is *very* damp. Once more let me *implore* you to return. No? Then I must positively leave you. But I will first render you all the little attentions in my power."

"The Amontillado!" ejaculated my friend, not yet recovered from his astonishment.

"True," I replied; "the Amontillado."

As I said these words I busied myself among the pile of bones of which I have before spoken. Throwing them aside, I soon uncovered a quantity of building stone and mortar. With these materials and with the aid of my trowel, I began vigorously to wall up the entrance of the niche.

I had scarcely laid the first tier of the masonry when I discovered that the intoxication of Fortunato had in great measure worn off. The earliest indication I had of this was a low moaning cry from the depth of the recess. It was *not* the cry of a drunken man. There was then a long and obstinate silence. I laid the second tier, and the third, and the fourth; and then I heard the furious vibration of the chain. The noise lasted for several minutes, during which, that I might hearken to it with the more satisfaction, I ceased my labours and sat down upon the bones. When at last the clanking subsided, I resumed the trowel, and finished without interruption the fifth, the sixth, and the seventh tier. The wall was now nearly upon a level with my breast. I again paused, and holding the flambeaux over the mason-work, threw a few feeble rays upon the figure within.

A succession of loud and shrill screams, bursting suddenly from the throat of the chained form, seemed to thrust me violently back. For a brief moment I hesitated, I trembled. Unsheathing my rapier, I began to grope with it about the recess; but the thought of an instant reassured me. I placed my hand upon the solid fabric of the catacombs, and felt satisfied. I reapproached the wall. I replied to the yells of him who clamoured. I reechoed, I aided, I surpassed them in volume and in strength. I did this, and the clamourer grew still.

It was now midnight, and my task was drawing to a close. I had completed the eighth, the ninth and the tenth tier. I had finished a portion of the last and the eleventh; there remained but a single stone to be fitted and plastered in. I struggled with its weight; I placed it partially in its destined position. But now there came from out the niche a low laugh that erected the hairs upon my head. It was succeeded by a sad voice, which I had difficulty in recognizing as that of the noble Fortunato. The voice said—

"Ha! ha! ha!—he! he! he!—a very good joke, indeed— an excellent jest. We will have many a rich laugh about it at the palazzo—he! he! he!—over our wine—he! he! he!"

"The Amontillado!" I said.

"He! he! he!—he! he! he!—yes, the Amontillado. But is it not getting late? Will not they be awaiting us at the palazzo—the Lady Fortunato and the rest? Let us be gone."

"Yes," I said, "let us be gone."

"For the love of God, Montresor!"

"Yes," I said, "for the love of God!"

But to these words I hearkened in vain for a reply. I grew impatient. I called aloud—

"Fortunato!"

No answer. I called again—

"Fortunato!"

No answer still. I thrust a torch through the remaining aperture and let it fall within. There came forth in return only a jingling of the bells. My heart grew sick; it was the dampness of the catacombs that made it so. I hastened to make an end of my labour. I forced the last stone into its position; I plastered it up. Against the new masonry I re-erected the old rampart of bones. For the half of a century no mortal has disturbed them. *In pace requiescat!*

HOP-FROG:
OR,
THE EIGHT CHAINED OURANG-OUTANGS

I never knew any one so keenly alive to a joke as the king was. He seemed to live only for joking. To tell a good story of the joke kind, and to tell it well, was the surest road to his favor. Thus it happened that his seven ministers were all noted for their accomplishments as jokers. They all took after the king, too, in being large, corpulent, oily men, as well as inimitable jokers. Whether people grow fat by joking, or whether there is something in fat itself which predisposes to a joke, I have never been quite able to determine; but certain it is that a lean joker is a *rara avis in terris*.

About the refinements, or, as he called them, the 'ghosts' of wit, the king troubled himself very little. He had an especial admiration for *breadth* in a jest, and would often put up with *length*, for the sake of it. Over-niceties wearied him. He would have preferred Rabelais's 'Gargantua,' to the 'Zadig' of Voltaire: and, upon the whole, practical jokes suited his taste far better than verbal ones.

At the date of my narrative, professing jesters had not altogether gone out of fashion at court. Several of the great continental 'powers' still retained their 'fools,' who wore motley, with caps and bells, and who were expected to be always ready with sharp witticisms, at a moment's notice, in consideration of the crumbs that fell from the royal table.

Our king, as a matter of course, retained his 'fool.' The

fact is, he *required* something in the way of folly—if only to counterbalance the heavy wisdom of the seven wise men who were his ministers—not to mention himself.

His fool, or professional jester, was not *only* a fool, however. His value was trebled in the eyes of the king, by the fact of his being also a dwarf and a cripple. Dwarfs were as common at court, in those days, as fools; and many monarchs would have found it difficult to get through their days (days are rather longer at court than elsewhere) without both a jester to laugh *with*, and a dwarf to laugh *at*. But, as I have already observed, your jesters, in ninety-nine cases out of a hundred, are fat, sound and unwieldy—so that it was no small source of self-gratulation with our king that, in Hop-Frog (this was the fool's name), he possessed a triplicate treasure in one person.

I believe the name 'Hop-Frog' was *not* that given to the dwarf by his sponsors at baptism, but it was conferred upon him, by general consent of the seven ministers, on account of his inability to walk as other men do. In fact, Hop-Frog could only get along by a sort of interjectional gait—something between a leap and a wriggle—a movement that afforded illimitable amusement, and of course consolation, to the king; for (notwithstanding the protuberance of his stomach and a constitutional swelling of the head) the king, by his whole court, was accounted a capital figure.

But although Hop-Frog, through the distortion of his legs, could move only with great pain and difficulty along a road or floor, the prodigious muscular power which nature seemed to have bestowed upon his arms, by way of compensation for deficiency in the lower limbs, enabled him to perform many feats of wonderful dexterity, where trees or ropes were in question, or anything else to climb. At such exercises he certainly much more resembled a squirrel, or a small monkey, than a frog.

I am not able to say, with precision, from what country Hop-Frog originally came. It was from some barbarous region, however, that no person ever heard of—a vast distance from the court of our king. Hop-Frog, and a young girl very little less dwarfish than himself (although of exquisite proportions, and a marvellous dancer), had been forcibly carried off from their respective homes in adjoining provinces, and sent as presents to the king, by one of his ever-victorious generals.

Under these circumstances, it is not to be wondered at that a close intimacy arose between the two little captives. Indeed, they soon became sworn friends. Hop-Frog, who, although he made a great deal of sport, was by no means popular, had it not in his power to render Trippetta many services; but *she*, on account of her grace and exquisite beauty (although a dwarf), was universally admired and petted: so she possessed much influence; and never failed to use it, whenever she could, for the benefit of Hop-Frog.

On some grand state occasion—I forget what—the king determined to have a masquerade; and whenever a masquerade, or anything of that kind, occurred at our court, then the talents both of Hop-Frog and Trippetta were sure to be called in play. Hop-Frog, in especial, was so inventive in the way of getting up pageants, suggesting novel characters, and arranging costumes, for masked balls, that nothing could be done, it seems, without his assistance.

The night appointed for the *fête* had arrived. A gorgeous hall had been fitted up, under Trippetta's eye, with every kind of device which could possibly give *éclât* to a masquerade. The whole court was in a fever of expectation. As for costumes and characters, it might well be supposed that everybody had come to a decision on such points. Many had made up their minds (as to what *rôles* they should assume) a week, or even a month, in advance; and, in fact, there was not a particle of indecision anywhere—except in the case of the king and his seven ministers. Why *they* hesitated I never could tell, unless they did it by way of a joke. More probably, they found it difficult, on account of being so fat, to make up their minds. At all events, time flew; and, as a last resource, they sent for Trippetta and Hop-Frog.

When the two little friends obeyed the summons of the king, they found him sitting at his wine with the seven members of his cabinet council; but the monarch appeared to be in a very ill humor. He knew that Hop-Frog was not fond of wine; for it excited the poor cripple almost to madness; and madness is no comfortable feeling. But the king loved his practical jokes, and took pleasure in forcing Hop-Frog to drink and (as the king called it) 'to be merry.'

'Come here, Hop-Frog,' said he, as the jester and his friend entered the room: 'swallow this bumper to the health of your absent friends [here Hop-Frog sighed], and then let us have the benefit of your invention. We want characters—*characters*, man—something novel—out of the way. We are wearied with this everlasting sameness. Come, drink! the wine will brighten your wits.'

Hop-Frog endeavored, as usual, to get up a jest in reply to these advances from the king; but the effort was too much. It happened to be the poor dwarf's birthday, and the command to drink to his 'absent friends' forced the tears to his eyes. Many large, bitter drops fell into the goblet as he took it, humbly, from the hand of the tyrant.

'Ah! ha! ha! ha!' roared the latter, as the dwarf reluctantly drained the beaker.—'See what a glass of good wine can do! Why, your eyes are shining already!'

Poor fellow! his large eyes *gleamed*, rather than shone; for the effect of wine on his excitable brain was not more powerful than instantaneous. He placed the goblet nervously on the table, and looked round upon the company with a half-insane stare. They all seemed highly amused at the success of the king's '*joke*.'

'And now to business,' said the prime minister, a *very* fat man.

'Yes,' said the king; 'come, Hop-Frog, lend us your assistance. Characters, my fine fellow; we stand in need of characters—all of us—ha! ha! ha!' and as this was seriously meant for a joke, his laugh was chorused by the seven.

Hop-Frog also laughed, although feebly and somewhat vacantly.

'Come, come,' said the king, impatiently, 'have you nothing to suggest?'

'I am endeavoring to think of something *novel*,' replied the dwarf, abstractedly, for he was quite bewildered by the wine.

'Endeavoring!' cried the tyrant, fiercely; 'what do you mean by *that*? Ah, I perceive. You are sulky, and want more wine. Here, drink this!' and he poured out another goblet full and offered it to the cripple, who merely gazed at it, gasping for breath.

'Drink, I say!' shouted the monster, 'or by the fiends—'

The dwarf hesitated. The king grew purple with rage. The courtiers smirked. Trippetta, pale as a corpse, advanced to the monarch's seat, and, falling on her knees before him, implored him to spare her friend.

The tyrant regarded her, for some moments, in evident wonder at her audacity. He seemed quite at a loss what to do or say—how most becomingly to express his indignation. At last, without uttering a syllable, he pushed her violently from him, and threw the contents of the brimming goblet in her face.

The poor girl got up as best she could, and, not daring even to sigh, resumed her position at the foot of the table.

There was a dead silence for about half a minute, during which the falling of a leaf, or of a feather, might have been heard. It was interrupted by a low, but harsh and protracted *grating* sound which seemed to come at once from every corner of the room.

'What—what—*what* are you making that noise for?' demanded the king, turning furiously to the dwarf.

The latter seemed to have recovered, in great measure, from his intoxication, and looking fixedly but quietly into the tyrant's face, merely ejaculated:

'I—I? How could it have been me?'

'The sound appeared to come from without,' observed one of the courtiers. 'I fancy it was the parrot at the window, whetting his bill upon the cage-wires.'

'True,' replied the monarch, as if much relieved by the suggestion; 'but on the honor of a knight, I could have sworn that it was the gritting of this vagabond's teeth.'

Hereupon the dwarf laughed (the king was too confirmed a joker to object to any one's laughing), and displayed a set of large, powerful, and very repulsive teeth. Moreover, he avowed his perfect willingness to swallow as much wine as desired. The monarch was pacified; and having drained another bumper, with no very perceptible ill effect, Hop-Frog entered at once, and with spirit, into the plans for the masquerade.

'I cannot tell what was the association of idea,' observed he, very tranquilly, and as if he had never tasted wine in his life, 'but *just after* your majesty had struck the girl and thrown the wine in her face—*just after* your majesty had done this, and while the parrot was making that odd noise outside the window, there came into my mind a capital diversion—one of my own country frolics —often enacted among us, at our masquerades: but here it will be new altogether. Unfortunately, however, it requires a company of eight persons, and—'

'Here we *are!*' cried the king, laughing at his acute discovery of the coincidence; 'eight to a fraction—I and my seven ministers. Come! what is the diversion?'

'We call it,' replied the cripple, 'the Eight Chained Ourang-Outangs, and it really is excellent sport if well enacted.'

'We will enact it,' remarked the king, drawing himself up, and lowering his eyelids.

'The beauty of the game,' continued Hop-Frog, 'lies in the fright it occasions among the women.'

'Capital!' roared in chorus the monarch and his ministry.

'I will equip you as ourang-outangs,' proceeded the dwarf; 'leave all that to me. The resemblance shall be so striking, that the company of masqueraders will take you for real beasts—and of course, they will be as much terrified as astonished.'

'O, this is exquisite!' exclaimed the king. 'Hop-Frog! I will make a man of you.'

'The chains are for the purpose of increasing the confusion by their jangling. You are supposed to have escaped, *en masse*, from your keepers. Your majesty cannot conceive the *effect* produced, at a masquerade, by eight chained ourang-outangs, imagined to be real ones by most of the company; and rushing in, with savage cries, among the crowd of delicately and gorgeously habited men and women. The *contrast* is inimitable.'

'It *must* be,' said the king: and the council arose hurriedly (as it was growing late), to put in execution the scheme of Hop-Frog.

His mode of equipping the party as ourang-outangs was very simple, but effective enough for his purposes. The animals in question had, at the epoch of my story, very rarely been seen in any part of the civilized world; and as the imitations made by the dwarf were sufficiently beast-like and more than sufficiently hideous, their truthfulness to nature was thus thought to be secured.

The king and his ministers were first encased in tight-fitting stockinet shirts and drawers. They were then saturated with tar. At this stage of the process, some one of the party suggested feathers; but the suggestion was at once overruled by the dwarf, who soon convinced the eight, by ocular demonstration, that the hair of such a brute as the ourang-outang was much more efficiently represented by *flax*. A thick coating of this latter was accordingly plastered upon the coating of tar. A long chain was now procured. First, it was passed about the waist of the king, *and tied*; then about another of the party, and also tied; then about all successively, in the same manner. When this chaining arrangement was complete, and the party stood as far apart from each other as possible, they formed a circle; and, to make all things appear natural, Hop-Frog passed the residue of the chain, in two diameters, at right angles, across the circle, after the fashion adopted, at the present day, by those who capture Chimpanzees, or other large apes, in Borneo.

The grand salon in which the masquerade was to take place, was a circular room, very lofty, and receiving the light of the sun only through a single window at top. At night (the season for which the apartment was especially designed) it was illuminated principally by a large chandelier, depending by a chain from the centre of the skylight, and lowered, or elevated, by means of a counterbalance as usual; but (in order not to look unsightly) this latter passed outside the cupola and over the roof.

The arrangements of the room had been left to Trippetta's superintendence; but, in some particulars, it seems, she had been guided by the calmer judgment of her friend the dwarf. At his suggestion it was that, on this occasion, the chandelier was removed. Its waxen drippings (which, in weather so warm, it was quite impossible to prevent) would have been seriously detrimental to the rich dresses of the guests, who, on account of the crowded state of the salon, could not *all* be expected to keep from out its centre; that is to say, from under the chandelier. Additional sconces were set in various parts of the hall, out of the way; and a flambeau emitting sweet odor was placed in the right hand of each of the Caryatides that stood against the wall; some fifty or sixty altogether.

The eight ourang-outangs, taking Hop-Frog's advice, waited patiently until midnight (when the room was thoroughly filled with masqueraders) before making their appearance. No sooner had the clock ceased striking, however, than they rushed, or rather rolled in, all together; for the impediment of their chains caused most of the party to fall, and all to stumble as they entered.

The excitement among the masqueraders was prodigious, and filled the heart of the king with glee. As had been anticipated, there were not a few of the guests who supposed the ferocious-looking creatures to be beasts of *some* kind in reality, if not precisely ourang-outangs. Many of the women swooned with affright; and had not the king taken the precaution to exclude all weapons from the salon, his party might soon have expiated their frolic in their blood. As it was, a general rush was made for the doors; but the king had ordered them to be locked immediately upon his entrance; and, at the dwarf's suggestion, the keys had been deposited with *him*.

While the tumult was at its height, and each masquerader attentive only to his own safety—(for, in fact, there was much *real* danger from the pressure of the excited crowd), the chain by which the chandelier ordinarily hung, and which had been drawn up on its removal, might have been seen very gradually to descend, until its hooked extremity came within three feet of the floor.

Soon after this, the king and his seven friends, having reeled about the hall in all directions, found themselves, at length, in its centre, and, of course, in immediate contact with the chain. While they were thus situated, the dwarf, who had followed closely at their heels, inciting them to keep up the commotion, took hold of their own chain at the intersection of the two portions which crossed the circle diametrically and at right angles. Here, with the rapidity of thought, he inserted the hook from which the chandelier had been wont to depend; and, in an instant, by some unseen agency, the chandelier-chain was drawn so far upward as to take the hook out of reach, and, as an inevitable consequence, to drag the ourang-outangs together in close connection, and face to face.

The masqueraders, by this time, had recovered, in some measure, from their alarm; and, beginning to regard the whole matter as a well-contrived pleasantry, set up a loud shout of laughter at the predicament of the apes.

'Leave them to *me!*' now screamed Hop-Frog; his shrill voice making itself easily heard through all the din. 'Leave them to *me.* I fancy *I* know them. If I can only get a good look at them, I can soon tell who they are.'

Here, scrambling over the heads of the crowd, he managed to get to the wall; when, seizing a flambeau from one of the Caryatides, he returned, as he went, to the centre of the room; leaping, with the agility of a monkey, upon the king's head, and thence clambered a few feet up the chain; holding down the torch to examine the group of ourang-outangs, and still screaming, '*I* shall soon find out who they are!'

And now, while the whole assembly (the apes included) were convulsed with laughter, the jester suddenly uttered a shrill whistle; when the chain flew violently up for about thirty feet; dragging with it the dismayed and struggling ourang-outangs, and leaving them suspended in midair between the sky-light and the floor. Hop-Frog, clinging to the chain as it rose, still maintaining his relative position in respect to the eight maskers, and still (as if nothing were the matter) continued to thrust his torch down towards them, as though endeavoring to discover who they were.

So thoroughly astonished were the whole company at this ascent, that a dead silence, of about a minute's duration, ensued. It was broken by just such a low, harsh, *grating* sound as had before attracted the attention of the king and his councillors, when the former threw the wine in the face of Trippetta. But, on the present occasion, there could be no question as to *whence* the sound issued. It came from the fang-like teeth of the dwarf, who ground them and gnashed them as he foamed at the mouth, and glared, with an expression of maniacal rage, into the up-turned countenances of the king and his seven companions.

'Ah, ha!' said at length the infuriated jester. 'Ah, ha! I begin to see who these people *are*, now.' Here, pretending to scrutinize the king more closely, he held the flambeau to the flaxen coat which enveloped him, and which instantly burst into a sheet of vivid flame. In less than half a minute the whole eight ourang-outangs were blazing fiercely, amid the shrieks of the multitude who gazed at them from below, horror-stricken, and without the power to render them the slightest assistance.

At length the flames, suddenly increasing in virulence, forced the jester to climb higher up the chain, to be out of their reach; and, as he made this movement, the crowd again sank, for a brief instant, into silence. The dwarf seized his opportunity and once more spoke:

'I now see *distinctly*,' he said, 'what manner of people these maskers are. They are a great king and his seven privy councillors—a king who does not scruple to strike a defenceless girl, and his seven councillors who abet him in the outrage. As for myself, I am simply Hop-Frog, the jester—and *this is my last jest*.'

Owing to the high combustibility of both the flax and the tar to which it adhered, the dwarf had scarcely made an end of his brief speech before the work of vengeance was complete. The eight corpses swung in their chains, a fetid, blackened, hideous, and indistinguishable mass. The cripple hurled his torch at them, clambered leisurely to the ceiling, and disappeared through the sky-light.

It is supposed that Trippetta, stationed on the roof of the salon, had been the accomplice of her friend in his fiery revenge, and that, together, they effected their escape to their own country: for neither was seen again.

CRITICISM

III

CRITICISM

REVIEW OF
TWICE-TOLD TALES
by Nathaniel Hawthorne

Twice-Told Tales. By Nathaniel Hawthorne. Two Volumes. Boston: James Munroe and Co:

We said a few hurried words about Mr. Hawthorne in our last number, with the design of speaking more fully in the present. We are still, however, pressed for room, and must necessarily discuss his volumes more briefly and more at random than their high merits deserve.

The book professes to be a collection of *tales*, yet is, in two respects, misnamed. These pieces are now in their third republication, and, of course, are thrice-told. Moreover, they are by no means *all* tales, either in the ordinary or in the legitimate understanding of the term. Many of them are pure essays, for example, "Sights from a Steeple," "Sunday at Home," "Little Annie's Ramble," "A Rill from the Town-Pump," "The Toll-Gatherer's Day," "The Haunted Mind," "The Sister Years," "Snow-Flakes," "Night Sketches," and "Foot-Prints on the Sea-Shore." We mention these matters chiefly on account of their discrepancy with that marked precision and finish by which the body of the work is distinguished.

Of the Essays just named, we must be content to speak in brief. They are each and all beautiful, without being characterised by the polish and adaptation so visible in the tales proper. A painter would at once note their leading or predominant feature, and style it *repose*. There is no attempt at effect. All is quiet, thoughtful, subdued. Yet this repose may exist simultaneously with high originality of thought; and Mr. Hawthorne has demonstrated the fact. At every turn we meet with novel combinations; yet these combinations never surpass the limits of the quiet. We are soothed as we read; and withal is a calm astonishment that ideas so apparently obvious have never occurred or been presented to us before. Herein our author differs materially from Lamb or Hunt or Hazlitt—who, with vivid originality of manner and expression, have less of the true novelty of thought than is generally supposed, and whose originality, at best, has an uneasy and meretricious quaintness, replete with startling effects unfounded in nature, and inducing trains of reflection which lead to no satisfactory result. The Essays of Hawthorne have much of the character of Irving, with more of originality, and less of finish; while, compared with the Spectator, they have a vast superiority at all points. The Spectator, Mr. Irving, and Mr. Hawthorne have in common that tranquil and subdued manner which we have chosen to denominate *repose*; but, in the case of the two former, this repose is attained rather by the absence of novel combination, or of originality, than otherwise, and consists chiefly in the calm, quiet, unostentatious expression of commonplace thoughts, in an unambitious unadulterated Saxon. In them, by strong effort, we are made to conceive the absence of all. In the essays before us the absence of effort is too obvious to be mistaken, and a strong under-current of *suggestion* runs continuously beneath the upper stream of the tranquil thesis. In short, these effusions of Mr. Hawthorne are the product of a truly imaginative intellect, restrained, and in some measure repressed, by fastidiousness of taste, by constitutional melancholy and by indolence.

But it is of his tales that we desire principally to speak. The tale proper, in our opinion, affords unquestionably the fairest field for the exercise of the loftiest talent, which can be afforded by the wide domains of mere prose. Were we bidden to say how the highest genius could be most advantageously employed for the best display of its own powers, we should answer, without hesitation—in the composition of a rhymed poem, not to exceed in length what might be perused in an hour. Within this limit alone can the highest order of true poetry exist. We need only here say, upon this topic, that, in almost all classes of composition, the unity of effect or impression is a point of the greatest importance. It is clear, moreover, that this unity cannot be thoroughly preserved in productions whose perusal cannot be completed at one sitting. We may continue the reading of a prose composition, from the very nature of prose itself, much longer than we can persevere, to any good purpose, in the perusal of a poem. This latter, if truly fulfilling the demands of the poetic sentiment, induces an exaltation of the soul which cannot be long sustained. All high excitements are necessarily transient. Thus a long poem is a paradox. And, without unity of impression, the deepest effects cannot be brought about. Epics were the offspring of an imperfect sense of Art, and their reign is no more. A poem *too* brief may produce a vivid, but never an intense or enduring impression. Without a certain continuity of effort—without a certain duration or repetition of purpose—the soul is never deeply moved. There must be the dropping of the water upon the rock. De Béranger has wrought brilliant things—pungent and spirit-stirring—but, like all immassive bodies, they lack *momentum*, and thus fail to satisfy the Poetic Sentiment. They sparkle and excite, but, from want of continuity, fail deeply to impress. Extreme brevity will degenerate into epigrammatism; but the sin of extreme length is even more unpardonable. *In medio tutissimus ibis.*

Were we called upon however to designate that class of composition which, next to such a poem as we have suggested, should best fulfil the demands of high genius—should offer it the most advantageous field of exertion—we should unhesitatingly speak of the prose tale, as Mr.

Hawthorne has here exemplified it. We allude to the short prose narrative, requiring from a half-hour to one or two hours in its perusal. The ordinary novel is objectionable, from its length, for reasons already stated in substance. As it cannot be read at one sitting, it deprives itself, of course, of the immense force derivable from *totality*. Worldly interests intervening during the pauses of perusal, modify, annul, or counteract, in a greater or less degree, the impressions of the book. But simple cessation in reading would, of itself, be sufficient to destroy the true unity. In the brief tale, however, the author is enabled to carry out the fulness of his intention, be it what it may. During the hour of perusal the soul of the reader is at the writer's control. There are no external or extrinsic influences—resulting from weariness or interruption.

A skilful literary artist has constructed a tale. If wise, he has not fashioned his thoughts to accommodate his incidents; but having conceived, with deliberate care, a certain unique or single *effect* to be wrought out, he then invents such incidents—he then combines such events as may best aid him in establishing this preconceived effect. If his very initial sentence tend not to the outbringing of this effect, then he has failed in his first step. In the whole composition there should be no word written, of which the tendency, direct or indirect, is not to the one pre-established design. And by such means, with such care and skill, a picture is at length painted which leaves in the mind of him who contemplates it with a kindred heart, a sense of the fullest satisfaction. The idea of the tale has been presented unblemished, because undisturbed; and this is an end unattainable by the novel. Undue brevity is just as exceptionable here as in the poem; but undue length is yet more to be avoided.

We have said that the tale has a point of superiority even over the poem. In fact, while the *rhythm* of this latter is an essential aid in the development of the poem's highest idea—the idea of the Beautiful—the artificialities of this rhythm are an inseparable bar to the development of all points of thought or expression which have their basis in *Truth*. But Truth is often, and in very great degree, the aim of the tale. Some of the finest tales are tales of ratiocination. Thus the field of this species of composition, if not in so elevated a region on the mountain of Mind, is a table-land of far vaster extent than the domain of the mere poem. Its products are never so rich, but infinitely more numerous, and more appreciable by the mass of mankind. The writer of the prose tale, in short, may bring to his theme a vast variety of modes or inflections of thought and expression—(the ratiocinative, for example, the sarcastic or the humorous) which are not only antagonistical to the nature of the poem, but absolutely forbidden by one of its most peculiar and indispensable adjuncts; we allude of course, to rhythm. It may be added, here, *par parenthèse*, that the author who aims at the purely beautiful in a prose tale is laboring at great disadvantage. For Beauty can be better treated in the poem. Not so with terror, or passion, or horror, or a multitude of such other points. And here it will be seen how full of prejudice are the usual animadversions against those *tales of effect* many fine examples of which were found in the earlier numbers of Blackwood. The impressions produced were wrought in a legitimate sphere of action, and constituted a legitimate although sometimes an exaggerated interest. They were relished by every man of genius: although there were found many men of genius who condemned them without just ground. The true critic will but demand that the design intended be accomplished, to the fullest extent, by the means most advantageously applicable.

We have very few American tales of real merit—we may say, indeed, none, with the exception of "The Tales of a Traveller" of Washington Irving, and these "Twice-Told Tales" of Mr. Hawthorne. Some of the pieces of Mr. John

Neal abound in vigor and originality; but in general, his compositions of this class are excessively diffuse, extravagant, and indicative of an imperfect sentiment of Art. Articles at random are, now and then, met with in our periodicals which might be advantageously compared with the best effusions of the British magazines; but, upon the whole, we are far behind our progenitors in this department of literature.

Of Mr. Hawthorne's Tales we would say, emphatically, that they belong to the highest region of Art—an Art subservient to genius of a very lofty order. We had supposed, with good reason for so supposing, that he had been thrust into his present position by one of the impudent *cliques* which beset our literature, and whose pretensions it is our full purpose to expose at the earliest opportunity; but we have been most agreeably mistaken. We know of few compositions which the critic can more honestly commend than these "Twice-Told Tales." As Americans, we feel proud of the book.

Mr. Hawthorne's distinctive trait is invention, creation, imagination, originality—a trait which, in the literature of fiction, is positively worth all the rest. But the nature of originality, so far as regards its manifestation in letters, is but imperfectly understood. The inventive or original mind as frequently displays itself in novelty of *tone* as in novelty of *matter*. Mr. Hawthorne is original at *all* points.

It would be a matter of some difficulty to designate the best of these tales; we repeat that, without exception, they are beautiful. "Wakefield" is remarkable for the skill with which an old idea—a well-known incident—is worked up or discussed. A man of whims conceives the purpose of quitting his wife and residing *incognito*, for twenty years, in her immediate neighborhood. Something of this kind actually happened in London. The force of Mr. Hawthorne's tale lies in the analysis of the motives which must or might have impelled the husband to such folly, in the first instance, with the possible causes of his perseverance. Upon this thesis a sketch of singular power has been constructed.

"The Wedding Knell" is full of the boldest imagination —an imagination fully controlled by taste. The most captious critic could find no flaw in this production.

"The Minister's Black Veil" is a masterly composition of which the sole defect is that to the rabble its exquisite skill will be *caviare*. The *obvious* meaning of this article will be found to smother its insinuated one. The *moral* put into the mouth of the dying minister will be supposed to convey the *true* import of the narrative; and that a crime of dark dye, (having reference to the "young lady") has been committed, is a point which only minds congenial with that of the author will perceive.

"Mr. Higginbotham's Catastrophe" is vividly original and managed most dexterously.

"Dr. Heidegger's Experiment" is exceedingly well imagined, and executed with surpassing ability. The artist breathes in every line of it.

"The White Old Maid" is objectionable, even more than the "Minister's Black Veil," on the score of its mysticism. Even with the thoughtful and analytic, there will be much trouble in penetrating its entire import.

"The Hollow of the Three Hills" we would quote in full, had we space;—not as evincing higher talent than any of the other pieces, but as affording an excellent example of the author's peculiar ability. The subject is commonplace. A witch subjects the Distant and the Past to the view of a mourner. It has been the fashion to describe, in such cases, a mirror in which the images of the absent appear; or a cloud of smoke is made to arise, and thence the figures are gradually unfolded. Mr. Hawthorne has wonderfully heightened his effect by making the ear, in place of the eye, the medium by which the fantasy is conveyed. The head of the mourner is enveloped in the cloak of the witch, and within its magic folds there arise sounds which have an all-sufficient intelligence. Throughout this article also, the artist is conspicuous—not more in positive than in negative merits. Not only is all done that should be done, but (what perhaps is an end with more difficulty attained) there is nothing done which should not be. Every word *tells*, and there is not a word which does *not* tell.

In "Howe's Masquerade" we observe something which resembles a plagiarism—but which *may* be a very flattering coincidence of thought. We quote the passage in question.

> *With a dark flush of wrath* upon his brow they saw the general *draw his sword* and *advance to meet* the figure *in the cloak* before the latter had stepped one pace upon the floor.
>
> '*Villain, unmuffle yourself*,' cried he, 'you pass **no** farther!'
>
> "The figure, without blenching a hair's breadth from the sword which was pointed at this breast, made a solemn pause, and *lowered the cape of the cloak* from his face, yet not sufficiently for the spectators to catch a glimpse of it. But Sir Willaim Howe had evidently seen enough. The sternness of his countenance gave place to a look of wild amazement, if not horror, while he recoiled several steps from the figure, *and let fall his sword* upon the floor. [See vol. 2, page 20.]

The idea here is, that the figure in the cloak is the phantom or reduplication of Sir William Howe; but in an article called "William Wilson," one of the "Tales of the Grotesque and Arabesque," we have not only the same idea, but the same idea similarly presented in several respects. We quote two paragraphs, which our readers may compare with what has been already given. We have italicized, above, the immediate particulars of resemblance.

The brief moment in which I averted my eyes had been sufficient to produce, apparently, a material change in the arrangement at the upper or farther end of the room. A large mirror, it appeared to me, now stood where none had been perceptible before: and as I stepped up to it in extremity of terror, mine own image, but with features all pale and dabbled in blood, *advanced* with a feeble and tottering gait to meet me.

Thus it appeared I say, but was not. It was Wilson, who then stood before me in the agonies of dissolution. Not a line in all the marked and singular lineaments of that face which was not even identically mine own. *His mask and cloak lay where he had thrown them, upon the floor.* [Vol. 2. p. 57.]

Here it will be observed that, not only are the two general conceptions identical, but there are various *points* of similarity. In each case the figure seen is the wraith or duplication of the beholder. In each case the scene is a masquerade. In each case the figure is cloaked. In each, there is a quarrel—that is to say, angry words pass between the parties. In each the beholder is enraged. In each the cloak and sword fall upon the floor. The "villain, unmuffle yourself," of Mr. H. is precisely paralleled by a passage at page 56 of "William Wilson."

In the way of objection we have scarcely a word to say of these tales. There is, perhaps, a somewhat too general or prevalent *tone*—a tone of melancholy and mysticism. The subjects are insufficiently varied. There is not so much of *versatility* evinced as we might well be warranted in expecting from the high powers of Mr. Hawthorne. But beyond these trivial exceptions we have really none to make. The style is purity itself. Force abounds. High imagination gleams from every page. Mr. Hawthorne is a man of the truest genius. We only regret that the limits of our Magazine will not permit us to pay him that full tribute of com-

mendation, which, under other circumstances, we should
be so eager to pay.

THE PHILOSOPHY
OF COMPOSITION

Charles Dickens, in a note now lying before me, alluding
to an examination I once made of the mechanism of "Barnaby Rudge," says—"By the way, are you aware that
Godwin wrote his 'Caleb Williams' backwards? He first
involved his hero in a web of difficulties, forming the
second volume, and then, for the first, cast about him for
some mode of accounting for what had been done."

I cannot think this the *precise* mode of procedure on
the part of Godwin—and indeed what he himself acknowl-
edges, is not altogether in accordance with Mr. Dickens'
idea—but the author of "Caleb Williams" was too good
an artist not to perceive the advantage derivable from at
least a somewhat similar process. Nothing is more clear
than that every plot, worth the name, must be elaborated
to its *dénouement* before any thing be attempted with
the pen. It is only with the *dénouement* constantly in
view that we can give a plot its indispensable air of consequence, or causation, by making the incidents, and
especially the tone at all points, tend to the development
of the intention.

There is a radical error, I think, in the usual mode of
constructing a story. Either history affords a thesis—or
one is suggested by an incident of the day—or, at best,
the author sets himself to work in the combination of
striking events to form merely the basis of his narrative—
designing, generally, to fill in with description, dialogue,

or authorial comment, whatever crevices of fact, or action, may, from page to page, render themselves apparent.

I prefer commencing with the consideration of an *effect*. Keeping originality *always* in view—for he is false to himself who ventures to dispense with so obvious and so easily attainable a source of interest—I say to myself, in the first place, "Of the innumerable effects, or impressions, of which the heart, the intellect, or (more generally) the soul is susceptible, what one shall I, on the present occasion, select?" Having chosen a novel, first, and secondly a vivid effect, I consider whether it can best be wrought by incident or tone—whether by ordinary incidents and peculiar tone, or the converse, or by peculiarity both of incident and tone—afterward looking about me (or rather within) for such combinations of event, or tone, as shall best aid me in the construction of the effect.

I have often thought how interesting a magazine paper might be written by any author who would—that is to say, who could—detail, step by step, the processes by which any of his compositions attained its ultimate point of completion. Why such a paper has never been given to the world, I am much at a loss to say—but, perhaps, the authorial vanity has had more to do with the omission than any one other cause. Most writers—poets in especial—prefer having it understood that they compose by a species of fine frenzy—an ecstatic intuition—and would positively shudder at letting the public take a peep behind the scenes, at the elaborate and vacillating crudities of thought—at the true purposes seized only at the last moment—at the innumerable glimpses of idea that arrived not at the maturity of full view—at the fully matured fancies discarded in despair as unmanageable—at the cautious selections and rejections—at the painful erasures and interpolations—in a word, at the wheels and pinions—the tackle for scene-shifting—the step-ladders and demon-traps—the cock's feathers, the red paint and the black patches, which, in ninety-nine cases out of the hundred, constitute the properties of the literary *histrio*.

I am aware, on the other hand, that the case is by no means common, in which an author is at all in condition to retrace the steps by which his conclusions have been attained. In general, suggestions, having arisen pell-mell, are pursued and forgotten in a similar manner.

For my own part, I have neither sympathy with the repugnance alluded to, nor, at any time, the least difficulty in recalling to mind the progressive steps of any of my compositions; and, since the interest of an analysis, or reconstruction, such as I have considered a *desideratum*, is quite independent of any real or fancied interest in the thing analyzed, it will not be regarded as a breach of decorum on my part to show the *modus operandi* by which some one of my own works was put together. I select "The Raven," as the most generally known. It is my design to render it manifest that no one point in its composition is referrible either to accident or intuition— that the work proceeded, step by step, to its completion with the precision and rigid consequence of a mathematical problem.

Let us dismiss, as irrelevant to the poem *per se*, the circumstance— or say the necessity—which, in the first place, gave rise to the intention of composing a poem that should suit at once the popular and the critical taste.

We commence, then, with this intention.

The initial consideration was that of extent. If any literary work is too long to be read at one sitting, we must be content to dispense with the immensely important effect derivable from unity of impression—for, if two sittings be required, the affairs of the world interfere, and every thing like totality is at once destroyed. But since, *ceteris paribus*, no poet can afford to dispense with *any thing* that may advance his design, it but remains to be

seen whether there is, in extent, any advantage to counterbalance the loss of unity which attends it. Here I say
no, at once. What we term a long poem is, in fact, merely
a succession of brief ones—that is to say, of brief poetical
effects. It is needless to demonstrate that a poem is such,
only inasmuch as it intensely excites, by elevating, the
soul; and all intense excitements are, through a psychal
necessity, brief. For this reason, at least one half of the
"Paradise Lost" is essentially prose—a succession of poetical excitements interspersed, *inevitably*, with corresponding depressions—the whole being deprived, through the
extremeness of its length, of the vastly important artistic
element, totality, or unity, of effect.

It appears evident, then, that there is a distinct limit,
as regards length, to all works of literary art—the limit of
a single sitting—and that, although in certain classes of
prose composition, such as "Robinson Crusoe" (demanding no unity,) this limit may be advantageously overpassed, it can never properly be overpassed in a poem.
Within this limit, the extent of a poem may be made to
bear mathematical relation to its merit—in other words,
to the excitement or elevation—again in other words,
to the degree of the true poetical effect which it is capable
of inducing; for it is clear that the brevity must be in direct ratio to the intensity of the intended effect:—this,
with one proviso—that a certain degree of duration is
absolutely requisite for the production of any effect at all.

Holding in view these considerations, as well as that
degree of excitement which I deemed not above the popular, while not below the critical, taste, I reached at once
what I conceived the proper *length* for my intended poem
—a length of about one hundred lines. It is, in fact, a
hundred and eight.

My next thought concerned the choice of an impression, or effect, to be conveyed: and here I may as well observe that, throughout the construction, I kept steadily in

view the design of rendering the work *universally* appreciable. I should be carried too far out of my immediate topic were I to demonstrate a point upon which I have repeatedly insisted, and which, with the poetical, stands not in the slightest need of demonstration—the point, I mean, that Beauty is the sole legitimate province of the poem. A few words, however, in elucidation of my real meaning, which some of my friends have evinced a disposition to misrepresent. That pleasure which is at once the most intense, the most elevating, and the most pure, is, I believe, found in the contemplation of the beautiful. When, indeed, men speak of Beauty, they mean, precisely, not a quality, as is supposed, but an effect—they refer, in short, just to that intense and pure elevation of *soul—not* of intellect, or of heart—upon which I have commented, and which is experienced in consequence of contemplating "the beautiful." Now I designate Beauty as the province of the poem, merely because it is an obvious rule of Art that effects should be made to spring from direct causes— that objects should be attained through means best adapted for their attainment—no one as yet having been weak enough to deny that the peculiar elevation alluded to, is *most readily* attained in the poem. Now the object, Truth, or the satisfaction of the intellect, and the object, Passion, or the excitement of the heart, are, although attainable, to a certain extent, in poetry, far more readily attainable in prose. Truth, in fact, demands a precision, and Passion, a *homeliness* (the truly passionate will comprehend me) which are absolutely antagonistic to that Beauty which, I maintain, is the excitement, or pleasurable elevation, of the soul. It by no means follows from any thing here said, that passion, or even truth, may not be introduced, and even profitably introduced, into a poem—for they may serve in elucidation, or aid the general effect, as do discords in music, by contrast—but the true artist will always contrive, first, to tone them into proper subservience to the predominant aim, and, secondly, to enveil them, as far as possible, in that Beauty which is the atmosphere and the essence of the poem.

Regarding, then, Beauty as my province, my next question referred to the *tone* of its highest manifestation—and all experience has shown that this tone is one of *sadness*. Beauty of whatever kind, in its supreme development, invariably excites the sensitive soul to tears. Melancholy is thus the most legitimate of all the poetical tones.

The length, the province, and the tone, being thus determined, I betook myself to ordinary induction, with the view of obtaining some artistic piquancy which might serve me as a key-note in the construction of the poem— some pivot upon which the whole structure might turn. In carefully thinking over all the usual artistic effects—or more properly *points*, in the theatrical sense—I did not fail to perceive immediately that no one had been so universally employed as that of the *refrain*. The universality of its employment sufficed to assure me of its intrinsic value, and spared me the necessity of submitting it to analysis. I considered it, however, with regard to its susceptibility of improvement, and soon saw it to be in a primitive condition. As commonly used, the *refrain*, or burden, not only is limited to lyric verse, but depends for its impression upon the force of monotone—both in sound and thought. The pleasure is deduced solely from the sense of identity—of repetition. I resolved to diversify, and so vastly heighten, the effect, by adhering, in general, to the monotone of sound, while I continually varied that of thought: that is to say, I determined to produce continuously novel effects, by the variation *of the application* of the *refrain*—the *refrain* itself remaining, for the most part, unvaried.

These points being settled, I next bethought me of the *nature* of my *refrain*. Since its application was to be repeatedly varied, it was clear that the *refrain* itself must be brief, for there would have been an insurmountable difficulty in frequent variations of application in any sentence of length. In proportion to the brevity of the sentence, would, of course, be the facility of the variation. This led me at once to a single word as the best *refrain*.

The question now arose as to the *character* of the word. Having made up my mind to a *refrain*, the division of the poem into stanzas was, of course, a corollary: the *refrain* forming the close to each stanza. That such a close, to have force, must be sonorous and susceptible of protracted emphasis, admitted no doubt: and these considerations inevitably led me to the long *o* as the most sonorous vowel, in connection with *r* as the most producible consonant.

The sound of the *refrain* being thus determined, it became necessary to select a word embodying this sound, and at the same time in the fullest possible keeping with that melancholy which I had predetermined as the tone of the poem. In such a search it would have been absolutely impossible to overlook the word "Nevermore." In fact, it was the very first which presented itself.

The next *desideratum* was a pretext for the continuous use of the one word "nevermore." In observing the difficulty which I at once found in inventing a sufficiently plausible reason for its continuous repetition, I did not fail to perceive that this difficulty arose solely from the pre-assumption that the word was to be so continuously or monotonously spoken by *a human* being—I did not fail to perceive, in short, that the difficulty lay in the reconciliation of this monotony with the exercise of reason on the part of the creature repeating the word. Here, then, immediately arose the idea of a *non*-reasoning creature capable of speech; and, very naturally, a parrot, in the first instance, suggested itself, but was superseded forthwith by a Raven, as equally capable of speech, and infinitely more in keeping with the intended *tone*.

I had now gone so far as the conception of a Raven—

the bird of ill omen—monotonously repeating the one word, "Nevermore," at the conclusion of each stanza, in a poem of melancholy tone, and in length about one hundred lines. Now, never losing sight of the object *supremeness*, or perfection, at all points, I asked myself—"Of all melancholy topics, what, according to the *universal* understanding of mankind, is the *most* melancholy?" Death—was the obvious reply. "And when," I said, "is this most melancholy of topics most poetical?" From what I have already explained at some length, the answer, here also, is obvious—"When it most closely allies itself to *Beauty*: the death, then, of a beautiful woman is, unquestionably, the most poetical topic in the world—and equally is it beyond doubt that the lips best suited for such topic are those of a bereaved lover."

I had now to combine the two ideas, of a lover lamenting his deceased mistress and a Raven continuously repeating the word "Nevermore"—I had to combine these, bearing in mind my design of varying, at every turn, the *application* of the word repeated; but the only intelligible mode of such combination is that of imagining the Raven employing the word in answer to the queries of the lover. And here it was that I saw at once the opportunity afforded for the effect on which I had been depending—that is to say, the effect of the *variation of application*. I saw that I could make the first query propounded by the lover—the first query to which the Raven should reply "Nevermore"—that I could make this first query a commonplace one—the second less so—the third still less, and so on—until at length the lover, startled from his original *nonchalance* by the melancholy character of the word itself—by its frequent repetition—and by a consideration of the ominous reputation of the fowl that uttered it—is at length excited to superstition, and wildly propounds queries of a far different character—queries whose solution he has passionately at heart—propounds them half in superstition and half in that species of despair which delights in self-torture—propounds them not altogether .because he believes in the prophetic or demoniac character of the bird (which, reason assures him, is merely repeating a lesson learned by rote) but because he experiences a phrenzied pleasure in so modeling his questions as to receive from the *expected* "Nevermore" the most delicious because the most intolerable of sorrow. Perceiving the opportunity thus afforded me—or, more strictly, thus forced upon me in the progress of the construction—I first established in mind the climax, or concluding query—that to which "Nevermore" should be in the last place an answer—that in reply to which this word "Nevermore" should involve the utmost conceivable amount of sorrow and despair.

Here then the poem may be said to have its beginning —at the end, where all works of art should begin—for it was here, at this point of my preconsiderations, that I first put pen to paper in the composition of the stanza:

"Prophet," said I, "thing of evil! prophet still if bird or devil!
By that heaven that bends above us—by that God we both adore,
Tell this soul with sorrow laden, if within the distant Aidenn,
It shall clasp a sainted maiden whom the angels name Lenore—
Clasp a rare and radiant maiden whom the angels name Lenore."
              Quoth the raven "Nevermore."

I composed this stanza, at this point, first that, by establishing the climax, I might the better vary and graduate, as regards seriousness and importance, the preceding queries of the lover—and, secondly, that I might definitely settle the rhythm, the metré, and the length and general arrangement of the stanza—as well as graduate the stanzas which were to precede, so that none of them might surpass this in rhythmical effect. Had I been able, in the subsequent composition, to construct more vigorous stanzas, I should, without scruple, have purposely enfeebled them, so as not to interfere with the climacteric effect.

And here I may as well say a few words of the versification. My first object (as usual) was originality. The extent to which this has been neglected, in versification, is one of the most unaccountable things in the world. Admitting that there is little possibility of variety in mere *rhythm*, it is still clear that the possible varieties of metre and stanza are absolutely infinite—and yet, *for centuries, no man, in verse, has ever done, or ever seemed to think of doing, an original thing*. The fact is, originality (unless in minds of very unusual force) is by no means a matter, as some suppose, of impulse or intuition. In general, to be found, it must be elaborately sought, and although a positive merit of the highest class, demands in its attainment less of invention than negation.

Of course, I pretend to no originality in either the rhythm or metre of "The Raven." The former is trochaic —the latter is octameter acatalectic, alternating with heptameter catalectic repeated in the refrain of the fifth verse, and terminating with tetrameter catalectic. Less pedantically—the feet employed throughout (trochees) consist of a long syllable followed by a short: the first line of the stanza consists of eight of these feet—the second of seven and a half (in effect two-thirds)—the third of eight—the fourth of seven and a half—the fifth the same—the sixth three and a half. Now, each of these lines, taken individually, has been employed before, and what originality "The Raven" has, is in their *combination into stanzas*; nothing even remotely approaching this combination has ever been attempted. The effect of this originality of combination is aided by other unusual, and some altogether novel effects, arising from an extension of the application of the principles of rhyme and alliteration.

The next point to be considered was the mode of bringing together the lover and the Raven—and the first branch of this consideration was the *locale*. For this the most natural suggestion might seem to be a forest, or the fields—but it has always appeared to me that a close *circumscription of space* is absolutely necessary to the effect of insulated incident:—it has the force of a frame to a picture. It has an indisputable moral power in keeping concentrated the attention, and, of course, must not be confounded with mere unity of place.

I determined, then, to place the lover in his chamber—in a chamber rendered sacred to him by memories of her who had frequented it. The room is represented as richly furnished—this in mere pursuance of the ideas I have already explained on the subject of Beauty, as the sole true poetical thesis.

The *locale* being thus determined, I had now to introduce the bird—and the thought of introducing him through the window, was inevitable. The idea of making the lover suppose, in the first instance, that the flapping of the wings of the bird against the shutter, is a "tapping" at the door, originated in a wish to increase, by prolonging, the reader's curiosity, and in a desire to admit the incidental effect arising from the lover's throwing open the door, finding all dark, and thence adopting the half-fancy that it was the spirit of his mistress that knocked.

I made the night tempestuous, first, to account for the Raven's seeking admission, and secondly, for the effect of contrast with the (physical) serenity within the chamber.

I made the bird alight on the bust of Pallas, also for the effect of contrast between the marble and the plumage —it being understood that the bust was absolutely *sug-*

gested by the bird—the bust of *Pallas* being chosen, first, as most in keeping with the scholarship of the lover, and, secondly, for the sonorousness of the word, Pallas, itself.

About the middle of the poem, also, I have availed myself of the force of contrast, with a view of deepening the ultimate impression. For example, an air of the fantastic—approaching as nearly to the ludicrous as was admissible—is given to the Raven's entrance. He comes in "with many a flirt and flutter."

Not the *least obeisance made he*—not a moment stopped
  or stayed he,
But with mien of lord or lady, perched above my chamber
  door.

In the two stanzas which follow, the design is more obviously carried out:—

Then this ebony bird beguiling my sad fancy into smiling
By the *grave and stern decorum of the countenance it
  wore.*
"Though thy *crest be shorn and shaven* thou," I said, "art
  sure no craven,
Ghastly grim and ancient Raven wandering from the
  nightly shore—
Tell me what thy lordly name is on the Night's Plutonian
  shore!"
        Quoth the Raven "Nevermore."

Much I marvelled *this ungainly fowl* to hear discourse so
  plainly,
Though its answer little meaning—little relevancy bore;
For we cannot help agreeing that no living human being
*Ever yet was blessed with seeing bird above his chamber
  door*—
*Bird or beast upon the sculptured bust above his chamber
  door,*
        With such name as "Nevermore."

The effect of the *dénouement* being thus provided for, I immediately drop the fantastic for a tone of the most profound seriousness:—this tone commencing in the stanza directly following the one last quoted, with the line,

But the Raven, sitting lonely on that placid bust, spoke only, etc.

From this epoch the lover no longer jests—no longer sees any thing even of the fantastic in the Raven's demeanor. He speaks of him as a "grim, ungainly, ghastly, gaunt, and ominous bird of yore," and feels the "fiery eyes" burning into his "bosom's core." This revolution of thought, or fancy, on the lover's part, is intended to induce a similar one on the part of the reader—to bring the mind into a proper frame for the *dénouement*— which is now brought about as rapidly and as *directly* as possible.

With the *dénouement* proper—with the Raven's reply, "Nevermore," to the lover's final demand if he shall meet his mistress in another world—the poem, in its obvious phase, that of a simple narrative, may be said to have its completion. So far, every thing is within the limits of the accountable—of the real. A raven, having learned by rote the single word "Nevermore," and having escaped from the custody of its owner, is driven, at midnight, through the violence of a storm, to seek admission at a window from which a light still gleams—the chamber-window of a student, occupied half in poring over a volume, half in dreaming of a beloved mistress deceased. The casement being thrown open at the fluttering of the bird's wings, the bird itself perches on the most convenient seat out of the immediate reach of the student, who, amused by the incident and the oddity of the visiter's demeanor, demands of it, in jest and without looking for a reply, its name. The raven addressed, answers with its customary word, "Nevermore"—a word which finds immediate echo in the melancholy heart of the student, who, giving utterance aloud to certain thoughts suggested by the occasion, is again startled by the fowl's repetition of "Nevermore." The student now guesses the state of the case, but is impelled, as I have before explained, by the human thirst for self-torture, and in part by superstition, to propound such queries to the bird as will bring him, the lover, the most of the luxury of sorrow, through the anticipated answer "Nevermore." With the indulgence, to the utmost extreme, of this self-torture, the narration, in what I have termed its first or obvious phase, has a natural termination, and so far there has been no overstepping of the limits of the real.

But in subjects so handled, however skilfully, or with however vivid an array of incident, there is always a certain hardness or nakedness, which repels the artistical eye. Two things are invariably required—first, some amount of complexity, or more properly, adaptation; and, secondly, some amount of suggestiveness—some undercurrent, however indefinite of meaning. It is this latter, in especial, which imparts to a work of art so much of that *richness* (to borrow from colloquy a forcible term) which we are too fond of confounding with *the ideal*. It is the *excess* of the suggested meaning—it is the rendering this the upper instead of the undercurrent of the theme—which turns into prose (and that of the very flattest kind) the so called poetry of the so called transcendentalists.

Holding these opinions, I added the two concluding stanzas of the poem—their suggestiveness being thus made to pervade all the narrative which has preceded them. The undercurrent of meaning is rendered first apparent in the lines—

"Take thy beak from out *my heart,* and take thy form
   from off my door!"
        Quoth the Raven "Nevermore!"

It will be observed that the words, "from out my
heart," involve the first metaphorical expression in the
poem. They, with the answer, "Nevermore," dispose
the mind to seek a moral in all that has been previously
narrated. The reader begins now to regard the Raven as
emblematical—but it is not until the very last line of
the very last stanza, that the intention of making him
emblematical of *Mournful and Never-ending Remembrance* is permitted distinctly to be seen:

And the Raven, never flitting, still is sitting, still is sitting,
On the pallid bust of Pallas just above my chamber door;
And his eyes have all the seeming of a demon's that is
   dreaming,
And the lamplight o'er him streaming throws his shadow
   on the floor;
And my soul *from out that shadow* that lies floating on the
   floor
        Shall be lifted—nevermore.

Excerpts From
THE POETIC PRINCIPLE

In speaking of the Poetic Principle, I have no design to
be either thorough or profound. While discussing, very
much at random, the essentiality of what we call Poetry,
my principal purpose will be to cite for consideration,
some few of those minor English or American poems
which best suit my own taste, or which, upon my own
fancy, have left the most definite impression. By "minor

poems" I mean, of course, poems of little length. And here, in the beginning, permit me to say a few words in regard to a somewhat peculiar principle, which, whether rightfully or wrongfully, has always had its influence in my own critical estimate of the poem. I hold that a long poem does not exist. I maintain that the phrase, "a long poem," is simply a flat contradiction in terms.

I need scarcely observe that a poem deserves its title only inasmuch as it excites, by elevating the soul. The value of the poem is in the ratio of this elevating excitement. But all excitements are, through a psychal necessity, transient. That degree of excitement which would entitle a poem to be so called at all, cannot be sustained throughout a composition of any great length. After the lapse of half an hour, at the very utmost, it flags—fails—a revulsion ensues—and then the poem is, in effect, and in fact, no longer such.

There are, no doubt, many who have found difficulty in reconciling the critical dictum that the "Paradise Lost" is to be devoutly admired throughout, with the absolute impossibility of maintaining for it, during perusal, the amount of enthusiasm which that critical dictum would demand. This great work, in fact, is to be regarded as poetical, only when, losing sight of that vital requisite in all works of Art, Unity, we view it merely as a series of minor poems. If, to preserve its Unity—its totality of effect or impression—we read it (as would be necessary) at a single sitting, the result is but a constant alternation of excitement and depression. After a passage of what we feel to be true poetry, there follows, inevitably, a passage of platitude which no critical pre-judgment can force us to admire; but if, upon completing the work, we read it again, omitting the first book—that is to say, commencing with the second—we shall be surprised at now finding that admirable which we before condemned—that damnable which we had previously so much admired.

It follows from all this that the ultimate, aggregate, or absolute effect of even the best epic under the sun, is a nullity:—and this is precisely the fact.

In regard to the Iliad, we have, if not positive proof, at least very good reason for believing it intended as a series of lyrics; but, granting the epic intention, I can say only that the work is based in an imperfect sense of art. The modern epic is, of the supposititious ancient model, but an inconsiderate and blindfold imitation. But the day of these artistic anomalies is over. If, at any time, any very long poem *were* popular in reality, which I doubt, it is at least clear that no very long poem will ever be popular again.

That the extent of a poetical work is, *cæteris paribus*, the measure of its merit, seems undoubtedly, when we thus state it, a proposition sufficiently absurd—yet we are indebted for it to the Quarterly Reviews. Surely there can be nothing in mere *size*, abstractly considered—there can be nothing in mere *bulk*, so far as a volume is concerned, which has so continuously elicited admiration from these saturnine pamphlets! A mountain, to be sure, by the mere sentiment of physical magnitude which it conveys, *does* impress us with a sense of the sublime—but no man is impressed after *this* fashion by the material grandeur of even "The Columbiad." Even the Quarterlies have not instructed us to be so impressed by it. *As yet*, they have not *insisted* on our estimating Lamartine by the cubic foot, or Pollock by the pound—but what else are we to *infer* from their continual prating about "sustained effort?" If, by "sustained effort," any little gentleman has accomplished an epic, let us frankly commend him for the effort—if this indeed be a thing commendable—but let us forbear praising the epic on the effort's account. It is to be hoped that common sense, in the time to come, will prefer deciding upon a work of art, rather by the impression it makes, by the effect it produces, than by the time it took to impress the effect, or by the amount of "sustained effort" which had been found necessary in effecting the impression. The fact is, that perseverance is one thing, and genius quite another; nor can all the Quarterlies in Christendom confound them. By and by, this proposition, with many which I have been just urging, will be received as self-evident. In the mean time, by being generally condemned as falsities, they will not be essentially damaged as truths.

On the other hand, it is clear that a poem may be improperly brief. Undue brevity degenerates into mere epigrammatism. A _very_ short poem, while now and then producing a brilliant or vivid, never produces a profound or enduring effect. There must be the steady pressing down of the stamp upon the wax. De Béranger has wrought innumerable things, pungent and spirit-stirring; but, in general, they have been too imponderous to stamp themselves deeply into the public attention; and thus, as so many feathers of fancy, have been blown aloft only to be whistled down the wind. . . .

While the epic mania—while the idea that, to merit in poetry, prolixity is indispensable—has, for some years past, been gradually dying out of the public mind, by mere dint of its own absurdity—we find it succeeded by a heresy too palpably false to be long tolerated, but one which, in the brief period it has already endured, may be said to have accomplished more in the corruption of our Poetical Literature than all its other enemies combined. I allude to the heresy of _The Didactic_. It has been assumed, tacitly and avowedly, directly and indirectly, that the ultimate object of all Poetry is Truth. Every poem, it is said, should inculcate a moral; and by this moral is the poetical merit of the work to be adjudged. We Americans, especially, have patronised this happy idea; and we Bostonians, very especially, have developed it in full. We have taken it into our heads that to write a poem simply for the poem's sake, and to acknowledge such to have been our design, would be to confess ourselves radically wanting in the true Poetic dignity and force:—but the simple fact is, that, would we but permit ourselves to look into our own souls, we should immediately there discover that under the sun there neither exists nor *can* exist any work more thoroughly dignified—more supremely noble than this very poem—this poem *per se*—this poem which is a poem and nothing more—this poem written solely for the poem's sake.

With as deep a reverence for the True as ever inspired the bosom of man, I would, nevertheless, limit, in some measure, its modes of inculcation. I would limit to enforce them. I would not enfeeble them by dissipation. The demands of Truth are severe. She has no sympathy with the myrtles. All *that* which is so indispensable in Song, is precisely all *that* with which *she* has nothing whatever to do. It is but making her a flaunting paradox, to wreathe her in gems and flowers. In enforcing a truth, we need severity rather than efflorescence of language. We must be simple, precise, terse. We must be cool, calm, unimpassioned. In a word, we must be in that mood which, as nearly as possible, is the exact converse of the poetical. *He* must be blind, indeed, who does not perceive the radical and chasmal differences between the truthful and the poetical modes of inculcation. He must be theory-mad beyond redemption who, in spite of these differences, shall still persist in attempting to reconcile the obstinate oils and waters of Poetry and Truth.

Dividing the world of mind into its three most immediately obvious distinctions, we have the Pure Intellect, Taste, and the Moral Sense. I place Taste in the middle, because it is just this position, which, in the mind, it occupies. It holds intimate relations with either extreme; but from the Moral Sense is separated by so faint a difference that Aristotle has not hesitated to place some of its operations among the virtues themselves. Nevertheless, we find the *offices* of the trio marked with a sufficient distinction. Just as the Intellect concerns itself with Truth, so Taste informs us of the Beautiful while the Moral Sense is regardful of Duty. Of this latter, while Conscience teaches the obligation, and Reason the expediency, Taste contents herself with displaying the charms: —waging war upon Vice solely on the ground of her deformity—her disproportion—her animosity to the fitting, to the appropriate, to the harmonious—in a word, to Beauty.

An immortal instinct, deep within the spirit of man, is thus, plainly, a sense of the Beautiful. This it is which administers to his delight in the manifold forms, and sounds, and odours, and sentiments amid which he exists. And just as the lily is repeated in the lake, or the eyes of Amaryllis in the mirror, so is the mere oral or written repetition of these forms, and sounds, and colours, and odours, and sentiments, a duplicate source of delight. But this mere repetition is not poetry. He who shall simply sing, with however glowing enthusiasm, or with however vivid a truth of description, of the sights, and sounds, and odours, and colours, and sentiments, which greet *him* in common with all mankind—he, I say, has yet failed to prove his divine title. There is still a something in the distance which he has been unable to attain. We have still a thirst unquenchable, to allay which he has not shown us the crystal springs. This thirst belongs to the immortality of Man. It is at once a consequence and an indication of his perennial existence. It is the desire of the moth for the star. It is no mere appreciation of the Beauty before us—but a wild effort to reach the Beauty above. Inspired by an ecstatic prescience of the glories beyond the grave, we struggle, by multiform combinations among the things and thoughts of Time, to attain a portion of that Loveliness whose very elements, perhaps, appertain to eternity alone. And thus when by Poetry—or when by Music, the most entrancing of the Poetic moods —we find ourselves melted into tears—we weep then—not as the Abbaté Gravina supposes—through excess of pleasure, but through a certain, petulant, impatient sorrow at our inability to grasp *now*, wholly, here on earth, at once and for ever, those divine and rapturous joys, of which *through* the poem, or *through* the music, we attain but brief and indeterminate glimpses.

The struggle to apprehend the supernal Loveliness—this struggle, on the part of souls fittingly constituted—has given to the world all *that* which it (the world) has ever been enabled at once to understand and *to feel* as poetic.

The Poetic Sentiment, of course, may develop itself in various modes—in Painting, in Sculpture, in Architecture, in the Dance—very especially in Music—and very peculiarly, and with a wide field, in the composition of the Landscape Garden. Our present theme, however, has regard only to its manifestation in words. And here let me speak briefly on the topic of rhythm. Contenting myself with the certainty that Music, in its various modes of metre, rhythm, and rhyme, is of so vast a moment in Poetry as never to be wisely rejected—is so vitally important an adjunct, that he is simply silly who declines its assistance, I will not now pause to maintain its absolute essentiality. It is in Music, perhaps, that the soul most nearly attains the great end for which, when inspired with the Poetic Sentiment, it struggles—the creation of supernal Beauty. It *may* be, indeed, that here this sublime end is, now and then, attained *in fact*. We are often made to feel, with a shivering delight, that from an earthly harp are stricken notes which *cannot* have been unfamiliar to the angels. And thus there can be little doubt that in the union of Poetry with Music in its popular sense, we shall find the widest field for the Poetic development. The old Bards and Minnesingers had advantages which we do not possess—and Thomas Moore, singing his own songs, was, in the most legitimate manner, perfecting them as poems.

To recapitulate, then:—I would define, in brief, the Poetry of words as *The Rhythmical Creation of Beauty*. Its sole arbiter is Taste. With the Intellect or with the Conscience, it has only collateral relations. Unless incidentally, it has no concern whatever either with Duty or with Truth.

A few words, however, in explanation. *That* pleasure which is at once the most pure, the most elevating, and the most intense, is derived, I maintain, from the contemplation of the Beautiful. In the contemplation of Beauty we alone find it possible to attain that pleasurable elevation, or excitement, *of the Soul*, which we recognise as the Poetic Sentiment, and which is so easily distinguished from Truth, which is the satisfaction of the Reason, or from Passion, which is the excitement of the Heart. I make Beauty, therefore—using the word as inclusive of the sublime—I make Beauty the province of the poem, simply because it is an obvious rule of Art that effects should be made to spring as directly as possible from their causes:—no one as yet having been weak enough to deny that the peculiar elevation in question is at least *most readily* attainable in the poem. It by no means follows, however, that the incitements of Passion, or the precepts of Duty, or even the lessons of Truth, may not be introduced into a poem, and with advantage; for they may subserve, incidentally, in various ways, the general purposes of the work:—but the true artist will always contrive to tone them down in proper subjection to that *Beauty* which is the atmosphere and the real essence of the poem. . . .

Thus, although in a very cursory and imperfect manner, I have endeavoured to convey to you my conception of the Poetic Principle. It has been my purpose to suggest that, while this Principle itself is, strictly and simply, the Human Aspiration for Supernal Beauty, the manifestation of the Principle is always found in *an elevating excitement of the Soul*—quite independent of that passion which is the intoxication of the Heart—or of that Truth which is the satisfaction of the Reason. For, in regard to Passion, alas! its tendency is to degrade, rather than to elevate the Soul. Love, on the contrary—Love—the true, the divine Eros—the Uranian, as distinguished from the Dionæan Venus—is unquestionably the purest and truest of all poetical themes. And in regard to Truth—if, to be sure, through the attainment of a truth, we are led to perceive a harmony where none was apparent before, we experience, at once, the true poetical effect—but this effect is referable to the harmony alone, and not in the least degree to the truth which merely served to render the harmony manifest.

We shall reach, however, more immediately a distinct conception of what the true Poetry is, by mere reference to a few of the simple elements which induce in the Poet himself the true poetical effect. He recognises the ambrosia which nourishes his soul, in the bright orbs that shine in Heaven—in the volutes of the flower—in the clustering of low shrubberies—in the waving of the grain-fields—in the slanting of tall, Eastern trees—in the blue distance of mountains—in the grouping of clouds—in the twinkling of half-hidden brooks—in the gleaming of silver rivers—in the repose of sequestered lakes—in the star-mirroring depths of lonely wells. He perceives it in the songs of birds—in the harp of Æolus—in the sighing of the night wind—in the repining voice of the forest—in the surf that complains to the shore—in the fresh breath of the woods—in the scent of the violet—in the voluptuous perfume of the hyacinth—in the suggestive odour that comes to him, at eventide, from far-distant, undiscovered islands, over dim oceans, illimit-able and unexplored. He owns it in all noble thoughts—in all unworldly motives—in all holy impulses—in all chivalrous, generous, and self-sacrificing deeds. He feels it in the beauty of woman—in the grace of her step—in the lustre of her eye—in the melody of her voice—in her soft laughter—in her sigh—in the harmony of the rustling of her robes. He deeply feels it in her winning endearments—in her burning enthusiasms—in her gentle charities—in her meek and devotional endurances—but above all—ah, far above all—he kneels to it—he worships it in the faith, in the purity, in the strength, in the alto-gether divine majesty—of her *love*. . . .

Bibliography

Scholarship and criticism on Poe is extensive, numbering well over 1500 items. Such a large number of critical studies is indicative of the interest in Poe over the last 140 years, and is to be expected for a major literary figure. The following bibliographical survey presents relatively few of these, but comprise a solid core of significant scholarly and critical works available in English.

I

Among the many editions of Poe's works, a half-dozen are of special note. The first collected edition of Poe's writings was edited by the man who blackened Poe's moral character and literary reputation so thoroughly that it was to be a century before the truth would begin to emerge. Rufus Wilmot Griswold and others collaborated on *Works of Edgar Allan Poe, with Notices of His Life and Genius*, 4 vols (New York: J. S. Redfield, 1850–56). Griswold's notorious "Memoir" appears in Volume III, and the edition contains unauthorized alterations. The first edition that can be considered generally reliable, although incomplete and sometimes inaccurate, is E. C. Stedman and George Woodberry's *The Works of Edgar Allan Poe*, newly collected and edited, with a Memoir, Critical Introductions, and Notes, 10 vols (Chicago: Stone & Kimball, 1894–95). And the edition is one to which many scholarly studies refer. The long-time standard edition, however, with variants and notes, is James A. Harrison's *The Complete Works of Edgar Allan Poe*, 17 vols (New York: Thomas Y. Crowell & Co., 1902). The Harrison edition contains a good biography in Volume I; but the edition is somewhat out of date and presumably will be superceded by Thomas Ollive Mabbott's *Collected Works of Edgar Allan Poe*, multi-volumed, in progress (Cambridge: Harvard University Press, 1969–   ). The first volume, the *Poems*, of Mabbott's long-awaited Harvard edition appeared in 1969. Over half of the first volume is commentary, notes, and variants, including the "Annals," a factual chronology of Poe's life and career. (Another important edition of the poems, with extensive notes and commentary, is Killis Campbell's *The Poems of Edgar Allan Poe* (Boston: Ginn & Co., 1917).)

The best edition of Poe's correspondence is John Ward Ostrom's *The Letters of Edgar Allan Poe*, 2 vols (Cambridge: Harvard University Press, 1948), reissued with a supplement

(New York: Gordian Press, 1966). Unfortunately only Poe's side of the correspondence is printed, but Ostrom's edition will remain standard until the Mabbott *Collected Works* appears with much of both sides of the correspondence. (An incomplete but useful collection of letters both to and from Poe comprises Volume XVII of the Harrison *Complete Works*.)

Three useful indexes to Poe's works are available. Bradford A. Booth and Claude E. Jones, *A Concordance to the Poetical Works of Edgar Allan Poe* (Baltimore: Johns Hopkins Press, 1941) is thorough. J. Lasley Dameron and Louis Charles Stagg, *An Index to Poe's Critical Vocabulary* (Hartford: Transcendental Books, 1966) is based on Poe's critical writings as collected in the Harrison *Complete Works*. A thorough index to Harrison is Burton R. Pollin, *Dictionary of Names and Titles in Poe's Collected [sic] Works* (New York: Da Capo Books, 1968).

II

The bibliographical record of Poe's publications, massively detailed yet still incomplete, is essentially contained in three volumes: Charles F. Heartman and James R. Canny, *A Bibliography of First Printings of the Writings of Edgar Allan Poe* (1940; rev. ed. Hattiesburg, Miss.: The Book Farm, 1943); John W. Robertson, *Bibliography of the Writings of Edgar A. Poe and Commentary on the Bibliography of Edgar A. Poe* (both 1934; reissued in one volume (New York: Kraus Reprint Co., 1969). These and other bibliographical studies are lucidly surveyed and appraised by G. Thomas Tanselle in "The State of Poe Bibliography," *Poe Newsletter*, II (1969), 1–3.

A good introduction to the problems and achievements of secondary bibliography—the criticism on Poe—is the trenchant appraisal of J. Albert Robbins, "The State of Poe Studies," *Poe Newsletter*, I (1968), 1–2. Besides commentary on the weaknesses of Poe scholarship, Robbins offers a pragmatic list of suggested readings for the "intelligent and earnest student—undergraduate, graduate, or layman—who wishes to get at Poe with a minimum of frustration and waste of time." Robbins has also published the *Checklist of Edgar Allan Poe* (Columbia, Ohio: Charles E. Merrill Co., 1969), a selected bibliography of Poe criticism arranged according to Poe's works. A useful essay on the most important studies of Poe up to 1955 is Jay B. Hubbell's chapter on Poe in *Eight American Authors: A Review of Research and Criticism*, edited by Floyd Stovall (New York: Modern Language Association of America, 1956). This volume was reissued in 1963 with an added checklist of studies 1955–1962, compiled by J. Chesley Matthews (New York: W. W. Norton); further revision and updating of the entire volume is now in progress. A *Complete Bibliography of Poe Criticism, 1827–1967* is in progress under the direction of J. Lasley Dameron; the first result of the project is

Dameron's *Edgar Allan Poe: A Checklist of Criticism 1942–1960* (Charlottesville: Bibliographical Society of the University of Virginia, 1966).' A useful but error-plagued bibliographical survey, dealing with Poe's reputation, is Haldeen Braddy, *Glorious Incense: The Fulfillment of Edgar Allan Poe* (1953; 2nd ed. Port Washington, N.Y.: Kennikat Press, 1968).

Bibliographies for recent studies include Richard P. Benton's "Current Bibliography on Edgar Allan Poe," *Emerson Society Quarterly*, No. 38 (I Quarter 1965), 144–147; No. 47 (II Quarter 1967), 84–87; and "Edgar Allan Poe: Current Bibliography," *Poe Newsletter*, II (1969), 4–12. Benton's first two bibliographies in *ESQ* cover the years 1963–1966. His fuller, third bibliography in *Poe Newsletter* covers the years 1966–1968 and is annotated; this bibliography continues annually in *Poe Newsletter*. An annual critical review of the year's work in Poe studies is J. Albert Robbins, "Poe and Nineteenth-Century Poetry," in *American Literary Scholarship: An Annual*, covering the years 1963–1967 (Durham, N.C.: Duke University Press, 1965–   ), and continued by Patrick F. Quinn (1968–   ). A more limited critical survey is Claude Richard's "Poe Studies in Europe," *Poe Newsletter*, II (1969), 20–23, the first installment of which focused on France. This continuing review-essay, besides evaluating current studies, attempts to make works in foreign languages and journals more accessible to English-speaking readers.

III

The definitive biography of Poe is Arthur Hobson Quinn, *Edgar Allan Poe: A Critical Biography* (New York: Appleton-Century-Crofts, 1941). Quinn cleared up many of the inaccuracies surrounding Poe, showed Griswold to have lied, exposed alterations and forgeries in Poe's letters, and added a sizable quantity of new data to the factual circumstances of Poe's life. Quinn's critically unsophisticated judgments on Poe's writings, however, mar what is otherwise a first-rate scholarly work. Two recent biographies, even though they contain little that is new, warrant mention for their balance and readability. William Bittner's *Poe: A Biography* (Boston: Little, Brown & Co., 1962) is a very good introduction to Poe, though his biographical interpretation of Poe's works must be read with some caution. Edward Wagenknecht's *Edgar Allan Poe: The Man Behind the Legend* (New York: Oxford University Press, 1963) is helpfully organized into chapters on Poe's attitudes toward "Life," "Living," "Learning," "Art," "Love," and "God." Another recent biographically oriented study is John Walsh's *Poe the Detective: The Curious Circumstances Behind "The Mystery of Marie Roget"* (New Brunswick, N.J.: Rutgers University Press, 1968), an interesting piece of scholarly detective work on how Poe creatively transmuted the facts of an actual murder into one of his most famous stories.

Several of the older biographies are still worth reading. George E. Woodberry's *Edgar Allan Poe* (1885), revised and expanded as *The Life of Edgar Allan Poe*, 2 vols (Boston: Houghton Mifflin, 1909), is revealing in its mild moral antagonism. Mary E. Phillips' *Edgar Allan Poe: the Man*, 2 vols (Chicago and Philadelphia: John C. Winston, 1926), despite the turgid style, is massively researched. Hervey Allen's *Israfel: The Life and Times of Edgar Allan Poe*, 2 vols (New York: George H. Doran (Doubleday), 1926; rev. ed. New York: Rinehart & Co., 1934) is a trifle romanticized but contains some legitimate oral tradition about Poe.

Two biographical approaches to Poe's writings are of special critical importance. Marie Bonaparte in *Edgar Poe: Étude psychoanalytique*, 2 vols (1933), translated by John Rodker as *The Life and Works of Edgar Poe: A Psycho-Analytic Interpretation* (London: Imago Publishing Co., 1949), sees anal eroticism and frustrated Oedipal desires as the basis of Poe's work. Her method is to examine the symbols of Poe's writings in the light of Freud's work with dream symbolism. All in all, her method is somewhat mechanical, and she has a tendency to force evidence into her theoretical scheme. But unlike Joseph Wood Krutch's well-known but weak psychoanalytic study (1926), Bonaparte's book, for all its faults, is strangely provocative and insightful. N. Bryllion Fagin's *The Histrionic Mr. Poe* (Baltimore: Johns Hopkins Press, 1949) is a biographical interpretation of Poe's works organized around the theme of role-playing. Fagin sees Poe as a frustrated actor who threw himself into the role of each of his characters, drawing upon the "emotional reservoir within himself." Fagin's book is the best of all such biographically oriented "critical" studies.

IV

Among the many full-length critical studies of Poe's writings, five stand out as especially significant. Perhaps the best introductory work of criticism is Geoffrey Rans' *Edgar Allan Poe* (Edinburgh and London: Oliver & Boyd, 1965), which presents Poe's work in the context of his esthetics and philosophy and which offers incisive evaluations of Poe scholarship. A study emphasizing Poe's works in the context of Romantic philosophy and esthetics is Edward H. Davidson's *Poe: A Critical Study* (Cambridge: Harvard University Press, 1957), one of the three best critical books on Poe yet produced. A provocative and insightful study of America's three great Dark Romanticists is Harry Levin's *The Power of Blackness: Hawthorne, Poe, Melville* (New York: Alfred A. Knopf, 1958), but some commentary is unevidenced and the book is not without a few errors of fact. Floyd Stovall's *Edgar Poe the Poet: Essays Old and New on the Man and His Work* (Charlottesville: University Press of Virginia, 1969), recording

Stovall's forty years of Poe study, brings together a number of good essays. Finally, the reader must not miss Patrick F. Quinn's *The French Face of Edgar Poe* (Carbondale: Southern Illinois Press, 1957), for, in an effort to account for the fascination Poe holds for the French, Quinn produces the most insightful extended criticism of Poe's works now extant. Readers interested in the French aspect of Poe's impact, however, will want also to consult Célestin P. Cambiaire's *The Influence of Edgar Allan Poe in France* (1927; reprinted New York: Haskell House, 1970), Lois and Francis E. Hyslop's *Baudelaire on Poe: Critical Papers* (State College, Penn.: Bald Eagle Press, 1952), T. S. Eliot's *From Poe to Valéry* (1949, reprinted in *To Criticize the Critic*, New York: Harcourt Brace, 1965), and Joseph Chiari's *"Symbolisme" from Poe to Mallarmé: the Growth of a Myth* (London: Rockliff, 1956).

Two other general critical studies, both introductory, should also be mentioned. Vincent Buranelli's *Edgar Allan Poe* (New York: Twayne Publishing Co., 1961) is an uneven study of themes in Poe's works, and ranges from the insightful to the inaccurate. Arthur Ransome's older work, *Edgar Allan Poe: A Critical Study* (1910; London: Stephen Swift, 1912), is a consistently lucid study emphasizing Poe's "unconcluded search" for an esthetic epistemology.

Three historically oriented works which deal not only with Poe's intellectual tradition but also with the important matter of his specific reading are Killis Campbell's *The Mind of Poe and Other Studies* (Cambridge: Harvard University Press, 1933), Burton R. Pollin's *Discoveries in Poe* (Notre Dame, Ind.: University of Notre Dame Press, 1970), and Margaret Alterton's *Origins of Poe's Critical Theory* (Iowa City: University of Iowa Humanistic Series, 1925). Alterton's study of the European sources and general context of Poe's literary theories may be supplemented with Edd Winfield Parks' *Edgar Allan Poe as Literary Critic* (1964), which emphasizes the influence of Poe's experience as an editor upon his critical theories. A much fuller and more important treatment of these and other matters is Robert D. Jacobs' *Poe: Journalist & Critic* (Baton Rouge, La.: University of Louisiana Press, 1969). Four other studies of the publishing conditions and the state of journalism in Poe's day should also be consulted. Perry Miller's *The Raven and the Whale: The War of Words and Wits in the Era of Poe and Melville* (1956) is a comprehensive study of the early nineteenth-century literary wars in America. Sidney P. Moss's *Poe's Literary Battles: The Critic in the Context of His Literary Milieu* (Durham, N.C.: Duke University Press, 1963), is an excellent and very readable study of Poe as a "magazinist" who waged brilliant critical warfare against the literary cliques of New York and New England. Moss's edition of some of the documents, *Poe's Major Crisis: His Libel Suit and*

New York's Literary World (Durham, N.C.: Duke University Press, 1970), may also be consulted. And Michael Allen's *Poe and the British Magazine Tradition* (New York: Oxford University Press, 1969) is a lucid, if incompletely researched, study of Poe's adoption of the literary modes and conventions of the British magazine writers and editors.

V

The periodical literature on Poe is too extensive to be dealt with more than summarily here. Three collections of critical essays are available, however. Perhaps the best is Eric W. Carlson's *The Recognition of Edgar Allan Poe: Selected Criticism Since 1829* (Ann Arbor: University of Michigan Press, 1966), a chronological selection of essays that reflect Poe's critical reception. But also useful are Robert Regan's *Poe: A Collection of Critical Essays* (Englewood Cliffs, N.J.: Prentice-Hall, 1967), which contains twelve good articles on a variety of aspects of Poe, and Thomas Woodson's *Twentieth Century Interpretations of "The Fall of the House of Usher"* (Englewood Cliffs, N.J.: Prentice-Hall, 1969).

Those who wish to pursue further the kind of revaluation of Poe offered in the introductory essays to this volume will want to consult essays by the following critics (for guidance to their locations, see the bibliographies listed in Section II):

For general essays: Roger Asselineau, Leslie Fiedler, Clark Griffith, Leon Howard, D. H. Lawrence, D. E. S. Maxwell, Joel Porte, Allen Tate, Richard Wilbur, Ivor Winters.

For moral, religious, philosophical, and esthetic aspects of Poe's world view: Robert M. Adams, Robert Daniel, Jay L. Halio, David H. Hirsch, George Kelley, James Lundquist, Richard A. Levine, Joseph J. Moldenhauer, Charles O'Donnell, Patrick F. Quinn, Joseph Roppolo, Allen Tate, G. R. Thompson, Kermit Vanderbilt, Richard Wilbur, Margaret Yonce.

For differing views of Poe's uses of the occult and the Gothic: Darrel Abel, J. O. Bailey, Richard P. Benton, Walter Blair, Doris Falk, James Gargano, Joseph M. Garrison, Clark Griffith, John S. Hill, Eugene R. Kanjo, Sidney E. Lind, Stephen Mooney, John E. Reilly, E. Arthur Robinson, James Schroeter, Donald B. Stauffer, G. R. Thompson, I. M. Walker.

For Poe's comic face: Richard P. Benton, Kenneth L. Daughrity, Eliot Glassheim, Harriet Holman, Terence Martin, Stephen Mooney, Claude Richard, William Whipple, James Southall Wilson.

VI

In the nearly five years since this book was first published, criticism on Poe has continued at a steadily increasing rate. Among the newer essays, the reader may wish to consult the following. For general essays and essays on the moral, religious, philosophical, and esthetic aspects of Poe's world view: Eric W. Carlson, Alice Chandler, Roger Forclaz, Sidney P. Moss. For differing views of Poe's uses of the occult and the Gothic: Gerald M. Garmon, Benjamin F. Fisher, Maurice Lévy, Barton Levi St. Armand, Joel Salzberg. For Poe's comic face: Alexander Hammond, Evelyn Hinz, David Ketterer, Robert Kierly, Robert Regan. New anthologies of reprinted criticism include William L. Howarth's *Twentieth Century Interpretations of Poe's Tales* (Englewood Cliffs, N.J.: Prentice-Hall, 1971), Eric W. Carlson's *Edgar Allan Poe: "The Fall of the House of Usher"* (Columbus, Ohio: Charles E. Merrill Literary Casebook Series, 1971), David B. Kesterson's *Critics on Poe* (Coral Gables, Fla.: Univ. of Miami Press, 1973). A collection of translations of French critics of Poe, Jean Alexander's *Affidavits of Genius* (Port Washington, N.Y.: Kennikat, 1971), supplements the Hyslop volume and other studies cited in Section IV of this bibliography. New bilingual editions of *Arthur Gordon Pym*, Baudelaire's translations of Poe's tales, and Baudelaire's famous essays have appeared, the first edited by Roger Asselineau (Paris: Aubier Montaigne, 1973), the second by W. T. Bandy (New York: Schocken, 1971), and the third also by Bandy (Toronto: Univ. of Toronto Press, 1973). Poe's reputation in Scandinavia is the subject of Carl L. Anderson's *Poe in Northlight* (Durham, N.C.: Duke Univ. Press, 1973). A useful collection of original essays, well representing the range of current views on Poe, is Richard P. Veler's *Papers on Poe* (Springfield, Ohio: Chantry Music Press of Wittenberg University, 1972). Robert L. Gale's *Plots and Characters in the Fiction and Poetry of Edgar Allan Poe* (Hamden, Conn.: Archon, 1970) is well done.

Four new critical studies have appeared. Daniel Hoffman's *Poe Poe Poe Poe Poe Poe Poe* (Garden City, New York: Doubleday, 1972) is an eccentric Freudian and Jungian reading of Poe's tales and poems. Stuart Levine's *Edgar Poe: Seer and Craftsman* (Deland, Fla.: Everett/Edwards, 1972), also written in an exaggeratedly familiar style, tries with only limited success to reconcile the apparent schism between Romantic seerism and analytic workmanship in Poe. David Halliburton, in *Edgar Allan Poe: A Phenomenological View* (Princeton, N.J.: Princeton Univ. Press, 1973), tries to delineate a unified pattern of experience in Poe's poems and tales by focusing on psychological and material phenomena recurring in these works; one of the most ambitious of recent critical studies, the book is flawed by a cumbersome methodology and jargon. G. R. Thompson's *Poe's Fiction: Romantic Irony in the Gothic Tales* (Madison: Univ. of Wisconsin Press, 1973) argues at full length the thesis presented in the introduction to the present book—a thesis that has been variously received by other Poe scholars.

Chronology

1809   Boston. Born January 19th.

1811   Richmond, Virginia. Poe's mother dies in December,
        leaving three small children to be cared for by friends. Edgar
        Poe is taken into the home of John Allan, a Richmond
        merchant.

1815–20 London. Attends classical academies in England while
        Allan attends to business interests.

1820–25 Richmond. The Allans return to America in 1820. Poe
        attends two Richmond academies, where he excells in lan-
        guages, sports, and pranks. Composes several verse satires in
        couplets, all now lost save "O, Tempora! O, Mores!"

1826   Charlottesville. Enters the University of Virginia, distin-
        guishes himself in ancient and modern Romance languages;
        gambles away $2000. Allan refuses to pay the debt and with-
        draws Poe from the University.

1827–28 Boston and Charleston. Enlists in the United States
        Army as "Edgar A. Perry" and is assigned to Fort Independ-
        ence in Boston Harbor. By summer, he sees his first work in
        print—a small volume of less than a dozen pieces, *Tamerlane
        and Other Poems* "By a Bostonian," which, in addition to
        the title work, includes such poems as "Dreams," "Visit of
        the Dead," "Evening Star," "Imitation" (revised as "A
        Dream Within A Dream"). In November 1827, Poe's unit
        is transferred South.

1829   Richmond, Philadelphia, and Baltimore. In April, a few
        weeks after the death of Mrs. Allan, Poe leaves the Army.
        Finds a publisher for a slightly augmented edition of his
        poems in Baltimore, where he lives for awhile with relatives.
        In December, *Al Aaraaf, Tamerlane, and Minor Poems* ap-
        pears with a half-dozen new works added to the revised
        Tamerlane poems, including the ironic "Sonnet—To Science,"
        the burlesque "Fairy-Land," and a verse "Preface" (later to
        be expanded as a serio-comic "Introduction" for the 1831
        edition of poems, and yet later to be reduced as "Ro-
        mance").

1830   West Point. Enters West Point; again excells in languages.
        Becomes known among the cadets for his comic verses about

the officers. John Allan meanwhile remarries, and discovers a letter in which Poe comments "Mr. A. is not very often sober" (dated May 3, 1830), whereupon he severs relations with Poe.

1831   New York and Baltimore. Without an allowance from Allan, Poe arranges to "disobey orders" (apparently involving nothing more than missing class and church) so as to obtain his release from the Army. *Poems: Second Edition* "By Edgar A. Poe" is published in New York in the spring; includes extensive revisions of "Tamerlane," "Al Aaraaf," and other early poems, as well as a half-dozen new poems: "To Helen," "Israfel," "The Doomed City" (later revised as "The City in the Sea"), "Irene" (later revised as "The Sleeper"), "A Paean" (revised as "Lenore"), and "The Valley Nis" (revised as "The Valley of Unrest"). The volume also includes a prose introduction titled "Letter to Mr. —— ——," which expounds a high Romantic view of art. Joins his aunt, Maria Clemm, and her daughter, Virginia, in Baltimore. Submits several tales in a contest announced by the *Philadelphia Saturday Courier*.

1832   Baltimore. The *Courier* publishes five of his satiric and burlesque tales at regular intervals from January to December: "Metzengerstein," "The Duke de L'Omelette," "A Tale of Jerusalem," "A Decided Loss" (the first version of "Loss of Breath"), and "The Bargain Lost" (the first version of "Bon-Bon").

1833–34   Baltimore. In the summer of 1833, Poe submits another group of tales in a contest sponsored by the *Baltimore Saturday Visiter*; these are first series of the never-published collection of parodies Poe intended to call *The Tales of the Folio Club*, at this time including in addition to the five *Courier* stories: "Some Passages in the Life of a Lion" ("Lionizing"), "The Visionary" (later revised as "The Assignation"), "Shadow," "Epimanes" ("Four Beasts in One"), "Siope" ("Silence"), and "MS. Found in a Bottle." "MS. Found in a Bottle" wins first prize of $50 and "The Coliseum" wins second place in the poetry competition; both are printed in the *Visiter* in October 1833. Sells "The Visionary" to *Godey's Lady's Book*, which appears in January 1834, Poe's first publication in a journal of wide circulation. In March 1834, John Allan dies, in his will omitting any mention of Poe.

1835   Richmond. Becomes associated with the *Messenger* in March; contributes a large number of works to its pages during the year: several poems; the first part of a verse drama, *Politian*; and five new tales, the Gothic "Morella," the Gothic burlesque "Berenice," the comic "Hans Phaal," the satiric "King Pest," and the pseudo-Gothic "Shadow." In addition, he writes a column on current literary events and over thirty reviews. Among the reviews is a demolition of Theodore S. Fay's novel *Norman Leslie*. Such reviews, combined with his continuing attacks on the Northern "literary cliques," begin to earn Poe the title of the "tomahawk man." Circulation of the *Messenger* increases dramatically. Meanwhile, in Baltimore, Maria Clemm hints that Virginia may be taken into the home of a cousin, and Poe promptly writes to ask for Virginia's hand in marriage. In September, he returns to Baltimore where he may have secretly married Virginia. In October, Poe brings Virginia and Mrs. Clemm to Richmond. In December, White offers Poe the editorship of the now prospering *Messenger*.

1836 Richmond. In May, Poe publicly marries Virginia Clemm, still not yet fourteen. His continuing labors to make the *Messenger* a leading critical journal are indicated by the large number of reviews he writes for it in the course of the year —over eighty. Among them is another blistering satire, the review of Morris Matson's novel *Paul Ulric*; other reviews include, besides attacks on writers now forgotten, two reviews praising the earliest work of Dickens, and exercises in critical definition.

1837–38 New York and Philadelphia. Quarrels with White over his low salary in January 1837; resigns from the *Messenger* and takes his small family to New York. Spends the next two years free-lancing in New York and Philadelphia before finding another editorship. Publishes poems and stories, including the comic tale "Von Jung the Mystic," the Gothic tale "Ligeia," and the two satiric companion stories "How to Write a Blackwood Article" and "The Scythe of Time" (later retitled "A Predicament"). In July 1838, his only novel, *The Narrative of Arthur Gordon Pym*, which had been published serially in the *Messenger* in 1837, is published in New York as a book.

1839 Philadelphia. Becomes associated with William Burton and in May becomes an associate editor of *Burton's Gentleman's Magazine*, contributing one signed feature each month as well as writing most of the reviews. His first contributions include the satiric tale "The Man That Was Used Up" and the Gothic tales "The Fall of the House of Usher" and "William Wilson." Becomes involved in a dubious textbook enterprise, Wyatt's *The Conchologist's First Book*. Begins his first series of solutions to cryptograms in *Alexander's Weekly Messenger*.

1840 Philadelphia. Publishes *Tales of the Grotesque and Arabesque*, reprinting twenty-four of his tales with the addition of an unpublished comic tale, "Why the Little Frenchman

Wears his Hand in a Sling." Quarrels with William Burton and is discharged. In an effort to establish his own journal, he sends out a "Prospectus for *The Penn Magazine*," but does not find sufficient financial support. Publishes "Sonnet —Silence," the satiric tale "The Businessman," and the hoax "The Journal of Julius Rodman." In November, Burton sells his magazine to George Graham, who unites it with his own magazine, *The Casket*, to form *Graham's Magazine*. Despite his quarrel with Poe earlier in the year, Burton apparently recommends him to Graham, and in December Poe contributes the Gothic tale "The Man of the Crowd" to the first issue of the "new" magazine.

1841 Philadelphia. Becomes an associate editor of *Graham's*. Contributes the ratiocinative story "The Murders in the Rue Morgue," the Gothic adventure "A Descent Into the Maelström," the dark idyll "The Island of the Fay," the ironic "Colloquy of Monos and Una," and the satiric "Never Bet the Devil Your Head." Also continues to publish elsewhere, notably "Eleonora" in *The Gift*, while in the *Saturday Evening Post* predicting the outcome of Dickens' *Barnaby Rudge* from the first installment.

1842 Philadelphia. In January, Virginia hemorrhages, the first serious sign of the illness that is to take her life in five years. Meets Dickens. Resigns from *Graham's* after a quarrel over the editorship. Works on a new, two-volume collection of stories in which comic works are carefully alternated with the serious works, to be titled *Phantasy-Pieces*, in imitation of the German *Phantasiestücke*, but never published. In the fall, publishes "The Pit and the Pendulum," "The Landscape Garden," and "The Mystery of Marie Roget."

1843 Philadelphia. Becomes associated with James Russell Lowell's new magazine *The Pioneer*, publishing in its pages "Lenore," "The Tell-Tale Heart," and an essay on English verse (later to become "The Rationale of Verse"). The magazine lasts for only three issues, however, and Poe again tries to establish his own independent journal, now to be called *The Stylus*, and again fails. In June, "The Gold Bug" wins a $100 prize in the Philadelphia *Dollar Newspaper* and is widely reprinted. Encouraged by the overnight success of the tale, Graham begins "publication in parts" of *The Prose Romances of Edgar A. Poe*, the first number containing the serious "Murders in the Rue Morgue" paired with the comic "The Man That Was Used Up." In the fall, the Gothic tale "The Black Cat" is followed by the comic tales "The Elk" and "Diddling Considered As One of the Exact Sciences." Begins lecture circuit in November with the "Poets and Poetry of America."

1844 Philadelphia and New York. Continues his lectures on American poetry while contributing to a variety of magazines; notable are the comic tale "The Spectacles" and the occult "Tale of the Ragged Mountains." Gets a job as copy editor for the *New York Evening Mirror* and moves his family to New York, punctuating his arrival with a successful hoax in the *New York Sun* about a balloon journey across the Atlantic. Continues to publish prolifically in a variety of journals; the serio-comic tales "The Premature Burial," "Mesmeric Revelation," and "The Oblong Box," and the comic satire "The Angel of the Odd" are followed by the ratiocinative "Purloined Letter," in turn followed by " 'Thou Art the Man'," a parody of the genre of the detective story which he has just helped popularize, if not invent, over the last three years; this followed by "The Literary Life of Thingum Bob," a satire on Graham and other editors. In December, he begins the *Marginalia* in the *Democratic Review*, a continuing series of random, brief comments, on reading, writing, and the quirks of life.

1845 New York. In January, "The Raven" appears in the *Evening Mirror*. Continues his lecture tour. Publishes the satiric stories "The Thousand and Second Tale of Scheherazade" and "Some Words with a Mummy," followed by the "philosophical" tale "The Power of Words," and the serio-comic "Imp of Perverse." Becomes associated with the *Broadway Journal*. Reprints in it many of his poems and stories, as well as contributing over sixty literary essays and reviews. Begins the "Little Longfellow War," a series of five articles accusing Longfellow, one of the most popular literary figures of the day, of plagiarism. In June, Evert Duyckinck selects twelve of Poe's stories and publishes them through the New York firm of Wiley and Putnam as *Tales*. In October, continuing his lectures and readings, Poe reads "Al Aaraaf" to the Boston Lyceum as a hoax. Meanwhile, the editors of *Broadway Journal* had quarreled, prompting Poe to borrow heavily from friends, so that at last he finds himself, however briefly, owner and editor of his own magazine. Continues to publish in various magazines; notably the satiric tale "The System of Dr. Tarr and Prof. Fether" and the serio-comic "Facts in the Case of M. Valdemar." At the end of the year, Wiley and Putnam brings out *The Raven and Other Poems*.

1846 New York. A winter illness forces Poe to cease publication of *Broadway Journal*, which had lost money during 1845. Contributes the serio-comic tale "The Sphinx" and the half tongue-in-cheek essay "Philosophy of Composition" to other journals. Begins in May "The Literati of New York City" in *Godey's*, a series of mildly satiric sketches of well-known New

York writers, including Thomas Dunn English, who replies angrily in the *Evening Mirror*. Poe rejoins in July, at the same time bringing suit against the *Mirror*, which had printed several other attacks on him. Although he is to win this libel suit next February, Godey ceases the feature with the sixth installment in November. Poe concludes the year with "The Cask of Amontillado."

1847 New York. In January, Virginia dies, ushering in Poe's least productive year, during which he suffers from deep depression and seeks solace in heavy drinking. All that he completes besides revised versions of the 1842 Hawthorne review and "The Landscape Garden" is two poems: one to Marie Louise Shew ("M. L. S."), the woman who had nursed Virginia during her last illness; the other "Ulalume," published in December.

1848 New York. In February, delivers a lecture titled "The Universe," at the New York Society Library, an essay on the principle of death and annihilation as part of the design of the universe, which he reworks for book publication in July as *Eureka*. Attempts a series of romantic liaisons: with Marie Louise Shew early in the year, with Annie Richmond at midyear, and with Sarah Helen Whitman at the end of the year. Mrs. Whitman, widowed, becomes engaged to Poe briefly but breaks it off. In the fall, in deep depression, he may have taken a very large dose of laudanum. Meanwhile, "The Rationale of Verse" and the second "To Helen" (for Helen Whitman) appear. In December, reads "The Poetic Principle" as a lecture in Providence.

1849 New York, Richmond, and Baltimore. Although he continues to contribute to a variety of magazines, his main outlet is the *Boston Flag of Our Union*, a popular weekly. In it from March to July, he publishes three poems, including the ironic "Eldorado" and "For Annie," and four tales, the seriocomic "Hop-Frog," the Gold Rush hoax "Von Kempelen and His Discovery," the satire "X-ing a Paragrab," and the idyll "Landor's Cottage." Spends two months in Richmond in the summer, where he proposes to Sarah Elmira Royster Shelton, his boyhood sweetheart (now widowed), and apparently is accepted. Goes to Baltimore at the end of September, where he seems to have gone on a drinking spree. Found semi-conscious outside a polling booth on October 3rd. Dies Sunday morning, October 7th, "of congestion of the brain"—a brain lesion, perhaps complicated by intestinal inflammation, a weak heart, and diabetes. His death is followed by Griswold's slanderous obituary notice, and by publication of two of his best loved poems, both dealing with the final triumph of death: "Annabel Lee" on October 9th, and "The Bells" early in November.